Critical acclaim for Peter James

'A well-paced thriller that delivers maximum emotional torture'
Chicago Tribune

'Grippingly intriguing from start to finish'
James Herbert

'Too many horror stories go over the top into fantasy land, but *Dreamer* is set in the recognisable world . . . I guarantee you more than a frisson of fear'
Daily Express

'A thought-provoking menacer that's completely technological and genuinely frightening about the power of future communications'
Time Out

'This compulsive story is a tale of the search for immortality . . . I cannot remember when I last read a novel I enjoyed so much'
Sunday Telegraph

'Gripping . . . plotting is ingenious . . . in its evocation of how a glossy cocoon of worldly success can be unravelled by one bad decision it reminds me of Tom Wolfe's *Bonfire of the Vanities*'
The Times

'Peter James, Britain's closest equivalent to Stephen King'
Sunday Times

'The suspense holds on every page, right to the end . . .'
She

Peter James was educated at Charterhouse and then at film school. He lived in North America for a number of years, working as a screen writer and film producer (his projects included the award-winning *Dead of Night*) before returning to England. His previous novels, including the number-one bestseller *Possession*, have been translated into twenty-eight languages. All his novels reflect his deep interest in medicine, science and the paranormal. He has recently produced several films including the BAFTA-nominated *The Merchant of Venice*, starring Al Pacino, Jeremy Irons and Joseph Fiennes, and *The Bridge of San Luis Rey*, starring Robert De Niro, Kathy Bates and Harvey Keitel. He also co-created the hit Channel 4 series *Bedsitcom*, which was nominated for a Rose d'Or. Peter James lives near Brighton in Sussex. Visit his website at www.peterjames.com.

By Peter James

Dead Letter Drop
Atom Bomb Angel
Billionaire
Possession
Dreamer
Sweet Heart
Twilight
Prophecy
Alchemist
Host
The Truth
Denial
Faith
Dead Simple
Looking Good Dead
Not Dead Enough

CHILDREN'S NOVEL

Getting Wired!

PETER JAMES

DREAMER
SWEET HEART

Dreamer
First published in Great Britain by Victor Gollancz in 1989

Sweet Heart
First published in Great Britain by Victor Gollancz in 1990

This omnibus edition published in 2011
by Orion Books Ltd
Orion House, 5 Upper St Martin's Lane
London WC2H 9EA

An Hachette UK Company

A CIP catalogue record for this book is available
from the British Library.

ISBN 9781407234236

Printed and bound in Great Britain by Clays Ltd, St Ives plc

www.orionbooks.co.uk

DREAMER

*To my mother, and to the memory of
my father – an absent friend*

Acknowledgements

My immense indebtedness to Jon Thurley, agent, friend and unflickering beacon of sanity in the lonely abyss, and to my editor Joanna Goldsworthy, for her encouragement, guidance and unswerving belief.

Many people have generously helped me in my research, both with their time and their wisdom, and among them very special thanks is owed to Dr David Stafford-Clark, Dr Keith Hearne, Barbara Garwell, Dr Robert Morris, Edinburgh University, Canon Dominic Walker OGS, David Berglas, Eleanor O'Keeffe, Society for Psychical Research, Tony Reynolds, Dr Duncan Stewart, Laurie Drury, Richard Howorth, Charlie Edmunds, Peter Rawlings, Rob Kempson, Roger W. Moore, Mike and Sally Oliver, Serina Larive, Berkley Wingfield-Digby and Ken Grundy (mad bastard of the mountains!).

My thanks also to the numerous readers of *Homes & Gardens* and *Psychic News* who responded to my requests for experiences of premonitions; to the *Hampstead and Highgate Express* for their kind permission to quote from an article on dreams; to Grafton Books for permission to quote from Tom Chetwynd's *Dictionary for Dreamers* (Paladin); and to Faber and Faber Ltd for permission to quote from No. 12 from 'Choruses and Songs' by W.H. Auden taken from *The English Auden* edited by Edward Mendelson.

My gratitude to my mother and my sister and everyone at Cornelia James for tolerating my long absences so supportively and in particular to my secretary Peggy

Fletcher for slaving so often and so hard over a hot photocopier.

And my deepest thanks to my wife Georgina, researcher, critic, proof-reader and chief stoker, who kept me going.

P.J.

Happy the hare at morning, for she cannot read
The Hunter's waking thoughts. Lucky the leaf
Unable to predict the fall . . .

W.H. AUDEN

1

The scream was carried towards her by the gust of wind, then whiplashed away, leaving her face smarting with the sting of grit and shock.

She stopped and listened. Another gust shook a few more early autumn leaves down from the trees, and dealt them out across the field. Then she heard the scream again.

A single piercing scream of utter terror that cut through her like a knife.

Go, it said. Get away.

Go while you have the chance!

Run!

For a moment, Sam hesitated. Then she sprinted towards it.

A small girl, slight, a few days past seven, her fringe of dark brown hair slipped down over her eyes and she tossed it back, irritated, then tripped over a flint stone in the dusty track and stumbled.

She stopped, panting, and stared around at the furrows of brown soil that stretched away from her across the barren field, at the woods that bordered two sides of it, and the barn beyond the gate at the far end, listening as the fresh gust came, but it brought only the sound of a creaking hinge. She ran again, faster this time, dodging the loose stones and bricks and ruts, the sandy soil kicking up in spurts under her.

'I'm coming,' she said, slowing again, catching her breath, stopping and bending to retie the lace of her left sneaker, then sprinting again. 'Nearly,' she said, 'Nearly there.'

She paused a short distance from Crow's barn, and hesitated. Huge, dark, in a state of neglect, with half its door missing, she could see through into the blackness of its interior. It was OK to go in with a friend, but not alone. Alone it was scary. When she played around here, and visited her secret places, she kept a safe distance from the barn, sufficiently far that nothing lurking in that blackness could leap out and grab her. The half door swung out a few inches and the hinge creaked again, like a wounded animal. There was a bang above her, then another, and she jumped, then breathed out again as she saw a loose flap of corrugated iron above lift and drop in the wind, banging loudly.

Slowly, nervously, she stepped past a strip of rotting wood, past a buckled rusted bicycle wheel and through the doorway into the black silence. The air was thick with the smell of rotting straw, and a duller, flatter smell of urine. There was another smell too, some smell she could not define, but which made her flesh creep, made her want to turn and run; a strange, frightening scent, of danger.

She felt as if the scream she had heard was still echoing in here.

She peered around in the gloom at the empty trough, the obsolete threshing machine and a section of an old plough lying on the floor in a shaft of dusty light. An old ladder lay hooked in place up to the hayloft, and as she stared up into an even blacker darkness, she heard a noise coming from up there; a whisper.

Her head spun in terror.

Then she heard a whooping sound as if someone was inflating a dinghy with a footpump, a strange tortured whooping, then a low pitiful moan.

'Noo.'

Then the whooping again.

Sam ran to the ladder and began to climb, ignoring its bending, its flexing, and the fear that at any moment it might snap in two; ignoring the blackness into which she was climbing. She reached the top and scrambled out onto the rough wooden joists and the thick dust, wincing as a splinter slid deep into her finger.

'No! Oo! *No!* Please no. Please . . .'

The voice turned into a strangled choking. She heard the pumping sound, much louder now, and a human grunt that accompanied it, and she heard a girl's voice hoarse, struggling for breath, pleading.

'Stop. Please stop. Please stop. No. Oh – h. Oh – h'

Her hand touched something round and hard, something plastic with a cord coming from it, something that felt like a switch. She pulled it and a bare bulb lit up inches above her head. She blinked and saw straw bales piled high in front of her with a thin dark gap like a corridor running between them.

For a moment, there was complete silence. Then a whimper, cut short. Shaking with fear she followed her shadow slowly down between the bales of dry acrid straw that stretched to the ceiling, stepping carefully on the joists, until her shadow became indistinguishable from the rest of the darkness.

There was another gasp, right in front of her, a sharp snapping sound, and one more terrible gasp that faded away into complete silence. She froze, her heart thumping, petrified as a figure rose up out of the darkness and began stumbling towards her, his hands reaching out for her, and she began to back away in slow steps, finding the joists, trembling, touching the rough straw to steady herself as she went, staring wide-eyed at the figure that followed her out of the shadows and was getting clearer with every step.

So clear she could now see it was not shadow that hid

3

his face, but a hood. A black hood, with slits for the eyes, the nose, the mouth.

She could see his hands too now; could see the deformed right hand, with just the thumb and the little finger, coming out of the darkness at her like a claw.

She tripped and fell backwards underneath the light bulb. She rolled, scrambled to her feet and tried to step back, but stumbled again, and felt a crunch as her foot went through the rotten flooring.

'You little bitch. What the fuck you doing here?'

She felt his hands clamp around her neck, felt the hand with just the thumb and finger, strong, incredibly strong, like a steel pincer, and her face was filled with the stench of onions and sweat; old stale sweat as if it had been in his clothes for weeks and was now being released, and fresh, raw onions, so sharp she could feel her eyes water from them.

'I – I was—' She froze as the grip of the hands tightened around her neck, squeezing the bones, crushing them. She jerked back, then she stumbled and he stumbled with her and they crashed to the floor. There was an agonising pain across her back, but she was free, she realised. She rolled, heard him grunt again, rolled some more and struggled to her feet. She felt his hand grab her sweater, pulling, and she wriggled, trying to tear free, then tripped again and fell.

As she tried to get up, his hand gripped her shoulder and spun her over, then he was lying on top of her, knees either side, pinioning her body down, and she felt the stench of his breath, the raw onions like a warm foul wind.

'Like to be fucked, would you, little one?' He laughed, and she stared up at his black hood, lit clearly by the bulb above it, seeing the glint of his eyes and his rotten broken teeth through the slits. He leaned back

4

tugging open his belt. The loose corrugated iron flap lifted above them in the wind, lighting them up with daylight for an instant, then banged loudly back down. He glanced up, and Sam sprang at him, clawing at his face with her hands, jamming her fingers into his eyes. The fingers of her left hand sank in deeper than she had thought they could, and she felt a hideous damp gelatinous sensation, then heard a rattling from the floor, like a rolling marble.

A hand crashed across her cheek. 'You little fucking bitch, what you done to it? What you done?'

She stared up, trembling, pulling her hand away from the sightless socket that was raw red, weeping, the eyebrows turned in on themselves. She felt him lean back, groping with his hands, and as he did so she pulled a leg free and kicked him hard in the face. He jerked his head back sharply, smashing it against the bulb which shattered, and they were in complete darkness. She rolled away, scrambling feverishly towards the hatch, then she felt her shoulders grabbed again and she was flung backwards, felt him jumping onto her. She kicked again, yelling, thrashing out, punching, feeling his breath closer, until his face was inches from hers, and a sudden shaft of light came in as the loose flap above them lifted again, lighting clearly the red sightless eye socket that was inches from her face.

'Help me!'

'Sam?'

'Help me!'

'Sam? Sam?'

She thrashed violently, and suddenly she was free of his clutches, falling, then rolling wildly into soft ground, in different light; she tried to get up but fell forward, and rolled frantically again. 'Help me, help me, help me!'

'Sam?'

The voice was soft. She saw light again, from beside her, from an open door, then a figure standing over her, silhouetted.

'No!' she screamed and rolled again.

'Sam. It's OK. It's OK.'

Different, she realised. Different.

'You've been having a bad dream. A nightmare.'

Nightmare? She gulped in air. Stared up at the figure. A girl. She could see the light from the landing glowing softly through her long, fair hair. She heard the click of a switch, then another click.

'The bulb must have gone,' said the girl's voice. A gentle voice. Annie's voice. 'You've been having a nightmare, you poor thing.'

She saw Annie walk towards her and lean down. She heard another click and her bedside Snoopy lamp came on. Snoopy grinned at her. It was all right. The babysitter was looking up at the ceiling, her fair hair trailing below her freckled face. Sam looked up too, and saw that the light bulb had shattered. A single jagged piece of glass remained in the socket.

'How did that happen, Sam?'

Sam stared up at the socket and said nothing.

'Sam?'

'He broke it.' She saw the frown on Annie's face.

'Who, Sam? Who broke it?'

Sam heard raised voices downstairs, then music. The TV, she realised. 'Slider,' she said. 'Slider broke it.'

'Slider?' Annie looked down at her, puzzled, and tugged the strap of her corduroy dungarees back over her shoulder. 'Who's Slider, Sam?'

'What are you watching?'

'Watching?'

'On the television.'

6

'Some film – I don't know what it is – I fell asleep. You've been cut. You've got glass in your hair and on your forehead. And your finger. It's everywhere.' She shook her head. 'I left it on. It must have—' She stared around again. 'Must have exploded. Don't move a sec.' Carefully, she picked the glass out of Sam's hair.

'Are Mummy and Daddy back yet, Annie?'

'Not yet. I expect they're having fun.' She yawned.

'You won't go until Mummy and Daddy get back, will you?'

'Of course not, Sam. They'll be back soon.'

'Where've they gone?'

'To London. To a ball.'

'Mummy looked like a princess, didn't she?'

Annie smiled. 'It was a lovely dress. There.' She walked over to the wastepaper bin, stooping on the way and picking something up from the carpet. 'Bits of glass everywhere. Put your slippers on if you walk around. I'll get a dustpan and brush.'

Sam heard the light tinkle of the glass dropping into the bin, then the sharp shrill of the front door bell. It made her jump.

'It must be your parents. They've forgotten their key.'

Sam listened to Annie walking down the stairs and the sound of the front door opening, waiting to hear her parents' voices, but there was a strange silence. She wondered if the film on the television had finished. She heard the click of the door closing, and there was another silence. Then she heard the soft murmur of a man's voice; unfamiliar. There was another man's voice as well that she did not recognise. Puzzled, she slipped out of bed, tiptoed across to her door, and peeked cautiously down the stairs.

Annie was talking to two policemen who were standing awkwardly, holding their caps.

7

Something was wrong, Sam knew. Something was terribly wrong. She strained her ears, but it was as if someone had turned off the volume, and all she could do was watch them mouthing silent words.

Then Annie turned away from the policemen and walked slowly, grimly, up the stairs while the policemen stayed down in the hall, still holding their caps.

She sat Sam down on the bed, pulling the blankets up around her like a shawl. She dabbed Sam's cheek with a handkerchief, picked some more pieces of glass from her hair, laid them down on the bedside table and then stared at her with her large, sad eyes. Sam saw a tear trickling down her cheek. She had never seen a grown-up cry before.

Annie took Sam's hands in hers and squeezed them gently, then she looked Sam directly in the eyes. 'Your Mummy and Daddy have had an accident in the car, Sam. They aren't coming home any more. They've – gone to heaven.'

Sam did not dream of the hooded man again for twenty-five years. By then he was only a dim memory in her mind. Something that had been a part of her childhood, like the toys she had forgotten and the rusting swing and the secret places that now had housing estates with neat lawns built all over them. Something she thought had gone for ever.

But he had not forgotten her.

2

Sam tapped out a row of figures onto her computer terminal, then sat back wearily and closed her eyes for a moment, the insides of her head banging and crashing like the vacuum cleaner in the corridor outside. She looked at her watch. Six-twenty. Wednesday, 22nd January. Christ, time went fast. It only seemed a few days since Christmas.

She swivelled her chair and stared through her own reflection in the window at the fine needle spray of rain that was falling silently through the darkness of the fast-emptying streets of Covent Garden outside. The wettest rain of all, the type that seemed to come at you from all sides, got inside your clothes, inside your skin, it even seemed to come up out of the pavement at you.

A draught of cold air blew steadily through the glass onto her neck and she hunched her shoulders against it, then rubbed her hands together. The heating had gone off and the office felt cold. She stared at the story board propped up beside the VDU. One coloured frame showed a sketch of a palm-fringed beach. The next showed a man and a woman in designer swimwear and designer suntans bursting out of the sea. In the next frame the woman was biting a chocolate bar which the man was holding.

'Castaway. To be eaten alone . . . or shared with a *very* good friend.'

The office had white walls and black furniture, and a skeletal green plant cowering in the corner that resisted all her efforts to make it flourish. She'd watered it, talked to it, played music to it, bathed its leaves in milk – and it stank foul for days – moved it closer to the window, further away from the window, moved it to just about every position in the room where it was possible to put a plant; but it never changed, never actually died so that they could throw it out, but never looked how it was supposed to so that it was worth keeping. Claire, with whom she shared the office, told

9

her she reckoned it was a *house* plant, not an *office* plant. Claire had strange views on a lot of things.

The walls were covered in schedules and pinboards with memos and Polaroids and product shots and there were two desks, her own which was vaguely orderly, and Claire's, which was neat, pristine, irritatingly tidy. Claire always arranged it like that every evening before she left with a smug expression on her face, almost as if to imply she might or might not be coming back.

Sam heard the cleaner coming closer down the corridor, clunk, bang, thump, and she squeezed her eyes shut against her headache which she could scarcely distinguish from the banshee howl of the vacuum cleaner. The door opened and the roar became a thousand times worse. She looked up fit to scream if Rosa was going to try and come and vacuum in here, then she smiled as her boss, Ken Shepperd, came in and closed the door behind him.

'Hi. Sorry, I'd have been down earlier, but I had a—' He waved his right hand in the air, then circled it around as if he were winding a ball of string.

'It's OK,' she said. 'I just need to know who you're going to have to light the Castaway shoot.'

'You look pale. Feeling OK?'

'Bit of a headache. I think it may be this VDU. I'm going to get one of those filters for it.'

'I've got some aspirins.'

'It's OK, thanks.'

He walked across the office towards her, a restless man in his mid-forties in the clothes of a college student, his steely hair tousled, permanently in need of a cut, his face comfortable and creased like his denim shirt, his sharp blue eyes smiling good-naturedly. He stopped by Claire's desk.

'Tidy, isn't she?'

Sam grinned. 'Is that a hint?'

'How are you finding her?'

Claire had only been with them a few weeks. Lara, her predecessor, had left without any warning. One Monday she failed to appear and sent in a letter the next day saying she was suffering from nervous strain and her doctor had advised her to work in a less stressful environment.

'She's all right,' Sam said. 'She doesn't talk much.'

'You complained that Lara nattered too much. Maybe Claire'll cope better with the pressure.'

Sam shrugged.

'What's that look on your face mean?'

She shrugged again. 'I thought she was nice when she started – but – I don't know.'

'Give her time. She's quite efficient.'

'Yes, sir!'

He walked over and stood behind Sam's desk, staring down at the story board. 'Joncie,' he said. 'I want Joncie to light it.'

'Shall I book him?'

'Pencil him in.'

'Who do you want if he's not available?'

'I've mentioned it already to him.' He squinted down at the board. 'Castaway. Daft name for a chocolate bar.'

'I think it's all right.'

He glanced down the sequence of coloured frames, and read out aloud. 'Like a coconut, Castaway has the goodness on the inside.' He stepped back, patted his stomach and repeated the line again, in a deep bass voice. Sam laughed.

'Castaway,' he boomed. 'The chocolate bar that won't melt in the sun . . . Castaway, the world's first pre-digested food. You don't even need to eat it – just buy it and throw it straight down the lavatory.'

Sam grinned and shook her head. Ken lit a cigarette and the sweet smell tortured her. She watched him prowl around the office, staring at the schedules on the walls; eighteen commercials already booked for this year; they'd made forty-three last year. Ken charged a fee of ten thousand pounds a day for directing and the firm took a percentage of the total production cost. If he weren't still paying off his debts and his wife, he'd be a rich man by now. And if he could keep his temper and his eye for the changing fashions, he would be eventually.

'You're going to behave at the meeting tomorrow, aren't you?'

'Behave?' he said.

'Yes.' She grinned.

He nodded like a reluctant schoolboy.

'Big bucks, Ken.'

'Done the budget?'

'Just going to print it out.'

He looked at his watch, a heavy macho brute of a watch festooned with important-looking knobs, water-proof to five hundred metres (handy for the bathtub, Sam once told him). 'Fancy a quick jar?'

'No thanks. I want to get back in time to bath Nicky. I was late last night.'

'Only a quick one.'

'Hot date?'

He pointed a finger downwards. 'Snooker. Got a couple of new lads from Lowe Howard-Spinks coming over. Business, Sam,' he said, noticing her expression.

'Business!' she mocked.

The wipers of the elderly E-Type Jaguar smeared the rain into a translucent film across the windscreen, making it hard to see. She drove fast, worried Nicky might already be in bed, straining forward to see the road ahead, past the Tower of London, its battlements illuminated in a bright fuzz of light and mist, into London's docklands and slowed as she turned into Wapping High Street, trying not to shake the twenty-five-year-old car too much on the cobblestones. She passed a block of dark, unfinished apartments, and a large illuminated sign which said SHOW FLATS, and another which said RIVERSIDE HOMES – RIVERSIDE LIFESTYLES. Buy a lifestyle, she thought. I'll have a pound of salami, two melons and a lifestyle please.

She drove down the dark street, so dark it could have been a hundred years ago, and turned right past a warehouse into an unlit parking lot. She smelled the oily, salty tang of the Thames as she climbed out, hitched her briefcase from the passenger seat and locked the door carefully. She hurried across the lot through the driving rain, glancing warily at the shadows, and flinched at the sudden rattle of a hoarding in the freshening wind.

She climbed the steps into the porch and the automatic light came on with a crisp, metallic click. She punched in the code on the lock, then went inside, closing the door behind her. Her footsteps echoed as she walked in the dim light across the stone floor of the lobby, past the exposed steel girders that were painted bright red, and the two huge oak casks that were recessed into the wall. Warehouse. You could never forget it had once been a warehouse, a huge grimy Victorian Gothic warehouse.

She went into the lift that you had to go into in darkness, because the light only came on when the doors shut. Creepy. Creepy and slow. She leaned against the wall of the lift as it slowly shuffled up the four floors.

13

Lucky there weren't any more, she thought, or you could eat your dinner going up in it. Then it stopped with a jerk that always unbalanced her, and she walked down the corridor to her front door, unlocked it and went into their huge flat. Nicky came racing down the hallway towards her, his shirt hanging over the top of his trousers, his blond hair flopping over his face.

'Mummy! Yippee!'

She bent down and hugged him and he put his arms around her and kissed her firmly on each cheek, then he looked up at her solemnly. 'I'm a 'vestor now.'

'A vestor, Tiger?'

''Vestor! I got a porthole.'

'Porthole?' she asked, baffled.

'Yeah! I made three pounds today.'

'Three pounds? That's clever. How did you make three pounds?'

'From my porthole. Daddy showed me how.'

'What's your porthole?'

He took her hand. 'Come on, I'll show you.' He looked up at her, triumph in his wide blue eyes. 'We're going for it.'

'Are you?'

'Yeah!'

' "Yes", darling, not "yeah".'

'Yeah!' he teased, tugging his hand free and running down the corridor, turning his head back fleetingly. 'Yeah!'

She put down her briefcase, took off her coat, and followed him across the huge hallway and down the corridor to his bedroom.

'Daddy! Daddy! Show Mummy how much money we've made.' Nicky stood beside his father, who was kneeling on the red carpet in front of his little computer, a cigarette smouldering in the ashtray beside him, holding his whisky tumbler in one hand and tapping the keyboard with his other. A tall, powerfully built man, even kneeling he dwarfed the cluttered room. He turned and looked at her and smiled his nothing-has-changed-has-it? smile. 'Hi, Bugs.'

She stared at him for a moment, at his handsome, almost old-fashioned face, the sort of face that belonged more to Forties Hollywood than Eighties London, his slicked-back blond hair, his pink shirt opened at the collar, his checked braces and pin-striped trousers. Stared at the man she used to love so much, who now felt almost like a stranger.

'Good day?' he said.

'Fine.' She leaned down, more for Nicky's benefit than for anything else, brushed her cheek cursorily against his, feeling his evening stubble, and mouthed a blank kiss, like a goldfish. 'You?'

'Bit slow. Market's a bit cautious.'

'Show her, Daddy.' Nicky put his arm around his father's back, and patted him excitedly.

'We've made him a little portfolio. Put a few shares in and I'll update them each day from the Market.'

'Great,' she said flatly. 'What are we going to have? The world's youngest Yuppie?'

'Yippie!' said Nicky, jumping up and down. 'We got bats.'

'BAT, Tiger, British American Tobacco.'

The floor, shelves and windowsill were strewn with toys, mostly cars and lorries. He was nuts about cars. A monkey holding a pair of cymbals was lying across the forecourt of a Lego garage, and a robot looked as if it was about to leap off the windowsill. Her husband tapped some more figures out on the keyboard, and Nicky watched intently.

Nicky.

15

Nicky sensed that something had gone bad between his Mummy and his Daddy, and with a child's intuition knew his Daddy was in some way responsible. It had seemed to make him even closer to Richard. If that was possible.

His father's son. He'd nearly killed her when he was born, but he'd never really be her son. Always his father's. They were close, so close. Cars. Planes. Lego. Games. Boating. Fishing. Guns. And now the computer they'd given him for Christmas. It was always Richard who taught him, Richard who understood his toys, Richard who knew how to play with them. Richard was his mate.

'American Express down two and a half.'

'Does that mean we've lost money?'

'Afraid so.'

'Aww.'

'Bathtime, Nicky.'

'Aww – just a few minutes more.'

'No, come on, you're late already. Start running it. Mummy's going to change.' Sam went out of the room and saw Nicky's nanny coming out of the kitchen. 'Hello Helen.'

'Good evening, Mrs Curtis,' Helen smiled nervously, unsure of herself as always.

'Everything OK?'

'Fine, thank you. He's had a nice day. He did well at school. They're very pleased with his arithmetic.'

'Good. Must have got that from his father – I'm hopeless at it.'

Sam went into their bedroom and felt the same cold-ness she had felt in the office; it seemed to be following her around. She stared at the bright, warm colours of the painting of the reclining nude on the wall, with her massive breasts and earthy clump of pubes and sly grin that she woke up and stared at every morning. Richard liked her. Insisted on having her there. She sat down on the four-postered bed, tugged off her shoes and leaned back for a moment. Her face stared back down from the mirrored panel on the top of the bed, her hair plastered down by the rain, her face white, much too white. Mirrors. Richard had a thing about mirrors.

She stared back at the painting of the nude. Was that what the tart in the office looked like? She wondered. The tart Richard had disappeared with off to a hotel in Torquay? Did she have big tits and a sly grin?

Bitch, she thought, anger and sadness mixing around inside her. It had all been all right. Fine. Great. A neat, ordered world. Happy times. Everything going well. Everything had been just fine.

Until she found out about that. It felt as if a plug had been pulled out from inside her and everything had drained away.

She sat on the edge of Nicky's tiny bed and flicked over the pages of *Fungus the Bogeyman* on his bedside table. 'Shall I read?'

'No.' He looked quite hurt. 'Tell me a story. You tell the best stories.'

She glanced around the room. 'You promised me you were going to tidy up. All those new things you got for Christmas are going to get broken.' She stood up and walked over to a cupboard door which was ajar and opened it further. A plastic airliner fell out, and the tail section snapped off and cartwheeled along the carpet. Nicky looked as if he was about to cry.

'That was silly. Who put that in there like that?' She knelt down.

Nicky said nothing.

'Was it you?'

Slowly, he pursed his lips.

'Maybe Daddy'll be able to fix it for you tomorrow.' She lifted the pieces off the floor and put them on a chair, then sat back beside him.

'It's my birthday on Sunday, isn't it, Mummy?'

'Yes, Tiger.'

'Am I going to get more presents?'

'Not if you don't tidy these up.'

'I will. I promise.'

'Anyway, you had lots of presents for Christmas.'

'Christmas was ages ago!'

'Four weeks, Tiger.'

His face fell. 'That's not fair.'

She was taken aback at how sad he looked, and stroked his cheek lightly with her hand. 'Yes, you're going to have more presents.'

Bribes. I'm buying his love. Buying my own child's love.

Shit.

'Yippee!' He pummelled the sides of his bed excitedly.

'Come on now, calm down. It's Wednesday. You've got four more days.'

'Three more.'

She laughed. 'OK. Three and a half.' Her headache was feeling a bit better.

Nicky puffed out his cheeks and contorted his face, deep in thought, counting on his fingers. 'Three and a quarter. Tell me a story now. Tell me a story about dragons.'

'You've had one about dragons. I told you last night.'

He sat back expectantly, blinking his large blue eyes. 'Go on, Mummy. Pretend it isn't finished. Pretend the dragon comes back to life and chases the man that killed him.'

'OK. Once upon a time in a land called Nicky-Not-Here-Land, there lived a horrible man.'

'Why was he horrible?'

'Because he was.'

'What did he look like?'

'Horrible.'

He lay back, and was asleep before she had finished. She stood up and he opened his eyes. She bent down and kissed him.

'Night, Tiger.'

'You didn't finish the story!'

Caught, she realised. Sharp. Kids were razor sharp. 'I'll finish tomorrow. All right?'

'All right,' he said sleepily.

'Night night.'

'Night night, Mummy.'

'Do you want the light on or off?'

He hesitated. 'On please.'

She blew him a kiss and closed the door quietly behind her.

Sam watched Harrison Ford dancing with Kelly Mc-Gillis in the headlights of his beat-up station waggon on the television screen. Her eyes smarted and she felt a surge of sadness for all that she – or they – had lost. For all that could never be the same again.

Richard slouched on the sofa in front of the television, whisky tumbler filled to its invariable four-finger measure beside him, and the bottle of Teacher's a few inches further away, almost empty. The gas log fire flickered in the grate the far side of him, and Sam shivered in the draught that blew in from the Thames through the plate-glass windows that stretched the entire width of the flat's living area.

The lighting in the room was low: just two table lamps were on, and there was a soft orange glow from the streetlighting across the river in Bermondsey. Sam turned her gaze away from the television and continued on around the oak refectory table, setting a red wine goblet at each place. 'How many glasses do you want out, Richard?'

'Uh?'

'Glasses. How many do you want out? I'm laying the table for tomorrow.'

'There's going to be eleven of us.'

'How many glasses each?' she said, slightly irritated.

'Three. We're having Chablis and claret. Folatières '83, Philippe Leclerc, then Calon Ségur '62. That's the last of my '62s. And a Sauternes – really good one – Coutet de Barsac, '71.' He picked up the tumbler and drained half of it, then lit a cigarette. 'Harrison Ford,' he said, blinking at the screen. 'Bloody good movie this.' He drained the glass, placed his four fingers carefully around the base, and poured the remainder of the whisky from the bottle. 'You'll like the Chablis.'

'Good,' she said.

'Archie's a real wine man, know what I mean? First growth, no shit. Three hundred quid a bottle touch for lunch – Lafites and all that stuff. Style! You'll like Archie. He's a good boy.'

'I think we should put one for Perrier as well. Everyone always wants it.' She looked at him, but he was engrossed again in the television. 'Are you serving port?'

'Yah.'

'I'll put port glasses out as well.'

'He's a big player, Archie.'

'Then you should have a nice game with him.'

'City, Sam. He's a big player in the City.'

'Perhaps he can teach Nicky something, too,' She

went over to the cabinet in the corner, and pulled out more glasses. The wind was howling outside, slapping the black water of the Thames against the piers below and shaking the rigging of the yachts. She could see the glints of light on the waves, the dark hulls of the lighters moored midstream. Bleak, she thought, turning away and carrying the tray to the table. 'Is this famous Andreas definitely coming?'

'Oh – er – yah.' Richard shifted about on the sofa and took a gulp of his whisky.

'So I'm finally going to meet him. What's his surname again?'

'Berensen.'

'Does he have a place in London?'

'No, he's just over on business.'

'From Switzerland? What exactly does he do? He's some sort of a banker, isn't he?'

Richard scratched the back of his head. 'Ah – yah – a banker.'

'A real gnome?'

'Yah.' Richard laughed, slightly uncomfortably. 'Actually he's quite tall.'

'Is he your biggest client now?'

'Yah. Sort of, I suppose.' He was sounding evasive, Sam thought, frowning. 'How's work?' he asked.

'Hectic. I should still be there now.'

'That guy Ken's making you work too hard. All this travelling you're doing is crazy. You're travelling too much, you know, Bugs.' He turned round.

His face, which had always looked fit and lean, had been sallow and lined lately, much older than his thirty-three years, and in the flickering light from the screen and the fire she suddenly caught a glimpse of what he would look like when he was old, when he no longer had the strength and energy that animated him and he started to shrivel and cave in, like a ghoul from a horror movie. It frightened her. Ageing frightened her.

'I have to travel.'

He drained two fingers of whisky and dragged hard on his cigarette again. The smell tantalised her, tempted her, and her refusal to weaken was making her irritated.

'I don't think you're spending enough time with Nicky,' he said.

'I spent three years with him, Richard. I quit my career for him.'

He leaned over and crushed his cigarette out. 'Dealer's choice, darling.'

'What do you mean?'

'It was your choice.'

'Our choice,' she said. 'I gave up three years. What did you give up? Why don't you give up three years?'

'Don't be ridiculous.'

'I'm not being ridiculous.'

'Bugs, I don't mind you working, but what you're doing is crazy. You're working all hours of the day and night, you bring your work home, half the time you spend roaring around Europe, jumping on and off aeroplanes. You're always off somewhere. France. Holland. Germany. Spain. Bulgaria. You went to Bulgaria about six times last year. I think you're ignoring Nicky. You're not being a good mother to him.'

The anger that was rising inside her went flat, as if it had been lanced, and she felt a sharp pang of guilt. She sat down on the dining chair, feeling limp, as something uncomfortable echoed from her own childhood.

She thought about her own childhood and how life had dumped on her then. She thought about her marriage and her happiness and the forgetting that had happened. Perhaps she had forgotten too much? Maybe it wasn't only children that could feel neglected and unwanted. Maybe adults could too. Maybe that's why it had happened.

3

'Something's wrong.'

'What's wrong?'

'Something.'

Sam heard the voices, low, murmuring, muted, like a snatch of conversation from across the room at a cocktail party, and stiffened. She turned around, craning her neck over the back of her seat, trying to see where they had come from, but the man and the woman behind her were asleep. She listened, but could hear only the sound of the aircraft's engines: a distant churning, like a dishwasher. Then the cycle changed, and she felt the plane begin to sink down into the cloud below.

Flying never normally bothered her, but suddenly she felt nervous. She stared uneasily at the trails of rain that streaked the window, and the swirling grey beyond. Landing. Her hands felt clammy with perspiration, and she realised she was shivering.

She wanted to put the clock back, not be on the plane at all. Stupid, unnecessary trip, she thought. Richard was right, she was jumping on and off too many planes. She wished she had not jumped on this one. Bucket seats; trying to save Ken money. Charter airlines took risks, someone told her. Calm down, Sam, she said to herself. Calm down.

There was a ping, and the 'No Smoking' sign lit up on the panel in front of her. Then another bell, higher pitched, faintly musical, like the gong of an elevator announcing its arrival. Beng-bong. The sound irritated her.

'This is Captain Walker.' His matey voice irritated her as well. There was a hum and a screech and a loud click. 'We've started our descent and expect to be on the apron in about twenty-five minutes. The weather in Sofia is cold – one degree Celsius and it's snowing. We hope you have enjoyed your flight with us and that you have a pleasant stay in Bulgaria. On behalf of us all, I'd like to thank you for flying Chartair, and hope you choose to fly with us again.' His voice was tired, clipped ex-RAF English. He was having to make the effort to sound friendly, and not as if it was just another charter flight, which it was; not as if he was tired and bored with dumping another load of cheap tourists in another cheap resort.

A little girl's head popped over the seat back in front of her. 'Hallo,' she said.

'Hallo,' Sam replied.

The girl's head disappeared and she heard giggling. 'I said hallo to the lady behind!'

Perspiration was trickling down Sam's face and she felt sick. She unbuckled her belt, slid across the empty seats beside her and walked unsteadily along the aisle which was sloping away from her, down towards the toilets, pushing against the seat backs to prevent herself from running forwards, waiting to be challenged by a stewardess, but they were busy stowing the duty frees and had not noticed her.

She reached the front of the aeroplane, still shaking, and was surprised to see the door to the flight deck was open. She stared through at the orange dials of the instruments and the captain and the first officer, in their white shirts, in their seats.

The first officer turned his head towards the captain, and she could hear him speak, clearly.

'Derek,' he said, 'there is definitely something wrong.'

The captain flicked a switch beside him, and spoke loudly and dearly. 'This is Chartair Six-Two-Four. Confirm we are on initial approach.'

A voice crackled back, sharp, tinny, with a precise, broken English accent. 'Chartair Six-Two-Four. This is Sofia tower. We confirm initial approach. Runway Two-One. We have visibility of only two hundred metres – check your landing minima.'

'Sofia tower. Chartair Six-Two-Four. Confirming runway Two-One.'

The captain leaned forward in his seat and adjusted a dial on the instrument panel. The first officer stared around. She could see the worry on his face, could feel his fear, as if it were a blanket of ice.

The microphone crackled again, and she heard the voice, more urgent. 'Chartair Six-Two-Four. We have you identified on radar. You are too low. I say again too low. Climb to seven thousand feet immediately.'

'We are at seven thousand feet,' said the captain calmly, a trace of weariness in his voice as if the man in the tower had become infected with the same irrational fear as the first officer.

'We have you identified on radar,' said the controller. 'You are at four thousand five hundred. Check your altimeter setting.' His voice rose in excitement and panic. 'Climb. Climb immediately! Discontinue your approach. I say again, discontinue your approach!'

'I have seven thousand reading on both altimeters. Please check your radar.' There was irritability creeping through the calm.

'Climb, Derek,' the first officer shouted. 'The mountains, for Chrissake. Fucking climb!'

'We're clear. The mountains are five thousand ceiling.'

There was a sharp click and the toilet door in front of her opened. A man stood there, in a black hood with slits for his eyes and mouth.

She reeled back, and he clamped a black leather-gloved hand over her mouth, cracking her head back hard against the bulkhead. She smelled the leather of the glove, new fresh leather, flung her head violently away, tried to scream, tried to back away, felt a lever behind her jamming into her back; then the black leather glove came over her face again and she ducked, heard a tremendous bang and the hissing of air, then suddenly she was out of the aircraft, spinning wildly in the turbulence, and the deafening howling of the freezing wind and the engines, spinning through a crazed icy vortex, falling, falling, falling through a blackness that seemed to go on for ever.

Then she was free of it, floating in the cold grey cloud as if it was water. She could push her arms and move through it. She went further away, swimming effortlessly, until she could see the silver Boeing in the distance, cloud swirling around it like tendrils of weed as it flew into the dark grey shape that loomed upwards in front of it, a shape that was barely discernible from the cloud.

At first there was silence. The aircraft seemed to go on for a long time into the solid wall of the mountain, and she wondered for a moment whether it was her imagination, or just a strangely shaped cloud. Then the tail section flew away and began to cartwheel downwards. It bounced up for an instant off a ridge, and something began to spray out of it, like champagne, and float down behind it. Luggage, she realised with a sickening feeling.

It bounced again, rose up, and did a half-turn in slow

motion. The stream of suitcases that followed bounced in the same place, deflecting in the same way, except some of them burst open leaving a wake of fluttering clothes.

A solitary passenger, strapped in his seat, flew up through the clothes, followed by another, then a third, their limbs shaking about like toys emptying from a child's cupboard as they plummeted back down.

There was a boom, and a ball of flame rose high up above. A fiercely blazing object joined the dance down the mountainside, showering sparks into the greyness all around it. An engine. It ploughed into the snow below her, hissing. Near it she could see the tail section, a stubby dark silhouette resting on the white snow, the top of the tail fin bent over at a right angle, the word 'Chartair' clearly visible, and part of the emblem of a prancing tiger and letters next to it G.Z.T.A.E.

And then there was a silence that frightened her. The cloud swirled around her, until she could no longer see the ground, until she could no longer tell whether she was lying face down or up. Panic began to grip her. She wanted to see Nicky, to hold him, squeeze him. She wanted to hug Richard, tell him she was sorry, tell him she forgave him, tell him she was sorry she had worked so damned hard. 'Where are you?' She turned her body over, then over again, trying to break away from the cold grey tendrils that were entwined around her. 'Let me go. Please let me go and see them. Just five minutes. Please. That's all. Five minutes.'

They tightened around her.

'Let me go!'

The air was getting warmer now, stifling; it was getting harder to breathe. 'Let me go!' she screamed, punching out with her fists, swirling, twisting.

She felt a cool breeze on her face.

'Bugs?'

Richard's voice, she thought, puzzled.

'Bugs?'

She saw a flat pool of light, and Richard standing near her in a striped shirt and paisley boxer shorts.

Different. The light was different. A dial blinked at her, orange like the dial of the aircraft, 0500. 0500. 0501.

'OK, Bugs?'

Richard was standing over her.

'OK Bugs?' he said again.

She nodded. 'Yes – I—'

He frowned, then struggled with the floppy arm of his shirt, and she heard the pop as the cufflink pierced the starch. Gold links with his initials on one side and his family crest on the other. Her wedding present to him. They'd come in a small wine-coloured box, and cost £216. Odd, the details you could remember. She stared at the reclining nude on the wall, at her face in the mirror above the bed, at the light streaming in from the bathroom door.

'A dream,' she said. 'I was having a dream.'

'You were making a horrible sound, really horrible.' He turned away toward the wall mirror, and knotted his tie. As he pulled it tight, she felt something pull tight around her own throat. Dread seeped through her, hung around her, filled the room. The black hood with the slits came out of the door at her and the black leather glove clamped over her mouth. She shivered.

Richard struggled into his trousers, disentangled his red braces and pulled on his silver armbands. She had loved to watch him dress when they had first started sleeping together. He was fastidious about his clothes. Shirts with double cuffs; trousers with buttons for braces. Proper trousers, he called them. She wanted to hold him suddenly, to hug him, feel him, to make sure he was real, still there; that her world was intact.

And then the revulsion as she remembered and she shrank back in the bed away from him, and shook with a sudden spasm of – fear?

'What were you dreaming about?'

'It – I – nothing. Just a nightmare.'

You're afraid to tell it, she thought.

Afraid that if you tell it—

'Must dash.' He leaned down to kiss her, and she smelled the coconut shampoo in his damp hair, his sweet Paco Rabanne aftershave and the strong trace of last night's garlic through the minty toothpaste on his breath. She felt a soft wet kiss on her cheek.

'Busy day?' she said, wanting him to stay just a moment longer.

'Japan. I reckon Tokyo's about to start going bonkers.'

'Don't be late. It would be nice if you could help me get things ready tonight.'

'Oh Christ, yah. Our dinner party.'

'It's for your clients, Richard.'

'I'll be back in good time.'

The front door opened, then slammed shut. She dosed her eyes but opened them again, afraid of going back to sleep. She looked at the clock again. 0509. In a quarter of an hour he would be at his desk, chatting to Tokyo. Dealing. The Nikkei Dow. Gambling on equities, warrants, options, futures, currencies. So many variables. So many imponderables. He'd got angry with her once when she told him his job was like being a croupier in a high-tech casino.

The door opened and Nicky came padding sleepily in.

'Hallo, Tiger. You're up early.'

'I can't sleep.'

She put her hand out and tousled his hair. Soft, real. He shied away just a fraction, then put his head under her hand again for more.

'Give Mummy a kiss.'

Damp. It felt like a miniature version of Richard's. 'Why can't you sleep, Tiger?'

'I had a nightmare.'

'What was it about?'

'It was about a horrible man. A monster.'

She sat up and hugged him. 'That's because I told you a story about one, isn't it?'

He nodded solemnly. He was a serious child sometimes. Always thinking things through.

'He ate me.'

She stared at the forlorn expression on his face. 'I bet you tasted good.'

He stamped his foot on the carpet. 'Don't. That's not funny.'

'Mummy's got to get ready. Want to sleep in our bed?'

'No.' He wandered off, shuffling his slippers across the floor. As he went, she saw the aircraft sliding silently into the solid wall of the mountain. The tail section cartwheeling down. The luggage spewing out. The boom, and the ball of flame. She slipped unsteadily out of bed and walked to the bathroom, shivering, from the images, from the chill air, from the dark cloud of foreboding that hung over her.

A bad dream, that's all. Forget it.

She heard the thump of the engines of a launch going by, up river; deep, steady, rhythmic.

Then realised it wasn't a launch at all. It was her own heartbeat.

4

Sam sat in the reception of Urquhart Simeon Mcpherson, holding the Castaway story board on the sofa beside her, watching Ken pacing restlessly up and down, hands sunk into the pockets of his battered leather coat over his denim jacket and blue jeans, his black boots immaculately shiny: his uniform. Scruffy clothes, but always immaculate boots.

Two girls came in through the door chatting, nodded at the receptionist and went down a corridor. A helmeted despatch rider with 'Rand Riders' printed on his back waded in and thrust a package over the counter; he stood waiting for the signature, bandy-legged in his body-hugging leathers, like an insect from outer space.

Ken sat on the arm of the sofa, above her. 'You all right?'

'Fine,' she said.

'You look a bit tense.'

'I'm fine,' she repeated. 'Waiting like this always feels like being back at school. Waiting to see teacher.'

He pulled a pack of Marlboro from his jacket pocket, and shook out a cigarette. He clicked his battered Zippo and inhaled deeply, then ran a hand through his hair.

'Production meetings,' he said grimly.

Sam smiled. 'I know you don't like them.'

'That copywriter – Jake wozzizname – gives me the creeps.'

'He's all right,' Sam said.

'He gives you the creeps too?'

'No.'

'Something's given you the creeps.' He looked at her quizzically.

31

She felt her face redden, and turned away. 'Maybe I'm a bit tired. Early start.'

'What you doing this weekend?'

'Nicky's birthday party on Sunday.'

'Six?'

She nodded.

'Having a big one?'

'Nineteen of them. We're having Charlie Chaplin films and a Punch and Judy.'

'All his smart little friends?' He tilted back his head and peered down his nose, feigning an aristocratic accent. 'Rupert . . . Julian . . . Henrietta. Dominic, Hamish, Inigo and Charlotte?'

'And the Honourable Sarah Hamilton-Deeley.'

'Ay say. The Honourable Sarah Hamilton-Deeley. Sounds ripping good fun.' He dropped the accent and stroked his chin. 'Hope you think of me, down at the chip shop roughing it with the hoi polloi.'

Sam grinned, then saw something sad in his face. She wondered sometimes whether he liked his independence, or whether he would like to be married again, have kids. She realised how little she knew about him, about the private Ken Shepperd. Here in this environment, where part of him belonged, part of him was comfortable, yet another part of him seemed to yearn to be somewhere else, doing something else, away from the bullshit and the glitz; a man snared by his mistakes and his success.

'I'll save you a jelly,' she said.

'With a jelly baby in it?'

'Of course.'

He looked up at the ceiling, then the walls. 'It's a poxy room this. Do you know what their billings were last year?'

'Eighty-two million.'

32

'And they can't even get themselves a decent reception area.'

Sam stared down at the table sprinkled with magazines and newspapers. *Campaign*. *Marketing*. *Media Week*. *The Times*. The *Independent*. The *Financial Times*. The carpet had been specially woven with the agency's logo of concentric squares receding forever inside each other, like a television picture of a television picture of a television picture. A huge version of the logo dominated the rear wall, surrounded by framed ads, wrappers and packaging. A Ferrari gleamed in the shine of a patent leather shoe on a girl's foot. A man with a dazzling wholesome smile held up a toothbrush. A can of old-fashioned rice pudding was several feet high, Warhol-style.

'I think it's quite smart,' she said.

'Sorry to keep you.' Charlie Edmunds came into the room, tall, almost gangly, with a floppy mop of fair hair. He stood in his cavalry twills, Hush Puppies and Jermyn Street shirt like an overgrown schoolboy. God, people were starting to look so young, and they concentrated so hard on not being young. The young were all earnest, serious, like Charlie, trying to act like forty-year-olds. And the forty-year-olds desperately wanted to be in their early twenties. 'Sam, nice to see you. Ken. Looking well.'

They followed him up a flight of stairs, along a corridor and into a windowless room with blue fabric wallcovering, and a long blue table in Scandinavian wood with matching chairs. There was an open Filofax on the table, several coloured sketches and photographs. In the middle of the table were a cluster of Castaway bars in silver foil wrapping with lagoon-blue writing. The room had a fresh, woody smell, and there was a soft monotone hiss from a heating duct.

33

'The others'll be here in a moment,' said Charlie. 'Sorry to drag you over at such short notice, but this is an account we've pitched very hard for and they've decided to pull this particular product launch forwards, so we haven't a lot of time.' As if to underline this, he looked down at his slim Omega wristwatch.

Sam glanced at her own watch, then up at an abstract painting on the wall. It was no doubt deep and meaningful; everything inside the portals of Urquhart Simeon Mcpherson was deep and meaningful and done for a reason, but its immediate identity eluded her. The colours reminded her vaguely of a bedroom in a Holiday Inn. The door opened and two men came in. One, in his mid-twenties, was short, belligerent-looking and thin as a drainpipe. He wore a black unstructured jacket over a black collarless shirt and shiny black tapered trousers. His dark hair was cropped short at the front and hung in a long mane down the back, and his face was long and thin, as if it had been crushed between two elevator doors. His nose, also long and thin, appeared to be bolted to his face by his eyes which were much too close together. The other man, slightly older, was dressed in baggy white; the sides of his head were shorn to stubble and he had a thick clump of hair on top. He wore round granny glasses, and looked slightly better fed and better humoured.

Sam had met them several times. They always reminded her of a couple of beat poets who hadn't yet been discovered.

'Jake, Zurbrick – you know Sam and Ken,' said Charlie.

They nodded at each other. Zurbrick, the art director, smiled genially, shook their hands, adjusted his glasses and dug his hands in his pockets, and Jake, the copywriter, nodded once, curtly, exuding seriousness and a faint air of superiority.

They sat down and Sam put the story board on the table, opened her briefcase and pulled out her Filofax and her budget folder.

'Right,' said Charlie. 'You've – ah – you've both seen the story board—' He leaned forward and picked up a Castaway bar. 'And the – ah – product.' He seemed nervous in the company of the other two.

Sam picked up a pencil on the table in front of her and tapped it lightly on the Urquhart Simeon Mcpherson monogrammed memo pad which had also been provided.

'How's the budget looking, Sam?'

'It's a bit over.' She pulled it out of the folder and passed it across to him. He glanced down and turned to the total. 'Oh yah, that's OK. They'll live with that. There's going to be one suit going as well – have to budget that in, first class – and for the recce too.'

'Who's the suit?' said Ken.

'The marketing director of Grand Spey Foods. He's all right, Ken,' he said quickly. 'Won't give you any trouble.'

'All suits give trouble.'

'I think he's got a bit of crumpet out there.' Charlie smiled. 'You won't see much of him.'

Ken grunted noncommittally.

Sam saw the diminutive Jake sitting with his hands on the table as if he was waiting to be fed, eyeing Ken disdainfully. She knew what he was thinking. *You're an old fart*, he was thinking. *We should be using a younger director.*

'You've shot in the Seychelles before, Ken, haven't you?' said Charlie.

He nodded.

Charlie had warned her that Jake had been against Ken, that he wanted Tom Land, a twenty-four-year-old whizz-kid director.

'What's it like?'

Ken stared at Jake. 'Poisonous spiders. Snakes. Massive land crabs. Hostile natives.'

Jake blanched, and his face twitched. Charlie grinned.

'And gorgeous women,' said Zurbrick in his Brummy accent.

'We have to make a presentation at the client's headquarters in a fortnight. They've asked for the director and producer to be present.' Charlie looked at Ken, and he nodded.

'Where are they?'

'Just outside Leeds.'

The weather in Sofia is cold – one degree Celsius and it's snowing. We hope you have enjoyed your flight with us and that you have a pleasant stay in Bulgaria.

'All right with you, Sam?'

Charlie's voice was distant. She looked up with a start.

'All right with you, Sam?'

'I'm sorry?'

They were all looking at her oddly.

'Leeds? Presentation?'

'Fine,' she said. 'Yes, no problem.' She pulled herself up in her chair, smiled at Charlie, Zurbrick and then at Jake, who stared back like a bird interrupted from picking flesh off a carcass.

'The script and story board you have is still rough, of course,' said Zurbrick, 'but it's the pivot for the whole campaign. We're looking for great subtlety combined with high impact.'

Sam scanned the scenes on the story board.

'The big difference with this product – the unique selling point – is the health angle. It's not going to be perceived just as a sweet, it's going to be pitched as a Personal Nourishment System.'

'A *what*?' said Ken.

'A Personal Nourishment System.'

'I seem to remember when I was young, we used to call them chocolate bars,' Ken said.

Jake stared at Ken as if he was a relic in a museum. 'Chocolate bars,' he said, 'went out with the ark. We're talking concepts here. We're talking a breakthrough.' He was jigging up and down in his chair, then he jammed his elbow down on the table and leaned forward intently. 'This campaign is going to be in the text books in ten years' time.'

'This is different, Ken, very different, Ken,' said Zurbrick. 'It's got everything you need. The client believes it's the first confection to contain a totally self-sufficient diet. It's got a full daily vitamin programme. Protein. Glucose. Organic coconut. Coconut's high in nutrients. Roughage. It helps avoid wrinkles, senility, sunburn. Gives you energy. All you need with this is water.'

'Just water?'

He nodded.

'You could live on these?' said Ken.

'Absolutely.'

Ken shook his head. Sam shot him a warning glance.

'The big trick with this bar,' said Zurbrick, 'is that the biscuit part is on the outside. It's brilliant. You take it in the heat, and the chocolate can't melt, can't go sticky. It's eater-friendly. The wrapping's airtight, watertight. It's a real serious survival food. It isn't just a chocolate bar – it's a Nineteen Nineties High-Tech food. It's state-of-the-art nutrition.'

Ken looked at him as if he was mad.

'Two angles, Ken. One, the contents – they're amazing. Two, the image. Castaways are eaten by successful people.'

'We're talking energy,' said Jake. 'Energy and youth. Street cred,' he said, staring pointedly at Ken. 'We don't want this looking like some bloody Bounty ad from the Sixties, we don't want Robinson Crusoe's desert island. We're talking twenty-first century, y'know? This is a twenty-first century desert island. We don't want it looking like a bloody desert island at all, we want it to look like it's something from space. This is young high-aspirant food. Street cred food. We're pitching this at the people who don't have time for lunch. We're going to change society with this food. Remember Gordon Gekko? Michael Douglas? When he said 'lunch is for wimps'? Castaway is lunch. It's the *new* lunch.' He jabbed his finger forward, his eyes twitching as if they had come loose. 'This is what we're pitching. This is what the script is all about. This is the way I've written it.'

Sam glanced down at her memo pad. She had drawn a picture of an aeroplane.

'Eater-friendly. Shit. What a load of crap. What does eater-hostile food do? Bite you back?' Ken shook his head. 'They believe it, Sam, don't they? They really believe it!' He switched on the windscreen wipers.

Sam watched them, stubby, jerky, slightly clumsy; they more than anything betrayed the Bentley's age, she thought.

'Personal Nourishment Systems,' he said. 'The psychology's all wrong, that's what worries me. People need to eat together, need to sit around a table. What are we going to end up with? A world full of isolated morons wandering around with their Walkmans eating their Personal Nourishment Systems?'

She smiled. 'I thought it tasted quite nice.'

'Tasted like a Bounty with biscuit.'

The wiper in front of her smeared the water without wiping it away. Watching the road ahead was like staring through frosted glass. She saw ripples of movement, streaks of brake lights, traffic lights, distorted pedestrians like huge upright fish.

SALE. SALE. SALE. The signs flashed out at her from the windows of Kensington High Street. Ken leaned over and pulled a packet of chewing gum from the glove locker. 'Want some?'

'No, thanks.'

'Traffic's bad. We should have gone down the Cromwell Road.' He unwrapped a stick of Juicy Fruit and put it in his mouth.

She smelt the sweet smell for an instant, and then it was gone. She stared down the long, midnight blue bonnet. Brake lights, shop lights, traffic lights. Dark grey sky. Dismal. The last few bargains in the shops, then in a week or so they would be dressing the models with their summer clothes, stiff mannequins with silly gazes in bright bikinis and summer frocks. In February. Daft.

It was strange sitting so high up, in the deep wide seat, like an armchair. Her feet were buried in the soft lambswool carpet and she smelled the rich smell of the reupholstered leather. Her uncle had a car that was high off the ground and smelled of leather. A Rover. She always sat in the back, while her uncle and aunt sat without talking in the front. Sunday afternoons. The ritual drive in the country from their dull house in Croydon. Staring at fields like those in which once she had run free and played. Where once . . . but that had been a long time ago and the memory was forgotten.

Leather. The smell of the leather glove in the dream. So clear. The black hood with the slits. A shiver rippled through her. The nerve was still there, raw, exposed. You could never really forget; only paper over the cracks.

When her parents had died, her aunt and uncle had inherited her without much grace, without much enthusiasm. They hadn't wanted her. She was an intrusion into their lives, into their flat childless tranquillity.

Her uncle was a morose man with a droopy moustache, irritated by everything: a noise, by lights left on, by the morning news. He shuffled interminably around the gloomy house tapping the barometer and muttering about the weather, although he never did anything that would have been affected by it. Sat in his armchair picking at his stamp collection with his tweezers, occasionally looking up. 'A Vancouver Island ten cents blue. Interesting.' Then he'd return to his silence.

Her aunt was a cold, humourless woman, who forever blamed God for her lot in life and went to church every Sunday to thank him for it. She was going through life amassing credits for the next life. She had one for marrying her husband. One for taking on Sam. One for having the vicar and his wife round for tea. One for joining the Samaritans – God knows what advice she dispensed – one for taking a purse she found in the street to the police. She had over three hundred credits written in a notebook Sam had once discovered. That had been twenty years ago. Sam wondered how many more she had added since.

The past was a strange place. Images changed with time. It tried to deceive you with its jerky black and white movies, with its faded photographs, its rust, wrinkles, its stubby wipers. Tried to pretend it had always been that way. Made it difficult to remember that everything was modern once; that everything around her now, in the street, in the shop windows, would be old one day, too.

The rain rattled hard for a second, then faded, as if a child had thrown a handful of pebbles. She turned and glanced out of the side window. The black print on the news vendor's billboard flashed at her like a single frame of a film and was gone.

'Stop, Ken!'

'Stop what?'

'Stop the car, for Christ's sake! Stop the car!' she yelled, groping for the door handle, pulling it, pushing open the door as he found a gap in front of a taxi and pulled into the kerb. There was the ring of a bicycle bell, and a cyclist swerved, scraping his wheel along the kerb, shouting angrily.

She fell out of the car, stumbled onto the pavement, and ran back to the news vendor. '*Standard*,' she said, grabbing the paper, pulling her purse out of her bag, fumbling, trying to open it, rattling the coins, spilling them around her. Then she stopped, oblivious to the stinging iciness of the rain, and stared down at the front page headline.

163 DEAD IN BULGARIA AIR DISASTER

Underneath was a photograph. The tail section of the aircraft, a dark silhouette resting on snow, the top of the tail-fin bent over at a right angle and part of the Chartair prancing tiger emblem clearly visible with letters next to it.

G.Z.T.A.E.

Chartair Six-Two-Four, she mouthed silently to herself, watching the newsprint darkening from the rain.

'Bulgaria has confirmed that a Boeing 727 belonging

to Chartair crashed this morning with the loss of all 155 passengers and eight crew. Full details have still not been released, but the plane is believed to have crashed into mountains whilst trying to land in poor visibility.'

She did not need to read any further. Turning, she walked slowly back to the waiting car.

She knew exactly what had happened.

'What is it?' dimly, she heard Ken's voice. 'Sam? . . . Hallo? . . . Anybody home?'

She pulled the Bentley's door closed, and stared again at the headlines and the photograph.

'What is it, Sam? What's the matter? Do you know someone on that plane?'

She looked ahead blankly, then pulled her handkerchief out of her bag and wiped the water away from her face. She felt more trickling down her cheeks and wiped that away too. Immediately they were wet again. She closed her eyes tightly, felt her chest heaving and sniffed hard, trying to stop the sobbing, but she could not.

She felt Ken's hand, tender, lightly on her wrist. 'Who was it?' he said. 'Who was on that plane?'

She sat in silence for a long while, listening to the rain and the sound of the traffic passing by.

'Me,' she said. 'I was on that plane.'

5

'Up their bottoms.'

'No!'

'It's true. They do.'

'I don't believe you.'

Richard picked up his wine glass, grinning drunkenly,

and swirled his wine around. 'They stick gerbils up their bottoms.'

'Honestly?'

Sam watched Sarah Rowntree's bright pampered face through the silver candelabra. The lights of a boat slipped past the window; she could hear the faint throbbing of its engine above the chatter.

'They put them in plastic bags then stick them up their bottoms.'

'I can't believe it!'

A draught of cold air, stronger than the others, bent the candle flames, and she watched the light dancing off the diamonds, the cutlery, the glistening cheeks. Friends. Dinner parties. She loved giving dinner parties.

Normally.

Her favourite way of entertaining. Cocktail parties were a hassle: small talk, good for prospecting business, that was all. Supper parties were as bad. You ended up perched on the end of an armchair, attempting to eat from a paper plate, with a dip on the side that didn't fit your wine glass, a paper plate that was always too small and bent when you tried to cut your ham and dumped your food on the floor if you were lucky and in your lap if you weren't.

Dinner parties were the civilised way. A few friends. Good food. Good conversation.

Normally.

Not tonight.

Tonight nothing fitted. Neither the food, nor the guests, nor her dress which was driving her nuts. The bouillabaisse starter had mostly disintegrated. Harriet O'Connell announced she had become allergic to fish, blaming pollution, and Guy Rowntree said he didn't eat garlic, so they'd split the one avocado she'd found in the fruit bowl.

The venison looked as if it had been cremated. The juniper berries in the casserole had fused into a thick, bitter sludge and the sauce had separated, drifting around on top like an oil slick.

And how the hell was she to know that juniper berries murdered claret?

It was Archie, on her right, who told her, informed her, lectured her. Archie Cruickshank – *You'll like Archie – he's a good boy . . . a big player – a real wine man, know what I mean?* – Archie with his wide blotchy face and his veins popping out, his fat belly and his pudgy fingers and his nose inside his wine glass like a pig sniffing for truffles. Archie had bored her and Bamford O'Connell, sitting on her left, rigid with vintages. ''78's much better than the '83.'

'Oh really?'

'Oh yes, absolutely. Shouldn't be drinking these '83s for at least another five years.'

'No?'

'The '82s are very underrated. Depends on the grower, of course.'

'Of course.'

He held his goblet up to the light and peered at it, keeping it at a distance as though it contained raw sewage. 'Pity about the claret. Assertive little wine, the '62. Should have been drunk a year or two ago, of course – but ruined by the juniper berries anyway. Give it such a metallic taste. Surprised Richard didn't warn you about that.'

'Yes, well, he's full of secrets.'

'Thought he was a bit of a connoisseur?'

She felt a breeze blow again, and sensed the huge medieval iron chandelier above them move a fraction. She looked up. It had light bulbs now, turned down low, in place of the thick candles it had once held. Then she looked along the table at the guests: at Andreas, down towards the far end, near Richard. Andreas Berensen, the Swiss banker who sat, hardly talking, watching, smiling silently to himself as if he was above all this. Tall, stiff, athletic-looking, in his late forties or early fifties, a cold, rather correct face with a high forehead, his fair hair neatly groomed each side of his head but thinned to a light fuzz on top. And a black leather glove on his right hand which he had not taken off. He picked up his wine glass and drank, caught Sam's eye, gave a smile that was almost a smirk and put his glass back down.

She felt the cold shiver again. The same cold shiver when he had come in the door and shaken her hand, shaken it with the black leather glove. Like the glove in the dream. Daft. Don't be daft.

Christ.

So much was churning through her mind. Guilt. Anger. I could have saved them she'd said to Ken, and he'd looked back at her gently and told her hundreds of people had dreams about air disasters and there was nothing she could have done; told her that if she'd rung the airline they'd have treated her the way they treated hundreds of cranks that called them every week.

But the anger raged on inside her. Anger and bewilderment.

Why? How? Did I really dream it?

The back of her dress was making her angry too; she couldn't get it comfortable, couldn't get it to sit right without pulling in one direction. She wriggled her shoulders, tried to ease the back up. She'd already gone out, once, to her bedroom, and ripped out the shoulder pads. Now she felt she wanted to go and put them back in. She wriggled her shoulders around again and felt the label scratching the base of her neck.

45

Archie shoved the rim of his Sauternes against his damp lips, tilted it and made a noise like a draining bathtub. A thin rivulet of wine dribbled down onto his tie. He had food all over him as well. She wondered if his wife dumped him in the washing machine when they got home. 'This is good,' he said condescendingly. 'Really quite good indeed. Gets mugged by the trifle, of course.'

She glanced at Bamford O'Connell, sitting on her left. One of Richard's oldest friends. With his raffish, centre-parted hair, his crimson velvet jacket and ancient yellow silk bow-tie, he looked more like an Edwardian dandy than a psychiatrist. His wife, Harriet, frumpily bohemian, who always looked as if she ought to be wearing sandals even when she wasn't, was sitting in the middle of the table, lecturing Peter Rawlings, a stockbroker, on ecological responsibility. Green Awareness.

'You see all we are is sponge, we're just sponges,' she informed him in her shrill, earnest, church bazaar voice. 'We absorb our environment like sponges.'

'There's a Futures market in sponges,' Peter Rawlings murmured.

It had been a mistake putting them next to each other. They had nothing in common and he was looking bored. She wished she had him on her right instead of Archie Cruickshank who was now slouched in his chair, staring thoughtfully at the ceiling and making an unpleasant slurping sound.

Archie. Every business had its share of ghastly people who had to be – teeth-clenchedly – tolerated, humoured, fawned over. She had her share too. Like Jake, the copywriter.

Sucking up, they called it at school. Nothing changed. You went through life sucking up. Then you arrived in heaven, clutching your notebook full of credits, like

46

Aunt Angela, for the Biggest Suck Up of all. Hey God, that was a great place you made. Only seven days? Wow. How did you do it? You made a few little booboos, but they're minor really they are, didn't matter – well, OK, it would have been nice if you hadn't taken my Mummy and Daddy and dumped me with two of the most miserable people you could find, it would have been nice if I hadn't had four miscarriages and then nearly been killed by my little Nicky, and if you hadn't nuked Hiroshima. It would have been nice if my husband hadn't bonked that little—

It would have been nice if that aeroplane hadn't crashed.

Her throat tightened and her stomach knotted with fear. It seemed suddenly that the volume control in her head had been switched off, and she could see everyone but not hear them.

She felt icily cold. Alone.

163 DEAD IN BULGARIA AIR DISASTER

Everyone in the room had stopped in freeze-frame. Then the movie started again. Her ears felt hot. Boiling. Archie began to eat his trifle. Other than lecturing her on wine he had asked her nothing about herself except to inquire how many children she had, three times so far. His wife, with peroxided hair and enormous boobs, was at the far end of the table trying to wrest Richard's attention away from Andreas. She looked more like a stripper than the wife of a banker.

'This is wonderful trifle, Sam,' Bamford O'Connell said in his rich Dublin brogue.

'Thank you.' She smiled, and nearly blurted out, 'Actually it's Marks and Sparks,' but just managed to stop herself. It had worked fine. She had taken it out of the container and bashed it about a bit.

A short, compact ball of energy, with a wildly

expressive bon-viveur face, O'Connell attacked another spoonful with gusto. He made life seem like a feast, whether it was eating, drinking, talking, or even sitting. Absorbed in studying others, he gave the appearance that life seemed a treat, an endless supply of pleasures. Catching her eye, he raised his glass. 'A little toast to you for all your efforts.'

She smiled again, and wondered if he could see her face reddening. He was quick, full of charm, and razor sharp beneath his mask of eccentricity. She could never forget that he was a psychiatrist, was always conscious of every movement, every gesture she made in his presence, wondering what it signalled to him, what inadequacies, what secret yearnings, what secret fears she was beaming out from the way she cut her food or held her glass or turned and touched a friend.

'Alive?' said a voice down the far end. 'Are they alive?'

She glared at Richard to change the subject, but he looked away, exchanged a poorly camouflaged grin with Andreas, then looked at the blonde. 'Yah, of course. Apparently when they wriggle around, it's very erotic – if you like that sort of thing.'

'I think it's disgusting,' said Sheila Rawlings.

'I bet you get worse things than that told to you by your patients, don't you, Bamford?' said Peter Rawlings, abandoning Harriet in a cloud of environmentally hostile cigarette smoke.

O'Connell smiled and caught Sam's eye, showing her he understood. He turned his glass around in his hands. 'I do. For sure I do.' He winked at Sam. 'That's why we put our patients on couches – so they can't see our faces when they tell us these things.'

'Who does this thing with gerbils?' said Archie's wife,

her eyes wide open, eyelids batting like beaks of hungry birds.

'Gays in America,' said Richard.

The phone rang.

Richard jumped up, walked across to his desk and picked it up. There was a silence for a moment as everyone watched him.

'Harry, gorgeous!' he said loudly. 'Fine, darling, it's a good line. No, I haven't – had to leave early . . . yah . . . it's definitely going to be a new ulcer drug. Unwind the hedge. Sell the warrant if you've got a natural buyer at a 10% premium to the ADR. What about Sony?'

'Richard,' Sam called across. 'Can't you ring him back?'

He covered the mouthpiece, and raised a finger.

Bamford O'Connell pushed his tumbling hair back away from his forehead. 'There's no peace for the wicked,' he said to Sam.

'Fifty-five and a half, did you say? What's the FX rate?' He tapped out a series of numbers on his calculator, then glanced at Andreas. 'Yah, okay, go for it. Buy me 150,000 shares' worth. Bye, darling. Talk to you tomorrow. Bye.' Richard hung up, switched on his Reuters terminal and tapped on the keyboard.

Sam glared at him furiously.

'Richard—' Peter Rawlings said. 'Where's IBM trading?'

'Hang on a sec.' Richard tapped the keyboard again. 'Shit, New York's going bananas.'

Archie looked round anxiously, then back at Sam, clearly tempted to go and see for himself but thinking better of it. Only Andreas showed no concern; he sat staring ahead, sipping his wine and smiling a cold, contented smile. Maybe Swiss bankers knew it all long

49

before everyone else? Considered English money men to be their puppets?

'Bid 124 5/8. Offer 125 7/8,' Richard shouted out, then looked quizically at Andreas. Andreas gave him a brief nod of reassurance.

Sam got up from the table, conscious of the eyes on her, and walked over to Richard. 'Turn it off,' she hissed. 'At once.'

'I want to see if we're pushing the stock.'

'I don't care. I want it off. Now.'

She marched back to the table, all smiles, and started to clear away the pudding bowls.

'Can you get the cheese, please, Richard?' she said, carrying a stack out to the kitchen and putting it by the dishwasher. She switched the coffee percolator on. Richard followed her out with the rest. 'Brilliant bouillabaisse,' he said. 'That was seriously moreish.'

'It was dreadful. The venison was a complete disaster. Why's that man Andreas wearing a glove?'

'Always wears it.'

'It's creepy.'

'It's all right. I think he's had some accident – got an ugly scar on it, or something.' He put his hands on her shoulders. 'You're very uptight, Bugs. Relax.'

She shook herself free and tinned to face him. 'You're very drunk.'

'I'm all right.'

'You're behaving appallingly. Embarrassing everyone. We've had to put up with you wittering on about gerbils up bottoms, with your lecture on how Catherine the Great died being screwed by a horse, and with your going off and sitting down to work.'

'And you've been like a stuffed dummy all evening. You're not chatting; you're sitting at the end of the table staring into space. Don't you feel well?'

50

'I'm fine.'

'You look bloody awful. You've been looking white as a sheet all evening. I think you should see the quack.'

'I told you, I'm very spooked by that air disaster.'

'Oh come on, Bugs, you haven't turned into a fucking oracle.'

She glared back at him. Strangers. Two complete strangers. She could no more talk to him about anything important these days than talk to someone she met on a bus. It would be easier to talk to a stranger on a bus. She turned and went back into the room. Richard sat back in his place, and the blonde immediately oozed towards him. 'Have you ever tried it with a gerbil?' she said.

He lit a cigarette and inhaled loudly. 'No. Sam doesn't go in for kinky sex too much.' He saw Sam's face and looked away hastily. 'Actually, she's too busy dreaming these days.'

'Wildly erotic ones?'

'No – all about aeroplanes crashing. Reckons she dreamed about the one that went down in Bulgaria today.'

Sam caught Andreas's eye again; caught the cold, almost knowing smirk.

'I reckon she was dreaming of my penis. Hey, Bamford,' Richard shouted. 'Didn't Freud think aeroplanes were schlonkers?'

'Aren't you going to offer any port, Richard?' she said, trying to articulate clearly, hoping they couldn't hear the quavering in her voice.

Bamford O'Connell turned to her, and smiled a sympathetic smile that told her not to worry, not to be upset, that Richard was a fine chap really, and was just a bit sozzled.

'Port, ah, yes. Got some really good stuff. Warres '63. Archie?'

'Delicious cheese, this creamy one,' said the banker's wife in an equally creamy voice.

It comes from the breasts of fat blonde women she heard a voice in her head saying, and had to bite her lip to avoid blurting it out. 'Cambozola,' she said tartly, then remembered who she was, why she was here, and put on her forced smile again. 'Nice, isn't it?'

'How's the stately home coming along, Sam?' said O'Connell.

'It's hardly a stately home. It's just an old farmhouse.'

'I thought it was quite historic, with a ghost or something?'

She shook her head. 'I don't think so.'

'Moving, are you?' said Archie, his sudden interest startling her.

'We used to have a little weekend cottage and we bought something a bit bigger, but it got quite badly damaged in the hurricane.'

''Tis a good idea to get away from London,' said O'Connell. 'Have a break from the muggers.'

'The country's full of muggers, too,' said Richard. 'They drive around on tractors.'

Sam fetched the coffee and began pouring it out. O'Connell passed the cups down for her.

'Thanks,' she said, when he had finished.

'Are you all right, Sam?' he asked.

'Yes – I—' her voice trailed away.

'You're looking a bit peaky. Are you working hard?'

'No more than usual. I had a bit of a shock today, that's all.'

'What was that?'

'I—' She felt her face reddening. 'I . . . do you – do you know much about dreams, Bamford?'

'Dreams? Anyone who'd tell you they know a lot

about dreams would be lying. I probably know as much as anybody. Who do you ask?'

'Do you use them in your work?'

'Sure I do. They're very important – but there's still an awful lot we don't understand about them.'

'Adam's penis – the forbidden fruit,' Richard expounded. 'It's obvious. The serpent. Classic Freud. It was Adam's schlonker.'

'How clever,' cooed the blonde. 'I've never thought of that.'

Sam sipped her Perrier, then turned the glass around in her hands and looked at the psychiatrist. 'Do you think it's possible to – dream the future?' she said, feeling slightly self-conscious.

'Precognition?'

'Is that what it's called?'

'Do you mean dream events that actually happen?'

'Yes.'

He picked up his glass and sipped his port with such an expression of pleasure she wondered if she was missing out not having any. 'Fine stuff, this,' he said. 'Fine port. I'm going to have one hell of a headache tomorrow. Is that precognition?'

She tilted her head: 'I'm being serious, Bamford.'

He smiled, then frowned. 'Is this to do with the air disaster on the news this evening? What Richard was just talking about?'

She nodded.

He studied her. 'I have patients that see the future all the time.'

'Really?'

'They think so.'

'And do they?'

'I'd be a rich man, wouldn't I? I'd get them to tell me

53

the winners of horse races. I could sell investment tips to Richard. We'd clean up on the Market.'

There was a loud pop above her and Sam felt a sharp pain in her hand. She let out a shriek, and stared down. Slivers of glass littered the table all around her. A large shard stuck out of her Perrier water. A small stain of blood spread across her index finger. She looked around, disoriented. Everyone was staring up at the chandelier.

'How odd,' someone said.

'Must have been some paint on it; paint can do that,' said another voice.

'Must be one of those current surges,' someone else said. 'You know, in the commercial breaks everyone rushes to the loo. It overloads the electrical circuits.'

'But it's after midnight.'

Sam stared up at the chandelier. One of the bulbs had exploded; there was a solitary jagged shard left sticking out of the socket.

A cold prickle of fear swept through her. The pop echoed around her head, faded then came back louder, carrying with it a dim memory from the past that was fuzzy and unclear.

She frowned and looked down: at the grapes on the cheeseboard, at the tiny slivers of broken glass that glinted in the candlelight, at the knuckleduster jewels on the blonde's podgy fingers, at the dark empty silence of the flat beyond the table. The memory pricked through her mind like the pain of the prick in her finger. Then, once more, she caught Andreas's eye; he curled his gloved fingers around his glass and smiled at her.

6

Sam heard the sound of a tap and the vigorous brushing of teeth, and turned over in bed with the uncomfortable realisation that a new day had arrived without the previous one having departed. She opened her eyes slowly; they felt raw, bound with wire. A shaft of light spilled out of the bathroom door and was mopped up by the grey darkness, the lingering, theatrical darkness of early morning in winter. She could almost feel someone's hand on the dimmer lever, slowly moving it.

Cue daylight!

Enter Richard, stage right, from bathroom. He wears a navy towelling dressing gown from which his legs stick out, white and hairy. His blond hair is wet and slicked back, and there is a spot of blood on his chin where he has nicked a zit. He stretches back his lips to reveal shining white teeth.

Cut to product shot.

ZING! The toothpaste that more and more dentists are recommending.

ZING! The ecologically sound way to brush your teeth. Yes, folks! Because when you've finished the paste, you can eat the tube!

Yet another Personal Nourishment System brought to you by the manufacturers of Napalm. Plaque removed. Foliage decimated. Faces peeled away.

Sam jumped, shivering.

Someone walking over your grave, her aunt used to say grimly.

She tried to switch off the weird commercial that was playing in her mind in her twilight half-awake state. The hypnopompic state, she had read in an article once.

Hypnogogic and hypnopompic, when you saw weird things as you drifted off to sleep or woke up.

She relaxed for a moment, but then felt a sense of gloom creeping around her, enveloping her. Something bad. Like waking up after you got drunk and knowing you'd done something you regretted. Only it wasn't that. It was something worse, this time. She tried to think but it eluded her. Her index finger was hurting like hell. She freed it from under the sheet and peeled off the thin strip of Elastoplast bound around it. There was a crash which shook the room.

'Bugger.'

She looked up, blinking against the brightness of the bedside lamp which Richard had switched on, and saw him lying on his face on the floor, his legs piniored together inside his trousers. He hauled himself up onto his hands and stared around the room, with a puzzled expression.

'Are you OK?' She glanced at the clock. 0544. He was late.

'Think I'm still a bit pissed.' He rolled over, sat on the floor, tugged his trousers off, then pulled them on again slowly, getting each foot down the correct leg this time.

'I'm not surprised, the way you and Bamford were carrying on.'

He rubbed his head and screwed up his eyes. 'We drank nearly two bottles of that port.'

'Why don't you have a lie-in?'

'Japan's going bananas.'

'It can probably go bananas without you.'

'Could be up four hundred points by now.' He sat down on the bed, screwed up his eyes and wiped his face with his hands. 'I've got a mega hangover,' he said. 'A serious wipe-out.'

He stumbled into his shoes, kissed her and she smelled the fumes on his breath.

'I wouldn't drive,' she said. Take a taxi.'

'I'll be all right. Fucking good evening,' he said. 'Great scoff.'

There was a click, and then the room went dark. She lay back and closed her eyes again. She heard the front door slam and the room was very silent, suddenly. So quiet you could hear a pin drop.

Or a light bulb explode.

She fell into a deep sleep.

She was woken by the roar of a bulldozer outside. A launch travelling fast up-river, crunching through the water. Someone was whistling 'Colonel Bogey'. She slipped her feet out onto the thick carpet and sat on the edge of the bed staring at them; the varnish on her toenails was chipped. A few traces of hairs showed on her calves; time for another waxing; she smelled the foul smell of the wax, and still had the small yellowy mark on the front of her shin where the idiot girl had burnt her last time.

There was the sound of a pneumatic drill, then a louder noise, from above: an aeroplane coming into the City Airport a few hundred yards up the river.

She caught a glimpse of herself in the mirror on the wall, and sat up straighter.

Deportment, young lady.

She ran her hands into her long brown hair and squeezed it tightly; she lifted it up and let it flop back down, giving herself a sideways glance in the mirror. Nice hair, rich, brown, chic.

Chic.

She could smile about it now, because it no longer mattered. But the sting had stayed with her for years.

That morning in London thirteen – fourteen – years

57

ago, when her aunt had taken her, under silent protest, to the Lucy Clayton modelling school.

'It'll do you good,' her aunt had said. 'Give you confidence.'

She could still see the withering scorn on the reedy interviewer's face. 'You're too small,' she had said. 'Much too small. Five-foot five, are you? We need five-foot seven here. At least five-foot seven, I'm afraid.' She had pushed Sam's face around as if she were a horse. 'Quite a nice face dear, very English Rose. You're really quite pretty, dear, quite chic.' The woman had said the word disdainfully, as if it were a deformity, not a compliment. 'Chic, but not *beautiful*.' Then the woman had turned to her aunt. 'Nice legs. Probably her best feature. Not long enough, of course, to be a leg model.'

Sam padded across the carpet and pulled the curtain open a fraction. It was a flat grey morning out there, a good hour yet from full light. She stared out at the brown water of the Thames, stretching out into the distance like a grubby tarpaulin. A grimy black and white police launch droned through it, rocking sharply, cutting it like a blunt knife. An empty lighter shifted about restlessly, moored to an enormous rusting black buoy. She heard the cry of a gull and saw the shadow of a bird, swooping low, slamming the surface of the water for an instant. The cold seeped through the glass and through her skin, and she hugged herself with her arms, rubbing her hands up and down them.

A duet of drills hammered in the building site below. A workman in a donkey jacket and orange hard hat walked slowly across the site, through the stark glare of the floodlighting, carefully picking his path, heading towards a fire burning in a black oil drum. Another workman somewhere out of sight was still whistling, this time ragged strains of 'Waltzing Matilda'.

58

At the edge of the site a bulldozer reversed, dug, swivelled, dumped, behind a hoarding with huge red letters. RIVERSIDE DEVELOPMENT. RIVERSIDE LIFESTYLES. The workman stopped, knelt down and pawed at the ground with his hand. He pulled something out, stared at it, rubbed it with his finger, then tossed it away over his shoulder.

Sam saw the ball of flame rising high into the sky, the engine showering sparks, bouncing, dancing.

The image froze for an instant in front of her and she could hear nothing. Silence.

Her finger was stinging as if there was a sliver of glass inside the skin and she put it in her mouth and sucked it hard. She saw the cold smile on Andreas Berensen's face. The fingers of his leather glove curling around the glass. Richard had been fawning over him: filling his glass first, asking his opinion first on each of the wines. Toadying. Sucking up. Richard never used to be like this. He used to be interested in her, used to be a proud man; Richard never used to suck up to anyone.

The cacophony outside started again, louder, deafeningly loud. Thought for the Day was beginning on the radio; she heard the cheery voice of Rabbi Blue, rich as treacle. 'I wonder,' he said, 'how many people remember their dreams? I wonder sometimes whether God has dreams?'

Clothes. Dressing. Image. What to wear today? She yawned, tried to concentrate, to focus on the day ahead. A first cut screening this morning, then lunch with Ken. She went into the shower, felt the fine spray, turned the temperature down cold. The needles of water drummed against her skin, hard, hurting. She came out and dried herself vigorously.

Better. Heavy dose of negative ions. One per cent better. What time had they gone to bed? Three? Four?

Port. Coffee. More port. More coffee. Andreas had left first, when Richard and Bamford started telling jokes. Harriet had lectured her on the state of the world. Harriet was worried about plastic; it gave out gases; you could get cancer just from sitting on a vinyl car seat.

She opened her wardrobe. First cuts: tense, tense, tense. Who was going to be at the screening? Hawksmuir. Horrible Hawksmuir. Jake yesterday and Hawksmuir today. Her two least favourite people. Dress to kill. It was a John Galliano and Cornelia James day, she decided.

She winced at the pain in her finger. From one tiny cut? Then she winced again from the sudden sharp pain she now felt in her head that went down her neck, deep into her stomach. She felt as if she had been slit open by a filleting knife. Weird. She felt weird. Seriously weird.

She put on a Galliano two piece. Battle dress. Fashion, she thought. Fashion was bewildering. As soon as you got the hang of it, it changed. She pulled out a stunning Cornelia James shawl and draped it around her shoulders.

Better. Great. Terrific.

She took a handkerchief out of a drawer, a small white handkerchief with French lace edging and her initials, S.C. embroidered in blue in one corner, and put it in her handbag. She tugged a comb through her hair, studied herself in the mirror then smiled, pleased with the effect. 'Zap!' she said. 'Kapow!' She clapped her hands together and walked out of the bedroom, wondering why those words had suddenly come into her head.

'No, you'll never get away with it,' said a voice with a deep American accent.

She heard Nicky giggle. There were several explosions.

'Not this time, Batman.'

KAPOW! SOCK! BIFF! BAM! ZAP!

'We'll see about that!'

Nicky and Helen were sitting at the table, watching the television. Nicky was holding his spoon in the air and milk was trickling down into his shirt cuff. Helen, spellbound, hadn't noticed, and Sam felt a flash of irritation. She grabbed the spoon and staunched the flow of milk with a kitchen towel.

Helen stood up. 'Sorry, Mrs Curtis – I—'

'OK,' Sam said, slightly coolly, giving Nicky back his spoon. Then she turned off the television.

'Aww!' said Nicky.

Helen sat down again, blushing.

'Nicky's watching too much television, Helen. He shouldn't be watching it while he's eating.' She smiled at Helen, realising she had sounded fierce, trying to reassure her.

'Sorry,' Helen said again.

Sam sat down at the table and poured out some orange juice. Nicky eyed her sulkily.

'What's happening at school today, Tiger?'

The Esso ads had worked on Nicky. When he was four he was a tiger. Ran around on all fours. Pounced. Hid in cupboards with a freebie tiger's tail sticking out. 'Tiger in here! Tiger in here!'

He stretched out his arm, seized the Sugar Puffs pack and poured a second helping sloppily into his bowl, spilling them all around. Without bothering to pour any milk, he shovelled cereal into his mouth.

'Grumpy, this morning?' Sam asked.

'I didn't sleep very well.'

'Mummy's tired today too.'

Mummy feels like shit.

'You were making noises,' he said.

'Did we keep you awake? I'm sorry.'

He shoved in more cereal, chewing with his mouth open.

'Thought you were a Tiger, not a camel.'

He closed his mouth and continued chewing, then stretched out and took a mouthful of juice. 'Batman,' he said. 'I want Batman.'

'Too much television is not good for you.'

'You make television.'

'Just the ads.'

'Ads are yucky. You made the ads for that new cereal. It's yuck. It tastes like dog's do.'

'And how do you know what dog's do tastes like?'

'It tastes of yuck.'

She caught Helen's eye. Helen looked at her with the uncertainty of a child looking at her teacher. Sam finished her juice and glanced at her watch. Eight-fifteen.

'Mummy's late. She's got to go.'

She went through into the living area to switch on the answering machine, and stared around the huge room with a faint feeling of dismay. The refectory dining table was still covered in coffee cups, half-empty glasses, overflowing ashtrays, butter dishes, and napkins strewn around like confetti. Two half-full bottles of Perrier water were missing their caps; she walked over and rummaged around for them. She found the stopper of the port decanter and put that on. A sliver of glass sparkled at her from an open salt cellar. She looked up warily at the iron chandelier. The one jagged shard of glass was still in the socket. The rest of the bulbs were fine, except that they were still on. She walked over to the wall and switched them off.

The room was filled with a grey light that hung heavily, thick with the smell of stale smoke and evaporating alcohol, a greyness that seeped into her skin like damp, that would make her clothes and her hair smell of cigar smoke if she stayed much longer. She glanced around at Richard's roll-top desk in the corner, his computer terminal beside it, at the grand piano with an antique opium-smoking kit on the lid, the two sofas down the far end by the television and the gas-log fire, the armorial shields on the bare brick walls, the swords, the medieval artefacts, the huge copper ladle for pouring gold that Richard had bought when the Royal Mint was being demolished. Richard's things, relics of his family's bloody past, portraits of dead ancestors, scrolls with thick red seals. Bare bricks and oak. A man's flat. It always had been and always would be. A helicopter roared past outside, a dark shadow passing the window.

'Bye, Tiger.' She stood by the front door, struggling into her coat.

Nicky came out of the kitchen. 'Bye,' he said flatly, walking towards his room.

'Hey! Tiger!'

He stopped and turned.

'Don't I get a kiss goodbye?'

He hesitated for a moment, then trotted over to her. 'All right,' he said. 'I'll forgive you. This time.'

'And if you're very good, I'll forgive you.'

'What for?'

'For being rude to your mummy.'

He pouted, then kissed her, and put his arms around her neck. 'I'm sorry, Mummy.' He kissed her again then turned and scampered off.

'Have a good day at school.'

'Friday! Yippee!'

Sam opened the front door and picked the *Daily Mail* off the mat. She turned to her horoscope. Pisces.

'Travel may bring surprises. Avoid arguments today,

however much a close colleague may irritate you. Both today and the weekend will be unsettling and may tax even your very strong inner resources.'

Thank you very much. Hope you have a nice day too. She put the paper inside her briefcase, closed the door behind her and walked down the dark hall, four floors up in the cold stone building that was still at the moment in the middle of nowhere. Another few years and there would be a thriving metropolis all around: colour, light, people, shops. Right now it was a mess; it was hard to tell what they were putting up from what they were pulling down.

She went out into the street, into the light that was a brighter shade of grey, into the smells of diesel oil and burning tar and the salty tang of the river. She felt the faintly gritty taste of dust in her mouth and heard the distant clatter of a train, the hissing of pneumatics, the rumble of a cement mixer.

Horoscopes. Who cared about horoscopes? Who cared about dreams? About light bulbs?

The grey E-Type was covered in a light coating of dust that had settled on it since yesterday, and their elderly Range Rover next to it had virtually changed colour under the stuff. She climbed into the Jaguar, pushed the key into the ignition and switched it on. The red warning light appeared and the fuel pump ticked furiously. She pushed up the choke lever and pressed the starter button.

The engine turned over several times, whining, snuffling, then fired with a sharp bang, and rumbled into life. The rev counter flickered wildly then settled down. She flipped down the screenwasher toggle, switched on the wipers, pushed the stubby gear lever into first, struggled with the handbrake, then gripped the thin wood-rimmed steering wheel and eased the car forward, listening to its engine sucking and grumbling like an old man woken from a comfortable sleep. The three small wipers smeared the salt and dust into a translucent film, and she gave the screen another squirt.

She heaved on the wheel, pulling out around a parked lorry into Wapping High Street, then released it, feeling it spin through her hands so fast she had to be careful not to let it burn them. Old things. Retro. Ken's idea. Heavily into retro. Run old cars as company cars. Smart image, good investment. She stopped at the main road, waiting for a gap in the traffic. A bus stopped in front of her, blocking her, and she glared at the driver who was looking fixedly ahead; like a carthorse in blinkers, she thought angrily.

Then she saw the poster on the side of the bus, staring her in the face as if it was taunting her, silver with an aeroplane and a blue prancing tiger, and the words boldly emblazoned.

'CHARTAIR – A GREAT LITTLE AIRLINE . . . NOW A GREAT BIG ONE!'

7

She parked and hurried across Covent Garden towards her club. There was just time for a quick swim. She tried to swim every morning before work, unless she had an early meeting or was travelling, and she wanted to swim badly today, to try to wake up some more, to clear the fuzziness out of her head.

She felt a bit better as she left the club, slightly more human but not much, walked down the narrow street and across the huge open square, past the old covered market building of Covent Garden, among the pigeons and the street cleaners who had the place to themselves for another hour yet. A gust of cold icy wind whiplashed her damp hair, and a piece of paper scudded along past her feet like a wounded bird.

DREAMS!

The word rippled through the glass of the shop window.

UNLOCK YOUR OWN SECRET WORLD!

DREAMS. DREAMS. DREAMS.

The window was filled with books on dreams.

DREAMS – YOUR MAGIC MIRROR.

THE POWER OF DREAMS.

THE A–Z OF DREAMS.

One of the small alternative bookshops she passed every day without noticing. She glanced at her watch, 9.20. She tried the door and was faintly surprised that it opened. She went in and the shop was filled with a crisp, pristine papery smell. New jackets, fresh print; it was a good smell. Books. She loved books.

A tall man in a black polo-neck glided noiselessly across the floor, his head swivelling from side to side like a robot. He stopped a few feet from Sam, inclined his head and raised his eyebrows. He looked clean, scrubbed, and smelt of organic soap.

'Dreams,' said Sam. 'I'm—' She felt flustered for a moment. He was making her nervous. He was the sort of man she should be asking for the complete works of Marcel Proust. 'I'm interested in something on dreams.'

'Mmm,' He rotated and glided across the floor, and made a wide, sweeping arc with his arm at a row of shelves, all labelled 'Dreams'. He turned around. 'Is it anything particular?' He spoke in a studied, hushed public-library whisper, and his breath smelt of peppermints. He ran his finger along the spines as if he were caressing a sleeping girl's back, then stopped and tapped

66

one lightly. He pulled it out and held it in the air. 'This is a possibility. Are you a student?'

'No,' said Sam, feeling flattered. No, but I'd like to be. I'd like to look like one, and be as carefree as one. And be as young as one. An Oxford man, are you? Me? I was educated at the University of Life. Know it? Turn first left down the Bitter Vale Of Tears. Graduated to Thompson's. Never heard of it? J. Walter Thompson. Started as a secretary. Then became a production assistant. By the time I was twenty-six I had been made a junior producer (sounds the bizz, eh?). Then I gave it all up for a sprog. Oh, yes, working again now. Working and dreaming. Had a dream about an air disaster, actually – you probably read about it – that one in Bulgaria? I could have saved them all. Should have rung up the airline, shouldn't I? EVERYBODY OFF, BOYS, THIS ONE'S A GONER!

Would you have done?

Shit. I'm going nuts. 'No – I – I'm a layman. I'm just interested in – er – dream interpretation.'

He replaced it with a slingshot flick of his wrist, and arched his back a fraction. 'Ahh, hmm, let me see, I think, yes, this you'd probably get on with awfully well,' he said, as if he'd known her all his life. He pulled out a slim paperback with a picture of an eyeball and a fish on the front cover. 'Yes, this is the one. *What Your Dreams Really Say*.'

Sam glanced at the back cover. 'Dr Colin Hare, lecturer in Psychology at the University of Hull, has made Freud, Jung and other great interpreters of dreams accessible to the layman in this concise dictionary of dream symbolism.'

' "It lives beside my bed . . . essential waking reading." ' *The Times*.

She flipped through the index, then turned to the page headed 'Aeroplane', and scanned through.

'Flying: The longing to lift off, get out of a rut. Erection and sexual fantasies. Aeroplane = phallus. Can also = womb.'

She looked through some more pages.

'Swimming. Often means sex. The struggle with basic impulses or other problems. Can literally mean worry about keeping your head above water.'

She turned again to the review quotes on the back cover, reading them for reassurance. 'Fine,' she said. 'I'll take it.'

She left the shop, folded the paper bag around the book and put it into her handbag. She walked through the closed bric-a-brac stalls and crossed the street to the office, a narrow building sandwiched between a publisher and a shop that sold surgical appliances.

The ground floor windows had black Venetian blinds, with the blow-up of a strip of celluloid running across, and the words 'Ken Shepperd Productions' repeated between the frames. She pushed open the heavy chromium-framed Deco door, and went into the stark airiness of the reception atrium.

Sections of motor cars stuck out from the white walls, like strange modern sculptures. The front three feet of a red Alfa Romeo. The tail section of a Volkswagen Beetle. The seats in the waiting area were old leather car seats set into clear perspex pedestals, and the receptionist sat, looking slightly daft Sam always thought, behind the steering wheel of the sawn-off front end of a white convertible Cadillac Eldorado.

'Morning, Lucy.'

The receptionist stopped typing and looked up, a bleary-eyed confection of mohair sweater, blotched makeup and streaked wild hair, which she tried to shake away from her face, without success. 'Oh, yah, hi.' She paused. 'Yah, morning. Gosh.' She smiled sleepily. 'Someone called.'

'Anyone in particular?'

Sam watched Lucy scrabbling through a pile of message slips. She looked as though she'd had even less sleep than herself. 'Ah, somewhere here – yah. Rob Kempson, from Praiseworthy – wants you to come in for a brief – either—' She peered at the note. 'Yah, Monday or Tuesday morning. Could you call him as soon as poss? Yah – gosh – no others so far.'

Sam took the slip and blinked, her eyes feeling slightly gritty, stinging from the chlorine in the pool and from tiredness. She walked past the life-size wax-work of Ken slouched in a wicker chair behind Lucy, presiding over his emporium from behind the copy of the *Daily Mail* that was changed every day, and glanced down warily, as she always did, to check that he wasn't playing a macabre joke by sitting there in person, as he had done once. The waxwork sculptor had captured the details well: the denim shirt and the curling hair, black turning to grey, and the slightly ragged, slightly dented I'm-going-to-one-day-change-the-world-before-it-changes-me-face. Everything except the eyes which stared blankly, lifelessly, unlike his real sharp blue eyes.

Windows of the soul. Strange things, eyes.

The waxy sheen of his skin wasn't like him either. The waxy sheen that did not smell of tobacco and talc and hairs and clothes and booze; the sculpture smelt of nothing and was cold to touch, shiny and hard.

This is what he would look like when he was dead.

She climbed the elegant staircase, past more sections of cars: the rear of an old London taxi recessed into the wall, with the door removed so you could sit in it if you wanted, the slatted, cobalt blue bonnet of a Bugatti, held to the wall by leather straps.

The building was on three storeys, with a basement. Ken's office was at the top, in the eaves, and his snooker room was in the basement which was also their viewing room. Sam's office was on the first floor, and there was a tiny office further along occupied by Drummond, their gofer.

She walked down the landing and into the stark black and white of the office she shared with their PA, who was sitting at her desk in a thick sweet fug of cigarette smoke.

'Morning, Claire.'

Claire had a maddening habit of never saying 'good morning'. Some days she did not even look up, and if Sam was in the office first, Claire would come in silently and sit down. Today she swept her short layered hair back from her round, pug-like face, and smiled. It was her favourite bad-news-coming smile. 'Can you guess what?'

Sam looked down at her and raised her eyebrows. She seemed to get a kick out of announcing problems.

'Giraffes! He wants four giraffes!'

The smoke was making Sam's eyes even sorer, and her finger was hurting like hell. 'Who wants four giraffes?'

'Ken.'

'Is he starting a zoo?'

'I don't know.' She shook her head. 'I give up. I really give up. Where on earth can I get four giraffes from?'

'Harrods,' said Sam, taking advantage of the stunned silence her remark brought to get past Claire's desk to her own safe haven by the window. And air, fresh air, however cold it might be. She pushed the window open and stared out.

'Harrods?' said Claire.

'Yes. They sell everything.' Sam watched a mummer dressed in black sitting on the kerb, drinking coffee from a thermos, then turned round and sat down at her desk. 'Try some of the animal companies in the Knowledge,' she said, picking up the phone and shuffling through her mail with her free hand.

'There's another problem. This one's a real disaster. It's the Polar night.'

'Bears?' said Sam, punching the dial buttons.

'No! Darkness. The Polar night. Didn't anyone realise?'

'Realise what?'

'The quote we've done for the fish fingers shoot – you know, JWT – the Superfingers – the trawler going past an iceberg? In the Arctic?'

Sam nodded, listening to the voice at the other end of her phone. 'Can I speak to Rob Kempson, please?'

'It's the Polar night, Darkness! No one's thought of that.'

'Could you tell him I returned his call, please. I'll be here for another half-hour, then back this afternoon.' She looked up at Claire. 'Studio, Claire. It'll be a studio shoot.'

'It's got to be location. The client specifically wants the Arctic.' She lit a new cigarette and flapped the smoke away with her hand. 'I don't know. I give up. I really give up.'

The door opened and Drummond shuffled in, tall, thin, hunched and dopey, like a sleepwalking anglepoise. 'New showreel,' he said, and sniffed, staring around the room as if he had just arrived in outer space. He held up a hard grey plastic box. 'Where do you want it?'

71

'It's got the BMW in, hasn't it, Drummond?' Sam said.

He nodded and sniffed again. 'And the Bacardi.'

'Leave it here, I want to see it. Ken and I both need to check it.'

'Do you know anything about giraffes?' asked Claire.

'Giraffes?'

'Yes, giraffes.'

Drummond gazed at her blankly, a drip running from his coke-addled nose. 'They don't dream much.'

'Dream?' Claire said.

'They only dream about half an hour a night. Shows they're not very smart.'

'Are you an expert on dreams, Drummond?' said Sam.

'Me?' He looked around the room, as if to check that he was the Drummond she was addressing. 'Weird things, dreams. Heavy duty. Inner Space.' He frowned, put the U-matic cassette on Sam's desk, then wandered out of the room.

'Mrs Wolf said this was going to be a bad month,' said Claire.

'Wolf?' said Sam dimly. 'Wolves. Giraffes. There seem to be a lot of animals around this morning.'

'My clairvoyant. Mrs Wolf.' Claire picked up the phone and started dialling.

Sam went out down the corridor to the coffee machine and poured herself a cup. She blew away the steam, took a couple of sips, then went back to her office and buzzed Ken on the intercom. 'We ought to leave in five minutes. We're due at the cutting room at 10.30.'

'I thought we were screening here.'

'Hawksmuir always wants to see the first cut on the cutting table. Do you want to walk or shall I call a taxi?'

'We'll leg it. Pick you up on the way down.'

Sam looked at Claire. 'Is she accurate, your clairvoyant?'

'Yes, she's very good. She told me Roger and I would split up.'

'Does she ever give you good news?'

'Sometimes.' Claire smiled, and stared up at the ceiling, her eyes shrinking back into their fleshy sockets and glazing over, almost as if she was going into a trance. 'Sometimes she gives me very good news.'

They stood in the small windowless cutting room, surrounded by racks of film cans, loose strips of celluloid and sticky labels, millions of them, attached to everything in sight and written all over with marker pens, and stared down at the small screen of the Steenbeck editing table.

Tony Riley, their editor, killed the overhead light, and the machine rolled with faint hum and a click of sprockets. The cream bonnet of a car appeared on the screen, long, stylish, vintage. A hand came into view and turned up the volume on the dashboard radio.

I'm in paradise . . . I'm in paradise . . . I'm in paradise. Sam mentally sang the words of the song that hadn't yet been recorded, the hard beat that would play over this. The camera pulled back to reveal a young, trendy man driving a large Fifties convertible Mercedes through the night. He was drumming the steering wheel with his hands in time to the beat of the music, and driving very slowly, no more than crawling speed. The camera showed a close-up of his face, slick, cocky, hedonistic, then cut to the view ahead. A long, narrow street, full of elegant houses with open doorways down both sides.

Leaning out of each doorway was a girl, dressed

73

erotically. As he drove slowly though, eyeing them, they came forward, seductively brushing the car with their hands, their feet, with the fronds of a whip, raising their gowns a fraction, showing their stockings, their garters. He turned from side to side in his seat, humming the tune.

I'm in paradise . . . I'm in paradise . . . I'm in paradise . . .

There was a cut to a hospital bed, with a man lying in it, being wheeled along the street by two orderlies in white. The girls recoiled in horror as the bed passed through, and stood in frozen silence, watching as it was brought to a halt in front of the Mercedes. The camera zoomed in on a gaunt, desperately ill young man. He was just recognisable as the same man who had been driving the Mercedes.

'Heaven or hell—' The words ran through her head automatically. 'Don't leave the choice to someone else. Use a condom.' The camera tracked past the bed and showed the Mercedes again, abandoned at the side of the road, burning fiercely. Ahead down the street, more cars were on fire and flames were leaping from the houses.

The machine clicked off and the overhead light clicked on.

Silence. Always a bloody silence.

Director's first cut.

The script according to Ken Shepperd. International award-winning director. Twenty grand's worth of fee.

The silence got longer.

We came in on budget, Sam thought. My contribution. Iron rod rule over Ken who would cheerfully have blown it, blown the profit.

To get it even righter than right.

Tom Hawksmuir, tall, sour copywriter, with a crop of blond hair twenty years too young for his booze-lined face, Euan Driver and Bentley Hewes. The agency Creative Team.

Hawksmuir punted the first missile. 'Looks like he's driving the Merc out of a fucking showroom.'

'The girl with the boa feather – didn't you shoot a close-up, Ken, when she climbs on the bonnet and tries to straddle the star?' said Bentley Hewes.

'Wouldn't get that through the IBA in a million years,' Ken said.

Cigarettes lit up. Ken. Tom. Tony Riley. Three out of six smoking. She wanted one too. So badly. The smoke irritated her nose and she sneezed. She opened her handbag and rummaged for her handkerchief; it wasn't there. Strange, she thought, rummaging again, unzipping the inside pockets and checking those too. She remembered clearly taking out the handkerchief, the one with her initials embroidered on; could have sworn she'd put it in her bag.

'The girls,' said Hawksmuir, 'they simply don't look like tarts. They look like sweet little girls from next door in fancy dress.'

'I thought that's the point,' Ken said, slowly, tersely.

'The script said tarts. Hookers, prostitutes. Not little girls dressed up in their mother's finery for a laugh.' Hawksmuir stared penetratingly at Sam. 'What do you think of the girls, Sam? Do you think they're sexy?' He gave her a leering smile. 'What do women find sexy in other women?'

'I thought the point of the commercial was to hit teenagers, Tom,' she said, finding she too was having to make an effort to stay calm. 'I don't think many teenagers go to prostitutes. They sleep with the girls next door, and they think that that's safe. We've tried to use girls that we felt teenagers, male and female, would relate to.'

'Let's go back to that girl in the boa.'
'Let's have another run through.'

'Let's get pissed, said Ken, as they walked back down Wardour Street. It had turned into a fine, clear day, cold in the blustery wind; crisp. They ducked into the trattoria. It was early. Clean pink tablecloths and shiny cutlery, bread rolls and grissini sticks in their packets, neat, undisturbed.

Sam still felt unsteady when she left the office shortly after six, the stale, caraway taste of the kümmel they had drunk with the coffee lingering in her mouth. She tried to work out how much they had had: two bottles of wine, maybe three, then the liqueur, two glasses, at least. 'Clear your head,' Ken had said.

Clear it? Christ. She screwed up her eyes and blinked, and the lights of the early London evening all shifted to the left. There was a dull ache in her stomach, a sharp cheese-knife pain down the centre of her forehead and she was shaking slightly from too many cups of coffee.

She stumbled over a paving stone. The sharp cold air was making her worse, she realised, as she walked unsteadily towards the car park. She wondered for a moment whether she was all right to drive, stopped, and decided she definitely was not. She saw a 'Hire' sign bearing down out of the dark, and tripped forward with her arm raised.

'Wapping High Street,' she said to the driver. 'Sixty-four.' She wondered if she was slurring her words. The rear seat seemed to rise up to meet her before she had got to it, and she sat down with a sharp thump. Oblivion. For a time in the restaurant, there had been oblivion, and it had felt good, felt marvellous, felt as if she was standing on the top of the world.

Ken hadn't mocked her dream. He was interested, wanted to hear all she could remember, helped her compare it to the events that had been reported in the news, on the television, on the radio. He didn't have an explanation, but he believed her. Coincidence, he had said finally, trying to reassure her. It was nice just to be believed.

Now the oblivion had mostly faded and she was remembering again.

She stared out at the news-vendor's hoarding, dimly lit by the street lamp above it, and listened to the rattle of the taxi's engine as it waited to pull out into the Strand.

AIR DISASTER – PILOT ERROR!

Yes. Now they knew too. They should have rung her and she could have told them. All the grisly details.

Me? Sure, what you want to know? I was there. Eye witness account!

This is Sam Curtis. News At Ten. In Bulgaria.

She sat back and peered out at the lights, the lights that passed, blinked, dazzled and were gone; lights that lit up the mannequins in the shops and threw shadows across the pavement through which people hurried against the cold, against the drizzle, against the clock. Did they all dream too? she wondered, feeling a sudden wave of nausea. She swallowed hard and held her breath, and the wave passed. She closed her eyes and drifted into a jumbled morass of thought.

Then she noticed the taxi had stopped.

'Sixty-four?' said a voice.

She opened her eyes, confused, blinking in the darkness. She felt an enormous weight of tiredness, too tired almost to get out of the taxi. She glanced at the red digits of the meter. £3.75. She pulled a banknote out of her handbag and pushed it through the glass. 'Make it four pounds fifty.'

He took it and sat in silence for a moment, then turned around and thrust something back through the partition window at her. 'I'd rather have money.'

She felt a thin, stiff piece of card. 'What's this?' she asked.

'It's what you gave me.'

'I gave you a—' She paused, and blinked again as the interior light came on and stared down at what she was holding.

An orange and white airline boarding card, with the word CHARTAIR printed on it and the number, slightly crooked, that had been stuck on afterwards. 35A.

'I didn't – this . . . I didn't give you this – I' She looked up baffled, trying to see the taxi driver's face in the darkness of his cab. Then his own interior light came on, and she could see clearly.

She felt the shock ripple through her, picking her up from her seat like a surging wave and dumping her hard on the floor. She lay there, humiliated, still not wanting to believe, looked again at the boarding card, confused, trembling with fear, then back up at the hooded face that was staring at her, the mouth and one eye grinning malevolently through the slits, the other eye nothing but a livid red socket with the lashes bent inwards.

8

Time froze.

She saw the smile, the hatred; the determination.

Oh Christ, somebody out there help me. Please.

She shot a brief glance through the taxi's window at the darkness, wondering if she could out-run him. The

78

street was quiet and there were alleyways and hoardings and empty buildings. If he caught her he could take her to any of a hundred places where she would not be found for days.

He was chuckling, enjoying his own private joke, watching her, grinning at her. Taunting her.

She stared at the boarding card, then up again, trying to understand, trying to get her brain to work properly, to make sense. She was in a taxi. She must be safe. Surely.

She shot out her hand and tugged hard on the door handle.

But it would not move.

She threw all her weight onto it. Still nothing. She stared up at him angrily, and he was roaring with laughter. She crawled to her knees and tried to pull down the window, and the metal flap sheared away, cutting her finger. She dived across the other side, and tried that door handle too. But she knew, even before she reached it, that it would not move. She scrambled back, grabbed the other door handle again and shook it wildly.

'Help! Let me out! Let me out!'

'Lady?'

'Help me!'

'Lady?'

She shook the handle again.

'Lady? Are you all right lady?'

The voice cut through the darkness, puzzled, gentle.

'Lady?'

She stared, blinking at the pool of orange light. Street lamp, she thought.

'Are you all right, lady?'

She heard the rattle of the taxi's engine, and a man with a kind face, in a peaked cap and moustache, was staring down at her worriedly from the driver's seat.

79

She suddenly realised she was lying on the floor, felt it shaking, could smell the rubber matting. She was clutching the door handle. 'I—' Her head swam with confusion and she thought for a moment she was going to pass out. She closed her eyes tightly, then opened them again. 'I'm sorry,' she said. 'I . . . had – I—'

He came round and opened the door for her, then helped her to her feet and out of the cab. 'I thought you was having a funny turn in there for a moment.'

'I'm sorry,' she said again, beginning to feel foolish as she became more conscious. 'I fell asleep . . . I was having a – dream. How much do I owe?'

'Three seventy-five,' he said. 'Do you want an 'and to your doorstep?'

Three seventy-five, she thought vaguely. Same as in the dream. 'No, fine. I'll be fine, thank you.' She handed him a fiver. Make it four-fifty—' She hesitated. 'I've been a nuisance. Keep the change, please.'

She turned and hurried away up the steps into the porch, heard the dick as she broke the beam and the automatic light came on, silently and obediently. She tapped out the combination code and turned around. She saw, through the darkness, the face of the driver as he reset his meter then switched off his interior light.

She stood and waited for him to drive off, shaking, her mind blurred with fear.

9

The woman's shadow fell across the gravestone, blocking the dim glow of light from the distant church window. The wind shook the trees, rattling the branches like bones, and carried faint strains of hymns from the choir practice; the woman was panting.

Tall, heavy boned, in her early seventies, she was unused to running, and it took her a while to catch her breath and for the pain in her chest to subside, took her a while for the excitement that bubbled like a cauldron inside her to calm enough so she could speak.

Her shadow bobbed over the words, revealing them for a moment, then blotting them out again.

'BILLY WOLF. 1938–1964.'

She knelt, as was her custom, closed her eyes tightly and murmured a rapid sequence of inaudible prayers. She rocked backwards and forwards, murmuring faster and faster until the words became a single high-pitched keening, and thick tears brimmed in her eyes, blinding her. Then she remained in silence, with her eyes tightly shut, until she could no longer contain her excitement. She opened her eyes and stood up.

'I've brought you a present, Billy,' she said in a guttural mid-European accent. 'You're going to be very pleased with me. So pleased! I know you are. Look, Billy!' She pulled the handkerchief from her old beaten-up handbag and held it out to the gravestone.

'It's hers, Billy! This'll do, won't it?' She beamed. 'I know you're pleased. It's taken so long to find her. The uncle and aunt adopted her, you see. They changed her name, took her a long way away. But we've found her again now. Little bitch. We're all right, now, Billy.' She held the handkerchief up once more, smiled at it, then folded it and put it carefully away in her bag. 'We've got everything, Billy.

'We're going to get her now.'

10

'Hey look at that! Ferrari – wow! Go faster, race it Mummy! Aww!'

The tail of the red sports car disappeared into the distance.

'Why are you driving so slowly, Mummy?'

'We're doing eighty, Tiger.'

'That's not very fast.'

'It's ten over the speed limit.'

'Was that man breaking the law then?'

'Yes.'

'Daddy breaks the law. He did one hundred and thirty-five last Saturday. Hey! Here's Daddy. Ohh.'

Sam glanced at Nicky in the rear-view mirror of the Range Rover, his face pressed against the window.

'It's not Daddy. It's just like Daddy's. Except Daddy's is a faster one. Why are we turning off?'

'We have to go shopping.'

'Oh noo! Do you like shopping, Helen?'

Helen looked round. 'Depends what I'm buying, Nicky.'

'How can anybody like shopping?'

'And now coming up before the news is the weekend weather report for Sussex and the South Downs. And it's going to be dry and windy with a possibility of gales . . . so hold onto your hats and your wigs and let's take you back to the summer of '67. The Kinks. "Sunny Afternoon".'

She drove into the parking lot of Safeways, the song stirring some vague pleasant memory inside her. They each took a trolley and marched in. Nicky sideswiped a display of alcohol-free lager, then crashed head-on with another trolley and got them so firmly locked together they both had to be abandoned. He swung on a barrier, trod in someone's basket and climbed a mountain of Heinz Baked Beans – 4p OFF! – which disintegrated under him.

She drove out with a feeling of relief.

'Are we having burgers?'

'Yes.'

'And sausages?'

'Yes.'

'Goodee!'

She braked hard and the tyres squealed as the Range Rover slewed to a halt throwing Helen forward against her seat belt.

'Sorry,' Sam said, staring up at the red traffic light. She turned around to Nicky, strapped into the rear seat. 'Okay, Tiger?'

He nodded, intently studying the cars crossing the intersection. 'Ford, Ford, Datsun, Rover, Toyota, Ford, Citroën, Porsche! Is Daddy going to be there, Mummy?'

'He'll be there tonight. He's gone shooting.'

'I want to go shooting. He promised to take me shooting.'

'Perhaps he'll take you tomorrow.' Shooting. She screwed up her nose, wishing Richard wouldn't encourage him. She wanted Nicky to be brought up in the country, and cultivated friends in London who had places in the country, as well as trying hard to make friends locally. The only thing she did not like about the country was shooting. She accepted it, but always uneasily. She turned back around and looked up at the road signs. LEWES BRIGHTON EASTBOURNE TUNBRIDGE WELLS. The light changed, she pushed the gear lever forward and let out the clutch.

'Vauxhall, Austin, Volkswagen, Jaguar, Ford, Honda, Volkswagen, Fiat . . .'

'Hey! Give us a break, Tiger.' Car names. He knew every single one.

'Is the goose going to be there, Mummy?'

'On the farm? I expect so.'

'Would a goose peck you?'

'Yes.'

'Would it kill you?'

She smiled. 'No.'

'Would it eat you if it did kill you?'

The black hood with the knife slits stared out through the taxi driver's partition.

'It wouldn't kill you.'

The raw livid eye socket.

Nothing. They were nothing. Old images from old dreams. They meant nothing; forget them. The mind playing tricks. Been upset over Richard's affair – probably triggering it off.

And the dream of the air disaster?

Coincidence. Ken was right. Coincidence, Leaving it behind her now. Leaving it all like a vanishing speck in the rear-view mirror. The country was the place she loved. Great to get away from London. The whole weekend. Nicky's party. Hard work but fun. The weekend was going to be great, would heal the wounds.

She turned off the main road into a narrow lane with a tall hedgerow on each side. A pheasant scurried along like a lame old woman. It was difficult to get used to the lane being much brighter now, since the hurricane last October. The trees that had made it dark had mostly gone. Everywhere you looked in the countryside you saw broken trees, uprooted trees, as if a giant had clumped through kicking things over for fun.

'I know where we are now! I know where we are now!'

She drove in through a narrow broken-down gate-

way, across a cattle grid, past a sign marked FARM
LANE, OLD MANOR FARM, LANE HOUSE, and
forked onto a ribbon of crumbling concrete like a
causeway across the ploughed field. The Range Rover
lurched through a pothole, dipped again, the suspension
crashing, the steering wheel kicking hard in her hands.
A faint smell of mud, manure and damp straw per-
meated through the closed windows.

'This is a silly road,' said Nicky.

She turned left again on the far side of the field, past
the front of the farm with its cluster of outhouses, barns
and silos, and down a steep hill. The rooftop of the
house came into view first then disappeared behind
some fir trees. They wound down past a tumbledown
barn, which always made something creep inside her,
round to the front of the house.

The house had been fine when they'd bought it and
they could have lived in it as it was, but Richard didn't
think it was grand enough. He had had it gutted, rooms
knocked through, new mouldings on the walls and
ceilings, a swimming pool dug out, a hard tennis court
laid. Money pouring out like water; money she didn't
know they had. Money that Andreas seemed to magic-
ally provide through deals she did not understand.
Andreas, the Swiss banker whom Richard had be-
friended, had become obsessed with, talked to on the
phone constantly when he was at home, fawned over
when he had come to dinner. She wondered whether
Richard had begun to change when the money started to
roll; or was it when he had started going with the tart in
the office? Or was it Andreas? Andreas whom she had
finally met two nights ago. With his black leather glove.

They'd lost part of the roof in the hurricane and it
was still being fixed now. Rusty scaffolding clung to the
wall at one end, a sheet of bright blue tarpaulin flapping

85

from it in the wind. Something about the scaffolding did not look right to her – it seemed to have come loose, seemed to be swaying.

The house was a Victorian farmhouse. The farmer lost both his legs in an accident, and had gassed himself in the tumbledown barn with the exhaust fumes of his car. His widow had sold off the farm and moved away; they'd only heard the story after they'd bought the house and she wondered if she would have tried to dissuade Richard had she known. Since she had heard the history, she always felt the house had a slightly melancholic feeling to it. It was the inside she liked most: the large, elegant rooms, some which they had made even larger, large enough to entertain in style, but not so large the place wouldn't feel like a home.

She swung the steering wheel to avoid a crater in the crumbling driveway. 'That's a job you can have, Tiger,' she said, more brightly than she felt. 'You can fill in the holes.'

'No.'

'Why not, Nicky?' said Helen.

'Umm. Coz there might be fish in them.'

The gravel of the circular drive rattled against the underside of the Range Rover, thick wall-to-wall gravel that the wheels sank into up to their hubs. She pulled on the handbrake and switched off the engine. Silence. Peace. She felt a gust of wind rock the car. Nicky tugged excitedly at his door handle. 'Birthday tomorrow! Yeah!'

'You're looking forward to it, aren't you?' said Helen.

'Yeah!'

'"Yes", darling, "yes", not "yeah". Okay?'

He hesitated, then grinned impudently at his mother. 'Yeah!' he said. 'Yeah! Yeah!' He jumped down and ran across the drive.

Sam looked at Helen, shaking her head and smiling. Helen blushed. 'I'm sorry,' she said. 'I'm trying to get him out of it. He's very strong willed.'

'Like his father,' Sam said, opening her door and stepping down. The wind tugged her hair, pulling her backwards, and a piece of grit blew into her right eye making it smart. She blinked hard, dabbing it with her handkerchief, then opened the tailgate.

She paused for a moment and stared at the view. Straight down over the fields down to the banks of the River Ouse, the open fields beyond, and the South Downs in the distance beyond that. To the right, the spires and walls of Lewes, the chalk bluffs and the ruined castle perched on the hill. Even on a bleak, blustery January morning, with the flattened trees with their roots in the air, it was stunning. Exhilarating. She wished she could put her wellies on and walk off into it right now, as she turned and hefted the first box of groceries towards the house, glancing up at the scaffolding again and the blue sheeting that flapped and cracked like a backing sail.

She opened the door and the smell of fresh paint engulfed her. She sniffed it, and it felt good. Helen followed her in, holding a bulging brown bag.

'God it's cold!' Sam carried the box through and dumped it on the kitchen table. She stared proudly at her brand new navy Aga, and switched it on, listening to the tick of its oil pump, then the whoof of its flame. She opened the cupboard and switched on the central heating. There was a clunk, a rattle, a tick, another whoof, and the slatted door began to vibrate.

She went back outside, crossing with Helen who was bringing in a case of Cokes. Nicky was following her, struggling under the weight of a carrier bag. She smiled.

'Can you manage, Tiger?'

He nodded a grim determined nod, and she took another box and followed him in, her feet scrunching on the gravel, watching him tenderly as he put his carrier down, then picked it up again. Such a tiny chap, but he hadn't seemed so tiny when he was born.

Caesarian. The idiot gynaecologist hadn't realised her cervix was too small for him.

No, Jesusgoddamn no! Oh my Christ!

A great job you did, Mr brilliant gynaecologist. Mr Framm. Mr smooth-talking great bedside manners Framm. Brilliant bit of surgery on me. What did you use? A shovel?

No more children? Won't be able to? Great. Triff. Thanks very much.

You could sue him someone had said, but what was the point? It wouldn't bring her another child.

Sue. Everyone sues everyone. Join the lepers with their begging bowls outside the Halls of Justice. Sue. Sue. Sue. You leave people alone these days; you don't dare touch; don't dare lift them bleeding to death out of the wrecks of cars in case they sue you for doing it wrong.

Nicky put the carrier down on the kitchen floor. 'I'm going to check my base now, make sure that's all right. I've got work to do in it.'

The barn was where he had his secret base; at least he wasn't scared of barns, she thought, watching him scamper off. He'd have asked Richard to come and check it out with him, but not her. She was all right for the odd game, the odd bit of amusement when he was bored, for putting him to bed and telling him stories, but it was Richard that he really liked to be with. Richard, who took him fishing, played with his cars, taught him to swim and use a computer and sail a boat. Some things you couldn't change no matter what you did. It was good that they loved each other so much. Except some-times she felt left out. Sometimes she felt as lonely as when she had been a child unwanted by her aunt and uncle.

She went back outside, heaved another box of gro-ceries out of the tailgate and carried it through the fresh blustery air. It could all be so good here. Was all just beginning to feel so good. And then. Richard. Oh you stupid sod!

She lugged her suitcase inside and tramped up the filthy dust sheet that covered the staircase. 'I thought they were going to finish painting the stairs. They are blighters, these builders.'

There was so much to be done. So much potential. So much you could do – if you had the enthusiasm. ENTHUSIASM. It had been there when they'd bought the place. Yes-yes-yes. The estate agent had given them the key and let them go back for the second viewing alone and they'd made love on the bare dusty floor.

Yes, please. Can we really afford this?

Sure we can, Bugs.

Yes, please.

Last June.

She walked past the dust sheets stretching away down the dark corridor, the ladders, the tins of paint, the rolls of lining paper, into the bedroom and put the case down on the floor. Mirrors. On all the walls. On the doors of the massive mahogany wardrobe they'd acquired with the house. There was one on order to go up on the ceiling. What did he like looking at so much? His own hairy bum?

She walked over and gazed out of the window at the thickening cloud and the swirling leaves. She watched the wind blowing, in the grass, in the trees, in the ripples on the distant river.

Slider.

The black hood stared out at her through the glass partition.

The orange and white boarding card.

Seat 35A.

She heard a click behind her, a gentle click like a door closing, and she felt a sudden fear clam around her like a cold mist. She stared on out through the window, at nothing but a blur. Someone or something had come into the room and was standing right behind her. So close, she could almost feel breathing down her neck.

She shook her head, trembling, and gripped the radiator beneath the sill tightly, so tightly she could feel the ribbing cutting into her hands. She wanted to turn, now, turn and face whoever it was. But she could not.

'Yes?' she said, instead.

There was silence.

'What do you want?' she articulated clearly, loudly.

Still there was silence.

She spun round, filled for an instant with a mad boldness. But there was nothing. Nothing except her reflection.

She sat down shakily on the white candlewick bed-spread and took the page from Friday's *Daily Mail* out of her handbag. She looked at the large photograph of the tailplane in the snow, and the smaller inset photograph of a Boeing 727, with the tiny caption underneath: 'Similar to the one that crashed.'

She turned the page, staring at the photographs of the pilot and co-pilot, one smiling, one stem. Neither the names nor the faces registered anything with her. She looked down the column until she found what she wanted: the emergency phone numbers.

She picked up the telephone and dialled. The number rang for a long time before it was answered.

'Is that Chartair?' she said, feeling foolish.

'Yes it is,' said a woman's voice.

'I wonder if you could give me some information about the . . . crash?'

'Is it about a relative, madam?'

'Er – not—' Sam felt flushed, afraid what the woman might think. That she was a crank with a ghoulish interest. 'I think perhaps I had a relative on the plane,' she said, knowing that her lie did not sound convincing.

'Could you let me have the person's name?' said the woman, her voice becoming impatient.

'I have the seat number. 35A.'

'35A? Your relative was travelling in 35A?'

Sam wanted to hang up. The tone of the woman's voice was flattening her. 'Yes,' she said. 'I think so.'

'Wouldn't have been on this plane. There were only thirty-two rows.'

'I'm sorry,' said Sam. 'So sorry – I must have . . .'

'Do you have a name?'

'Name?'

'Of your relative.'

'I'm sorry,' Sam said. 'I've made a mistake. I don't think they . . . he . . . were . . . was on that plane at all.' She hung up feeling hot, flustered, watching her reflection in the mirror putting the phone back on the bedside table.

35A.

She tossed the numbers around in her head, added them together, subtracted them, said them over to herself, trying to find some clue. She pulled the book she had bought out of her handbag and shook it out of its crumpled paper bag.

What Your Dreams Really Say.

She stared at the eyeball and the fish on the cover, then glanced at the biography of the author inside.

'Dr Colin Hare Ph.D., D.Sc. A Fellow of the British Psychological Society. Winner of the University of London Carpenter Medal for "great innovative work". Considered Britain's leading authority on dreams, he lectures extensively throughout the world.'

She flicked through a few pages, then turned to the index. Hood. Hood. '*Hood*, see Mask.'

'To dream of yourself or others wearing a hood or a mask can be a warning of deception by someone you trust.

'It may alternatively indicate an aspect of your personality.'

That was all. She looked up 'Numbers' and turned to the page.

'Three: The male genitals. Father, mother, child. The Trinity.

'Five: The flesh. The body. Life.

'Any letters of the alphabet indicate pleasant news on the way.'

'Mumbo jumbo,' she muttered. Some people could do *The Times* crossword in four minutes. Not her; never. Riddles. Puzzles. She'd never been any good at them. Thicko Sam.

She heard the rattle of water inside the radiator, and felt a sharp cold draught down the back of her neck. She was frightened again, felt goosepimples on her shoulders, her arms, on her thighs. The door of the room swung open a fraction with a click, half closed then opened again, click, click.

There was a louder click from her right and the mirrored door of the wardrobe swung slowly open. Her heart crashed around inside her chest as she stared, paralysed for a moment, into its dark interior. The metal coat hangers clanged together, gently, chiming.

There was a splitting crack of wood above her, then

another, as if someone was walking over the joists. The whole room seemed to be coming alive around her.

She went out onto the landing, hurried along it and halfway down the stairs, then stopped, and stared back up, trying to compose herself. She could still hear the coat hangers chiming as if they were being played like musical triangles.

11

'Seventeen, eighteen, nineteen.' She looked quizzically at Helen.

'Yes. I make it nineteen.'

The long trestle table in the dining room was covered with a bright tablecloth, nineteen paper plates, pink and yellow napkins, red and blue striped paper cups. The walls were festooned with balloons and ribbons, and there was a large banner along one saying 'Happy Birthday Nicky.'

'Looks wonderful, doesn't it?' Helen's voice tingled with excitement, and Sam smiled, pleased for her. Pleased that she could be so thrilled at something so simple, and hoping the feeling would rub onto Nicky. Nice, old-fashioned, simple.

'Great,' she said absently, watching Helen rub her hands together gleefully, like a child. She was a child, really. Nineteen. Her funny spiky hair, and her thick North Country accent, and her superstitions. Seeing omens in everything. Don't look at a new moon through glass. Turn money over in your pocket. Say 'grey hares' on the last night of the month and 'white rabbits' in the morning. She frowned uncertainly, hoping Helen wasn't going to riddle Nicky with fears and guilt and make him cranky.

Like people who dreamed of air disasters.

She felt a breeze on her face, and heard the wind again rattling the windows. The house seemed to let in draughts as a leaky boat took in water. She walked through the hallway, and stared at the bare floorboards of the staircase, wondering if it had looked better with the dust sheets on, and smelled the wood smoke from the newly lit fire that was roaring and spitting in the drawing room.

With the fire lit and Richard back the house seemed OK, fine; it had been the wind that had scared her, the wind and the central heating starting up; the house had been empty for five years, it was all damp, it was bound to creak and crack and make strange sounds when the heating came on and the wood dried out. Richard had explained to her before. It all made sense; sure. It was fine. It had been her imagination in the bedroom, the wind and her imagination and the drying out house.

She opened the kitchen door and saw him sitting at the table, his shotgun spread out in bits. Nicky, standing beside him, his face streaked in gun oil, was polishing the stock. Richard rammed the cleaning rod down through one barrel, then the other.

'Honestly, Richard! Not on the table!'

He closed one eye, and squinted at her through each barrel in turn. 'Going to have to have these re-ground. Pitting. Can't understand it.' He poured some oil onto a rag, then began to wipe the barrels.

'Didn't you hear me? I don't want that on the table. We have to eat on that.'

'It's all right.' He studied the triggers for a moment, then inserted the can between them. 'Only a bit of oil.'

She heard the clunk as he squeezed the can and bit her lip, feeling guilty suddenly.

Domestic bliss. The family all together. Something

she'd never had; one of the few things you could give to a child that mattered. She pulled a couple of newspapers out of a cupboard, and smiled down at him. 'Slip these underneath.'

He glanced at them. 'I've read them.'

'Richard,' she said reproachfully.

'Look, Mummy!' Nicky held up the shining stock.

'That looks wonderful, Tiger. Time for your bath now.'

'Daddy said we can go shooting tomorrow, coz it's my birthday.'

'If you've got time. You're going to have a busy day tomorrow.'

Nicky's face fell, and he turned to his father. 'We will have time, Daddy, won't we?'

Richard smiled. ''Course we will. Let's have a kiss goodnight.'

Sam watched him hug his father, arms around his neck, the simple, total, uncomplicated love of a child. Crazy with love. She'd been crazy with love for Richard too. Loved him, admired him, respected him. For ten years. Until.

'Will you tell me the story you told me the other night, Mummy? About the man who killed the dragon, and the dragon came back to life?'

'You want that one again?'

'Tell it again. Do! Please!'

The man who killed the dragon and lived happily ever after.

Happily ever after, Childhood's greatest myth.

'Go and run your bath, Tiger, and Mummy'll be up.'

Nicky scampered off.

'He's exhausting,' Sam said.

''Night, Tiger.' Richard put the gun barrels down and refilled his whisky glass, wrapping his hand around it, getting the level exactly to the top of his fourth finger. He took the glass to the tap and ran in some water. 'You look nice, Bugs,' he said tenderly. 'Like that jumper on you.'

She glanced down, to check what she was wearing. 'Thanks.'

'I—' He hesitated, then dug his hand into his corduroy pocket and pulled out a small package. 'I—' He blushed – 'got you a little present.'

'For me?'

He held it out to her; it had classy foil giftwrap, but clumsily done, and crumpled, with far too much sellotape which she picked away carefully with her nail. Inside there was a small slim leather box that looked old. She looked at Richard uncertainly, and he nodded at her. She lifted the lid and saw an elderly looking Rolex watch, with a slim rectangular face and twin dials.

'It's – er – genuine – antique. Thirties. I thought – your retro stuff – go with the image—'

'It's the bizz,' she said, lifting it out. 'Very trendy. It's – beautiful.' She kissed him. 'it's lovely.' She removed her own watch, put it on the table and strapped on the Rolex.

'You have to wind it, of course.'

'Yes. Funny, two dials – so you can tell the time in different parts of the world? For early jetsetters?'

'One's for the hour hand, the other's minutes.'

She smiled. 'Ah.'

'Should improve your street cred.'

'Should do.'

'Like it?'

'Yes. It's wonderful – it—'

He sat back down at the table. His eyes were watering. He was crying. 'I'm sorry, Bugs. I've made such a

96

hash. I – I've really—' He bowed his head slightly and rested it in his hands. 'I love you, you know, I really love you. I don't want to lose you.'

She went to him, put her arms round him and held him tight for a moment, cradling his head, and blinking away her own tears of sadness. Sadness for what had happened, for how he felt; sadness that even in her arms part of him felt like a stranger. She stroked his face. 'It's a lovely watch. It must have cost a fortune.'

'I wanted to get you something very special.'

'You're spending a lot of money these days.'

He sniffed. ''S all right. Into some good deals. Andreas reckons we'll be fine as long as nothing happens to the Japanese market.'

'Is it likely to?'

He drew away from her and took a hard pull on his whisky. She stared at him, and thought she could see a faint trace of worry in his face. 'Is it likely to?' she repeated gently.

He sniffed again. 'No.' But she sensed an element of his usual confidence missing. 'How long have you been dealing with Andreas?'

He shrugged. ''Bout eight or nine months.'

'He seems to have helped you make a lot of money.'

'Yah's a good bloke.' He flushed slightly.

'Do you trust him?'

'Straight as a die.'

'Is he?'

He nodded.

'Doesn't sail close to the wind?'

'No – he's—' He hesitated – 'actually, he's – ah – quite cautious. He's a director of a bank. Quite a substantial outfit.' He scratched the back of his head awkwardly. 'Why are you—?'

'I just thought he was a bit odd, that's all.'

97

'The Swiss tend to be a bit cold.'

'How was the shoot?' she asked.

'Good bag.' He looked relieved that she had changed the subject. 'Hundred and eighty pheasants. Brought some back. Think I'm going to build a proper game larder.'

She began to turn the winder of her watch carefully, backwards and forwards; it had been years since she'd wound a watch, she realised.

'You've got the Punch and Judy organized, haven't you, Bugs?'

'Yes.'

'What time's kick-off?'

'Three o'clock. You'd better get the projector set up. You won't have much time tomorrow, since you've got to fetch your mother.'

'The old goat.' He took another large pull on his drink. 'She's getting past her sell-by date.'

'Nicky might say that about you and I one day.'

'Probably will.'

'Doesn't that bother you?'

He shrugged. 'No.'

She kissed him again on his cheek. 'I'll go and tell Nicky his story.' She went out of the room and closed the door, blew her nose and wiped her own tears away. She climbed the stairs slowly, turning her mind back to the story of the man who killed the dragon and the dragon came back to life, except this time it turned into two dragons, and the man killed both of them and then it turned into four and he killed them too. Killed them dead.

12

'Oobie, joobie, joobie! Who's a naughty girl, then?'

Sam stared at the candy-striped stand; Punch swivelled around in his pointed hat, with his great hooked nose, rapped his baton down hard on his tiny stage and screeched:

'Naughty, naughty, naughty, naughty. Who's been a naughty girl, then?'

One of the children shouted out, 'Nicky's mummy has!'

Punch swaggered up and down along the stage, repeating to himself, 'Nicky's mummy's been naughty, has she? Nicky's mummy's been naughty, has she? We'll have to see about that, won't we?'

'Yeah!' came the chorus.

'Ooobie, joobie, joobie, who's been a naughty girl, then?' He swivelled and stared directly at Sam, leaning forward over the stage and curling and uncurling his index finger at her; it was a long finger, out of proportion with the size of the puppet, and the action unsettled her.

'Oobie, joobie, joobie,' he repeated over and over, curling and uncurling, leaning closer; the children were silent now, sensing an atmosphere. 'I think she ought to be punished, don't you, children?'

'Yeah!'

Punch stood upright and rapped the stage with his baton again. 'Who thought she was on an aeroplane?' He cackled with laughter.

Sam smarted with anger, with bafflement.

'Naughty! Naughty! Naughty!'

The baton came down. Whack, whack, whack. Harder, this time with real menace.

'Who's going to have to be punished then?'

'Nicky's mummy!' came the chorus.

Stop this. I want to stop this. Get him out of there. He's mad.

'We could beat her with a stick!' he screeched, then ducked down out of sight. 'Or we could . . .'

He reappeared.

But now he was wearing a black hood with slits cut into it.

Sam tried to back away, tried pushing herself on the carpet, but she was wedged against something, something hard, soft; the sofa, she realised.

She could see his lips smiling through the hood, then he winked, and his left eyeball shot out, hit the floor and rolled across the carpet, rattled onto the bare floorboards, bouncing against the skirting board and carrying on rolling, rattling like a cannonball.

The children shrieked with laughter.

He lifted something shiny, metallic up over the floor of the stage.

She shivered.

Shotgun.

He raised it up swiftly and aimed at her.

'*No!*' she screamed.

She saw the spurts of flame from the barrel and felt a sharp sting on her cheek.

The lights went out, and for a moment she was covered in darkness, sticky, cloying blackness that pressed against her eyes, her ears, forced its way into her mouth. Then a row of red digits appeared above her, and she blinked, startled by their brightness.

0415.

The darkness was becoming tinged with red, as if the light was bleeding into it. She heard a sharp snort beside her, a gurgling sound and several more snorts. Then Richard's voice.

'Wassermarrer?'

She felt a chill breeze. Dream, she thought. Dream. 0416.

Light poured out of the clock like blood into a bath. She heard Richard's voice again. 'What the fuck was that?' Heard the sound of his arm sliding through the bedclothes, a loud clank, the sound of water spilling, 'Shit', then the click of the light, which blinded her for a moment.

'Jesus,' he said.

He was staring up at the ceiling. Cracks ran out in all directions across it, like veins in an old woman's hand.

Like glass that had been hit by a bullet. She shivered.

Right above her head, a small chunk of plaster was missing completely. Her cheek was hurting like hell, she realised. Gingerly, she put her finger to her face, and felt the hard, flaky plaster crumble between her fingers as she touched it.

Richard leapt out of bed, horrified. 'It's fucking coming down. Get out of here!' He struggled into his dressing gown and she climbed out of bed too, and pulled her own dressing gown on. The ceiling seemed to be moving, breathing, sagging, cracking more as she looked at it. It looked like eggshell now, like a hard-boiled egg that had been dropped and the shell had cracked all around it.

'It's the water that got in after the fucking hurricane,' Richard said as she followed him out into the corridor. 'The survey said the roof had been leaking and the loft above our room had damp. The central heating's drying it out and the joists are warping.'

They ran down the corridor and checked Nicky's room, and then Helen's room, snapping their lights on, saying 'It's OK, it's OK,' then snapping the lights off again and closing the doors.

'Are their rooms safe, Richard?'

'They look fine. The roof was badly holed above our room – ours is probably the worst.'

There were no beds in the spare rooms yet, so they lugged sheets and blankets downstairs and made makeshift beds up on the two sofas in the drawing room. Richard stoked up the fire, got it going and piled logs onto it, and she lay on the sofa, snugly wrapped up now, her heart not thumping quite so badly, and watched the leaping flickering flames. Watched them as they slowly faded and died and dawn began to break outside.

13

The frost scrunched under her feet, and she rubbed her hands together against the icy air. The sun hung low in the sky over the Downs, pale, weak, as if it had been left on all night. The river slid past below her, dark brown, silent, like the fear that was sliding through her.

She touched the graze on her cheek gingerly and looked down at the mark on her finger which had now almost gone. There was a muffled pop, like the bursting of a paper bag, then another; she turned and saw Nicky running flat out across the lawn towards a small grey ball of fluff that was rolling about, flapping.

'It's not dead, Daddy! It's not dead!'

She saw him poke a hand forward nervously, then jump back, watched Richard striding over, gun crooked under his arm. Teaching him to shoot, already. Promised him a gun for his ninth birthday. Guns. Killing things. Hunting. Would the world ever change if children were taught to follow old instincts? Or was it foolish to ignore them, to try to pretend they no longer existed? Choices. So many choices to make in bringing up a child. So many decisions that could change or forever affect them. Decisions. Who the hell was equipped to make them?

She glanced at her Rolex. It was five past one. 'Richard,' she called out, 'we'd better have lunch.' She sighed. Her few moments of respite were over. The five minutes she had managed to grab for herself in the midst of the preparations. The rest of the day was going to be chaos. She yawned. Her back ached slightly, but nothing much. It had been OK on the sofa. It would have been even more OK if she could have had another twelve hours of sleep.

Oobie, joobie, joobie.

The weird taunt echoed in her head, and Punch's finger curled out towards her, curled, uncurled.

Oobie joobie joobie. The taunt seemed to hang in the air around her, then dissolve.

The whole damned ceiling could have come down.

Did that trigger the dream? she wondered. In that split second that the plaster struck? Was that how dreams worked? Did they all happen in a fraction of a second?

'Mummy! We shot a pigeon.'

'Very clever, darling.' She glanced down at the litter of wrapping paper on the kitchen floor, at the remote controlled car, already with a bit broken off. The BMX was in the garden, lying on its side. 'Don't you like your bike?'

His eyes lit up. 'Yeah!'

'It's not going to do it much good lying out in the garden. The grass is wet.'

'I'm going to use it again this afternoon. I am.'

'You shouldn't let it stay wet.'

'I'll dry it, I promise.'

'You won't.'

'I will. I promise I will.'

'Promises are important, Tiger. Never make a promise you can't keep. OK?'

He looked away. 'Yes,' he mouthed silently. 'Richard!' she called. 'Come on, lunch!' She could hear him on the telephone.

'Yah!' he shouted. 'Just a sec.'

She dug the ladle into the stew, and tipped a small portion onto Nicky's plate.

Richard came in.

'Who were you talking to?'

'Oh. Andreas. Just a—' He picked up the wine bottle which Sam had already uncorked. 'Are you having some wine, Mummy?' Richard hovered over his mother with the bottle.

Sam stared at her mother-in-law's thin wrinkled face, with her make-up too thick and her hair elegantly coiffed, too black. She always dressed well in expensive clothes that were now slightly frayed, not because she could not afford new ones, or to have them mended, but because she simply wasn't aware. It always seemed strange, his calling her Mummy. She wondered if Nicky would still be calling her Mummy when she was old like that.

'Wine, Mummy? Would you like some wine?' Richard repeated, louder.

'Coffee, I think,' she said. 'Do you do espresso?'

'We're going to have lunch first,' said Richard patiently, more patiently than usual.

His mother turned towards him. 'Your father'll have some wine, I expect. He's late.' She opened her handbag and scrabbled about in it, slowly, deliberately, warily, like a dog scratching away the earth over a hidden bone.

She pulled out a compact, clicked it open, and examined her lips. She took out a lipstick, and twisted the stem.

Sam and Richard exchanged a glance. His father had been dead for eight years.

'Would you like some stew, Mummy?'

'I'll have a cigarette now, I think, darling.'

'We're going to eat first, Joan,' Sam said, kindly but firmly.

Her mother-in-law frowned, puzzled.

'Have you thanked Granny for your present?' asked Sam.

Nicky looked forlornly at her. 'I only got handkerchiefs.'

'Handkerchiefs are jolly useful,' said Helen.

'Granny,' said Nicky, turning to her. 'We shot a pigeon.'

She rolled her tongue over her lips, then carefully put the lipstick back into the bag. She pulled out her cigarettes, and extricated one from the pack.

'Mummy, we're still eating,' said Richard, irritated.

'When's his birthday?' she said. 'Sometime soon, isn't it?'

'Today,' Sam said. 'It's today.'

Her mother-in-law frowned again and looked at her watch. 'Usually home by now.' She looked up at Richard. 'Probably in a meeting.'

'I'm sure he won't mind if you start without him,' said Sam. 'Why don't you have some stew?'

'Pigeons are naughty. Daddy's going to give me a gun when I'm – er – when I'm nine.'

'Elbows off, Tiger.' She turned to Richard. 'Do you think we should call the Punch and Judy man? He should have been here by now. Said he'd be here by one.'

'Looking forward to your party, Nicky?' asked Helen.

'Umm,' he said thoughtfully. 'Yes.'

They heard the sound of a car and Sam looked out of the window. A small, elderly Ford pulled up. 'Thank God,' she said, hurrying out of the room, as if she was afraid he might change his mind and go away.

He stood apologetically on the front doorstep, an unassuming little man in a drab suit and a thick mackintosh, with two huge suitcases.

'I'm so sorry I'm late,' he said. 'So terribly sorry.' He smiled, exposing a row of crooked rotting teeth, yellow and brown, and his breath was foul, as if he had been smoking a pipe. 'My wife's not well, I had to wait for the doctor.' He looked afraid. There was fear in his eyes.

'I'm sorry,' she said.

'Thank you. It's one of those—' He paused. 'I'm sorry,' he said. 'I'm here to be cheerful, to make the party go.' He smiled again and she could see he had been crying.

She felt a tug on her pullover and saw Nicky standing there.

'This is the Punch and Judy man, Tiger.'

'Hallo, young man. Happy birthday.'

Nicky looked suspiciously up at him.

'Say hallo, Tiger.' But Nicky said nothing. The man was thin and pale, with a slightly translucent skin; his head was almost bald on top, with a few strands pulled over and plastered down. He looked like a forgotten toy. 'Do you want a hand with your bags?'

'No, no, oh no, no, I can manage, thank you.' He picked up the two enormous cases and staggered forward, breathing hard. Sam saw tiny beads of sweat on his forehead, and she shivered suddenly. He made her feel uncomfortable. This little man who could make children laugh and scream and cry, this little man with his sick wife and his suitcases full of puppets.

What a life, she thought, what a life, to turn up every day on strangers' doorsteps. Did he love children? Or was he weird? As she stared at him she felt afraid, as if the man was carrying death into her house, carrying it in his two big heavy suitcases.

Nicky was looking at her anxiously. He stretched up towards her and spoke in a quiet, conspiratorial voice. 'Mummy, he doesn't look like Punch and Judy.'

'I'm sorry we're a bit early.'

'No, that's fine, really.' Sam smiled, staring at the woman, trying to think of her name. The wife of a City friend of Richard's. They owned a stately pile somewhere near here.

'It was very nice of you to invite Edgar.'

Sam looked down dubiously at the scowling child. A brat. It was stamped all over his face. 'Delighted,' she said.

'I trod in cow shit this morning,' Edgar said.

'Darling!' said his mother. 'I don't think Mrs Curtis wants to know about that.'

'I'll just get Nicky.' Sam looked around. 'Tiger! Come and meet your first guest!'

Helen appeared, holding Nicky gently by the arm, coaxing him along.

'This is Edgar,' said Sam.

'Give him his present.'

Edgar thrust out a small package. 'I trod in cow shit this morning.'

'Edgar!' said his mother.

'What do you say, Nicky?'

Nicky went bright red. 'Umm. Thank you very much. We shot a pigeon this morning,' he added.

'Shall we open that later, Nicky?' said Helen, lifting the package. 'We'll put them all together so we don't get in a muddle.'

'Why don't you show Edgar your presents, Tiger?' said Sam. She smiled at his mother. 'Would you like to come in!'

'Thanks, no. Have to dash. Be back at six?'

'OK. Bye.' Sam closed the door.

'I want to shoot a pigeon,' Edgar said.

'We're having a party now, Edgar,' she said. 'You can come back one day and go shooting with Nicky and his father if you like.'

'I want to shoot one now.'

'Nicky has got a radio controlled car. Would you like to see that?'

The child stamped his foot. 'Pigeon,' he said. 'Eeeeee, urrrrr, grrrmmmm.' He sprinted off across the hall, then stopped and glared through the kitchen doorway. He marched in and across to Richard, who was reading a paper. 'Urr.' He said. 'Grrremmmm.'

Richard carried on reading.

'Urrrr. Grrremmmmm.'

Richard glanced over the top of his paper. 'Sod off,' he said.

'Urrrrr,' said the child, screwing up his face. 'Urrrr, urrrr. I want to shoot a pigeon.'

'Ask her, she'll take you.' Richard nodded at his mother, who was studying her face in her compact through a stream of cigarette smoke, and carried on reading.

Edgar put up his hand and tugged the paper down sharply, ripping it. 'I want to shoot a pigeon.' He stamped his foot.

Richard shot out his hand and grabbed the boy's ear.

'Ow!'

Shoving the paper aside, he stood up, twisting his ear harder, and marched him out of the kitchen.

'Owwwww! Arrrrrrr!'

He gave one final tweak for good measure.

'Richard, what are you doing?'

'Little bastard,' he said.

Edgar stood in the hallway, bawling, as Richard walked back into the kitchen. Sam stormed in after him. 'What have you done to that child?'

'Little bastard tore my paper.'

'Did you hit him?'

'No, but I will do next time.'

The doorbell rang.

'Oh God,' she said. 'Three o'clock, it's meant to start. Why are they all coming early? Can you shove the sausages in the oven? The bottom right-hand.'

'I'll put that little bastard in if he comes in here.'

'Shall I get the door, Mrs Curtis?'

'Thank you, Helen.' She looked back at Richard. 'Have you put the gun away?'

'Yes.'

'What's your mother doing?'

'She wants to know when we're having lunch. Bloody daft bringing her here.'

'It is her grandson's birthday.'

'You'd better remind her.'

'She's not completely gaga. She did buy him a present, and a nice card.'

'I wanna go home,' Edgar bawled.

'Hi Sam!' a voice called. Sam went back into the hall.

'Vicki!' She dashed over. 'Come in.'

'I've got to collect Peter from sailing.'

109

'Hallo, Willie.' Sam looked down at the slightly lost-looking child.

'Thank you very much,' she heard Nicky whisper, holding another brightly coloured package.

'Rowie!' Nicky's godmother.

'Sam! Mmmn!' Their cheeks collided and they each blew kisses out into the air.

'How are you, darling?'

'Fine. Great.' Sam tousled the hair of Rowie's stern little boy.

'Hallo, Justin.'

'Hallo, Auntie Sam.'

'This is daft, Sam. We live a mile away from each other in London, almost in the next-door village down here, and the only time we see each other is at kids' parties! How about lunch this week – Tuesday any good?'

'Sure. Why don't we have lunch at the club? A swim and a sauna? They have a good salad bar now.'

Another car was pulling up. Chaos; she felt bewildered for a moment. Then she saw the Punch and Judy man come down the stairs and walk through into the drawing room, quietly, meekly, gliding. Like a ghost, she thought.

14

'Sausage, Celia?'

The little girl raised her pig-tailed head. 'I don't eat sausages. My mummy says they're common.'

Sam stared at her, flummoxed for a moment, then moved on down the table with the heavy tray, listening to the babble. 'Sausage, Willie?'

'Yes, please.'

'I always have prawns at my parties,' said Celia loudly, to no one in particular.

Richard followed, with a tray of hot quiche.

'I don't eat quiche,' she heard Celia say.

'You'll get spots if you don't eat quiche,' he said.

She puffed up haughtily in her pink frock. 'My mummy says I'm going to be very beautiful. I'm going to be a model.'

'Are we having a film? Are we having a film?' said an excited voice Sam did not recognise. She stared at Nicky at the head of the table, in an orange paper crown, fists sunk into a half-eaten burger, ketchup, and relish oozing out the sides of it, his face and new jumper streaked in the stuff, like a Jackson Pollock painting.

'What film? What film?'

She looked at her watch. Just past four.

Babble. A child blew a plastic bugle. Another blew a low-pitched whistle, from which a strip of coloured paper uncurled. A little girl ran excitedly into the room, sat down and began whispering to her friend, who then rushed out. Sam saw the Punch and Judy man standing in the doorway, and she nodded at him.

'OK, everyone! Punch and Judy time!'

There were excited squeals, and a couple of groans.

'Can we all go next door, please.'

She herded them through into the drawing room and tried to get them seated on the floor in front of the candy-striped Punch and Judy stand. It was wobbling a bit and she could see the side move every few moments as the man shuffled around inside, sorting his things out. She watched it warily for a moment, traces of last night's dream echoing around her head as she listened to the babble. Helen wandered through the kids, dishing out lollipops.

'There's a real man inside there.'

''Course there isn't.'

'How do you know?'

'I looked.'

'How could you look? You're not tall enough.'

'I bet I am.'

'I bet you're not.'

One small girl sat on her own, slightly away from the rest, with her hands over her eyes.

Sam went out into the kitchen. Her mother-in-law was staring into her compact mirror, caking more make-up onto her nose, a thin thread of smoke rising from a mound of lipstick-covered butts in the ashtray beside her.

'Joan,' Sam said, 'the Punch and Judy's about to start. Would you like to see it?'

'Punch and Judy, dear?' She frowned. 'No, I think I'd prefer to stay in here. My lipstick's a bit smudged.'

'It looks very nice. I'm sure Nicky would like it if you came in.'

Her mother-in-law began to rummage in her bag again, the dog scratching through the earth for its bone.

There was a ripple of laughter from the drawing room. 'See you in a minute.' She walked across the hall, and paused in the doorway of the drawing room. The Art Deco clock on the mantelpiece caught her eye. Coming up to four-fifteen.

The time seemed familiar for some reason.

'Oobie, joobie, joobie! Who's a naughty boy, then?'

'Oh no I'm not!' squawked Punch, his soft pointed hat and hooked nose appearing over the top of the tiny stage.

'Oobie, joobie, joobie! Naughty, naughty, naughty!'

The words sent a prickle of anxiety through her.

'Oh no I'm not!'

'Oh yes you are!' shrieked Mrs Punch, dancing up and down in her gaudy frock.

'Oh no I'm not!'

'Oh yes you are!'

'Come on children, I'm not naughty am I?'

'Oh yes he is!'

Sam looked over the sea of faces, some grinning, some with lollipop sticks poking out of their lips. The girls in their party frocks, the boys in their shirts, mostly grubby already, and short trousers slightly dishevelled from the games. What sort of people would they become when they grew up? You could tell the meek and the assertive, the bullies and thinkers. Christ, they all had a long way to go before – before what? Before they could begin to understand? Look at me – I'm a grown up – thirty-two – and I don't even begin to understand. Maybe life wasn't about understanding at all? Maybe there was something else. We all charged through, looking in the wrong cupboards and missed the point. Would these children one day become old and baffled and still be opening and shutting cupboards? Rummaging through handbags for – cigarettes? For – the key to life? Like Richard's mother in the kitchen? No, not any more. We're entering the Age of Aquarius. It'll all make SENSE. The new UNDERSTANDING.

''Ere, children, help me. If you think I'm not naughty, shout out with me, all right? OH NO I'M NOT!'

'Oh no you're not!' There was a faltering chorus, uncertain, slightly embarrassed.

'Don't listen to him!' shrieked Mrs Punch. 'Say, "OH YES YOU ARE!"'

She stared at Nicky, sitting there, rapt. He was a nice chap, she thought; he cared, even now; he'd grow up to be a caring person.

'OH YES YOU ARE!'

She was vaguely conscious of the door opening at the far end of the room.

'That wasn't very loud!'

'OH YES YOU ARE!'

Something wasn't right.

Something was making her feel very frightened.

'Come on, louder!'

'OH YES YOU ARE!'

She saw the smile on his face first, forty feet across the room, the smile of a demon, not a small child. In an instant it was gone, and instead there was a laughing boy, a greedy little boy who has got his way and is happy, for a fleeting moment, until he becomes bored again. He was laughing, laughing to himself, laughing while the blood stopped flowing inside her and was turning to ice.

'Edgar,' she said, mouthing the word. 'Edgar!' she shouted against the sea of voices that were rooting for Mrs Punch.

'Edgar!' she shouted again, against the sea of voices that were now rooting for Mr Punch. 'Put it down! For God's sake put it down!'

It couldn't be loaded. Impossible. Richard was careful. He couldn't be that foolish.

'Edgar!'

He stood by the door, staggering under the weight of the shotgun like a drunken miniature gunfighter.

The finger.

Curling in the night.

4.15.

The clock. In the bedroom. When she had woken up.

4.15.

The clock on the mantelpiece.

4.15.

The finger on the trigger.

Oobie, joobie, joobie.

'*Edgar!*' She took a step forward.

The gun swept wildly across the backs of the children, up at her, up at the ceiling, then down at the children again.

'I'm going to shoot pigeons now.' She heard the words clearly, across the room, through all the noise, as clearly as if he was standing next to her.

The barrel was swinging up towards her.

'*Edgar, be careful! Put it down!*'

Pointing straight at her.

'OH NO I'M NOT!'

'OH YES YOU ARE!'

'EDGAR PUT IT DOWN.'

She could see straight into them, straight down both barrels, even from here.

'OH NO I'M NOT!'

Shut up. For God's sake shut up, you fool. Can't you see? Haven't you got peep holes in your damned box?

'Whack whack, ouch!'

'You hit me and I'll hit you.'

'DOWN, EDGAR, DOWN, PUT IT DOWN.'

'Oh no you won't.'

'Oh yes I will!'

She heard a solitary giggle.

His finger closed around the trigger.

'EDGAR!'

She stared down desperately at Nicky, tried to walk towards him, to get Nicky out of the way, to stop Edgar.

Whack.

'Ouch.'

'Where's he gone? Where's he gone?'

'HE'S BEHIND YOU!'

Mrs Punch spun round. 'Oh no he isn't!'

'OH YES HE IS!'

She spun round again. 'Oh no he isn't!'

'OH YES HE IS!'

Sam saw the spurt of flame from the barrel, and dived for the floor. Saw Edgar catapult backwards; the puzzled look on his face. Saw the gun in slow motion float upwards then drop silently to the ground, slowly, fluttering like a huge feather.

She spun around and saw what looked like snow suspended in the air all around the striped stand. Something hurtled along the floor, rattling loudly, bounced off the skirting board and stopped by her feet. Punch's head. It lay, grinning at her imbecilically, with one eye and part of its cheek missing.

Then the bang reached her, rippled through her like a shock wave, throwing her sideways, deafening her, like hands clapped over her ears so all she could hear was a faint ringing.

She saw the laughter fall from the faces, like masks that had dropped off. She scanned the room frantically. Nicky sat with his mouth open, holding his lollipop in his hand. She scrambled to her feet and stepped through the motionless children that were frozen like ornaments, and knelt down, flinging her arms around Nicky, hugging him. 'OK, Tiger! You OK?'

She looked around wildly as he nodded. 'Richard,' she said. 'Richard!' Conscious of saying the word, but unable to hear it. But he was already there, wading across the room as if someone had pushed the slow button on a video.

She could smell the acrid cordite now. Her ears cleared, and she heard a child sobbing. Nicky was still staring up at the stage, with its ripped-open canopy and the shreds of cloth that were floating down from it, as if he was waiting for Punch to pop back up and grin.

The candy-striped box shook once, then again, then moved several inches to the left. Then it moved again, drunkenly.

Oh God no, she thought.

Then it stopped moving and the Punch and Judy man came out, bewildered, his face sheet white, and staggered around the room with his arms outstretched in front of him. 'Police,' he said. 'Please fetch the police.' Then he staggered out into the hall.

Richard marched grimly across the room, holding his shotgun in his hand. Another child began to cry, then another.

Sam stood up and rushed out after the Punch and Judy man. 'Are you all right?' she asked.

'Police,' he said. 'Police! Fetch the police! The police!' He windmilled his arms.

'Are you all right?'

He stamped his foot like a child. 'I want the police!'

'I'll – I'll call them,' Sam said, backing away slowly. She felt Richard's cautioning hand on her arm, and he nodded for her to go back into the room.

'Shall we – play a game – everyone?' she heard Helen say, as she walked into the sea of shocked faces and the babble of tears, and through to the rear of the room. Edgar was sitting on the floor in the doorway, screaming, and she knelt down.

'Are you all right?' she said.

He carried on screaming.

She waited until he subsided. 'Are you all right?'

'My arm hurts.' Then he screamed again. 'It hurts!'

'Let me have a look at it.'

He shook his head and she grabbed his arm, furious. 'Let me see it.'

He looked up at her startled, and stopped screaming.

Sullenly he held it out. She tested it carefully. 'It's fine. You've just bashed it, that's all. Maybe that'll teach you not to play with guns.'

He stayed on the floor and glowered at her, as she walked back into the drawing room, looking down at the children, then again at the ripped canopy. There was a nasty peppered area on the new wallpaper, and she saw the edge of one curtain had also been damaged. She gazed around the rest of the room, at the clock on the mantelpiece. Twenty past four.

Oobie, joobie, joobie.

The pink curling finger.

She closed her eyes for a moment, hoping this too was a dream and that she could wake up and nothing had happened.

'Musical bumps!' said Helen. 'We'll play musical bumps!'

She opened her eyes. Helen was trying, trying so hard. 'Musical bumps,' Sam echoed. 'Good idea!' Trying to smile, trying to beam and look cheerful, staring down into the blank numbness and suspicion and fear, and she knew even without the cold silence that greeted her that you couldn't fool children with a cheery smile. Dragons did not die and people did not live happily ever after. But you had to try, because perhaps, sometimes, life was about trying.

Good idea!' she repeated. 'We'll play musical bumps!'

15

'Hi – Vivien, isn't it? Sorry, Virginia – of course! Look, I'm terribly sorry – Simon's a bit upset. We've had a bit of an . . . nobody's hurt, it's all right . . . accident with a – one of the children got hold of my husband's – but it's fine. Really—' Simon's mother's face had gone sea-sick white. 'Fine, really. He's OK – fine—'

Simon shuffled out of the house, his hair limp like his face, holding a silver foil balloon with the words 'THANKS FOR COMING TO NICKY'S PARTY!' printed on it in mauve letters, which bobbed above his head as he walked.

I had a dream about it, you know; yes! This is the second time actually. Last time was a little worse – 163 people snuffed it.

Stop looking like that, you snotty cow. I'm not loopy. I'm not a crank.

So I dreamed it? What did you want me to do? Cancel the party? Sorry Tiger, no more parties. Mummy has nasty dreams?

Anyhow, I didn't think it was a premonition – pre-cognition – what d'you call it? Seeing-the-future dream because a chunk of plaster came down and hit me on the face. So that's what I thought had caused the dream. I thought that after the aircraft dream, then Slider in the taxi, I was all spooked up. I just thought – hell – that was a weird dream. The dream book tells you that guns are phalluses – yup, schlonkers, and shooting is sexual aggression.

So I worked it all out . . . you see Richard and I aren't exactly what you'd call—

Thoughts shovelled through her mind as she walked across Covent Garden. It was a fine, sharp, cold Monday morning, and the fresh air was waking her up. She'd felt too tired to go for her early swim and was regretting it now. Her head was muzzy, sore with tossing in bed through the night watching an endless movie of threatening images: of Punch and guns and Slider grinning and people coming out of doorways and popping out of lift hatches, all wearing black hoods, and

119

eggshell cracks rippling across ceilings, and roofs coming down, smothering her, burying her in a dark void, burying her and Slider together, him on top of her, with the eyeless socket staring at her, laughing at her.

She pushed open the Art Deco door and went into the office. She felt disoriented. There were girls all around, on the sofas, on the chairs, and others standing. They had shoulder bags and clutch bags and big leatherette portfolios, and were dressed in battered macs or flak jackets or great puffy coats like eiderdowns wrapped around them over the tops of their jeans and boots; smoking, chewing, hair-tossing girls who looked hopefully at her as if she was a magician that had come to free them from the wicked witch.

Shit. Casting session.

Need that this morning like a hole in the head.

Midnight Sun.

Kapow!

For-hair-that-comes-alive-after-dark.

Boom!

Midnight Sun.

For-people-who-come-alive-after-dark.

Zap! Biff! Klap-klap-klap!

Midnight Sun.

Very-special-shampoo-for-very-special-hair.

Midnight Sun.

Very special shampoo.

For very special people.

'Morning Lucy. Ken in?'

'Gosh – ah – yah.'

'Anyone from the agency here yet?'

'Gosh – ah – no.'

Lucy looked as though she had been to a children's tea party, too, and had got ketchup and relish over her face and in her hair, except it was dye in her hair and make-up on her face, blodged, smudged and much too much.

'Good weekend?'

Lucy yawned. 'Yah, Bit heavy.'

Sam glanced around at some of the girls, walked past Ken's waxwork with its fresh *Daily Mail* and went up the three flights of stairs to his office. She rapped on the door and went in.

It was more like a lair than an office. Clients did not come up here; they were seen down in the basement with the snooker table and screening theatre and the full up-front image. The office under the steeply sloping caves was plain, simple. A comfortable sofa, two easy chairs, the walls covered in framed photographs of awards, of location shots: Ken in action, waving his arms, stabbing a finger, sitting in a chair, reflecting in the shadow of a crane dolly, Ken shaking hands with or issuing orders to a plethora of personalities, mostly minor familiar faces from the commercials on the box, and a few more famous ones, like Orson Welles, Robert Morley, Frank Bruno, John Cleese. The right-hand wall was dominated by a movie poster, a gaudy yellow and green high-tech mish-mash.

'ADLANTIS! THE LOST WORLD OF THE 20TH CENTURY!' proclaimed the title.

Ken had nearly lost his house because of that movie. Three years ago, when she'd first joined him, it had been touch and go. Cash flows, projections, interminable meetings with his bank manager that he reported to her, quite openly, afterwards. He'd been bust. Seriously bust. Over two million in the hole. He'd spent it on his dream, on his burning ambition, on his big break into the movie business. He'd put all the money he had and all the money he could borrow, hocked everything, the house and all, for his big break.

ADLANTIS! THE LOST WORLD OF THE 20TH CENTURY!

Five thousand years after civilisation is wiped off the face of the earth by thermo-nuclear war, primitive life starts up again on the planet earth . . . Centuries later, Ignav Flotum IIIrd, a Borodovian monk on an archaeological dig, discovers an old tin can . . . Convinced this is a time capsule deliberately left behind by another age it is opened in grand ceremony . . . to reveal . . . a television commercial director's showreel. From this reel a picture of late twentieth-century society is gradually pieced together. They conclude that since most of the movies only run for thirty seconds and the longest for only one minute, the concentration span of twentieth-century man must have been extremely low, thus contributing to his downfall, in spite of the clear socio-economic messages portrayed by these movies.

The movie had never been completed, and Ken had always been slightly evasive about the reasons. Sometimes it was because the leading actor had been a raving egomaniac. Sometimes the weather had been to blame. Sometimes the pressure of the executives from the studio that had partnered him but had never come up with all the dough they had promised. But mostly, she felt, it had never been finished because he had lost heart in it long before the money had ever run out. He promised to show her what there was of it, one day, but she wondered if he ever really would.

At least his house had been saved, his huge Victorian house on the edge of Clapham Common filled with weird objects, things he had collected, suits of armour, bizarre pictures, a tumbledown miniature Roman temple folly in the garden. He loved the house, had put years of thought and effort into making it something stunning, wild, with a Byzantine bathroom and medieval dining room and Baroque drawing room with a minstrel's gallery. Crazy, nuts – but stunning. The house had the space to take it without the styles clashing. The furniture was beautiful. It was a fun place. He lived in it on his own, from choice. His divorce had been a long time ago and the wounds had been deep. There were girls around, sure, always someone in tow, some bright young hopeful, more intelligent than the average but kept at a distance, kept at bay, kept out of his heart which was a strictly private place.

He was sitting behind his desk reading a letter, looking as if he had just got in, his denim jacket still on and a scarf hanging around his neck. He glanced up and smiled. 'Got my jelly baby?'

'Jelly baby?'

'From Nicky's party. You promised.'

'Oh – shit – I—'

'What time's the casting session meant to start?'

'Nine-thirty.'

'Anyone here yet?'

'Some of the talent. No one from Saatchi's.'

He looked at her. 'Christ, you look terrible. Are you OK?'

She nodded and swallowed hard.

'How did the party go?'

She turned away, wishing she hadn't come up here now, not wanting him to see the tears. She gazed at a photograph of Ken on his hands and knees, trying to show a sheepdog how to eat its food. She heard his intercom buzz sharply, then again. It gave a longer more insistent buzz and then was silent. She heard it buzz in another office, somewhere else in the building, and then she felt a hand lightly on her shoulder.

'What happened, Sam? Is it the air crash? Is the shock hitting you?'

She felt the tears running freely down her cheeks, and squeezed her eyes tighter, fighting. 'It's horrible, Ken. Oh Christ, it's horrible.'

'What's horrible?' he asked gently.

'It's happened again.'

'What's happened?'

She shook her head. 'Another dream. I had another dream.'

The intercom buzzed again and Ken answered it. 'OK,' he said, and put the phone back down. 'Everyone's here – we'll have to get down. Want to tell me later? We'll have a drink? This afternoon – after it's over?'

She sniffed. 'Thanks. I'll be down in a minute. Just have to make a quick phone call.'

She opened the door.

'Sam, don't worry. Everything'll be OK.'

She nodded, unconvinced.

'You haven't really had a break for a long time – you even came in over the Christmas hols. Why don't you take a few days off? Go away with Richard somewhere?'

'I'm OK. Thanks.'

'You need a holiday, Sam. Everyone does. Go skiing or something – have a break. Hey, I nearly forgot, I read this in a magazine and cut it out for you. It's about dreams.'

'Thanks.' She took it and put it in her handbag. 'I'm sorry I forgot your jelly baby,' she said, then went out and down the stairs.

Drummond was walking along the corridor, studying the label on a box he was carrying.

'Hallo.' He paused, as if trying to remember her name. 'Sam,' he added as if it was an afterthought.

'Hallo, Drummond.'

'Good weekend?'

'Fine.' She smiled wearily.

'How're the dreams?'

'Dreams?'

'Giraffes. You were dreaming about giraffes, or something.' He frowned and stared at the label again, mystified.

'I thought you'd said they don't dream much.'

'They don't.'

'I'd like to be a giraffe,' she said, opening the door and going into her office.

Smoke swirled around her, blue, thick Monday morning smoke, like mist. Claire seemed to need twice as many cigarettes on a Monday. 'Morning, Claire.'

Claire was concentrating on a script she was reading. Sam thought she detected the briefest nod, but wasn't sure. She opened the window sharply to release the fumes, to release her irritation at Claire, then changed the paper in the blotter on her desk.

'Good weekend?' said Sam, trying to force some conversation.

Claire glanced up for a second. 'All right.' Then read again.

She wondered what Claire did in the evenings, at weekends. All she knew was that she'd had a boyfriend called Roger with whom she'd split up, and that she lived in West London. Getting her to talk about her private life was like trying to pry open a superglued clam. She glanced down at her thick pile of post. It would have to wait.

'I've put the hotel details on your desk, Sam,' Claire said suddenly.

'Hotel?'

'Leeds. The Castaway presentation. You're doing it Friday week at nine in the morning. You asked me to book a hotel for the Thursday night.'

'Oh yes, thanks.' She quickly sifted through the post, the memos, costings to be done, the calls to be returned, checking for anything urgent, feeling tired and tensed up, wishing she had gone for her morning swim. Everyone talked about shrinks these days, about new stress ailments, yuppie flu: yuppie syndrome, she'd read somewhere. Maybe she had yuppie syndrome, whatever that was.

She saw the plane flying into the mountain. The finger curling in the night. Edgar coming into the room with the gun. Something cold trickled slowly through her, like a finger tracing its way down a frosted window. She shuddered, and pulled out a phone directory.

She found the number of Bamford O'Connell's Harley Street practice, and dialled it. A brisk pleasant woman answered.

'Is it possible to speak to Dr O'Connell?'

'May I ask who's calling please?'

'It's Mrs Curtis. I'm – we're – friends of his.'

He came on the line only seconds later, surprising her. 'Sam?' His thick Irish brogue was full of warmth.

'I'm sorry to call you at work, Bamford. I wondered if it was possible to see you – professionally.'

'That was a great evening last week.'

'Thanks.'

'You'd like to have a chat about something?'

'Please. I – it's about what we were discussing at dinner.'

'What was that?'

She looked at Claire, then down at her desk. 'Dreams. I've had another. I—'

126

'Would you like to come round to the flat this evening?'

Claire stopped reading and listened, without looking up.

'Is it possible to see you privately?' Sam felt herself getting flustered.

'Sure, come here, see me here. Is it very urgent?'

Yes, it's urgent as hell. 'No, I—'

'If it's urgent, I could try and make a few minutes today. Otherwise, Thursday morning, twelve o'clock. I'd have a bit more time then.'

'Thursday would be fine. Thanks, Bamford,' she said. 'I really appreciate it.'

As she went out of the office and closed the door, Claire turned around and smiled.

Sam went down the stairs slowly, thinking. The entrance atrium was packed with girls now, there was a babble of chatter, a haze of smoke and perfume, a small dog yapped excitedly and the switchboard was warbling while Lucy ignored it, phone to her ear, deep in some personal conversation. The front door opened and a man came in, fast, determined, pushing his way through the throng of girls, staring straight at Sam, walking towards her, striding; a great bully of a man dressed in black with a hood over his face, his eyes barely visible through the two thin slits.

She felt her legs buckling and a cold flushing sensation in her stomach; her head spun. She crashed against Ken's waxwork, saw the newspaper crumple and thought dimly, Damn, he'll be annoyed, as she stumbled, grabbing the cold, icy cold hand for support, felt something give, felt the whole arm tear away at the shoulder, and she staggered forward holding the hand as if it was a child she was taking across a road, staggered forward holding the hand with the severed arm attached to it, through the horrified faces and the screams of the girls, bounced off the wall, off Lucy's white Cadillac door, as she tried to stop, to back away, to turn and run from the man with the black hood and the eye slits, but she kept stumbling forwards, through the girls that were backing away open-mouthed . . . smart, pretty, beautiful girls staring at the arm, wide-eyed with horror, then her feet ran into each other and she fell forwards, making a slight whinnying sound.

Help me. Get me away from him. Oh Christ stop staring, don't you understand?

He was standing over her, in baggy black trousers and a grimy jacket and a black balaclava against the cold. He was holding a crash helmet in one gauntleted hand and a jiffy bag in the other, which he dropped as he knelt down to help her to her feet.

'Orl right, doll?' he asked. He smelled of leather and tobacco and a faint hint of hot engine oil.

'Fine, thanks – I . . .' She stood swaying, staring blankly around at the silent faces that stared back, listening to the yapping of the dog.

'Ssh, Bonzo! Quiet!'

'Sam! – Gosh, Sam. You OK?'

'Yes, I—'

'Ken Shepperd Productions?' said the man in the balaclava, holding out the jiffy bag. 'Need a signature.'

Sam stared down at the severed arm on the floor, at the sea of faces, at the crumpled newspaper. She picked up the arm and carried it back to the waxwork. 'Lucy, if you've got a moment . . .' She was conscious she was talking slowly, almost as if she was sitting on the ceiling, looking down at herself speaking. 'Perhaps you could nip out . . . and get a new *Daily Mail*.' She peered inside the shirt-sleeve and saw the jagged hole below his shoulder. She put the arm limply in his lap, then turned and went down the stairs to the basement.

16

The water hissed and spat; she felt the rush of heat in her nostrils, and rivulets of sweat running down her face and her body. She glanced at the thermometer, which was still rising, leaned back on her towel on the hard wooden slats and breathed in the scorching steam that was thick with the smell of pine.

'Any more?' Rowie stood, holding the small wooden bucket, naked and running with sweat too, her ginger hair matted to her head, her breasts hanging down, a hint of sag, of droop. She would have to be careful, Sam thought, she could easily run to fat. Was beginning to show signs already: her freckled skin was looking creamy, slightly puffy, around her neck, her arms, her thighs, and the great ugly stretch marks that seemed to be getting more noticeable.

Rowie. Partner in crime through five years of school. Sam had been chief bridesmaid at Rowie's wedding; she'd been flung the bouquet and caught it, and the superstition had come good. She'd met Richard and they got married eight months later.

Rowie. Life had come easy for her. Boyfriends, marriage, children, four of them, no effort. Everything progressed for her, straight, easy, linear; took life as it came and it had always come good.

'I feel guilty,' she once confided to Sam. 'I don't know why I have such a nice life.'

There was always a storm somewhere, or a disaster or a tragedy, waiting to happen, but so far it never had.

The only glitch had been discovering her third child was dyslexic, and that was being sorted out.

Sam looked at Rowie's body again. You are running to fat. Good. Hooray. Great. You're going to be plump and waddly in a few years' time.

Christ.

She felt a wave of shock at the malevolence of her thoughts. Did she wish fatness on her? Disaster? Was she really fond of her or jealous as hell? She stared down at her own body, good firm breasts, just right. They wouldn't get limp and saggy. She looked at her thighs and her legs, firm, skinny almost, like her wrists.

It must be like fucking a skeleton.

Richard had said that once about an anorexic-looking model who had walked past them on a beach. Did he think that of her too? Christ, it was hard to get the balance right.

A great fat shapeless hulk of a woman in a bathing hat came into the sauna, gave a surly nod and studied the thermometer.

Don't you dare put any more water on, Sam thought, watching her. Great tree-trunk thighs, a Mr Bibendum stomach and breasts like empty sacks. She had no bum at all, just the huge flab of her back which ran into her thighs; shapeless, as if God had dumped her on earth without having finished making her.

I don't ever want to look like that. No thanks. Skinny lib.

They plunged and shrieked and showered and the Big Hulk followed them, dampening their chat to nothing in particular. Sam showed Rowie where her leg had got burned from the careless waxing, and Rowie told her they'd taken the kids skiing over Christmas and she'd got a bruise on her bum that had only just gone. Then they dressed and went and helped themselves to gazpacho and tuna salads filled with beanshoots and pulses and nuts and seeds and other strange things neither of them recognised which would probably make their stomachs fizz and rumble all afternoon, sat down in a quiet corner, free now from the Big Hulk, and clinked their glasses of organic apple juice together.

'Cheers!'

They each smiled.

'Gosh, it's been ages,' Rowie said.

'Since before Christmas, actually. Not since September.'

'September? That long?'

'Before the hurricane. I'm certain.'

'Time. I don't know what happens to it. New watch? It's wonderful.'

'Richard gave it to me – to improve my street cred.'

'It's gorgeous. God, you know what Suzy said to me last Saturday? She said, "Don't come shopping with me, Mum, you ruin my street cred." Eleven. She's only eleven!'

Sam grinned. 'You can blame it all on commercials.'

Then there was a silence. A long flat silence in which all her thoughts began to pile up and cut away her elation at seeing Rowie again, and crush her down. Rowie split open her granary roll and dabbed a piece in her gazpacho, like a nurse swabbing a wound, thought Sam suddenly, and shivered.

'How's Richard?'

'Oh, he's . . . you know. Fine. Busy, I—' She shook her head, staring into Rowie's face the way she might have stared into a mirror.

'Oh God,' said Rowie, as she saw the trickle from Sam's eye, and heard Sam make short jerking sounds, her face contorted as if someone was pulling a wire tight around her neck.

They sat in silence while Sam tried to compose herself. She split open her roll as well, dunked a piece in the soup and felt the fierce taste of onions and tomato and garlic in her mouth.

'What's happened?'

Sam picked up her spoon and poked around in the soup bowl. She hadn't talked about it; not to anyone. Because . . . because it made her feel such a fool. Maybe Rowie knew anyway and was just being nice? Everyone else did; the Pearces and the Garforth-Westwards and the Pickerings and the . . . shit, oh shit, oh shit. She looked up.

'The boys – Roddy and Guy and that lot – have a shoot in Scotland the first week in January, every year. Richard always goes with them. He went off this year as usual, except two days after he'd gone, at six o'clock on a Sunday evening, I got a call from the police. I thought they were phoning to tell me he was dead or had an accident. It was horrible. They gave me the registration number of his BMW and asked who owned it.' She stared intently at Rowie's puzzled face, then jammed her elbows on the table and leaned forward, feeling better now she was actually talking about it. 'His car had been parked on a double yellow line outside a hotel in Torquay since Friday evening. They'd towed it away and it hadn't been claimed, so they'd been worried it had been stolen.' She gazed quizzically at Rowie.

'Naturally.' Rowie stared back, and realisation dawned slowly across her face. 'Oh God – you mean?'

Sam nodded. 'Yes. With a girl from his office – some hot-shot little Eurobond dealer.' She gazed down at her soup and rolled the spoon over. 'Unfortunately, I didn't immediately twig. I assumed his car had been stolen and dumped, so I rang the boys – I got their number in Scotland from Juliet – to speak to him.' She shook her head. 'Can you imagine what a fool I felt? How small I felt? His friends – our friends – they knew. They were trying to cover up for him like a bunch of school kids.'

'Christ. You poor thing, Sam. You must have felt an absolute—'

'I did.'

'What did Richard say?'

'Not a lot.'

'And he hadn't noticed his car was missing from Friday night to Sunday afternoon? What on earth was he—' Rowie stopped in mid-sentence. 'Oh, Sam, I'm sorry.'

Sam sighed. 'I thought our marriage was – you know – something very special, that we – that it was all going—' She grimaced and stared down at the table-cloth. 'I thought at least we respected each other. It's just . . . I don't know, the way he did it – the timing – I think Christmas is a special time. Am I being ridiculous?'

Rowie smiled and shook her head.

'All this thing about Aids. That's been bothering me too. I mean God knows where she's been.' She shook her head. 'But it's our friends – that's what's really got me. Christ, I saw some of them over Christmas. They knew then that he wasn't going shooting with them and I bet the girls knew too. I haven't heard a dicky from any of them since.'

Rowie sipped her juice, and spoke over the top of her glass.

'These things happen, Sam.'

'You always think they happen to other people.'

'It doesn't necessarily mean much. To Richard. It doesn't mean that he doesn't still love you very much, not necessarily; a lot of people have affairs just for sex.'

'I know. Part of me says it's daft to get so angry – that

133

all men have affairs, and it's part of married life, and another part feels that I don't want to touch him ever again. We haven't made love since. The thought of it makes me feel ill.' She stared at Rowie. 'Is that normal?'

'I don't know, Sam. All marriages are different. I always thought you had a good marriage.'

'Yes. I did too.' Sam shrugged. 'Richard just seems to have changed recently.'

'In what way?'

'It's hard to describe, exactly. He's started to make a lot of money – big money – the last eight or nine months. He's become very pally with a Swiss banker chap who I think's very weird, but that may just be me. He really fawns over him; rings him all the time to consult him on things. Speaks to him more than he speaks to me.' She swallowed some soup. 'The gun at the party . . . he would never have left his gun lying around before. He used to be quite a patient man, but he's become very snappy. He was quite brutal to Edgar before the party started.'

'Maybe he's worried. Everyone in the City's been very twitchy since the Crash. Did he lose much?'

'He said Andreas warned him it was going to happen, so he was OK.'

'Andreas?'

'The Swiss guy.'

'Have you ever been tempted to have an affair?' Rowie asked.

'No. You get gropers at parties, but they just turn me off. Have you?'

Rowie smirked and ate more bread. 'It's been going on for years,' she said.

Sam felt as if someone had pulled a plug out inside her. The whole established order of the world seemed to be turning on its head. 'Who with?'

'A black guy.'

'*What?*'

'My aerobics teacher.'

'You're kidding.'

'It's – strictly sex only,' Rowie said. 'You know, I didn't think women were meant to feel that way, but we have this great thing.' She smiled apologetically, and looked sheepish, as if wondering whether she should have told her after all.

'I thought you had a good marriage,' Sam said. 'Special, like ours.'

'Other pastures always look greener. Yup. Our marriage is fine. But James works all the time, and I just started getting . . . I don't know—' She smiled again. 'I'm not in a very good position to pass moral judgements, am I?'

'Is anybody?' Sam pushed her soup bowl aside and picked at her salad. 'How's Justin? Was he very upset after the party?'

'No,' Rowie said. 'He thinks it was all very exciting, that it was all part of the Punch and Judy show. How about Nicky?'

'I think he's very shocked still. Richard keeps going on about how resilient kids are, but I'm not so sure.'

Richard had paid the Punch and Judy man five hundred pounds to keep him from calling the police.

'*I don't want you to teach Nicky to shoot any more.*'

'*It wasn't his fault.*'

'*I keep thinking what might have happened. Just a few inches lower and he would have killed that man – or Nicky – or any of the children.*'

'*It was mother's bloody fault.*'

'*Don't be ridiculous.*'

'*It was. Leaving a cigarette burning on the hall table. Christ, if I hadn't seen that the bloody house would*'

135

*have gone up. I was so angry, I just forgot about the
gun, I suppose. That's what I must have done . . . I still
can't believe it. I always lock it away, and put the
cartridges on top of the wardrobe. I was sure I had
done that. Certain.'*

She'd tried to tell him she had dreamed it and he'd
told her not to be ridiculous.

'I'm not sure how resilient adults are either,' Rowie
said.

They stayed and talked until it was past three, about
men and life and kids and people they used to know and
didn't any more but bumped into or heard of from time
to time. Sam tried to ease the subject of dreams in,
wanted to talk to her, wanted to say 'I dreamed it
would happen' but the chance didn't come and there
wasn't a break in the conversation where she could
bring it in without feeling foolish.

Rowie suggested Sam took the afternoon off and they
went shopping. Hell, how many afternoons had Sam
taken off in the past three years, and surely everything
could wait until tomorrow? So they went shopping.
They tramped Covent Garden, then went across to
South Molton Street and each bought stuff the other
admired, and thought would look great, and Sam
wondered why she was bothering to look great for
Richard, and why Rowie was bothering to look great
for James, and when Rowie bought a really zany track-
suit number she knew that was not for James's benefit at
all.

Then suddenly Sam found the chance and told Rowie,
and instead of making her feel a fool Rowie said she
could understand; that *she* could tell when things
were going to happen herself, she told Sam; she got
FEELINGS. She had an aunt who was very psychic,

who always had the same dream the night before there was going to be a death in the family: she'd see a stranger in the distance walk on a beach at low tide and go into the sea and disappear, and the next day a member of the family would die, but she could never tell who.

They had drinks in a wine bar they stumbled across in Hanover Square, and then more drinks, a bottle or so of Chardonnay. It was good. Sam wondered if Archie at her dinner party would have approved of it. They got pissed, really, seriously, pissed, until they were clinking glasses and giggling like schoolgirls, and Rowie told her not to worry, everyone had FEELINGS about things from time to time and some people had stronger FEELINGS than others, but Sam was fine, she wasn't going nuts, and a hooded man from the past wasn't coming to get her. She was probably shaken up by Richard's affair and it was triggering off all sorts of unpleasant things in her mind.

That was all.

So go home.

Relax!

OK?

Sam grinned and started walking to clear her head, feeling vaguely guilty, but not that guilty, that it was late and she hadn't rung Richard and she'd missed Nicky's bedtime. She hadn't made up her mind whether to collect her car or take a taxi, and knew she shouldn't try to drive because she was smashed, but somehow she found herself in Covent Garden when the rain started to come down as if a tray of water had been tipped out of the sky, and there wasn't a taxi in sight, so she sprinted for the car park.

17

The rain seemed to stop as abruptly as it started, leaving the London night in a shiny black lacquer on which spangles of light danced, winked, glinted. She glanced out of her side window and could see the reflection of the Jaguar on the black tarmac as clear as if she was driving beside a lake.

A Belisha beacon winked at her and she stopped. A man hurried over the crossing holding a broken umbrella.

THE NORTH. M1

She frowned. North. She was going north. Christ, she was sloshed. What was the time? What the hell was the time? London seemed quiet, too quiet. She stared at the clock, and could hear it ticking loudly, suddenly, like a grandfather clock.

Quarter to ten.

It felt like 4 a.m.

Quarter to ten. Christ. Had she and Rowie been drinking all this time?

She came into Swiss Cottage, and a car hooted angrily on her inside.

'Oh sod off,' she shouted into the dark, swinging the steering wheel, then heard the angry horn of a taxi right beside her. She braked cautiously and blinked, the lights blurring together. Slow down. Got to slow down. Wrong direction. Got to head for the City.

But she turned further away, going up Fitzjohn's Avenue towards Hampstead. A white Ford Capri, sitting up on huge wheels, drew alongside her and a yobbo gave her the thumbs up. She turned away contemptuously, then dropped down into second gear and floored the accelerator. She felt the tail of the Jaguar snake as the rear wheels spun, then eased off, felt the tyres bite, heard the roar of the engine, felt the surge of power as she accelerated forwards. She pulled right across, overtaking in the oncoming lane, saw headlights coming down the hill towards her, closer. The engine was screaming, she changed into third and missed the gear. There was an angry grating and the car began to slow down, the headlights almost on top of her now. She was still stabbing the gear lever, trying to find the gate, and jerked the wheel hard to the left. The lorry passed her, inches away, shaking her with its vibration and its slipstream.

Shit.

Then she saw the police car coming down the hill, slowing, as if it was looking for somewhere to turn and come after her.

Stop.

Stop, she thought. Got to stop.

Don't be stupid. Get away!

She swung right, without indicating, into a side road and accelerated down it. It came out into a busy street, brightly lit, with shops, restaurants, cafés, pubs. Hampstead High Street.

Shit.

She turned left, then saw another side street on her right, and turned into it. It had trees, cars parked down both sides and large terraced houses. She looked at her mirror for signs of a car following. Nothing. She slowed right down, crawling along, until she found a gap, and pulled into it. She switched off the ignition, then the lights, and breathed out. Quiet. So quiet, she thought.

She climbed out of the car into the strange translucent light and looked up, hazily, at the full moon that was burning down between the branches of the trees. Bright, she thought, brighter than the sun. She walked along the road then stepped onto the kerb to avoid a car which came thundering down, far too fast, as if it had been deliberately trying to hit her, and she stood for a moment, watching its tail lights disappear.

She glared up at the brilliant moon again, then walked on down the road, afraid of the shadows of the trees, like dark pools of blood. Afraid of the trees themselves that seemed to be watching her, and afraid of the brilliant light of the moon in the open that lit her up, exposing her like a startled rabbit caught in a car's headlamps.

She breathed a sigh of relief as she came out into Hampstead High Street. Cars. People. Noise. The glare of the moon was diffused by the streetlights, by the lights from the shop windows. She felt safe now and looked around for a taxi. Two passed in succession, both carrying passengers. A greasy-looking man in a Japanese sports car slowed down, peering at her. She turned away and noticed a red, circular tube sign a short distance away. She glanced once more up and down for a taxi, then walked up the street and into the station.

It was grimy, draughty, and seemed to be empty, apart from the woman in the ticket office, who stared at Sam through the Plexiglass window. A severe, elderly woman with her hair raked sharply back, her face caked in make-up and her lips a brilliant ruby red. Something about her reminded Sam of her aunt.

'Wapping,' Sam said. 'I'd like a ticket to Wapping.'

'Return?' said the woman sternly, as if it was a reprimand.

'No, I just . . . I just want to go there.' She was conscious that she was still drunk, slurring her words, stumbling over them, and her mind raced, trying to find the word she wanted, but it ducked away elusively, like a child dodging behind dark trees. 'I don't want to come back.'

'We don't do one-way from this station,' the woman said, her head not moving as she spoke. 'No singles.'

Single. That was the word. Single. Why had it been so difficult? she wondered.

'I'll have a double then,' said Sam and, almost immediately, the make-up on the woman's face began to crack, and her lips parted and widened. For an instant, Sam was frightened as the woman's expression changed and her mouth widened even more, then her shoulders began to shake up and down and her eyes sparkled. She was laughing. Sam realised; she was roaring with laughter. At her joke.

'Have a double!' said the woman. 'Have a double.' She roared again, and Sam grinned happily, feeling warm, warm deep inside.

'Funny. That was so funny.' She winked at Sam and jerked her head. 'Go on, that was so funny I couldn't give you a ticket after that.' She jerked her head, 'Go on. If the inspector catches you, tell 'im Beryl said it was all right.'

'I ought to pay you,' said Sam.

'Nah.' She jerked her head again, and Sam walked off past her and through the empty barrier.

She found herself facing a bank of lifts, with large steel doors, more like goods lifts than passenger lifts.

She pushed the button for the lift and waited. Faintly, behind her, she heard a peal of cackling laughter from the woman in the ticket office, and smiled to herself. The woman laughed again and the tone changed slightly, as if she was laughing at her rather than with her. Then she saw the sign in front of her, red letters on white board, huge. So huge, she wondered how she could have missed it: OUT OF ORDER.

She walked to the staircase, and then began to descend the stone steps that spiralled down, around a steel-cased shaft, listening to the clacking echo of her footsteps. WARNING. DEEPEST STATION IN LONDON. 300 STEPS. USE ONLY IN EMERGENCY. Somewhere in the distance she heard a clank and a rattle, and the sound of voices. The wall stayed relentlessly constant, unrelieved even by graffiti. Grimy drab tiles.

Christ. Like going down into a public lavatory.

The sign was right, the stairs seemed as if they would go on for ever, and she wondered how far down she was now. It felt deep, very deep, but there were no markers, no clues, just the same monotonous downward spiral, around the shaft. She passed a cigarette butt that looked as if it had been recently stamped out. It was getting darker, she realised. Further away from the moon. The colour seemed to be going from the tiles, and the temperature was getting colder.

Then she felt the jerk of a hand around her neck.

For a split second she was furious, then fear surged through her, paralysing her.

No. Not me. Please not me.

She was pulled backwards so sharply she thought her spine was going to snap, and she cried out in pain. She felt something in her neck, pushing in, crushing the bone and pushing out the air, choking her. She felt the hand, hard, rough, over her mouth, crushing her lips against her teeth, and tasted blood. She tried wildly to bite the hand, felt it jammed up against her nose. It smelled of onions.

Like Slider.

Please God it's Slider. Please God this is a dream and I can wake up.

She heard a door open, and felt herself being dragged

through. She tried to kick, to break her mouth free and shout, then she was pulled again and her feet slid away completely from under her, and she was arched backwards, violently, her scream of pain trapped in her throat.

The light faded completely, and she heard the clang of a door closing.

She was in pitch darkness. Herself and her attacker.

She heard his breathing, hoarse, panting. Malevolent.

Help me. Please. Don't let this be happening.

She felt a hand, rough, calloused, sliding up her thigh. She struggled wildly, but could not move. The fingers reached the top of her tights, and she felt them rummage harshly through her pubic hairs for an instant, then thrust up deep inside her, his fingernails cutting her like a knife, and she wanted to scream, but still the hand was over her face.

Oh God, no you bastard, let me go. No, *no*.

Then she felt her panties tugged down, and heard them ripping.

She tried to bite again, tried to wriggle, but his grip was like a vice, and every movement was agony. She stared, wide-eyed, into the darkness. There was a click then a whirring sound somewhere in the room. Think. Think, for Christ's sake. Self defence. Hurt him. Fingers in his eyes. His eyes. Which way was he facing?

She could hear him breathing heavily, grunting, like a pig. She felt a cold draught of wind up between her legs, then the fingers thrust in even further, so hard they were going to split her apart, heard the pop of a button, then the sound of a zipper. Her assailant was moving, slowly, cautiously, preparing himself.

No. God no. Please God no.

'Kiss me. Tell me you love me,' he said in a bland North London accent, and she felt his mouth nuzzling her ear. 'Tell me you love me,' he repeated, in a seductive French accent this time, nuzzling her ear again, and she jerked away, from the wetness of his mouth, from the stench of cigarettes and beer and onions on his breath. The fingers slipped out, probed gently through her pubic hair, caressing. 'Tell me you love me,' he said again, harshly. Then there was silence as she stared around the dark, her heart crashing, her brain racing, thinking, thinking, listening to his panting, which was getting louder, faster.

Outside she heard footsteps, and she felt her assailant grow tense, the hand over her mouth tighten.

Help me. Please help me.

The footsteps passed by, two or three people. She heard someone call out, someone laugh, someone shout something back. They faded away. There was a deep rumble, and the floor trembled slightly for a moment.

'Tell me you love me,' he said. 'Tell me you love me.'

She felt the hand lift away a fraction, enough to let her speak, and she lunged out with her mouth, as wide open as she could stretch it, and bit, hard, tried to bite a chunk out of his hand.

'You bitch!'

As his grip released, she sprang away from him, kicking out, smashing with her fist, then kicked again, felt something soft, heard a groan, then her head smashed into the wall and she bounced off, dazed.

'You cunt bitch!'

She kicked out again, as hard as she could, scrabbling with her hand to find the door, then kicked again, hit air, could not see his shadow in the darkness. She felt a hand grab her hair and lunged forward with her finger, felt something soft, gelatinous, and he screamed. She thrust forward, kicking out wildly again, pushing with her finger and again he screamed. The grip on her hair slackened.

Door handle. It was in her hand. She pulled, and the door opened and she fell out onto the stone staircase. 'Help!' she tried to scream, but it only came out as a whisper. 'Help me. Oh God help me!' She scrambled up the steps. Christ, run, for God's sake. Run. She tried, but she couldn't even raise her leg to the next step up. She heard the door opening behind her. Run, run! She pushed forward against the air that was like a wall. Help! She tried to scream again, but nothing would come out.

She grabbed the hand rail, trying to pull herself up the staircase, but it was steep, too steep. She pulled again, feeling her arm muscles tearing against the strain, against the force that was preventing her.

'Cunt bitch.'

She tried again, but still she could not move.

The hand closed around her neck, and she was jerked violently back.

She lashed out with her elbows, but her arms were being held tightly and she could scarcely move them. 'No!' she screamed. 'No! No! No!'

She jammed her feet down onto the steps, trying to get a purchase, but it was no use. She was being dragged back down, back to the dark room.

'No! No! No!'

'Bugs?'

'No!'

'Bugs?'

'No!'

'Sam?'

The voice had changed, was gentle now. A different voice.

'Bugs, are you OK?'

She felt a cold draught blow across her face.

'Bugs, darling?'

She felt the sweat pouring down her face.

'Bugs?'

Her whole body was drenched, and she shivered.

'Bugs?'

She heard the rustle of sheets, the clank of a bed spring, then a click and there was brilliant white light that dazzled her, brighter even than the moon.

'You OK, Bugs?'

Richard's face, close, so close she could not focus.

'Horrible. It was horrible.'

'You were screaming,' he said.

'Sorry. I'm sorry.' She eased herself up in the bed, and sat, her heart pounding.

'Probably the booze,' he said.

'The booze?' She was aware of a sharp ache in her head.

Jumbled memories jostled in her mind. Christ, how much had she drunk? How had she got home? She tried to remember, panicking. There was just a blur.

'You were pissed as a fart.'

'I'm sorry,' she said blankly.

'It was bloody funny. The way you kept telling Julian not to worry.'

'Julian?'

'Holland.'

Holland, she thought. Julian Holland. Edgar's father. She remembered now. He had been in the flat when she had arrived home. 'I felt sorry for him.'

'I think he thought you'd flipped. You virtually sat on him, and kept telling him it was all your fault, because you'd ignored your dream.'

Dream. She shivered. 'He looked so – so unhappy. So guilty.'

'Can hardly expect him to be jumping up and down for joy.'

'It was nice of him to come round.'

'I played squash with him. He wanted some exercise.'

'Did I thank him for the flowers?'

'About a hundred times.'

She stared at the curtains, flapping gently in the draught. 'They're grubby,' she said.

'Grubby? The flowers?'

'The curtains. We'll have to get them cleaned soon. We've never had them cleaned.' Her head ached and her mouth was parched. She smelled onions again. Hot warm onions and booze and stale smoke. 'Have you been eating onions?'

'Yah. Pickled. We had fish and chips and pickled onions. They were seriously good. From that place – that little parade of shops.'

'You played squash and then had fish and chips?'

'Yah.'

'I thought you were trying to lose weight.' She sipped her water, then closed her eyes tightly against the light and felt herself back, suddenly, in the dark room. She shuddered and sat up, afraid to go to sleep.

'OK?'

'Fine,' she said. 'I'm fine. I think I'll just – read – for a while.'

18

Bamford O'Connell's waiting room smelled of furniture polish and musty fabric, like every medical waiting room Sam had ever been in. *Tatler*, *The Field*, *Country Life*, *Yachts & Yachting* and *Homes & Gardens* had been laid out neatly. Too neatly, fanatically neatly. She wondered if they had been laid out by the patient who was closeted with O'Connell now, behind the closed door.

I've got this thing about tidiness, Doctor. I've just tidied up your waiting room. If there's someone out there untidying the magazines, I'm going to chop their head off with a machete. You will understand?

Of course. If that's what you feel you must do. It's important not to repress your feelings.

It would be a good thing if I did chop her head off, wouldn't it? Stop her dreaming.

Yes it would.

I could take her head home in a plastic bag and stick it on a spike in the garden. And every morning I could say to her 'Naughty, naughty, naughty, who had another bad dream last night?'

Someone with a ballpoint pen had added tiny round glasses and a goatee beard to the model on the front of *Vogue*, making her look like a rather sinister Sigmund Freud.

The door behind her opened, startling her, and she heard Bamford O'Connell's voice, slightly softer than usual, with less of an Irish accent. 'Sam, hallo. Come in.'

The psychiatrist was wearing a sober Prince of Wales check suit and serious tortoiseshell glasses. The eccentrically dressed bon viveur of the dinner table had changed into a studious man of authority. Only the centre parting and the hair that was too long remained of the private Bamford she knew. She found the change to this new persona oddly reassuring, as if it put a distance between her and Bamford the friend.

He closed the heavy, panelled, privacy-assured door with a firm click, and the sudden silence of his consulting room startled her. She wondered if it was soundproofed. Like eyes adjusting to light, her ears slowly adjusted to the stillness that was only faintly disturbed by the hissing of car tyres from the rain-soaked Harley Street three floors down, and from the gentle, more constant hissing of the wall-mounted gas fire.

The room was neat, elegant, sparse, with a mahogany desk, an oak bookcase, two comfortable reproduction Victorian armchairs, a chaise longue, and a large painting on the wall that looked like rhubarb in a thunderstorm.

'Sit yourself down, Sam.' He pointed to one of the armchairs. 'Great evening that was, last week. Wonderful fun.'

'Good. It was nice seeing you both. Harriet's looking well.'

He sat down behind his desk, the window framing him in a landscape of rooftops, grey sky and falling rain; heavy, steady rain, the sort of wet Sunday afternoon rain you saw falling in movies and through French windows on theatre sets. He tugged his jacket sleeves up a fraction to reveal a smart watch with a crocodile skin strap, and neat sapphire cufflinks. 'So, to what do I owe this great honour?'

'I need some help – advice. It's professional, this visit. I want to pay you for it.'

'You'll do no such thing.'

'Please, Bamford, I want to.'

'I won't hear of it. Anyhow, I shouldn't be seeing you without a referral from your doctor.' He winked. 'Tell me.'

She looked down at the carpet, expensive, pure wool, mushroom coloured, then up again. 'We were talking at dinner – about dreams . . . premonitions.'

'That air disaster in Bulgaria,' he said. 'You'd dreamed about it.'

'Yes.' She paused, glanced up at the light bulb

hanging from the ceiling and felt a cold chill. 'I – I had another dream.' She stared at the bulb again. 'Over the weekend . . . which came true.'

He tilted his head slightly and interlocked his fingers. 'Tell me about both the dreams.'

She told him of the air disaster dream, and the Punch and Judy dream, and Punch appearing with a black hood and the shotgun, and what happened subsequently. He sat in silence staring at her so intently he was beginning to make her squirm. He seemed to be reading her face like someone reading the small print on a policy.

'This black hood that was in both dreams – do you have any associations with it?'

She sat still for a moment, then nodded.

'What are they?'

She looked down at her fingers. 'It's . . . something from childhood. I – It's a long story.'

He smiled encouragingly. 'We've got plenty of time.'

'There was a boy in our village,' Sam began. 'I suppose you could call him the village idiot, except he wasn't comical. He was nasty . . . malevolent, evil. He lived with his mother in a farmhouse just outside the village. It was a creepy place – quite big, isolated. There were always rumours of weird things going on there.'

'What sort of things?'

'I don't know. Black magic, that sort of thing. His mother was sort of . . . a witch, I suppose. She was foreign. My aunt and uncle used to talk about her occasionally, and the rumour was that she was the wife or the mistress of a German warlock who was into ritual killing, and that Slider was his son, but—' She shrugged – 'that was village gossip, probably. She was certainly very weird. Reclusive. There were a lot of strange goings on at the farm. A friend who lived in the village told me

150

years later that the woman had had an incestuous relationship with her son, but I don't know how she knew that.' Sam smiled, 'You get a lot of strange gossip coming out of a small community. She – the woman – got pregnant, had a daughter, but no one ever saw her. I don't know whether it was by her son. There were rumours of ritual orgies and God knows what else. All the children were always told to keep well away. The house had a very creepy feel. I can still remember it very clearly. People's pets used to disappear – dogs and things – and they always said that Slider had got them.'

'Slider?'

'That was his nickname. He had a glass eye which he used to slide in and out. He'd walk down the High Street and when he saw anyone he'd slide it out and wave it at them. It was all red, livid, behind, and his eyelashes used to bend in the wrong way.' She looked up at O'Connell, but he showed no reaction. 'Sometimes he put a small onion in his eye instead. He'd take it out, wave it at someone, chew it, then spit it out.'

O'Connell frowned slightly.

'No one knew how he'd lost it. The rumour was that a cat he was torturing had scratched it out, through I think he'd been in a car accident and had lost it then. There were rumours that he used to torture animals – the pets that he'd taken. After he died and his mother moved away the garden was dug up. Apparently it was like an ossuary.'

'How old was he?'

'Early twenties, I suppose. He also had another deformity. On one hand he only had one finger and a thumb; it was withered – horrible – almost like pincers.'

'Was that from an accident?'

'I don't know. I think it was something he was born with.'

'How did he die?'

Years, she thought. I haven't talked about this for years. Not to anyone. The fear had been so strong that she'd never even told Richard. In case . . . in case just telling it brought it all back. She felt something moving towards her, a shadow like a cloud, or a wave that was piling up behind her; she shivered, and stared at O'Connell again, for courage, for reassurance.

'I killed him.'

There was a long silence. 'You killed him?' he said finally.

Sam nodded and bit her lower lip. Talking about this . . . weird. She thought it had all faded away; thought that if she forgot it all for long enough, it might be as if it never had happened. Thought that after twenty-five years she was safe, finally. Safe from Slider.

'You murdered him?'

'No . . . I – I was playing out in the fields, and I heard this scream coming from a barn. It was quite isolated, almost derelict – hardly ever used. I ran over to it and heard noises up in the hayloft – horrible strangling noises – so I climbed up the ladder and saw him – Slider – wearing this black hood . . . strangling – he'd just raped and strangled a girl.

'He chased me across the loft, then got on top of me. I didn't know who he was at that moment, because of the hood, but I knew he was going to kill me. I bit him, and kicked and somehow I gouged him in the eye and his eyeball flew out. He got even madder, then . . . I don't remember exactly what happened but part of the loft was rotten, and he fell through and got impaled on an old machine on the ground.' She was shaking now, shaking so hard that even when she clenched her hands together she could not keep them still. 'There was a metal bit – a sort of spar – that had gone right through his neck. I could see him staring up at me; there was blood all around him. It was dark in the loft, because the light bulb had broken – it had got broken in the struggle. There was myself and the girl that was dead. I knew she was dead – I don't know why, but I knew – but I didn't know if Slider was dead or OK. He still had the hood on, and all I could see was the one eye looking out of the slit at me. I didn't know if he was going to climb up off the machine suddenly and come and kill me . . . And I didn't dare go down because—'

'What happened?'

'I stayed up there. I'd worked out that somehow I could stop him from climbing the ladder – I would throw bales of straw on him if he tried – but he still didn't move. Then it got pitch dark and I couldn't see him any more, and that got even more frightening. Then, later, I heard voices, saw torches, and I heard my father. I just screamed and screamed.'

'And Slider was dead?'

'Yes.'

'Who was the other girl?'

'Someone from the village. I didn't really know her. She was older than me – in her teens.'

'How old were you?'

'Seven.'

'That's quite a memory to carry from childhood, Sam.'

'There's more,' she said. She looked down at her wrist and began to toy with her watch strap. 'After this happened, I started dreaming of Slider.'

'One would have expected you to,' said O'Connell.

'I used to have the same recurring dream. That I heard the scream and went to the barn and climbed up into the loft, and Slider would come out of the darkness at me.

Except he didn't die in the dream. He was always about to get me – lying on top of me, with his one eye missing and just this red socket coming closer – then I'd wake up, and something bad would happen.'

'Such as what?'

'It started small. The first time I had the dream, my hamster died the next day. Then, each time, it seemed to get worse. I'd get sick, or my mother was having a baby and lost it. Then last time I had the dream I woke up and . . . my parents had been killed in a car crash.'

'That was all when you were seven?'

'Yes.'

'And you didn't have the dream again after that?'

'No . . . it was almost as if he'd got what he wanted, I suppose – got his revenge.'

'Could you tell at all from your dreams what sort of bad things were going to happen?'

'No.'

'And now you're getting the image of this Slider with these two dreams?'

'There have actually been three dreams with him in.' She told him of her dream in the taxi. 'I had a very weird dream the night before also,' she smiled. 'You probably think I'm cracking up.'

'Tell me it.'

She told him about her dream of Hampstead underground. When she finished, it was still impossible to read his reaction.

'This hooded man – Slider – was this the man in your dream down the underground?'

'I don't know – I didn't think so. I couldn't see his face, but there didn't seem to be a mask – except—' She tailed off. 'He smelled of onions.'

'You look very tired Sam. Are you on any medication?'

'No.'

'Not sleeping pills? Tranquillisers?'

'No. Nothing.'

'Does Richard know you're here?'

She hesitated. 'No . . . I'd be grateful if you didn't—'

'Of course.'

She stared into his expressionless eyes then away at the expanse of polished wood on the top of his desk, with nothing on it except a gold pen, lying flat. Then she glanced down at her fingers. Biting her nails, she thought, looking at her thumb, with part of the skin bitten away as well. Ugly.

'I wondered if there were any pills you could give me that would stop me from dreaming.' She was picking at it, picking, picking. Stop. She tried, then began to pick again.

He pushed out his lower lip, then tapped his gold pen with his fingers. 'There are inhibitor drugs, but they have a lot of side effects. They'll cut down your dreaming at night but you'll start having day dreams, hallucinations, instead. Tell me, Sam, if you're seeing the future, what are you really frightened of? Isn't it helpful? Can't you use this information?'

'It's not like that. It's as if . . . as if I'm making these things happen by dreaming about them.'

'You caused the plane to crash?'

She nodded.

'And it wouldn't have crashed if you hadn't dreamed it?'

She felt her face redden slightly, and shrugged.

'These dreams you had as a child after this hooded man was killed – how soon after the dreams did things happen?'

She racked her brains back in time. Hazy. Childhood was just a mass of images. Like dents in an old desk they became smoothed over the years, part of a familiar landscape, and you couldn't remember the order in which they came, no matter how hard you tried. 'It varied, I suppose.'

'A day? A week? Several months?'

She heard the cry of her own voice.

'*Mummy!*' Hugging. Crying.

'*It's all right, darling.*'

'It was always soon. The next day, or a few days.'

'Did you ever have anything bad happen when you hadn't had dreams?'

'I – I suppose so, yes.'

Silence.

I see what you're saying.

She picked again, tore away a piece of skin and it hurt.

'There's an air disaster in the news every few weeks, Sam. If you dream of an air disaster, it's almost bound to come true.'

'Not with all the details in my dream, surely?'

'Did you write them down? Before you heard of the disaster?'

'No.'

'I know you're an intelligent girl, Sam, but you're very tense at the moment. Do you think there's any chance at all you might be crediting your dream with more detail than was in it? That you might be making the dream fit the facts?'

'No.'

'Look at the other dreams for the moment – your hooded fellow in the taxi who gave you a boarding card. That doesn't seem to me to be anything prophetic. You found out that there was no such seat number on the plane, didn't you?'

'Yes, I did.'

'35A, wasn't it? Those numbers might have some other significance. Do they mean anything to you?'

'No.'

'They'll be in your dream for a reason. Everything in our dreams is there for a reason, but you can only get to understand them if you go through analysis.' He smiled. 'Don't look so worried.'

'Do you think I should go to an analyst?'

'If you feel your dreams are disturbing you to the point where they're affecting the quality of your life, then it's something you could consider.'

'What would an analyst do?'

'He would try to uncover the anxieties that are causing these dreams. Try to find the root of them. Bring them to the surface. Help you to understand why you are having them.'

She picked at a different nail. 'I still think that I've – that these things have been premonitions, Bamford.'

He pulled open a drawer on the right of the desk then pushed it back in again, without appearing to take anything out. Then he did the same with the left-hand drawer. Like an organist setting his stops, she thought. 'Let's have a look at the Punch and Judy dream: Punch disappears, reappears in a black hood and fires a shotgun at you. You wake up and a chunk of plaster has fallen on you from the wall. Is that right?'

'From the ceiling.'

'The next day a kid gets hold of your husband's gun and fires it during the Punch and Judy show.' He picked up his gold pen and rolled it between his neatly manicured fingers. 'Well, there are connections, for sure, but I don't think you could have foretold what was going to happen from that dream. I don't think anybody could. Let's turn it around a bit, Sam. How did a boy of six get hold of a loaded gun?'

'Richard—' She hesitated. 'We're not sure. Richard thinks he must have left it out. He normally keeps it upstairs, with the cartridges on top of a wardrobe so it's out of Nicky's reach.'

He nodded. 'So he might have put it away?'

'It's possible, but unlikely. The boy said he found it against a wall.'

O'Connell leaned forward. 'You see, Sam, it could well be that dream was telling you something, but not in the way you think. Consider this as an alternative: you gave up your career for Nicky, and because his birth was difficult you couldn't have any more children. Maybe you feel anger at him. Maybe deep in your subconscious you feel that if you didn't have him around—?'

Sam stared, flabbergasted for a moment, anger building up inside her. 'Are you saying it was me? That I gave him the gun?'

'I'm not saying for a moment you do feel that way, but I want to show you the possible alternatives, areas that an analyst would probe, trying to find the real reason for that dream. Your dreams indicate to me you have problems that you've got to get to grips with. By dismissing them as premonitions, you are ignoring their real meanings, brushing them away under the carpet. It's much easier to put them down as premonitions than to face their real truths.'

'Don't you think you're trying to dismiss everything with a cosy Freudian explanation?' she said coldly.

'I'm not trying to dismiss anything. But you need to understand what dreams are really about, Sam.' He put the gold pen neatly down on the desk and steadied it to prevent it from rolling. 'Our lives are a constant balance between sanity and madness. Most of us get by all right. We keep our emotions under control when we're awake, but they all come pouring out in our dreams when we're asleep: jealousies, pain, thwartings, grief, anger, desires, and the past. Most importantly, the past.' He realised the pen was distracting her, and put it away in a drawer. 'Daddy's having it off with my mummy and I'd like to do that, but if he catches me, he'll cut my goolies off . . . Or in your case, Daddy's got a huge donger and I've only got a tiny clitoris, so I'm inferior . . . you know? The primal scene and all that stuff?'

She smiled weakly.

'The dream you had about going down the underground . . . you've told it very well. You've made it sound like a narrative. I could follow the story easily.' He raised his hands. 'But I don't understand a thing about it. You see, it's probably full of symbols that are personal to you.' He paused and looked awkward suddenly. He shifted about in his chair, then leaned forward, put his elbows on his desk and rested his chin on his hands.

'Sam,' he said softly. 'Do you mind if I ask you something very personal? If you don't want to answer that's perfectly all right.'

'No – of course.'

'I couldn't help noticing at dinner that things seemed very strained between you and Richard.'

Her face reddened.

'Are things all right between you?'

Penis starvation. Of course. That's unhinged me. That's why I have these nutty dreams. Of course!

He leaned back, without taking his eyes off her. 'I think you would find it much easier to talk to a stranger. Would you like to see a member of my unit at Guy's who without harassing you in any way would help you to sort it out?'

'I don't know.'

'If your dreams are bothering you to the point where you feel they're affecting the quality of your life, then you should consider it. Equally, they might all just go away.'

'They're not going to go away,' she said.

'Why do you think that?'

'I don't know. It's just a feeling.'

'Would you like me to recommend someone?'

'I wish I could believe you, Bamford. I wish I could believe all that analysis stuff. But I know I'm having premonitions. I could have saved the lives of those people.'

'Forget premonitions, Sam. They're nothing more than lucky guesses. That's all. Don't get caught up down that alleyway.'

She felt a flash of anger. 'Why not? Nicky could have been shot – any of those children could have been. I might have been able to prevent it.'

He shook his head gently, and it inflamed her anger even more. 'Whatever you decided, Sam, let me give you one piece of advice. Stay away from the hokum guys.' He tapped his head. 'It's all in here. It doesn't matter what anyone else says. I know. The medical profession knows.'

'God you're a smug bastard,' she said.

He did not react at all. There was a long silence, in which he continued to stare at her, and she felt her face getting hotter and redder, sorry she had said that, guilty that she'd taken so much of his time and had spat it back in his face.

'Sam,' he said, 'you've come to me for help, for advice. I've given it to you. What do you want me to do? Tell you to go and see a clairvoyant? A medium? Send you off to a dream group? To a parapsychologist? I want to help you, not make things worse.'

'If you want to help me, Bamford, you've first got to believe me.'

He pushed each of the sleeves of his jacket up in turn, scratched his nose, then put his elbows back on the desk.

'I'll tell you what I believe. I believe that *you* genuinely believe you are having premonitions.'

'And you think they're just delusions?' She stared at him, the anger flaring again. 'Do you want someone else to die? Will that prove it?'

He sat back in his chair and rested his hands on the arms. 'Hooded men,' he said. 'Your hooded fellow – Slider?'

She nodded sullenly.

'Sam, you're a grown woman. You're a mother and a successful businesswoman. And you're still dreaming of your childhood bogeyman. There's no living person I know of who can foretell the future consistently. There never has been. There are lucky guesses and intelligent guesses, and sometimes the brain whirrs away during our sleep and presents probabilities to us. That's all. Your big ugly hooded fellow who stinks of onions is frightening the hell out of you, and you think you're being haunted by the ghost of someone who died twenty-five years ago. Some creature that comes to you in your dreams and is trying to destroy you. If he wants to destroy you, then why does he keep tipping you off? Giving you warnings?'

She felt cold again, cold and empty and all twisted up. She stared up at the light bulb then out through the window at the rooftops and the leaden sky. 'Maybe it's some game he's playing. Some macabre game to sort of . . . torment me . . . You know? Just playing with me – until he's ready.'

'We're all haunted by ghosts, Sam; but they're not

spirits, or demons that have come back from the grave. They are our own personal fears, anxieties.' He tapped his head again. 'We need to get inside there, Sam, and pluck him out. That's what an analyst would do.'

She stared at him then shook her head. 'I wish you were right, Bamford.' She screwed up her eyes tightly.

Christ I wish you were right.

19

Sam sat in front of her dressing table, putting on her make-up. She was wearing the black lace bra, panties and suspenders that Richard had given her for Christmas the year before. She wondered if he would remember, and she wondered why she was wearing them now. A signal? An olive branch?

She eyed herself, then leaned closer to the mirror examining the crow's-feet around her eyes; they were getting more pronounced all the time. This is it, girl, all downhill from here. Be a Wrinkly soon; then a Crumbly. Then . . . nothing at all. The void. Godless black nothingness. She touched the lines lightly, stretched the skin, making them disappear for an instant, then stared again at the photograph of Richard and herself on a yacht in Greece; the year after their wedding; nine years ago. They looked so young and carefree then. How much softer her face was, how much fresher. Now a new line seemed to appear every day. She frowned into the mirror and a row of wrinkles popped out along her skin that she had never seen before.

Maybe it was the photograph that was changing, not her face? Maybe her face had always been like that and the photograph was receding into the past? Showing a woman who was getting younger and younger. So young sometimes she seemed like a total stranger. She unscrewed her lipstick.

Bamford O'Connell. Was he right? Maybe. Maybe. She shrugged at herself, and pushed her hair back away from her face. No grey hairs yet, but they'd be along soon.

Do you think there's any chance at all you might be crediting your dream with more detail than was in it? That you might be making the dream fit the facts?

No. No way, absolutely not. Surely not?

Oh shit. You're screwing up my head, Bamford. I had it all there, in sequence. Don't mix it up for me, just because I don't fit into any of your neat boxes.

'Where are you going, Mummy?'

She saw Nicky in the mirror, standing in the door-way, and turned around, smiling. 'We're going out to a dinner party.'

'Whose party?'

'The Howorths'. Do you remember them?'

'Are we going to the country?'

Sam carefully traced the lipstick across her lips. 'Uh huh.'

'Is it the weekend tomorrow?'

'Tomorrow's Friday. Come and give Mummy a kiss.'

Nicky trotted over, and she stroked his hair.

'Top of your class in arithmetic again today?'

'Yes, I was.'

'That's very clever. Mummy used to come bottom in arithmetic.'

He looked around suddenly, at the sound of the front door, then sprinted out of the room. 'Daddy! Daddy! Daddy!'

'Hi, Tiger!' she heard Richard say out in the hallway.

'Daddy! Can we set the Scalectrix up? We haven't had that set up since Christmas. Can we do it tonight?'

163

'Stop bloody whining at me.'

'Please, Daddy, can we set it up?'

'Jesus, Tiger! Bloody leave off, will you?'

Richard stormed into the bedroom and kicked the door shut behind him. 'Fucking whingeing on and on at me. What the hell are you wearing that for? You look like a whore.'

'You gave it to me.'

'Been fucking Ken in it?'

She stood up, livid. 'Are you drunk?'

'No, I'm not fucking drunk, but I'm going to get fucking drunk.' He charged out of the room, and Sam stared, bewildered, after him. The rage. She'd never seen him in a rage like this. He came back into the room with a whisky tumbler in his hand and slammed the door again.

'What's the matter with you?' she asked.

'Get those fucking whore clothes off and put something decent on.'

The menace in his voice frightened her. He was like a madman.

'I thought you liked—'

He marched over, grabbed the bra and ripped it away, so hard it tore, burning her flesh in the process. She shrieked in pain, then slapped him hard, really hard, on the face. 'You bastard.'

He blinked, and stared at her, and for a moment she thought he was going to come at her, going to come at her and kill her. But instead he blinked again, as if half waking from a trance, backed away and sat down on the bed. He drank some of his whisky then bent down and untied his laces. He kicked off his shoes, swallowed more whisky and lay back, closing his eyes. 'What time are we due there?'

'Eight,' she said.

She pulled the rest of the bra away, eyeing him warily and took a new one out of a drawer. 'Don't you think you'd better have some coffee rather than whisky?'

He said nothing.

She removed her lace panties, screwed them up and dropped them in the waste bin, and put on some fresh ones which matched the bra. She put on her dress, in silence, took her evening handbag out of the cupboard, and looked in her daytime bag. She noticed an envelope in amongst all the junk, and took it out. There was a magazine cutting inside it, which she unfolded and glanced at, puzzled.

'DREAMS – BEHIND CLOSED EYES THE FUTURE OPENS UP.'

Ken. Ken had given it to her on Monday and she'd forgotten about it. She went out of the bedroom, holding the article, and closed the door. She heard Nicky's bath running, and went into his bedroom. He was sitting sulkily on his bed. She went over and sat down beside him. 'Daddy's had a bad day, Tiger.'

'He promised we could play Scalectrix tonight.'

'We have to go out tonight.'

'He shouted at me. I didn't do anything wrong.' He began to cry and she held him tight. 'I'll play Scalectrix with you until Daddy's ready.'

'No,' he sobbed. 'Got to set it up. Only Daddy knows how to set it up.'

Helen came in, 'Bath's ready, Nicky.'

'Have your bath, Tiger, and I'll tell you a quick story before we go.'

He stood up, his face long and wet and walked slowly over to the door. Sam followed him out, then went down the corridor through into the living area and sat down on a sofa in front of the television. She was quivering with the pent-up anger and confusion inside her. This was a new Richard, something completely different; something she did not know how to handle. Maybe it was he that needed to see Bamford O'Connell, not her? Maybe the Market had been bad today. He was grumpy sometimes when the Market was bad. But never like this. She looked down at the article and began to read.

Dreams should be taken far more seriously than they are, claims David Abner, a clinical psychologist at Guy's Hospital who believes that not only are dreams a rich source of creativity, but they also offer valuable insight into personal and psychological problems, as well as, on occasions, a glimpse into the future.

Perhaps the most famous of all 'premonition' dreams was that of the Biblical Pharaoh, whose dream of seven fat cows being swallowed by seven thin cows enabled Egypt to conserve food over seven good years and stave off potential famine over seven poor succeeding harvests.

More recent figures, too, have been profoundly affected by their dreams. Hitler was saved by one of his, when as corporal in the First World War, his nightmare of being engulfed by debris caused him to wake up and dash outside, only for a shell to land on his bunker seconds later and kill all the sleeping occupants.

Dreams have inspired great inventors. Elias Howe invented the sewing machine after he dreamed of natives throwing spears with eye-shaped holes at their tips, and thus solved the problem of where to put the hole in the needle.

And in religion, leaders have taken the view that God speaks to his prophets through dreams. 'Many people still believe that today, and I'm sure to some degree it is still true, whatever God is, that dreams can be seen as messages from the universe,' says Abner. 'It seems that some people are receiving stations. Jung called it 'Collective Unconscious'. Whatever the explanation, whether it is ultimately scientific or spiritual, there is no question that in dreams some people seem to tune into a field of insight not open to the waking, conscious mind.'

In the next few months, Abner and a fellow group of dream therapists are planning to set up a phone-in 'dreamline', where people can both instantly have premonitions registered, and discuss their dreams with therapists working through the night.

In the meantime, people interested in learning more about their dreams can join in a series of dream groups being set up under his auspices. Phone 01–435–0702 for details.

Sod you, Bamford. Sam picked up the phone. Sod you and your stay away from the hokum guys. Sod you and your damned arrogance, she thought, as she heard the phone ring and a man's voice answer, a soft, laid-back American accent.

'Dave Abner.'

'I, er—' She felt foolish and looked around, making sure no one had come into the room. 'I read an article in – er – about your—'

There was a silence, followed by a distant 'Uh-huh', then a pause, 'Which article was that?'

'Someone cut it out. I'm not sure where from – about your dream groups.'

'Oh yeah, I remember.' He sounded bored. 'This number's wrong. They shouldn't have put this number. They should have put Tanya's.'

'Tanya?'

'Tanya Jacobson. She's doing the dream group right now. I'll give you her number.'

She dialled the new number, and a husky woman's voice answered, harassed, somewhat breathless. 'Hallo?'

'Could I speak to Tanya Jacobson, please?'

'Yes, speaking,' the reply came, somewhat irritable, and for a moment Sam was tempted to drop the receiver back down.

'David Abner gave me your number,' said Sam nervously. 'I read an article about your dream groups, and I wondered—'

'You'd like to join our group?' The woman's voice had changed, become friendlier. 'You've called at just the right time. This is an amazing coincidence! We're looking for one woman to complete the group. Listen, we're starting a new group next Monday night. Is that too soon?'

'No,' Sam said.

'Wow! Wonderful! You sound wonderful. I get feelings, you know, vibes. You get them too?'

'Yes,' said Sam hesitantly, dubiously. Feelings, Feelings. Everyone seemed to have feelings these days.

'OK, what's your name?'

'Mrs Curtis.'

'So formal. Wow. What's your Christian name?'

'Sam.'

'Sam, that's nice. You're going to fit in wonderfully. We start at seven-thirty. If you come a little early, you can have coffee, meet everyone. I'll give you the address. Do you know Hampstead?'

'Hampstead?'

'We're very near the tube.'

A chill went through her.

'Tube?' Sam felt herself shaking. She wanted to hang up, now, hang up and forget it.

Hampstead.

The tube.

'Hallo, Sam? You still there?'

Hampstead. Near the tube. The words banged around inside her head. *Hampstead. Near the tube.*

'Willoughby Road. Do you know Willoughby Road?'

'I can find it,' she heard her own voice say, as if spoken by a stranger.

'Off the High Street. You come out of the tube, turn left, and just walk down.'

'I'll drive,' said Sam. 'I'll be coming by car.'

She hung up. The room seemed cold, suddenly, and the wind rattled the windows. Rattled them like an angry stranger who was trying to get in. A stranger. Like Richard. Christ, what the hell was wrong with him? She heard the thump of the engines of a large ship heading upstream, then another gust of wind shrieked through the rigging of the moored yachts, rattling the halyards that were loose, and strumming the ones that were tight, tight as guitar strings.

Tight as her own nerves.

20

The rain which had been falling hard all day finally stopped just as she left the office, and in the darkness the roads were streaky kaleidoscopes of reflections of brake lights, indicators, street lamps. Puddles of glinting black water butted up against the gutters, as if left behind by a falling tide, and cars sluiced through them, throwing the water up like bow spray. A Belisha beacon flashed on-off-on-off, its beam sneaking across the road towards her, and she stopped. A man hurried over the crossing holding a broken umbrella.

Exactly as she had seen in her dream.

She felt her stomach tensing. Everything. The rain, the darkness, the reflections were exactly as she had seen in her dream. It was unfolding like a replay. She wanted to stop, turn around; go home. Instead she drove on up Avenue Road, biting her lip, drawn by some force she could not stop. Drawn as if the dream insisted on replaying itself to her; as if it had a mind of its own.

As if it was challenging her.

She blinked hard, wondering for a moment whether she was awake now.

Ten past seven.

She glanced anxiously at the clock and wished she had left more time, but she had sat in her office, reluctant to leave, waiting until the last moment when she had to make the decision to go or forget it. She had to find the place yet, and park. *If you come a little early, you can have coffee, meet everyone.*

THE NORTH. M1.

She drove into the Swiss Cottage one-way system, and a car hooted angrily on her inside. 'Sod you.' She swung the Jaguar's steering wheel, then heard the angry horn of a taxi right beside her. She braked cautiously and blinked, as water splashed onto her windscreen. She switched on the wipers, and everything blurred for a moment. She pulled over into the right-hand lane, and headed up Fitzjohn's Avenue towards Hampstead. A white Ford Capri sitting up on huge wheels drew up on her inside and a yobbo gave her the thumbs up.

She shivered. No, she thought. It wasn't possible. It could not be happening.

The same white Ford Capri as she had seen in her dream. The same yobbo. Making the same gesture.

Don't be ridiculous, she told herself. Coincidence. That's all. She turned away contemptuously, then dropped down into second gear and floored the accelerator.

She heard the roar of the engine, felt the tail of the Jaguar snake as the rear wheels spun, then eased off, felt the tyres bite and the surge of power as she accelerated forwards.

There was a car moving slowly in front, and she pulled right across, overtaking in the oncoming lane. Headlights were coming down the hill towards her and ice-cold fear swept through her.

No. Please God, no.

The lorry from the dream. Bearing down.

She heard her own engine screaming, slammed the gear lever forward and there was a fierce clacking and the stick kicked violently in her hand. The car began to slow down, the headlights almost on top of her now. She stabbed the gear lever forward again, and jerked the wheel hard to the left. The lorry passed her, inches away, shaking her with its vibration and slipstream.

Shit.

She saw the police car coming down the hill, slowing, as if it was looking for somewhere to turn and come after her, and she felt a cold hand around her forehead, tightening like a vice.

The dream. It was the dream. Exactly, everything. She wanted to stop, turn around, go back. She turned right, drove down the street that could have been the one she had driven down in her dream, but might not have been, and then left into Hampstead High Street. On her right, almost immediately, she saw the same tree-lined street from her dream, no doubting this one, and found herself turning automatically, as if it was drawing her into it.

Willoughby Road.

It was the street she wanted.

She stared, disbelieving, at the sign, then heard the toot of a horn behind her and drove forward, peering through the side window, trying to read the numbers.

There was a gap in the line of parked cars halfway down the street; exactly where she had parked in her dream. She stopped the Jaguar and reversed into it, then got out and looked around. A droplet of water hit her on the forehead, and she put up her hand in surprise. The dark evening had a stillness to it that she found eerie, as if all was not quite right, as if something was about to happen and the night was waiting.

Don't be ridiculous, she told herself as she looked at the doorways, trying to read the numbers. Then she smiled wryly as if she had discovered some private joke: she was parked right outside the address she had been, given. Number 56.

She went in through the open gateway and down the faded mosaic steps to the basement. At the bottom were a couple of dustbins, several empty cardboard packing boxes, and a cluster of empty milk bottles. There was a small plastic push-button with an illuminated plastic panel beside it which read 'Dream Studies Centre.'

She stared at the button, unable to push it. She wanted to turn and run back to the car and drive away. Something had drawn her here that did not feel good. Something that was making her tremble and feel sick and scared. She shuddered. Her stomach felt as if it was being wound through a mangle.

What would Bamford say? Perhaps it was all to do with fear of the dream group. The similarities in the drive here had been coincidence, and her fear of going down the tube steps was really her fear of coming down these steps, into the unknown.

She raised her finger and pushed the button gently, so gently she hoped it might not ring. It rasped back at her, inches from her face, piercing, shrill, as if it was angry it had been disturbed.

'Hi. You must be Sam.'

'Yes.'

'You found us?'

'Yes. Fine. It was easy.'

'Terrific. Wow! Wonderful. I'm Tanya Jacobson.' A small plump bundle of energy in a shapeless brown smock and black woollen leggings, with a wild frizz of hair and a scrubbed, earnest-looking face that was definitely a make-up free zone. A lump of crystal hung from a cord around her neck and her pudgy fingers were covered in chunky rings with large, gaudy stones. She gave Sam's hand a short friendly shake. 'Come in.'

Sam followed her down a dingy corridor and into a small room with battered chairs lined around the walls and a bare pine coffee table in the middle.

'Have a seat, Sam. I just want to have a quick talk before we go in.' The woman sat down, tucked her feet under her chair and rested her head on her hands, fixing her gaze on Sam.

'Nice face, Sam. I should think you're a really kind person. Am I right?'

Sam blushed. 'I don't know.'

'Have you been in a dream group before?'

'No.'

Tanya Jacobson nodded her head up and down in a straight line. 'Are you married?'

'Yes.'

'Does your husband know you're here?'

'No.'

Tanya Jacobson looked mildly surprised. 'OK. Fine. That's fine.' She raised her head off her chin then lowered it back down again. 'What do you do, Sam?'

'I work for a company that makes television commercials.'

The woman smiled. 'Right. Wow. So you're the one that's to blame?'

Sam smiled back, thinly.

'Tell me, why do you want to join a dream group?'

She shrugged. 'I don't know much about it. I've been having some very strange dreams which seem to keep coming true. I read the article and I thought I'd give you a call.'

'You think you're having premonitions?'

'Yes.'

The woman sat up eagerly, like a puppy wanting to please, thought Sam. 'Good! You can tell the group. Now tonight you can see how you feel, how you resonate with everyone. If you feel good then we hope you'll join us permanently.'

'Permanently?'

'For the life of the group. Normally about two years. We meet every Monday, and it's—' She looked embarrassed – 'nine pounds a session. Do you think you can live with that?'

'Two years seems a long time.'

'Dreams take a long time to work through, Sam. We have to get the dynamics going. You'll understand. I think you're really going to be good.' She patted Sam's hand. 'You have a slight disadvantage, because the rest of the group has been together for some weeks, and they're resonating nicely. It's going to take you time to resonate.'

'Does . . . does everyone here have premonitions?' Sam asked.

'Well, we're a group, Sam. I'm a psychotherapist, OK? A psychologist. What we do is work our dreams through. Premonitions, precognitions . . . that's all a little bit—' She tilted her head from side to side – 'a little bit fringe, OK? We're trying here to really connect with our dreams, go with them, free associate, get some good dynamics going. OK? Shall we go through?'

Sam followed her out down the short corridor. She did not like the answer she had been given, the string of heavy jargon. The paper had said they were studying premonitions, but this woman, Tanya Jacobson, seemed to be dismissing them.

They went into a large square room that smelled of stale cigarette smoke and old furniture, except there was hardly any furniture in the room. A bare light bulb hung from the ceiling. There were no chairs, but old, battered cushions, bean bags and poufs were spread around the floor in a large circle. Several people were lying sprawled out on them, leaning against the walls, their feet stretched out across the threadbare carpet. She felt hostility at her presence. She wanted to turn and walk out.

'OK, this is Sam, everyone. We'll go round in turn. This is Barry – he leads the group with me. Barry, this is Sam.'

A lanky man lay stretched out in a shiny black karate suit, his feet bare, his limp, shiny black hair brushed forward in a Beatle fringe over his eyebrows. His eyes were closed and he was muttering intently to himself. He raised an arm like an Indian chieftain, without opening his eyes. 'Good to meet you, Sam,' he mumbled, then continued with his private muttering.

'And this is Anthea.'

A woman in her fifties was coiled up in a corner, staring at her, blinking slowly like a basking snake. She was wearing a homemade jumper and grimy jeans, and had long red hair that hung down to her waist, and which covered her arms and her chest like a rug. The woman gave her the faintest acknowledgement, then gazed up at the ceiling with a puzzled look, as if she had just felt a drop of rainwater.

'Hi, I'm Gail.' A pretty blonde-haired girl introduced

herself in a New England accent. She looked smart and elegant, and rich in her white silk blouse, velvet headband and Cartier wristwatch.

'Hallo.'

She smiled gently, sympathetically at Sam. 'It's pretty difficult, huh, the first time?'

Sam smiled and nodded.

A voice in a flat northern accent said 'Clive,' and an aggressive-looking man in his late thirties, with short, tousled, prematurely greying hair stood up and shook her hand grimly, as if it was a duty to be got over with like having an injection, then sat down again and hunched up inside his baggy jumper.

'Find yourself some space that feels good, Sam. Would you like some tea? We have camomile or dandelion, or there's coffee – Hag or Nescafé.'

'Nescafé, please.' said Sam.

'Do you take milk, sugar?'

'Milk please. No sugar.'

The basking snake uncoiled a little, and the man in the baggy jumper leaned back and stretched his arms. *Keep away*, they were saying, *Keep out!*

Sam sat down well away from them on an empty stretch of cushions near the door. 'We're just waiting for one more – Sadie – then we'll be complete for tonight,' Tanya called out. 'Roger's rung to say he has flu, so he won't be making it. I told him we'd be keeping mental space for him.'

Sam looked around the room. There was a frosted glass curtainless window high off the ground, a wall-mounted convector heater, a small table with a telephone on top of an answering machine, and a pine dresser that was being used as a bookcase and dumping ground for coffee mugs and full ashtrays.

The walls were painted in faded white Artex, and

there was a closed off serving hatch with a dusty red Buddha, that looked like a half-melted candle, on the ledge in front. There was one solitary picture on the walls, a framed print of a languid eighteenth-century boy reclining on a bed and gazing at an ornament he was holding.

Tanya Jacobson came back into the room, and handed Sam a scalding mug.

'Keeping your distance, are you, Sam? Keeping your space?'

Sam was uncertain whether she had done something wrong or given away some important clue about her personality. She felt awkward, uncomfortable; and unwanted. She heard the clatter of an electric heater, and the click of the door closing.

'Sadie's late again,' said Tanya. 'I think she has a problem with her timekeeping. She has a lot of dreams about clocks.'

'And sex,' said the man in the baggy sweater. 'She seems to have a lot of dreams about sex.'

'I think she has a bit of a problem about sex,' said the American girl.

Tanya nodded her head noncommittally, with the faintest trace of a sympathetic smile. 'We all have problems. That's what the group is for. Now Sam, the way we introduce someone new to the group is to get them to tell a dream. Did you bring one with you?'

'One with me? I haven't written any down – no.'

Tanya tapped her head. 'In there, Sam. Is there a dream you can remember that you'd like to tell the group?'

Sam shrugged. 'I—' She looked around. The basking snake in the corner appeared to have gone to sleep. The man in the baggy jumper was staring fixedly at the wall ahead, and she wondered if he was sulking because he hadn't been asked to tell a dream. The American girl smiled intently at her and gave her a nod of encouragement.

The door opened and in came a tiny woman with a figure like a rugger ball and a prim face that was heavily caked in make-up, only partially visible behind a curtain of limp brown hair. She mouthed a silent apology, checked her bright red lipstick with her tongue, then sat down primly on a pouf and opened her handbag with a loud click. She rummaged in it, pulled out a pack of cigarettes, a lighter and a small tin, from which she removed the lid, and set it down on the floor beside her. She looked like a goblin perched on the pouf, Sam thought, and wondered what she was going to do with the tin.

'Sadie, we have a new member in our group tonight. Sam, this is Sadie. Sam's going to tell us a dream. It doesn't matter if it's an old dream, Sam.'

Sadie smiled at Sam, a long, lingering smile that Sam first mistook for warmth, but then realised, as it continued, was a warning shot across her bows.

She turned away, confused, and heard the click of the woman's cigarette lighter, and her sharp, smug, intake of smoke.

'Did you remember a dream you had last night, Sam?' said Tanya Jacobson.

She felt her face reddening. 'No – I – I don't think I dreamed last night. At least I—' She stared helplessly around the room. It was wrong. All wrong. She saw the American girl, nodding encouragingly, willing her on.

You poor deluded sod, she thought.

What do you want me to do? Tell you to go and see a clairvoyant? A medium? Send you off to a dream group? I want to help you, not make things worse.

She saw Sadie squatting on her pouf and caught the

slight narrowing of her eyes. *Don't take up much time*, she was saying. *I have important dreams to tell.*

'Last week, er—' Sam faltered. 'Last Tuesday night, I had a dream that . . . that seems to be coming true. At least, some of it.'

'Would you like to tell us about it?'

Sam told them her dream of Hampstead tube station, feeling foolish, talking at their blank faces, at the blank wall, talking whilst Tanya Jacobson sat on her cushion, rocking backwards and forwards with her eyes closed, and whilst Sadie squatted on her pouf, puffing on her cigarette and tapping the ash into the tin she had brought. She wondered whether anyone was taking in a word she said.

When she had finished the silence continued. The American girl leaned back and gazed at the ceiling, and the man in the baggy jumper stared at the wall ahead.

Tanya Jacobson appeared to take several deep breaths, then opened her eyes. 'Okay, Sam, the first thing I want you to do is to free associate.'

'Pardon?' said Sam.

'I want you to tell me anything that comes into your mind about the dream.'

'Replay.' Sam said.

'Replay?'

'Yes. The journey here – it was exactly as I dreamed it. Coming here was like a replay of the dream.'

Tanya stared at her with a faintly disinterested look on her face. 'Don't get too stuck on that for a moment. There's a lot going on in that dream. Is there another reason why you dreamed Hampstead? Did you ever live here? Or know anyone that lived here?'

'No.'

'It was very filmic,' the American girl said suddenly. 'There was a very Buñuel feel to the first part. Then, when you went down those steps, it was like a tunnel, it gave me the feeling of – you know? The Harry Lime movie. *The Third Man.*'

Anthea uncoiled a fraction in the corner, and raised her head. 'Sewers,' she said slowly, articulating very precisely, as if she were teaching a foreigner to speak English.

'Sewers?' echoed Tanya Jacobson.

'Sewers,' she repeated. 'Gail's got it wrong. It wasn't tunnels, it was sewers.'

'I'm not connecting with you, Anthea,' said Tanya.

'Oh for God's sake.' Her voice was getting louder, deeper, more haughty. 'In the film. *The Third Man*. It was sewers they went down, not tunnels.' She lowered her head and began to coil back up again.

'That was a good movie.' Barry spoke without opening his eyes. He scratched the side of his left leg with the toes of his right foot. 'Orson Welles.'

'And Joseph Cotten,' said the American girl.

'Vagina,' said the man in the baggy jumper gruffly. 'I'm getting a vagina.' He sat upright and clasped his hands together, staring at Sam. He had a face that might once have been kindly, but now had a hardened, slightly embittered look. 'You're going down inside this vagina and you're finding something horrible there. There's this man that grabs you, takes you into this dark room where there's no light, and he's trying to strangle you, rape you. I'm getting this very strong feeling that you hate men.'

'Don't you think it could be pre-existence, Clive?' said Tanya Jacobson.

He frowned, then sat back and dug his hands into his pockets. 'Pre-existence,' he said. 'Hmm.'

Tanya Jacobson threw her head back, then tilted it forwards again. 'You know what's coming through to

me? We've got several different dreams here. The journey. The buying the ticket. The travelling down the
steps. Now the travelling down, I'm connecting very
strongly with pre-existence, you know. Like birth rever-
sal.'

Sam tried to make sense of the jargon. She stared at
the print on the wall of the man looking at the ornament. He looked puzzled too.

'You mean she's going back into her mother's
womb?' said the American girl.

Tanya gave three sharp nods of her head as if she was
trying to shake water out of her hair. 'She's going down
into this sort of tunnel, then suddenly she gets pulled
into this dark room. In birth it would be the opposite.'
Tanya stared at Sam. 'In birth, you start inside the
womb, then you move down the tunnel, then the doctor
or whoever delivers you pulls you out.' She patted her
chest. 'I'm getting strong feelings that you're dreaming
about going back to the womb. It's a nice safe place in
there, you don't have to do anything. It's nice and warm
and snug. It would be a good place to escape to. No
traumas in there. No premonitions. Are you connecting,
Sam?'

'I'm not sure,' she said hesitantly.

'What sort of birth did you have, Sam? Traumatic?
Caesarian or something like that, or was it normal?'

She shrugged. 'I don't know. I never—' She trailed off
and Tanya smiled, reasurringly.

'It's a big shock, being born,' Tanya said. 'It never
leaves us. Keeps coming back in our dreams.'

Wide. So wide of the mark, Sam thought.

'Is that connecting with you, Sam?'

'No,' she said apologetically.

'Do you know this man?' said Barry, his eyes still
shut.

Do I? Slider? Was he Slider? Onions? Christ, do I want to get into all that? That's why you're here. I know. But.

'No.'

'He could be your animus,' said the American girl.

'Do you know about animus and anima?' asked Tanya.

'No,' said Sam.

'Jung said we have an opposite self which appears sometimes in our dreams. If you're a man, you see a strange woman who is your dream self, and if you're a woman, then a strange man. He could be your animus. Do you feel violent towards anyone? Towards yourself?'

She shook her head.

There was a long silence. Tanya Jacobson sat back with her eyes closed. Then she opened them again. 'Let's try and free associate a bit more. This person was trying to rape you in the dream. Think about rape. Free associate. Just say anything that comes into your mind.'

Sam looked around the room, then at the picture once more. Her heart felt heavy. The heater continued to rattle, and somewhere above she heard the muted shrill of a doorbell.

'Slider,' she said.

The man in the baggy jumper turned his head towards her, studying her thoughtfully, and the American girl smiled.

'Who is Slider, Sam?' said Tanya Jacobson. 'Do you want to tell us about Slider?'

She told them the full story of how she had discovered Slider, and how he had died, and how she had kept on dreaming until her parents had died.

When she had finished, there was a silence that seemed to go on for ever.

'That's awful,' the American girl said. 'That's really awful. It's made me feel all creepy.'

There was another long silence.

'How did you feel about it, Sam?' said Tanya Jacobson.

The words were like a distant echo, and she looked around, baffled, wondering if they were really addressed to her. She saw Sadie, on the pouf, and for a moment she thought she was perched on a mountain ledge.

'I can't remember, really. Numb, I suppose for a long time. I felt that he had done it, that he had killed them. I didn't dream of him again for a long time.'

'Why do you think that was?' Tanya said.

'I suppose my parents dying was the worst possible thing. There wasn't anything worse that he could do.'

Tanya nodded. 'Who brought you up after this, Sam?' she said.

'An uncle and aunt.'

'Were they nice?'

'No. They resented me. They were very cold people.'

'Did you ever tell them about Slider?'

'No.'

'Have you ever told anyone, Sam?' said Tanya.

'No.' She hesitated, remembering she had told Bamford O'Connell.

'What about your husband?'

'No.'

'What happened when you dreamed of him again?' Gail asked. 'How long after was it?'

Sam stared at her. 'Twenty-five years after. It was two weeks ago.'

'Wow,' Tanya Jacobson said. 'You're holding a lot inside you, aren't you? All bottled up. Can't tell your uncle and aunt. Can't tell your husband. But it's going to come out in your dreams, Sam, it always does.' She leaned forwards. 'You see, Sam, it doesn't matter what we try and hide from the world – we can't hide things from ourselves. It all comes out in our dreams, and it keeps on coming out until we face them, deal with them. But it's good, Sam. It's good that it's come to the surface, because you can deal with it now. You're going to have to face it, talk about it more, then he'll go away.' Tanya clasped her hands together dramatically. 'You have to meet your monster, Sam. We all have our personal monsters that come to us in our dreams. One of the things we try to do here is to meet them, and understand them. Then they go away.'

Sam stared back at her, then glanced at her watch. Were the others getting impatient? She wondered. She could see Sadie glaring down at her own watch then back at her, puffing angrily on her cigarette. 'Would someone else like to have a go – I've had rather a lot of time.'

'Don't worry about the others for a moment, Sam. This is your dream. Let's worry about you. I don't think we're ready to move on yet. OK?'

Sam suddenly felt very emotional, on the verge of weeping. She looked around and saw friends looking back. Even some of the hostility of Sadie's gaze seemed to have softened. Safe. She was safe here.

'Do you have any other associations?'

Sam closed her eyes, wondering if she dared. She opened them and looked around. It was beginning to seem easy to talk. 'Yes . . . my husband.' She felt her face reddening. 'The man in the dream smelled of onions. When I woke up, I could smell onions on my husband's breath.'

'And you associated him with the rapist?' said Tanya.

Sam bit her lip. 'He's been having an affair.'

'Wow!' Tanya clapped her hands together. 'I think

you're really beginning to connect!' She rocked backwards and forwards. 'We've got a whole bag, here, haven't we? This hooded man – Slider – you know, he's really strange for me. I'm connecting with the hood – like a mask. I think that part of what you are seeing in him is some dark side of yourself. You know? You can't let your real self show, can't let your feelings show, you keep them all safely hidden behind the mask. I think he represents so many things for you. Part of him is nasty adult, your cold uncle and aunt, they're a threat to you, taken away your nice, kind, warm parents and given you this cold resentment, this total lovelessness.' She shook her head, then stared hard back at Sam. 'Think of your description of him, Sam. The hood, the one eye – what else does that remind you of? You know? What does that make you think of?'

Sam tried to think, but could not concentrate.

'The old one-eyed trouser snake? It makes me think of a penis, Sam. A giant penis.'

Sam's heart sank. Did all analysis end up down the same road, at the same place? Did everything end up with a penis?

'You've been violated, Sam, haven't you? Your childhood was violated by this man, now your adulthood is being violated again by your husband. Does this resonate?'

Sam felt irritated suddenly. Crap. This was all crap. 'I'm sure it all fits very neatly, but I think that's a side issue. The point is that I had a premonition – about the Bulgaria air disaster. I dreamed it the night before it happened. There was someone in the dream with Slider's hood on his head. The next day, I dreamed of him again, in a taxi. It's as if he's linked with each of the premonitions. I don't know – like a sort of a harbinger. I feel that more bad things are going to happen. I had a second premonition a few days later, and he appeared again.'

Tanya raised her eyebrows. 'Sam, dismissing a dream as a premonition is the easy route. I think you're using that as an excuse not to face the real meaning of the dreams. I'm not saying that you don't have premonitions, or what you think are premonitions, but I'm not connecting with them. I don't think they matter.'

'They matter to me.'

'OK! They matter to you.' Tanya glanced at her watch. 'There's one other thing I want you to think about which could be important: this man chasing you. You were trying to run up the stairs from him and you couldn't move. Being chased by the opposite sex can mean that you fancy someone, but feel guilty about it – that you don't dare respond to the overtures. Am I touching any nerves?'

'I – I don't know. I don't think so.'

'Are you happy if we leave it there for a moment?'

Sam shrugged.

'OK, there's plenty for you to think about there,' Tanya said. 'Has anyone else brought a dream?'

'Yes,' Sadie said, almost bursting.

'Would you like to tell us, Sadie?'

'It's another of my sex dreams.'

Sam detected a faintly irritable sigh from the man in the baggy sweater, and tried to remember his name. Ian? Colin?

Sadie dipped into her handbag and pulled out a thick notebook. She leaved through pages of handwriting, then stopped. 'This was last Monday night, after the group. I was in this big old room, up in an attic – it was like my parents' house, but it was much bigger, and there was this little old lady in the corner, all wrinkled, sort of watching me. She was doing tapestry, but she was trying to embroider this sheet of metal with a drill.

'Anyhow, I was lying naked on this bed, and I was manacled, and I realised that she was the one who had manacled me, and the metal sheet turned into a scoreboard, and she was going to be scoring.' She looked smugly around the room and took a cigarette out of her pack. 'Clive came in the room. I didn't recognise him at first, then I realised he had on that baggy sweater he always wears.'

Sam looked at him, and saw him almost fuming with rage. Clive, that was his name.

'He started making love to me, but he wasn't satisfying me, so I told him he'd have to go to the back of the queue and try again later. Then this young boy from the office came in, and told me he'd been fancying me like mad for months and he really wanted to be my toyboy.'

The dream seemed to go on interminably. The young boy from her office. Robert Redford. Prince Philip. Jack Nicholson. John McEnroe. Paul Hogan, Richard Gere. All, it seemed, had desired her secretly for much of their lives. All had been unable to satisfy her.

Finally, everyone was standing up. The two hours had passed. Sam had resonated well, she was told. 'Do you think you're more in touch with your feelings?' Tanya asked her.

'Yes, I think so,' she said dubiously.

Everyone was embarrassed about handing over their money, and it changed hands quickly, silently, almost shadily, like contraband, as if acknowledgement would somehow debase what they were going through.

'So you're going to come next week, Sam?' Tanya asked.

Barry still lay on the floor in his black karate suit,

187

with his eyes closed. He raised his right arm. 'Bye Good meeting you.'

She wondered if he had ever once opened his eyes to look at her, and whether he would recognise her again.

'Yes,' Sam said.

'You keep a lot inside you, don't you?'

'I suppose so.'

'We'll have to get it out,' Tanya said. 'It's going to take a long time. Just don't get sidetracked into those pre-monitions, Sam. We don't dream the future—' She tapped her head through her frizz of hair. 'But we make connections. We meet our monsters. Forget the manifest, Sam. You've got to connect with your deep psyche.'

'I'd like to believe you,' Sam said.

'You will, you'll believe me.'

She walked out and up the basement steps, with her thoughts a churning vortex. Reassurance. It felt good to be reassured, to be told the answers. Schoolteachers told you the answers, too. They knew the answers to many things.

But not always the ones that mattered.

You have to meet your monster, Sam.

Kill the dragon. Kill him dead.

She went outside into the dark night.

Went out to her monster.

21

The night seemed mild, more like summer than early February, and the group dispersed silently into it, with scarcely a 'good bye'. She looked up at the sky, as she climbed into the Jaguar. The branches of the trees were like cardboard cut-out silhouettes against the brightness of the full moon.

She turned the ignition key, listened to the tick of the fuel pump, then pushed the starter. The engine turned over, then died. She pushed the choke lever up and tried again, keeping the starter button pushed hard in, listening to the churning of the engine, the hiss of the air intakes, the whine of the starter motor.

She took her hand off the button, and the noise faded away. There was the clicking of a ratchet, then silence. She slid the choke down to halfway, then tried again. Still nothing. She looked at the clock.

Quarter to ten.

She switched the ignition off, switched it back on and tried again. Again the engine turned over lifelessly.

'Come on, don't do this to me. I've got an early start.'

She sat, and blinked hard. She felt completely drained and a little foolish. Christ, what had she said? What had made her blurt all that out? To total strangers. To a bunch of loonies. What had they thought of her? Who cared? Probably more than they had thought of Sadie and her drivelling fantasies.

She tried again and kept on trying until she heard the battery beginning to die, and then she stopped, and looked at the clock again. If she phoned the RAC how long would they take? she wondered. An hour at least. Possibly two or three. She had a breakfast meeting at quarter to eight in the morning, and did not want to arrive shattered. The car was OK here, safe. She could send Drummond up to sort it out in the morning.

She shivered, and did not know why.

She locked the car and as she did so she heard the squeal of tyres and the roar of an engine. She looked up and saw a car hurtling down the street, its lights on full beam, making straight towards her.

Like in the dream, she thought, panicking, running

around the back of the Jaguar onto the kerb, watching the car thunder past.

Like in the bloody dream.

She shivered again.

We don't dream the future . . . but we make connections. We meet our monsters. Forget the manifest, Sam. You've got to connect with your deep psyche.

She walked down the street, feeling nervous of the shadows of the trees, like dark pools of blood, and afraid of the brilliant light of the moon in the open that lit her up, exposing her like a startled rabbit caught in a car's headlamps.

The dream. It was all like the dream.

As she crossed the next pool of light, it faded suddenly, as if it had been extinguished. There was a patter, like tiny feet, then a splodge of cold water hit her forehead.

Rain. She felt relieved. It had not rained in this part of the dream.

The downpour followed quickly, within seconds, and she wondered whether to run back to the car and get her umbrella. But she was only a short distance from the High Street, and saw a taxi cross in front of her.

'Taxi!' she shouted and ran, but it had gone by the time she got there. She stood there as the rain became even heavier, drenching her, staring at the blurring headlights, tail lights, searching for a yellow 'For Hire' sign.

Another taxi rattled past, its tyres sluicing, shadows of people huddled in the back, then another, also taken. She felt her hair plastering down on her forehead and her coat becoming heavy from the water. Some way up the hill she saw the tube sign. For a moment she hesitated, gazed down the street and then up at the lines of lights. No taxis.

It wasn't raining in the dream.

You'll be OK.

No, Sam. No.

Oh shit.

You have to meet your monster.

Dream. It was just a dream.

It's much easier to put them down as premonitions than to face their real truths.

Vagina. I'm getting a vagina.

You mean she's going back into her mother's womb?

Of course. Didn't everybody?

Maybe they did.

She ran towards the tube station, then stopped. Don't be so bloody stupid.

Scaredy cat! Scaredy cat! Scaredy cat!

Me?

Scaredy cat! Scaredy cat! Scaredy cat!

Actually, I don't take tubes any more – well – you know, muggers and all that. Richard doesn't like it.

Scaredy cat!

She ran on again, towards the sign.

You're not going to go down there, Sam!

Oh yes I am.

Oh no you're not!

Oh yes I am.

Oh no you're not!

Oh piss off.

She ran inside, past several people huddling in the entrance, into the chill dry smell of dust and staleness, and stared around at the ticket machines.

Out of order. Out of order. The third one seemed to be working and she opened her bag, pulled out her purse, then hesitated, trying to find Wapping on the list of stations, but could not.

She walked over to the ticket office, trembling, wondering if the same woman from her dream was going to be sitting there. She felt relieved when she saw a young man, with a heavy beard.

'Single to Wapping, please.'

'The lifts aren't working,' he said, raising his eyebrows.

'I'm sorry?'

'The lifts. We've got a problem with the power.'

'I can walk.'

He frowned. 'Have you been here before?'

'No.'

'It's a long way down.'

She felt a prickle of anxiety. 'I—' She paused. 'I don't mind.'

He shrugged. 'Ninety pence. Turn right.' He pointed with his hand.

She took the ticket, and walked through the unattended barrier. There was a sign at the head of the stairs.

THE LIFT SHAFT AT THIS STATION IS THE DEEPEST IN LONDON. 300 STEPS. USE ONLY IN EMERGENCY.

The grimy tiled walls were familiar, like the walls of a public lavatory; like the walls in the dream. She stared at the steel-cased shaft in the middle of the staircase exactly as she had seen it in her dream.

Christ, how the hell did I dream this so accurately?

Maybe I've been here before? A long time ago?

Must have been.

She was shaking.

Relax! This is a tube station. Everyone uses the tube.

She listened, hoping some more people would come so they could walk down together. There were brisk footsteps, and two men, deep in conversation started down the staircase. She heard more footsteps behind and the chatter of foreign students. A huge crowd of them, Italian, stylish careless, chattering excitedly, laughing, energy, enthusiasm. Life. She started walking down with them, hurrying, to stay in their midst, not to be left behind on her own.

They were halfway down when she felt something snap, and her handbag fell to the ground. It bounced and rolled over down several steps; her Filofax fell out, and burst open, scattering paper all around.

Shit.

She knelt down, as the students stepped carefully through everything, without the pitch of their chatter altering. She crammed the sheaves of paper back untidily, hurrying, feeling foolish, then looked at the broken strap of her handbag. A rivet had sheared. Then she became aware of the silence. She was shivering from her soaking clothes, from the draught, and from fear, she realised, stuffing the Filofax back into her bag. The chatter of the students had already faded, and she was alone. Turn around, she thought, turn around and go back up.

She looked up and then down. Each was as dark and silent and menacing as the other.

You have to meet your monster.

Was this what Tanya Jacobson meant?

Here?

She stood and listened and the chatter of the Italians was gone completely.

Calm, Sam. Calm. Just go on down. You'll be fine.

She tucked her bag under her arm, took one step down, then another and heard the sharp echo of the shuffle of her feet.

It wasn't raining in the dream.

The ticket collector was a woman in the dream.

Dream. Just a dream. That's all.

She began, slowly, to walk down further, until she had completed one spiral and then another. Deep below her she heard the faint rumble of a train.

In the dream there hadn't been any other people. There were plenty of people around tonight, surely there were? She walked down further, tiptoeing, trying to walk silently so there was no echo, so that no one could hear, so that if he was there waiting then – Christ, she thought, her coat was rustling, her handbag rubbing against it. She stopped again and listened. There was another faint rumble, then silence. How many steps now? How far had she come? She felt the back of her neck prickle. Someone had crept down after her. Someone was standing behind her.

She spun round.

No one.

She felt her heart beating, beating so loudly she could almost hear it. Come on, Sám. Meet your monster. Meet your monster.

And what the hell did you do when you met him?

Hit him with your bag and try to out-run him? Out-run him to where? To an empty platform?

She stood and stared fearfully back up the steps, then continued on down, slowly, trying to be silent, and knowing she wasn't.

I must be nearly at the bottom, she thought. How many steps? Three hundred. She walked down some more, counting. Five. Six. Seven. God it was a long process. She could not even be halfway down yet, she calculated.

Then she froze.

Right beneath her, only yards away, she heard the shuffle of a foot.

She listened again, motionless.

Someone was standing below her, breathing heavily, panting.

She heard the scrape of a foot again.

Yards away.

Then she saw the shadow on the wall.

Stationary. Moving very slightly.

Someone standing very still, trying not to be seen.

Someone waiting for her.

The grimy walls seemed to be closing in around her. She felt ice cold water running through her.

Then the shadow began to rise up the stairs towards her, swiftly, determined. It grew larger, darker.

She heard footsteps, like drum beats. And a man grunting.

Grunting like a pig.

She turned and ran, tripping.

No. Help me. For Christ's sake help me.

She stumbled and fell, bashed her knee, picked herself up, threw herself up more steps, grabbed the handrail, pulled herself on up.

She bounced off the wall on her right, then stumbled across, her shoulder crashing painfully into the rail on her left. Her lungs were searing, but she ran on, hearing breathing behind her, footsteps behind her, the grunting, the shadow chasing her own, touching it then falling back.

Then she was at the top and running, out through the barrier, through the people sheltering in the entrance and out into the pelting rain and the lights of the street.

She leaned against the wall, gasping for breath, swallowing deep gulps of air, feeling her heart crashing inside her chest. She doubled up in agony as a stitch gripped her stomach, and stayed there shaking as the rain washed the perspiration from her face.

She pulled off her gloves, and let the rain cool her hands, staring up at it thankfully.

She stayed a long time, until she had become little more than part of the furniture of the street; invisible; just a huddled thing, another of the derelicts of any big city you stepped past a bit faster and made sure you did not look at. She limped down the street, her ankle hurting like hell, towards a telephone booth she could see in the distance.

She thumbed through the book, and found the number of the RAC.

'May I have your membership number?' the girl said tartly.

'My card's in the car. We have a company membership. Ken Shepperd Productions.'

She hung on for a long time before the girl came back. When she did she sounded surly, disbelieving, reluctant. 'If you wait with your car, we'll get someone there when we can.'

'How long will that be?'

'At least an hour. We have a lot of call-outs at the moment.'

She climbed wearily back into the Jaguar, locked the doors, and sat gazing blankly ahead. She closed her eyes, her brain churning, wondering whether she had imagined it. She saw the shadow moving, heard the shuffle of feet, the breathing, the grunting, the shadow following her up the steps. She shuddered and stared fearfully out of the window, at the dark, and switched on the radio.

She snapped it off again almost immediately, afraid suddenly of not being able to hear the sounds outside, and sat and waited in silence, thinking about the dream group and about Bamford and about the shadow that had come up the steps towards her.

And if Bamford was right? And Tanya Jacobson?

If the shadow had been in her own mind?

If. If. They probably were right.

Damn them.

Nutty as a fruitcake, old boy.

My wife?

Sam?

Got a brick missing from the load, I'm afraid.

The rattle of an engine startled her; she felt the beam of a spotlight, and saw the breakdown truck pulled up alongside her. The driver waved, and she raised her hand in acknowledgement. She unlocked the door, with a stiff, frozen hand, and climbed out. The rain had stopped, but the air felt cold.

'Won't start?' said the man. Young, chirpy.

'No.'

'Nice car. Ought to be in a museum.'

'It's been very reliable.'

'It's the electrics in these old Jags. They ought to be rewired – complete new loom – that's usually the problem.' He slipped into the driver's seat, turned the ignition and pushed the starter motor.

The engine fired immediately. He revved it several times whilst she stood, in numb disbelief in a cloud of thick, oily exhaust. He revved it again, hard, too hard, she thought, but beyond caring, then he stuck his head out. 'You probably flooded it. Sounds fine. Very sweet.'

She shook her head slowly. 'No. I didn't flood it.'

He shrugged.

'There's another reason,' she said.

'Loose connection?'

She shook her head. 'No.'

The RAC man frowned. 'Temperamental, is she?'

'Temperamental,' she echoed, looking away. Somewhere in a room above them she heard a faint tinkle of laughter, then a man's voice, raucous, and another tinkle of laughter. She heard the clicking of a bicycle, and the creak of brakes, and saw an elegantly dressed woman dismount, and carry the bicycle up the steps of number 54.

'Can I have your card, and I'll just get your signature.'

'I'm sorry,' she said. 'I'm sorry you've been bothered.'

He ducked into his cab and pulled out a clipboard. 'Probably flooded. Happens all the time. What's this got? Triple SUs?'

'Pardon?'

'SU carbs?'

'I don't know.'

'Flooded, most likely.'

She pulled the card out of the glove locker and handed it to him. It would have been easy to have agreed with him. Yes, I flooded it. How silly of me. But it hadn't been that. Nor a loose connection.

It hadn't been anything that a mechanic could have dealt with.

22

It was after midnight when she arrived home, and the hall was in darkness. She closed the front door quietly and took off her soaking wet coat. She could see a dim pool of light through in the living area, and walked down the corridor.

Richard was hunched over his desk, in front of his Reuters screen, whisky tumbler and bottle of Teacher's beside him. He turned his head.

'Look wet,' he slurred.

And you looked smashed out of your brains. 'It's pelting.' She walked over and kissed his cheek. 'Still working?'

'Andreas said there was going to be some action tonight. Reckoned there could be some big movements.'

He blearily rubbed his nose, poured out another four fingers, then tapped his keyboard and leaned forward as if trying to focus on the screen. He frowned at the changing figures. 'Where've been?'

'Oh – we've got a problem over a shoot. Fish fingers – Superfingers – the client wants it done on location in the Arctic, and we're trying to persuade them to do it here in a studio.' She was glad he wasn't looking at her; she had never been good at lying. 'Then the car wouldn't start.'

'Bloody ridiculous car to poddle round London in. I tell you, that bloke Ken's got a serious ego problem.'

'It's nothing to do with ego. He likes old cars; they're a good investment and a good image.'

'Especially when they break down in the middle of the night.' He frowned again at the screen.

She stared out of the window, watching the rain sheeting down onto the dark silhouettes of the restless lighters and the black water of the river. At least the aggression had gone, that strange violent temper he'd arrived home with when he'd ripped her bra. Her slap seemed to have done something and he'd been calm since; testy, but calm.

'Jon Goff rang. They've got some theatre tickets for Thursday, to see some new Ayckbourn thing.'

'Damn, I want to see that. Can't, Thursday. That's the night I have to go to Leeds. We've got a presentation on Friday morning.'

He squinted at some figures, then checked something on a pad on his desk. 'Jesus!' he shouted at the screen, his voice an agonised roar. 'You can't fucking do that! How can you?' He crashed his fist down on his desk. 'How can you fucking do that?'

'Ssh,' Sam said. 'You don't have to shout like that. Nicky—'

'Fuck Nicky. Jesus Christ. What's the Market fucking doing? Andreas never gets it wrong! What do they think they're playing at? Tokyo told me they thought New York looked cheap.' He glared belligerently at the screen cluttered with endless rows of figures and the strange names and symbols. Jargon. Language. A language that was as alien to her as the language of the dream group would have been to him.

She stayed, standing silently behind him for several minutes, watching as he drank more, tapped in more commands, cursed some more. He seemed to have forgotten she was there, seemed oblivious to anything outside of the small screen with its green symbols.

She left him and went to undress, and lay in bed for a long time, with the light on, thinking. Thinking about Richard and what was troubling him and wishing they could talk more openly, wishing she could tell him about her dreams without him sneering and wishing he could tell her what was wrong. She thought about Bamford O'Connell, about the dream group. She churned through the air disaster, the shooting, going down the steps of Hampstead tube station. She looked at the clock. 0215. Richard still had not come to bed.

Bamford O'Connell and Tanya Jacobson had now both said the same thing.

In my mind.

What had been coming up the tube station stairs? Her own imagination?

She heard the click of the shower door, then the sound of running water. Odd, she thought dimly. Odd Richard having a shower before he came to bed. She thought again of the steps and the shadow, thought about it for the hundred millionth time.

Nothing. There was nothing. Why the hell didn't I go on down?

Meet your monster.

Not me. I'm scared.

Scaredy cat, scaredy cat!

'Bye, Bugs.'

She smelt the minty toothpaste, and felt his kiss. She sat up with a start. 'What's the time?'

'Twenty-five past six. I'm late.'

'It's morning?'

Richard's eyes were bloodshot, and his face was pasty white. Hers probably was too.

'I'm playing squash tonight.'

'Will you want supper?'

'Yah – be in about nine.'

'OK.'

The door closed.

Morning. She hadn't dreamed. Had she slept? She slid out of bed feeling strangely alert, fresh. Must be a good biorhythm day. I feel great. Terrific. I'm resonating.

It's going to take you time to resonate, Sam.

Wow, Sam, you really resonated well.

I did?

Resonate, she thought as the hard droplets of water of the shower stung her face, and the soap stung her eyes. Resonate! She smiled. She felt light, carefree, as if a weight had been lifted from her. Watch out, Slider, I'm resonating. I'm going to get you, you horrible slit-eyed creep.

She dressed and went into the hallway. Helen came out of her room in her dressing gown. 'Good morning, Mrs Curtis. You're off early today.'

'Yes, I've got a breakfast meeting. What's Nicky got on at school?'

'An outing. They're going to London Zoo.'

Sam walked through into Nicky's room. He was just beginning to wake up, and she kissed him lightly on the forehead. 'See you this evening, Tiger.'

He looked up at her dozily, a sad expression on his face. 'Why are you going now, Mummy?'

'Mummy has to go in early today.' She felt a twinge of guilt. What was he feeling? she wondered. Unwanted? A nuisance? Someone in the way of her career? Bamford O'Connell's words flashed at her.

You gave up your career for Nicky . . . Maybe you feel anger at him. Maybe deep in your subconscious you feel that if you didn't have him around—?

She stared down at Nicky, reluctant to leave him, wanting to hug him, wanting to take him to the zoo herself, to show him the giraffes and love him. Wanting him never to feel for one instant the way she had felt throughout most of her childhood. 'See you this evening,' she said, turning reluctantly.

'Will you be late tonight, Mummy?'

'No.'

'Promise?'

She laughed. 'I promise.'

'You didn't tell me a story last night.'

'Mummy was a little late last night.'

'Will you tell me one tonight?'

'Yes.'

'About the dragon? Will you tell me that one again?'

She smiled and nodded, stroked his hair, kissed him again, then went out and down the hallway and put on her coat, which was damp.

It was still fairly dark outside, made worse by a swirling mist that was thick with drizzle. A glum paperboy in a sou'wester was standing in front of the mail boxes, sifting through the papers.

'Flat Eleven,' Sam said. 'Have you got them?'

The lenses of his glasses were running with water. He peered helplessly through them.

'Don't worry,' she said, and hurried to her car.

Her energy faded fast, and by the time she got to the office after her meeting she felt tired and sticky; grungy. The hotel dining room had been hot, stuffy. Everyone had sat drinking too much coffee, crunching toast, bleary-eyed, surrounded by the smells of aftershave, fried eggs and kippers. What the hell had the meeting been about? Nothing, that was what it had been about. The suits at Mcphersons wanted Ken to understand the importance of this commercial, the significance of being invited to Leeds to make the presentation. Earnest, serious hellos. Positive handshakes. This wasn't going to be no ordinary commercial. No, sir. The coming of Christ was an insignificant blot in the annals of time compared to the new Coming. The Dawning of A Great New Era. CASTAWAY. The first Personal Nourishment System. The Twenty-first Century Food. Food that Resonates.

The ashtray was filled with fresh, lipsticky butts, and the smoke haze was thick. Claire was hammering on her typewriter, head bent low in concentration.

'Morning, Claire.'

Claire lifted her hand a few inches in acknowledgement and carried on her frenetic typing.

'What are you typing?'

'I'm just doing this for Ken,' she said, almost furtively.

'What is it?' said Sam, getting increasingly infuriated.

'They don't want the giraffes.'

'What?' Sam opened the window and breathed in a lungful of wet Covent Garden mist.

'They're cancelling.'

'The whole shoot?' Sam said, alarmed.

'No. They've decided to use pantomime giraffes. They're worried about the animal rights people.'

'Booze, cigarettes, animal rights, exploiting women . . . for God's sake, we're not going to be able to make commercials about anything.' Sam sat down at her desk and slit open the top letter. It was informing her of an increase in lab charges.

Claire shook a cigarette out of the pack and looked slyly at Sam. 'Horrible, that thing on the news. Did you hear it?'

'What thing?' said Sam absently, concentrating on the letter.

'That poor woman.'

'Woman?'

'Last night. The one who was murdered.'

She read the first paragraph again, irritated by Claire's chatter, trying to calculate the true cost of the increase.

'It was on the radio this morning. Hampstead tube station.'

Sam looked up with a start. 'What, Claire? What are you talking about?'

'Last night. A woman was raped and murdered at Hampstead tube station. It was on the news this morning. Makes you wonder where you're safe, doesn't it?'

The room seemed to be dissolving around her. She felt her legs shaking and a sharp acidic sensation in her throat.

Claire began typing again.

'Hampstead, did you say? Hampstead tube?'

Claire did not seem to hear her.

'Jesus.' She looked at her watch. It was twenty past eleven. She went outside, across to the news vendor and stood by his stand in the driving rain with no coat on as the first edition of the *Standard* was dumped by the delivery van, and the vendor untied the string, slowly, agonisingly slowly.

She read the headlines again, then again, stared at each word of the bold black type in turn, as if she was afraid to read on, as if by reading on it might all suddenly come true and she would find she was the girl who had been—

RAPED AND MURDERED ON THE UNDER-GROUND.

Oh Christ.

Oh sweet Jesus, no.

She was only dimly aware of the world that was continuing around her. A taxi dropped someone off. Two people hurried past under an umbrella. A van was unloading parcels.

Then she saw the photograph underneath.

Saw the woman's face smiling out at her, as if she was smiling at her and no one else. As if there was a secret understanding in that smile.

She reeled sideways, crashed into the vendor who smelled like a damp sack, apologised, held onto the news stand and stared again, numb with shock, at the photograph.

Please, no. Please let this be a dream.

She walked back slowly, crying with misery, help-lessness, shame, guilt. Guilt. Guilt. Scaredy cat, scaredy cat, could have saved her! Could have saved her! Could have saved her!

Her.

She'd been talking to her only minutes before.

It wasn't true. It couldn't be. It had to be a—

She blundered in through the office door and knocked Drummond, who was coming out, flying. The box he was carrying fell to the ground with a sharp crack and rolled into the gutter. 'Sorry,' she said. 'Sorry. Sorry.'

She walked past Ken's waxwork – the arm had been glued back on although the angle looked odd – and up to her office. She sat back at her desk and put the wet and soggy paper down and stared again at the photograph, then the words, then the photograph again.

A thirty-seven-year-old mother of a young child was brutally raped and murdered at Hampstead Underground Station last night.

Tanya Jacobson, a psychotherapist, was found dead in a boiler room halfway down the notoriously deep stairwell shortly after ten o'clock by a maintenance electrician. Ticket clerk, John Barker, had warned Mrs Jacobson earlier that the lifts were out of service and that the steps went very deep.

Premonitions, precognition . . . that's all a little bit – fringe, OK? We're trying here to really connect with our dreams, go with them, free associate, get some good dynamics going.

She looked up and saw Claire watching her. 'I know her,' Sam said bleakly. 'I was with her just – before – she was . . . I went to this—'

The dark room. Knickers being ripped down. Hands around the neck. The stench of onions.

Tell me you love me.

Cunt bitch.

No. Please, no. Don't kill me. Please don't kill me – I have a child – please—

Sam felt an icy coldness torrenting through her, deep inside. She closed her eyes then opened them again. 'It must have been minutes—' She paused. 'I could have prevented it,' she said.

Claire looked up at her, and frowned.

Sam thought again of the grunting, and the dark shadow that came up the stairs towards her. 'I ought to call the police,' she said. 'Tell them I was there.'

'Did you see anything?'

'Yes – I . . . I don't know,' she sighed.

She stood up abruptly and wandered around the office, clenching her hands. She walked over to the window and stared out at the sheeting rain, at puddles, at awnings, at black umbrellas and at an old man who was sifting through the contents of a litter bin.

Dead.

Terrific. Wow! Wonderful. I'm Tanya Jacobson.

Tanya Jacobson. Sam felt the coldness of the draught on her hands, and water from her wet hair running down her face.

Just don't get sidetracked into those premonitions, Sam. We don't dream the future – but we make connections. We meet our monsters.

'I dreamed it,' she said.

Sam, dismissing a dream as a premonition is the easy route. I think you're using that as an excuse not to face the real meaning of the dreams.

Maybe it was the other way around? Were they using the psychology route to avoid facing up to premonitions?

Christ. There must be someone who—?

She felt the heat from the radiator rise up through the cold draught, as she continued to stare out through the window. 'That clairvoyant you go to, Claire. Why do you go to her?'

'Mrs Wolf?'

'Yes.' Sam turned around. 'What do you go to her for?'

'I go to her for guidance.'

'Is she accurate?'

Claire swept her hair back with her hands and looked sharply up at the ceiling, as if the answer was written there. 'Yes, she's – very accurate. She's very accurate indeed.'

'Does she help you to understand things?'

'She's very good at . . . helping people to understand things.'

'Would she see me, do you think?'

'Oh yes, I'm sure she would. You can just go along. You don't even need an appointment, although it's best to make one. Wednesdays. She's always there Wednesdays.'

23

The shop was in a narrow street in Bloomsbury. She could see the sign halfway along on the other side. 'THE WHOLE MIND AND BODY CENTRE.' It was painted blue, and she sensed weird vibes coming out from it even from this distance. She glanced at her watch. Fifteen minutes early.

There was a smaller sign in the window of the shop, a stand-up card which she read when she got closer.

EVA WOLF, CLAIRVOYANT
SITTING TODAY.

Another on top of a neat stack of pyramids proclaimed THE WONDER OF PYRAMIDS! There was also a row of rock crystals, several packs of Tarot cards, an assortment of books – *Realise Your Full Psychic Potential* said one, *Understand Magik*, said another – and a silver four-leafed clover charm bracelet wrapped around a sign which said THE PERFECT VALENTINE GIFT!

The interior of the shop was, like the sign, blue, with blue-tinted fluorescent lights throwing down harsh light across the shelves and the open floor. Designer occult, she thought. She went inside and the feeling of hostility almost overwhelmed her. She wanted to turn and run – from the heat of the blue fluorescents and the smell of joss sticks and the glare of a woman who looked up at her from behind a half-dismantled cash register.

Was she Mrs Wolf?

Her red hair was pulled back tight across her scalp, her skin tight over her face, as if she'd been affected by some freak pull of the moon. She wore a black polo neck sweater which showed her nipples dearly, like two black spikes.

Sam turned away and looked around. There were several crystal balls on a shelf in front of her. A rack of meditation cassettes, more pyramids, astrological charts, shelves stacked with candles, some of them black, a pouch with several small stones laid on it, a display of herbal sleep tinctures, and all the time the smell . . . the joss sticks, yes, but something else, something weird. Seriously weird, she thought, the fluorescent lights burning down on her scalp like sun-ray lamps.

The woman was bent over the cash register, picking at it with a screwdriver like someone trying to get the meat out of a lobster.

'Excuse me?'

The woman looked up. 'Yes?' It seemed to come out without her mouth moving, almost without a sound, almost as if she had imagined it. She felt strangely disoriented.

'I have an appointment with Mrs Wolf.'

The woman skewered the cash register again. 'Through the books. Downstairs.' Without looking up this time; again the mouth had not moved.

Sam walked through to the back of the shop, past a stack of pocket books and hesitated at the top of the stairs.

Cut and run.

Don't be silly.

Claire comes here. It's fine. Maybe that woman just had a row with her boyfriend or something? Or her girlfriend? She went down a steep, narrow staircase into the basement, which was an extension of the books section. A man with a pigtail, dressed in black, was restocking the shelves. There were books all around, piled on tables, on shelves, in dumpbins. Past them on the far wall she saw an arrow pointing down a short corridor to a door.

'Eva Wolf, Clairvoyant', was handwritten in large script and underneath in smaller writing it said:

CLAIRVOYANT SITTINGS. 30 Mins.   £12
PALM READINGS   £10
AURA READINGS   £10
TAROT   £12
PRIVATE SEANCES BY ARRANGEMENT

The door was slightly ajar and a guttural mid-European voice called out from behind it. 'Is that Mrs Peterson? You are rather late. I have another appointment.'

'No, I'm Mrs Curtis.'

There was a silence. 'I don't think Mrs Peterson is coming today. Come in, please. Come in.'

Sam pushed open the door and went into a room that wasn't much bigger than a toilet cubicle. The bare brick walls were painted the same blue as everywhere else and a single blue light bulb hung overhead. The room smelt faintly of joss sticks and strongly of a noxiously sweet perfume. Mrs Wolf was seated behind a tiny round table, which she dwarfed, wearing a dark polo neck sweater and an unfastened afghan waistcoat. She sat bolt upright, a tall, heavy-boned woman in her early-seventies, her stiff face daubed with gaudy make-up, and poker-straight wiry grey hair that hung down around it and over her forehead in a fringe. Her eyes stared at Sam from their shadowy sockets, like wary creatures of the deep.

'Please shut the door behind you. Put your coat on the hook.'

Sam did so and sat down. The woman took her hand quickly, snatchily, like a bird taking food, and held it firmly in her own large hand; it was hard, calloused, as if she spent her spare time digging potatoes, and her nails were unvarnished and had dirt underneath them. There was an old Bible on the table, wrapped in cracked cellophane, and a coffee cup with lipstick on the rim.

The woman stared at her, as if she had been expecting something quite different and Sam felt awkward, too close, as if her personal space was being invaded.

'It was a sitting you wanted?'

'What I really want is – just to talk. I want some advice . . . I'll pay for your time.'

The woman did not react. 'You've half an hour. You may make what use of it you like.'

They sat in silence for a moment and Sam felt increasingly uncomfortable. She heard footsteps upstairs and the faint sound of an extractor fan; she looked at the woman's stiff, serious face and saw she had two warts, and a mole with a hair growing out of it. The face seemed to stiffen even more and slowly, almost imperceptibly, she began to quiver; Sam felt her hand trembling.

'I've been having what I suppose are premonitions . . . in my dreams. It started a couple of weeks ago. I—' She heard her own voice tailing away. What did she want to hear? she thought suddenly. Why had she come here at all? She felt a rising surge of fear inside her.

Stay away from the hokum guys.

'I was hoping you might help me to understand why these are happening.'

Mrs Wolf was giving her the distinct impression that she wasn't really interested. 'That would be the spirits telling you things.'

'Spirits?'

'It all comes from the spirits.'

'Ah.'

'It's all part of God's love for us.'

'Ah.'

Mrs Wolf's expression mellowed; she leaned forward and patted the Bible tenderly, affectionately, as if it was a baby she had just been suckling. 'The Good Lord is always watching over us; He doesn't mind if you are Christian or Jewish, because there is room for everyone in the Kingdom of God.' She smiled a distant, private smile. 'He still understands and He tells me to tell you that He's keeping room for you. Any time you want to enter into Him He will receive you.'

Very reasonable of Him.

'Kindness. He's so full of kindness. Kindness and love.'

'That's why he killed my parents.'

'He's asking us to say a prayer together. A little prayer for protection and understanding and then we'll say the Lord's Prayer.'

The clairvoyant closed her eyes and held Sam's hand a little tighter. Too tight; she was crushing it.

'Gracious Spirit, as we join together here, we ask for blessing upon all of those who come from Spirit to be with us and we ask a blessing, please, for Mrs Curtis. Now, Father, we ask for protection and we know that when we come to Thee, as we stand in Thy grace, we are indeed protected from all of earth's conditions. If we could come to You more often, we would find that peace and tranquillity that exists only in Your presence . . .' There was no feeling of sincerity in the woman's words; she could have been reading from a telephone directory. It was almost as if she was . . . mocking?

Claire believed this woman? Swore by this woman?

Give her a chance.

'Amen.' The clairvoyant stared hard at Sam.

'Amen,' Sam said, half under her breath.

The woman's hand was cold. Uncomfortably cold; how could she be that cold?

'I'm getting a connection with advertising. Would you understand that?'

You know that. I told you when I made the appointment that Claire had recommended me. 'Yes,' Sam said.

'I'm being shown two people in Spirit – could be your grandparents. No, they're younger. Could they be your parents?'

Sam frowned.

'Died when you were quite young, did they?'

Had Claire told her this?

'I'm being told there was a break in your career – a young child involved – but that was in the past?'

Sam nodded, reluctantly.

'I see difficulties with a man at the moment. This is a very ambitious man, and I'm shown his heart being torn. Pulled in two directions. I don't know if it's between you and work, or between you and another woman. Does that mean anything?'

Sam nodded again.

She tightened her icy grip on Sam's hand even more, so much that Sam winced, but the woman ignored her, closed her eyes tightly and started breathing in hard, short bursts. Sam stared, her hand in agony, and to her horror saw sweat beginning to pour down the woman's face. She wondered if this was a trance.

RAPED AND MURDERED ON THE UNDER-GROUND.

Last night she had lain in bed reading until she was too tired even to turn the pages any more. She had felt herself going down the dark steps, waiting for the shadow, and when she finally saw it and had turned to run, she had not been able to move, and had stood and screamed. Then Richard had grunted and asked her if she was OK.

No, damn you. I am not O.K. And you don't believe me, do you? You don't believe that I was down there, down the tube station, minutes before it happened.

Had a lucky escape didn't you, Bugs?

That was all he'd said. Big grin on his face.

He thought it was funny?

Mrs Wolf's eyes opened and they were filled with a strange, uncomprehending fear. They closed again and she was still drawing short, almost desperate, breaths. She spoke slowly, almost as if she was sleeptalking. 'Do – you – know – a – man – with – only – one—' Then the panting started again, and the woman began shaking her head from side to side and whimpering, 'No – no – no – no—'

The room was becoming icily cold. Sam could see steam from the woman's breath, thick vapour that hung in the air. She felt goose-pimples running down her arms, down her back and a churning feeling in her stomach.

There was a strange rumbling sound, like a distant tube train, except it seemed to be coming from above them, not below. As she listened to it, she felt the coldness in the room seeping through her, turning everything inside her to ice.

There was a sharp ping above them.

The light went out.

Sam snapped her neck back, staring up, trying to see the bulb, then looked around wildly in the sudden pitch-black darkness.

The clairvoyant continued to pant and whimper. Then her grip began to slacken, and Sam felt the temperature in the room warming.

'I think we'd better stop,' Mrs Wolf said. 'I think we'd better stop.' She was still breathing heavily.

'Please tell me . . . please tell me what's going on,' Sam whispered.

'There's . . . I—' She heard the rustle of the woman's clothes in the darkness. 'They won't show me anything. Nothing.'

'Why? I don't understand.'

'It's better if you don't.'

'I want to know.'

'There'll be no charge. I can't give it to you. I can't give you what you want.' The woman's chair scraped back.

'Why not? Please explain—'

'You want to know what's going on? The future? I can't see. I can't show you.'

'Why can't you?'

'I can't. Open the door. We must open the door!'

'Why can't you?' Sam's voice was rising.

'Because there's nothing there,' the woman said.

'What do you mean?'

'There's nothing there.'

'You mean you can't see anything?'

'Nothing.'

'What . . . what does that mean?'

The clairvoyant's voice was trembling. 'No more future. It means – that you don't have any future.'

Sam felt her hand released; heard the woman move; the sound of the door opening and dim light from the corridor filled the room.

'There's no charge,' said the woman. 'Just go. Get out!'

'Please—' Sam said. 'Please just explain. Tell me—'

'Out, get out! Get out!' the woman cried. 'Get out! No charge, just get out!' She was screaming now. 'What have you brought with you? Take it away. We don't want it here. Take it, get out, get out!'

Sam stared up at the bulb. It was intact, but blackened. She stood up, stunned, her mind numbed.

'Get out of here!' the woman hissed again. 'Take it away. Take it with you.'

Sam backed away out of the room and down the corridor, past the man with the pigtail who glared malevolently. She climbed the stairs and saw the woman with the pulled-back red hair still skewering the cash register, glance up and follow her with her eyes.

Sam stumbled through the shop and out into the street, her brain a vortex of confusion. It was a cold, sharp afternoon, the sky a watery blue, with the sun already setting. Four o'clock. A waiter came out of a Greek restaurant across the road and locked the door behind him. Two men strode past chatting, one rubbing his hands against the cold.

She began to walk as fast as she could away from the shop, from Mrs Wolf, away from the woman with the pulled-back face, blinded by the raging confusion in her mind. She kept bumping into people, then saw an object in front blocking her path and stepped around it, off the pavement, onto the road.

There was a howl of brakes and she looked up, startled, at the taxi that was stopped inches from her.

The driver's head came out of his window, a cloth cap

with clumps of hair either side. 'Woz wiv you then? Woz your fuckin' game? Trying to get yourself bloody killed?'

'Sorry,' she said. 'Sorry.'

Through the blur of her tears she saw a small park across the road; she went into it and sat down on a bench.

She lowered her head into her arms, and thought for a moment she was going to be sick. She could feel the world turning like a huge fairground wheel, accelerating, spinning her round, making her giddy, then rising up and trying to tip her onto the grass. She held onto the seat, held on tightly; held on because she knew she was tilted so far over now that if she let go she would fall out into space.

No more future . . . you don't have any future.

OK. I want to wake up now. Dream over.

Two barristers walked down the path in front of her, in their gowns and wigs; she watched them, hoping they might turn into frogs or giraffes, or take their clothes off and leap in the air so would know it was a dream for sure, but they simply carried on walking, talking.

She stared up at an advertising hoarding on the side of a high-rise office. Huge bold letters, already illuminated for the falling darkness. Huge bold letters that beamed at her as if they were taunting her.

SAFEGUARD YOUR FUTURE WITH THE GUARDIAN ROYAL.

24

The heavy traffic streaming north was gradually thinning the further away they got from London. They could have been on another planet or travelling through space, Sam thought, staring out through the windscreen. Just blackness peppered with drifting red lights and occasional orange blinking lights and the rushing of wind, and bridges that passed overhead and seemed to suspend time for a fraction of a second, and signs that came out of the dark then flipped away again past the windscreen.

NORTHAMPTON. COVENTRY. LEICESTER. LOUGHBOROUGH 10. SERVICES 15.

Lightning forked across the sky and a few blobs of water hit the windscreen. The interior of the Bentley was dark, just the weak glow of the dials on the dashboard and the radio which was on but was turned down too low to hear. Ken had been quiet, uncharacteristically quiet; they had both been quiet.

'It was Claire who suggested her?' he asked suddenly.

'Yes.'

'She's been to her?'

'I think she goes quite often; she swears by her.'

'Did you tell Claire what she said?'

'No. I don't find her very easy to talk to.'

'You don't like her very much, do you?'

'I think she's a bit weird.'

'She's quite efficient.'

'How much do you know about Claire, Ken?'

'Not a lot. Lives in Ealing. Used to live in South Africa. Worked for a small commercials company there for eight years.'

'Do you know what she was doing for them?'

'Same as what she's doing now.'

'I don't think she knows very much about the business.'

'She had good references.'

'Did you check them?'

'No. She said the company had gone bust. It was at

218

the same time she split up with a boyfriend, which is why she decided to come back to England. You don't think the references are false, surely?'

'No, I'm sure they're fine. I think I'm just very . . . I guess freaked out by everything that's been happening.'

'You need to get away, Sam. Can't you and Richard go off somewhere for a few days?'

'He doesn't seem to like going away these days.'

'I'd like to go round there and give that cow a bloody thrashing. The Whole Mind and Body Centre,' he said contemptuously. 'Load of sodding con artists, that's all. Loonies. Dream groups, clairvoyants, shrinks—' He glanced in his mirror and moved across into the nearside lane. 'Perhaps we ought to try to find a witch doctor. Maybe they've got one in Leeds.'

She smiled.

'What are we going to do with you, Sam?'

'You needn't worry. I don't have any future.'

'Of course you have a sodding future.' He took his hand off the wheel and touched her arm lightly. 'I want you to have a future. It's crap, Sam. Look, none of us has any future. In the long run we'll all be dead – so what's she saying? You're going to be dead in a hundred years? Was she any more specific than that?'

'Why do you think she said what she did? I thought these people – if they saw something bad – weren't supposed to tell you.'

He shrugged. 'There are some very weird people in the world, Sam. Maybe she just didn't like you . . . was envious that you are young and pretty and thought she'd scare the hell out of you for fun.'

She saw another fork of lightning streak through the sky, then vanish. Like a light bulb going out.

Pop.

Ping.

Light bulbs.

Light bulbs went all the time, didn't they? If you had something sticky on them, like paint, then they could explode. Couldn't they?

The woman with the pulled-back face.

Mrs Wolf.

Weirdos. Ken was right. They conned Claire. But they hadn't conned her. Oh no. Great trick that, the light bulb trick. Works a treat, hey? Every one a winner.

Another sign drifted out of the darkness towards them.

LEEDS

Another sign followed it, black and white this time.

163 DEAD IN BULGARIA AIR DISASTER.

Then another swirled out of the darkness, bending, curling, like a sheet of newsprint.

RAPED AND MURDERED ON THE UNDER-GROUND.

It was coming straight at them, hit the windscreen and flattened out like the wing of a giant insect. Ken switched the wipers on and the blades smoothed it out like a poster on a billboard, so that she could see it clearly, read it clearly, see Tanya Jacobson's face staring through the glass at her, smiling, winking.

Are you resonating, Sam?

Sam shrieked.

'Sam? You OK?'

Ken's voice. She blinked hard and stared ahead. Nothing. No newspaper. Just the blackness and the tail lights and the wipers clearing the spots of rain, and a new light now, a tiny winking light on the dash. They were turning off.

'Fine,' she said. 'I'm sorry. I was dozing.'

The hotel was only a short distance from the motorway, and there was a battery of signs so no one could miss it.

TROPICANA GOLF & COUNTRY CLUB.
TROPICANA INDOOR POOL AND GRILL
   BAR – OPEN TO NON RESIDENTS.
PARADISE ISLAND CREOLE RESTAURANT.
PARADISE DISCO.

The palm tree emblem was emblazoned on the two entrance columns and bedecked in fairy lights shining out through the rain, which was falling harder now. It was emblazoned again, forty foot high, on the wall above the entrance porch. Country club, Sam thought. You'd never get permission to build a twenty-storey hotel in the middle of the countryside, but a country club: that was a different matter. Image. Packaging. Labels. You could do anything you wanted if you knew the right label to stick on it.

RESIDENTIAL GUESTS ENTRANCE.
GOLF CLUB.
PARKING.

They followed the arrows that were in the shape of palm fronds down an avenue lined with trees and bushes to the main entrance. As they pulled up outside the door, Sam stared around uneasily at the darkness, feeling a sudden frisson of fear.

'Looks a bit naff,' Ken said.

She gazed at the copper palm tree above the porch, then around again at the darkness.

'What's the matter?'

'Nothing.' She smiled. 'It's fine.'

The entrance lobby was festooned with tropical plants, bright lights, rattan furniture, and painted a lush tropical green. A girl in a matching tropical green dress, with a small gold palm tree engraved with the name 'Mandy' pinned to her chest, tilted a mouthful of gleaming white teeth at them.

'Good evening, Madam, good evening, Sir. Do you have a reservation?'

'Yes, we're in the Grand Spey Foods party.'

'Ah.' She looked down and rummaged through a sheaf of paper. 'Mr and Mrs—?'

'Mr Shepperd and Mrs Curtis.'

'There's a message for you from a Mr Edmunds. They have been delayed in London and won't be here until late. If they don't see you tonight, they'll meet you in the foyer at eight-fifteen in the morning.'

'Thanks,' said Ken. He turned to Sam. 'Let's dump our stuff in our rooms then have some dinner.'

A cocky teenage porter with bum-fluff on his upper lip, and 'Bill' pinned to his chest, showed Sam to her room first and Ken went with them. Sam was on the nineteenth floor. 'Get a lovely view of the motorway,' Bill snickered, unlocking the door.

It was a small fresh bedroom with bamboo furniture and bright green drapes and bedspread, a carpet with a rush matting pattern and on the wall was a print of a Gauguin painting she vaguely recognised of a black man and beautiful black woman sitting on the floor of an art gallery.

'Quarter of an hour?' said Ken.

'Fine.'

They went out and closed the door, and she pushed the brass buttons on her suitcase; the locks opened with sharp clicks.

Shit. Did she really bring all this stuff? For one night? She untied the straps and sifted through the layers of flattened clothing. Thick sweater. Had she really packed that? And another? Three different outfits? Nuts, nuts, nuts. It was hot and stuffy in the room. She went over to the window, pulled back the curtain and saw a balcony. She unlocked the door and stepped out onto it.

She felt the cool air, refreshing, could hear the rain falling through the darkness, and see the motorway stretching away into the distance like a never-ending neon sign. She looked down and saw the roof of the swimming pool directly beneath her, a huge octagonal-shaped glass dome over a pool set in a brightly lit indoor tropical garden. There was a thin haze of condensation on the glass making everything slightly fuzzy. She watched a fair-haired woman with a fine figure slowly stretch out on a deck chair under a sun lamp, and toss her hair back. To the side of the pool was a wooden bar with a coconut matting roof, where several people sat wearing nothing but swimming costumes. She wondered what the temperature was in there.

She leaned against the balcony rail trying to get a better view and it seemed to move a fraction under her weight. She stepped back nervously, stretched out her hand and tested it. It was fine, rigid. Standing at arm's length, she pushed harder against it. It was still fine. Had she imagined it? Come on, Sam, pull yourself together. Nervous of everything. Relax. She went back to the rail and put her full weight on it, defiantly. She even gave it a shove with her bum, just to see.

25

'Island In The Sun' came round for the third time on the Paradise Island Restaurant muzak. It was suffocatingly hot, as if the hotel was determined to spare no detail in maintaining the illusion of the Indian Ocean on this damp green strip of countryside sandwiched between the motorways.

The walls were uneven and painted white, with bits of fishermen's netting hanging from them. A model wooden schooner sat on a high shelf. Sam's mouth was feeling hot and blasted from a Creole fish curry, and she sipped some mineral water. Ken lit a cigarette. There were blotches of sweat on his denim shirt, around his chest and on his brow.

'You're looking a bit more cheerful,' he said, picking up his glass. 'Cheers.'

'Cheers,' she said. 'I must remember to keep on smiling. I keep forgetting.'

'Yeah, well – it's not a bad thing. It's very dangerous to be too cheerful.'

'Oh yes?'

'I think sometimes we ought to put people in hospital for feeling cheerful. We'd have a far safer world if everyone was miserable, depressed; cheerful people are dangerous – blinkered optimists all bloody bashing on regardless. Don't worry, old boy, it's all going to be fine, eh what?'

She grinned. 'You're probably right.'

'Want any pud?' he asked, looking around for a waiter.

'No, thanks.'

'In a year or two's time, they won't have to bother with menus in restaurants – they'll just be serving everyone Castaway bars. How would you like it served, Madam? In its wrapper? On a plate? Would you like us to cut it for you? To eat it for you?' He dabbed his forehead with his napkin. 'I'm sweltering. They ought to warn you to bring tropical clothes when you come here. Fancy a quick walk? Get some air?'

They went out of a side entrance. The lightning and the rain had stopped and there was a mild breeze which felt good. They walked down a path towards the golf course, and it got increasingly dark as the lights from the hotel windows faded behind them. Then the path stopped and they walked on the soft wet grass of the golf course itself, treading carefully, in now almost pitch darkness.

Ken took her hand and held it firmly, comfortably, protectively. Safe. She felt safe with him. He squeezed her hand, and she felt a good warm feeling inside.

Two silhouettes came out of the darkness towards them. Sam saw the glow of a cigarette, heard a whisper and a giggle, then they passed.

'Do you believe in the supernatural, Ken?'

He was silent for a long time. 'I'd never rule anything out, Sam,' he said finally. 'Half the scientists who've ever lived have ended up being proved wrong. Scientists, doctors, they can be arrogant buggers. Who knows? Who knows anything? When electricity was invented, scientists ran around screaming that it was impossible, that it did not exist, that it was all an illusion, the work of the devil – whilst businessmen went out and made lamps.'

She smiled.

'I don't know about seeing the future. The way you're seeing things . . . it's weird. I don't know if it's supernatural, or whether you're seeing through some time warp. Or is it just odd coincidences? Know what the Indonesians used to do?'

'No.'

'They used to read the future in the entrails of chickens. I saw it on TV. It looked disgusting.'

She giggled, suddenly feeling light-headed. 'Did it work?'

'It seemed to work for them. How would Richard feel if you started doing that?'

'He'd—' She shivered, suddenly feeling cold. 'Let's turn back.'

'Actually, my father – he didn't exactly have

premonitions, but he used to get . . . feelings about things. The Blacks, he used to call them. 'I've got the Blacks coming, boy. A big Black.'

'What did he do when he had them?'

'He got quite nervous. He was a superstitious man, and he used to be doubly careful. Sometimes something bad happened and sometimes it didn't.'

They walked around towards the front of the hotel, past the outside of the swimming pool, and Sam glanced up at the towering hulk of the building, up towards her room, then around again at the darkness. It felt almost as if someone else was out there in the darkness with them, someone who they could not see but who was listening to them, watching them.

'What did your father do for a living?'

'Spent his life out on strike, mostly. Silly bugger. Print worker on a newspaper in Nottingham. Red Harry, they called him. He was going to lead the revolution. He was going to be the Russians' number one in England. "Won't be long now, boy!" he used to shout at me across the breakfast table. "They'll be 'ere any day now, boy!"'

'What happened to him?' Sam asked.

'Eventually got kicked out of his job. The lads supported him for a few weeks, then they drifted back to work. He got very bitter about it. He got bitter that the Russians never came, as well. He died bitter as hell. I remember my aunt coming up to me at the funeral. "'Ee was a luvly man, your Dah. A luvly man. 'Ee never did anyone any 'aarrm."' He squeezed her hand again. 'What a bloody epitaph, eh? She hadn't the guts to say he was a stupid fart who pissed his life away.'

'Is that how you remember him?'

'No. I'd left home before he got the boot. When I knew him, he still had his fire and his enthusiasm. Used to read me bedtime stories about the Russian Revolution. He couldn't understand it when I went into advertising. Wouldn't speak to me for years.'

'Sad.'

'Still, I don't expect my epitaph'll be much better.'

'Why not?'

'I used to be a bit like my dad. I thought I could change the world. I wasn't an agitator, but I thought I could change it through being creative, through movies. Instead, all I do is feed the system. Feed it with ads for chocolate bars and Japanese cars and wholemeal bread. That's what's going to be on my epitaph. "Here lies Ken Shepperd. He made more wholemeal bread commercials than anyone else. Tough and gritty with nowt taken out. The man who gave the world *wholemeal dreams*." '

She laughed, and they reached the hotel door.

'Let's have a drink,' Ken said and they went through to the Paradise Bar and Disco and sat in a dark corner table. A group of salesmen were at a nearby table. One was telling a joke and the others were tittering, and a woman, too old for her long blonde hair and the mini skirt she was wearing, sat on her own at the bar. Ken glanced at her, caught Sam's eye and winked. 'Shall we buy Jake a present? Have her waiting in his room?' He signalled the waiter over and ordered a bottle of Krug. 'Courtesy of Grand Spey,' he said. 'Want to dance?'

She looked at him, surprised. 'Sure.'

He took both her wrists and led her onto the dance floor, pulling her gently towards him. She felt a tingle of excitement in her throat, and it ran down her neck into her stomach.

'When A Man Loves A Woman' was playing, and he stared at her, quizzically, and moved a fraction closer.

No, Sam.

Big danger.

Her arms were throbbing, and she felt a trickle of perspiration run down the back of her neck. He tilted his head forward and their lips touched gently dusting each other. She jerked back as if she had had an electric shock, then gave him a brief peck and put her cheek firmly against his. She felt the roughness of his stubble, smelled his cologne and his hair shampoo and the clean earthy smell of his sweat through his denim shirt.

They danced, their cheeks together, and she glanced around warily for a moment in case Charlie Edmunds or either of the others or anyone else she knew might be in the room, but there was no one other than the group of salesmen roaring at another joke and the hooker at the bar smoking a cigarette.

She felt Ken's hands stroking her back, firmly, suggestively, and she remembered suddenly another time that she thought she had forgotten for ever. The cold, sharp night. The rich smell of leather from the car's seats. The light sensuous touch of the boy's hand just above her stocking on her goosepimpled thigh, and the car's radio playing hot steamy midnight passion music, 'Je T'Aime, Je T'Aime'. The windows were steamed up, and she remembered thinking that there might be a Peeping Tom lurking out there in the dark. She remembered vividly the sound of tearing paper, the oily rubbery smell of the Durex, the rustling of clothes and the awkward grunts. Then lying back, moments later, with a deadweight on top of her, saying to her 'How was it? Was it good? God it was great!' It was? She wasn't even sure whether anything had happened, whether he had come, or whether he'd had whatever it was called – premature something or other?

Sandy. She could remember his name, but his face was gone. Fair hair, that was all. The rest was a blur.

The music stopped and she pulled her face away. Their eyes met. 'I find you very attractive, Ken. Don't tempt me.'

'Me? I'm just dancing,' he said, but his eyes stayed locked on hers. 'I'd like to sleep with you.'

She shook her head. 'We've got a great relationship, Ken. Let's not—' She shrugged. 'I have to be strong right now, I have to be strong and keep my head clear – somehow.' She hugged him tight, 'I'm sure that making love with you would be the most wonderful thing in the world, but I can't, OK?' She nipped the tip of his ear gently with her teeth, then pulled away. 'Let's sit down and have a drink.'

The champagne was on the table, and he poured some out. They clinked glasses and drank, and Ken lit another cigarette.

'I thought that things between you and Richard—' he began.

'They're not that great,' she said. 'I don't know what's the matter with him. He's changed so much in the past few months.'

'How do you mean?'

'He's a different person. I don't know whether it's—' She stared down into the bubbles. 'There's a rather weird man he's become terribly pally with. I don't know if this chap's got some hold over him . . . like a Svengali.'

Ken frowned sceptically.

'I mean it, Ken. He's always on the phone to him. He used to back his own judgement – always seemed to do all right – then this guy, Andreas Berensen, gave him some advice or tips last year which came good and Richard made a lot of dough, and now he virtually won't go to the loo without asking his permission.'

'Who is this Andreas Berensen?'

229

'He's a director of one of those Swiss banks.' She shrugged and drank some more. 'Maybe I'm just being neurotic about him. Maybe it's not him at all – maybe it's me. Maybe Richard just doesn't find me attractive any more. He's drinking a hell of a lot. I sometimes wonder if he's having a nervous breakdown.' She smiled sadly. 'I – I feel it's important that I've just got to be around. I've got to be strong.'

'Richard's a lucky guy.'

'Having a loony for a wife?'

'You're not a loony, Sam. You're a great, terrific, wonderful girl. OK?'

'Yes, boss.'

Ken grinned and Sam glanced around the room again.

'You look nervous about something, Sam.'

'No. Just seeing if the others—'

'Seeing if teacher's arrived to send us all to bed? Nothing really changes in life, does it?'

'Don't you think so?'

'No.'

'Don't you think we—' She tilted her head back to look at him from further away – 'we get harder?'

' "She thought love was nothing more than the contact between two skins – but she still cried when I left." '

'Françoise Sagan?'

'You read her too?'

'I used to be into glib philosophy.'

'And what are you into now? Reality?'

'No,' she said. 'I'm beginning to think I've had enough reality. I've had reality all my life. I think I deserve a bit of fantasy.'

Ken grinned again. 'I'm sorry. I should have worn my Superman costume.'

She touched his shoulder lightly. 'How did the ad go? "You only had to look at the label"?'

He stared back hard at her. 'What the hell are we going to do with you? There must be some experts in premonitions – there's experts in bloody everything – there must be people who aren't cranks and aren't sceptics. Some organisation, maybe, or at some university. Your shrink friend you went to sounds like a conceited berk. Have you rung him and told him about Hampstead?'

'No. I still don't think he'd believe me.'

'What did you tell the fuzz? Didn't they come round and interview you?'

'They just wanted a statement – what time I was down there, who I saw. They told me I was sensible not going on down those stairs.'

'Did you tell them about your dream?'

'I didn't think that—'

'I can imagine him reading it out in court.' He put on a thick North London accent. 'The – er – witness, yer honour, saw it all in a dream, you see. She reckons it were done by this geyser wot wears a black 'ood and died twenty-five years ago.'

She laughed, uneasily. 'Did your father do anything about his premonitions? Did he ever see anyone about them?'

'No, never. He just accepted it. His family came from a mining background – they're a superstitious lot, miners – they just accept things, without questioning them too much.' He stood up and took her wrist. 'Let's have one more dance.'

He held her tightly on the dance floor. 'Sure you don't want to change your mind?'

'I'm an old woman, Ken. An old woman who's losing her marbles. I thought you only went for young glammy models?'

He kissed her cheek tenderly. 'Really old, aren't you,

231

Sam? Can hear your joints creaking and your bones rattling.'

She punched his stomach playfully with her fist.

'It's me,' he said. 'I'm the one that's getting old. Past forty and it's all downhill.'

'Does it worry you, age?'

'I keep noticing things. Tiny physiological changes. My skin getting saggy; hairs sprouting in odd places. My memory going. I talk to people sometimes and forget who it is I'm talking to. They'll probably find me one day asleep under a railway arch, wrapped up in newspapers. "Silly old bugger, don't remember who he is, keeps prattlin' on about wholemeal bread and chocolate bars. Yeah? Well maybe he's hungry. Don't look as if he's eaten in days."'

She giggled. 'Come on, it's bedtime.'

'Alone?'

'Alone,' she said firmly.

26

A single sharp rasping sound woke her.

Doorbell.

She opened her eyes and it rang again.

Doorbell.

The room was filled with strange yellowy light. Like sepia.

It rang again.

Coming, I'm coming. Christ, Richard why don't you answer?

She put out her hand and felt him lying there, on the wrong side. What on earth?

Oh Christ.

The door bell rang again, but it wasn't the doorbell, it

was the rasping snore of the man asleep on the wrong side of the bed.

Ken.

Oh Christ. No, surely not? Surely she hadn't?

He was still there. It would have been easier if he'd slunk away in the darkness and they could have met at the breakfast table and pretended it hadn't happened.

Maybe.

He was still there and he was snoring and it was early morning. Daylight. Her mouth tasted foul. Her stomach churned over, rumbled, tensed up. She lay still not daring to make any more movement, not wanting to wake him, not until she had had time to think. It was all there in the morning light, everything that you could hide from and curl up from in the darkness. Darkness. Darkness was a place where you could pretend that nothing was real. She wondered how she was going to face Ken, and she felt a feeling of sadness and stupidity as if everything she had worked so hard for, the past three years, she had thrown away in one night. She stared numbly at the ceiling, wishing she could push the clock back a few hours, to last night.

What was it going to be like? What were they going to say to each other? Was he going to tell her this morning that it would be silly for her to go on working for him? Or would he let it ride, let it come to its own conclusions? Long stony silences in the office. Biting remarks. Casting sessions when she would study his reaction to each model, the pangs of jealousy eating her insides. And finally clearing out her desk. Was that what the future held in store?

Just his head was visible under the rumpled sheet, his hair tousled, the brown stubble on his jaw, mouth slightly open and the rasping snore. She wondered if he was dreaming now; what did other people dream? She listened to the heater clattering, ticking and blowing, and stared at the Gauguin print on the wall, at the woman with the one bared breast, firm, pointed, and she looked down at her own breasts and they seemed small and sagging in comparison.

Must brush my teeth before he wakes. She slipped quietly out of the bed and felt a flutter of anxiety as he stirred, but he settled down again and continued snoring. She walked silently across the carpet, opened the balcony doors and slipped through the curtains into the first weak rays of the dawn sun. The sky was a mixture of greys and yellows, and the air smelled fresh, moist, strangely warm, you could almost believe you were in the Indian Ocean, she thought. Even the motorway seemed further away, empty, silent, like a canal. A low mist hung over the ground, and through it she could see some of the contours of the golf course, the grass shimmering with water.

The sun seemed to be getting brighter as she stood there, and she felt the thin warmth of its rays now on her naked body. It gave her a curious sense of freedom, and she was surprised that she was not feeling self-conscious about being naked.

I have a lover.

The feelings inside her were weird. She felt light, almost lighter than air for a moment, then slow and ponderous, heavy as lead. Something had changed inside her; something that had happened in the night had changed for ever in a way she knew she was going to understand, but did not yet.

She stared down at her breasts, and at her dark pubic hairs, the ends tinged a gingery gold by the sunlight. Her whole body became bathed in a gingery blonde glow, as if she was standing under a huge lamp.

She leaned against the wet balcony rail, and looked

down. The lights inside the glass dome were on; a workman, who looked tiny from here, was vacuuming the pool which also looked tiny, like a tear drop. A waiter ambled towards the poolside bar carrying a crate of beer bottles which clinked together noisily, and she was surprised how clearly she could hear them through the glass and nineteen storeys up.

The fair-haired woman whom she recognised from yesterday strode into the pool area, holding a towel and a book. She stretched the towel out on one of the recliners under a sun lamp, and settled herself down into it. Sam leaned further forward, to see what was directly beneath, and the balcony seemed to wobble.

Loose, it was loose.

No it's not, it's your imagination. Go on, try it again.

She stepped back nervously.

Scaredy cat! Scaredy cat! Scaredy cat!

The rail is loose.

Scaredy cat!

They slap these junk hotels up. What do they care about safety? The rail is loose.

Scaredy cat!

She went slowly, cautiously, back over to it, and peered over the edge. Christ. The drop down.

Vertigo.

She took a pace back, her head spinning.

Scaredy cat!

I am not afraid. Damn it, I am not afraid. I'm not some crank who's scared of balcony rails. She marched forward, gripped the rail firmly with both hands and looked downwards.

There was a sharp, rending crack and the entire balcony tilted forwards, throwing her against the rail.

No. Oh Christ, no.

The rail was holding the entire weight of her body.

235

'Ken! Help! Help!'

There was another crack and it tilted some more.

She turned her head. The balcony door was above her now, several feet above her.

'Ken!'

She was whimpering.

Oh God help me. 'Ken! Ken!'

There was another crack and she lurched further forwards, almost overbalancing. Don't look down. Don't look down. Don't move. Gently. Gently. She tried to turn, to climb back up on the sheer slippery floor, but the angle was too steep and each time she moved she felt the balcony lurch further downwards.

Help me, someone.

The woman below was stretched out under the sun lamp, directly beneath her.

I'm going to fall on you. Get out of the way!

The waiter carried another crate of beer towards the bar.

Look up. Please look up.

'Help!'

A tight rasping whisper.

'Ken! Help me.'

She was swaying now. The rail was making splintering cracking sounds. She could feel it giving beneath her. She tried to push away, but it just sagged further.

She looked desperately back up at the door. 'Ken!' she called. 'Ken!'

Then she saw him coming, and her heart leapt. OK, it was going to be OK, he'd know what to do. The balcony lurched again and she screamed.

'I can't hang on.'

He came through the door, Ken, stark naked, except he had a hood over his face, a black hood with knife slits.

'Ken? Are you mad? No games, Ken. No – no – no—.'

There was a deafening rending, tearing sound.

Ken stood there, watching her.

Smiling. His lips smiling through the slit.

There was one more lurch, a ferocious snap, then she was falling, plummeting, hurtling down.

She felt her stomach crash up inside her throat. Clutching the rail still. The glass dome got bigger, bigger, the air screamed at her. The woman, she thought. The woman. I'm going to kill the woman.

'No. No!'

She heard a buzzing sound, sharp, insistent.

Darkness. Darkness all around. Filled with the buzzing.

She was cold, drenched with – water from the pool?

The buzzing again.

A strange clattering sound above her. Heating duct?

The darkness. The void.

The buzzing sound.

Telephone?

She put out her hand. Nothing.

It buzzed again.

She tried the other side, felt something hard, heard a sharp clatter, felt the unfamiliar receiver in her hand.

'Your early morning call, Madam.'

'Wasser? Thank – thank you – I—' But the operator had hung up.

Christ.

The terror began to subside and her head swirled in confusion. She groped with her hand for the light switch, found it, pressed it and the light beside her bed lit up, dazzling her for a moment. She spun round and looked at the right-handed side of the bed, then sighed with relief: it was undisturbed; the pillows were fresh, undented. She closed her eyes, gulping in air, feeling the cold, plunge pool cold, of the sweat on her body.

Thank God. She was conscious she was mouthing the words. She slipped out of bed, went over to the window and opened the curtains. It was still dark outside, dark and raining. She walked across the room and into the bathroom, turned on the tap and stared at her frightened face in the mirror.

It was another one, she knew. The same feeling, the same vividness.

The same as the other dreams that had come true.

27

She stared out of the Bentley's window, through the weak reflection of her own face at the blackness beyond. The void. Nothingness.

Hell was the void where you could scream for ever and no one could hear you. A void where it was always cold and where you never grew any older and never died and never escaped. For ever.

Charlie Edmunds and Jake and Zurbrick from Urquhart Simeon Mcpherson had all been having breakfast when she'd gone down in the morning, and she had not been able to tell Ken about the balcony dream until now that they were on their way back to London. She left out that he'd been in bed with her.

The day had gone well. Grand Spey Foods had liked the Castaway commercials, and had liked Ken. They would recce in April and shoot in May, three commercials, back to back; the budget had been approved at over six hundred thousand pounds.

She told Ken how she had gone out on the balcony when she'd first arrived and thought it was loose then, but had checked it and it seemed all right, and he'd told her she shouldn't be spooked by the dream, that maybe there had been a tiny bit of looseness and it was her survival instincts warning her. Maybe the same instincts that had warned her about the gun being left around and the rapist in Hampstead.

'It could be that you've got sharp antennae, like rabbits' ears. Like Bugs Bunny.'

'Richard calls me Bugs.'

'Maybe that's why.'

'He says that sometimes when I'm thinking I stick my front teeth out, like a rabbit.'

'I hadn't noticed.'

'Maybe you never see me thinking!'

'I suppose "Bugs" is better than "Jaws".'

'Thanks a lot!'

Ken drove for some minutes in silence, then lit a cigarette. 'I don't know about the air disaster – maybe that's coincidence – but the other two . . . maybe someone up there likes you.'

'My fairy godmother?'

He smiled. 'I favour the sharp antennae.'

'You're beginning to sound like Bamford.'

'Bamford?'

'Our shrink friend.'

Ken said nothing. He inhaled on his cigarette and tapped the rim of the steering wheel.

'Do you ever think about death?' she asked.

'Sometimes.'

'Are you afraid of it?'

'I'm much more afraid of life.'

'What do you mean?'

He tilted his head back. 'Afraid of going to my grave, I suppose, without having put anything back.' He wound his window down a fraction and flicked some ash out. 'I

239

feel that when we live, we're constantly taking things – burning up petrol, polluting the atmosphere, decimating forests, you know. Always taking. I think we all need to put something back into the world in return. That we ought to try and leave it a better place than when we arrived. I don't feel I've done that yet.'

'You're funny.' She smiled, and felt his hand on hers, squeezing gently. 'Nice funny. You think a lot, don't you?'

'Maybe I think too much. What are you doing over the weekend?'

'Going to the country. Richard's shooting tomorrow and we're going to a dinner party tomorrow night. Then on Sunday – nothing, I hope. What about you?'

'I'm off to Spain in the morning. The Jerez shoot.'

'Yes, of course. How long are you away for?'

'Back Wednesday, if we stick to schedule.'

'What are Spanish crews like?'

'They're OK. You've got quite a few quotes to do.'

'It's going to be a busy year.' She laid her head against the soft leather, closed her eyes and listened to the faint swooshing of the tyres and the sounds of the traffic on the motorway all around them. Her toes were warm, roasting warm from the heater, and she felt very tired now; she dozed.

She woke up with a start as the Bentley bumped along Wapping High Street.

'You've had a good kip,' Ken said.

'I'm sorry, I wasn't much company.' Then she saw the two police cars parked in the street outside the warehouse; she glanced at Ken and their eyes met and she saw him frown, but he said nothing. She looked at the cars again, one with the City of London Police crest emblazoned on the door, the other unmarked, apart from two discreet aerials.

Ken helped her in with her suitcase and stood watching as the elevator door closed, and nodded, without saying, that he would wait a few minutes, in case.

Christ.

She knew.

She was absolutely certain as she stood in the gloomy light of the lift, listening to it shuffle and clank slowly upwards. It stopped with its usual sharp jerk, and her suitcase fell over with a bang. She lugged it down the corridor, then stood outside the door to the flat, rummaging through her handbag for her keys. There was a stillness about the whole building, a quiet uneasy calm as if neighbours all around were waiting silently, watching through their spyholes.

When she opened the door, Nicky came hurtling down the hall like a missile. 'Mummy!'

Not his normal gleeful greeting, but an angry, confused cry for help.

'Tiger! What is it Tiger?'

He was close to tears. 'They cut open Teddy.'

She felt a strange feeling of unreality, as if she wasn't really here, but was imagining it. Dreaming it. 'Teddy? Cut open? Who cut—?' Then she saw a policeman come out of Nicky's room.

Helen followed in his wake, walking slowly.

'What's happened, Helen?' Sam asked. 'Have we been burgled?'

Helen shook her head slowly. She was in shock.

Sam felt a sharp twist of fear in her stomach. Was this real? Was she really here? The door frame seemed to slide towards her, and struck her hard on the arm. She stumbled into the hallway, putting her hand out to steady herself, and held onto the edge of the coat stand. 'Helen? What is it?'

'They pulled all his tummy out,' Nicky started crying, and his face swirled in front of her.

'Burgled? Have we been burgled? Where's my husband?'

The policeman walked down the corridor towards her and stared at her, embarrassed. He was young, about twenty, she thought, tall and gangly. 'Mrs Curtis?'

'Yes.'

'I think – er – the Inspector . . . perhaps you'd better have a word with him. Or your husband.' He pointed down towards the living area, then backed away and walked towards her bedroom.

'Why are you going in there?'

'The Inspector,' he said. 'He'll explain.'

'I don't want you going in there.' She rested her hands on Nicky's shoulders.

The policeman went bright red. 'I'm afraid we have a warrant, Mrs Curtis.'

'A what?'

'A search warrant.'

'What are you—'

Christ.

Was this another dream? Another nightmare? Was Slider going to come down the corridor?

A search warrant.

'What are you looking for?' she asked.

'I think it would be best if you spoke to the Inspector, Madam.'

'I want to see it.'

'The Inspector—'

'You're not going in there until I've seen it.' She turned to Helen. 'Don't let him in there.' She knelt down and kissed Nicky. 'One second, darling. Wait here, and don't let that man go in my bedroom.'

'He cut open my teddy, he did,' Nicky sobbed.

'I'll cut him open,' Sam said, glaring at the policeman and sounding as if she meant it. She stormed down the corridor, then stopped as she saw another policeman on his knees in the kitchen, peering underneath the dishwasher with a torch. Pots, pans, plates, dishes had all been pulled out of the cupboards and stacked on the work surfaces, and something snapped inside her.

'Get out!' she screamed. 'Get out of my kitchen!' She grabbed a drawer, any drawer, and yanked it out; it was full of knives and spatulas and whisks and wooden spoons and she hurled it at him. It flew across the room, showering its contents out, hit the wall above him and fell down onto his head with a hard crack, hurting him. From the way he groaned, hurting him a lot.

'Sam.'

Richard grabbed her arm. 'You've got to let them.' He turned to the constable on the floor who was rubbing his head and staring at his finger. 'Are you OK?'

The constable screwed up his eyes. 'Could you get her out of here, please?'

Richard led her through the living area.

There were two men in the room. One was standing by the refectory table, in a brown suit with bell-bottom trousers and a sixties Beatle-cut hairstyle, tying up bundles of documents with red ribbon. The other was kneeling down in front of Richard's desk, pulling more documents out of a drawer, mustard socks and white hairless legs sticking out of his grey suit trousers. He glanced over his shoulder and then stood up, a burly man who might have been a bit of a boxer ten years before, with a greedy face and eyes that bulged out slightly, giving him the expression of a well-fed frog. His suit was too small, and crumpled, and his shirt collar was loosened, his tie halfway down his chest. He gazed at Sam in a faintly patronising way, as if he did not have to bother with her, as if she too was a child whose teddy bear he could order to be ripped open. 'This the missus?'

Richard nodded, eyeing Sam like a cornered animal. Then he stiffened, tried to smile a reassuring everything's-fine smile but it flashed across his face like a nervous twitch. 'Bugs, this is Inspector – er?'

'Milton. Like the poet. Detective Inspector Milton.'

'Good evening,' she said.'

'Company Fraud Department, City of London Police.' He jerked a thumb at the man in the brown suit. 'Detective Sergeant Wheeler.' Wheeler carried on binding the documents without looking round.

Fraud Department.

Sam stared, baffled for a moment.

Images flashed at her. Richard's behaviour. His strange late hours bent over his computer screen. The money for the new house. The Rolex. The booze.

Something trickled through her, cold, unpleasant.

Detective Inspector Milton looked at her contemptuously. I could eat you for breakfast and fart you out into the pond, lady, so don't mess with me.

'Nice flat, Mrs Curtis,' he said, in a snide, nasal voice. 'I was brought up round here. My parents used to live around the corner. Couldn't afford the rents now, of course, could they? Still, I suppose that's progress.'

'I want to see your ID and your warrant.'

He fished his wallet out of his pocket and opened it one-handedly in a well-worn movement, holding it up so the lady could see it clearly, read it clearly, let the lady have all the time she needs, just like the rule book says.

By the book, lady, know what I mean? Doing all this by the book. Know your types. Smart bastards. Well

244

we're smarter these days, Feet may still be big, but now our brains are big too. It's our hearts that have got smaller.

The photo showed a younger, thinner version of his face, with a startled expression and his eyes bulging even more. Then he snapped the wallet shut, put it back into his inside pocket and with the same hand, pulled out a sheet of paper which he handed to her. There was a crest on the top, several rows of formal type, their address and a signature at the bottom. R. Fenner. Magistrate. He folded it up and put it back in his pocket.

'Perhaps you could tell me why you're here?'

He scratched his nose with his finger. 'I expect your husband'll tell you later, if you ask him nicely.' He fingered the top of Richard's desk. 'Beautiful furniture. Cost a few bob that desk, eh? You people make me sick, Mrs Curtis. Yuppies. You ought to be on the stage, you should. You'd be good playing the indignant wife, you know that? Bet you like spending your husband's money for him, but your hands wouldn't be dirty, would they? Bet your nose is clean as a whistle. Bet if I looked up your nostrils there wouldn't be a bogey in sight. Be like looking up the barrels of a brand new Purdey.'

'Have you rung Bob Storer?' Sam asked Richard.

'He's on his way over.' He shook a cigarette out. 'Nothing we can do, Bugs. Just got to let them get on with it.'

She glared back at the Inspector. 'I don't care what bits of paper you've got with you. You don't ever speak to me like that again.' She turned to Richard. 'Can we have a word in private?' She walked out of the room.

Helen was standing in the hallway. 'It's Nicky's bathtime. Do you think it'll be all right if I bath him?'

'You'd better let them check down the plughole first.'

Helen nodded, uncertain whether Sam was being funny or serious.

Sam went outside into the passageway, waited until Richard had joined her, then closed the front door. 'What's going on, Richard? What on earth is this all about?'

There was a clang behind her and she spun round. Ken was standing in the elevator door. 'OK, Sam? Is everything—'

'It's fine. Thanks. Fine. I – I'll see you – er—'

'Thursday.'

She smiled thinly, watched the door slide shut and heard the clunk and whine of the elevator descending, then looked back at Richard. 'What is it, Richard?'

'It's nothing,' he said. 'Really.'

'Nothing? The Fraud Squad crawling all over our flat? You can tell me, for Christ's sake.'

'It's OK, Bugs.' He tapped some ash onto the floor. 'They're just sniffing around, that's all.'

'Sniffing around?' She stared at him. 'What have you done?'

'Nothing.'

'The police don't rip open teddy bears unless they think there's something inside them.'

He shrugged. 'Bit of aggro from the Surveillance Department of the Securities Association. The aftermath of Guinness, I suppose. All that insider dealing stuff. They're still trawling their nets.' He looked away evasively.

'Are you mixed up in all that?'

'No. Of course not.' He took a deep drag on his cigarette. 'Everyone's jittery about insider dealing. I've put a few clients into a deal which happened to hit the big time and the Securities boys can't believe it was luck.'

'There's more, isn't there, Richard?' she said. 'There's more to it than that.'

'No. Not really.'

'Are you going to be arrested?'

'No.' His face went bright red. His cigarette was almost down to the filter. He held it between his fingertips like a workman, dragged hard again and inhaled deeply. 'Not yet, anyway.'

28

Sunday morning. She lay in bed watching Richard dress, with Nicky, warm, curled up beside her. Nicky who kept waking the last two nights and running into their room, terrified the nasty man with his big knife was going to come back. He'd slept between them, and she'd lain awake mostly, listening to his breathing and his occasional funny little whimpers, and it made her feel safe having him there.

Bastards.

Inspector Milton. Milton, like the poet. Come to take your paradise away, lady. Oh yes, I'm one smart bastard, you see. One smart bastard with a great big chip.

> Wisest men
> Have erred, and by bad women been deceived;
> And shall again, pretend they ne'er so wise.

She glanced at the clock. 7.45.

Did you ever read him, your namesake, you great frog-eyed bastard? You smug creep who left a little boy terrified. Happy? Happy that my son's met a real live bogeyman? Who ripped his teddy bear open with a knife? Brave. Oh so brave.

247

Smug. Jesus, so smug. Walking out with your card board boxes filled with papers, all neatly tied in red ribbon by your gawky friend in his time-warp suit.

Nicky was awake now; blinking, his eyelids making little scratching sounds against the bedclothes.

'Bye, Bugs.'

She looked at Richard and felt his anguish. She lifted up her hand and touched his face. 'Drive safely. When will you be back?'

''Bout midday,' he said in a voice so heavy he could scarcely lift it out of his mouth. 'Bye, Tiger.' He ran a hand across Nicky's head.

'Are you going shooting, Daddy?'

'No, Tiger.'

'You said I could come with you today. You said we could go shooting today.'

'We will do. This afternoon, OK?'

'Where are you going now?'

'I have to do some business.'

'Can't I come with you? Where are you going?'

London Airport. To meet Andreas. To sign some documents.

She heard the bedroom door open and close, then the front door, the scrunch of gravel, the roar of the BMW's engine. She looked up at the ceiling, freshly plastered and painted; the builders had got that done fast enough, at least in the bedroom. They'd found rot in all the ceilings and there were ladders, planks, gaping holes, and more scaffolding up outside because they'd had to agree that the roof couldn't be bodged any more. There'd have to be a new roof and Richard had said the money was fine, all fine. Until Milton (like the poet) had turned up on Friday.

Nicky was sleeping again and she dozed. A while later

Nicky stirred then got out of bed, but she scarcely noticed because now she was slipping into deep, tired sleep and stayed asleep until nearly ten.

When she opened her eyes and saw full daylight through a chink in the curtains she stared at it blankly, flatly, feeling limp like an old busted tyre that had run flat too long and had finally come off the rim. No energy. Wiped.

She went down to the kitchen and made some coffee. Helen came in.

'Morning, Mrs Curtis.'

Sam smiled. 'Sleep well?'

'Yes. So quiet here. It's like home.'

'Where's Nicky?'

'He went outside a while ago.'

She went over to the fridge and poured out some orange juice. She sipped it and it hit her stomach harshly, acidly, made it twinge.

'Mummy!'

The scream sounded like the wail of a siren.

'*Mum-mee!*'

They flung themselves out of the kitchen through the side door.

'MUM-MEE!'

They stared around, up, down, across the fields, down towards the river.

The river?

Sam started sprinting down towards it.

'MUM-MEE. MUM-MEE. MUM-MEE!'

She stopped dead and spun round. Above her. Up. On top of the scaffold.

A dreadful creaking sound.

Tearing, rending.

Oh my God Jesus, no. Christ, no. No. No.

Arms around the new scaffold as if he was hugging it

because he loved it and not because he knew that if he let go he would be dead.

It had come loose from the wall of the house and was swaying like a broken crane, tilting, shrieking and creaking, one way then the other, it bashed against the wall, nearly throwing him free, then swung away again, so far this time she was certain it would topple over, but instead it swung back and smashed against the wall again, harder this time, chipping chunks of brickwork away, clanging, the sound echoing down through the pipes.

Sam sprinted over to the base, tried to hold it with her hands, Helen stood beside her and tried too but they had no chance of holding it. It tilted even more over, and some of the base lifted up from the ground right beside her, then it righted again for a moment, smashing and clanging back against the wall.

Sam ran around the side, to the old scaffold that was still attached, and began to climb.

Her hand numbing on the ice cold rusted metal, she hauled herself up, ignoring the ladder up the inside of it, felt the wind blowing as she climbed and the structure vibrating.

'*MummyMummyMummy!*

I'm coming. Coming. Coming.

She felt a muscle pull in her thigh, and her hand cut on something sharp. A slipper fell away from her foot. She heard the creaking, clanging, behind her, turned, saw Nicky now only feet away, then his face was in front of hers, so close she could touch it, then he swung away out of reach. Oh Christ, no, please no . . . so far surely it was going to topple this time, then he swung back towards her.

'Darling, give me your hand . . . here, take it, mine, that's right, that's right!'

She clenched her hand over his, clenched it so hard she was never going to let go again. He started pulling away from her, and she pulled harder, could feel his arm stretching. 'Hold on, Tiger, just hold on!'

Stretching more. The pain was unbearable. He was coming loose – careful – be careful – pulling him off it.

Then she felt herself moving.

No.

There was a sharp crack.

No.

A splintering sound.

The scaffolding was bouncing, like a spring.

Let go, let go, let go.

Falling.

She let go his hand in terror, in disbelief.

The wall was moving away. Nicky moving away, staring at her, his face frozen. Sideways, going over sideways.

No.

It was her that was going over.

The ground was rushing towards her.

Falling.

She spun, desperately trying to push back, but it was too late, far too late.

She felt the inside of her head rotating, then the ground hurtled at her, slammed into her, smashed her stomach up into her spine. She felt a tremendous windedness, heard a click from her jaw, smelt wet grass, mud. There was a strange muffled clanging sound all around her. Like church bells.

'Bugs?'

The ground was soft.

It moved underneath her as if it was sprung.

Bedclothes.

A dream. It had been a – Richard staring at her, the light was odd, different.

'How are you feeling, Bugs?'

She frowned. Her head ached like hell. She moved and her arm ached too. Her tongue was stinging; she could taste blood in her mouth.

'Nicky,' she said. 'Where's Nicky?'

'Nicky's fine. He's just a bit bruised.'

Nicky peered down at her, wide open eyes, serious. God he looked so serious sometimes. She put an arm up to stroke him. The movement hurt, and she winced.

'How are you feeling, Mrs Curtis?'

A stranger's voice, a man, pleasant, standing over the bed in a white smock with a stethoscope curling out of the pocket, looking intently at her.

'I—' The room seemed to spin around.

'You've got concussion.' He glanced at his watch. 'You've been unconscious for over three hours.'

Three hours? No, he'd got it wrong. There must have – it had just . . . 'Where am I?'

'You're in the Sussex County Hospital, in Brighton.'

'Hospital?'

'Yes, I'm afraid you had a very nasty fall. We've X-rayed you and given you a scan. You're fine. No bones broken, but I think you're going to feel a bit jarred and sore.' He smiled, a pleasant reassuring good-bedside-manners smile. He was young. Younger than her. 'You've been very lucky, I think, the height you fell from. Fortunate we've had so much rain, it must have made the ground very soft.' He smiled again. 'I'll come back and see you in a little while.'

'Thank you,' she mouthed, but nothing came out. She felt disoriented. Sunlight was shining into the room, weak winter sunlight and she could see the sky. She had no idea of the time; it felt like afternoon.

The door closed, then there was a clanking sound. She felt the bed sinking.

'Tiger, don't do that,' Richard said. 'You're winding Mummy down.'

She heard footsteps, then Nicky's voice, excited. 'I can see the sea!'

She stared at the white ceiling and the light bulb above her head. She pushed her tongue around inside her mouth. It was sore along the top; she tasted the blood again.

Scaffold.

I was on scaffold.

She looked back at Richard, watched him with damp frightened eyes. He sat down beside her and held her hand.

'I'll sue those fucking builders.'

She shook her head, slowly, carefully. 'It wasn't – not their fault—'

'It was coming away from the wall. Could have crashed down on anyone. Could have killed anyone underneath it.'

'Nicky shouldn't have—'

'Scaffolding's meant for climbing up. That's what it's for.' He sniffed. 'How are you feeling?'

'My head hurts.'

'They thought you'd fractured your skull.'

'How did your meeting—?'

'Fine. All going to be fine.'

253

She squeezed his hand.

''S a good hospital,' he said. 'They want to keep you in overnight. The doctor said you can leave in the morning.'

'It's Sunday, isn't it?'

'Yes.'

'I've got a meeting in the morning.'

'I'll call Ken. The doctor doesn't want you to go back to work for a day or so.'

'Ken's away. Could you call Claire? Tell her – or Lucy.'

'Sure.'

'What's out here, Daddy?'

'The corridor, Tiger. That's where we came in.'

Nicky leaned over the bed. 'I'm sorry, Mummy.'

She smiled at him. His eyes were red from crying.

'Give Mummy a kiss.'

He leaned over and gave her a nervous peck as if he shouldn't give her a long one in case it hurt. 'I only went up to see if there was a nest.'

'Did you find one?'

'No. Are you coming home now?'

'Tomorrow.'

'Oh. Can we stay with you?'

'You stay with Daddy tonight.'

He slid away from the bed. 'I'm going exploring.'

'Don't go out there, Tiger,' Richard said.

'I won't go very far.'

She heard the door open and shut, and felt Richard stroking her hand. He bent towards her a fraction and spoke quietly, as if he did not want to be overheard. 'I have to go to Switzerland, Bugs, on business – Montreux. I thought maybe you'd like to come. We could go on to Zermatt, have a few days' skiing.'

254

Zermatt. They went to Zermatt the first Christmas they were married.

'I have to go in the next week or so. I thought maybe next weekend.'

She stared into his anxious eyes. 'What have you got to do?'

He glanced around nervously. 'I've got a bit of dosh stashed away in a bank over there. I want to make sure that it's safe if the going gets rough . . . make sure we can keep paying the mortgage, and Nicky's school fees.'

'I've got my job, if anything—'

'Yes, I know, but there's no point in—'

'Don't do anything illegal in Switzerland, will you, Richard?'

'No, it's fine. Andreas has sorted everything out. I just have to move a bit snappily before—'

'Before?'

He shrugged. 'I don't know. No one really knows. It'll take the police a while to sift through everything. They're raiding people all over the shop. They've done Archie as well. It might be several months, but it could only be a couple of weeks.'

'How much trouble are you really in?'

He got up from the bed and walked over to the window. ''S not serious. Get a fine or something,' he said evasively.

'That inspector – Milton – kept saying you wouldn't have such a nice view from a prison cell.'

'Frighteners, that's all. Talking big. He was all mouth.'

'He was horrible.'

He came back over and sat down. She felt fully awake now, though her head was aching badly, fully awake and churned as hell. She was sorry for him, really sorry for the first time since she'd arrived back and found the police. Sorry for him and torn up and twisted inside. Christ, it had all been so fine until – the tart? The dream of the aeroplane? Now it all seemed to be collapsing around her.

Like scaffold.

'Think you could get away?' he asked.

'I'll have to check my Filofax. At home.'

'Be nice if you came.'

Richard and Nicky stayed until she'd had supper and the nurse came in to give her a pill to help her sleep.

'I'm whacked,' she said. 'I'm not going to need any help sleeping.' But she took the pill anyway, and it made her feel better, gave her a strange surge of excitement.

Hope.

Answers. There were answers. There were answers to why it was all happening. You just had to look in the right place, that was all, find the secret button or maybe some magic code word. Go away, Slider, I command thee. Into thy dungeon, Oh foul beast. Slink away in disgrace and ne'er darken my doorstep again. You foul cursed creature of darkness.

Out, out, vile jelly.

What the hell was in the pill? She felt smashed, euphoric. Then a great wave of tiredness picked her up, and she floated along with it until it gently lowered her back down.

She slept.

30

They kept her in hospital until late Monday afternoon, when Richard collected her and drove her to London. She arrived at the office on Tuesday with a dull head-ache, and Claire looked up as she came in. That was something, she thought, Claire actually looking up; progress.

'How are you?'

'OK,' she said.

She wished Ken was in, that he wasn't away filming in Spain, that she could go up and tell him, tell him about her antennae, sharp, so sharp. Too damned sharp. She picked up the top letter on the pile on her desk.

It was a brief but courteous note from the secretary of the Royal Yacht Squadron. 'The committee regrets that it cannot permit its premises to be depicted in advertisements, regardless of the singular merits of your particular project.'

Damn.

It was a great script. The crusty old buffer sitting outside the clubhouse pulling out his spectacles and a packet of condoms falling out of his pocket with them.

You can't teach an old sea dog new tricks. But you can kill him with a new disease. Wear a condom. It's an admiral thing to do.

She picked up the next letter, then put it down again. Her hands trembling, her eyes damp. Fear. It seeped through her, deep inside her, cold as melting ice. She opened her handbag and pulled out *What Your Dreams Really Say*, and glanced again at the brief biography of the author, then picked up the phone and dialled Directory Enquiries.

'I'd like the number for Hull University, please.' Sam covered the mouthpiece. 'I dreamed it. I dreamed I fell – from a balcony.'

Claire gazed back at her without replying for a moment . . . almost – almost, it struck Sam, as if she thought it was amusing.

The operator gave her the number and she wrote it down.

'How did you like Mrs Wolf?' Claire asked.

'I thought she was weird.'

'She's very accurate, I find. Didn't you?'

'I hope not,' Sam said, staring down at the number, and dialling it.

'Hull University,' said the voice that answered the phone.

'I'd like to speak to Dr Colin Hare in the Psychology Department, please.'

'Putting you through.'

'Psychology,' said a man's voice, abrupt, slightly irritable.

'Could I speak to Dr Hare?'

'May I ask who's calling?'

'Yes, my name is—' Sam saw Claire watching her, and felt uncomfortable – 'Mrs Curtis.'

'Can I tell him what it is about?'

'Yes, she said, 'It's about his work on dreams. I just wondered if it was possible to have a word?'

'He's on a call at the moment.'

'May I hold?'

'Yes. You can hold.'

'Thank you.' She looked at Claire. 'I've got a splitting headache. Would you mind nipping down to the chemist on the Strand and getting me some Disprin?'

'Sure, I'll just finish this—'

'Now,' Sam said, more snappily than she had meant.

Claire stood up slowly. Sam handed her a fiver, and Claire walked out of the room.

'Yes, hello?' A gentle, slightly nervous voice.

'Is that Dr Hare?'

'Speaking.'

'I'm sorry to – er – bother you . . . I'm calling you because I'm desperate. I need help.' Her voice was

258

faltering, breaking up and tears were coming in and choking the words in her throat.

'Tell me,' he said patiently, as if he had all the time in the world to listen. 'Do tell me.'

'I'm – things are happening. My dreams . . . I'm having—'

Calm down, Sam, for God's sake! Take it gently. *Don't sound like a fruitcake.*

'I keep having dreams which come true, but I can't read them. They're slightly different . . . I think I might even be making the future happen. Does that sound daft?'

'Well, I – could you give me a bit more detail?'

'Would it be possible to come and see you? Nobody believes me. I really need to talk to someone who knows about dreams. If I could just have half an hour of your time?' She felt a bit calmer. 'I don't think I can really explain it that well over the phone, but I think my life is in danger. And my family, and other people. I just need someone who can maybe explain a few things about dreams to me. If you don't have the time yourself, perhaps you could suggest someone?'

'I'd be happy to have a chat. Precognitory dreams are something we are studying here at the moment, so you've called at a good time . . . Unfortunately it'll have to be in April or May, as I'm off to the States on Friday for about two months, lecturing. Perhaps I could contact you when I get back?'

She clutched the phone hard in her hand. 'I must see you before you go. Please. I can't – I – I could be dead by then.'

Idiot.

Stupid thing to say.

'Oh dear,' he said. There was a silence. 'That does sound very drastic.'

'I'm sorry,' she said, 'I don't want to sound dramatic – but it's true.'

'I could see you late tomorrow afternoon. Is that any good?'

'Yes, I—'

'Where are you phoning from?'

'London.'

'It's a bit of a journey.'

'I don't mind.'

'How old are you?'

'Old?'

'Yes.'

'Thirty-two – well – almost thirty-three.'

'Ah, good, yes – we are studying subjects in exactly your age group. Ah – if you came up, would you – ah – be prepared – ah – to spend a night in our sleep laboratory – it's very pleasant – at the university – it's just like a hotel bedroom – apart from the wiring of course. It would help us – and it might help you?'

'I'd try anything.'

'I know that we have a – ah – vacancy in the laboratory tomorrow. That would tie in rather well.' He had begun to sound quite enthusiastic. 'I'm going to be – yes – I – I'm at my flat tomorrow afternoon – just opposite the university – perhaps – if you come there – we can have a quiet chat – first?'

He gave her the directions and she repeated them carefully, writing them down, thanking him again and hung up, then looked at her Filofax for any meetings she would have to cancel. She felt a surge of excitement, of hope. Maybe a simple answer. Or would he just say the same too? Sharp antennae and coincidences?

She picked up the next letter on the pile, and opened it.

On the floor below, the front door swung shut behind

Claire as she walked out into the street, and crossed over towards the chemist.

31

She stared out of the window of the train, at the Humber river seeping through the drab countryside like ink spilt across a school desk, and at a cluster of brick chimney stacks on the horizon, like tent poles supporting the dark canopy of sky.

A man walking down the corridor, stopped and peered in at her, stared for some moments and moved on, then the train went into a tunnel and she felt scared, scared that the door might slide open and he would come into the compartment in a dark hood. The tunnel roared around them, echoing, thundering, then they came back into the light, past a level crossing with a line of traffic waiting for them.

Wednesday afternoon. Had the dream group met again on Monday? Led by Barry, the silent man in the black karate suit? Had they met and discussed her dream? What the hell did they all think? That she was some kind of a witch? Or had it not occurred to any of them to connect the dream? Were they all too busy resonating?

The man walked back, peered into her compartment again and she glared at him venomously. Go away. Go away Slider or whoever the hell you are. Leave me alone. Piss off. He hesitated, turned around, and walked off.

It could be that you've got sharp antennae, like rabbits' ears. Like Bugs Bunny.

Sure, of course, Ken. Doesn't everyone who dreams of a balcony collapsing know what that really means?

Surely Freud knew? And Jung? It said in *What Your Dreams Really Say* that balcony was a mother's breast. Of course. Mother died. I lost her breast. Simple. And of course Freud knew that balcony = scaffold. Plain as daylight, old boy.

It's much easier to put them down as premonitions than to face their real truths.

Of course.

Richard thought she was nuts coming up here. Told her that concussion did strange things to the mind and she needed rest, peace and quiet, told her to take it easy for a few days so she'd feel fit and strong for Switzerland. Told her Switzerland would make her feel better. Sure. It would stop her premonitions, and make his business better and mend their marriage. Switzerland was full of magical properties.

The problem was that when you tried to tell people about your premonitions, after they had come true, they thought you were a little batty. Poor old Sam. Fell off a scaffold onto her head. Never been the same since. Of course, she was already slightly unhinged by her husband's affair . . .

Real truths?

In the distance she saw a stream of lorries crossing a suspension bridge. They passed a bunkering station, a lightship in the middle of the estuary, a row of cranes hunched against the sky like old men with fishing rods, then the train slowed, and the word HULL flashed past the window.

The real truth was that children could have been shot, and it was lucky that they had not been. That she could have been raped and murdered and had escaped because she had dreamed it. That she was damned nearly killed on the scaffold because – because . . . because she'd failed to recognise something from the dream of the balcony?

The real truth was that 163 people on the aircraft might still be alive. That Tanya Jacobson might still be alive. Whilst Bamford talked about Freud, about jealousies, pains, thwartings, about penis envy, about cosy things that he was comfortable with. Cosy things that explained everything. And nothing. Cosiness. Dream groups. Steps down into the tube station. The vagina. That was all. It didn't matter that you got raped and murdered, as long as you understood the dream. As long as it resonated.

The taxi dropped her outside a row of 1930s semi-detached houses opposite the main gates of Hull University. 'Bell not working. Please come up to first floor and shout,' said the handwritten note on the door.

She hefted her small overnight case up the narrow staircase and onto a dark, gloomy landing. A door opened behind her.

'Mrs Curtis?'

She turned around and saw a short, bearded man in his forties. He was wearing crumpled corduroy trousers and an Arran sweater and had straggly, untidy hair, which he was making worse by rummaging a finger through, as though he was searching for something he had left in there. He had a piece of sticking plaster above his right eye.

'Dr Hare?'

'Ah!' He had the embarrassed, faintly disorientated air of a man who has walked into a ladies' washroom by mistake. 'Yes. Ah – Colin, please.'

She smiled. 'Sam.'

'Sam, right.' He windmilled his arms and looked up at the ceiling as if worried it was about to collapse on him. 'Bulb's gone again, I'm afraid.'

Sam felt a fleeting chill. Another one.

Come on girl, don't be daft. Can't get spooked up every time a light bulb goes.

Hare clapped his hands together and rubbed them. 'Good. Your train – I thought you'd be here a bit earlier. Late, was it?'

'Yes, I'm afraid so.'

'Well – er – come in. I'm afraid it's a bit of a – rather embarrassing, actually – probably as well. I was just starting to tidy up—'

She followed him into a large bedsitting room, and recoiled in shock.

It seemed as if a hurricane had just passed through.

Clothes were strewn everywhere, books lay on the floor, some opened, their covers bent back. There was a spidery coffee stain in the centre of one wall, and following it down she saw a broken cup lying against the skirting board. A smashed compact disc player was tangled with the wreckage of a standard lamp. A radio was on the floor, its casing shattered and its wiring and batteries spewed out; above it, a chunk of plaster was missing from the wall. An elderly Olivetti typewriter lay upside down on the floor near a broken wooden table, and sheets of manuscript littered the place like confetti. The window looking out onto a dull neat garden had a crack right across it.

He raised his arms helplessly in the air. 'I apologise. Terrible mess, I'm afraid. My—' He hunched his shoulders. 'My wife and I, we just had a bit of a fight. Divorce, you see.' He rummaged in his hair again, then lightly tested the plaster above his eye, staring around with a bewildered expression. 'I'm not quite sure how I'm going to explain all this to my landlady.' He checked his beard carefully with his fingers, then closed the door behind him and locked it. 'Just in case she comes back. She's rather possessive, you see. I'm sorry.'

'Can I give you a hand clearing up?' Sam asked. What on earth could they have had a such a fight about in this crummy room? Had he walked out on her? Shacked up here with a mistress? Was he a little raver underneath his ramshackle academic exterior? Her eye caught a colour photograph on the mantelpiece above an electric fire of two little girls in school uniform. The glass on that was cracked too.

He transferred a pile of books and junk from one side of an ancient sofa to the other, then took her coat, and hung it over his arm. He hovered, tugged at his pullover, scratched his beard and checked both flaps of his shirt collar.

'I really appreciate your seeing me at such short notice,' she said.

He took the coat off his arm, held it up in the air and stared at it, like a conjurer who has got his tricks confused. I'll just hang it up. I'll be all right in a minute. I'm, a bit flustered, you see. Would you like tea?'

'Thank you.'

'There's coffee if you'd rather.'

'I'd prefer coffee.'

'Yes. Good. I'll just – if you want to use the – it's down the corridor.' He walked across the room to the kitchenette, almost on tiptoe, as if trying to compensate for the noise he must have made earlier.

She listened to him foraging through the crockery, heard the sound of a fridge door, then the shriek of a kettle, as she looked around at the hopeless mess. Maybe this is what you were supposed to do when you discovered your husband was having an affair? Smash everything up?

He came back into the room carrying a tray with two steaming mugs, and a plate scattered with biscuits.

Something crunched under his feet, and he looked down lamely at a smashed cassette.

'Coffee, you said?'

'Thanks.' She took the mug, raised it to her lips, and blew on it to cool it. It did not smell like coffee. She sniffed again, trying not to let him notice. It was tea.

'I'll put these biscuits here. You must be hungry. It's a long trip.' He sat down opposite her, perching on the edge of his chair.

'I thought your book was very good.'

His eyes widened, and he smiled. 'Ah. *What Your Dreams Really Say*?'

'It's very interesting.'

'You found it helpful?'

'Yes, I did. Well, some of it.'

'It's all right, as far as it goes. They edited an awful lot out. Just stuck to the classic interpretations. I didn't have any space for premonitions. That'll be in the next one.' He stirred his tea and glanced nervously towards the door. Sam wondered whether his wife would come bursting through at any moment wielding an axe; and how she would cope with the demented woman if she did.

He looked at his watch. 'Have to keep an eye on the time – Laszlo likes people to get settled in early.' He saw her frown. 'The dream laboratory. We'll go over there in about half an hour. I've arranged for you to have supper in the canteen.'

'Everyone seems to ridicule the idea of premonitions,' she said.

'Of course they do, it makes them feel safe. If they rubbish a thing in their own minds, then it can't pose any threat to them.' He put his teaspoon down. 'They think parapsychologists are cranks. I'm a scientist, that's all. I'm a scientist who won't be blinkered.' He looked at his watch again. 'Let's talk about you. You told me on the phone that you feel your life is in danger.'

'Yes.'

'Do you mind if I tape our conversation?'

She shook her head, and he ducked an arm into the debris and pulled out a small recorder. He switched it on, put it on the table in front of her and tested it with a hint of triumph in his face, as if he had scored a point over his wife by finding something she had not destroyed. He crossed his arms and leaned back in the chair. 'Why don't you start by telling me everything you think I should hear, then we'll go to the laboratory and monitor your sleep and dream patterns, see if we spot anything unusual. We could have a discussion tomorrow. I have a meeting in the morning, but lunch is free. Could you stay until then?'

'Yes. Thank you.'

'Good. Well—' He waved at her to start.

She told him the full story, while he sat nodding his head, grunting from time to time, and continually crossing and uncrossing his arms as if he was practising a new form of semaphore.

'What a shame that these weren't all logged in advance,' he said. 'They sound very interesting examples. Two of them seem very clearly precognitive: the air disaster – I know several people who saw that one – and the murder of that poor woman in Hampstead. By precognitive I mean that you clearly saw into the future. The others seem rather more premonitory – warning dreams, but not—' He wrung his hands together – 'not quite so specific. Good examples, though, very good examples.' He raised a finger, leaned forward and switched off the tape. 'Tell me. This hooded man – Slider – he's linked in some way with each dream?'

'Yes.' She smiled at him uncertainly, almost disbelievingly. She had been expecting him to mock, pull them apart. But he didn't.

He believed her.

And she realised now she wished he didn't.

'I don't think you should be frightened, Sam. You obviously have a remarkable gift.'

'I don't want it. I want to get rid of it. I just want to lead a normal life.'

He smiled, as if it were a private joke. 'A normal life. Have you ever considered the possibility that life without premonitions is an abnormal life? Dreams and premonitions have helped shape the world. Calpurnia saw Caesar's death in a dream. She could have saved his life – if only he hadn't ridiculed her. Even the Bible says that all events are foreshadowed.'

He picked a careful path over towards the windows. There was a sickening crunch under his foot. 'Bloody woman,' he muttered. He reached the window and looked out. 'Sam, sixth sense – psychic awareness, whatever you like to call it – is a part of normal life. It's as much a part as eating, drinking, breathing, thinking. We suppress it because society thinks it doesn't need it, that it's smarter to teach a child to use the phone than to transmit a message by telepathy.'

'Why would someone suddenly become psychic?'

'I don't believe anyone does *suddenly* become psychic. We are all born with these powers but they fade out very quickly in most of us, because we don't use them. Our society actively discourages us from using them, as you've been discovering from the people you've been to for help.' He turned round. 'Most people are afraid of being ridiculed, so they leave it at that, don't give their psychic abilities any chance to develop. But these powers don't go away; we still have them. Some of us have the ability to use them instinctively; some of us need a clonk on the head to re-activate them.' He shrugged. 'They're there. We are all born with them, as much as we are born with arms and legs.'

'I don't remember having a clonk on the head.'

'You don't have to be dropped on your head. A trauma can do it just as well. Look at yourself – someone tried to rape and kill you when you were a little girl, a ghastly man in a black hood . . . you lost both your parents together. Pretty big traumas.'

'But these dreams stopped after my parents died. Stopped for twenty-five years. What's started them again?'

'Well, that's what we have to try to discover. There's some trigger – something obviously linked with this hooded one-eyed man. Perhaps we'll learn something from the laboratory.' He looked at his watch again, as if he was anxious to get out of the room.

Anxious in case his wife came back?

'I think we'd better get across now. We can continue talking.' He stood up, fetched her coat, helped her into it, then insisted on carrying her overnight bag.

It was dark outside and beginning to snow. They stopped at the kerb, waiting for a gap in the thundering traffic, the howling, blattering heavy rush hour traffic, cars heading home and trucks heading to the docks, wipers clacking, lights glaring, gears grinding, and he shouted at her, above the roar, 'If you tried to walk across this road with your eyes shut, you'd be knocked down and killed. Yet most of us travel through life with our minds shut.'

The slipstream of a lorry buffeted her sideways and her lungs filled with foul diesel exhaust. Another dark shape loomed down the road, blasting the night with its exhaust, its tyres churning the white flecks of snow to pulp and flinging slush up at them. They sprinted across and walked in through the gates of the university.

She felt envious of the students they passed in the harsh glare of the campus lights, thinking she'd like to be a student now, that she'd like to be young and starting it all again. A boy and girl passed them, talking earnestly, clumping along in their Doc Martens. Street fashion. Street cred. She would look ridiculous in Doc Martens, she thought. She would *feel* ridiculous in them.

Students. Target market. Future As, Bs, Cs. Consumers. Future yuppies. Come autumn, you'll all be eating Castaways.

They went across the quadrangle, in through a door and up two flights of stone stairs.

'I'm afraid it's not much, but it's quite comfortable,' Colin Hare said as they walked across the second floor landing. He pushed open a door and turned on the light, then stepped aside.

It was a neat, small bedroom, with a wide single bed that looked as if it was fresh out of a furniture store, and an unmarked beige carpet. There was a wardrobe, chest of drawers, television and a wash basin. The room smelt new. The curtains were drawn, and the navy-blue counterpane on the bed had been turned down. It could have been a hotel bedroom anywhere in the world, except for the cluster of wires dangling from a pod on the wall above the bed.

It scared her.

Something about it wasn't right, and she did not know what. It was like a show bedroom with fake walls on the furniture floor of a department store. It wasn't real. It would be like undressing and going to bed in a shop window. Only it wasn't that either.

Something else. She shivered. Tell him 'no thanks'. Tell him you have to go now.

Why? He's trying to help.

That's what you think.

'It's quite different to what I had imagined,' she said. 'It's very ordinary looking. Nice. Much nicer than half the hotel rooms I've stayed in.'

'We need it to feel normal for people.'

'I thought I was going to be in a glass booth.'

'No, we don't need to watch you whilst you're asleep. We get all the information we need from the printout. I'll show you the monitoring room.'

As they came out of the door, a studious-looking girl holding a bundle of papers walked past. 'Good evening, Dr Hare,' she said in a Scottish accent.

'Ah, good evening, Jane. This is Mrs Curtis – a new subject.'

Subject. Like a laboratory frog in formaldehyde?

'Good evening,' said the girl politely, before disappearing down the stairs.

'She's one of our researchers, doing a post-grad at the moment. I'll show you my office,' Hare said. 'I prefer to see people out of the office. It's quieter.' They went across the hallway, and he pushed open the door to a chaotic room littered with papers, computer terminals and overstuffed filing trays; it wasn't much tidier than his bed-sitting room.

They went further down the hallway and into a small brightly lit room with a battery of electrical equipment, computer screens, and two massive graph plotters. A young man in his late twenties was poring over sheets of graph paper. He had dark, Slavic features with heavy black rings around his eyes. He shovelled a handful of jet black hair off his forehead and studied something intently. His hair tumbled forward again and he shovelled it back again, mildly irritated.

'Laszlo, can I introduce you?'

The man looked round at them and rubbed his eyes blearily, as if he was grumpy at being interrupted. 'Mrs Curtis?' he said, in an abrupt, disinterested voice. Sam wondered if he had been the person who answered the phone yesterday.

She smiled. 'Yes.'

'Good,' he grunted, then yawned.

She frowned. There was a silence.

'Er – Laszlo calls this place the Hull Hilton,' said Hare, sensing the awkwardness.

'Ah,' she said.

Laszlo turned back to his graph, and began studying it again. 'Have you ever been in a sleep laboratory before, Mrs Curtis?' he said, without looking up.

'No,' she said.

'No problem.' He made a mark on the graph with a pen, pursing his lips in concentration. 'You don't have to do anything. Just sleep.' He giggled, an unexpected, high-pitched, boyish giggle. 'Just sleep. Have dreams. You have the fun, we do the work. That's right, Dr Hare?' He addressed the professor by his surname as if it was a joke.

Hare turned to Sam. 'People don't realise quite how boring dream research is,' he said. 'One of us has to sit in here all night, watching the graph. It's pretty intrusive on the private life of the investigator.'

Sam wondered if that was why he had got divorced. 'Can't you leave me sleeping, then read through it in the morning?'

'No. We have to keep an eye on the plotter. Pens run out, the paper has to be replaced.' He picked up a sheet of graph paper, on which she could see eight rows of blue lines, some zig-zagging, some squiggling. 'Each of these is just twenty seconds of sleep. We get through two and a half thousand sheets in a night's sleep. We need to interact with the sleeper. If we see some unusual activity, we want to wake them up right away, find out what was going on. And the other thing we do is this—' He smiled proudly, and tapped a small control panel with a row of gauges and switches on it. 'Lucid dreams,' he said. 'Do you ever have lucid dreams?'

'What are those?' she asked.

'When you become aware in a dream that you are dreaming?'

'I've had one,' she said. 'A long time ago.'

'Yes? And were you able to do anything about it?'

'What do you mean?'

'Were you able to control the dream? Manipulate it?'

'No. I just knew that I was dreaming.'

'Do you know much about sleep? About dreaming?'

Sam shrugged. 'Not really, I suppose.'

'How often do you dream?'

'Normally?'

'Yes.'

'I don't know – once or twice a week.'

'No. You dream every night. All human beings do. In eight hours of sleep, you'll have between three to five dream periods, starting from ten to fifteen minutes long and increasing to about thirty to forty minutes. But you probably won't remember any of them. You'll only re-member them if you wake up either in the middle of a dream or immediately after.' He showed her a wodge of printout sheets. 'You're looking sceptical. It's all here. If you stayed long enough, I could prove it to you.'

She watched the jagged lines, as he ran his finger along each one in turn. 'That's low-voltage flat stuff from the front of the brain – not much activity during sleep. That spidery one is the Rapid Eye Movement Scan, REMS. Your eyes blink very fast when you are dreaming. These are other regions of the brain: respiration, cardiovascular activity, body temperature.' He scratched his head. 'You see, when you remember a dream, fine, great, we can analyse it, log it, see if any parts come true. But what about all those dreams you don't remember? Those five periods every night? Two or three hours a night, of which you maybe remember a few seconds once a week? What's happening then? We know you're dreaming, but what are you doing? What's happening to you?' He tapped his head. 'What's going on in there? Are you having premonitions that we're missing because you don't remember the dreams? Are you out of your body, out on the astral? Travelling in time? If you could become aware that you are having a dream, then you might be able to remember it. You could wake up at the end and tell it. We have a microphone in the bedroom and a voice-activated tape recorder.'

'You can really do that?'

'There's a big bonus. If you can be aware that you are dreaming, then you can control your dream.'

'How do you make someone aware they are dreaming?'

He pointed to the grey control box. 'This sends out an extremely low voltage electrical signal. We wire it to the subject's median nerve, and when we see that they've entered the dream state, we fire the signal. What it does is let that person be aware he or she is dreaming – without waking up. Then they can take charge of their dream.'

'And if they were on a plane that was crashing, could they save it?'

Hare dug his hands into his pockets. 'It may help to identify the difference between a precognitive dream and a dream that is simply a nightmare.'

'If you stop the plane crashing, then it's just a nightmare?'

'We don't know, but that's the sort of area we're researching. You might be an excellent subject for that. When I get back from America—'

'It's good for your fantasies,' said Laszlo, without looking up from his work. 'You're having some dull old dream, then you get the buzz that you're dreaming. You can have anything in the world that you want. You want to shack up with Tom Cruise, you just imagine him, and away you go!' He looked up. 'You begin to wonder what's so smart about being awake.'

'I've been wondering that for some time,' Sam said.

32

Sam ate supper in the canteen on a formica-topped table, amid the chatter and bustle of the students and the smell of chips and batter and tinned oxtail soup of the day. Then she went to bed just the way she would have in any hotel room, except the bathroom was not en suite, but across the corridor, which was awkward.

Hare and Laszlo came in and wired her up, wished her sweet dreams, then went out and closed the door.

She sat up in the bed and turned the pages of *Vogue*. Smart women stared back at her, cold arrogance on their chiselled faces, preening at her in their finery as if she was a mirror. Elegance. She wondered how elegant she looked now, with the wires taped all over head. A girl in a negligee sat on the shiny black bonnet of a Porsche. Two male models looked disdainfully at her, a father and son pose, the old man in tweeds, on a shooting stick, the son in a sharply cut suit.

'Old Men Dream Dreams, Young Men See Visions,' said the caption beneath.

She put the magazine down on the bedside table, had

a sip of water, then turned out the bedside light. She settled down slowly, carefully, making sure she did not dislodge any wires. Her head hurt where the wires were pulling her hair, but she did not dare touch them. The bed was comfortable, soft, more comfy than her own. There was a chill draught from the window which she had left open a fraction, and she heard footsteps in the quadrangle below.

'Ouch. Keith, you bastard!'

'No!' a girl screamed, giggled, then screamed again. 'No, I didn't mean it, no, not down my neck! Oh, you bastard!'

They were clearing away in the canteen somewhere near by. Clattering trays, cutlery. Taps were running. A record played faintly in the distance, Buddy Holly's 'Every Day'. Christ, it was going to be hard getting to sleep tonight. Strange noises. The greasy smell of chips from the canteen. The painful tugging of her hair.

Premonitions.

Hare believed her. But. There was something odd about Hare. Something not quite right. And about Laszlo.

Were they both sitting in the lab now, in front of the plotter, watching her brainwaves? What had Hare talked about whilst they were wiring her up? Five stages of sleep. Stage one, the hypnagogic state. Hypnagogic.

When you're just beginning to drift away. You often see strange faces, weird faces, scary images.

Then there was stage two – deeper sleep; stage three – when the body was shut down; stage four – deep sleep, the mind a blank; and then stage five – REM sleep. Dreaming.

She hadn't even gone into stage one sleep yet.

She turned over again restlessly, fumbled for the control panel above the headboard, and pushed a switch. The television came on. She wondered how her brainwaves were going to look now, as she blinked at the sudden brightness of the screen and watched a commercial she did not recognise.

A long shot of a mountain, covered in snow, the sun bursting over the peak. In the distance was a tiny speck, coming towards them; then a sign flashed across the screen.

'AROLEID.'

The sign vanished and the speck got closer, and the sign flashed again.

'AROLEID.'

It strobed on and off, intercut with the speck that was getting bigger all the time, until it filled the screen.

'AROLEID,' said a voice she vaguely recognised, in a whisper followed by a laugh. 'AROLEID.'

She frowned. Aroleid? What on earth was Aroleid? She switched off the television and stared up at the ceiling, and saw the blades of a large fan revolving slowly, like a propeller. Strange, she thought, she had not noticed it before. It was cold in the room, cold in the bed. She wondered why the fan had been switched on.

The door of her room opened, then closed quietly. She heard someone breathing, the clink of a key, and the distinct click of a lock sliding home.

Someone locking it from the inside.

She stared, trembling, into the darkness. 'Who's there?' she said. Who the hell was it? Dr Hare? Laszlo? Why had they locked the door? 'Who is it? Who's that?'

Silence.

She could see someone standing by the door, a dark shadow, almost motionless, but not quite. A dark shadow that she could hear breathing.

'Dr Hare?'

Her voice was sounding strange, constricted. Christ.

Who was here, in this building? How loudly would she have to shout to be heard? What was showing on the plotter now?

Surely they would see it?

Unless.

Laszlo?

Christ, no.

The shape began to move towards her.

'We'll see how this looks on the graph,' said a voice she knew. The same voice on the commercial on the television a few moments ago. Not Dr Hare's. Nor Laszlo's.

She felt pressure on the sheet under her chin, then the bedclothes were ripped away. She screamed, a short, gargled scream, and felt a gloved hand over her mouth.

'Calm down, you silly bitch. I'm just going to fuck you, that's all. You'll like it. You'll love it.'

She stared up at the dark shape. There was a click and the bedside light came on and she blinked at Slider standing over the bed in a metallic green jump suit, like a motorcycle racing suit, thick black gauntlets, and goggles over the eye slits of his black hood.

She shrank back, and saw his mouth grinning through its slit.

He held something out towards her, offering it to her, something orange and white: an airline boarding card. He waved it over her eyes so that she could read it, clearly.

CHARTAIR 35A.

'You'll be needing this. Very soon. You shouldn't leave it lying around in the back of taxis. That's careless, so very careless.' He let go of it and she watched it flutter down onto her chest. 'Oh look, it's fallen!' He leered at her. 'You're slow, aren't you, bitch? So slow. The fall. From the balcony? Good, wasn't it?'

He grinned again, showing all his filthy broken teeth. 'There's more to come. So much more. So much further to fall. You've got the really big fall to come.'

She watched him, as he strutted over to the wash basin and picked up her toothpaste. He unscrewed the cap, held the tube up. 'Like games, do you? Puzzles? Riddles? See what you think of this!' He began to squeeze out the toothpaste. It fell in long streams onto the carpet as he rolled up the tube until it was empty, and then dropped it onto the floor. 'Messy stuff, toothpaste. Don't bother with it myself.'

This is a dream, she thought; surely this is a dream? A lucid dream?

'What have you got all those wires on your head for?' he asked. 'Trying to beat me with high tech? Stupid little bitch, aren't you? It's time you had a lesson. I think I'm going to give you one.'

Lucid dream. I'm having a lucid dream.

If you can be aware that you are dreaming, you can control your dream.

'No,' she said, surprised at how firm she sounded. 'I don't want a lesson. I'm going to give you something. I'm going to give you a Castaway bar.'

He looked puzzled.

Concentrate. Castaway bar. Castaway bar!

One appeared in her hand.

I can have anything in the world that I want, she thought suddenly. She thrust it out to him. 'Eat it,' she said.

He walked over and took it, and she sat up in bed, watching him unwrap it and bite a piece off.

'What do you think of it?'

'It's all right,' he said. 'It tastes a bit like a Bounty with biscuit.'

'That's what Ken said.'

'He said the same?'

'Yes.'

He smiled.

She felt a surge of confidence. 'I want you to tell me why you keep coming back to me, Slider. What do you want? Why don't you leave me alone?'

He licked his fingers. 'It was good, that bar.'

'Like another?'

'No.'

'It's no problem to get you another. I can fill the whole room with them if you want.'

'You could fill the room with Castaway bars?'

'Yes. And I could make you disappear if I wanted. But I don't want to do that. Not yet. I want to know what you want. I want to know why I'm having these dreams.'

He raised his arms, and looked surprised. 'I'm your friend, Sam.' He sat down beside her. 'I'm your friend, that's why! You're having them to protect you. I'm showing you the future to warn you of danger. You've got to learn to trust me.' He put an arm around her and squeezed her gently. 'I'm your friend. See? Happy?'

'Great.'

He smiled. 'Great! This is great. You thought I wasn't your friend?'

'Yes.'

He chuckled. 'Ridiculous. That's crazy.'

She felt him heaving up and down as he began to laugh, and she laughed with him. They sat together, laughing almost helplessly for a long while. Then they sat in silence, peaceful silence.

'Listen, Sam, you mustn't worry about the future. It's all taken care of. All the details.' He squeezed her again, then jumped up from the bed, went over to the door and opened it.

'Don't go,' she said.

'I'm not going. I want to see if the papers have come.' He opened the door and stooped down, then turned around, holding up *The Times*. 'It's a good place this, isn't it?'

'Yes,' she said. 'Wonderful.'

He pushed his goggles up onto his forehead, opened *The Times* and scanned through it, then he folded the pages back, came over to the bed and sat down again. 'I told you I'd taken care of all the details. Look!' He held the pages in front of her.

ANNOUNCEMENTS AND PERSONAL.

She looked up at him, at the eyes through the slits, the eyes which suddenly looked so cold and hard she could not tell which was the glass one.

'Come on,' he said, becoming insistent. 'Have a look, see for yourself – see the column?'

'Deaths,' she read, and began to tremble as she followed his finger down the column, a long, neatly manicured nail. Too long, like a talon.

'Look, there!' His voice was filled with childish glee. 'Can you see?'

She froze.

'CURTIS. Tragically. Samantha (Sam) Ruth. Aged 32. Beloved wife of Richard and loving mother of Nicky. Funeral service private. Family flowers only.'

'The date,' she dimly heard him say. 'The only thing they left out.'

She felt a sharp draught of air, and a sheet of the newspaper suddenly blew away onto the floor, then another sheet, as if caught in a ferocious gust. She heard the roar of an engine, felt her hair whipping her face, saw the curtains crashing wildly. She looked up, petrified, at the cciling. The fan was spinning wildly, huge, black and menacing, spinning and clattering, the noise turning into a deafening roar that made her put her hands over her ears.

No!

The wind ripped at the bedclothes and tore them off the bed, hurling them across the room like pieces of paper.

'No. Oh God, no!' she screamed, as the glass of water beside her exploded like a grenade, showering her in sharp stinging shards.

The doors of the wardrobe suddenly flew open and her clothes hurled out onto the floor. The light bulb on her bedside light exploded, and the room went dark.

'Oh God help me.'

'You little bitch. Think you're going to beat me with high tech? Think you could make me disappear just by thinking about it?'

She was flung out of the bed and smashed into the ceiling, then felt herself falling down, falling through a freezing swirling vortex, tumbling head over heels through a debris of glass and furniture which cut and stung, and then she crashed into the ground, hard; so hard, she was unable to move.

There was a brilliant white light, which dazzled her and she closed her eyes against it.

'Sam?'

She shivered. Cold, it was so cold.

'Sam?'

She smelt a strange, unfamiliar, dusty smell, and opened her eyes. She saw a beige fuzz. A strange beige fuzz, lying on top of her, crushing her. She was bitterly cold.

'Jesus Christ,' said a man's voice.

'Are you all right, Sam?'

Dr Hare, she thought. It sounded like Dr Hare.

She pushed the fuzz of beige, but it would not move.

'Have you hurt yourself?' said Colin Hare's voice.

I don't know, she wanted to say. I don't know. 'Please get this thing off me.' She pushed the beige fuzz again. Then she realised. It was the carpet.

She was lying face down on the floor.

'Jesus Christ.' Laszlo's voice.

'We'll lift her back onto the bed.'

She felt hands, awkward, fumbling hands, then the fuzz was lifted away and she saw the white ceiling. No fan, she thought vaguely, then heard the creak of springs and felt the softness of the bed. Hare's face was close to hers, searching, worried. Laszlo's dark-ringed eyes probed her with a strange incomprehension that frightened her.

'Are you all right?' said Hare.

She gave a weak nod.

'She looks cold, Laszlo. Let's put the bedclothes back over her.'

She watched him turn and walk across the room. Laszlo was still staring down at her. Why? He seemed to be saying. Why?

Hare bent down, scooping up a sheet from the floor, Christ. The mess.

The room looked as if it had been destroyed.

Glass, clothes, bits of furniture were strewn all around. The window was smashed and the curtain rail had been ripped away from the wall. There was a thin trail of something white underneath the wash basin. A chair was lying lopsided against a wall, one of its legs buckled under it, like an old man who has fallen and can't get up. Her bedside table was lying on top of the wardrobe.

No. It was not possible.

Hare came back towards her, dragging an armful of

bedclothes. He dropped them down, disentangled a sheet, then draped it over her gently.

Like a flag over a dead soldier.

I'm dead. I'm dead. That's why he's looking at me like that.

'Take the other end, Laszlo. Tuck it in firmly.'

'Am I all right?' she asked.

Hare was studying her carefully. She felt the bed tilt slightly, first one side, then the other, then Hare stooped down again, and she felt the weight of a blanket. Warmth.

'I want to wake up now,' she said, and she caught a brief nervous glance between Hare and Laszlo.

Hare smiled thinly. 'You are awake now, Sam. You had a bad—' He paused and raised his hands in the air.

'Lucid,' she said. 'I had a lucid dream.'

'Ah,' said Hare. 'Yes – I—'

'Toothpaste. He squeezed my toothpaste. Is it there?'

'Your toothpaste?'

'On the wash basin.'

He looked over at the basin, then down at the carpet beneath it. The trail of white toothpaste spelled out a word in large, clear writing.

AROLEID.

Hare knelt, touched the toothpaste with his finger, then picked up something and held it out. It was the toothpaste tube, empty, rolled flat.

'He was here,' she said, staring wide-eyed at the writing. 'He did that.'

'Who, Sam?'

'Slider.'

He gazed around the room again.

'I didn't do all this,' she said. 'Not on my own. And I couldn't have reached . . . not with the wires—' She raised her hands and felt the wires. They were all still in place.

Hare looked back down at her, his eyes darting about her face, then at Laszlo.

'How's the graph?' she said, feeling anger suddenly, anger and confusion and fear and shock battling it out inside her head. 'Everything's fine, is it? Showing sweet dreams? Any abnormalities?'

Hare turned to Laszlo. 'I think we'd better – ah – disconnect.'

Laszlo smirked and raised his eyebrows.

Sam watched them both.

What the hell's up with you two? Is this some kind of a game? Think it's funny? Great hocus-pocus? Christ. Then she realised: he was smirking, but it wasn't humour, no, not at all. He was grimacing. He just looked like he was smirking when he was grimacing. Hare didn't think it was funny either. He was shaking like a leaf, like a rabbit.

Like someone seriously shit scared.

She looked away, around the room, then back at Hare again. Could see the terror in his eyes.

And suddenly she understood why.

33

She'd stayed awake most of the rest of the night, in numb silence. Hare had sat in the room with her, hunched in a chair much like he was hunched in a chair now opposite her in the pub, by the window that looked out on the main road outside the university.

AROLEID.

What the hell did Aroleid mean? Was it an anagram? DIE LORA? DIE ORAL? Riddles. No good at riddles.

285

AROLEID.
You've got the really big fall to come.

Falling? Was it something to do with falling? Hare was blinking quizzically. God, the poor sod looked awful. Couldn't have slept at all. Not in a chair. He said something to her, but the pub was filling up with its lunchtime trade, and it was getting harder to hear his soft voice above the babble of conversation and the roar of the traffic outside. 'Pardon?'

'I hope you didn't mind coming here?'

'It's fine,' she said, relieved not to be in his bedsitting room, not in that room. That was clear. Clear as daylight. Jesus. Fine cold jets of water sprayed her insides; needle sharp they hurt, stung, flooding her with icy coldness that got into her blood and filled everywhere in her body. She looked at him, into his tired, frightened eyes, and took a deep breath.

'It wasn't your wife, was it, who smashed your room up?' she said.

He sat for a long time in silence, before he finally replied. 'No,' he said.

'It was someone – some *thing* that didn't want you to help me, wasn't it?'

He continued staring. Staring right through her. As if he was watching some private movie. Then he raised his shoulders and nodded lamely, eyes wide open, like a frightened animal. So frightened it scared her too. His mouth twitched, and he locked his fingers together, then pulled them apart, slowly, one at a time.

'There is a scientific explanation.' He picked up his glass shakily and drank some beer, then wiped his beard with the back of his hand. 'Disturbances . . . energy.' He nodded as if that was it. Simple.

'I'm not quite with you.'

He seemed reluctant to go on and hesitated, locked

his fingers again, then unlocked them. 'Our brain waves give out terrific energy. Incredible energy – particularly if we are in any state of excitement – I—' He stopped whilst a waitress brought over their lasagnes and set them down. Steam rose up between them.

'Anxiety – that sort of thing – can transmit. It's possible, of course, that I picked up your anxiety and the energy set off a chain reaction in the energy patterns of my room affecting the electro-magnetic polarisation of the – ah – molecules in . . . It's what is sometimes called the poltergeist phenomenon.'

'Doesn't poltergeist mean "angry spirit"?'

'Well literally it means "noisy spirit". In German.' He dug his fork warily into his lasagne, as if worried it might be booby-trapped. 'They do good food.'

'Looks delicious,' she said flatly. She lifted up a forkful of scalding microwaved pasta, but she had no appetite, and lowered it.

'If you come up again, I'd like you to meet other people who have premonitions – to know that you are not alone.' He put his fork down and sipped his beer, gazing at her with his worried eyes. 'I'd be grateful if you would come up, or I could come down to Sussex. I really would like to make further studies. Most fascinating – it could be most valuable.'

'Have other people had as many as me?'

He seemed to relax a fraction. 'Oh yes, I—' He paused – 'I would say yes.' He frowned. 'It's a question of logging your future ones now, isn't it? Seeing which of those come true.'

'What I want to know is where do premonitions – precognitions, whatever you call it – come from?'

'Ah. Well, that's the big one. That's what we are trying to discover here. We are working on three theories. We are not looking at anything that can be dismissed as coincidence, or self-fulfilling prophecy; we are studying case histories only of people who genuinely seem able to see into the future . . . Real time. Does that mean anything to you?'

Sam shook her head.

He turned a layer of cheese over with his fork, peering at the meat it uncovered, swivelled round to study the crowd of people behind them, a rag-bag mixture of businessmen, students, building labourers, then turned back to her.

'Real time is the theory that you tune into people's thoughts, telepathically – unintentionally, of course. You see, you may have tuned into the pilot, telepathically. Maybe he had a drink problem, or some other problem, and he knew the plane was going to crash when he next flew to Bulgaria. Perhaps he was going to do it deliberately – commit suicide. Perhaps you picked those signals up.'

'Read his mind?'

'Yes. Picked up his thoughts. Even the sort of dialogue he knew he would have with his co-pilot.' He smiled. 'The child who fired the shotgun and the rapist in the underground station – you could have tuned into them, into their thoughts, in your dream state.'

She felt an uncomfortable tightening in her throat, and stared down at her fingernails. They were looking worse. 'If I'm picking things up telepathically, why don't I get more things – your thoughts, my husband's, people walking down the street?'

'The air is full of signals – radio signals, light waves, sound waves. We only pick up a narrow band of them. Either our brain is incapable of receiving the rest, or it filters them out, keeping only what we need. It's possible something's gone wrong with your filtering system and in your sleep you're picking up bits of thought from other people.'

'Would they show on your graphs?'

'We're hoping so. We're hoping we may find some common irregularity in people who have premonitions.'

'What about mine, last night?'

'Unfortunately, we didn't record you for long enough. The only thing was you – when you went to sleep, you did seem to go into REM sleep quickly – but that often happens in a strange environment.'

'How does this telepathy theory explain my balcony dream?'

'Dreams can be very obscure. Premonitive or pre-cognitive dreams get mixed up with the dream processes and buried in symbols. It's one of our biggest difficulties, to separate it all out. The true meanings are often concealed, and need interpreting. I'm sure far more people have premonitions than ever realise it, because they don't analyse their dreams.'

'What symbols do you mean between the balcony and scaffold?'

'Well, falling – in a woman – often relates to falling to – ah – yielding to sexual advances—' He fidgeted with his hands. 'Ah – intercourse.'

Good old Sigmund. Knew you couldn't keep out of this.

She felt her face going bright red.

The dream was nothing to do with the scaffold.

Was it?

She saw him looking quizzically, saw from his expression that he realised he had touched a nerve.

'Symbolism . . .' he said, trying to move on quickly. 'It's not always correct, you see.'

'What are the other theories?'

'The supernatural, of course.' He prodded his lasagne

with his fork, pricking it all over, as if trying to let the steam out. As if trying to exorcise the steam.

'Do you believe in the supernatural?'

'Ah.' He turned the fork over in his hand. 'I'm a scientist. Officially we're not allowed to believe in the supernatural.'

'And unofficially?'

'It's a question of definition.'

'Do you believe in ghosts?'

He scratched his beard then his cheek and lowered his head a fraction. 'I don't have any – evidence – of a connection between ghosts and precognition.'

'What about Slider?'

'You think he's a ghost – a spirit – haunting you from the past?'

'What do you think?'

He plucked up sudden courage and put a forkful of lasagne in his mouth. A tiny morsel fell away and tumbled through his beard like an acrobat in a safety net. He chewed thoughtfully. 'I think he's very interesting. Most bogeymen get left behind in childhood. He could simply be an embodiment of your fears. That whenever you are afraid – whenever your brain picks up danger – it translates it into this grotesque image. It's saying to you "Slider, watch out," as if it was saying "Red Alert".'

'So when he appears in a dream, I know that I have to be careful – that something's going to come true?'

'It seems that way, doesn't it?' He dug some more lasagne with his fork. 'I think it's important for you to try to work things out, to find the meanings. There's a paper I've written on just this. I'll nip over and get you a copy. I think you'll find it helpful.'

'Thank you.'

He smiled. 'The other theory we are working on and

feel has currency is the time warp theory. Do you understand time, at all?'

'Vaguely, I suppose.'

'I won't blind you with science, but we believe there do exist different spheres and planes – different dimensions of time – and that in the dream state some people tune into those—' He raised his hands – 'by design or by accident we don't know.' He toyed with his shirt collar. 'You are frightened that our hooded man is a ghost of someone from the past, haunting you, but I would tend to take the view from what you have told me that he's not a ghost from the past at all. I think it is possible that he's someone in the present, now, who is bothering you, worrying you – someone that you are associating with this Slider.'

She felt the coldness again, much more now, spreading out around her body just beneath her skin. She saw that the table was shaking, then realised that it was her hands holding onto the edge of it that were making it do that. Her legs were crashing together. Everything seemed to have gone out of focus.

'What—' Her voice was trembling. 'What sort of person?'

He was looking at her anxiously. 'Someone you know, perhaps, who makes you feel uncomfortable? Someone you don't like, or don't trust? Someone who reminds you of this hooded one-eyed man? I don't know. I don't want to put thoughts into your mind. It's just a possibility that you're seeing something bad connected with this man.' He shrugged. 'It may be nothing.'

Andreas? she thought. Andreas? Tell him about Andreas? No, stupid. There's no connection.

'Maybe Hampstead?' he said. 'Maybe you saw him in Hampstead – or someone who resembled him? Reminded you of him?' He checked his watch. 'Just a

291

theory, of course. You've got a train to catch. I'll just nip over quickly and get that paper for you. Two minutes.'

He drained his beer, stood up and hurried out of the pub. She watched him through the window as he ran to the edge of the pavement and waited for a gap in the stream of lorries, then she looked down at her lasagne, and cut a piece with her fork.

There was a fierce squeal of brakes, and a thud like a sledgehammer hitting a sack of potatoes. She spun around and looked back out of the window, and saw Hare hurtle up in the air then disappear. She heard slithering tyres and a dull metallic bang, then more slithering and another bang.

Someone screamed.

Herself.

Then someone else. She leapt up from her seat, sending her chair crashing backwards, ran, barged into someone, knocking their drink flying. 'Sorry, so sorry.' Out of the way! Oh please get out of the way! She lunged for the door. 'Excuse me, excuse me. Colin!' She burst out of the door, then stood and blinked.

Hare was standing on the pavement, waiting to cross.

'Dr Hare! Colin! Colin! Don't!'

There was a gap in the traffic and he sprinted out into the middle of the road.

'No! Dr Hare! No!'

She saw the truck. Heard the fierce squeal of brakes, and the thud, like a sledgehammer hitting a sack of potatoes, and Hare disappeared. She heard slithering tyres and a dull metallic bang, then more slithering and another bang.

'Dr Hare! Colin! No. No, please God, *nooo*.'

The door behind her opened and she heard footsteps.

Car doors were opening. Someone hooted. She heard the hiss of air brakes. The rattle of a diesel engine.

She inched forward, clutching her thighs with her hands, then sprinted over, pushed past the crowd that was already forming, looked, saw his body face down, his head somewhere underneath the massive wheel of the artic, a stain of blood and – something else – spreading out beside it.

She turned away, staggered, bumped into someone, apologised, knelt down and vomited violently.

34

The room was warm and the tea was hot and sweet, treacly sweet, and she sipped some down, felt it slipping down her throat and into her stomach, felt the warmth of its spreading out inside her, then she had to put the mug down because it was too hot to hold. She put it on the vinyl table top beside the words which looked freshly carved into it.

FUCK ALL PIGS.

She was surprised it hadn't been noticed and covered up or removed. Perhaps it happened all the time? Then as she watched them, they changed.

AROLEID.

The police officer smiled at her from across the table, a big teddy bear of man in his blue serge jacket and his silver buttons and a coating of dandruff on both shoulders, and a face that looked as though it would like to change the world but didn't know how.

'Drink some more, love, drink it all up. It'll make you feel better.'

Sam nodded and picked the cup up again, but she was shaking too much and hot tea slopped over the rim and scalded her hands. She put it back down and a puddle spread out around it. 'Sorry. So sorry.'

'Doesn't matter, love. Let it cool a bit.'

She fumbled in her bag, pulled out her handkerchief and wiped her hands, then dabbed her mouth. She'd rinsed it out, but she could still taste the bile. She looked around the room: small, dull, an interview room with hard lecture hall chairs, green paint on the walls, flaking, chipped, a big chunk missing on the far side – was that where they had banged some punk's head while they were interviewing him?

The police officer read through her statement again slowly out aloud to her. 'Anything else you'd like to add, love?'

Yes.

I caused it.

I killed Tanya Jacobson, and now Dr Hare. They both died because – because they might have been able to help me?

So why hadn't Bamford O'Connell died? Because he hadn't tried? Had Ken tried?

'All right, love?'

She sat up with a start, blinking. 'Sorry. I—'

'Would you like to lie down somewhere, for a while?'

She felt her stomach heave. 'I'll be all right, thank you. I should get back to – back down – to London.'

'There's someone come from the university to run you to the station.'

'Thank you. That's – very – kind.'

He pushed the statement across the table to her. 'If you wouldn't mind just signing that. I don't know if the coroner will want you for the inquest. He'll write if he does.'

She followed him out into the front of the police station and to her surprise saw Laszlo sitting, waiting.

He stood up, his face ashen, the black rings around his eyes even more pronounced, and as she saw him she began to cry. She felt the kindly pat of the police officer's arm on her shoulder and heard him speak.

'She's suffering from shock, I'm afraid. I have suggested we run her up to the hospital, but she wants to get back to London.'

Then she was outside in the bright cold light, climbing into Laszlo's beat-up 2CV Citroën. He clipped her seat belt and closed her door for her, then got in himself and started the engine. She listened to its high-pitched lawn-mower whine.

'Thank you,' she said.

'I think there are trains quite often.'

'Yes.'

He drove in silence for a few minutes. 'Terrible,' he said suddenly. 'This is so terrible.'

'Yes.'

'He was the whole department. He knew so much. It was all just beginning.'

'Nice. He was so nice.' She felt tears running down her cheeks and didn't brother to wipe them

'He was a very dedicated man. Maybe he was too dedicated.'

'What do you mean?'

He turned and glanced at her. 'You know what I mean.' He braked at a traffic light.

She looked at him, but there was nothing in his face, just an emptiness as if he'd put up a sign which said 'SORRY, CLOSED FOR THE SEASON, GONE AWAY.'

'I feel responsible,' she said. 'I feel that I caused it.'

'No,' he said, and the sharpness of his reply surprised her. The light changed and they drove on. 'You know what they say, Mrs Curtis. You know the expression. "If you can't stand the heat get out of the kitchen".'

'What do you mean?'

'If seeing the future frightens you, don't go looking for it.'

She stared numbly ahead. Her head was pounding and her stomach was heaving again. 'I'm not looking for it.'

'Why have you come here then?'

'Because I want to stop. I want to stop seeing the future. I don't want to see it any more.'

'You've gone too far down the road. You can't stop.'

'Why not?'

'Existence is full of crossover points, Mrs Curtis. Countries have boundaries. Life has a boundary of death. The earth's gravity has a boundary beyond which it cannot pull. When you start to look into the paranormal you remain a spectator up to a certain boundary. When you cross over that, you become a participant. Do you understand?'

She frowned at him, trembling.

'When you are looking into the future, you are look-ing beyond the earth's plane, Mrs Curtis. If you look long enough, you cross that boundary and you become part of the future.'

'I – I don't really understand.'

'I think you do. You understand the forces that are around you, that you brought into the laboratory last night. I could see on your face that you understood.'

'I didn't understand last night.'

'Didn't you?' he said, almost bitterly.

'Do you think I deliberately killed Dr Hare? Do you think that I—?'

They pulled into the station and she wished that they hadn't arrived. Laszlo wanted her out, out of his car, his town, his life, wanted her out as fast as he could make her go. 'I think you have a bad energy force around you, Mrs Curtis. It's . . . maybe making bad things happen because it's confusing things, confusing people.'

'What energy force? Where's it coming from?'

He switched off the engine and unclipped his seat belt. 'I think there is a train in about five minutes. If you hurry.'

She climbed out of the car and he lifted her overnight bag off the back seat and carried it into the station for her. 'You have your ticket?'

She nodded.

'That platform there.'

'Can I ask you just one thing, please?'

He said nothing.

'If this is how you feel about seeing the future, why have you been working with Dr Hare?'

'Because I thought that I wanted to know,' he said, and turned away. He stopped and half turned back round. 'I was wrong.'

She watched him walk out of the station without looking at her again, heard the slam of a car door and the lawnmower whine of a 2CV engine, and the crash of the gears. As if he could not drive away fast enough.

35

It was eight o'clock in the evening when she got back to Wapping. Richard hadn't come home yet; Helen was in her room watching television and Nicky was lying in bed, awake, looking miserable. She sat down beside him and hugged him hard, but his face did not change.

'I don't want you and Daddy to go away again, Mummy. It's not fair. You're always away.'

'It's only a week, Tiger. Mummy and Daddy have got to spend some time together.' She hugged him again, and kissed his forehead. It was a cold dry night and a strong wind was blowing, nearly a gale, and the water was slapping around in the river outside. She looked down at him, and wished she could tell him the truth: that she didn't want to go away either, that she was worried about leaving him alone, even though he would be staying with friends and would have a good time with them. She didn't want to tell him that she was scared to go.

Scared as hell.

She told him a story, then started another one and he finally fell asleep. She went out, closing the door behind her and walked through into the living area. The phone started to ring and she went over to Richard's desk and answered it.

'Yes? Hallo?'

'Sam?'

'Ken!' She felt excitement surging through her. 'Ken! You're back!'

'How's everything?'

'Oh – everything is – well – it's—' But suddenly she couldn't speak any more; her voice seemed to catch in her throat and her eyes flooded with tears. She began shaking, shaking so much she dropped the phone. It hit the floor and a bit chipped off the mouthpiece. She bent down and picked it up.

'Sam? Sam? What's up? Are you OK? On your own? Want me to come over? Want to come over here?' he asked when she did not reply. 'Or meet somewhere?'

'I'll—' She forced the words out – 'I'll come over. Be there as soon as I—' She hung up and sniffed, staring bleakly out through the window. Then she dried her

298

eyes and knocked on Helen's door to tell her she was going out.

She sat at the traffic light at the edge of Clapham Common and the Jaguar's engine died on her. She pressed the starter button and it rumbled into life again, and she blipped the accelerator hard: there was a crackling roar and a cloud of oily blue smoke swirled through the darkness around her. Haven't taken the car for a decent run for weeks, she thought, blipping it again. It backfired with a loud bang, crackled and chucked out even more smoke as she accelerated when the lights changed, then she slowed down, turned into the driveway of the huge Victorian monstrosity of a house and pulled up behind the Bentley.

The front door opened as she climbed out of the car.

'Ken!' She flung her arms around him and hugged him hard, showering him in tears from her madly blinking eyes.

'Sam! What's—?' He held onto her tightly and hugged her back. She broke away and he looked at her. 'Christ, what's happened? You—' He hesitated. 'Come on, let's get you a drink.'

'Are you alone?'

He smiled. 'Yes. Only got back from Spain an hour ago. I rang you because I won't be in tomorrow – have to go down to Bristol.' He closed the front door and she followed him through the hallway, with its two suits of armour, glancing warily at the eye slits, past another waxwork of Ken sitting in a wicker chair – had he bought up a job lot? – and a ten-foot-high surreal picture of a wild pig leaping between two mountain peaks, past a juke box and into the drawing room with its minstrels' gallery and a Wurlitzer on the floor underneath, and more big paintings, a Hockney and a

Lichtenstein and a spoof Picasso portrait of Arianna Stassinopoulos Huffington by Georges Sheridan, and the roaring fire in the Adam fireplace which Ken had salvaged from somewhere or other. The television was on; *Miami Vice*, it looked like.

She sat down on a high-backed antique sofa that swallowed her up, and Ken went out of the room for a minute, then came back in with a tumbler in his hand. 'This is a really fine malt. Islay. You'll like it. Get it down you.'

She drank some, and then some more and it burned some of the churning out of her stomach.

'How was Spain?' she asked, looking down into the glass.

'Fine. Went well.' He lit a cigarette and sat down on the equally huge sofa opposite her.

'I shouldn't be here,' she said, 'it's dangerous, you see – for you—' Then the tears exploded as if a pipe had burst somewhere in her head.

Ken came and sat down beside her. She looked at him through her streaming eyes.

'I'm frightened for you, Ken. I think you could be – I think you've got to be really careful.'

'Careful of what?'

'I have a bad energy force around me,' she blurted.

He put his arm around her. 'Have you had another dream?' he asked gently.

'Sharp antennae,' she said, and she told him about the fall from the scaffold and her trip to Hull, told him everything that happened, and all she could remember of what Hare and Laszlo had said.

He sipped his drink and stubbed out his cigarette, blowing the last lungful of smoke up at the fresco of plump naked cherubs on the ceiling. 'You think this Dr Hare was killed because he was trying to help you? That his flat got smashed up by some spirit, as a warning, and because he ignored the warning he was killed?'

Sam watched the flickering flames of the fire, and nodded. 'I'm not sure how much more of any of this I can take.'

'You're having a rough time of it, aren't you? The scaffold – all this in Hull.' He squeezed her shoulders. 'I think we've got to try to take a balanced view on everything. I know it all seems horrific, but the human mind is a strange thing, Sam; we're very susceptible. It's still possible that a lot of what's going on is getting over dramatised.'

'You're beginning to sound like Bamford O'Connell.'

He smiled. 'Not quite as bad. I do believe you've had some premonitions – the aeroplane and the tube station – but the balcony is pretty iffy, Sam. This man getting run over – Dr Hare – is horrendous, but you said how dangerous that road was, that he was flaked out after a night awake and had drunk a pint of beer. We have to try to keep a balanced view, that's all.'

She pressed her lips tightly together and said nothing. Ken leaned his head back against the cushions. 'Or I deal!'

'Pardon?'

'Or I deal!'

'Or you deal?'

'Aroleid? That word? "Or I deal" – it's an anagram.'

'Or I deal? Doesn't mean anything to me.'

He clicked his fingers. 'Got it! "I reload!"'

'I reload,' she echoed.

'This Slider – he was wearing a green motorcycling suit, and gave you an airline ticket? Chartair?'

'Yes. The same one he gave me in the taxi after we had lunch. You know, after the Chartair disaster. I remember the seat number. 35A. And he said that I was wrong to think the scaffold was the big fall.'

Ken looked hard at her. 'It seems that it's more likely a bad dream connected with the disaster and your fall. You're bound to keep thinking about it.'

'I can accept that, I suppose. I can accept that much more easily than—' She turned the glass around in her hands.

They sat in silence. 'OK. So what are we going to do with you now? Wrap you up in cotton wool until the dreams all go away? Putting you in a padded cell would seem the safest for everyone.' He grinned, then saw she was not smiling, not smiling at all, but nodding in agreement. He touched her cheek with his knuckles. 'You're going to be OK, Sam, you're one of life's survivors.'

'Oh yes?'

'Look—' He lit another cigarette. 'I think you may have made a mistake dashing off up to Hull so soon after your fall.'

'Why?'

'This may sound hard, and it's not meant to: I think you are panicking. You've got yourself into a state, and you've got to let yourself come down out of it. I think you need to go away. As I said last week, have a holiday. Try to forget about it all. Really relax.'

'I'm going on Saturday. Skiing for a week with Richard. I've sorted everything out in the office. Is that OK?'

'Of course. But you've got to relax, OK? Take a hard look at everything and see if it still looks the same afterwards – I think you'll find it won't.'

'I hope you're right,' she said.

'So do I. Come on, I'll buy you some dinner – I bet you haven't eaten. Are you hungry?'

'Not really.'

'You should eat something.'

'I'll take you. I'll treat you.'

'It's a deal.' He stood up and drained his glass. 'Be a great Scrabble word that.'

'What word?'

'Aroleid. Makes a lot of words. I thought of another: Redial.'

'That's not using all the letters.'

'Did your hooded motorcyclist tell you you had to?'

Sam looked at him anxiously. 'Please, Ken. Be careful.'

They went out into the hallway and he slipped up the visor of one of the suits of armour. 'It's OK, Sam. I've got my own hooded men with slits for eyes. They'll kick yours to pieces if he tries messing around here.'

He let go of the visor and it shut with a loud clang.

36

GATWICK AIRPORT.

The blue and white motorway sign with its symbol of an aeroplane flashed past.

'Out of the way, you prick!' Richard pressed the horn, flashed his lights, then accelerated hard as the car in front finally moved over. Sam watched the BMW's wipers shovelling the cold February rain off the windscreen. There was a loud slap and spray from a lorry blinded them for a moment.

The same dream. Thursday night, and again last night. The fan on the ceiling, rotating, getting faster, faster. The fan she had dreamed of in the laboratory. The fan that was like a propeller. Then she would wake, shivering, in a sweat. That was all. Just that. It had stayed with her all yesterday and all of today.

She'd sent flowers to Colin Hare's funeral. She

thought about writing a note, but in the end she'd asked them to put her name on the card and nothing else.

There was a deafening roar and a Jumbo sank down towards them. Flaps and undercarriage lowered, it passed slowly overhead and down out of sight behind some warehouses. She waited for an explosion, for a dull boom and sheeting flame; but there was nothing.

Richard braked, then accelerated again.

'You're driving fast,' she said.

'We're late.' He pressed the horn, angrily blasting at a car that pulled out in front of them. 'I got a couple of bucket seats. I couldn't get us on a schedule as everything to Geneva was booked. The whole world's going skiing these days. 'S all right – it's a good airline.'

'Which one?'

'Chartair . . . Come on, you arsehole, move over.'

Chartair.

Chartair.

She stared through the windscreen at the black blades of the wipers scything backwards and forwards.

Like propellers.

'Do airliners have propellers?' she asked.

'Only small planes do.'

'So the sort of plane we're going on wouldn't have any?'

'They haven't for about thirty years.'

'I thought they had tiny little propellers, inside the engines.'

'They have fan blades. To compress the air.'

Fan blades.

She heard the clicking of the indicator, and saw the turn-off ahead.

'I wish we were taking Nicky,' she said, 'He's old enough to start skiing now.'

'Next year,' Richard said.

Next year. Would there be a next year? 'I feel lousy leaving him alone again. All I ever seem to do is leave him.'

'He'll be OK. Fine. He's an independent little chap.'

Independent. That was what her uncle and aunt used to say about her. Their way of justifying ignoring her. *Oh you needn't worry about Samantha. She's an independent little girl.*

She thought of the plane taking off in the teeming rain, taking off into the swirling grey sky. The vortex. You swirled through the vortex into the void. You stayed in the void for ever.

The car slowed, then accelerated up the ramp. 'We're fucking late. I'll drop you. Grab a porter or a trolley and get checked in while I park.'

She wheeled the trolley through the jam-packed departure concourse, steered it through lines of people who were queuing in every direction, so many queues they all seemed to meet together somewhere in the middle in a solid wedge of baggage and anoraks and fraying tempers. An old man was driven through them in a buggy, leaning back under his panama hat, looking around with a bewildered expression as if he thought he was in a rickshaw in another century.

Please don't fly, she wanted to shout. Not today. You'll be dead. Some of you. It's dangerous today. She bit her lip. Relax, for Christ's sake. Millions of planes, every day. Everyone flies. Like a bus; only safer.

Beng-bong. 'Will Mr Gordon Camping please go to the Airport Information Desk.'

She saw the row of Chartair check-in counters, saw signs on the wall saying GENEVA, MALAGA, VENICE, and joined the shortest queue. Come on, come on. She looked at her watch. The queue moved forward a fraction and a man with a face like a nodding dog rammed her legs from behind. She turned round to glare, but he hadn't noticed and a moment later he did it again. She spun round, angrily, wincing in pain.

'Why don't you have a driving lesson?' she said.

'Can I have your tickets please, Madam? Madam? Madam?'

Sam fumbled in her bag and pulled out the small folder. She put it down on the desk top.

The girl pulled the tickets out and frowned. 'You're late for that flight. It closed twenty minutes ago.'

'I – the – traffic—' she said lamely.

The girl reached under her desk and pulled out a phone. 'I'll have to ring through.'

Sam stood, waiting, looking around to see if Richard had arrived yet. No sign of him.

'All right,' said the girl. 'You're lucky. How many pieces are you checking through?'

'Two.' Sam heaved the bags onto the conveyor and the girl glanced at the weight on her dial. She peeled two numbers off the chart in front of her, stuck them onto two orange and white boarding cards, and handed them to Sam.

Sam glanced down and saw the number on the top one.

35A.

No.

Joke.

The check-in desk came towards her, banged her knees. She stumbled backwards, tripped over the nodding dog's trolley, grabbed his shoulder and sent his cases flying.

The check-in girl was watching her strangely, oddly, hostile.

Sam's face was burning hot. 'I'm sorry . . . is it possible . . . different seats?'

'Absolutely not,' said the girl. 'The flight is completely full.'

Sam saw the bags beginning to move along the conveyor, and she lunged forward and grabbed them, pulling them back onto the floor.

'They're checked through, Madam,' said the girl.

Her mouth tasted as if she had bitten into a lemon, and she screwed up her eyes, feeling spikes shooting into her brain like splinters of glass, and held onto the desk top for support.

The girl was looking at her as if she was mad.

Don't you realise? You stupid dumb check-in girl? Your plane's going to crash? They're all going to be . . .

'You can have these back,' Sam said. 'I'm afraid – you see – we can't go.'

'We can't resell the tickets for you, and they are not transferable.'

'Fine, that's fine.' Sam dumped the boarding cards on the desk top, heaved the cases back onto her trolley, and started to battle her way back across the concourse.

She saw Richard, sprinting, dodging through the crowds, dressed as if he was off for a day's shooting, in his sleeveless puffa, striped shirt and green cords, his face sweating.

'Hi,' he said. 'What's up?'

She felt her face redden, then a tear roll down her cheek.

'Oh, shit. We've missed it?'

Sam nodded.

He looked at his watch. 'Forty minutes. It doesn't take off for another forty minutes. This is fucking ridiculous. I'll get the manager. I've met the fucking guy who owns this airline. Tom Chartwell – he's a friend of Archie's. I'll sort them out.'

'No.'

'What do you mean?'

'I don't want to.'

'Want to what?'

'I don't want to get on the plane.'

'What do you mean?'

She lowered her head, and pulled out her handkerchief. She squeezed her eyes shut against her tears, against her hopeless feeling of foolishness. 'I can't do it.' She waited for his explosion. Instead, she felt his arms around her, warm and gentle.

'You really are in a bad way, aren't you? I thought that – the two of us going away together, y'know?' He sighed.

Someone barged into them, and apologised. She scarcely noticed. 'I want to,' she said. 'I do want to. But I can't get on that plane. Something's going to happen to it.'

There was a loud pop and the sound of splintering glass, right behind her.

She shrieked and spun round. Then she closed her eyes and breathed in, as she saw a man kneel down and stare ruefully at the golden brown liquid gushing from his dropped duty-free bag.

'Are you going to tell them?'

'Tell them?'

'Yes,' Richard said, almost shouting. 'Tell them.'

She dabbed her eyes.

'Are you, Bugs?' he said harshly. 'Are you going to bloody tell them? Why don't you go and announce it over the tannoy? Tell them. Chartair flight CA29 is going to fucking crash?'

She tried to think it through. Tried to imagine walking up to Airport Information. 'Excuse me. I've had a dream a couple of times . . . well, actually about your plane that crashed – the one in Bulgaria. Well, you won't believe it, but I think this one's a-goner too. You see, Slider, this hooded bogeyman has turned up twice, in two dreams, with this boarding card. 35A. Well, you see – that's the card I was given for this flight, so it's obvious, isn't it?'

'We could drive, Richard,' she said. 'I don't mind, if you're tired, doing the driving.'

'Have you dreamed this plane's going to crash?' he asked.

'I can't get on it.'

'Is it going to crash?'

'I don't know.'

'Are you going to tell someone?'

'Something's going to happen, but I don't know what. I don't know if it's going to crash – or—'

'Bugs, I've got to get to Switzerland. I have to be there Monday morning. Things are getting—' He looked around nervously at a policeman who was standing near them, and lowered his voice. 'I could end up with everything bloody frozen; I've got to move quickly now. If you don't want to come, I'll go on my own.'

'I do want to come . . . it's twenty to three now. We could be in Dover in a couple of hours, take the ferry or the Hovercraft, drive through the night and we could be in Geneva by two or three in the morning. It's Sunday tomorrow, and you haven't got to be there until Monday.'

'Montreux,' he said.

'It's only a short way further.'

'I was looking forward to a nice day tomorrow. I was hoping we could take a boat out on the lake.'

'We can,' she said.

'Are we all right to drive?'

'What do you mean?'

'No weird dreams about driving?'

309

She wiped her eyes again. 'No.'

She waited whilst he went to fetch the BMW and watched the cars and taxis that pulled up, emptying out people who put their arms up against the sheeting rain and sprinted for trolleys. There was a mocking laugh right behind her.

Slider's laugh.

She turned around. A man's suitcase had burst open, spilling its contents over the floor. He knelt down to scoop them up, and his companion laughed again. An unpleasant gloating laugh that went on and on, getting louder, until it was so loud it was deafening her and she couldn't stand it any longer. She pushed her trolley away through the crowds, pushed it along the pavement, until she was past the shelter of the awning and on her own, a solitary figure drenched in the torrenting rain and in her fear.

37

The bed felt strange. Huge. Soft. Too soft. She moved slightly, heard the clank of a spring and felt a slight reverberation somewhere beneath her.

There was a warmth and brightness in the light that flooded into the room soaking up her waking fears. Headlights strobing past. Stiff policemen at the border. *Non!* You are the woman who dreams. You are not welcome in Switzerland. Why are you coming here? Please go away. Take your dreams away with you.

We are coming to ski.

You are not coming to ski. You are coming to fiddle with the great Swiss banking system.

Sunlight streamed in through the gap in the curtains and lit up a section of the wall to her right. There was a faint whirring sound above her and a gentle draught of air. She looked up and saw the blades of a fan turning slowly.

She pulled herself up in bed a fraction, watching the fan warily, then fumbled on her bedside table for her watch. She felt the base of a lamp, then the leather strap, and picked up the Rolex, holding it dangling in front of her face, staring at the twin dials. It took her a moment to work it out. Eleven-forty. She had a slight headache, she realised, heaving herself further up and taking a sip of water, the same ache she seemed to have had for weeks, a dull pain that sometimes got turned up and was sharper, but never stopped. Her back was aching too, from the soft mattress, far too soft. It felt as if the bed had half collapsed under her.

The noise of the fan altered slightly, became a fraction louder, and she looked up at it again. It seemed to be wobbling as if it were loose.

She wondered where Richard was. The door to the bathroom was ajar but she could not hear any sounds from in there. She sipped some more water and looked around the room. A huge elegant room, grand and comfortably old-fashioned. Louis XIV furniture. A frieze of a bas-relief moulding around the ceiling. Soft pastel colours. A glass chandelier over the dressing table.

The noise above her became louder still, and she was nervous suddenly that the fan was going to fall down on top of her. Great. Terrific. Get killed by a ceiling fan that falls on you. She watched it, feeling increasingly uncomfortable. It was spinning faster; the draught was turning into a bitter howling blast. Her top sheet began to flap.

Christ.

It was wobbling more now and it still seemed to be

accelerating. Lines began to appear in the ceiling all around it, like veins in an old woman's hands. They got thicker, wider, and the ceiling began to sag, to swell. It looked like a huge cracked eggshell. Bits of the plaster fell away, crashing down around her, spraying fine white powder all around. The fan lurched drunkenly, and dropped several feet.

She screamed.

It hung at a weird angle, the blades only inches above her head now. Wiring spewed out all around it, the ceiling sagging, more chunks of white plaster tumbling all around her, the icy wind from the blades whipping her hair against her face, making her eyes smart and her lips hurt; the blades sagged more, lowering every second, lowering down towards her.

She threw herself sideways, rolling in terror to get away, but the sheets wrapped around her like nets, winding tighter as she rolled. She flung her weight against the side of the bed, feeling the chunks of plaster dropping around her, damp, icy cold, striking her head, her neck; she pulled, twisted wildly and flung herself sideways again; she felt the bedclothes give, and then she was free, falling. She tried too late to put her arms out, and hit the carpet hard with her face, painfully, rolled across and kept rolling until she crashed into the skirting board.

Then there was complete silence.

She lay back, gulping down air, feeling the perspiration trickling down her face and her body. There was a jangle of keys, and the sound of a door opening. A deep woman's voice, embarrassed, said '*Excusez-moi.*' and the door was shut hastily.

A spring clanked, and she felt a slight reverberation somewhere beneath her. Something felt odd, strange, not quite right.

Bed? Was she still in bed? The fan was still clattering, but it was quieter now. She opened her eyes and stared fearfully around. The room was filled with soft warm light, diffused through the heavy curtains. Everything was normal, calm. There was no wreckage. Nothing damaged. She glanced warily up at the ceiling, frowned, blinked. There was no fan. No cracked plaster. Just a crystal chandelier and elegant moulding. But she could still hear a fan.

Puzzled, she tried to put her hand out to the light switch, but could not move it. It was caught up in the sheet. Her whole body seemed caught up in it, as if it had been tied around her like a straitjacket. She sat up with a start, panicking, then realised it was just trapped underneath her, and she pulled it free.

She heaved herself up a fraction then fumbled on her bedside table for her watch. She felt the base of a lamp, then the leather strap, and picked up the Rolex, holding it in front of her face, staring at the dials. Eleven-forty.

That had been the time in the dream. Had it been a dream? She looked around, feeling disorientated. Her head ached, she realised, heaving herself further up, and taking a sip of water. Her back was aching too, from the soft mattress, far too soft. It felt as if the bed had half collapsed under her.

The pitch of the fan changed slightly, and it began to make a clacking sound. She looked up at the ceiling again, then realised it was coming from the bathroom. She slid out of bed, padded across the soft carpet to the bathroom door and looked in at the massive white bathtub and twin basins. It smelled of soap and cologne and there was a warm damp haze. A huge white towel was lying on the marbled floor, and the bath was wet, as if it had recently been used. Richard's paisley dressing gown was hanging on a hook on the door. Then she saw the fan, a small extractor on the wall above the lavatory seat. It sounded much louder in here.

She glanced in the mirror at her face and was shocked how puffy and tired she looked. She switched off the light, and the fan's motor cut out; the blades hummed, clacked a couple of times then stopped.

The silence felt strange, uncomfortable. She wrapped a towel around herself and walked across the room, drew the curtains and looked out of the window. Quiet, everything's so quiet, she thought. She opened the window. It was mild, warm in the sunlight, more like spring than February. She leaned on the sill and stared out at Lake Geneva, at the vast expanse of water that felt more like an ocean than a lake, except it was completely flat, as if the water had been stretched taut between the shores, like a giant canvas. Beyond, through the hazy light, she could see the French Alps, snow-covered, with craggy brown patches. Somewhere over to the right, through the haze, was Lausanne. And beyond, out of sight, at the end of the lake, was Geneva.

Below her an elderly well-dressed man with a bright cravat was walking a tiny terrier down a wooden pontoon; he stopped to gaze at the speedboats and small yachts that were moored to it, motionless, like toys, then peered down at the water, studying it carefully, as if trying to spot something he had dropped. She smelt a sudden whiff of cigar smoke, then the tang of the lake, almost salty.

Her head twinged. What time had they arrived? She tried to remember. About three. They'd stood outside ringing the bell until an elderly, grumpy night porter had opened up, and grudgingly carried their bags in.

A church bell rang twice then faded away into the silence. Peace, she thought. Peace. She watched a boat, a long way out, a smudge moving through the haze.

They had listened to the BBC news on the car radio as they had driven down through the night, in case, just in case, and there had been nothing up to the last news at midnight. No air disaster. Nothing at all. Chartair Flight CA29 had probably taken off and landed, like any other flight.

But if she had been on it? What then?

She turned and looked up at the chandelier and where the fan had been in her dream. So real. God, it had seemed so real. Like all the others . . . she turned back to the lake. Its stillness unsettled her. She heard the rattle of a key and the door opening behind her.

'Hi, Bugs, you're awake.'

'Just woke up.'

'I've arranged a boat,' he said. 'This afternoon. I thought we'd go out for a row after lunch.'

'Fine. Nice.' She noticed the wodge of newspapers under his arm. 'Are those today's?'

'Yah.' He put them down. The *Sunday Times* and the *Mail on Sunday*.

'From England already?'

'The Swiss are efficient.'

She scanned the front page of the *Mail*, and began to leaf through it.

'There's nothing, Bugs.'

'Nothing?'

'No air crash. That was what you wanted, wasn't it?'

She stared hard, trying to find the traces of satisfaction on his face, so she could shout, get mad at him. But there was no satisfaction. There was nothing but worry in his face. For her.

38

The gentle splash of the oars was the only noise that broke the silence on the lake. She leaned back in the tiny boat and trailed her finger over the side through the water. Icy cold. She pulled it out and rubbed it, then looked up at the mountains in the distance towering high above them. Everything seemed huge against the tiny insignificance of the boat.

It had been warm when they'd started out, almost hot, but the afternoon sun was fast losing its strength and wisps of white mist were rolling over the lake. She shivered, and watched a duck paddling on its own, a few feet from them, as if it was in the middle of a village pond.

'How are you feeling?' Richard said, pulling on the oars.

'OK. Tired.'

He looked tired too. White. Like a marble bust. Like a waxwork.

Like a corpse.

He'd scarcely spoken at lunch; they'd sat like two strangers forced to share a table. She thinking it through her way, Richard thinking it through his way, twitching his nose, lighting his cigarettes, drinking too much; beer, then wine, then cognac. She was surprised he hadn't gone to sleep, had still wanted to go out on the lake, as if there was some mission in it.

Maybe he hoped they'd fall in love again out here? Maybe some dream in his mind, some image, lazy days punting on the Cam. Summer. Summer was fine for boating on lakes. Right now it was still high winter. High winter and it was bloody freezing.

She hunched her arms up around herself, not wanting

to break the illusion, not wanting to say, For Chrissakes let's get back before we die of pneumonia. Not romantic that, not romantic at all. Hell we're here to give it a chance. Give it your best shot. Heal the wounds. So let's shiver it out.

A thin white trail of foam slid past them.

Like toothpaste.

You little bitch. Think you're going to beat me with high tech?

'Are you getting cold, Bugs?'

'A little.' Somewhere in the distance she could hear a strain of music, Buddy Holly's 'Every Day', as if someone had suddenly turned the volume up on a radio. Then it stopped as abruptly as it had started. The same song had been playing on the radio in the dream lab. She tried to remember whether that had been in her dream, or when she had been awake.

'Want to head back?'

She stared at the mist. Thickening clouds of it rolling towards them.

'Yes,' she said, her mind churning. 'Let's go back.' She watched Richard rowing in his chunky sweater and his Ray-Ban glasses; trying to look young and trendy. He could never look young. She'd never have loved him if he had looked young. He had always looked middle-aged. Like a father. 'What time is your meeting tomorrow?'

'Nine.'

'Will it be long?'

'Just have to sign a few papers.'

'What papers?'

'Just some banking things.'

'What sort of banking things?'

He grinned slyly. 'My disappearing act.'

'Disappearing?'

317

'Yes, I – Andreas is – he's set up this whole nominee chain. Absolutely brilliant. The money's being shunted all over the world – from Switzerland to the Dutch Antilles, then to Panama, then Liechtenstein, then back to Switzerland. Goes to a different set of nominees each time.' He shrugged as he saw her frown. 'Everyone does it.'

'Everyone?'

'Yah. Covers it up. Bloody Fraud Squad couldn't find who really owned it in a million years – nor could Interpol. No one could.'

A ball of mist rolled between them, making him hazy, like a shadow. She felt its icy breath.

Like a ghost.

She shivered. In the distance she could hear a faint thumping sound, and she turned, peering into the mist that was thickening around them. Row faster, she wanted to say, but she did not want him to see that she was scared. 'When do you think you'll know about—?'

He completely disappeared for a second in the mist. 'They've arrested the senior partner of our US affiliate and offered him a reduced sentence if he talks.'

'I meant what I said. I could, you know, support us if—'

The thumping sound was getting louder, nearer.

'It's going to be all right, Bugs. It's really smart, what Andreas has come up with. We're going to be fine.'

The mist closed silently around them and she could feel its icy tendrils dampening her hair. Her voice trailed, sounding flat, dead. She felt afraid. Afraid of being in this tiny boat in the mist. Afraid of the thumping.

Then she heard the rustle of water and the thrashing of an engine; closing on them. Fast.

'Can you hear that?' she said.

Richard took his sunglasses off and tucked them into his pocket. He watched the mist with a worried frown.

'Can you row a bit faster?'

He looked around. 'I'm not sure of my bearings. This damned mist has come down fast. It'll probably clear in a minute – it's only patchy.'

'Row, for Christ's sake!' she screamed, half standing up, then fell back in the boat, rocking it wildly, so wildly some water poured in over the gunwale.

'Bugs, be careful, don't make any sudden movement like that.'

She felt the icy water soaking her feet. 'It's coming at us,' she said. 'It's coming straight at us. Can't you hear it?'

'Did you dream this too?'

'I don't know. I don't know what the hell I dream.'

The thumping roar became louder, and she saw Richard squint through the mist.

'It'll be all right,' he said, pulling again on the oars. 'We'll just keep going.'

She turned around, craning her neck, trying to see through the dense white cloud.

Propeller.

She shivered again.

Propeller.

Not a fan.

Not a plane's propeller.

A boat's.

Then she saw the huge black shadow, almost on top of them.

'Hey!' she yelled. '*Hey!*'

Water smashed over them, stinging, hurting, hard as bullets, the boat plunged sideways then pitched madly, catapulting her forward off her seat onto the floor. Her face slammed into Richard's legs. She heard the thumping roar of the engine, the thrashing of the propellers, grinding, churning the water into a mad wild spray, throwing up huge heavy chunks that crashed down onto them, like a waterfall. They rolled crazily.

We're going to turn over, she thought.

Then there was silence.

It had gone.

Vanished.

Complete silence, apart from the slapping of water as the boat rocked in the wake.

Water was streaming down her face, oily, filthy water that tasted of spent fuel and stung her eyes. Richard's cavalry twill trousers were sopping wet, and his hair plastered down over his forehead. 'Are you OK?' he asked.

The boat lurched sideways.

'Where is it?'

'What an arsehole. Going that speed through this.'

'I can't hear it. Where's it gone? What was it, Richard? What the hell was it?' She crawled back onto her knees, then carefully sat back down, wiping the water from her eyes and pushing her hair back.

'Some sort of speed boat.'

'Why can't we still hear it?'

'What do you mean?'

'It's – like – it's just vanished,' she said. 'Into thin air.' She peered into the swirling whiteness, shaking with cold, with fear. Then she heard the whirring of a starter motor, the sharp boom of a powerful engine close by, like thunder, and the sound of thrashing water.

A voice called out of the mist. '*Allo? Ça va? Allo?*'

The engine revved a fraction, then died again. '*Allo?*'

A massive dark shape appeared behind Richard, then the mist cleared and she could see it was the stern of a large smart powerboat. A man was standing behind the wheel in a tartan jacket and a baseball cap, looking anxiously down. '*Pardon. Je m'excuse.*'

Behind him was a cabin with smoked glass windows and wide-slatted Venetian blinds, and Sam could see a figure behind the blinds, a man peering at them.

'You fucking loony!' shouted Richard.

'*Je m'excuse – je m'excuse.*' The driver raised his hands. '*Ça va?*'

Richard waved his hand dismissively. '*Ça va, allez, allez, ça va.*'

Sam caught the eye of the man behind the blinds, caught the malevolent smirk, caught the features just enough to be almost sure.

It was Andreas Berensen.

The driver pushed his gear lever forward with a loud clunk, and as the boat burbled slowly away from them, the mist lifted for a moment and they could see the shore clearly in the distance. Then the mist dropped down again like a stage curtain and the boat and the shoreline were gone.

'Did you see him?' Sam asked.

'Him? Who?'

'Your friend.'

'My friend?'

'Yes, your friend. Did you see him?'

'What do you mean, Bugs? My friend?'

'Andreas. He was on the boat.'

'Don't be fucking ridiculous.'

'He was watching us. I saw him in the cabin.'

'You think he'd have just stayed in and not come out? Andreas?' He laughed. 'He'd have come out, wouldn't he? He's one of my best friends. Christ, Bugs, you've really got a thing about him. You don't like him, do you? There wasn't anyone else on the boat. It's your mind playing up again.'

'I didn't imagine it. There was someone in the cabin. I'm certain it was Andreas.'

Richard shrugged. 'You're being daft, Bugs. I really think that – maybe – when we get back you ought to go and see Bamford.'

She turned and stared angrily into the mist, and listened to the sound of the boat accelerating off into the distance. As the burble of its engine faded, she could hear another sound, like distant laughter that rolled slowly across the lake as if it had been carried by the wind.

Except there was no wind.

39

The sunlight strobed at them through the fir trees, and she watched the three-pointed star on the end of the bonnet flickering like a dancer in a silent movie. The scenery passed by soundlessly, as if she was in a cocoon. The air inside the car was thick with the smell of new leather and she caressed the soft hide of her seat gently with her fingers, ran them along sensuously.

The pass dipped sharply down to the right, and there were a series of warning signs – thick, squiggly lines, two arrows, one black, one red, and a large exclamation mark. Richard braked, and she braced her feet in the thick carpeting in the foot-well. Strange, to see him sitting on her left, driving, she thought, trying to remember the reason why they were in this Mercedes and not his own BMW. She stared again at the vivid green colour of the bonnet. Vile. A vile colour for such an expensive car. Yuck.

They squealed around a hairpin bend, passed a small hut with a sign advertising ice cream and Löwenbrau, then crossed over a narrow stone bridge. A yellow PTT bus passed going the other way.

'Don't you think the colour of this car is horrible?' she said.

'Haven't got time to worry about the colour,' he said, and accelerated hard, with an angry look on his face. She felt the tyres scrabbling on loose grit, heard them squeal as they bit onto a stretch of fresh tarmac and the Mercedes yawed slightly. The engine bellowed and the car surged up the hill, past a marker post and a row of trees with white rings around them. The trees ended and they hurtled up a section of twisting road with a rock face rising steeply up to the left and an unguarded drop to the right, down into the fast-flowing river that was getting smaller beneath them.

She looked at him anxiously, unsure why he was driving so fast, too fast for the road and the size of the car, as they moved over even closer to the edge making space for a massive truck that was thundering down from the opposite direction; she felt the blast of its slipstream rock the Mercedes.

They squealed around a double hairpin, and to her relief she saw there was now a low stone wall at the edge of the road. A few hundred yards further on the right was a small lay-by, with a sign indicating a panoramic view. She heard the faint blaring of horns. A red Volkswagen came fast down the other way, then a motorbike, its engine revving with a caterwauling howl, followed by a white van.

She heard the horns again, closer now, vicious, angry blasts, and something made her shiver. She could see the road curving out of sight ahead, and they passed a road sign with a black curving line and a warning 40 KPH underneath.

Her seat belt seemed to tighten on her, jerking her

back into the seat so hard she could not breathe. A juggernaut was hurtling out of the bend on their side of the road, straight at them, its horn blaring, trying desperately to pass another juggernaut on its inside. She heard the screeching of the Mercedes's braking tyres, saw Richard stare wildly, first at the rock face to their left then at the drop of several hundred feet to their right. The juggernaut was almost on top of them, she could see the driver in the cab wrestling with his wheel, the helplessness on his face as his vehicle began to slew out away from the one it was overtaking. A gap began to open up, and for a moment she thought they might be able to squeeze through it.

Might.

Then it swerved crazily back the other way, hit the juggernaut it was overtaking and rebounded straight at them.

The front of it seemed to rear up towards them, a huge shadow like the mouth of a giant hungry insect, and she tried to duck down under the instrument panel, but her seat belt jerked her up. She heard the thundering of its engine, the piercing banshee of its horn, its hissing squealing brakes, its slithering tyres, all orchestrated into a deafening terrifying cacophony of destruction.

She saw the three-pointed star flick backwards, then the massive bumper of the juggernaut exploded through the windscreen, and she threw her hands up in front of her face as if she was going to be able to push it away, hold it off with them. She felt herself catapulted up, forwards, and an agonising pain as her head smashed into something hard, sharp.

There was a grinding, grating roar, and a terrible screeching of rubber and metal, and then she was outside, standing at the roadside in the lay-by, she realised, puzzled, watching as the juggernaut careered on wildly down the road with the Mercedes jammed under its cab, like a beetle with a fly in its mouth. It slewed out towards the edge, the rear of the Mercedes smashing through the low wall, then they both plunged over, still locked together, tearing through the trees, banging like huge dustbins, crashing. Then there was silence as they fell, a long silence, and the light was fading around her, everything was going dim, until it became completely dark and she could see nothing.

Death.

This is death. Silence. Trapped in a dark void.

For ever.

The void.

For a moment, she felt sick. Sick and angry. Then she began to shudder. Help me someone. 'Richard!' she called out. 'Richard?'

Nothing.

There should have been sirens. Police. Ambulance. Fire engines. 'Help me someone!' She felt herself floating, suspended in something that did not feel like water or air. Void, she thought. This is the void.

'It's OK!'

A single whisper.

'It's OK, Sam!'

A figure glided towards her out of the darkness. Another figure in the void with her. Coming closer. Closer. She saw a glint of light on the metallic green racing suit, then his head.

No. Please God, no.

The head coming closer. The black hood. The livid red eyeless socket coming closer, closer, so close it was going to touch her cheek.

'*No!*'

'Bugs?'

'Help me. Oh God help me.'

'Bugs?'

Different voice.

Then the single bong of a church bell, and something stirred in the darkness beside her.

'Bugs? It's OK. You're OK.'

'Richard?' she said.

The room was cold, icy cold. Cold as hell. Her face was numb. There was a rustle, then the clank of a spring.

'OK, Bugs?' said Richard's voice sleepily. She heard another grunt then a louder rustle, and felt herself move slightly.

Gingerly she slid her right hand across and touched him, in disbelief. Warm flesh. Breathing. She touched him again and let her hand stay on him, squeezing the flesh, and he grunted again. Then she rolled over towards him, put out her other arm, and touched his shoulder with her hand. She held him tightly, trembling with fear, with relief, and kissed his back.

He stirred again.

'Make love to me,' she said.

40

She stood at the window and stared out at the lake, waiting for the porter to collect their suitcases.

A powerboat sped across the water, a long way out, so far she could scarcely hear its engine. She wondered if it was the one that had come out of the mist and nearly killed them.

There was a rap on the door, and she called out, '*Entrez!*'

The porter came in and picked up the cases and she followed him down the corridor to the elevator. The lobby was gloomy, chilly, with the same unruffled, faintly expectant air that the lobbies of grand hotels always seemed to have. A phone rang, muted, and was immediately answered. The hall porter stood at his station, eyeing his domain. A short neat man in thick glasses sat behind the cashier's desk, writing in a huge ledger. Behind the reception desk, one clerk was talking on the telephone and another was flicking idly through a brochure.

A young man in a sharp suit waited just inside the entrance, his shiny leather briefcase on the floor beside him, glaring impatiently at his watch. Near him a well-dressed elderly couple were sitting on a sofa, the man reading a newspaper, the woman working on a small tapestry. Sam sat down opposite them, and pulled her book out of her bag.

A tall elegant woman strode in through the revolving doors in a full-length fox coat with a string of pekinese dogs tangled around her feet. The hall porter stiffened deferentially, and addressed her in German. Sam wondered whether she was some actress she should have recognised, or the bored wife of a rich businessman. She watched her chat for a moment with the clerk who had been reading the brochure, then take her key and tow her train of dogs towards the elevators.

They'd made love last night for the first time since – since it had happened. Back to normal; it felt strange; everything had changed and yet nothing had. If he'd learned anything new from his office tart, he'd been careful not to show it. Same position, same technique, same dead weight. Same romantic words.

Shit, that was great Bugs.

Then asleep.

Well, it was three in the morning. Could you put back romance once it had gone? Romance, she thought, feeling a twist of sadness. She opened her book and turned to her place.

'We will meet again soon?' he asked, and she was quick to notice the question in his voice and could not resist the opportunity to tease him.

'Perhaps,' she said languidly, and was enormously pleased to see the frown that sprang across his forehead.

'Perhaps?' he said brusquely. 'Only perhaps?'

For her answer, she reached for his hand and kissed his fingers one by one.

'Hi, sorry about that,' said Richard breathlessly. She looked up and saw him hurrying across the lobby towards her, looking harassed. He kissed her on the cheek. 'What are you reading?'

She held up the cover. '*Daughters of the Storm* by Elizabeth Buchan. It's good. I'm enjoying it.'

'Are we packed?'

'Yes. You've been longer than you thought.'

'The car's broken down.'

'What's happened?'

'I got to the bank all right, then it wouldn't start when I left.'

'Is it OK now?'

'No. Something's wrong with the electrics, I think the computer's gone on the blink.'

'I've just checked out,' she said. 'Shall we check back in again?'

''S OK. Andreas has lent us his car.'

'Andreas?'

'Yah. He's going to come up and join us in Zermatt for a couple of days – says he knows some great off-piste runs. He'll bring the BMW if it's fixed, otherwise we'll pick it up on the way back.'

'That's very decent of him,' she said hesitantly.

'Yah's a good bloke. I told you.' He looked down. 'This all the luggage?'

'Yes. How did it go?'

'Fine.' He sniffed. 'No problems. As far as the Swiss banking system is concerned, Richard Curtis no longer exists.' He stooped to pick up the bags, and the porter sprinted across, snatching them away, then beamed triumphantly.

'Outside? Your car?'

They followed him out into the brilliant sunlight, and Richard pointed across the driveway to the car that was parked awkwardly with two wheels on the kerb; a shiny green Mercedes.

41

She turned and walked back into the lobby, sat down on the sofa and stared ahead, stared at nothing.

Richard followed her in. 'Bugs? What's the matter, Bugs?' He sat down beside her. 'What's up?'

'I – don't want to go in that car.'

'What do you mean?'

She continued staring ahead numbly.

'Why not Bugs? It's almost brand new.'

'The colour,' she said.

'The colour? Do you think I had a choice? It was fucking decent of Andreas to lend us it – his own car. It's only about a month old.'

'I had another dream!' she screamed at him, so loudly that everyone in the lobby heard. And she didn't care, thought they probably hadn't understood what she said and that it was just another couple having a row.

'Great. Another fucking dream!' He leaned over

329

towards her, and put his hands on the arm of the sofa.
'What did you dream, Bugs?'

'A – green Mercedes.'

'What do you want me to do? Go back to Andreas,
tell him "thanks a lot for the car, but my wife doesn't
like the colour"?'

She smiled. She wasn't quite sure whether it was
because she thought it was funny or it was nerves, but
she looked up at him and smiled again.

'Pull yourself together, Bugs. You didn't want to fly
out here because you thought the plane would crash.
Now you don't want to drive because . . . what do you
want to do? Stay here for the rest of your life?'

She followed him back out to the car, and he held up
the keys.

'Would you feel better if you drove?'

'No.' She climbed in and he slammed her door shut
for her.

Neither of them spoke for a long time as they headed
out of Montreux following the lake around, and then
down into the Rhône valley. Everything that had happened in the past weeks churned over in Sam's mind, the
advice she had been given, the explanations.

*It's important for you to try to work things out. To
try to find the meanings.*

Green Mercedes. Disappearing into the mouth of the
juggernaut.

Very Freudian.

You think so?

Bound to be.

Think it could symbolise a desire to rebirth?

Oh definitely.

*I'm getting the sexual act very strongly, Sam. Does
that resonate?*

Regular ding-dong.

She watched the sunlight glinting off the three-pointed star on the Mercedes's radiator. The car even smelled the same as the dream. Leather. Thick, rich, pungent leather. Like Ken's Bentley. Like her uncle's Rover.

Like the dream. Like the dream. Like the dream.

The dashboard was wood, immaculately polished, new.

Like a coffin.

Richard was on her left. The hideous green colour. The same colour. Designer puke.

He stretched out his arm and laid his hand on her thigh, patting it gently. 'Andreas says the snow's terrific at the moment. He was up there last weekend.'

'Good,' she said. 'Good.'

The vine terraces rose steeply up from the Rhône valley to their left, and the Alps towered down on them from the right, like a fortress wall. A wooden fruit stall flashed past, then a giant furniture mart. She felt her throat tightening and a deep numb sense of dread building in the car. She wanted to stop, get out, but instead she sat silently, thinking; trying to work through everything, as Hare had told her.

Green Mercedes. Disappearing into the mouth of the juggernaut. Sure. Plenty of interpretations. Bamford O'Connell and Tanya Jacobson and everyone in the dream group could have had a field day on the dream.

Except.

Closer. All the time closer. Drawing her, reeling her in.

To meet the monster?

She opened the glove compartment and looked in, looking to see if there were any clues about Andreas. Nothing. Just an assortment of classical music tapes, an owner's handbook and a clean, neatly folded duster.

Andreas; she picked at a hangnail. Andreas who had no wife or family. Richard thought he had been married once, some time ago, and that his wife had died, but he wasn't sure. Andreas. The enigma. Was it you peering out from the cabin of that boat? Were you trying to run us down? Ridiculous; not before the forms had been signed. So why didn't you come out and speak to your friend? Why did you stand and smirk? If it was you?

Maybe Richard was right; maybe Andreas was a nice guy and she was maligning him. Maybe.

The road narrowed and ran along beside a shallow rocky river; she watched a man and a small boy standing on the bank with their fishing rods. A cassette was sticking out of the tape deck and she pushed it in. A Beethoven piano sonata tinkled from the speakers and made her feel sad, reminded her of autumn.

The road curved away slightly from the river, and was now lined on either side with trees bowing across towards each other in a guard-of-honour salute, and the sun, low down behind them, flashed through them like a strobe.

Like the dream.

She glanced at the road ahead. The trees ended. Different trees to the dream. They were firs in the dream. The scenery was different, too.

'How did you meet Andreas, originally?'

'Rang me up; said I'd been recommended – wanted me to do some dealing for his bank.'

'Why's he being so . . . helpful?'

He rubbed his index finger and thumb together. 'Dinero. The Swiss will always be helpful for dinero – and he's just a good bloke as well.'

'You don't think that he's being too helpful?'

'What do you mean?'

'You don't think he has any – I don't know – any other motive?'

'Like what? Christ, you're so fucking suspicious, aren't you?'

'Is he involved in this insider dealing stuff?'

He shook his head.

'He got you dropped in it, but kept out himself?'

'Wasn't—' He hesitated – 'wasn't just him, Bugs, you know. I suppose that's what I get paid for doing – taking risks.'

'You don't get paid to break the law. Or did he pay you?'

He went bright red.

'Is that where all the money came from? To buy the house, and everything?'

He sniffed nervously, fumbling for his cigarettes. 'No, I told you. We – I – did rather well on a few deals.'

'What sort of deals?'

'Oh, you know – had a couple of good tips. Take-overs,' he said evasively, sniffing again, then braking as they approached a hairpin bend.

As they rounded it she saw a small hut with a sign advertising ice cream and Löwenbräu, then they crossed over a narrow stone bridge. A yellow PTT bus passed going the other way. Her throat tightened more. Richard accelerated hard with an angry look on his face. She felt the tyres scrabbling on loose grit, heard the squeal as they bit onto a stretch of fresh tarmac and the Mercedes yawed slightly. The engine bellowed and the car surged up the hill, past a marker post and a row of trees with white rings around them. 'You're being bloody stupid about this whole thing. I'm doing it for us,' he said, picking up his cigarettes and shaking one out.

To their left was a rock face rising straight up from the edge of the road, and to their right was an unguarded drop down into the fast-flowing river that was getting smaller beneath them.

Unfolding.

The dream was unfolding now.

Exactly.

Calm. Stay calm. Stay calm.

They moved over even closer to the edge as a massive truck thundered down past them, and she felt the blast of its slipstream rock the Mercedes.

'Richard, please drive a little slower.'

''S all right. I'm not going fast.' He lit his cigarette. 'Got a long way to go, and we've still got the fucking train journey up into the village.'

We're not going to get there, she wanted to say. We're going to get wiped out by a juggernaut. In a minute or two's time. We'll be dead. All over. Fini. Curtains. Snuffed out.

She felt a curious sense of euphoria suddenly. Of power.

Of freedom.

As if someone was telling her to relax, that the next few minutes did not matter, that nothing mattered any more. That the choice to live or die was hers. That dying would be nicer. So much fun. Live out the dream! Go for it! Be free!

She laughed. Silly. Stupid. To have been so worried.

'What's funny?'

Funny, The word echoed around. Funny. Then the shivers gripped her and she felt as if a million hoses were pumping iced water straight into the centre of her stomach. They squealed around a double hairpin, and she saw the low stone wall at the edge of the road.

I'm going to wake up in a minute, she thought. This is a lucid dream. I can control it.

She heard the faint blaring of horns, then a red Volkswagen came fast down the other way, followed by a motorbike, its engine revving with a caterwauling howl, followed by a white van.

The ones she had seen. Identical. The same colours.

She was shaking with terror.

Richard. She tried to speak, but nothing came out. 'Richard!' she shouted, but it only came out as a whisper. She heard the horns again, closer now, vicious angry blasts. She unbuckled her seat belt.

Lay-by. They were coming to the lay-by.

'Stop!' She threw herself at Richard, grabbing the wheel, and felt the Mercedes swerving wildly. Richard stamped on the brakes and the car squealed to a halt.

'For Christ's sake, have you gone fucking mad?' he yelled.

'Pull off the road,' she said. 'For God's sake!' Her voice was a weird, croaking whisper. 'Quickly!'

He glared at her, then accelerated harshly, squealing the tyres again, pulled over into the lay-by and stopped, flinging her forward. 'What the fuck are you playing at?'

'Out! Out! Get out!' She opened her door, flung herself out, tripped, grabbed the swinging door and stared wide-eyes down the steep wooded gorge towards the river.

In the distance she heard the roar of a juggernaut. Two juggernauts, closer, coming closer, hurtling down; any moment they would come around the corner, one overtaking the other. Coming, coming, coming. She turned and saw Richard standing beside the Mercedes, staring at her.

They're coming. You'll see. You'll see that I was right.

Where are you?

The roaring continued. Closer. Getting closer.

Richard walked around the back of the car towards

335

her. A car came around the corner, then another, a red
Porsche with skis on the roof, a small Renault, a BMW,
an Audi piled high with suitcases.

Come on.

Still the roaring.

Then she realised that it wasn't the roaring of juggernauts. It wasn't coming from the road at all.

It was the roaring of water in the gorge below.

She walked along the lay-by, listening to the loose
stones scrunching under her feet. A small truck droned
up the road past her followed by a line of cars, then
nothing again except for the sound of the gorge. She
walked to the wall and stared down the sheer rock face
through the trees at the frothing white water of the
river. She heard footsteps behind her, then felt his arm
around her waist.

'Maybe they should put me away,' she said.

'Maybe you should just forget your dreams, Bugs.'

42

They'd had to stop and put chains on the Mercedes for
the last ten miles. Richard had straggled and cursed for
the best part of an hour, whilst she'd hovered around in
the freezing cold and tried to help, and not been much
use. But it had been better than just sitting, waiting.
Anything was better than that.

Maybe Ken was right.

'You've got yourself into a state, and you've got to let
yourself come down out of it . . . Try to forget about it
all.

Yes.

Take a hard look at everything and see if it still looks
the same afterwards – I think you'll find it won't.

Yes. Yes, boss. Oh absolutely, sir.

Christ, I wish you were right.

Täsch was where the road ended. Richard lifted the cases out of the boot of the Mercedes and put them onto a luggage trolley. Sam stood in the snow and watched him drive off into the vast car park, the exhaust smoke trailing behind, thick and heavy in the bitterly cold afternoon air, the chains clattering and the tyres squeaking on the hard-packed snow.

The snow smelled good, smelled fresh and clean and lay everywhere. It was still falling, and tickled her face and made everything look like a Christmas card, made her think of snug log fires and roasting food, and wine, and laughter.

They were here. They'd got here. Got here because? Because the dreams had told her how? Because the plane would have crashed if they'd been on it? Because if she hadn't made Richard row like hell they would have been run down in the boat?

Because two juggernauts would have come round the bend if she hadn't made Richard pull off the road?

Sure they would have, Sam. By magic?

It was because we stopped that we survived.

Bullshit.

You know why you refuse to believe it, Richard? Because you're scared, that's why.

I'm not nuts, oh no. Slider's playing this game with me. 'Now you see me, now you don't.' 'He's standing right behind you . . . oh no he isn't.' 'Some dreams come true and some dreams don't.' It's a game, that's all; a game you have to win.

Because if you lose you die.

She stamped her feet to warm them up and dug her gloved hands deep inside her pockets. Richard hurried back towards her in his red anorak and his white moon boots, and they pushed the trolley together up the ramp to the funicular train to Zermatt.

The porter put their bags into the back of the electric buggy, then held the door open for them. They moved off from the station with a jerk, heading up the narrow Bahnhofstrasse, the buggy making a high-pitched whine. A stream of horse-drawn sleighs trotted past them the other way, bells jangling.

Money, she thought. You could smell it in the thick coats, in the fat chocolates and expensive watches that sparkled in the windows; you could smell it in the cigar smoke and coffee and *chocolat chaud* that hung in the frosty air along with the dung and the smell of horses; in the bustle, jostle, in the signs, Confiserie, Burgener, Chaussures, Seiler, Patek Philippe, Longines, in the smart skis rattling on smart shoulders, pink, green, Racing, Slalom, Géant and the clunking and crunching of unclipped boots. The Matterhorn rose like a monolith above the roofs of the hotels, the sun sinking down beside it, thin and dull, like a tarnished bauble in need of a polish.

Whymperstübe. Hotel Whymper. Named after the first Englishman to climb the Matterhorn. The graveyard under the bridge was full of them. So full they had run out of space. She shivered. Stone slabs sticking crookedly out of the snow like old men's teeth. Young Englishmen along with the local traders and local heroes, all just as dead as each other, all with their epitaphs. 'I chose to climb', she remembered on one, and she wondered what would be on her own.

'Hasn't changed much,' said Richard.

Nine years. It had been magical then. Like coming to a fairy tale. Snow and hot chocolate and soft pillows and laughter. Free. Taking the baker's sled and tobogganing through the streets at three in the morning. She had felt so free then. Free and silly and mad.

The buggy turned up the alleyway, braked to avoid two elderly women, then pulled up outside the Alex. They went to the reception desk and Richard filled out the forms, and the porter took their bags up to their room. It was simple and comfy with modern wooden furniture, plump pillows and a great thick duvet soft as snow. 'We ought to call Nicky,' she said.

'Yah.'

She went over to the window and stared out at a school opposite, the desks abandoned for the night. She could see a display of crayoned drawings pinned to a notice board. She tried to concentrate her mind. To think.

There were so many possibilities. Maybe that's why people ignored their premonitions: because once you started looking, trying to cover all the options, you would become a hermit, or go mad. Perhaps you couldn't escape. All you could do was delay, buy a few hours or days or weeks, a time of terror and confusion; a bonus not worth having.

The snow was falling more heavily, and she felt the warm air from the radiator on her face.

'How're you feeling, Bugs?'

She raised her eyebrows.

I'd feel a lot better if—

If you believed me; but you won't. Ken doesn't either; not really. Only two people do. One's dead; the other doesn't want to know.

Laszlo. Driving away from the station as fast as he could.

But you're not going to win, Slider. I'm not going to let you. She smiled wryly. I'm going to beat you. Doing OK so far, eh? I'm going to win. I promise.

Richard rolled over on the bed and pulled his cigarettes out of his anorak pocket. 'What are you smiling at?'

'How does that limerick go?' she said.

> ' "There was a young lady of Riga
> Who rode with a smile on a tiger. . .
> They returned from the ride
> With the lady inside
> And the smile on the face of the tiger." '

'Is that how you feel?'

'Life's a tiger,' she said. 'That's how I feel.'

'Cheers!'

'Cheers,' she said.

They clinked glasses. Richard swirled his wine around and took a large gulp. 'It's good being away on our own, don't you think?'

'Yes.'

'We never seem to talk when we're at home, do we?'

She sipped some wine. 'What would you like to talk about?'

He shrugged and yawned. 'Us, I suppose. We seem to have been through a bit of a thin patch—' He inhaled deeply on his cigarette and focused on something past her. She turned her head. There was a glitzy blonde sitting at a table with a portly man a good thirty years her senior.

'She's not that great,' Sam said.

'She's got good tits.'

'It's very flattering to sit here watching you ogle other women.'

He drank some more wine, then his face suddenly

became animated and he leapt up. 'Andreas! We weren't expecting you until tomorrow!'

She saw the banker walking stiffly towards them in a long fur-collared coat sprinkled with snow, his gloved hands by his side. She sensed a sudden chilly draught, as if he had left the outside door open, and felt goose-pimples breaking out on her flesh.

He nodded at her as he reached the table, a faint smirk on his lips; the same smirk she had seen through the slats of the blinds on the boat. She was certain.

'How are you!' Richard said effusively.

'Not much changed since this morning.' Andreas smiled coldly back at him, shook his hand, then fixed his eyes on Sam. 'Good evening, Mrs Curtis.'

'Good evening,' she said, as courteously as she could, staring back into his icy cold eyes that seemed to be laughing at her.

'So nice to see you again. I enjoyed meeting you at dinner very much. Such a pleasant evening.'

'Thank you. I'm glad you enjoyed yourself.'

'Sit down, join us,' Richard said, urgently signalling to a waiter for another chair.

'You have eaten, I think,' said Andreas. 'I have something then I join you.'

'No, absolutely not, you join us now,' Richard insisted. 'It doesn't matter. We're happy to sit while you eat. I'll get you a glass. Would you like some wine?'

'Thank you.' The banker pulled off his coat, and Richard scurried around, taking it from him then passing it on like a rugger ball to the waiter who brought the chair; he grabbed a glass from the empty table next to them, poured out some wine and put the glass down in front of Andreas. 'Just a local one, I'm afraid. Dole, nothing grand.'

'The local ones are the best to drink here,' Andreas

said, sitting down and locking his eyes onto Sam's again.

'Yes,' Richard said. 'Yes, of course, I'm sure you're right. We had some excellent wines last time we were here . . . Perhaps we should have a toast. To today! Let's have some champagne – bottle of Poo – we'll have some Bollers if they've got any. I'll get the wine list.' He grinned. 'Got to toast the – dematerialisation – of Richard Curtis.' He looked at Andreas for approval, and the banker looked away dismissively, like a dog bored with a puppy.

'They don't find anything wrong with your car.'

'What do you mean?' Richard waved at the waiter again. 'Could we have a menu – *un menu, et la carte des vins, s'il vous plaît.*' He turned back to Andreas. 'Nothing wrong?'

He shrugged. 'Maybe it is something – how you call it? – loose in the wiring or something. It's fine, now. Drives very nicely.'

Nothing wrong.

Sam felt the goosepimples crawling up her neck. Nothing wrong. Like the Jaguar in Hampstead. She shook, as if she had had an electric shock. Both Richard and Andreas looked at her.

'You all right, Bugs?'

'Fine. Just a bit cold.' She caught Andreas's eyes again, the cold blue eyes in that flat featureless face that appeared so unassuming until you looked closer; neat, dull, fair hair, but lost most of it on top, almost bald except for the light fuzz; he'd probably been quite handsome when he was in his twenties, in a rather stiff sort of way. He looked a fit man now, fit and athletic, and flashily dressed in his pink cashmere sweater, cream silk shirt, and the small silver medallion on his chest.

'Extraordinary,' Richard said. 'I suppose that's the

problem with these electronics. Get little glitches in them which come and go. Almost impossible to find.'

Then she saw it.

Saw it and realised.

Saw it as Andreas curled his gloved fingers around the bowl of his wine glass, the quick almost imperceptible flick of the thumb and the little finger, which she would have missed if she hadn't been looking hard, the click he had devised to make the middle three fingers move, to make them curl around the bowl.

To make them look as if they were real.

43

She thrashed violently, trying to free herself from the bedclothes that were over her head, heavy as sandbags, smothering her, trying to free herself and escape from the blades of the fan that were coming down towards her and the ceiling that was cracking like eggshell. She heaved the bedclothes away frantically, but they fell back, crushing her body, crushing her face, blocking her mouth, her nose. She was gulping, gasping for air, twisting, helplessly.

Trapped.

She tried to scream but the sheet came into her mouth.

Too late, she realised the sheets were holding her.

Preventing her from falling.

She was slipping free of them now, slipping out into the swirling vortex below her. She grabbed the corner of one, desperately, but it held her weight only for a fraction of a second, and then tore.

'Help!' Her voice echoed around her as if she was in a cave. Then she plummeted downwards, hurtled through the freezing cold air, bouncing, falling, spinning towards a tiny hole of darkness. She put her hands up, trying to ward it off, trying somehow to swim away from it.

'*No!*'

She hurtled into the hole, trying to grip the walls, but they were covered in smooth ice and her hands slid down them, burning from the cold, from the friction. There was whiteness below, and she could see the blades of the fan scything through the air, clattering louder as she tumbled down towards them, waiting for the impact, waiting to be cut into a thousand pieces.

'Fifty-five and a half seven. OK, hit that fucking bid. Sally, that's Mitsubishi Heavy five hundred at fifty-five and a half I sell. OK, now buy back the bloody stock!'

Richard's voice in the darkness.

'I'm talking big noughts, Harry. Big noughts. No. Serious. He's a major player, a triple-A client. We should hedge with futures. Five hundred contracts. Could be a squeeze on the market. I'm seven and a half bid for as many as they've got. Shit. It's moving away from us. Take the offer. For Christ's sake take the offer!'

His voice rambled on. She had never heard him talk in his sleep before. Never heard him talk in such a faltering, nervous voice.

The she heard children chanting.

> Humpty Dumpty sat on a wall,
> Humpty Dumpty had a great fall.
> All the King's horses and all the King's men,
> Couldn't put Humpty together again.

The children laughed, and she heard the laughter echoing, as if it was echoing around an empty classroom. It continued, getting louder. She slipped out of bed and immediately it stopped.

Puzzled, she walked across the room. Richard stirred and grunted behind her. She lifted the curtain and stared out. The whiteness of the snow on the ground filled the night with a strange translucence. A church bell chimed three o'clock. The school opposite was dark, silent, empty. She turned and went back to bed, pulled the duvet up around her and lay staring into the darkness.

A cold breath blew into her ear, and she heard a voice, soft, whispering, taunting. Slider's voice. Just one word.

'Aroleid.'

Then silence.

44

It was snowing hard as they trudged up the hill towards the Furi lift station with their skis over their shoulders. They passed a cowshed then a row of old chalet-style buildings, PENSION GARNI said the sign on each one.

'I thought you'd always been keen on Japanese warrants?' Richard said.

'Swiss franc ones only,' Andreas replied.

It was another language. As foreign as the languages of the country they were now in. French. German. Switzer-deutsch. Snatches of foreign languages all around. Two lanky men strode in front of them, one wearing a fluorescent yellow ski suit and bright yellow boots, the other in white, with bright pink boots. They talked loudly, their feet clumping, skis slung over their shoulders. They roared with laughter. Normal people. Out for a day's skiing. Going for it.

Going for it. Living in the fast lane. Flying at the sharp end. Style.

Death. Lying in a cellophane bag on a mortuary slab. Floating in the void. In the void where you could shout and no one could hear you. For ever.

For a moment, she did not care. She was tired of walking up the hill, tired of the snow tickling her face. Tired of being scared. She wanted to sit down. To sit down and sleep and not dream.

To sleep: perchance to dream: ay there's the rub. For in that sleep of death what dreams may come?

Did you go on dreaming after you were dead? In the void?

'You're quiet this morning, Bugs,' said Richard.

She blinked away the snow and trudged on, saying nothing, and looked again at Andreas's padded green skiing gloves.

I think it is possible that he's someone in the present, now, who is bothering you, worrying you – someone that you are associating with this Slider.

He's a banker, that's all. A banker with a bad hand. He's dry and arrogant; so are most bankers. What are you afraid he's going to do? Eat you? Turn you into a frog? Jump on you when Richard's not looking and rape you and slit your throat? Just because you imagine you saw him on that boat? He's doing you both a favour, be nice to him.

They crossed the wooden bridge over the river and then climbed up the steep steps to join the jostling queue into the ski-lift station. She shuffled slowly forwards behind Andreas and Richard in the air that was thick with garlic and suntan lotion and lip salve and perfume.

'Sony,' Richard said. 'Their seven-year warrants are a fucking good buy at the moment. Five times geared and a four percent premium.'

'I prefer Fujitsu,' said Andreas.

She could hear the machinery now, the whirring of the motors driving the massive cable, the scraping, sliding sound of the six-man gondolas unhooking, slowing, the metallic thump of their doors opening, the clatter of skiers pushing their skis into the racks then clambering in, the clunk of the doors shutting and the sudden roar of acceleration as the tiny cabins, like eggs, slid down the cable, gaining momentum, and through the gantry that locked them to the cable. She felt afraid of the gondolas, suddenly, afraid of the mountain, wanted to go back to the hotel.

Something hit her hard in the small of her back, and she spun round.

'*Entschuldigung.*' A woman was leaning forward, trying to push her skis back together, smiling apologetically, a flustered, messy-looking woman with two small girls in matching pink outfits.

She felt her skis being lifted out of her hand. She turned and saw Andreas placing them in the rack at the back of the gondola. He took her arm and propelled her in.

She looked around. 'Richard? Where's Richard?'

'He is going in front.'

There were four little Japanese boys in the gondola, watching them wide-eyed. Someone shouted outside, urgently, a torrent of Japanese, and the boys scampered out seconds before the door closed.

The gondola accelerated, unbalancing her, and she sat down hard on the plastic bench. Andreas sat down opposite her, holding his ski poles, fingers neatly curled around the handles, as they swung suspended on the cable just outside the mouth of the station, then began to glide upwards.

She looked out of the window. Flash bastard. His

ultra-modern ski suit, a metallic green racing suit, and goggles pushed up on his head. Wonder if you ski as flashily as you look? Probably do, damn you.

It was snowing even harder. The wind buffeted them and the visibility seemed to be going as the weather closed in around them. The gondola juddered and she looked anxiously around, listening to the rattling of the cable and the patter of the snow hitting the windows, and caught his eye. He was watching her and smiling drily to himself.

'The weather is not so good,' he said, his eyes still staring, penetrating.

'Not a nice day for boating,' she replied.

He did not flinch.

She looked away. 'Do you sail, Andreas? I should think Lake Geneva is a great place for sailing, or for power boating.' She looked sharply back at him; still no reaction.

'I am working too much. Skiing is my only relaxation.'

'If I lived in Montreux, I'd be out on the lake all the time. Very exhilarating on a cold Sunday afternoon to roar across water, wouldn't you think?'

'I would not know,' he said, turning towards the window as if he was bored with the conversation.

'It was Ratty in *The Wind in the Willows*, wasn't it, who said "There is nothing – absolutely nothing – half so much worth doing as simply messing about in boats." *The Wind in the Willows*. Did you ever read *The Wind in the Willows*?'

'I don't believe so.'

She searched his face, trying to read it, trying to read the signs from the way he shifted his position, from the way he turned his head to look out of the window again, from the way he clenched his fists just a fraction.

348

'Higher will be better. I think perhaps it will be above the cloud,' he said.

She glanced up nervously again as the cable rattled loudly through the runners of a pylon, and the gondola swayed. Through the window she could see the tops of the fir trees below.

There's more to come. So much further to fall. You've got the really big fall to come.

Who the hell are you, Andreas? Or is it me? She looked again at the fingers, then at his green suit; something seemed familiar about the suit.

The gondola stopped with a jerk, and swayed wildly. She felt the fear surge through her. A gust of wind caught them and tossed them sideways. The snow and the mist seemed to be getting even denser; she heard the wind wailing mournfully through a pylon, felt it shake them again and there was a creak above her head, then a sickening rending sound, like metal tearing. Andreas was smirking again, smirking at her fear.

The cabin lurched violently, twice, then the gondola began to move forwards. There was another tearing sound above them, and the gondola lurched again. There was a loud bang. A dark shadow fell across them and her heart jumped. There was an even louder bang and a tremendous jolt, and they swung backwards.

Then the doors opened with a hiss and a dull thump, and the banker stood up.

They had arrived at the station.

He lifted her skis from the rack and stood waiting for her. She swung herself out and jumped onto the ground. There was another bang as the next gondola arrived, crashing into their empty one. 'Thank you,' she said, and followed him over to Richard who was standing in the queue for the exit.

Richard turned around. 'I thought you were right

349

behind me. Got in a gondola with a bunch of Krauts. They didn't speak a word of English. Did you have a nice chat?'

'Your wife is very charming. Such a well-read lady.' Andreas smiled again at Sam, and she looked away, up at the ceiling of the lift station, at the dark churning wheels of the machinery, listening to its rattling and grinding. There was a clang as the next gondola arrived and thudded into the rear of the one in front.

It was here, she knew. Here on the mountain. Waiting.

45

'Sam!'

She heard Ken's voice echo around the mountain and turned with a start, looking up, scanning the slope she had just skied down. But there was no one. No one but Andreas in his metallic green suit waiting to start his descent, waiting until she had stopped so she would be sure not to miss it. She looked at Richard, but he did not seem to have heard anything.

Clear.

It had sounded so clear.

Like a warning.

'The sun's trying to break through,' said Richard.

She nodded and stared up again at the slope. At least they were in the lee of the wind here. Beyond the peak she could see the silhouette of the sun smouldering behind the clouds, like a cigarette burning through a tablecloth.

In the last hour, since lunch, the snow had stopped and the mist was starting to clear. They had gone higher at Andreas's suggestion, up to the top of the glacier to get above the worst of the weather, and he had been right. She heard the drone of the piste basher grinding up the glacier behind her, close, too close, and she turned and watched the huge red machine with its caterpillar tracks and rotating blades chomping through the snow. PISTENBULLY was emblazoned in large letters on its side. An orange warning light flashed on its roof, and its siren wailed, a short, monotone pulse, like a door hinge creaking in the wind.

Andreas launched himself off the top of a mogul, crouched low, dug his pole in, straightened his legs then bent them again, turned neatly, too damned neatly, straightened and bent his legs again, repeated his pole action and turned again, neat, snaking, even turns, his body flowing, rhythmic, exaggerating each movement as if he was giving a lesson. He headed down towards the rotating blades of the Pistenbully, in zigzagging tightly carved turns, his speed staying constant, keeping his head down.

As if he had not seen it, she thought, with a tremble of horror and excitement.

He turned again, accelerating hard away from it, then back again, straight into its path.

Straight towards the blades.

Then at the last moment he made one sharper even more stylised turn, crouched down low into a racing tuck and accelerated out of its path, straight at her, grinning demonically.

She stepped sideways, crossed her skis, lost her balance, and flailed out with her poles.

He swung into a sharp braking turn and skidded towards her, showering her with shards of cold snow.

She fell on her side with a jarring thump, and heard him roar with laughter. She dug her ski poles into the ground, and pushed herself upwards. Her skis slid away from under her and she fell back down, hard. Bastard; she glared up at him, then at Richard, who was standing with his glove off and his finger up his nose.

Andreas seemed to have come alive here on the slopes; as if he could make up for what he lacked in conversation by a virtuoso performance on his skis. He pushed his goggles up onto his forehead. 'Here, I help.' He leaned over, grabbed her arm in a vice-like grip, and heaved her back up. 'Hurts, doesn't it, to make the fall?' He stared, a piercing hard stare. 'We make a traverse here, into a very good powder bowl I will take you down. Not many people know it.' As he replaced his goggles, she looked at the hand he had used to pull her up, his right hand with the three useless fingers, and she remembered another time she had felt a grip like that, only once in her life, a very long time ago. He stretched his hands behind him and pulled the green hood up over his head, then launched himself off down the mountain and disappeared into a bank of mist.

Sam dusted the snow off her trousers. 'I don't want to ski with him any more, Richard.'

'He's a good skier,' he said defensively. 'Knows this area well. It's good to have a guide with this mist.'

'I don't care.'

'Actually, I think he rather fancies you.'

She stared at him in stunned silence. 'What am I, Richard? Part of your deal?'

He blushed, and scratched his ear. 'Don't be ridiculous. Just keep him sweet, that's all.'

'God,' she said. 'You used to be such a proud man.' She turned away, unable even to look at him, and began to ski down following the direction of the banker. She made a stiff, awkward turn, then another and stopped, her eyes smarting, anger and fear churning her up, fuzzing her brain.

She watched Richard hurtling down too fast as usual, in his hunched, slightly out-of-control style, and disappearing into the mist. She heard the rustling of more skis, and watched another couple ski past, the man slightly stiff, the woman elegant, flowing. The mist swallowed them as well, then there was silence. She was alone, suddenly, on the slope.

She looked around nervously. Her thigh hurt from the fall, and she was cold and wet. She wished she was home, in front of the fire, with Nicky playing on the rug.

Home was a cosy place. A safe place. Somewhere that no longer existed.

She blinked hard, pushed herself forwards half-heartedly, made a poor, jerky turn, then another, trying to get the rhythm, trying to get the enthusiasm. She felt the jar of an edge catching, and her skis crossed. The ground raced up towards her and hit her hard in the stomach, winding her.

'Shit,' she said. She was lying face down, one leg still in its ski jammed behind her, the other free. She crawled back to her feet, put her ski back on, and stared down into the mist that was fast rising up towards her.

Where were they?

'Richard?' she called.

Silence.

'Richard?' she shouted louder, but the mist sucked in her voice like blotting paper.

She eased her skis downhill and made two more turns, then stopped again. She saw a figure a short way below her, a dim silhouette, and skied down towards it. She got closer and saw the metallic green of Andreas's ski suit moving off again, turning sharply to the right. There was a shadow just below her, a piste marker post, with an arrow. She skied down. It was black, a black run, pointing the opposite direction to which Andreas had gone. There was something written on the marker, the name of the run, as there always was, and she peered closer.

AROLEID.

She stared, blinking in disbelief.

AROLEID.

The snow seemed to be swaying underneath her. Rocking her as if she was standing in a boat.

AROLEID.

Sweet Jesus, no.

AROLEID.

It was flashing at her, strobing, corning closer, closer, then it smacked her in the face and knocked her to the ground.

She lay there and stared up at it, numb with terror.

DIE ORAL!

DERAIL.

AIR DOLE.

OR I DEAL.

ORDEAL I.

REDIAL.

She heard a sound like a snigger and spun around. But there was nothing.

She scrambled back onto her skis and stared at the sign again.

AROLEID.

Pointing to the left. The solitary marker in the mist.

She stared into the mist, shaking. Terrified to stand here alone by the sign. Terrified to go. In any direction.

'Richard!' she shouted again, but no sound came out.

The cold gnawed at her fingers, her face, gnawed at her insides as if it was trying to eat its way through her. The mist was thickening and there was a weird dream-like quality to it.

It's OK.

Lucid dream.

I'm going to wake up in a minute.

Please God, I want to wake up.

She thought she heard a sound behind her and turned around. There was a silhouette just above her, like a person, but it seemed to disappear as she watched. The mist, she thought. Tricks with the eyes. 'Richard! Is that you?'

Nothing.

The mist was thickening again and the green suit had disappeared.

AROLEID.

To the left.

The sign Slider had shown her.

No way. No which way, thank you. She turned right, pushing herself off after Andreas, pushing herself away from the sign as quickly as she could. She was gathering speed now down an incline, then felt herself jerk forwards and almost fell as her skis ran from the firm piste into deep powder snow.

The green suit had disappeared completely, but she could see his tracks, and skied in them. 'Wait for me, you sod,' she muttered, turning with difficulty and nearly falling again, trying to remember her powder technique, but the snow was heavy and she missed the tracks, heard a sharp scraping under her skis, and almost lost her balance as she went over a buried rock. Christ. Wait. Wait for me!

The slope fell away and she shrieked as she accelerated sharply. She turned frantically, then turned again, hurtling down a steep unskied gully. She heard the scrape of another rock then slewed on a patch of ice, peering ahead, trying to see where she was going, to see the next bump before it rose up under her and threw her off balance. She stopped, inches from a massive bare rock, backed away, turned, skied over a bump that threw her up in the air, and she came down into deep wet powder, and started shooting up the side of the gully. She tried to turn. She hit another bump and swung around, bounced up hard, then saw Andreas's green suit just ahead. She turned again, then again and stopped, exhausted, gasping for breath, right behind him.

'Christ,' she said, panting. 'That was steep. Are you sure this is right?'

'Yes, this is right,' he said. 'But from here it gets even steeper. It's a good run, but you have to be a little careful.' He pushed his goggles up onto his forehead, and turned around.

Sam screamed.

The backs of her skis crossed and dug into the wall of the gully and she slid forward and jammed the points of her ski poles into the snow, gripped the handles hard, shaking her head, staring in wild disbelief.

Staring at the black hood with slits for the eyes, nose and mouth that he had over his face.

Staring at the metallic green suit.

Slider.

In the dream laboratory.

The metallic green suit.

That suit.

She turned around looking for Richard. Christ, where are you? Then she stared back at Andreas afraid to take her eyes off him, afraid in case—

He was smiling, enjoying himself, enjoying watching her shake. He touched the hood with his ski glove. 'Silk balaclava – very good for keeping the face warm. We go into deep powder soon. It sprays up and makes the face cold.'

Calm down.

For Christ's sake, calm down. Just a balaclava. Lots of skiers wear balaclavas.

Only a bloody balaclava!

Only a green metallic suit.

Coincidence. That's all.

He tugged his goggles back on and beckoned her with his hand.

She stared, not wanting to move, but her skis began to slip, and she had to jam her poles into the snow again to stop herself from skiing straight into him. She turned her head, staring back up the gully.

Richard. Please come.

The mist lifted a little and she could see how steep and narrow it was.

'It's lucky for you I stopped here,' he said, still smirking. 'You could have had a nasty fall.'

She saw a shape appear at the top. It was Richard. Her heart leapt with relief.

He started down, turned, crossed his skis and fell head first. She watched anxiously as he lifted his face out of the snow, then he waved at her.

She looked back at Andreas. Was this a dream? Was this a lucid dream?

I'd really like to wake up now. Except she knew this time she was awake.

'Come!' Andreas said. 'Come slowly, be very careful. I want to show you.'

I think it is possible that he's someone in the present, now, who is bothering you, worrying you – someone that you are associating with this Slider.

She edged forward, unable to take her eyes off his face, until she was beside him.

'Now look.' He pointed down.

She peered over the ledge she was now standing on; the gully opened onto a narrow couloir which dropped

357

away almost vertically. It was filled with rocks and loose snow, and its sides were rounded and covered in smooth ice, like the barrel of a cannon. It became narrower as it went down, finishing in a shelf that she could not see beyond.

'You must be very careful down this couloir, and not fall,' he said, grinning again. 'You won't stop if you fall. There is a bad drop at the end. You must turn immediately right and make a traverse. If you fall, you will go three hundred metres onto rocks.' He jump-turned and skied gleefully down as if he was on the nursery slope, swaying his arms, pumping his legs, leaping almost like a dancer, gaining speed, ignoring his own warning.

She turned and saw Richard getting ready to start down towards her again.

'Richard, be very careful here,' she called. 'Stop where I am – don't go too fast.'

He raised a hand in acknowledgement, and she set off down, slowly, petrified, turning awkwardly through the rocks and the rubble. She halted at the bottom, and froze. The slope below her became a sheer ice wall that fell away down into the mist below; she felt her head swim with vertigo, and inched back, away from it, turning around to warn Richard. He had stopped several yards above her. 'All right?' he shouted.

'Be careful. Be really careful here, it's a sheer drop.' She edged further backwards, afraid to turn around until she was several feet back up the couloir. Richard was still waiting for her to get clear. Silence, she thought. A frightening, terrible silence.

Where the hell was he taking her, this man? This creature. This thing. Whoever he was? She stared back up at the couloir. Christ, it would be a nightmare to climb that. It was four o'clock. The light would be going soon, particularly if the mist got worse again. The runs would be closing, and the pisteurs would be making their sweeps of the pistes. But not here. This wasn't a piste. They'd never get back up there before dark. The only way was to keep going down.

You have to meet your monster, Sam.

I'm meeting him, she thought, starting the traverse across the icy narrow ledge, with the sheer drop to death two feet away. She was gathering speed, she realised, and the ledge was too narrow to turn. She stemmed the skis outwards in a snowplough and began to slide out towards the edge.

She eased them back, parallel, and the icy ground was hurtling past faster, the wind whipping her face. Out of the corner of her eye she saw Andreas, laughing through his hood, then the ledge opened up into a huge slope and her skis ran off the ice into deep soft powder snow. She stopped and looked down. It was steep. Far steeper than she normally skied. The slope went down for several hundred feet then eased into a more gentle gradient, down to a lip. Beyond that seemed to be another sheer drop.

Somewhere above was the clatter of a circling helicopter; ski patrol, she thought, straining her eyes with sudden hope, but she could not see it.

A savage gust of wind blew, whipping the surface snow up into a bitter stinging mist that she had to turn her face away from. She stared up at the sky again, dark blue through her goggles, like deep silent water. The clattering was fading into the distance.

Behind her Richard's skis scraped on the ice; he had stopped at the lip and was peering down at the sheer ice wall.

'Where the hell are you taking us, Andreas?' he

shouted. 'We're not bloody mountaineers. Are you trying to fucking kill us?'

Andreas grinned at Sam, ignoring him. 'This snow is sitting on ice. You must not traverse. Make your descent straight down. Short turns. Follow in my tracks exactly. If you traverse, you could cut it away and it will avalanche. Follow me exactly. If you are not turning in the right place, you go over the lip at the bottom. There's another ice wall. Sheer.'

She stared down, then looked at him. The fear was paralysing her.

Andreas launched himself, compressing his body, exploding in a spray of powder, compressing again, exploding again, turning, sharp tight turns, controlling his speed. He compressed again, but came up oddly, twisting, tried to recover but he fell face forward, somersaulted and disappeared completely for a moment in a spray of snow. One hand emerged, then his head. He lifted himself up a fraction, and put his hands over his face.

She knew what she had to do, knew that she had to go now or she never would. She launched herself gingerly down, making the first turn, in Andreas's tracks, too slowly. She had not enough momentum and her upper ski caught in the heavy powder and nearly pulled her over. She jerked it free, panicking, and turned again, gathering speed now, too much. She turned again, then again, surging; she saw Andreas fifty yards below her, and beyond him the lip, a long way down. Don't look down. Don't fall. Her muscles were so clenched she was turning all wrong. She was trying to slow, but she was not slowing; she was accelerating.

Twenty feet above him she turned out of his tracks and began to traverse across the slope, accelerating fiercely now.

'Bugs!' she heard Richard scream. 'Don't traverse! Bugs! Turn, for God's sake, *turn*!'

The lip was rushing up.

She was going too fast to turn now.

'Bugs! Turn! Turn, Bugs! Fall over, for God's sake! Fall over!'

It was getting closer.

She screamed; tried to force her skis to turn. Tried right. Then left. The lip was hurtling towards her.

Then the snow exploded around her. Her neck cricked painfully and she was lying flat on her back, staring at the sky.

She heard Richard's voice, anxious.

'Bugs? You OK?'

She felt her heart thumping. She rolled over and the snow moved under her. 'Fine,' she shouted. 'I'm fine.' She pulled herself up, brushed the snow off her goggles and saw Richard looking fearfully down, first at her, then at the long cut she had made in the snow. Andreas, a hundred yards above her now, still had his hands over his face, and she saw blood running down his gloves.

'Andreas!' Richard shouted. 'Are you all right?'

The gradient was more gentle here and she was still some way from the lip. Both her skis had come off, and she hauled them out of the snow, laid them down, and reset the bindings. Richard waited. Andreas was sitting, his hands covering one eye, and she looked again at the diagonal line she had cut above him as she pushed her foot back into one ski, and trod down hard, trying to get the lock of the safety binding to snap home, her hands numb, her mind numb.

There was a sound like a clap of thunder, and she felt as if someone had kicked the soles of her feet. Cracks began to appear in the snow above her. They spread out, like veins.

Like eggshell, she thought.

There was a loud rumble, and the ground began to shake. The cracks spread out all around her, with a strange, terrifying sound, like a giant sheet of parchment being torn.

Like a giant eggshell cracking.

Like the ceiling of the hotel room.

She heard Richard's voice scream at her: 'Go, Bugs. *Go!*'

She tried to move, but she was frozen with fear.

Frozen as if she was in a nightmare.

'Go, Bugs!'

There was a whiplash crack and a chunk of snow slid away right beside her. She heard the roar of a breaking wave above her, and looked upwards; saw the cloud moving down the slope towards her, saw it in slow motion, boulders of ice and the foaming spray of snow.

She pushed herself forwards, trying to skate with the one ski she had on, her other foot sinking into the deep powder.

The roaring was becoming deafening now and she heard a mad howling wind, felt it blasting her. She was almost at the edge, almost, then the snow slid away under her and she was falling.

The wind tore at her face, its wailing banshee howl in her ears, then she felt the pressure pushing in on them.

She heard the drumming and thudding of falling rocks and ice all around her, a crazed, accelerating, terrifying cacophony, like a million footsteps racing down a tunnel. The clatter and rattle and howling, echoing, getting louder.

Swim. Try and keep to the surface.

She moved her arms. Something hit her on the head, blinding her with pain, then she was tumbling again.

She felt her hands sliding down something bitterly cold that was burning them.

The ice wall.

She was spinning.

Vortex, she thought.

The mad dark roaring was all around her. Something smacked into her cheek and hurt, then she was falling, free for a moment. She bounced off something hard, then something else again.

Then she stopped moving. She could hear the mad noise continuing all around, the drumming and rattling and howling, becoming more muffled, slowing down. Distant.

And then silence.

She lay in darkness. She closed her eyes tightly, then opened them again. But she could see nothing at all.

She tried to move her hands. They would not move.

She tried her legs – her head. It was as if she had been set in cement.

She began to tremble.

The void. The void that she had dreamed of when the Mercedes had crashed, and gone over the edge.

The void where she would never see Nicky again.

Nor Richard.

Nor anyone.

She felt the terror surge through her. Half an hour.

Half an hour was all you had if you were trapped in an avalanche. After that you were virtually given up for dead.

Where was she? How far down? How deep?

She felt the cold all around her.

And the silence.

This is death.

She tried to move. Her right hand felt loose, but something was trapping it.

The strap of the ski pole. She wriggled her hand, and it came free. She was able to touch her face. She ran her fingers over her forehead, her nose, her mouth. It is me. I am alive. She touched her cheek. It was stinging.

Which way up am I lying?

They had talked about avalanches so much in the past. Joked about them. Discussed what to do. They said that you crapped yourself in the fear. That was how the dogs found you. From the smell.

She wondered if she had done that.

How embarrassing. If they found you like—

Spit. Someone had once said that you should spit. If the spit landed on your face you knew you were lying on your back. She spat. Damp spots landed on her forehead.

'Help me!' she shouted. 'I'm here! I'm here!' But she could tell, from the flatness of the sound, that her voice was trapped with her inside the tomb.

At least I could be unconscious, she thought. At least I could have been knocked unconscious and allowed to die without waking up.

A drip fell on her face; then another. Melting snow.

Where was Andreas? Richard? Was Richard buried in it too?

They were way off the piste, down the side of the mountain. Would anyone even have seen the avalanche? She put her hand up and pushed. Hard as rock. She tried to scrape with her glove. It slid, uselessly.

Ski pole, she thought, putting her hand down and grasping the top of it. But it would not move.

Something sharp, metal. There must be something.

She pulled her glove off with her teeth, feeling another drip as she did so, and scraped at the snow with her fingers. Cold shards dropped onto her face, into her eyes. Her goggles must have come off, and she was suddenly annoyed that she had lost them. Maybe they'll find them? Maybe they'll find them even if they don't find me?

Identified by my goggles.

Her hand was getting cold. Conserve heat. She wriggled it back into her glove, then tried again to free the ski pole, yanking it, twisting it around, but it was jammed. She closed her eyes and punched the snow above her head, listening to the muffled thuds. It felt good to make a noise. To break the silence. The dark silence.

Could you breathe through ice? How much air did she have?

She heard a sound, like a handful of pebbles flung against a window. Right above her.

Her heart raced. They had found her. Found her!

Then nothing. She heard a faint echo. It could have been a footstep a few yards away, or an explosion way in the distance.

She punched the snow again, in anger, despair, closing her eyes against the falling slivers. It seemed to give a fraction, or was she imagining it? She punched as hard as she could, and suddenly her hand broke through. She felt a shower of snow over her face and down the inside of her sleeve. She wiped her face and opened her eyes.

Daylight.

Brilliant white daylight.

She stared at it through a small hole, barely wider than her fist.

'Hey! Help me!'

The daylight seeped into her tomb and she could see around her.

Could see that she was not alone.

That there was someone else in here with her.

Could see the livid red eye socket staring sightlessly through the slit in the blood-stained hood. Inches above her face. As she looked, another drop of blood fell from the socket down onto her cheek.

She screamed. And screamed again.

Andreas's hooded face inches above her, squeezed out of the roof of the tomb like a gargoyle. His mouth was open in a twisted smile and the eye socket gaped, stared at her, seeing as much as his good eye which was also staring at her from its slit, staring blankly, not moving or blinking.

Oh sweet Jesus no. No.

Then she saw the hand at the strange angle above her, as if it did not belong to the same person as the face; the hand, stripped of its glove, the deformed hand, withered, with just the thumb and the little finger, sticking motionless out of the snow like a claw.

She shook her head, trying to turn away, trying to look up through the tiny hole she had made at the daylight. Then the daylight darkened, and for a moment it vanished completely. The ground around her seemed to be drumming, shaking.

Oh God don't avalanche again. Don't move. Please.

She saw blades rotating above her.

A fan.

Black blades.

Descending down towards her, whirring madly.

Propeller.

The fan.

The ceiling cracking.

Eggshell.

The black blades.

Helicopter.

Then they began to move further away. The drumming stopped.

Helicopter.

Oh please come back. I'm here. Please come back.

But it had gone.

'Help!' she screamed. 'Help! Help me!'

She heard a scrabbling, rattling sound above her, and voices, excited. *'Ici! Ici! Ici!'*

There was a sudden, deafening rumble, and a shower of snow and ice fell onto her face. Andreas's face was shaking, vibrating as if he was laughing, the black hood lifting up and down as if he was still alive, still breathing, still mocking. The head was coming closer, nearer, inching down to her, inching down as if he was trying to kiss her.

No. No. No. No.

There was another rumble. Then the light went and she was in pitch darkness again.

Entombed in darkness and silence.

In the void.

In the void where you could scream for ever.

Her eye lashes touched something, soft, cold, damp, flicked backwards and forwards, making tiny scratching sounds as the face came closer, started pressing against her face.

She pushed her head away, swivelled it backwards and forwards, trying to drill into the ice behind, but all the time she could feel the face pressing more and more, the hard cheekbones through the silk pushing into the side of her own mouth, pushing harder and harder, grinding, as if their two heads had been put together inside a vice which was slowly being tightened.

The pain was getting worse. It was getting harder to breathe, she was gulping and choking, trying to think through the terror that was blinding her even more than the darkness.

You're smothering me.

You're crushing me.

You're hurting me so much.

Then she felt the explosion inside her head.

Like a light bulb.

And everything stopped.

46

A bald man smiled at her out of the darkness, and stretched his arms down towards her.

She shrank back, tried to kick out at him, but her legs wouldn't move. 'Leave me alone!' she screamed.

He blinked, startled, then smiled again, a gentle reassuring smile. Sam frowned. Different, she realised, quite different. Large warm eyes and a bushy black beard. 'It's OK, please, it's OK,' he said.

She watched him, puzzled. Puzzled by the vibration and the dull roaring din that echoed around as if she was inside a tin drum, and the curious smells of rope and oil and grease and exhaust fumes. She heard the snap of a shackle, the clank of a chain, and a voice shouting; the man with the beard shouted something back which was drowned. Someone squeezed her hand.

'It's OK, Bugs. You're fine. You're going to be OK.'

Richard.

She turned her head a fraction and saw fir trees slide past, then a blue wall of ice, then nothing but a grey haze, as if she had just caught the end of a home movie.

'How you feel?' The man with the bushy beard was leaning over her again.

'My leg hurts.'

'We give you something for it. Do you have allergies to any drug?'

She shook her head. It hurt to do that. 'Where am I?'

'In the helicopter. We will have you in hospital in Visp very quick now. Just we wait a few more moments.'

Her hand was squeezed again, and she felt her forehead being caressed. She closed her eyes and immediately felt sick. She opened them and saw Richard standing over her. He stroked her forehead. 'You're OK. You're going to be fine.'

Beside him she noticed the silhouette of the Matterhorn spin past in the distance. She sat up a fraction, ignoring the pain, remembering.

'Lie down, Bugs. Don't try to sit up.'

She could see a sheer wall of ice, steely blue, dropping away below a long gully. Near it, a wide strip was missing from the side of the mountain.

That was where she had been.

It went out of sight for a moment, then she could see it again clearly, just below her. They were level with the couloir, and she followed it across and down. The top part of the slope which had been covered in powder snow was now rock and mud. To the right, the rock and mud continued all the way down to the lip, and then gave way to the ice wall. To the left, the mud turned into snow, great chunks, like white boulders strewn across, piled up at the bottom making a wall several yards high that stopped just short of the lip; and further to the left, where the ice wall ended and there was a lesser gradient, the ice boulders carried on, stopping short of a second lip below.

On both the higher and lower lips men in brown clothing were trudging through the boulders, fanned out, taking short steps forward and pushing thin metal rods into the snow between each boulder. They raised their heads, moved forward and pierced again.

'Crazy,' said a voice behind her. She turned and saw

the man with the bushy beard look first at her, then at Richard. He shook his head and looked angry, angry and hurt. 'Crazy. You English. Crazy. Why you go skiing down there?' He tapped the side of his forehead with his finger. 'Crazy.'

'I—' But there was no fight in her. 'I'm sorry,' she said.

'I think you have very lucky.'

'Lucky?'

He gestured to the window, and shook his head again. 'You see there? The ice, the walls? It's impossible. Look where you are coming down.'

She could see clearly now. The whole side of the mountain dropped away sheer. If they had succeeded in getting down the slope that had avalanched, they would still . . .

The lip where Andreas had told her to turn ran on around the side for a few yards, then dipped steeply. They wouldn't have seen it from above when they were on it. They wouldn't have seen it until their skis had left it, and they were tumbling down the rock face that fell away sheer beneath it, down a thousand feet or more, into the rolling mist.

47

There was a knock on the door of her hospital room.

'*Entrez*,' she said.

A policeman came in, in his dark blue uniform and black holster, holding his cap in his hand. He closed the door behind him and nodded politely at her. He was short, trim, precise-looking, with neat dark hair and a neat thin moustache.

'Meeses Curtis?'

She nodded.

'Kaporal Julen from the Walliser Kantonspolizei,' he said.

'Hallo.'

'How are you feeling, Meeses Curtis?'

'OK, thank you.'

'You have the ribs broken, and the leg?'

'Two ribs, and my ankle.'

'I hope you do not mind, I would like to ask you some questions?' he said.

'No, of course.'

He pulled up a chair near the bed, and sat down, placing his cap in his lap. 'It is a bad thing, to get caught in an avalanche. We try to make safe on the pistes, but when people going away from the marked routes, without a guide—' He raised his hands in the air.

'Yes.'

'You know – this place where you were, there was no way down? If you 'ad not been taken wiz the avalanche, you would have moz certainly been killed. You could not have skied down further. Impossible to ski. Why did your 'usband take this route, down this couloir?'

'It wasn't my husband. It was Andreas.'

'Andreas?'

'A business colleague of my husband's. A Swiss. He claimed he knew the area well.'

He frowned. 'I do not understand.'

Something in the policeman's face unsettled her. 'He lives in Montreux and skis in Zermatt a lot, he told me.'

'Who is Andreas?'

'Andreas Berensen. He's a director of the Fürgen-Zuricher Bank, based in Montreux.'

'I don't think so, Meeses Curtis. The ski patrol helicopter see you at the top of the slope, juz before the avalanche. There were only two people.'

'Myself and Andreas. My husband was behind us. We got separated, you see, in the mist.'

He shook his head. 'Only two people,' he said firmly, raising his voice a fraction.

She felt a sudden frisson of fear. 'There were three of us—' Her mouth twitched into a nervous smile. 'There were three of us. Andreas was trapped with me – dead. I'm sure he was dead; his eye was all—' She saw the strange expression on the policeman's face and faltered.

He stared down at his hat, then up at her. 'Are you trying to make a joke with me?'

'A joke?' She flared in anger. 'A joke? You think I'm joking? That I think this is funny?'

He stood up and walked over to the window. 'You come from London?'

'Yes.'

'Nice city. I was there. On holidays. I visit Scotland Yard. Good. Very efficient, Scotland Yard. Always raining in London, yes?'

'Not always.'

He sat down again and placed his hat in his lap. 'You were skiing down this mountain with your husband and with Andreas Berensen?'

'Yes.'

'Broken two ribs; and you have the multiple break of the ankle?'

'Yes.'

'Otherwise you are all right?'

'Yes.'

'Concussion?'

'I don't think so.'

'I think perhaps concussion. Concussion or you are making jokes – or making excuses? You are trying to make blame on someone other for your stupidity.'

Her face was smarting. 'I'm sorry, I don't understand.'

'Don't you?' He thumped his chest, angrily. 'Me, I understand. Every year people dead in the mountains, stupid peoples, who ignore the piste markings, who think they can go off the piste without having to pay for the guide.'

'I'm sorry – I really don't understand what you are saying.'

He glared at her, furious now. 'I think you understand, Meeses Curtees; I think you and your husband understand very well.'

She closed her eyes. Riddles. Riddles. Was this some crazy new riddle? Some new game? 'Could you please explain to me exactly what you are saying? What you are insinuating?'

He drummed his fingers on his hat, then stopped abruptly and looked directly at her. 'Andreas Berensen, director of the Fürgen-Zuricher Bank . . . You and your husband were skiing with this man, yes? He was your guide, yes? You tell me this and your husband tell me this, yes?'

'Yes. Christ, he was buried with me in the avalanche. We were under the snow together. He'd – he must have fallen on his ski tips. His eye was gouged out. He was trapped with me – dead.'

'There was no one with you. I have spoken with the men who rescued you: nothing. They said there was no one with you when they found you. I have spoken to the Fürgen-Zuricher Bank, Meeses Curtees.' He looked at his hat then at Sam again and shook his head. 'They don't know any man of this name. They have never heard of Andreas Berensen. There is no one called Andreas Berensen who lives in Montreux. There is no one in Switzerland who is a director of a bank with this name. There is no one in Switzerland who even has a passport in this name.' He tapped his hat. 'You know why, Meeses Curtees? Because he does not exist, that is why.'

48

'Dead men don't climb out of avalanches, Sam.'

But dreamers wake up from dreams, she thought, glancing round the restaurant. Four businessmen sat at the next table studying the lunchtime menus. Although it seemed empty, there was an air of expectancy about the place. It was still early. In half an hour it would be full, Julio would be turning away the punters with a smile, a raised eyebrow, a humble peasant shrug. Scusa. Sorry. So sorry.

Ken leaned forward, in his crumpled denim shirt, studying her face carefully, and broke a roll in half, spraying crumbs over the tablecloth. The waiter swept the Orvieto from the table and poured it into their glasses with flourish, as if he was watering a couple of plants.

Ken shook out a cigarette and tapped the tipped end hard on his watch. 'Richard saw him swept away?'

'Yes.'

'And you were trapped with him?'

'I – thought so.'

'And he was above you?'

'Yes.'

'So the rescuers would have dug him out first?'

She nodded.

'And they saw nothing?'

She picked up her glass and drank some wine. 'No.'

He lit the cigarette, inhaled, and slowly blew smoke

out of his nostrils, rolling the cigarette around between his finger and thumb at the same time. 'So you imagined it?'

Her brain did not seem to want to work, did not seem to want to tackle the problem; the insides of her head felt flat, inert. 'Andreas must have been swept off the precipice – I suppose – and I was just imagining I was trapped with him. The bash I had on my head – perhaps that's what – it's just that it—'

Tiny crows' feet appeared either side of Ken's eyes as he smiled.

She shrugged. 'It seemed so real.'

'Being buried in an avalanche – must have been very frightening.'

'It was freaky. I thought I was going to die. I really thought, you know, that was it. When I saw his face – Andreas – I felt – I—' She glanced down at the table cloth, then across at the door where a knot of people were standing; Julio was helping a short fat man off with his coat, with clinical efficiency, as if he was peeling a large orange.

Ken raised his glass. 'It's good to have you back. I've missed you.'

'It's good to be back – I've missed—' She hesitated and blushed, and glanced away; she heard the clink of their glasses, and took a mouthful of wine, cold, steely, then winced as it touched a cracked filling.

'When are you planning to come back to work?'

'After lunch.'

'You're joking.'

'I'm serious. I'm starting again this afternoon. Ten days in a Swiss hospital is enough sitting around. I'm pretty nippy on my crutches.' She smiled. 'And I don't want Claire getting my job.'

He sniffed his wine, took a large sip, drew on his cigarette and carefully knocked the ash into the ashtray. He studied the tablecloth thoughtfully, then looked up at her. 'Claire's left.'

Sam stared at him, numb with surprise. She shivered, feeling cold, suddenly. Cold, damp; she wondered for a moment whether the heating was on in the restaurant. She eyed him carefully. 'Left? Claire?'

'Uh huh.'

'How – when?'

'She never turned up the day after your avalanche. I got a note two days later.'

'What – did it say?'

'Nothing. "I regret that I shall not be able to continue working for you." Signed, Claire Walker, brackets, Miss.'

'That was all?'

'Uh huh – really dumped us in it – you were right – I should have listened to you. The bloody cow.'

'And she hadn't said anything to you before?'

'Nope.'

'How on earth have you been coping – I mean – so you've had no one there—?'

'Drummond's been a good lad. We've got by.'

'Bloody bitch. God, she might have waited until I'd come back. You've always treated her fairly – just to walk out like that—'

He drew hard again on his cigarette, nodding, and blew the smoke away from her. 'That's staff, isn't it?' He picked up his glass and leaned back. 'So what's Richard going to do about his money?'

'He says the bank – in Montreux – is lying. He's had several meetings during the past few months with Andreas, actually at the bank – there's no question he was a director. It was obviously all part of the covering of tracks – it's been a bit too thorough – it seems that Andreas covered the tracks a little too well.'

'So Richard's hoist on his—?'

She nodded. 'His money has vanished. Gone.'

'What's he going to do?'

'He'd set all this up because he thought he was going to lose his job and that he might have his accounts frozen. But it looks as though that won't happen now – the case against him is being dropped. His solicitor told him last night.'

'What's the reason?'

She raised her eyebrows, and smiled a thin smile. 'Richard's not sure. It seems that one of the key prosecution witnesses has vanished.'

Ken looked hard at her, then dug his hand into his breast pocket and pulled out a buff envelope. 'This one?' He handed it across to her, and she took it, her eyes locked on his, frowning.

The envelope was not sealed; she slid her fingers inside and pulled out a black and white photograph, which she laid down on the tablecloth. It was a page of a book divided into three panels, a large one at the top and two smaller ones beneath. She glanced up at Ken and down again. Then she saw him. The bottom right hand panel. She leaned down, closer and felt a creeping sensation up the back of her scalp.

She saw the hand first, the small deformed hand, with just a thumb and little finger, the middle three fingers missing; then the face, the cold, rather correct face, with the high forehead, the fair hair neatly groomed either side of the head but thinned to a light fuzz on top. The only thing different was that he was wearing spectacles, round, metal rimmed, that had a dated look to them. He

377

was standing in front of a building, in a suit with all three buttons done up, and looked as if he was unhappy about the picture being taken.

'Andreas,' she said. 'That's Andreas.'

'How old is your Andreas?'

'Late forties – early fifties.'

'This one would be about ninety-five, if he was still alive. He hanged himself in a prison cell in Lyons in 1938.'

Her legs hit the underneath of the table, jolting it; her head suddenly felt boiling hot and for a moment she thought she was going to be sick. She put her hands flat on the table for support.

'I was watching a documentary on the box a couple of weeks ago, about evil, and black magic, and they showed a picture of this bloke – the hand – it reminded me of your chap you told me about.'

'Who is he, Ken?'

'Claus Wolf. He was a very weird German – heavily into black magic – got involved in several covens around Europe in the Twenties and Thirties. He had something going in Italy and got kicked out when Mussolini had a clean up, and moved to France. He married someone equally weird and they got into ritual sacrifice killings. He was arrested in Lyons, in 1938, on several murder charges, but his wife, Eva, who was eight months pregnant, fled, and is believed to have come to England, posing as a Jewish refugee. They had a four-year-old son she had to leave behind, who was eventually adopted by relatives in Switzerland.'

'And he's Andreas?'

'There can't be too many people with the same deformity.'

'This was all in the programme?'

'No. I know the producer – at the Beeb – so I rang him

and asked if he had any more gen – and he had a word with the researcher – and let me have the photo.'

She sat in silence for a moment, staring at the cold arrogant face. 'It's Wednesday, today.' She looked at her watch. 'Claire said she's always there on Wednesdays.'

'Who?'

'Bloomsbury – can we go to Bloomsbury?'

Ken stopped the Bentley outside the Whole Mind and Body Centre and Sam hobbled in. The woman with the pulled-back hair and pulled-back face was sitting behind her cash register.

'I'd like to see Mrs Wolf.'

'She's not here,' the woman said, with virtually no movement of her lips.

'I thought she always was on Wednesdays.'

'She's ill.'

'Do you know when she'll be here next?'

'She's very ill. I don't know if she'll ever be back.'

'I need to see her.'

'She doesn't want to see anybody.'

'Is it possible to have her address?'

'No,' said the woman. 'It is not possible.' She lowered her voice. 'Go away. Just get out, go away; don't come back. We don't want you here again.'

Sam hesitated. 'I – it's very important – I must—'

The woman half stood up, and for a moment Sam thought she was going to lunge at her. She backed away, stumbling, tripped on the doorstep and dropped a crutch. She leaned down, scooped it up, and looked again at the woman, who was standing upright now, her face filled with hatred, and hurried outside. She climbed into the Bentley, shaking, her face smarting. Ken put her crutches on the rear seat then closed her door. 'Any joy?'

379

'Christ, they're strange in there. She's ill and they don't think she's coming back – and they wouldn't give me her address.'

He was silent for a moment. 'I think I know it,' he said.

Sam looked at him in amazement. 'How? What do you mean?'

He started the car, without speaking.

'What do you mean, Ken?'

He raised a finger, and eased out into the mid-afternoon traffic.

They crawled up Tottenham Court Road, then turned left into Marylebone Road. She watched the lights and the silver flying spur mascot on the bonnet blankly, her mind fogged, unfocusing, a part of her still in the icy underground tomb. They went up the ramp of the Paddington overpass, and she glanced again at Ken, trying to find some clue in his expression. They turned off towards Shepherds Bush, came to the end of the expressway and joined the slow heavy traffic.

They went through Acton and into Ealing. Ken stopped twice and checked the A–Z, and they navigated a maze of back streets, finally stopping outside a crumbling Victorian mansion block.

He opened the door for her and helped her out of the car. 'I'll come with you, be your minder.'

'How do you know this is—?'

'I don't; but I think I'm right.' They looked at the names on the entryphone. It was written in pencil and faded so badly it was barely legible. '2 Wolf' was all it said.

She looked at Ken again, puzzled. 'I don't understand.'

'I think you will.'

She was about to press the buzzer, but Ken stopped her and, instead, pressed one for another flat.

'Harry? That you Harry?' said a grumpy old woman's voice.

'Parcel – special delivery,' Ken said, then the latch buzzed and he pushed open the front door, holding it for Sam.

The corridor was dark and dank and smelt of boiled cabbage; the linoleum on the floor had rucked up and was uneven to walk on.

'Wait here,' Sam said. 'It'll be better on my own.'

'You sure?'

She nodded and carried on into the gloom. She squinted at the first doorway on the right, which was number 1, then reached the far door, smelled a strong smell of cats, and saw the faded brass number 2 on the door. She hesitated for a moment, and listened. Somewhere behind her she could hear a television turned up much too loud. She glanced around, and pressed the buzzer; there was a grating metallic rasp which echoed around. Then a long silence. She was about to ring again, when she heard footsteps, firm, quick.

The door opened, and Claire stared out at her.

Sam blinked in disbelief.

Claire.

Claire staring at her, matter-of-factly, no trace of surprise.

As if she had been expected.

Sam stumbled back, confused. 'Claire?' she said.

'Why have you come here?' she said, icily.

'I – I thought – I – I wanted to see Mrs Wolf.'

'My mother has had a stroke and can't see anyone. Go away and leave us alone.'

'Your *mother*?' Sam shook her head, trembling. 'Your mother?'

'She had the stroke when she saw her son fall in the avalanche. She saw it all.'

'Saw it?'

'My mother sees a lot of things.'

'Where did he fall?'

'He went over a drop, fell a long way down, then through deep snow and onto a frozen lake. They will find him in the spring.'

Sam stared at her, unable to speak.

'You've killed both of her sons. Isn't that enough for you? Why don't you leave my family in peace now?'

The door closed firmly and she heard the sound of the safety chain. She stood in silence too shattered to move.

'Sam? You OK?'

She saw the red glow of Ken's cigarette. Slowly, she hobbled down the passage towards him.

'OK?'

She stopped in front of him. 'You were right,' she said. She tried to read his face in the dim light, then she heard a noise that sounded like a door handle behind her, and turned fearfully. But there was nothing.

She climbed into the car and sat in silence as they drove away, watching the lights of the traffic and the darkness.

'You've had no more dreams, since?' he said.

'No.'

'I wouldn't talk to anyone else. I wouldn't dig any further, Sam. Try to forget about it. It'll heal in time.'

'I wish I could believe that.'

'Don't you?'

She shook her head.

'If the mind's got the ability to see the future, Sam, then I'm sure it's got the ability to forget the past.'

'Maybe.'

'Forget it all. The hooded man's dead and buried.

Both of them are now. Bury him in your own mind, too.' He tossed his cigarette butt out of the window. 'Forget it. Forget the past. It's over. You've met your monster – isn't that what someone said to you?'

She nodded.

'You've met your monster – all your monsters – and you've beaten them.'

'Life's full of monsters, Ken.'

'Life's full of survivors, too.'

Maybe it was an hour later that Ken dropped her off at Wapping. Maybe it was several hours. She seemed to think they'd stopped and had a drink, or perhaps she was confusing that with another time. Her head was a blur of burning pain and she was shaking all over.

She went into the lift and pressed the button for the fourth floor and the door slid shut and the light came on and they began to move upwards, slowly, shuffling and clanging, it seemed to be going slower than ever. It stopped, with the same jerk that always unbalanced her, but this time it seemed even more vicious and she was thrown against the side.

There was a sharp pop, and the light went out. She felt the sting of glass on her face, and yelped.

Then there was silence. She waited for the door to open, but nothing happened.

She fumbled her fingers down the control panel, trying to find the round 'Door Open' button, her heart thumping. It ought to be at the bottom of the panel, she knew. She felt the indents of the floor selectors, reached the bottom one, then nothing. Just cold smooth metal. She moved her hand up, counting. Ground, First, Second, Third, Fourth, then smooth metal again. She pressed a button at random. Nothing. Tried another. Nothing. She gave the door a thump with her fist and heard the dull metallic boom echo around. She thumped it again.

Alarm bell, she thought. There was an alarm bell. Higher up; or was it the last button? She pushed each button in turn. Nothing. Nothing. Suddenly the door began to open, slowly, scraping, and her heart leaped with relief.

Then she screamed.

Screamed and fell back across the tiny lift.

Pressed herself hard against the wall as Claire came in through the door with a sickle in her hand, raised above her head.

'No! Claire, no!'

She flung her hands up and felt a raw terrible pain as the grimy, muddy blade sliced into her arm. She tried to fend Claire off with a crutch, but the demented woman tore it out of her hand and flung it, clattering, into the corridor.

'Richard!' she screamed, 'Oh my God Richard, help me!'

The blade smashed into her hand, slicing off fingers, then into her chest.

'Richard!'

It gouged into her chest again, searing her with pain, then it crashed into her head; she heard the clang; felt the agonising pain, closed her eyes, opened them again, saw Claire's face right up against hers, her eyes blood-shot, flooded with crazed pleasure, saw the hand rise up again, then a million red hot spikes were being ground into her skull.

Claire jerked sharply backwards; Sam saw her dimly, skidding across the floor, a hand holding her hair, shaking her head like a rag doll, saw her flung against the wall, a startled look in her eyes, saw the sickle smash into the wall, then drop out of her hand. Richard.

Richard shaking her, wild with rage, smashing her head into the wall, again, then again, until she slumped senseless onto the floor. He turned towards her.

'Bugs?'

Sam stumbled forwards, reeling. Richard was now a dim blur. She fell towards him.

'Bugs?'

There was silence.

'Bugs? You OK?'

The blood covered her face, poured down it, poured through her clothes.

'Bugs?'

Light came on. Brilliant dazzling white hospital light, a doctor staring into her face, and beyond him she saw the painting of a nude on the wall, and she realised it wasn't a doctor, but it was Richard.

'You're OK, Bugs, it's all right. You're OK.'

She ran her hand across her face and stared at it. Water. Perspiration; it was only perspiration. She stared at her hands; counted her fingers, slowly: they were all there; not a mark.

'Was that another?' he said. 'Was that another of your nightmares?'

She shook her head. 'No. It was different. Different.'

He leaned forward and kissed her on the forehead.

She was panting, she realised, panting and gulping down air. She lay back and listened to the sound of her own heartbeat pounding inside her chest that was as tight as a drumskin. 'It was different, this time. It was fine. Just a dream,' she said, loudly, clearly, as though she wanted the whole world to hear; as though, if she said it loudly and positively enough, she might even believe it herself. She closed her eyes for a moment, and saw Claire's head smash into the wall again, and again. Saw the glazed beaten expression in Claire's eyes as she

385

slumped to the floor. Then she looked back at Richard and smiled.

'It was just a dream.'

SWEET HEART

Acknowledgements

Research is essential to my novels and there are many people who in the writing of *Sweet Heart* generously gave me much more of their time and their knowledge than I ever asked of them. They include Eleanor O'Keeffe of the Society for Psychical Research, David and Anne Anderson who so kindly and enthusiastically allowed their beautiful home to be the model for Elmwood Mill, Jan Newton, David Venables and Bill McBryde of the Official Solicitor's Office, Simon Fraser of Fraser & Fraser, Vicki and Polar Lahaise, Mick Harris of Brighton Police, Ren Harris, Marie Helene Roussel, Linden Hardisty (who improved my tennis too!), Canon Dominic Walker OGS, The Venerable Michael Perry of 'The Christian Parapsychologist', Dr Duncan Stewart, Robert and Felicity Beard, Ian Wilson of Dean-Wilson, Sarina LaRive, Sue Ansell, Jill Bremer, Dr S. Domoney who successfully churned my stomach, Veronica Keen, and many more.

A special mention is due to my unflagging secretary, Peggy Fletcher, and my equally unflagging agent, Jon Thurley, and editor Joanna Goldsworthy. And to my mother, and to my sister, Genevieve for their constant support, and to my wife, Georgina, who redefined the boundaries of patience.

To Tim and Renée-Jean

'I prithee, sweetheart, canst thou tell me
Whether thou dost know
The bailiff's daughter of Islington?'
'She's dead, sir, long ago.'

(Ballad)

Chapter One

The dog scampered under the rotting gates.

'Peregrine!' the woman called. 'Peregrine! Come back at once!'

No one ever went in there, except for a few local tradesmen who privately admitted it gave them the creeps. Not even her dog, which was nosy and inquisitive and was always going in places he shouldn't, had ever gone in there before.

'Good boy! Come back!'

But her voice was drowned by the weir below. She waited a moment. 'Come on!' she called once more. 'Peregrine!'

Most of the days of her life she walked the dog down the lane, across the iron footbridge and up into the woods, always speeding her pace a little past the property and rarely even looking down at the derelict mill below, with the garden and house beyond with its strange old recluse.

She pushed open one of the tall gates and peered down the drive. Her Yorkshire terrier was running up the steps to the house. Without stopping at the top he nosed his way in through the front door, which was ajar.

'Peregrine!' she bellowed, appalled. 'Come back here! Peregrine!' She hurried down the drive.

The roar of water from the weir made the silence of

the house all the more menacing, and the gravel that scrunched under her feet felt as if it must have been put there to make a silent approach impossible. She stopped at the bottom of the steps, perspiring from the heat of the late summer morning. The house seemed larger from here, rising up the bank above her.

'Peregrine!' her voice was more conciliatory now. 'Peregrine!'

The terrier was barking inside the house, a steady insistent yapping, and she sensed eyes watching her from behind one of the dark mullioned windows; the eyes of the old woman with the hideously burned face.

She climbed the steps and stopped at the top to catch her breath. The dog yapped away inside. 'Peregrine!' she hissed, peering past the oak door into the gloomy hallway.

Then she noticed the milk stacked on the doorstep — five bottles, and a carton of eggs. Newspapers and letters were scattered over the floor inside the door. The house seemed still, felt still. She pressed the bell, but heard nothing; she tried again but it was dead. She rapped the brass hoop of the tarnished knocker, gently at first then harder, the full thud echoing, the dog's barking becoming even more insistent.

She pushed the door open wider with difficulty, the perished draught excluder jamming on the mountain of post, mostly junk mail, that had built up on the oak floor. She stepped in.

The hallway was small, dark, with a low ceiling and stone walls, and smelled unpleasant, of something that had gone off. There was a staircase ahead with a passageway beside it, and doors to the left and right of her. A sinister winged bust stood on an ornately carved table, and her reflection stared back through the dust on a spangled mirror on the wall. The dog was in the gloom at the end of the passageway; she could hear him

2

barking, but could not see him.

'Hello?' she called up the stairs. 'Hello?'

She glanced around, seeking movement, a shadow, and noticed the framed photographs covering the walls. Photographs of elegant women in fine dresses. Except their faces had been carefully burned away, leaving their elegantly coiffed hair, forties and fifties styles, around charred holes. She looked closer, startled. Horrible; the old woman was even barmier than she'd thought.

They gaped down at her, the walls of the passageway solid with them, all faceless. The terrier was pawing and scratching at the door at the end.

'Come here, damn you!' she whispered.

He turned to her, whined, then pawed again at the door. She knelt, grabbed his collar furiously, then felt a shadow fall over her shoulder. She spun round, but it was just the front door moving restlessly in the breeze. The smell was stronger here, vile. The dog whined again and tugged, as if it were trying to tell her something. She wanted to go, to get out of here, but the dog's insistence bothered her. She let go of him and knocked on the door with her knuckles. The dog yapped furiously.

She turned the handle, the door opened and the terrier bolted through. The smell rushed out. Strong, pungently strong. A stench of sour milk, unflushed lavatory and meat that had gone badly off.

'Struth.' She pinched her nose with her fingers. She heard flies buzzing and saw a whole haze of them as she walked in, and heard another sound, too, a faint rustling like expensive silk.

The room felt alive, yet at first there did not seem to be anyone in here. An old drying rack hung above the Aga; an ashtray filled with lipsticky butts lay on the table; an open tin of stew with hair growing out of it sat on the draining board. The fridge door was ajar. That explained the smell, she thought, relieved.

3

Then she saw the old woman's legs.

At first she thought that she was breathing. She was lying face down through the doorway into what looked like a boiler room. The muscles of her legs were moving, and her mouth and left eye, which was the one she could see, were moving too. So were her hands. Her neck rippled like a wheatfield in the wind.

She staggered backwards in shock and retched, but the horror held her throat so tightly nothing came out. The dog stood in front of the corpse barking excitedly. She slammed into the doorway in her panic, then ran down the passage, out through the front door and down the steps.

She could feel them on her own flesh, feel them rippling, chewing, as she hurried back up the drive, brushed them off her thighs, off her wrists, millions of imaginery white wriggling maggots tumbling on to the gravel as she hurried home to the telephone, gulping down the air, trying to flush out her lungs, hurrying because she could see in her mind the old woman staggering out through the door after her, maggots writhing, dropping from her eye sockets, her cheeks, her hands, like white rain, and could hear her screeching, 'Leave me alone! Let them be. Let them eat. It's only my body, my foul scarred body. My prison. They're freeing me. Can't you see, you old cow? They're freeing me!'

Chapter Two

Charley's bike had fallen over earlier in the day and the pedal now caught the chain guard with an irritating clack ... clack ... clack as she pedalled in her sodden clothes, head down against the fine June rain that hung like orange gauze over the sodium streetlights. A stream of cars sluiced past, then a lorry, too close, its filthy slipstream shoving her like an unseen hand in towards the kerb; she swerved.

A thumping beat of music rose up through the rain as a river boat, draped in bunting and lit up like a Christmas tree, churned through the inky water of the Thames and slid out of sight beneath her.

She rode across the roundabout, then up into the quiet of the Tonsleys and turned left into the Victorian terraced street, past the silent parked cars, smart GTIs and BMWs and a couple of Porsches. When they had first moved here, fifteen years ago, it had been a run-down area with derelict cars and mostly elderly people. As first-time buyers with no capital it had been all they could afford. Now it was Des-Res London, with sand-blasted façades and smart front doors and satellite dishes pinned to the rooftops like badges of an exclusive club.

As she dismounted she saw Tom's car parked a short way down the street and felt a beat of excitement. She still looked forward to seeing him at the end of each day; looked forward to seeing him as much as she had when they had first met, twenty years before, when she'd been sixteen; more, she thought sometimes. Especially after some of their arguments, increasingly frequent these days, when she was frightened she might come home to find a note on the table and his clothes packed and gone.

Rain lay on the dark pavement like varnish. She wheeled her bicycle up to the front door, unlocked it and parked the bike on the oak flooring of the hall.

Ben greeted her with a rubber dummy of Neil Kinnock's head in his mouth. 'Hallo, boy!' she said, kneeling and rubbing the golden retriever's chest vigorously with both hands. 'Good to see you boy! Yes it is! No, don't jump!' She shut the door. 'Hi!' she shouted. 'Hi!' Tom called from upstairs.

Charley shook water out of her hair, pulled off her cape, slung it over the newel post and glanced in the mirror.

'Shit!' Her streaky blonde hair was partly matted to her head and neck and partly sticking up in spikes, and her mascara had run down her right cheek. She pulled a face at herself, a charging Apache warrior expression, then prodded her hair with her fingers. 'Not great, huh?' she said to the retriever.

A trickle of rainwater ran down inside her pullover as she went upstairs, followed by Ben, and down the corridor into Tom's den.

The room was dark, cosy, lit with a single pool of light from the Anglepoise bent over the tidy desk. Tom was studying a sheaf of documents bound together with looped pink ribbon. He looked round. 'Hi.'

He was wearing a navy V-neck pullover over his striped shirt and had removed his tie. A tumbler of gin and tonic was by his right hand. He had open, un-cluttered good looks with a hint of brooding temper

6

simmering below the surface that rarely flared with other people, only with herself. A temper that could frighten her with its sudden rages, with the distance it put between them, frighten her because it could stay, like unsettled weather, for days. The way it was now.

'Working late?' she said, walking over and kissing him on the cheek.

'Someone has to earn the money.'

'Hey!' she said. 'That's not fair.'

He stared back down at the documents.

She watched him, flattened. 'Did you play squash?'

'No, had a crisis with a client. Husband's grabbed the kids — had to get an injunction. How was your day?'

'OK. I went to acupuncture, helped Laura in the shop, then we saw *Shirley Valentine*.'

'We've already seen it.'

'Laura hadn't. Anyone call?'

He yawned. 'No. How was the acupuncture?'

'Unpleasant; as always.' She sat on his lap and crooked her arm around his neck. 'Don't be bad tempered.'

He put his hand against her stomach. 'Does your acupuncturist think it's going to work?'

She shrugged. 'Yes, he does.'

'At thirty quid a go he would.'

She looked at his clean, manicured nails. He had always been meticulous about his appearance; even when they had no money at all he had always managed to turn out looking smart. She stole a glance at her own nails, bitten to the quick, and wished she could find the willpower to stop. He used to chide her about it constantly, now he only did when he was irritated by something else.

He wriggled. 'God, you're sopping!'

'The forecast was wrong.'

'I don't think you should be biking.'

'That's daft. Helps keep my figure.'

'Your figure's fine. Cycling's not very relaxing in London and you're meant to be relaxing.' She felt a twinge of anxiety as he yanked open a drawer, pulled a book out titled *Infertility* and tapped it. 'It says here that too much physical exercise worsens infertility problems. It dries everything up inside, or something. I'll read it out, if you like.'

Please don't let's row again tonight, she thought, standing up and walking across the small room. She gazed at the bookshelves, at the toy Ferrari she'd put in his Christmas stocking, at a copy of *Inner Gold*. She picked up a Rubik cube and gave it a gentle twist; dust flew off.

'Did you discuss it with the acupuncturist?'

A car hooted in the street outside; the cubes rotated with a soft crunch. 'He had some pretty crackpot theories,' she said.

'So do you.'

'They're not crackpot.'

'What about the crap therapy thing you went to with Laura. Rebirthing?'

'Rebirthing was good.'

'Great,' he said. 'One session of rebirthing and no sex for two months.' He rocked his drink from side to side, rattling the ice. 'You don't make babies without screwing — or didn't anyone tell you that?'

She was silent.

'You ought to get on and do this regressive hypnotism you keep talking about. You'll probably find you were a nun in a previous life.'

'Laura says —'

'I'm not interested what Laura says.' He drank some of his gin. 'Do you really discuss our sex life with your friends?'

Three yellows lined up down one side. She twisted the cube again. 'Don't you discuss it with yours?'

'There's not much to discuss. We don't have a sex life these days, we have scientific experiments. When did you last *enjoy* sex?'

She put the cube back on the shelf, walked over and kissed him again. 'Don't be like this, Tom. I always enjoy it. It's just that' — she bit her lip — 'time's running out.'

Tom's voice became a fraction gentler. 'Darling, everyone says you didn't conceive before because you worked too hard, because of tension. That's why you gave up work. No one said you have to give up sex.' He took her hand and squeezed it. 'Listen, there's a house I like the look of. The particulars arrived today.' He flipped open a file with a wodge of estate agents' particulars.

As she looked at the coloured photograph in the centre a fleeting sensation of familiarity rose inside her, then sank away like a shadow underwater. The photograph was fuzzily printed and the view of the house was partially obscured by shrubbery. Tudor, more a large cottage than a house, the lower half red brick and the upper plaster with wood beams. It had small mullioned windows and a steeply pitched roof tugged down over it like a hat that was too large. It seemed tired, neglected and rather melancholic.

ELMWOOD MILL, ELMWOOD, SUSSEX. A delightful 15th-century mill house in outstanding secluded position, with outbuildings including the original watermill and large brick barn. In need of some modernisation. About 3 acres. For sale by private treaty or auction at a date to be agreed.

'I think I — I've —' Her voice tailed away.

'You've what?' Tom said.

She shook her head. 'Nothing. I — I thought for a moment I knew the house.'

'What do you think of it?'

'It's very pretty.' She glanced through the particulars. 'Doesn't say a price — it's probably way out of reach.'

'I rang them up.' He smiled triumphantly. 'They're asking two-fifty, but they might take two twenty-five.'

'How come?'

'It's a complete wreck.'

'Just what we want!' she squealed, and Tom was suddenly touched by her glee and enthusiasm, by something that seemed rekindled inside her. A drop of rain water fell on his cheek, but he barely noticed. Even soaking wet she smelled nice. She always smelled nice; it was one of the things that had first attracted him to her. Her face was pretty with an impish toughness behind it, and there was an element of tomboy in her that had always appealed. Her body was slim, but strong and she could look dynamite in a mini and just as good in jeans. She wasn't beautiful, but she had a raw animal sexiness about her that was part of the chemistry between them. It had barely dimmed in all the time they had been together. Until now.

He should be patient and understanding, he knew; he should be sympathetic and caring. Instead he felt chewed up inside. He was guilty about his resentment against her childlessness (when maybe it was his fault — or at least partly his fault). Moving to the country. That was what they had both decided to do. Get out of London, out of the Big Smoke and the Big Hassle. It would be different in the country. It would come right there.

'I've made an appointment for tomorrow. There's some-one else keen, apparently,' he said. 'Three o'clock. OK?'

She nodded and looked down at the photograph. The sense of familiarity returned.

'Have you fed Ben?' she asked.

'Yup.'

'And Horace?'

'Rats, I forgot.'

'You never remember Horace.'

'Teach Horace to bark and I might.' He yawned and closed the file. 'I must get on.'

'How was the lasagne?'

He was already reading his documents. 'Fine.'

She went downstairs. Ben ran after her and over to the front door. 'Sorry, boy, I'm, not going out in that rain. I'm going to have a hot bath. You can go into the garden on your own.' She walked through to the kitchen and unlocked the back door. 'OK, boy!'

Ben sat down and sighed like an old man.

'God, you're a wimp!' She went to the dresser. 'Hi Horace, you don't mind getting wet, do you?' She pressed her face against the glass bowl. The magnified red carp swam over and watched her as if she were a good movie, mouth opening and shutting. 'Had a good day, have you?' She opened the lid of its food. 'How do you feel about moving to the country, Horace? It's a shitty old place, London, don't you think?' She dropped a pinch of food in and it spread through the water like a cloud of fallout. The fish swam unhurriedly to the surface and took its first glum bite.

Elmwood Mill.

Something stirred deep in her memory. Like a forgotten name on the top of the tongue it hung there, tantalising her, then slipped away.

She went upstairs and into the bathroom. As she turned the taps and water splashed out she felt, for some reason she did not understand, afraid.

Chapter Three

The property was by a lake at the end of a mile-long lane that sloped continuously downhill. They had passed only three other houses, the last over half a mile distant. Charley saw the green and white estate agent's board through the trees beside a crumbling brick wall which had jagged glass cemented along the top. Daylight glinted through the slats of the rotting wooden gates.

The appointment was for three o'clock. The car clock said 3.44.

'He must have buggered off,' Tom said.

Charley let Ben out. The golden retriever hurtled clumsily past her, shook himself, then bounded over and cocked his leg against the wall. Eight months old, still a puppy. They had got him when she'd given up full-time work.

The car ticked and pinged and smelled of hot oil. She stretched, feeling flat suddenly, and silently annoyed at Tom for picking her up so late. Always something. For over a year they'd been house-hunting, and every time something was not right. The rooms were too small or the neighbours were too close or someone else got interested and the price went too high. Both of them knew, but rarely spoke, of their need for a fresh start.

Black clouds like locomotives shunted through the blue sky. Gusting wind tugged at the roots of her hair. The foliage, lush from a long spell of heavy rain, bent in the wind and the sodden grass sparkled under the coarse sunlight. Moisture seeped into her shoes.

The lake stretched like a grubby carpet between the walls of trees around it, slapping its creases out against the banks. A solitary upturned skiff lay on a patch of grass in front of them under a faded sign nailed to a tree. 'PRIVATE. NO FISHING. MEMBERS ONLY.' Beyond it was a metal footbridge over a weir, and a path leading up into the woods.

A flock of starlings flew overhead. She felt the chill of the wind, more like March than June, and hugged her arms around herself. She heard the rattle of branches, the woodsaw rasp of a crow, the roar of water from the weir. Behind the sounds was an odd stillness after the bustle of London. Strange not to hear any traffic, or voices.

There was a sharp clank as Tom pushed the gate open, the metal bolt scraping through the gravel of the drive. He was unchanged from court, in his pinstriped suit and Burberry mackintosh. They must look odd together, she in her jeans and baggy pullover and bomber jacket.

Then her heart skipped as she stared down the sweeping drive at the cluster of buildings nestling in the hollow a hundred yards away, between mossy banks that rose up into the woods on either side. The house — a different view from the estate agent's photograph — a brick barn, and a dilapidated wooden water mill.

There was little sign of life. The windows were dark. Water tumbled from the weir into a brick-walled sluice pond below them. It frothed angrily around the motionless wheel and slid in a fast narrow stream through the garden, under an ornamental wooden bridge, past the barn and into a paddock beyond.

Excitement thumped inside her, although the house was smaller than she'd thought it would be, and in worse condition. Shadows boxed on the uneven roof as the wind punchballed the trees; an L-shaped single-storey extension seemed as if it might collapse at any moment on to the coal bunker and an oil tank beside it in a bed of nettles. Then she stiffened.

Something was missing.

She stared around, noticing something new all the time. A bird bath, a shed, a wheelbarrow, a hen run. Two uprooted oak trees leaned against one another on the front lawn, their branches interlocked like fighting dinosaurs.

The hollow had once been the river valley, she realised, before the river had been dammed to make the lake. Apart from the grass, which looked as if it had been cut, it was wild. There were some rhododendron bushes, a few desultory clusters of wild flowers, a small orchard.

Something was missing.

Her eyes were drawn to a level patch of scrub grass halfway up the bank above the barn, between the mill race and the woods. Her armpits were clammy; she felt dizzy and held on to Tom's arm.

'Are you OK?' he said.

Strands of hair thrashed her cheek. A bird chirruped.

The slapping of the waves on the lake. The tumbling water of the weir. The wind in the trees. The quiet. It was touching something, stirring something, like snatches of an old tune.

'Charley? Darling?' He shook her arm. 'Anyone home?'

'What?' She came back to earth with a jolt and felt disoriented for a moment. 'Sorry, I was just —' She smiled. 'It's wonderful.'

'Don't get your hopes too high. There's someone else interested, and we might hate the inside.'

'We won't!'

Ben tore down the drive and loped across the grassy bank.

'Ben!' she shouted.

'It's OK, the house is empty.'

'Why don't we phone the agent and tell him we're here now?'

'Let's go and have a look first.'

The sluice pond was deep and cold. Slime coated the wall. The thunder of water grew louder as they walked down and she felt a fine spray on her face.

'We'd be wanting to pee all the time,' Tom said.

Further on clear water flowed under the ornamental bridge and Charley thought how on warm summer evenings they could have supper, the two of them, by the stream. Bring her mother down on fine days. Convert the barn and maybe Tom's father could live there. If Tom and his father could stop hating each other.

The house seemed larger as they neared it, partly because it sat up above them. The front was the pretty view in the particulars. Elizabethan, one end slanted and the other square. The plaster of the upper floor was crumbling, the wooden beams were rotten and the brickwork of the ground floor was uneven. The windows were small and differing sizes.

They heard a car door. Ben ran back up the drive, barking. A man hurried in through the gates, short and purposeful, a blue folder tucked under his arm, hands and feet pointing outwards like a penguin. He paused to pat Ben, and was rewarded with muddy pawprints on his trousers. He hove to in front of them, puffing, a plump, dapper man in polished black loafers with shiny

15

pens in his breast pocket and alabaster skin.

'Mr and Mrs Witney? I'm sorry, so sorry to have kept you.' He leaned slightly backwards. Wind lifted the hair off his bald pate.

'We were a bit late ourselves,' Tom said.

'Ah yes, tricky to find the first time.' A Rotarian badge glinted smugly in the lapel of his grey suit. 'Budley, from Jonathan Rolls.' His fleshy fingers gave Charley's hand a sharp downward tug, as if it were a bell-pull. 'Moving out of London?'

'Yes.'

'Something like this comes on the market once in a decade.'

'Windows look bad,' Tom said.

'Reflected in the price. So little's been done for years.' He gave his signet ring a twist. 'Dates a long way back — to the Domesday Book. Been added to since, naturally.'

Charley stared up the mossy bank at the level patch of scrub, at the woods, at Ben playing happily, then at Tom, trying to read his face, but it was blank, giving nothing away.

'Wonderful place for children,' Mr Budley added.

Charley caught Tom's eye.

Tom tied Ben to the boot scraper at the bottom of the steps and they followed Mr Budley. The front door was oak with a tarnished lion's head knocker. The wind billowed Charley's jacket.

'How long has the house been empty?' Charley asked.

'Only about nine months. Miss Delvine passed away at the end of last summer,' Mr Budley said.

'Here?' said Charley. 'In the house?'

'Oh no, I don't believe so.'

'I always think it's a bit creepy when someone's actually died in a house,' Charley said.

16

'You know who she was, of course?'

'No.'

'Nancy Delvine.' He said the name in a reverential hush.

Charley repeated it blankly and glanced at Tom. He shrugged.

'The couturier,' Mr Budley said, making them feel for a moment they'd let him down. 'She was very famous in the forties.' He leaned towards them and lowered his voice. 'She made for royalty.' He allowed them time for this to sink in before pointing to a brass plaque above the door with a crude etching of a sun. 'The original fire insurance plaque from 1711. Steeped in history, this house.' He placed the key in the lock and turned it as if he were opening a pearl oyster.

The tiny entrance hall was strangely silent and smelled like a church. There were closed doors with iron latches to their right and left, a narrow staircase ahead, a dark passageway to the right of it. A winged bust stood on the hall table under a pockmarked mirror.

Mr Budley pressed a light switch. There was a sharp metallic click. Nothing happened. The grimy lampshade was fixed to the low-beamed ceiling above Charley's head. She could have changed the bulb without standing on tiptoe.

'The mains power,' Mr Budley said. 'It keeps tripping. The box is in the cellar. We might as well start there.'

They walked along the passageway, Tom's metal-capped shoes echoing on the bare boards. The walls, panelled in oak, were badly in need of a polish and seemed to press in on them. Dozens of picture hooks and nails stuck out of the panelling. Mr Budley stopped beside a door and noticed Charley's expression.

'Valuable paintings. Couldn't be left in an empty

17

house — the insurance.' He opened the door. Thick pipes ran above it. 'It's steep,' he warned, switching on a tiny torch.

Charley felt a draught that smelled of coal and damp as she followed him down the wooden staircase into pitch darkness. He shone the beam of his torch on a dusty electricity meter, then on a metal box with a large handle and a row of ancient ceramic fuses. There was a crackle and a flash of sparks, then a weak light filled the room.

Charley shrieked and clutched Tom. A group of bald, naked shop window mannequins on pedestals stared at them.

'Miss Delvine did some of her work here in the house.'

'God, they gave me a fright!' Charley looked warily around the rest of the cellar. The floor was brick, and uneven. There was a wine rack, a wooden wheelchair and a cast-iron safe. Beyond an opening in the far wall was pitch darkness.

Tom turned to the mannequins. 'All right class, sit down.'

Charley giggled uneasily. The mannequins gazed stonily.

'This lever—' Mr Budley pointed. 'There's a built-in voltage trip. For some reason the circuit keeps over-loading.'

'Seems pretty primitive,' Tom said.

'Needs rewiring.'

The first floor landing was lit by two candle bulbs in a gilded sconce on the wall. A pot stand with a dead plant sat in a narrow recess. The floor was on a slant, as was a window with tatty chintz curtains overlooking the rear garden. With the timber beams and low ceiling it felt like being on an old ship.

'Has anyone done a survey?' Tom asked.

'No. Not yet,' said Mr Budley, 'but there's no problem. Houses like this might tilt a bit but they're solid as rocks. I'd rather be in a house like this when the bomb drops than in any of the modern ones on our books.'

The master bedroom reminded Charley of a country house hotel they had once stayed in. It had beamed plaster walls and a huge carved oak bed with a grimy counterpane the colour of parchment. There was a maple wardrobe, a matching dressing table with a silver hairbrush and a comb and crystal bottles caked in dust. The room smelled strongly of rotting fabric and more faintly of musky perfume.

'East,' Mr Budley said. 'This room gets the morning sun.'

'Good size,' Charley said. 'Plenty of space to build in some fitted cupboards. It's got a nice feel to it, this room.' She stared out of the leaded-light window. The view across the lake was stunning.

'Is the furniture going?' Tom said.

Mr Budley nodded. 'If there's anything you are interested in I'm sure a price could be discussed.'

Behind them was a tiny door through which even Mr Budley had to duck. 'The ensuite bathroom is one of the features of the house,' he said. 'Wonderful taste, quite what you'd expect of a woman like Nancy Delvine.'

It was in hideous bright pink with gold-plated taps. There was an unpleasant carbolic stench, and mildew on the carpet.

'Here we have the airing cupboard and the upstairs lavatory. And this is the smallest spare room, ideal for a young child.' Mr Budley walked on ahead. 'This one is a much better size,' he said as he went into a room at the end of the landing. 'Miss Delvine's workroom,' He announced. 'To think she made garments for royalty actually here in this —'

19

His voice stopped suddenly. His eyes darted round at the treadle sewing machine, at the work surface under the window covered in cuttings of fabrics, bits of chalk and a pattern weighted down by large scissors, at the desk with a sketchpad and a vase full of crayons. There were two tailor's dummies, one bare with 'Stockman 12' stencilled on its midriff, the other partly covered in tattered black taffeta. Sketches were pinned haphazardly around the walls. A showcard of a model in a boa-trimmed hat, white gloves and an elegant dress had a large printed caption at the top: 'CHOSEN BY VOGUE'.

The room felt cold, icily cold. Charley pulled her jacket around her. A bunch of brown paper pattern cards swung gently on a butcher's hook hanging from the picture rail.

'This would make a good study, Tom,' she said. She went to the window. Her eye was drawn to the patch of scrub grass on the bank behind the barn. 'Were there stables here, Mr Budley?'

'Stables?' Mr Budley said. 'No, I — I don't believe so. You could build some, of course.' Hurriedly he ushered them out.

The kitchen was in custard yellow, the ceiling stained uneven ochre with nicotine and the light shade was full of dead flies. There was an Aga. Blackened and ancient in an ugly tiled recess, but an Aga.

'Nice to have breakfast in here,' Mr Budley said.

There was a deep enamel sink, a wooden draining board and dreary fitted cupboards. The floor was brick, which Charley liked. A slatted clothes rack was suspended from the ceiling on a pulley and cord system, a ragged tea towel draped over it. She pulled the cord. There was a creak and the rack wobbled precariously.

'Saves you hanging the laundry out on a wet day,' said Mr Budley.

'It might be nice to keep some of these old things, mightn't it, Tom? Make a feature out of them.'

'Keep the whole house as it is and save a fortune.' Tom winked at Mr Budley, and blew his nose.

'You could,' Mr Budley agreed. 'You could indeed.' He threw open the dining room door with a weary flourish. 'The mill owner was an important man in the community. This is reflected in the size of the reception room.'

It was larger than she expected, with a refectory table that had ten chairs and could have seated more. The beamed walls were wattle and daub, they were informed. There was a recess by the fireplace with a kneehole writing desk and chair. It would be good to have friends for dinner in this room. She pictured them around the table, the fire roaring.

They crossed the hallway. 'The drawing room,' Mr Budley said. His ebullience seemed to have left him.

The room must have been a fine one once and was dominated by the huge inglenook. The curtains across the French windows at the far end diffused the sunlight, and the rich warm glow masked much of the grime and faded colour. There was a peach-coloured sofa with shell-shaped cushions and several matching chairs, a cocktail cabinet that could have come from a state room of an ocean liner and an elegant chromium magazine rack.

It felt strange walking across the floor. Very strange. She had a curious sense of familiarity, and as she opened the curtains of the French windows she felt she had seen the same view before. The bank rose up to the right, the grass rippling in the wind. A chestnut horse was grazing in the paddock beyond the wooden fence. The feeling faded and left her wondering where it reminded her of.

Mr Budley was studying his watch, 'I — ah — have

clients waiting at another property. Would you think me terribly rude it I left you to see the grounds on your own? Or do you wish to go around the house again?'

Tom looked at Charley, then turned back to the estate agent. 'How much interest have you had? You mentioned someone might be offering this week, didn't you?'

Mr Budley glanced over his shoulder as if worried he was being spied on. 'Confidentially, I think an offer of two hundred and thirty would secure this.'

'It needs everything doing,' Tom said.

'Oh yes. No denying.' Mr Budley raised his hands. 'But with everything done it would be worth four to five hundred thousand, at least, with development potential — so much potential. Where can you find a property like this, so close to London yet so quiet? It's really very underpriced. If my wife and I were younger we'd buy this, no hesitation. How often can you buy beauty?' His eyes darted nervously again.

'I'll call you tomorrow,' Tom said.

'You'll make the right decision. I can tell you are people who make right decisions.'

They followed the agent down the steps and Charley held on to Ben as he hurried off up the drive.

Tom puffed out his stomach and covered his mouth with his hand. 'Nancy Delvine lived here!' he said, mimicking Mr Budley.

'Gosh? Really?' she mimicked back.

'Have you ever heard of her?'

'No.'

Charley let Ben go. He bounded towards the stream. A crow swooped down low over him.

'But you used to be in the rag trade.'

'So I don't think she can have been very famous.'

'Well,' Tom said, 'what do you think?'

'I think Mr Budley's a creep.'

'I don't imagine he comes with the house.'

Charley was silent for a moment. 'It's a wreck.'

'We wanted a wreck!'

'Do you like it?' she said.

'I love it! It's absolutely wonderful. I want to live here!'

'I like it too. It's just —'

'Just what?'

'I'm not sure about being so isolated.'

'Christ, we're much safer here than living in the middle of London.'

'I'll probably get used to it,' she said.

'We've got those people interested in Wandsworth so now's the chance. This place is a terrific buy, and if we end up not liking it we'll sell it at a profit in a year or two's time. But we're going to love it.' He clapped his hands together. 'It's what we need — a new beginning.'

'Yes,' she said uncertainly.

A shadow flitted on the ground in front of her. For a fleeting moment she thought it was the crow. Then she heard Tom's shout, saw him leap towards her, saw his hands raise up, felt them shove her sharply backwards. There was a crash on the ground beside her as though a table had been dropped, and a stinging pain in her leg.

She turned, white-faced, shaking. A large slate tile lay where she had been standing, shattered like a pane of glass. Blood dribbled out of the gash in her jeans leg and ran towards her ankle. Tom grabbed her wrist and pulled her further away from the house, out into the middle of the drive.

'You OK?' he said, tugging out his handkerchief and kneeling down.

She looked at the roof, then at the slate, her heart hammering. She winced as Tom pressed the handkerchief over the wound.

'Lethal,' he said. 'Christ, if that had hit you . . .'

23

She nodded silently, staring up again. 'Just the wind,' she said. Another shadow zigzagged towards her and she stepped back out of its path. But it was a sparrow, coming down to take an insect from the lawn.

Chapter Four

Charley opened the door of the cubicle and carried out the two small specimen jars. They felt warm and slightly tacky. Tom followed sheepishly, his cheeks flushed.

The row of people sitting in the low leatherette chairs looked up from their magazines and murmured conversations. Couples, husbands and wives in their twenties, thirties, even in their forties, with nervous faces, anxious faces, desperate faces, clutching their empty jars, waiting their turn, hopefuls all.

She walked selfconsciously down the carpeted corridor and knocked on the door marked 'Laboratory'.

'Come in.'

A young woman sat behind a small desk, writing on a pad with a fountain pen. The name on her lapel said Dr Stentor. She had short blonde hair, was about twenty-six years old and rather hearty. Charley handed her the jars.

'Well, these look jolly good, don't they?' she said in a booming voice. 'Did you manage the split ejaculate?'

Tom gave a single embarrassed nod. He hated this. He had turned up today, reluctantly dutiful, the way he might have attended a distant relative's funeral.

Dr Stentor tilted one of the jars so the grey fluid slid down the side. 'You got the first spurt in here?'

'I'm afraid some of it' — Charley blushed — 'got spilt.'

Dr Stentor squinted in the jar. 'Well, gosh, don't worry. There's enough here to fertilise half of England.' She gave an accusatory glance at Tom. 'That's if they're all right, of course. Jolly good, have a seat.'

They sat down while she went into another room. The telephone rang, three warbles in succession, then stopped. The office was bare, functional, greys and reds. A framed certificate hung on the wall.

'Is it today, your regression hypnosis thing?' Tom said.

'Yes.' Charley saw his smirk. 'Laura —' she began.

Tom raised his eyebrows. 'Laura what?'

'She knows someone who was having problems conceiving. She went to a regressive hypnotist and discovered she'd seen her children murdered in a previous life. She got pregnant very soon afterwards.'

'Tosh!'

'No harm in trying it.'

Tom took out his diary and checked a page. 'No. No harm.'

They sat in silence for a moment.

'What do you feel about the house, Tom?'

'Positive. You?'

'I like it, but it's a big undertaking and I'm still worried about it being so remote.'

'I think it's great it's remote. Peace and quiet! Who the hell wants neighbours?'

She looked at him uncertainly.

'Listen,' he said, 'if we lose our buyer it could be months before we get another chance of anything. At least let's make an offer.'

'OK.'

Dr Stenor returned and sat opposite them. 'Well, it's gone up. Around forty million. Perhaps the boxer shorts are helping.'

'I'm ...' Tom gritted his teeth. 'I'm still dunking them in cold water every day.'

'That's obviously helping too. It is possible for you to conceive with this sperm count. You only have one tube open, Mrs Witney, and it's not brilliant, but there is a chance. If you want to try an implant again we'd be very happy to do it, though we're booked until November. I'll send a report through to your doctor,' she went on. 'I wish there was some magical solution I could offer. Good luck.'

They took the lift down, the smart, plush, carpeted lift. 'It's encouraging isn't it?' Charley said, trying to break the awkward silence between them.

'Encouraging?'

'At least your count's gone up.' She took his hand and squeezed it. 'I feel fine about the house. I'm sure I'll like it. Will you call the agent?'

'Yes,' he snapped, pulling his hand away and digging it into his jacket pocket. 'I said I would.'

'I'll call him if you'd prefer.'

'I said I would.' He hunched up his shoulders and leaned against the wall of the lift like a sulking child. 'I'm not so sure about it now.'

'Why? Two minutes ago you couldn't wait.'

He shrugged. 'I have people come to me every day who've moved house because they thought it would save their marriages.'

'What's that meant to mean?'

He said nothing and she wished she had not asked the question, because she knew exactly what it meant.

Chapter Five

The engine roared gruffly as they accelerated. The black bonnet sloped upwards in front of her, its chromium radiator cap glinting coldly in the moonlight. The exhaust biffed twice as he changed gear, and the note of the engine became smoother.

The dull white lights of the instruments flickered and the thin needle of the speedometer jerkily moved past sixty ... seventy ... seventy-five. The thrills of the speed, of the night, tingled insider her. She felt indestructable as the car raced past sentinel hedgerows, the headlights unfurling a stark chiaroscuro world of light and shadow through the narrow windscreen.

It was like being in the cinema, except it was happening, she was part of it. She could feel the vibration of the car, the inky cold of the wind thrashing her hair around her face, could see the steely dots of the stars above, and smell the tang of wet grass that hung in the air, the perfume of the night.

She was afraid there would be a click, the ride would stop and she'd have to put another penny in the slot. She chewed the gum; the minty flavour had gone, but she still chewed ... because he had offered it to her ... because the girl in the film they had just seen had chewed gum ... because ...

'Who is in the car with you?'

The voice was American, a long way away. It belonged to another time.

The note of the engine changed again, the road dipped then rose and her stomach rose with it. Trees, telegraph poles, road signs flashed past. He braked harshly, the wheels locking up, the car snaking, the tyres yowling as they came into a sharp left-hander. She gripped the grab handle on the door, then relaxed as he accelerated again and sank back deep into the seat. Her body and the car and the road and the night seemed fused into one; the pit of her stomach was throbbing and she could not stop the smile on her face. She turned away, embarrassed, not wanting him to see, wanting to keep her excitement private. His hand left the wheel and squeezed her thigh, and she felt the wetness deep inside her.

Tonight. It would be tonight.

His hand lifted away and there was a grating crunch as he changed gear, then the hand came back, bolder, began to slide her skirt up until she felt his cold fingers on her naked flesh above her stockings.

'Oh,' she breathed, feigning shock, and wriggled slightly because she felt she should react, that she should not seem too keen.

Tonight. She was ready.

'Do you know his name? Can you tell me his name? Can you tell me your name?'

They squealed through a bend and the road widened into a long straight stretching out ahead like the dark water of a canal. The engine was straining and there was a loud protesting whine from somewhere beneath her as his fingers slid about her wetness and pulled away reluctantly as he put both hands back on the wheel. She heard the clunk of the gears and the note of the engine soften. The thrill was accelerating within her, some wild animal instinct aroused, a careless abandon.

His hand came back, one finger probing deep, and she parted her legs a little to give him more room, pressing against the leather seat, blinded by her hair in her eyes. She changed the angle of her head and her hair whipped away behind her.

'Where are you? Do you know where you are?'

The finger slid out and they went into a long curve that threw her against the coarse tweed of his jacket, the tyres squealing like piglets, then the road straightened and she wanted the finger back in again.

She was intoxicated with a raw energy. They snaked through another bend, almost flying now; a rabbit sat in the beam of the lights and the car thudded over it.

'Stop, please stop!'

'You what?'

'Stop. You hit a rabbit.'

'Don't be a stupid cow!' he shouted.

'Please. It may be in pain.' She imagined the rabbit lying in the road, its head twitching, legs and back smashed into the tarmac, fur and blood spread out. 'Please stop.'

He stood on the brakes and she lurched forward, her hands slamming against the dash, the tyres howling, the car snaking crazily. They stopped with a jerk, then reversed. She stared at the black lane behind them, and could see nothing.

'It were just a stone, yer silly cow,' he said. 'Just a stone. We didn't hit no rabbit.'

'I'm glad,' she said.

He turned towards her, kissed her, his hand slid up her thigh, the fingers probed inside, parting her, opening her wider. She smelled burnt rubber, leather, heard the rumble of the exhaust, the knocking rattle of the engine, felt the tweed of his sleeve brush her face. Their lips pressed together, their tongues duelling hungrily, the rubbery ball of her chewing gum rolling around. She tilted her head away, dug her fingers in her mouth and plucked it out. As their lips met again she

30

reached with her left hand towards the window, scrabbling to find the winder. The finger thrust even deeper and she moaned softly, her hand finding the dashboard, the glove locker, and she pushed the gum hard under it out of sight.

The finger worked up and down and strange sensations of pleasure exploded through her body. Her left hand was now on the flannel of his trousers, feeling the heat of his leg. It slid slowly across into the dip that was even warmer, and squeezed the bulging stiffness.

She fumbled for the metal tag of his zipper, pulled it. It stuck. She tugged at it and it opened and she slipped her hand inside, felt the soft cotton, something damp, then she was holding his hard flesh, large, huge, smoother than she'd imagined. She ran her thumb over the top, felt something slimy, slippery, traced her finger along the shaft.

He blew air down her neck and rolled over on to her, tugging her knickers down. She lifted her bottom, helped him, heard the buckle of his belt free.

The thingie.

No time.

His hands slid up her bare skin, under her bra, fondled her breasts clumsily, then gripped her ribs and began pushing his hardness inside her, shoving, thrusting it in, forcing it in. Too big for her; it wasn't going to fit. She thought it was going to split her apart, then it went deeper, rising right in her, thrusting up and down. Her stomach was juddering.

Oh. Oh. Oh. She was gasping. Oh. So good, So good. She pulled at his shoulders, touched his face, his hair, tugged his ears, feeling him further in, further in, pumping. A million pumps working inside her, his breath in her ear, his tongue, panting.

She screamed. Then again. She exploded, howling in wild ecstasy into the night.

Then silence.

Saw his eyes, close, staring, his lips smiling. Except they weren't his lips. It was a woman. Looking down at her.

'Charley? You OK?'

A soft American voice.

'You OK? You were pretty far gone, eh?'

Charley said nothing. Her whole body was burning with embarrassment and perspiration trickled into her hair.

The American woman's face was large like the rest of her, and heavily made up. It was encased in a shock of rusty hair, and clusters of silver balls the size of Christmas baubles hung from her ears. She was smiling encouragingly.

'Who were you, Charley? Who were you with? *What were you doing*?'

'I —' There was a minty taste in Charley's mouth. 'I was chewing gum,' she said.

She was lying on a bed. A red bulb burned overhead in a paper globe. She heard faint strains of a musical instrument which sounded like a sitar. The woman's tongue curled inside her painted lips like the stamen of a rose. Flavia. Charley remembered her name now. Flavia Montessore. She stared around the large dim room. Tapestries on the walls. Bookshelves. Sculptures. A rather grand, ornate room, eastern feeling.

'You were making love, right?' Flavia Montessore asked.

Charley hesitated, then nodded.

'That's terrific!' Flavia beamed. 'You know something? You're my first ever orgasm!'

Charley's hands were beneath the blanket covering her. She found she was still wearing her underwear.

'Don't look so worried,' Flavia Montessore said. 'You were having a good time. Going into past lives can be fun!'

'I — I've never had an erotic dream before.'

Flavia Montessore shook her head and the earrings jangled. 'It wasn't a dream, Charley, it was happening.' She had green eyes and bright green mascara. Her fingernails were green too. 'You were there. It was real. You regressed. You were reliving it. Boy, were you reliving it!'

'It was just a dream.'

'You were in a deep trance, Charley. You weren't dreaming. You were reliving something from a past life. Tell me about it, it'll help you remember too. Where were you?'

'I was in a car.'

'What sort of car?'

'A sports car.'

'What period? Nineteen twenties?'

'No. Later.'

'Do you know the make?'

'I was inside it all the time. I didn't see the outside. I don't know what it was.'

'Where were you? Which country?'

'England,' she said reluctantly. 'I was in the country-side.'

'Can you remember your name?'

'No.'

'The man you were making love with. What about his name?'

'I don't know.'

'You were chewing gum. What flavour was it?'

'It was Wrigley's Doublemint. I can still taste it. I took it out of my mouth and put it under the dash-board.'

'How old were you?'

'Young. My teens.'

'Have you ever been regressed before?'

'No.'

'You're a good subject. I think you could remember a great deal if we worked on it. When I come back from the States this winter I'd like to do some more work with you.'

'I thought past lives were hundreds of years ago, not this century,' she said.

Spangles of light danced in Flavia Montessore's earring. 'There are no rules, Charley. Some people have gaps of hundreds of years between lives, some thousands. Some have only a few years and some come back immediately. It depends on your karmic situation.' She smiled again.

Charley was finding it hard to take her seriously. She had always found it hard to believe in the idea of reincarnation, in spite of Laura's enthusiasm. The hypnotist's heavily made-up face reminded her of a seaside fortune teller. Deep inside was a feeling that she had somehow been tricked, conned.

Chapter Six

'This would go well.' Charley shook the silk square out to show its full design, then draped it around the woman's shoulders. The woman held it by the corners as if it were a grubby sack and stared at herself in the mirror. Her face was taut, like her hair. Charley winked at Laura. Laura gave her a cautionary frown.

'Cornelia James?' The woman looked down at the corner for the signature.

'Of course, madam,' Charley said.

'Does rather suit me, wouldn't you think?'

'Absolutely. And it gives you two outfits.' Charley removed the scarf with a conjuror's flourish. 'Without it, a simple day dress.' She draped the scarf back around, arranging it more strikingly. 'With it, you dress up. Perfect for a cocktail party or the theatre. You'll find it wonderfully cool to wear when it's hot.'

'And you think this blue really is my colour?'

Charley performed a ritual walk of approval, like a Red Indian round a totem pole. 'It definitely suits you. Your husband'll love it.'

'Boyfriend,' the woman said.

'He'll love it too.'

She paid with a platinum card that matched her hair and swept out into the Walton Street drizzle, the rope-handled carrier bearing the emblem of Laura's boutique rubbing against the crocodile scales of her Chanel handbag.

Laura closed the door behind her and tossed her imaginary hair back from her face, still not used to the fact that she'd had it cut short. She was attractive, with rather boyish features, and her cropped brown hair made her look even more masculine. A rack of linen jackets swayed in the draught behind her. The summer displays looked bright but uninviting against the June rain.

Charley clipped the American Express slip into the till. 'Lady Antonia Hever-Walsh, my dear, no less,' she said. 'What a cow.'

'She's a good customer,' Laura said tartly.

Charley wondered what had happened to Laura's sense of humour recently. She was normally far ruder than Charley about customers she did not like, which was understandable, since she had to put up with them for six days a week while for Charley, helping out in the boutique was a hobby.

A horn blared from the stationary traffic in the street. Someone under a red umbrella peered in through the window, then hurried on. Ella Fitzgerald's voice drifted from the speakers; Charley did not think it suited the gloomy afternoon.

'It wasn't a dream, Charley, your regression. No way. It would definitely have been a past life.'

'It was bloody embarrassing, I tell you. Having the only erotic whatever-it-was of my life in front of this woman.' Charley entered the sale in the ledger and flicked back a couple of pages. 'You haven't had a bad couple of weeks. Perhaps you've turned a corner.'

'Flavia Montessore's famous. She's rumoured to have regressed Nancy Reagan. She practices all over the United States. She's one of the top regressive hypnotists in the world.'

'How can you tell something's a past life and not a dream?' The traffic crawled forward. A warden walked past with her satchel. 'Didn't you say you were a Crusader in one life? How do you know it's not some story you read when you were a child and have forgotten about?'

'Because it was too vivid. There was detail I couldn't possibly have got from reading a school book.' Laura began to straighten out the pile of clothes Lady Antonia Hever-Walsh had tried on and discarded. 'I know people who've spoken languages they've never learned under regression.'

'And screwed people they've never met?'

Laura hooked the straps of a skirt onto a pine hanger. 'I've never got laid in regression.' She slipped the size cube over the hook.

'I wasn't in the past at all,' Charley said.

'You said you were in an old car.'

'Not that old. I'd say it was post-war.'

Laura was silent for a moment. 'The window's wrong. I think we should change it.' She hung the skirt on the rack. 'You don't know much about your past, do you? You don't know anything about your real parents, about your ancestors?'

'My real mother died in childbirth,' Charley said; the thought always disturbed her.

'How did your real father die?'

'He died of a broken heart.'

'*What?*'

'It's what my adoptive mother's always told me,' Charley said defensively.

'Do men die of broken hearts?'

'They can do.' Broken heart. Throughout her childhood that explanation had seemed fine, but the scorn on Laura's face made her doubt it and she wanted to change the subject. 'You know what I think the regression thing was? It was a horny dream, that's all. Tom and I have had sex once in the last two months,

37

after we got back from seeing the house for the first time. These things come out in dreams, don't they?'

'What's your acupunturist hoping to achieve by making you celibate?'

'He's trying to get the balance in my body sorted out so I'll be more receptive. Don't laugh, Laura. You're the one who suggested acupuncture.'

'They have weird ideas sometimes. Want some coffee?'

'I'm not meant to have any. Another of his things.'

'Tea?'

'That's a no-no too. Have you any juice?'

'Aqua Libra?'

'Sure. Have you ever heard of a couturier called Nancy Delvine?'

'Nancy Delvine? Rings a bell. Why?'

'She lived in Elmwood Mill.'

'Elmwood Mill? Oh, the house, right! Any news on it?'

'We should be exchanging on Wandsworth this week, and if we do we'll exchange on Elmwood.'

'Excited?'

'Yes.'

'You don't sound it.'

'I am. It's just — it's a big change.'

'I love the countryside. I'd move there if this place wasn't such a tie.' She went into the little room at the rear of the shop and emerged a few minutes later with a mug of coffee and a glass. She handed the glass to Charley and stirred her coffee.

'Flavia Montessore's worried about you,' she said at last. 'She rang me before she went to the airport this morning. I didn't really know whether I should tell you or not.'

'What do you mean, worried?'

'I don't know. She wasn't very precise. She said she

38

was picking up some bad vibes.'

'What about?' Charley said, suddenly alarmed.

'She thinks she ought to give you more regression when she gets back.'

'Sounds like a good con-trick.'

'She's not like that. She only regresses people she genuinely believes have had past lives.'

Charley smiled. 'The way I could only sell a dress to someone if I genuinely believed it suited them?' Like wallpaper over a crack, her smile masked her unease. She walked over to the window. Shapes passed outside blurred by the rain sliding down the glass. Blurred like her own past.

The unease had begun when she'd awoken on Flavia Montessore's bed. It had stayed with her through the night and throughout today. As if sediment deep inside her had been stirred and would not settle.

Chapter Seven

Charley changed the flowers in the vase in her adoptive mother's room, as she did every week. It was all she could do for her.

She shook the water from the stems of the carnations and dropped them into the waste bin. The sun streamed in through the window. It was hot in the room. Stifling. Charley paid the nursing home extra for the view over the park, a view her mother had never noticed and was unlikely to.

The white-haired woman lay silently in the bed that she refused to leave these days, the regular blink of her eyes every thirty seconds or so virtually the only sign that she was alive.

'Your favourite flowers, Mum. They look lovely, don't they?' She touched the cold cheek lightly with the back of her hand and held the roses up. There was the faint twitch of an eye muscle. Until a few months ago her mother might have uttered some incoherent words, but now Alzheimer's disease had claimed even those.

Small and functional, the room contained few of her mother's possessions. A couple of armchairs from her flat, a chest of drawers and the television that was never on. Two three-winged picture frames were on the bedside table, one showing Charley taking her first bath, Charley with a monkey on Brighton seafront, Charley in her wedding dress grinning exuberantly and Tom, subdued in a morning suit. There was a faint tang of urine, and stronger smells of disinfectant and fresh laundry.

Charley lifted the roses to her nose. Their scent brought a memory from childhood of her adoptive father pruning the bushes in the garden, and then another: they were in his greenhouse and he picked a ripe tomato and gave it to her. She bit into it and the seeds squirted on to his shirt and down her dress and they both laughed.

He had died when she was seven, of cancer. She remembered his eyes best, his large watery eyes that always looked so gently at her, eyes she could trust implicitly. They had looked out from his skeletal figure as he lay dying, and they looked out now from the other frame beside the bed.

Sadness welled for the frail woman who had worked so hard for many years to look after her, and was rewarded with Alzheimer's for her efforts.

All their money had gone in caring for her father, and after his death they had moved from the house to a flat. Her mother had etched a living making soft toys at home for a company in Walthamstow, and Charley had gone to sleep to the whirring of the sewing machine in the living room. In the holidays she had earned them extra money, sitting on the floor packing hair bows into plastic bags for the same company. There was a white van that came round twice a week to bring work and collect it. Their lives were run by the van's timetable.

After her mother had been admitted to the nursing home Charley had gone to clear out the flat in Streatham. She had listened to the rumble of traffic outside and the bawling of a baby on the floor above as she sifted through the drawers, pulling out tights that smelled faintly of perfume, a Du Maurier cigarette tin filled with hairpins, a brown envelope stuffed with early love letters between her adoptive parents. She had been searching for something, she wasn't sure what; some small affirmation of her past, some hint about her real parents, maybe a newsclipping of a death notice, or an obituary. But there was nothing.

She arranged her roses, their crimson and white petals like satin in the brilliant sunlight.

'Pretty, aren't they, Mum?' she said, then sat and held her mother's limp, bony hand, gripping it tightly, trying to find some warmth in it, wishing she could again snuggle into her arms.

Life seemed sad, finite and pointless when you could fit a person's possessions into a suitcase or a trunk or a crate. When you could simply pack away a life. A life that had probably once, like her own, been filled with hope and endless possibilities (expressed in the love letters), and gone nowhere.

She blinked away her tears. 'We're moving, Mum,' she said brightly. 'We've bought a house in the country. Elmwood Mill. Doesn't that sound romantic? It's got an old mill in the garden, and a real millstream, or race as it's called, and a barn, and an Aga in the kitchen, and we're going to have our own hens. I'll bring you eggs. Would you like that?'

Her mother's hand was trembling; it seemed to have gone colder, clammy.

'What's the matter, Mum? You needn't worry — it's only forty-five minutes on the train. I'll still see you just as often.'

The trembling was getting worse.

'You can come and stay with us. We've got plenty of room. How about it?' She looked at the old woman, alarmed. She was shaking, her face had gone even whiter and perspiration was streaming down it. 'It's OK, Mum, don't worry! It's no distance away at all! It won't take me any longer to get here from Elmwood than from Wandsworth.'

The door opened and a nurse came in, a beefy girl with a bucktoothed smile. 'Would you like some tea, Mrs Witney?'

'My mother seems a bit feverish,' Charley said standing up.

The nurse hurried over, felt her pulse then pressed the back of her hand against her forehead. 'She's on some new medication. I'll ask the doctor to come in.'

Charley lowered her voice. 'I think I've upset her. I told her we are moving to the country and maybe she thinks it means I won't be visiting her so often.'

The nurse gave her a reassuring smile. 'No, I really don't think she's able to register anything these days. I'm sure it's just a chill or a reaction to the medication. We'll get the doctor as quickly as we can.'

The nurse hurried out and Charley waited anxiously. In the park a woman was pushing an infant in an old black pram; the traffic rumbled and hooted. Charley turned. Her mother's eyes were closed, the trembling was subsiding. She was sleeping.

Chapter Eight

They moved on Wednesday 12th September.

Charley felt an air of unreality about the drive down from London. All her life she had wanted to live in the countryside, yet she could not quite tune into the fact that today, unlike the half-dozen previous occasions when Mr Budley had loaned them the key, she was no longer coming as a visitor.

The Citroën's engine drilled loudly, the air of the baking late summer day barely cooling her face through the sunroof. She overtook a tractor then slowed as she crested the hill, glancing in the mirror, waiting for the removals' pantechnicon to catch up. Tom's Audi, in front, slowed too.

'ELMWOOD. TWINNED WITH BEIZE-LES-AIX.' A groundsman was rolling the cricket pitch. A kid came out of a newsagents drinking a Coke and behind him a Wall's Ice Cream sign rocked in the breeze. She was already familiar with the mini-roundabout next to the petrol station, the sight of the church ahead up a steep lane and the bustling high street to the right, with bric-a-brac on the pavement in front of an antiques restorer. She'd seen a promising-looking butcher and found a good farm shop.

A mile past the village Tom turned off the main road and drove in through the gateway at the end of a cluster of farm buildings. Several signs were fixed in a line down one gatepost: MANOR HOUSE. THADWELL'S BARN. ROSE COTTAGE. ELMWOOD ANGLING CLUB. The bottom one, rotted and barely legible, said ELMWOOD MILL.

The pantechnicon loomed in Charley's mirror and she turned into the cloud of dust kicked up by the Audi. The little Citroën banged through a pothole with a jar that threw her up against her seat belt and she cast a worried glance at the cardboard box on the passenger floorwell.

The track dipped steeply, then levelled out past a large modern red-brick house in a garden that was still maturing. A blonde-haired woman in wellington boots and a bikini strode out of a loose box towards a Range Rover. In the garden was a swimming pool surrounded by stark white busts on Grecian columns. Naff. Tom had christened it Yuppie Towers.

There was a stagnant pond, then a wooden barn neatly converted into a house with a dilapidated corrugated iron workshop adjoining it that jutted out to the edge of the track. An elderly saloon car was parked on the hard, and through the open doors of the workshop she could see a pair of feet underneath a jacked-up car. The trail of dust from the Audi stung her eyes. The pantechnicon laboured behind.

There was one more building, a stark grey stone cottage with a white picket fence and a neat garden. An old bicycle leant against the wall and an ancient Morris Minor sat in the driveway. The track narrowed and dipped again, the tall straggly hedgerow on each side pressing in on the Citroën like the brushes of a car wash. She felt a twinge of claustrophobia. The hedgerows had grown rampantly in the past three weeks. A bramble clawed at the window and the aerial twanged and juddered.

A cow stared down over the hedge beside an old

bathtub that was its trough, then the light dimmed as the sun was blotted out by the interlocked branches of the woods rising up on either side. Among them cables swung between the telegraph poles that followed the track. Charley bit a nail. She'd seen too many movies about isolated houses where the wires had been cut.

She pulled her finger from her mouth. Ben whined. Remote. It was beginning to feel too remote. 'OK, boy! Nearly there —' She hesitated. 'Nearly home!'

Home.

It had been strange last night, with the carpets rolled up and the curtains down. Sad. Sad that a house could be your home one day and belong to a total stranger the next. Gone. Too late to turn back. The bridges were burnt. Tonight 14 Apstead Road would have new people under its roof, new voices, new laughter, new tears. They'd probably change the colour of the front door and pave over the front garden, and she and Tom would drive by in a couple of years and scarcely be able to pick out the house.

A trail of cuttings of leafy branches and brambles littered the track around the next bend. The hedgerow was cut in a neat flat-top style. In the next dip a short man in a tweed cap lowered his power trimmer and pressed himself into the hedge to let her pass. She waved an acknowledgement and Ben barked at him.

Tom was heaving a cool box out of the boot of the Audi as she pulled up and the pantechnicon inched its way through the gate pillars. As she climbed out of the car she heard the steady roaring of the weir and the mill race tumbling over the wheel. Ben ran around excitedly.

She opened the lid of the cardboard box and peered in. The perforated cling-film was still in place over the neck of the bowl, and Horace was swimming around happily enough. She felt a surge of relief. She had been frightened the fish might die during the journey. She wanted no omens.

The engine of the pantechnicon clattered then faded, and there was complete silence except for the sound of rushing water. The breeze died and the still air was hot in the sun; sheep bleated in the distance and there were two faint blasts from, possibly, a shotgun. A bird trilled. Her feet scrunched on the gravel. Ben began barking again.

A metal door slammed. Voices. A bumble bee zoomed towards her and she flinched. Tom called out, 'Any of you guys like a beer?'

She walked to the bank of the stream. Only about three feet wide and maybe a couple of feet deep, it was easily jumpable. The water moved swiftly, clear and fresh, and the bed was lined with pebbles and rounded stones. The shadow of a bird strobed across.

'Cor, it's all right, innit?' someone said. A beer can opened with a hiss. She looked at the other side of the bank, at the patch of scrub grass.

Stables.

The feeling remained each time she had come, nagged her from a dark recess of her mind that was just out of reach, taunting her.

The executors of Nancy Delvine had taken every light bulb, even the one in the cellar.

'Bastards!' Tom said angrily, and drove off to the village in search of an electrical shop. The removals men took their lunch break and sat by the stream with their sandwiches.

Charley carried Horace into the house and placed him safely on the draining board. 'Like your new home?' She screwed up her face at the custard yellow. 'Think we'll change the colour scheme. Any preferences?'

She walked around the house, her plimsoles squeaking on the bare wood. Without furniture, the rooms seemed smaller, lower-ceilinged and dingier. Light rectangles marked the walls where pictures had hung or cupboards had stood. They reminded her of a film about Hiroshima her mother had taken her to see as a child; it had shown shadows on the walls that were the remains of people who had been vaporised when the bomb dropped.

She climbed the steep staircase to the attic. Shafts of light from the one small window picked their way through the dust which hung as thick as sleet, tickling her nose and throat. There was a faintly unpleasant smell of something decomposing. It was hot and uncannily quiet. The only sound was the sharp ping ... ping ... ping of a single drop of water every half second on to something metallic. The room was empty, the boxes of junk under dust sheets had been cleared out. She walked across to the window, the hardboard floor sagging then springing back into place with a dull *boomf*, shedding small eddies of dust into the air.

Most dust came from human skin.

Weird. Weird thoughts coming into her head. Maybe it was part of moving. Moving was the second biggest trauma of married life. Or third. Something like that, Tom had told her.

There was a fine view out of the window over the lake and beyond. Maybe a couple of miles across the woods and down the valley on the far side, were the roof and chimneys of a large house.

It was going to be OK. Tom was right. It was beautiful here. Beautiful and peaceful.

A shadow moved across the wall, as if someone had walked behind her. She turned, but the attic was empty. It must have been a bird passing the window, she thought. Except the shadow had come from a different direction. She felt a prickle of unease and stepped to the left, then right, to see if the shadow could have been from herself.

A rattle above her head, like dice, startled her, then she heard the chirp of a bird. A man shouted, his voice faint. Another replied.

Boomf.

She looked round as the floorboard made a sound as if someone had trodden on it. Probably just springing back into place after she had walked over it, she realised, but she left the attic quickly.

As she went on to the first floor landing a thud echoed around the house. It was followed by several more in rapid succession.

Door knocker.

She hurried down the stairs. A tall man was standing at the front door wearing grimy overalls over a frayed collar and a ragged tie. He was in his early forties, she guessed. He had an unkempt beard and there were streaks of grease on his high gaunt cheeks. His straw hair looked as if it had been battered by a hurricane. She liked his face instantly. It had both a salt-of-the-earth trustworthiness and a hint of fiery nobility that reminded her of Russian aristocracy. His eyes were sharp, penetrating, but warmth and a hint of mischief danced in them like winter sun.

'I'm Hugh Boxer, your neighbour from up the lane. Thought I'd pop by and say hallo.' His voice was easy and cultured.

She held out her hand. 'Charley Witney.'

He wiped his grimy paw of a hand down his trouser leg and shook hers with a solid, positive grip. 'Welcome to the lane.'

'Thank you.' She smiled. 'Which is your house?'

'The barn. Thadwell's Barn.'

'With the old cars?'

His eyebrows were like miniature bales of straw, and his face crinkled as he smiled back. 'Some people in the country breed animals — I prefer cars. They don't need milking.'

She laughed. 'I think the barn — house — looks great.'

'Not bad for a cowshed, is it? Actually, the other thing I came to see you about was the car. I wondered if it would be OK to leave it for a day or two.'

'The car? I'm not with you, I'm afraid,' Charley said.

'Nancy Delvine's old Triumph Roadster. I bought it from the estate. It's in the barn, behind the straw bales.'

'I didn't know there was a car there. Is it something very rare?'

The removals men were unloading a sofa from the lorry.

'No,' Hugh Boxer said, 'not exactly. There are a few around. Ever watched *Bergerac*?'

She nodded.

'One of those. I don't think its been on the road for thirty years.'

'Do you collect them?'

'Sort of.' His eyes studied her more seriously for a fleeting moment, as if they were probing for something. It made her feel uncomfortable.

The removals men were humping the sofa up the steps behind him.

'It'll take me the best part of a day's work to move the bales. I'll try and do it sometime in the next week.'

'There's no problem. We're not using the barn for anything.'

They stepped aside. An arm of the sofa thumped into a doorpost. 'Where's this to go, missus?'

She pointed through to the drawing room. 'Anywhere in there.'

'I'll get out of your way,' Hugh Boxer said. 'If I can

be any help any time, anything you want to know, just give a shout.'

'That's kind of you ... Oh, who's the chap trimming the hedge in the lane?'

'Gideon. We all employ him. He'll be along to see you, I should think.'

'We were told.'

'The George and Dragon's the best pub for food. Turn right out of the lane and it's a mile straight on.'

'Thanks. You must come and have a drink when we're straight.'

'Have you got a lot to do?' he glanced past her into the interior of the house.

'Plenty.'

'Nice house. I always thought it was rather attractive.' He hesitated, as if he were about to say something else, then he turned away. She followed him down the steps and Ben bounded up. 'Hallo, chap!' he said, pausing to pat him. 'You're not much of a guard dog, are you?' He gave Charley a cheery wave, and strode off.

The barn had double doors, both halves rotten and held shut with bricks. She tugged one open. Something small scuttled across the concrete floor and disappeared into the shadows. There was a smell of straw and oil. The ancient sit-on lawnmower they had bought from the executors was in front of her, its grass collector unhooked and propped against the wall beside it. It was about the only thing they had wanted that the executors had been willing to sell at a reasonable price.

Halfway across the barn was a wall of straw bales, and a narrow gap to the right which she had not been through before. As she approached she could see an old work bench under a high window. She squeezed through into what appeared to be a derelict workshop.

It was dark, with one grimy window filtering out most of the light.

In the middle of the floor was a tarpaulin, old and heavily coated in dust, the shape of a car silhouetted beneath it. Her heart rose into her throat; there was something about it that made her hesitate. A sleeping monster that should not be disturbed.

There was a scratching sound in the rafters and a trickle of dust fell. Rats? Bats? The wall of straw towered over her. More shapes came into focus out of the gloom. An old metal table. A garden roller with its handle broken.

Leave it, a voice in her head whispered.

I'm not going to be spooked by my own damned barn!

She lifted a corner of the tarpaulin. It revealed the dull pitted chrome of a bumper and a black wing with a sidelight mounted on top. She tried to peel it back further, but it was heavy. She walked sideways, tugged it over the bonnet and saw the upright radiator sandwiched between two massive headlamps. There was a chromium cap on top of the radiator and a small round badge on the front with a coloured globe of the world and 'Triumph Motors' in tiny letters.

She stepped backwards, tugging the tarpaulin across the bodywork and over the canvas roof. Finally it came free and slithered into a crumpled heap on the floor. Her nostrils filled with a smell of metal, musty canvas, stale oil.

The car looked familiar.

Because of *Bergerac* on television. She had seen the detective series, knew the model. She circled it. A bulbous sports convertible with running boards and a stubby nose. There was a narrow window at the back of the roof, and two glass panels in the boot where the dickey seats were. The black paint was thick with dust and the tyres were flat. A cobweb was spun across a corner of the windscreen, and a tax disc was visible behind it. She leaned closer and could just make out the faded lettering. *Nov 53.*

She pressed down the passenger door handle and pulled; the door opened with a cracking sound, as if some seal of time had been broken, and the smell of old leather and rotting canvas rose up from the interior, engulfing her.

The silence was complete. She had a feeling of being an intruder. She squeezed in through the passenger door and sat on the bench seat. It was hard and upright. Knurled black knobs protruded from the wooden dashboard on metal stalks. Two round, white dials were mounted in the middle, the speedometer on her side. The large spoked steering wheel was almost touching her right arm, the tiny column change gear lever sticking out from it like an antenna. She pulled the door shut with a dull clunk and felt very enclosed, the roof inches above her head, the screen just in front of her nose.

She pushed herself further down in the seat and sat for a moment, uncomfortably aware of the silence. She could see the outline of the bonnet through the dust on the windscreen and the radiator cap at the end. She touched a knob on the dashboard, then gripped it in her fingers and twisted it; it was stiff and for a moment would not move. She twisted it harder, and the windscreen wiper blade lifted an inch and broke several strands of the spider's web. She let go of the knob, startled, and the blade dropped down. The spider ran up the screen and she could almost sense petulance in the motion. She put her hand on her lap guiltily.

She was trembling. The seat creaked, crackled, a spring twanged.

A spring released itself somewhere inside her too.

She knew this car. Not just from seeing one in the

television series. She had been in one like this before, travelled in it. She was certain it was the same make of car in which she had made love in her regression.

She could remember everything: the roughness of his tweed jacket, the gruff roar of the engine, the wind thrashing her hair, the harsh ride on the uneven surface, the engine straining, the biff of the exhaust as he changed gear, the minty taste of the gum in her mouth.

She remembered the erotic sensation of the finger inside her. The car slithering to a halt. The smell of burned rubber, fresh leather, the rumble of the exhaust, the knocking rattle of the engine, the bonnet shaking, vibrating, the tweed of his sleeve brushing her face, his mouth over hers, their lips pressed together, kissing hungrily. The rubbery ball of chewing gum she had plucked out of her mouth and pushed under the glove locker.

There was a crack like a pistol shot.

She sat up with a jerk, dripping with perspiration, a deep feeling of fear in the pit of her stomach. She shook her head but her hair, matted with sweat, barely moved. Rivulets ran down the back of her neck, her armpits; she was shaking. The car seemed to be shrinking around her, the air getting scarcer as if something was sucking it out.

She scrabbled for the door handle and as she did she realised she was holding something in her hand, something small and hard.

She stumbled out, grazing her leg on the top of the sill, but barely noticing. She stood and stared at the small hard object in her hand, took it over to the window, but it was too dark to see.

She hurried through the barn and outside, squinting against the dazzle of the brilliant light. She looked down. About half an inch across, dark grey and pitted like a miniature shrivelled brain. A tiny strip of wood veneer was stuck to one side.

It was an old dried piece of chewed gum.

Her hand shook, making the gum dance like spittle on a griddle. Then it fell. She looked down, tried to spot it, knelt, sifted through the gravel, rummaged her hands backwards and forwards. Over by the house she heard a shout, the sound of metal banging, the scrunch of feet; a laugh. She carried on rummaging, making a widening arc, but it had gone, swallowed by the pebbles the way the sea swallows a footprint in the sand.

A voice called, 'Mrs Witney? Hallo? Need to know where you want these packing cases!'

'Coming!' she shouted.

Hundreds of people chew gum in cars. Thousands. Millions. There was nothing special about finding gum in a car.

Nothing special at all.

Chapter Nine

Tom and Charley dined outside on the sheltered patio at the rear of the house, on a Chinese takeaway and a bottle of champagne, and watched the red ball of sun sink down behind the paddock, leaving its heat behind it in the dusk.

The days were getting noticeably shorter; in a few weeks the clocks would be going back, but now, in the balmy evening, winter seemed a long way away.

The grazing chestnut mare turned into a silhouette and slowly faded to black. Stars appeared in the metallic sky, bats flitted and the lights of planes coming into Gatwick winked.

They picked at the last grains of rice and strands of noodles and wrote a list of things to be done.

Later, in bed, they made love. But in a strange way it was more like a rite than a spontaneous act of passion. It reminded her of when they had made love on her wedding night after two years of living together. Both of them had been tired, flaked out, but they knew it ought to be done. Consummation.

They had consummated the move tonight for their own secret needs, hers to be held and to hold; to hold something real, to feel Tom, to feel life after the weirdness of the discovery, first of the car in the barn then the chewing gum. Reality.

She wondered what his need was. Wondered what

went through his mind when he made love to her so mechanically, so distantly. Who did he think about? Who did he fantasise she was?

The noises came after, through the open window. The noises of the night. Real darkness out there.

She could taste the minty gum in her mouth.

Ben padded restlessly around the room, growling at squeals, at shrieks, at the mournful wail of vixens.

It was two o'clock. She slipped out of bed and walked across the sloping wooden floor to the curtainless window. The new moon powered a faint tinfoil shine from the lake. Somewhere in the dark a small creature emitted a single shriek of terror, several more in fast succession, then one final shriek, louder and longer than the rest; there was a rustle of undergrowth, then silence. Mother Nature, Gaia, the Earth Goddess was there dealing the cards, keeping the chain going. Life and death. Replenishment. Recycling the living and the dead equally methodically.

Serial murderers were out there too. In the inky silence.

Tom had taken two weeks' holiday for the move, but he had to go to London in the morning. A wife had poured paint stripper over her husband's new car and had blinded his racing pigeons. Tom brought home stories of cruelty every day. Sometimes Charley thought there were few acts committed in the world crueller than those under the sanctity of marriage.

The water slid relentlessly over the slimy brickwork of the weir, crashing down into the dark spume of the sluice. It seemed to echo through the stillness, unreal; it all seemed unreal. She was afraid. She wanted to go home.

She had to keep reminding herself that she was home.

* * *

57

'Blimey, what you running here? A space station?' The Electricity Board man's eyes bulged from a thyroid complaint and there was sweat on his protruding forehead from the heat outside. He tapped his teeth with his biro.

'What do you mean?' Charley asked.

Footsteps from the hall above echoed around the cellar. Somewhere a drill whined. She looked at the man irritably. She was tired.

He held the printed pad so she could see the markings he had made. 'The quarterly average for the past year here has been five hundred units. This quarter it's gone up to seven *thousand*.'

'That's impossible. It's been empty for a year and we only moved in yesterday.' She watched the metal disc revolving. 'Is the meter faulty?'

'No, I've tested it. It's working fine. See how slowly it's going? You're not using much juice at the moment.'

'If there's a short circuit, could that —?'

'Must be. You've got a leak somewhere. You'd better get an electrician to sort it out. It's going to cost you a fortune otherwise.'

'We're having the house rewired. They're meant to be starting today.'

She was not sure he had heard her. He was checking the meter once more with a worried frown.

The Aga was smoking from every orifice, and Charley's eyes were smarting. A new telephone was on the pine dresser next to the answering machine, its neat green 'Telecom Approved' roundel hanging from a thread. The phone was red to match the new Aga — when they could afford it. For the time being, her hope of replacing the existing solid-fuel one was item 43 (or was it 53?) on the list of priorities she and Tom had written out last night. 'Central Heating' was at the top and 'Snooker

Room In Barn' was at the bottom (item 147). During the next twelve months, if they found nothing disastrously wrong with the house, they could afford up to item 21, 'Window Frames'. If Charley went back to full-time work, eventually, it would help. (Item 22, 'Double Glazing'.) For the time being the sacrifices were worth it. It was a good investment. On that point, Mr Budley, the estate agent, was right.

The telephone engineer poked his head round the kitchen door. 'Same place as the old one in the lounge?'

'Yes, with a long lead,' she said, scratching what felt like a mosquito bite on her shoulder.

'The cordless one in the bedroom?' He had an attachment clipped to his waist with a large dial on it.

She nodded and coughed.

The engineer looked at the Aga. 'Needs plenty of air. Leave the door open until the flames have caught. Me mum had one.'

'Open? Right, thank you, I'll try that. I'm making some tea, or would you prefer coffee?'

'Tea, white no sugar, ta.'

She opened the oven door as he suggested and backed away from the plume of smoke that billowed out. She picked up the kettle and turned the tap. It sicked a blob of rusty brown water into the stained sink, some of which splashed on to her T-shirt, hissed, made a brief sucking noise and was silent.

Bugger. The plumber, she realised, had just asked her where the stopcock was. She flapped away smoke. With that and the sun streaming in, it was baking hot. They needed blinds in here (item 148, she added, mentally).

There was an opened crate on the floor labelled in her handwriting 'kitchen'. Crumpled newspaper lay around it and the pile of crockery on the table was growing. A flame crackled in the Aga. She peered into the goldfish bowl. 'Hi, Horace, what's doing?' she said, feeling flat.

Ben padded in and gazed at her forlornly.

'Want a walk, boy?' She stroked his soft cream coat and he licked her hand. 'You've had a good morning's barking, haven't you? The builders, the electrician, the telephone man and the plumber.'

She filled the kettle from the mill race, which looked clear enough, and boiled the water twice.

The smoke from the Aga was dying down and the flames seemed to be gaining ground. While the tea was steeping she admired the flowers Laura had sent, the three cards from other friends and a telemessage from Michael Ohm, one of Tom's partners, which had arrived this morning.

There was no greeting from Tom's widower father, a London taxi driver who had desperately wanted his only son to be a success, to have a profession, not to be like him. When Tom had succeeded his father resented it in the way he resented everything he did not understand. He had lived in Hackney all his life, in a house two streets from where he was born. When Tom told him they were moving to the country, he had said they must be mad.

Ben bounded on ahead up the drive. The builders were unloading materials from a flatbed truck, and an aluminium ladder rested against the side of the house. A squirrel loped across the gravel into the shade between the house and the barn. Charley could hear cattle lowing, the drone of a tractor, the endless roar of the water and a fierce hammering from upstairs.

At the top of the drive she felt the cooling spray. The weir foamed water, but the lake was flat as a drumskin. Mallards were up-ended near the shore and somewhere close by a woodpecker drilled a tree.

She crossed the iron footbridge, looking down uncomfortably into the circular brick sluice pond. It reminded her of a mineshaft. On the other side of the bridge there were brambles and the remains of a fence which needed repairing. It was dangerous and someone could trip and tumble in. She walked quickly and turned to wait until Ben was safely past.

The path was dry and hard and curved upwards, left, climbing through the woods above the lake. The undergrowth grew denser and the trees were slender, mostly hornbeam, birch and elms. A large number were uprooted, probably from the winter storms or maybe the hurricane of eighty-seven. They lay where they had fallen, leaning against other trees or entombed in the creepers and brambles and nettles of the wild undergrowth.

Traces of a nightmare she had had during the night remained in her mind: a horse rearing up, opening its snarling mouth to reveal fangs chewing a piece of gum the size of a tennis ball, breathing hot minty breath at her then laughing a whinnying laugh. She had woken and tasted mint in her own mouth.

Chewing gum. In the car. It —

Her train of thought snapped as Ben stopped in front of her and she nearly tripped over him. He began barking, a more menacing bark than normal, and she felt a flash of unease. The bark deepened into a snarl and something moved ahead on the path.

A man hurrying, stumbling, very agitated, holding a fishing rod with a bag slung over his shoulder. He was wearing an old tweed suit with leather patches on the sleeves and gum boots. There was a strip of sticking plaster above his right eye, and a solitary trickle of sweat ran down his face like a tear. He was about sixty, tall and quite distinguished, but his state of anxiety was making him seem older. Ben's snarl grew louder. She grabbed his collar.

'I wonder if you'd mind terribly nipping down and telling Viola I'll be a bit late,' the man said without any introduction. 'I've lost my damned watch somewhere and I must go back and look for it.'

'Viola?' Charley said blankly.

The man blinked furiously. 'My wife!' he said. 'Mrs Letters.'

She wondered if he was a bit gaga.

'I must find my watch before someone pinches it. It has sentimental value, you know.'

'I'm sorry,' Charley said. 'We've only just moved in.' Ben jerked her forwards.

'Rose Cottage, up the lane! I'd be very grateful. Just tell her I'll be a bit late.' He raised a finger in acknowledgement, then turned and hurried back up the path.

Charley continued holding Ben. He was still snarling and his hackles were up, his eyes flickering with colour.

'What is it, boy? What's the matter?' She pulled him and he followed reluctantly. She waited until the man was well out of sight before she dared release him.

Rose Cottage. She had seen the name on the board at the entrance to the lane. It must be the stone cottage. Ben ran on ahead sniffing everything happily, his growls forgotten.

She came out of the shade and the sunlight struck her face, dazzling her. Ben cocked his leg on a bush. The potholed ground was dry and dusty and the hedges buzzed with insects. A swarm of midges hovered around her head and there was a strong smell of cows, an acrid smell of bindweed and the sweeter smell of mown grass.

The roof of the cottage came into view through the trees and a dog was yapping. A car door slammed, then a woman's voice boomed like a foghorn.

'Peregrine! Quiet —!'

Charley rounded the corner. The ancient Morris Minor estate was parked in the driveway of the cottage behind the picket fence and beside it was an old woman who had a cardboard groceries box under one arm and was holding the leash of a tiny Yorkshire terrier with the other.

Ben leapt forward playfully but the terrier replied with another volley of yaps. Charley grabbed Ben's collar and made him sit.

'Are you Mrs Letters?' she shouted above the terrier's yapping.

'Yes,' the woman shouted back. She was a no-nonsense country type in stout brown shoes, tweed skirt and rib-stitched pullover. Short and plump, she had a ruddy, booze-veined blancmange of a face and straight, grey hair which was parted and brushed in a distinctly masculine style.

'We've moved into the Mill. I'm Charley Witney.'

'Ah, knew you were coming sometime this week.' She glared at the dog and bellowed in a voice that could have stopped a battleship, 'Peregrine!' The dog was silent and she looked back at Charley. 'Viola Letters. Can't shake your hand, I'm afraid.'

'I have a message from your husband.'

The woman's expression became distinctly hostile and Charley felt daunted. She pointed towards the valley. 'I just met him and he asked me to tell you that he's lost his watch and he's going to be a bit late.'

'My husband?'

'In a tweed suit, with fishing tackle? Have I come to the right house?'

'Said he'd lost his watch?'

'Yes — I —' Charley hesitated. The woman was more than hostile; she was ferocious. 'He seemed rather confused. I think he may have hurt himself. He had a strip of elastoplast on his head.'

The terrier launched into another spate of yapping and the woman turned abruptly and walked into the house, dragging the dog so its feet skidded over the paving slabs. She closed the front door behind her with a slam.

Chapter Ten

The gardener turned up in the afternoon, small and chirpy with a hare lip, and tugged the peak of his cap respectfully.

'I'm Gideon,' he said with an adenoidal twang, 'like in the Bible.'

Charley smiled at him. 'You've done a good job with the hedge.'

'I wanted it to be nice for when you arrived,' he said, obviously pleased with the compliment. 'The old lady, she never wanted nothing done.'

'Why not?'

'I dunno; never saw her, 'cept rarely. She left me the money for cuttin' the hedge and the grass out the back door.'

'Didn't she ever go out?'

'Nope. Had everything delivered.'

'Why did she do that?'

'She were what you call a recluse. Mind, I'm not sorry. I know I'm not Robert Redford, but she really didn't look that great.' He glanced at the house. 'Is there's any jobs in the garden you want doing?'

There were plenty.

They walked around together, and agreed on a plot between the hen run and the paddock fence for the kitchen garden. The soil was moist and sandy, he told her, pretty well everything would grow. They could buy spring cabbage and broccoli plants, and he had some leeks to spare. They would be eating their own vegetables before the winter was over, he said.

She bluffed her way through a discussion about hens, helped by a book she had read called *Poultry Keeping Today* which she'd borrowed from Wandsworth library. Gideon knew where to buy good layers, but the run needed fixing first to make it fox-proof and he'd get on with it right away. He charged three pounds an hour and she paid him for the work he had done on the hedge. Eight hours, which sounded about right.

She tried to get him to tell her more about Nancy Delvine, but he did not seem to want to talk about her. He'd only seen the woman twice in ten years, and that was enough. Why, he would not say.

The first call Charley received, after the engineer had tested the equipment and gone, was from Laura.

The engineer had been right about the Aga. It had heated up and the smoke had gone. The musty smells of the kitchen faded a bit and the dominant one now was from the cartons of the Chinese takeaway in the rubbish sack. She had spent the last three hours opening crates, unpacking and moving furniture around. It would have to be moved again for the decorators and the carpets, but at least it was beginning to look vaguely like home.

'The flowers are wonderful,' Charley said, caressing the petals of a pink orchid.

'Got your green wellies out yet?'

'It's too hot.'

'You're lucky you're not in London. It's sweltering. No one's buying any winter clothes. How did the move go?'

'Fine. Great. You must come to Tom's birthday a fortnight on Saturday. We're going to have a barbecue, if it's warm enough.'

'Any dishy bachelors around?'

'Actually there's a rather nice chap down the lane.'

'Really?'

'I have a feeling he's single. If he is, I'll invite him.'

'Tom's going to be thirty-eight, isn't he?'

'And not very happy about it. Someone told him middle age starts at forty.'

'He doesn't look middle-aged.'

Hammering echoed around the house. 'Laura,' Charley began. 'Do you know when Flavia Montessore is going to be back in England?'

'In the autumn sometime.' Laura sounded surprised. 'Why?'

Charley toyed with the green tag hanging from the phone. 'I — I just wondered, that's all.' There was a clatter outside the window and the rungs of an aluminium ladder appeared. 'You know I said I was in a car?'

'Bonking. Yes.'

'I was chewing a bit of gum. I took it out of my mouth and stuck it under the dash —'

A pair of legs climbed past the window.

'I found . . .' Her voice trailed off, and she left foolish.

'Found what? Charley, what did you find?'

The ladder was shaking. 'The autumn. Do you mean October? Next month?'

'She usually calls me. I'll let you know.'

Rude, Charley thought, suddenly. Mrs Letters. Rose Cottage. Very rude to slam a door.

'If you want to see someone sooner I know a very good man called Ernest Gibbon. He does private sessions.'

She'd gone out of her way to give Mrs Letters the message, and she'd turned her back and slammed the door. Rude. Except it hadn't felt rude at the time, just odd. The woman had seemed upset. Upset by something more than a husband being late.

'I can give you his number,' Laura said. 'He's in south London.'

'Is he as good?'

'He's brilliant. Give him a try.'

'I might,' she said distractedly, and wrote the number down on the back of an envelope.

Tom arrived home in the evening and changed into a T-shirt and jeans. He thought three pounds an hour was fine for the gardener, but he would look after the lawn himself. Part of the fun of moving to the country was to work in the garden, he said.

He went in the barn and managed to get the huge old mower started, then sat on the seat and drove it with a terrible racket across the gravel and up the bank. It farted oily black smoke and the engine kept cutting then racing, jerking him about like a circus clown. Finally there was a loud bang and the engine stopped and would not start again. Tom climbed off doubled up with laughter and she felt, almost for the first time, that everything was going to work out.

'Let's find a pub,' Tom said. 'I fancy a beer and a steak.'

'The chap up the lane said the George and Dragon was the best for food.' She brushed hairs back from his forehead, and the evening sun danced deep in his slate blue eyes. He didn't look thirty-eight and she didn't feel thirty-six; she felt twenty-six, or maybe sixteen, when she'd first seen those eyes, gazed up at them from the sticky carpet where she'd fallen sloshed in the pub and seen them grinning down at her. 'Hallo, Joe Cool,' she'd said to the stranger, and then passed out on his shiny Chelsea boots.

The George and Dragon was an old coaching inn and the glass panel in the door displayed its credentials: 'Relais Routiers', 'Egon Ronay', 'Good Pub Guide,'

'Good Beer Guide'. The thin licensing strip across the lintel proclaimed the proprietor to be Victor L. Lubbin.

A roar of laughter froze as they went in. A bunch of labourers around a table glanced up then one said something and the laughter resumed. A solitary fruit machine stood against a wall. It winked its lights, flashed its signs, changed its colours and repeated a scale of musical notes every few seconds, its sole audience an old English sheepdog which lay on the floor eyeing it sleepily like a bored impresario at an audition.

The room had a low ceiling, yellowed from age and smoke, and massive timber beams. Ancient farm implements had been hung on the walls along with a dartboard. There were old-fashioned beer pumps and an unlit inglenook. Beside the dartboard were notices advertising a jumble sale, a steam traction rally, Morris Dancing — 'Morfydd's Maidens'.

A knot of three people stood at the far end of the bar. One Charley recognised, the tall frame of Hugh Boxer, their neighbour, raising a stubby pipe as a greeting. 'Hi!' he said.

He was wearing a crumpled checked shirt, a knitted tie and had an amiable smile on his bearded face, though there was the strong, authoritative presence she had felt before. The grease smears had gone and his hair had been tidied a bit.

Charley introduced Tom, and Hugh Boxer ordered them drinks and introduced them to the couple he was with. They were called Julian and Zoe Garfield-Hampsen, and lived in the red-brick house with the Grecian columns around the pool at the end of the lane. Yuppie Towers. Julian Garfield-Hampsen was tall, with a booming voice and a ruddy drinker's face. He wore a striped Jermyn Street shirt with corded cufflinks and smoothed his hand through his fair hair each time he spoke. He was probably about the same age as Tom, but he looked ten years older.

'How super to have another young couple in the lane!' Zoe said. She had a small, reedy voice and spoke slowly and precisely, which made her sound like a schoolgirl in an elocution lesson. She was the woman Charley had seen walking out of the stables in her bikini and wellington boots. 'Julian and I have always simply *adored* Elmwood Mill,' she added.

'We love it,' Charley said.

'It's super! The only thing that put us off buying it is it sits so low down and doesn't get much sun in the winter.'

'Spritzer.' Hugh Boxer handed Charley her glass. 'And a pint of Vic's best sludge.'

'Cheers.' Tom held his dark bitter up to the light, studied it for a moment, drank some and nodded approvingly at the landlord.

The landlord, a stocky, dour man with thinning black hair, made no response for a moment. He turned to take a tumbler from the small aluminium sink, then said, in a dry Midlands accent, 'Cricketing man, are you?'

'I used to play a bit,' Tom said surprised.

The landlord wiped the tumbler with a cloth. 'Sunday week,' he said. 'Ten o'clock, Elmwood Green. We've a charity match against Rodmell and we're two short.'

'I'm a bit rusty. I haven't played for a few years.'

'Bat or bowl?'

'I used to be a bit of a batsman, I suppose.'

'Put you down for opening bat?'

'Well I wouldn't — er —' But the landlord had already started to write his name on a list. 'Witney? With an *H* or without?'

'Without,' Tom said. 'I haven't got any pads or kit.'

70

'You get roped into everything down here,' Hugh said. 'They'll have you on every committee going within a month.'

'Viola Letters is doing the tea,' the landlord continued. 'I expect she'll be in touch with you, Mrs Witney.'

'Oh, right,' Charley said, taken aback but smiling.

'Do you do food at night?' Tom dug his fingers hungrily into a large bowl of peanuts on the bar.

'Restaurant's through there.' The landlord pointed. 'Last orders for food at nine forty-five.'

Tom shovelled more peanuts into his mouth. They had half an hour.

'Julian played last year, but he's hurt his shoulder,' Zoe said. 'How many children do you have?' she asked Charley.

'None, so far.' Charley's face always reddened at the question. 'We — we hope to start a family here.'

'Super!' The expression on Zoe's face said, *At your age?*

The Garfield-Hampsens had three children. They were called Orlando, Gervais and Camilla. Julian (Joo-Joo) was in computer software. Zoe evented-and-thinged on horses. Everything was *super*.

Charley caught Hugh Boxer's eye. 'Is that your lovely Jaguar outside? Tom's been ogling it since we first saw the house.'

'Tell him to pop in any time if he sees the workshop door open. I'm working on a beautiful old Bristol.' He tapped his pipe against the rim of an earthenware ashtray. There was something cosy about the sound. He dabbed his forehead with the back of his massive hand. 'It's close tonight.'

She felt the sticky heat too. 'It's clouding. The forecast is thunder.'

He struck a match and took several long sucks on the

pipe, then shook the match out. There was still grease under his nails.

'Is that your business, old cars?' Charley said.

He drew on his pipe and fired the smoke out through his nostrils. It rose up in a thick cloud around him. 'No. I'm a ley hunter,' he said, and took a sip of his whisky, cradling his glass in his hand.

'Ley hunter?' She caught the twinkle in the eyes; morning sunlight on an icy pond. Beneath the ice there seemed to be immense depth.

'Hugh's frightfully famous. He's our local celebrity,' said Zoe.

He waved his pipe dismissively. 'It's not true. Don't believe it.'

'It is!' She turned to Charley. 'He's been on television, radio, and in all the papers. He had a whole half page in the *Independent* with his photograph. They called him Britain's leading authority on ley lines.'

Hugh puffed on his pipe as if he were not part of the conversation.

'And he's had two books published.'

'What are their titles?'

The smoke smelled rich and sweet. Charley liked the smell of pipes.

'I shouldn't think you've heard of them,' Hugh said. '*The Secret Landscape*, and *Dowsing — the Straight Facts*.'

'He's absolutely brilliant. The books are fascinating.'

Tom and Julian Garfield-Hampsen were talking about property. 'We're trying to get permission to extend,' Julian said, and Zoe's attention switched to them.

'Were they bestsellers, these books?' Charley asked.

He sucked on the pipe again. 'No.' he grinned and raised his straw-bale brows. 'It's a very specialised subject. I don't sell many, just a few copies.'

'Is that how you make your living?'

'I earn my crust at the university. I lecture.'

'Which one?'

'Sussex.'

'I thought you didn't look like a garage mechanic. Do you lecture on ley lines?'

'No. Psychology. Ley lines are my hobby — for my sanity.'

'And old motor cars?'

'Anything old. Old cars. Old buildings. Old landscapes.' He shrugged, and looked closer at her, more penetratingly. His voice lowered and his face suddenly seemed more gaunt. 'Old spirits.' He tamped his pipe with his stubby thumb. He bit his nails too, she noticed with surprise. His eyes lifted from the pipe back to her. They stared intently. It was as though they were searching for something, as if they were trying to rub away an outer layer and peer through.

'What do you mean, old spirits?'

'Past lives. I can always tell someone else who's had past lives.'

'How?'

'Just by looking at them.' She felt something cold trickle through her, pricking at her like an electrical current.

'You mean reincarnation?'

He nodded.

'You believe in that?'

'Don't you?'

'No, I don't believe in it. I don't think it's possible.'

'I don't believe in divorce,' he said quietly. 'But my wife still left me.'

There was a silence between them.

'I'm sorry,' she said at last.

He smiled, but she saw the pain beneath the mask.

'Do you believe in regression?' she asked, sipping her spritzer.

'Regression hypnosis?'

'Yes.'

He took a match out of the box. 'There are a lot of meddlers, amateurs. Anyone can announce he's a hypnotist and set himself up in business.'

'The Triumph in our barn,' she said avoiding his eyes. 'How old is it?'

'The original log's missing. I'll have to check the chassis and engine numbers. They started making them in forty-eight.' He struck another match. 'Have you met Viola Letters yet, the grand old dame of the lane?'

There was a single flash of lightning. Conversation in the pub flickered for a brief instant then resumed.

'In Rose Cottage?'

He sucked the flame into the bowl of his pipe. 'That's her. Keeps a hawk-eye on what goes on.'

There were three more flashes.

'Do she and her husband not get on too well?'

He looked puzzled, then faintly amused. 'I didn't know they communicated.'

Charley felt her face reddening. 'What do you mean?'

Thunder crashed outside.

Hugh swirled his whisky around in his glass, then drank some. 'She's a widow,' he said. 'Her husband's been dead for nearly forty years.'

Chapter Eleven

The sky was clear again the next morning and the air felt fresh after the storm. Water dripped from the trees, an intermittent plat ... plat ... plat, and wisps of mist hung over the lake. It was just after eleven.

As Charley walked alone up the lane she heard a rumble ahead of her, and a tractor came around the corner towing an empty trailer. She stepped into the brambles to let it pass, and smiled up at the driver, an elderly wizened man. He stared fixedly ahead and drove past without acknowledging her. She watched him rattle on down the dip, surprised.

The Morris Minor was in the driveway and the Yorkshire terrier started yapping before Charley had pushed the gate open. She went hesitantly up the path. A ship's bell was fixed to the wall beside the front door. She searched for a knocker but could not see one, so she jangled the bell. The yapping intensified and a voice the other side of the door quietened it.

The door opened and Viola Letters stood there, half kneeling, holding the terrier by its collar, in the same stout shoes as yesterday, a tweed skirt too thick for the heat and an equally thick blouse. She looked up at Charley warily.

'I've come to apologise,' Charley said. The old woman's eyes were peering over the top of her cheeks like a crab staring out of wet sand, and the dog's eyes were black marbles sparkling with rage. 'I'm desperately sorry. I wasn't playing a trick. I didn't know your husband was dead.'

She pulled the dog back. 'Would you like to come in?' Her voice sounded like a deeper bark.

Charley stepped into the hall and the dog glared at her in an uneasy silence.

'Close the door. He'll relax then.'

Charley did so and the dog yapped angrily.

'Kitchen!' Mrs Letters dragged it into a room at the back, gave it a gentle slap on the bottom and shut the door on it.

'Sorry about that. He's normally fine with visitors. Getting a bit cantankerous in his old age,' her mouth opened and shut as she spoke like a secret door in the folds of flesh.

'He can probably smell our dog.'

The woman looked at her, suspicion returning to her face. 'You're Mrs Witney, you said.'

'Yes.' Charley noticed a strong waft of alcohol. 'I'm afraid I made a terrible mistake yesterday. I don't know how it happened, I must have misheard completely what the man said.'

Viola Letters was silent for a moment. 'Can I offer you a drink?' she said then.

There was a smell of linseed oil and polish in the house. It had a cared-for feeling, the walls painted in warm colours with contrasting white woodwork. There were fine antiques and almost every inch of wall was covered in paintings, mostly seascapes and portraits, and a number of amateurish landscapes in cheap frames.

Charley followed Mrs Letters through into the drawing room. A copy of the *Daily Telegraph* with the crossword filled in lay on a small Pembroke table. Viola Letters pointed her to a small Chesterfield. 'Gin and tonic?' she barked. 'Whisky and dry? Sherry?' She said everything in a raised voice, as if she was trying to make herself heard above an imaginary din.

There were Persian rugs on the floor and the tables were covered with lace tablecloths weighted down with silver snuff boxes, ivory animals and photograph frames. On the mantelpiece was a sepia photograph of a bearded Edwardian in naval uniform, his chest adorned with decorations, and on the floor, by the brass coal scuttle, was a small military drum.

'Actually, I'd love a soft drink, some mineral water or tap, please.' She had a strange metallic taste in her mouth, which she had noticed before.

'Water?' Viola Letters said the word as if it was a disease. 'Nonsense! Sun's almost over the yardarm. Pinkers? Scotch? What's your poison?'

'Perhaps just a small sherry?' Charley said, not wanting to offend her. She sat down.

'Expect we could rustle one up from ship's stores,' Viola Letters said, going over to a mahogany cabinet.

Something brushed against Charley's leg and miaowed. She lowered her hand to stroke it. She tickled between its ears and the back of its neck, then looked down. An eyeless socket in the side of the cat's face was pointing at her.

'We're a tight ship here, our little community. If I can be of any help just give me a call or pop over any time. There aren't many of us down here. I try to keep watch. We don't get too many strangers, but it's going to be a bit worse from now on: some fool journalist has written this up in a book of country walks. It's a public footpath down over the lake. Did you know?'

'It doesn't look as if it's used much.'

'It will be. We'll have hordes of bloody ramblers all over the place, I expect.'

There was something about the old woman that

seemed vaguely familiar, but Charley was not sure what. 'How long have you lived here?' she asked.

'Since nineteen fifty, but I'm not classed as a local. They're odd, the farming community. They don't trust anyone who moves here. You have to be born here. There are two farmers who won't even nod good morning to me, and I've seen them most days for the past forty years.'

'I saw one on my way today.'

'Most peculiar.' She lowered her voice. 'Interbreeding — a lot of that sort of thing round here.' She raised her voice again. 'You're Londoners?'

'Yes.'

'Well, you'll find country life a bit different. If there's anything you need to know — doctor, vet, what have you — just shout.'

'Thanks. I wondered if it's possible to get newspapers and milk delivered.'

'I'll give you the number of the dairy. There's a jolly good newsagent in Elmwood who delivers — darkies, of course, but one can't help that.'

The cat rubbed its eyeless socket against Charley's leg. She tried not to look at it.

'Nelson! Buzz off!' Viola Letters marched across the room clutching a massive schooner filled to the brim. 'There you go.' She went back to the cabinet, poured herself a tumbler of neat gin, splashed in some angostura and sat down opposite Charley. 'Cheers.'

'Cheers.' Charley sipped her sherry.

'Your husband's not a naval man, I suppose?'

'He's a lawyer. He specialises in divorce.'

There was a silence. In the kitchen the terrier began yapping.

Mrs Letters looked at her carefully. 'Sorry if I seemed rude yesterday, but you did give me the deuce of a shock.'

Charley sipped some sherry for courage. 'I must have misheard — got the wrong address — name —' Her voice tailed off.

The crab eyes slid up above the cheeks. 'No. I think you did see him, the old love.' She leaned forward, her face lighting up. 'Are you very psychic, dear?'

'No, I don't think so.'

Viola Letters fetched a photograph in a silver frame from another room and showed it to Charley. It was black and white, a tall, serious man, standing to attention in the uniform of a naval officer. The face was clear, and the resemblance to the man she had seen yesterday was strong. She had to look away, suddenly, as his stare began to make her feel uneasy. Sherry slopped over the rim of her glass on to her hand.

'It was the sticking plaster that convinced me,' Viola Letters said, reseating herself. 'Before he went up there he caught his forehead on a shelf, just above his right eye.'

Charley shivered. That was where the plaster had been.

'We were meant to be going to a luncheon and he'd gone fishing, promising to be back early. It seems he lost his watch. It had belonged to his father who'd been presented with it after the battle of Jutland and was of great sentimental value. He'd been a commander too.' She drank a mouthful of gin and swallowed as if it were fuel. 'He'd asked someone to pop down and tell me, just like you did, that he'd be late.' She blinked twice and smiled wanly. 'He was a fit man, never had any problems with his ticker before. I found him on the bank a couple of hours later. The doctor said he must have been dead for at least an hour by then.'

Charley felt icy mist swirling inside her. 'Has — anyone — ever — seen him — before?'

'No. About a year afterwards I went to see one of

these spiritualist people — a medium — but nothing came through. I hoped to find out if there was anything he had wanted to say.' She gulped some more gin. 'That thunderstorm yesterday,' she went on. 'Perhaps it was something to do with the atmospherics ... Still, it's jolly good to have some young blood in the lane,' she said, trying to brighten her face, to swallow her tears. 'We have a charity cricket match Sunday week, for the NSPCC. Don't suppose you could bake a couple of cakes?'

'Yes, of course.' She wanted to keep the conversation about Mrs Letter's husband going, but could not think what to say.

'Have you met everyone else in the lane?'

'I think so.'

'Delightful couple at the top in that rather vulgar house, Julian and Zoe Garfield-Hamsden. And Hugh Boxer, my neighbour in the barn. He's a dear. A brilliant man but a bit loopy.' She tapped her head. 'All these university professors are. Spends half his time wandering round with a couple of coat hangers looking for ley lines or some rubbish. Cheers!' She drained her glass.

'You have some nice paintings,' Charley said to fill the silence.

'My husband did several of them. He loved this part of the world and painted a lot locally.'

'I thought they looked familiar.'

'There's one that would interest you upstairs. I'll get it in a minute. It's a very nice one of Elmwood Mill.' She studied her glass, the crab eyes blinking slowly.

'Did you know Nancy Delvine?' Charley asked.

'No. Not at all.'

'What did she die of?'

'A stroke.'

'Had she been in hospital for a long time?'

'Hospital, dear?' The old woman looked at her. 'No, it was in the house. I found her. In the kitchen.'

Charley's mind raced aimlessly. She remembered the elusiveness on the estate agent's face. *Here? In the house?* Mr Budley's voice. *Oh no, I don't believe so.*

'Was she married?'

Viola Letters stood, rather hastily Charley thought. 'Can I get you a top up?'

'No, thank you. I've still got —'

The woman took the glass out of her hand. 'You haven't got a drop in that, not a drop.' She refilled Charley's glass and brought it back to her, brimming.

Charley gazed at it in horror. 'It's really a bit —' But the old woman had already set it down beside her and was on her way back to the cabinet. 'Thank you.'

Viola Letters splashed angostura into her gin and stirred it noisily. Charley's nose dipped involuntarily towards her sherry. She was feeling decidedly blotto.

'Dick loved the countryside. He was quite a sensitive old thing really, although they used to say he was tough in the Navy. I'll go and get that picture.'

Charley heard her walk up the stairs then across the floor above. The terrier yelped again, sorry for itself rather than angry now. She thought of the face in the photograph, the man yesterday in the woods. Tom had laughed at her dismissively, told her what she had told Viola Letters — that she must have mistaken what the man had said. But she had known in her heart she could not have mistaken everything. Not the name Letters, and the watch, and the address.

She hadn't told Tom about the gum. She knew he would have been even more scornful about that.

Viola Letters came back into the room holding a small framed painting. 'This is it.'

Charley took the painting. It was an oil of Elmwood Mill viewed from behind the bridge. The quality was good, clear, the detail immaculate. She studied the house and the mill, noticing its roof was in better condition than now. The picture blurred suddenly and she screwed up her eyes, trying to focus. Something was wrong, odd, different.

'When did he do this?' she asked, her voice trembling.

'Golly, now you're asking. He died in nineteen fifty-three, so before then, of course. Before the fire.'

Charley stared again, the picture shaking so much in her hands it was hard to see clearly. She tried to compose herself, to concentrate, brought it close to her face, stared harder, harder, at the building on the level patch of ground beyond the barn, the other side of the mill race, halfway up the bank. A large smart stable block.

The stable block that was missing.

Chapter Twelve

Beldale Avenue reminded Charley of the street in Finchley where she'd spent her early childhood, before her adoptive father had died and they'd had to move. A quiet south London backwash of unassuming semi-detached houses with pebbledash walls. Tidy. Orderly. Two delivery men were unloading a new washing machine from a yellow van. A mother pushed a baby in a pram. Three children raced each other down the pavement on BMX bikes.

She was surprised by the ordinariness. She had been expecting something different, although she did not know what. Something more secretive, sinister.

Number 39 had soup-brown walls, secondary double glazing and an almost smugly neat front garden presided over by a ceramic gnome with a grin on its face like an infant that has just dumped in its nappy. An old estate car was parked outside sagging on its springs, the rear window plastered with faded pennants of English counties.

As she ground through the traffic, Charley resented being in London again. She parked on the shaded side of the street and locked the Citroën with the windows open and the roof partially rolled back for Ben, who barked in protest at being left.

Tom had been as dismissive about Mrs Letters's husband as about everything else. It was Charley's mistaken identity, Viola Letters's wishful thinking, an imagined resemblance to an old faded photograph. 'Ghosts glide down corridors of houses late at night, rattling chains. They don't wander through woods at eleven in the morning carrying fishing rods,' he had said.

He had been equally dismissive about the stables. All old houses had stables, he had said. Elmwood Mill was bound to have had some.

They had worked on the house together over the weekend. Between them they had finished stripping the walls of the bedroom and decided on the colour. Tom had favoured Wedgewood blue. Charley thought that might feel cold in winter. They agreed on magnolia, then started on the largest spare room, which had been Nancy Delvine's workroom and would now become Tom's study. They had decided to leave the downstairs until after Tom's birthday party.

A curtain parted above her and she hesitated, tempted to go back to her car and drive off. It was Laura who had persuaded her to come. Or maybe she had persuaded herself. She did not know. Fear rippled through her, fear and curiosity and something else she did not understand. She felt clammy, too, and had the metallic taste in her mouth again. Her watch said 12.05. She was five minutes late.

Ernest Gibbon had not sounded how she had expected over the phone. No drama, no Flavia Montessore theatricals. He had not sounded anything much at all, other than a man who had been interrupted in the middle of the cricket match on the television. She had phoned him on Friday afternoon after speaking to Laura, and had been surprised he had been able to fit her in straight away on Monday morning.

The bell rang with a single chime and a tall, ponderous man in his late fifties opened the door. He was accompanied by a smell of boiled cabbage which made her nausea worse.

'Mr Gibbon?' she said.

He had a hangdog face, with droopy flesh that disappeared each side of his chin into mutton chop sideburns, and limp black hair that was centre-parted and a little too long, giving him a Dickensian air. He looked down at her through eyes distorted by the dense lenses of his tortoiseshell glasses. His dark suit had seen better days and his tartan tie was knotted too tightly, making the points of his shirt collar stick up slightly, and in spite of the heat he wore a cardigan. She glanced out of habit at his shoes. Her mother had told her you could always judge a man by his shoes. He was wearing wine-coloured corduroy carpet slippers.

'Yes. Mrs Witney?' he intoned in a flat, soporific voice that had no trace of emotions; he might have used the same tone to comment about the weather or to concur with a complaint about the punctuality of trains.

He held the door until she was inside, then closed it firmly. Unease rose inside her as he slid the safety chain across.

The hallway had a bright orange and brown patterned carpet; a porcelain spanish donkey in a straw hat was on a copper trolley in front of her. On the wall above it was a wooden crucifix.

'I'm afraid it's at the top.' She detected a faint wheeze after he spoke, as if he had a slight touch of emphysema, and as they climbed the staircase the wheezing became more distinct. 'Come far, have you?'

'From Sussex.'

Wooden plates with scenes of Switzerland relieved the grim Artex stair walls. He paused on the landing to get his breath. On this floor the house had a tired old smell, a milder version of the way Elmwood smelled at the moment, and it depressed her. Her stomach fluttered uncomfortably and she felt increasingly nervous, part of her wanting to pay him now, pay him for his time and go, forget about it.

He walked a few paces down the landing, opened a door and put his head in. 'My client's turned up, mother. You'll have to make your own tea. I've put your lunch out in the kitchen for you, and locked the front door if you have to answer it. See you later. Cheerio.'

Psycho. There was no mother. It was all an act.

Christ, calm down!

Ernest Gibbon climbed the next flight, the stairs creaking under his heavy plod, and then a third into a spartanly furnished attic room with the same orange and brown carpeting as the rest of the house. There was a divan with a microphone on a stalk above it, an office chair on castors and an untidy stack of hi-fi equipment and wiring. It was hot and stuffy.

'Lie down on the couch, please,' he said. 'Make yourself comfortable. Take off your shoes, loosen anything that's tight.' His instructions sounded as if he were reading out a shopping list.

She pushed off her white flats. 'Could we have the window open a little?'

'You'll find you'll cool down soon enough. Your body temperature will drop very low.' He went out and came back with a folded blanket which he put on the divan. Everything at the same unhurried pace. He walked across to the window, drew the flimsy curtains and the room darkened.

'Have you ever been regressed before, Mrs Witney?'

She stretched out, feeling awkward, regretting she had taken off her shoes because it made her feel more vulnerable. The pillow was lumpy. 'Yes, once.'

'My fee is thirty-five pounds if we're successful, fifteen if we're not. One in eight fail to regress. It will take two hours and we should get two or three previous lives on the first occasion. They are normally between thirty or three hundred years apart.' Another shopping list.

She glanced up at the microphone over her face masked in grey foam rubber. The divan smelled of vinyl.

'I tape each session and give you a copy. It's included in the price. Make yourself comfortable. It's important you are comfortable as you are going to be staying in the same position for a long time.'

Psycho. She felt a flash of panic. The mother was a rotting skeleton. He was going to ... then she heard the sound of a lavatory flushing below and relaxed a little.

'Is there anything you'd like to ask me before we begin? I can see that you are nervous.' He busied himself with his recording equipment, sorting out a tangle of wires. 'It is natural to be nervous. Going back into past lives means that we are opening up Pandora's boxes deep inside us.'

'Do all people have previous lives?'

He continued untangling the wires. 'Jesus Christ existed before he came to earth. He told us, "Before Abraham was, I am." The Bible has many mentions. Christianity is founded on life everlasting. In my Father's house there are many mansions. In our own lives are buried many past lives.' He pulled out a jackplug and pushed it into a different socket. 'Our present carnations are part of an ongoing process. Some people have deep traumas carried from previous lives. When they understand the cause, the traumas go.' He removed the wrapping on a new cassette, wrote slowly on the outside, then looked up at her. 'Do you have a particular trauma? A fear of anything?'

'Heights, I suppose.'

'You probably died in a fall in a previous life. We'll find it.'

The simplicity of his comment made her suspicious. It was too pat.

He pushed the cassette into the machine. 'Do you have a special reason for wanting to be regressed, Mrs Witney?'

'I — I've been getting a feeling of *déjà vu* about somewhere.'

'You feel as if you've been there before?'

She hesitated. 'Yes.'

He adjusted a flickering sound level light. 'Sometimes we access trace memories passed down through genes. Sometimes we transcend time. Sometimes we connect into the spirit world. The important thing is to feel free. Relax. Enjoy yourself. If there is anything uncomfortable or threatening you must tell me.'

'Why?'

The hypnotist pressed a button. There was a click and a loud whine. His voice and her own repeated: '... or threatening you must tell me.' 'Why?'

He pressed another button and she heard the shuffling of the tape rewinding, then another click. He stooped to inspect the machine. 'Because you'll be reliving all that happens. It will feel very real. Pain will feel real. Danger will feel real. It will be real.' He stood up. 'Comfy, are you? Get your hands comfy too.'

Charley wriggled around and he gently laid the blanket over her. 'I shall be putting you into an altered state of consciousness. You won't be asleep, but it will seem like it. When you come out you'll feel like you do after a nice Sunday lunch; lazy and relaxed.' He allowed the merest hint of a smile to show on his face for the first time, and it made him seem more human, made her feel safer. He walked ponderously over to the door and turned a dial on the wall.

The overhead light went out and a much dimmer red light came on. The hypnotist coughed and sat in the chair beside her. A train went by in the distance and he paused as if waiting for it to pass, then leaned towards her.

88

'Tell me your first name.'

'Charley.'

'I want you to look at the microphone. Concentrate on the microphone. Blank everything out of your mind except the microphone, Charley.'

She stared at it for a long time, aware of the silence, waiting for him to speak, waiting for something to happen. The silence continued. The microphone slipped out of focus, turned into two, then back into one. She wondered how long she had been looking at it. A minute? Two minutes? Five? Another train went by.

'Velvet, Charley. I want you to think of velvet, soft velvet all around. You are in a tent of velvet. Your eyes are feeling heavy. Everything is soft, Charley.' His voice droned, the tone unaltering. 'You are safe.'

She tried to imagine being in a cocoon of velvet.

'How old are you, Charley?'

The banality of the question surprised her. She glanced at him, saw the frown of disapproval, then looked back at the microphone. 'Thirty-six.'

'Close your eyes now. Think back to your thirtieth birthday. Can you remember what you did on your thirtieth birthday?'

She racked her brains. Thirty. Yes, she could remember that one, would never forget it. She opened her mouth, but it was difficult to speak; she had to strain to get the words out; they came out slowly, sounding slurred, almost as if someone else was speaking them.

Tom had taken her to dinner to a new Italian restaurant in Clapham to celebrate. They'd had a row, one of their worst rows ever, and Tom had stormed out of the restaurant, leaving her to pay the bill. She could feel the burning embarrassment now, six years later, could see the faces of the other diners, a woman with long blonde hair studying her disdainfully from across the restaurant as if she was an exhibit in a zoo, whispering to her dinner companions and the whole table chortling with laughter. Then it got even worse. When she opened her handbag and found she had not brought her purse. The manager had not let her leave, had locked the restaurant door and stood guard over her while she called Tom.

'Did he come back?'

'Yes.'

The microphone seemed to nod at her sympathetically.

'Go back in time, Charley. Go back to your twenty-first birthday. Can you remember your twenty-first birthday?'

Her eyelids drooped. She forced them open. Slowly they closed again and she felt herself sinking down through a soft darkness towards sleep. 'Camping.' The word seemed heavy. It rolled out of her mouth and dropped away into an abyss. 'Tom and I. In Wales. The Brecon Beacons. It rained and the fire wouldn't light. Had champagne ... a bottle of champagne in the tent. We were giggling and it collapsed. That's when he proposed to me.'

'Go back to sixteen now, Charley. Feel sixteen.'

Silence.

'You are sixteen. Look down at yourself, tell me what you are wearing.'

'A red miniskirt. White boots.'

'How is your hair?'

'It's long.'

'Do you like being sixteen?'

'Yes.'

'Why?'

'Because I'm going out with Tom.'

'Are you going out tonight?'

'Yes.'

'What are you going to do?'

Charley began to tremble. 'There's something bad.'

'What do you see?'

'Sharon Tate. People murdered. It's horrible.'

'Are you there?'

'No.'

'What are you doing?'

'I'm reading a paper. We're going out. To a movie.'

'What are you going to see?'

'*Easy Rider.*'

'Is Tom your boyfriend?'

'Yes.'

'When did you meet him?'

'On my birthday.'

'On your sixteenth birthday?'

'Yes.'

'Let's go back to your sixteenth birthday. Can you remember it?'

'Yes.' Her voice sounded slurry.

'Are you having a party?'

'In a pub — with Laura — other girlfriends, to celebrate. I'm really pissed.'

'What are you drinking?'

'Cuba Libre. He's laughing at me.'

'Who?'

'The fella. With the Beatle haircut.' She giggled. 'He thinks he's so cool. Joe Cool! He's laughing at me. I'm feeling sick now, going to be sick.' Her head spun.

Silence.

'Go back to your tenth birthday, Charley. Can you remember your tenth birthday?'

Images of childhood drifted past her, flashed at her briefly and floated away like roadsigns at night. Packing bows into plastic bags, her mother stitching stuffed toys, the television on loudly. *Emergency-Ward 10.* Vietnam. Hancock. Alf Garnett. *Juke Box Jury.*

Bonanza. Peyton Place. Kennedy was shot. Churchill was buried. Screeching Chinamen burned books. Man landed on the moon. She could smell the carpet of the sitting room floor where she lay for hours, dressing her doll, tending it, making it better when it was ill, the doll that needed her, depended on her, rolled its eyes obediently, gratefully. Florence Doll. Princess Margaret married Anthony Armstrong Jones. Florence Doll got married too. The ceremony was even grander. Florence Doll married Binky Bear who was the Head of the World.

'Your tenth birthday, Charley.'

The memory was indistinct. She was becoming aware of the room, aware of the hypnotist, and felt a trace of disappointment. She lay in silence for a moment. 'I think I'm awake,' she said.

'Your tenth birthday, Charley,' he repeated.

Damp animal smells filled her nostrils. 'The zoo. London Zoo ...' Her voice trailed off. She floated in silence again. She opened her eyes. The microphone was a blur and her whole body seemed weighted down with sandbags.

'Can you remember your fourth birthday?'

'*You careless girl! You stupid, stupid, careless girl.*'

'He's shouting at me.'

'Who is shouting at you?'

'My dad.'

'Why is he shouting at you?'

'I rode — bicycle — I got a red bicycle — into a bush. He's going to spank me and lock me in my room. My mum's crying. She's telling him it's my birthday, but he's still going to lock me in. It's the pills he's on. Mum says the pills for his illness make him angry.'

Tiredness drained her. Time faded. She was floating. It was pitch dark. She was scared. She tried to wake. She could not. She tried to sit up. Nothing moved.

'Relax, Charley.'

Her body and the darkness seemed to merge together.

'We're going back now, Charley, we're going back a long way further.' His calm voice drifted around her, seemed to fill her like air. 'We're going to go back now to before you were born. You are floating in darkness, floating in space, in the void, all is calm, peaceful, you have no worries, Charley, you are in spirit now, free, weightless, free of life.'

Dark silence carried her.

'You are in spirit now. You have a complete set of memories. The clock is running backwards. You are free to search for a memory in all time.'

The darkness swirled.

'Think about your previous life now, Charley. Remember your death. Remember how you died.'

Fear tightened around her. She began spinning, helpless, spinning in draining water, faster and faster like an insect being drawn down to the plughole; she was fighting, flailing, arms slithering, spinning faster still, being sucked down, down.

Then she was in brilliant white light. Sunlight, beating down, hard, tormenting her, sunlight pressing her against the hill, trying to crush her into the hill, to stub her out on it. Sadness filled her. An immense weight of sadness, and despair.

'Where are you?'

'On an 'ill.'

'How old are you?'

'I dunno.'

'What's your name?'

'I dunno.'

'Do you have brothers or sisters? Parents?'

'I dunno.'

'Do you recognise the hill?'

93

'No.'

'What's the colour of your hair?'

She pulled some strands out with her fingers. 'Brown.'

'Are you working? At school?'

'I dunno. I don't want to be here.'

'I presume you've had education? Where did you go to school?'

She looked up. She could see clouds through the trees. Tears were sliding down her face.

'Why are you crying?'

The ground was soft under her feet, too soft. She was sinking in. She stepped forwards and her left foot came free with a squelch. Her right foot was stuck. She pulled and it came out of her shoe, leaving that behind. She knelt down, put her hand into the boggy mud and pulled. 'My shoe. I'm wearing the wrong shoes. I oughter be in boots.'

'Why are you crying? Where are you?'

'Dunno.'

'How old are you? Tell me how old you are. When was your last birthday?'

'Dunno.' She pushed her foot back into the shoe, and stumbled on. Something bit into her hand, something sharp, hard-edged, something she could not let go. She fell and there was a sharp pain as it cut into her palm; she transferred it to her other hand, a small metal tin, and stood, forcing herself upwards, pushing the sky off her back as if it was a tent that had collapsed on to her. Something rattled inside the tin. Above she heard running water, splashing, cool water and she forced herself to go on, into trees, squelching on upwards.

'What are you carrying?'

The voice was distant in the sounds of the woods. She paused and stared around at the darkness of the trees. A rabbit was watching her. A crow. There was sudden complete silence as the chatter of the birds stopped. As the water stopped. It felt as if the whole animal kingdom was watching her. The track forked here, and she knew the way was to the right. She went on through thick bracken which crunched under her feet.

The rock loomed out of the trees, blurred through the tears that filled her eyes and streamed down her cheeks.

She reached the base of the rock, and the path was dry here, easier to walk on. As she carried on up around it she saw another rock, a strange upright rock indented in the centre, shaped like a heart.

She climbed towards it, puffing from exertion, sobbing gently. The huge granite rock at the edge of a small bluff looked as if it could topple over at any moment.

The track went underneath the overhang then around the back of the bluff on to the top. The rock looked heart-shaped from this side too, although less distinct, and even bigger than from below. It was a good eight feet high and six feet across. She knew it well. It was covered in carvings, initials, and she knew them too. *P loves E. Chris l. Lena. Mary-Wilf, Dan-Rosie. Arthur Edward loves Gwennie. D loves BJ.*

'Do you recognise any of the initials?'

She swallowed, stared down at *D loves BJ*, and squeezed the tin harder between her hands. Then she walked to the shrubbery behind the rock, knelt down, and for a while was blinded by her tears.

She scraped away the dead leaves and began to scoop a hole in the damp sandy earth. When it was nearly a foot deep, she laid the tin in, scraped the earth back over and spread the leaves out on top.

'Why are you burying it?'

She stood up and patted the earth down with her foot, then walked on through the shrubbery and down a steep bank towards a small waterfall. She began to feel spits of water on her face, her arms, her legs, and as she got closer, holding out her dirty hands, the spits turned to a fine continual spray that got heavier and wetter until she was standing in the waterfall itself, the fine spray drenching her, tiny needles of water coming harder and harder, so hard they were hurting now.

She tried to move away, but crashed into a wall. She spun round. Her face stared back from a mirror. 'Room,' she mouthed, but it was strange. Her face in the mirror did not move.

'I don't like this room,' she said.

'What room are you in?'

'I don't like this room. I don't want to be here.'

'Where is it?'

'I don't like it. I don't want to be here. Please, I don't want to be here. Please take me out.'

A figure loomed in the mirror behind her.

'No!'

The mirror exploded into spidery cracks. A jagged shard landed at her feet.

'GET ME OUT! GET ME OUT! OUT! PLEASE GET ME OUT!' She hammered with her fists. Terror throttled her, strangled her voice. 'OH QUICK, OUT! PLEASE GET ME OUT! PLEASE! OH PLEASE!'

A face looked at her anxiously. 'Charley. Wake up now. It's all right.'

The terror still surged. She was thrashing wildly.

'Charley, it's all right.'

The strange face. The centre parting. Mutton chops. Eyes like pinheads through the thick lenses. He disappeared. There was a click. Bright light flooded around her, then his face was over her again.

'It's all right, Charley. You are safe.'

She felt as if she was lying in the water. Rivulets ran down her face, over her neck, her shoulders, her stomach. She pulled her hands out and pushed away the blanket and immediately felt cooler. She lay still, exhausted, and looked up into the myopic eyes. 'What—?' It was an effort to speak. 'What happened?'

'Your past life. You were reliving something unpleasant, some bad experience,' he said gently. 'That's a good thing. It is only by reliving bad experiences in previous lives that we free ourselves of the traumas we have in this carnation.'

There was a choking lump of fear in her throat. 'It was awful,' she said. 'Horrible. It didn't make any sense — like a bad dream.'

'It wasn't a dream. You were in a past life.' He looked at his watch. 'I'm afraid we'll have to stop there. We've run over, and I have another appointment. I'll give you the tapes.'

'I thought ... I thought I had two hours.'

'It's three o'clock,' he said.

'Three? Impossible! Nearly three hours? I've only been a few minutes — ten minutes — it can't be —'

'It takes time, going into past lives; you were there a long time.'

She shook her head, bewildered, and tried to move, to get up, but she felt completely drained.

'We need to have another session,' he said. 'We should not leave it like this, with the wound open. We need to find out more.'

She stared at him, her mind jumbled.

'You were talking in quite a different voice. We need to find out who you were, what you were burying in the tin. We need to know what terrified you.'

'Why?' she mouthed. It came out a squeak of terror, like a hunted creature in the woods at night caught out in the open, away from its nest, its lair, its mother.

'Our past lives are part of our psyche, Charley. When we regress to them we stir that up, transcend the time bands. We don't want you start having trace memories, or suddenly being frightened and not knowing why. You may find that a lot of your fears now relate to this incident in your previous life. If we can see what happened, find out what caused it, it might help you.'

'And if we don't?'

'We shouldn't leave it,' he said. 'Not like this. I don't think that would be wise.'

He smiled with a smugness that disturbed her. She shivered as fear coursed through her veins.

'I still don't understand.'

'You will,' he said. 'You'll understand.'

Chapter Thirteen

'We've met before,' she said. 'In a previous life.' She tilted her glass towards her lips and stared into his eyes. 'We were lovers.'

He blushed, glanced away, then back; she was still staring. He raised his own glass and grinned. 'When?'

'It's lovely wine,' she said, the words running into each other.

'You're only thirty-eight once.'

'Are you sure?' She clinked her glass against his.

Charley watched Tom and Laura in the shadows of the hurricane lamps, at the end of the two tables they had joined together, and wondered what they were talking about so deeply. Laura in a white jacket, with a large quartz brooch, leaning towards him, her elbows on the table. Beautiful. She looked beautiful and Charley felt dowdy in comparison. She had been putting on weight since the move, just a little, and it annoyed her.

Smoke from the barbecue drifted over the table and Bob Dylan's voice sang softly from the speaker Tom had run from the drawing room. He always played old records on his birthday.

'Bats bonk upside down. Did you know that?' She heard Richard Howarth's voice, dimly, through the chatter.

'You're very brave, entertaining so soon,' said

Michael Ohm, sitting on her right. His Zapata moustache seemed to be getting thicker each time she saw him, as if to compensate for the widening bald patch in the centre of his head. He pushed his red-framed glasses back up his arched nose. One of Tom's partners. Trendy. Lawyers were starting to look like architects. Architects were looking like bankers. Change. Life shifted silently beneath you like sand.

She shivered. The heat of the Indian summer day had gone and a damp chill filled the darkness. People were putting on pullovers. Rubbing their hands. They would have to move inside soon.

Richard Howorth, Tom's best man, was here and his girlfriend, Louisa, an interior decorator. John Orpen, Tom's accountant, and his wife, Sue, were trying to prise conversation out of an extremely drunk Julian Garfield-Hampsen. Charley had suggested inviting Hugh for Laura, and Tom had thought it a good idea to invite Julian and Zoe as well; she was glad he was keen to make friends with the neighbours.

Laura was ignoring Hugh. Matchmaking for her was always difficult. She did not seem to know what she wanted herself. She had chucked away a marriage that could have been salvaged without ever really explaining to Charley why, and had fought fiercely for custody of her two girls, yet sent them to boarding school because she needed to concentrate on her shop.

Michael Ohm wiped soup from his moustache. 'How do you find it here compared to London?' he asked.

'Strange,' Charley replied. 'But it's nice getting to know Mother Nature. We actually had our own eggs for breakfast this morning — well, egg — but it's a start. We're planting all sorts of vegetables. Some of the local shops are hysterical. The grocer in the village sells only one kind of bread — sliced white. Can you believe it?'

'Geller is a con man! He's a complete fraud!'

The outburst came from Hugh Boxer at the other end of the table. He sat up in his chair, shoulders hunched inside his crumpled linen jacket, his eyes blazing fiercely, black crevasses scoring the gaunt skin of his face.

'How can you say that?' Zoe Garfield-Hampsen piped heatedly in her little girl voice, her breasts almost popping out of her low-cut dress in indignation. 'I've seen him with my own eyes. I've seen him do it!'

One hurricane lamp flickered, died for a second, came on again roaring fiercely, then Bob Dylan stopped abruptly in mid-chord; the table dimmed. Charley looked at the house. The lights had gone out. Then both the hurricane lamps went out as well, plunging them into darkness. She felt a blast of cold air as if a freezer door had been opened behind her. Someone howled; a ghostly wail.

'Mains trip,' Tom said. 'I'll do it. Won't take a sec.' There was the sound of a glass smashing. 'Ooops, bugger,' he cursed.

John Orpen clicked on his lighter and lifted the glass lid of the hurricane lamp in front of him. 'The wick's too low.' He relit it and turned it up.

Bob Dylan started singing again, several lights in the house came back on together and everyone cheered. Tom reappeared. 'We've had the place rewired,' he said, 'but they've done something wrong.'

'The trip's probably been set too sensitive,' Michael Ohm murmured.

'The soup was absolutely brilliant,' Sue said. 'Can you give me the recipe?'

Charley stood and began clearing the table.

Laura followed her into the kitchen with an armful of plates which she balanced precariously on the stack Charley put down. She looked at the clothes rack on the pulley and tugged the cord. The rack rose up and down,

101

then wobbled above them. Charley noticed she looked sloshed, and was surprised: Laura rarely drank much.

'S'beautiful place. You're so lucky! I'm incredibly envious!' She pulled the cord again, mildly irritating Charley, and the rack rose up and down with a creak. 'So tell me, how did it go with Ernest Gibbon? What did you think of him?'

Shadows from the rails of the rack swung across the floor as Charley loaded plates into the dishwasher. 'I thought he was a creep.'

'He's sweet!' Laura slurred indignantly. 'S'lovely man!'

'Tom's listened to the tapes — bits of them anyway. He says he was feeding me with thoughts.'

'He'd never do that. He's got a terrific reputation.'

'It struck me as a good con. He leaves you feeling terrified, so you want to go back to find out what happens next.'

Laura tugged the cord once more. 'No, I don't think he's like that.'

There was a wailing screech then a bang like a clap of thunder in the room.

Laura jumped back and crashed into the fridge.

Charley stared in shocked silence at the clothes rack; it was lying on the floor between them.

'Sorry,' Laura said, looking lamely at the cord. 'Forgot to hook it back.'

Tom turned the pork chops and sausages over on the barbecue. Fat spat and sizzled on the red coals. He prodded a couple of the jacket potatoes, gave each of the sweetcorns a half turn, blinking against the searing heat and the smoke, stood back unsteadily and had a gulp of his wine. He could see the glow of the lamps and the shadowy figures at the table fifty or so yards away, but the darkness and the booze made it hard to make out much more.

A pair of hands slipped around his waist. 'Hi,' she said, quietly, simply. He smelled her perfume, felt the light pressure of her hands.

'Not quite done yet,' he said, turning round.

Laura's eyes were locked on his, her mouth smiling quizzically in the faint glow of the coals. 'I like looking at you,' she whispered.

He smiled, embarrassed.

'I often see you across a room at a party, looking at me. I like it when you look at me.'

Her fingertips brushed against his, then her fingers curled around his, squeezing them gently. He glanced over towards the table. Shapes, just shadowy shapes; he and Laura would be shadowy shapes too. He hoped.

Laura stretched up on tiptoe and placed her lips against his, soft lips, much softer than Charley's, he thought, before pulling back, taking her wrist and leading her behind a tree. They kissed, longer this time, and he pressed her against the tree, filled with a sudden urge of drunken lust. He slipped his hand inside her jacket, inside her blouse, ran his fingers over her breasts while she ground her pelvis against his growing hardness. He drew away and squinted mischievously at her. 'What are we doing?'

'Having a snog.' She smiled petulantly then grasped the back of his head and kissed him again. His hand wandered under her skirt, over the nylon of her tights and the smooth skin of her stomach, then slid inside her tights and over the bare skin of her buttocks. He started trying to pull her tights down.

She shook her head, still keeping her lips to his, murmuring. 'Uh oh, no!'

He broke away and glanced furtively round the tree. 'We could have a quick knee trembler.'

'No!'

He fumbled with her tights.

'Stop it!' she said. 'I smell burning.'

He turned to the barbecue. Flames were leaping up around the chops. 'Shit!'

'I think I'd better get back and join the party,' Laura said. 'Which way's the loo?'

'The least grotty one's at the top of the stairs, turn left, second door on the right.'

They began to sing happy birthday as Charley brought the cake out. The baker in the village had made it. There was a legal-looking scroll on the top and the wording 'HAPPY BIRTHDAY TOM' visible through a forest of candles. The wind blew most of them out and Tom the rest. There was a roar of applause and raucous shouts of 'Speech!'

His face became a flickering blurr.

She felt a deep sense of unease. The smell of the barbecue disturbed her. Burning embers. The flames licking at the inky darkness. Silence pressed in around her. The smiling faces and the shouts and laughter faded.

She had been here before. Seen flames here before.

She saw the old man stumbling through the woods towards her. The girl climbing up towards the rock with the tin in her hand, crying.

'Penny for your thoughts.'

She looked round, startled. Hugh was sitting in Michael Ohm's seat and was grinning at her.

'Sorry,' she said. She shivered, rubbed her arms. 'It's cold. Do you think we should move inside?'

'Soon.'

'Do you remember what you were saying in the pub, Hugh, about old spirits?'

'Yes,' he said, taking out his pipe. 'OK if I —?'

'I love the smell, she said. 'Have you ever been regressed into past lives?'

'Under hypnosis?'

'Yes.'

He bit the stem and cocked his head slightly, his eyes narrowing. He lowered his voice. 'I told you, there are a lot of amateurs around. Don't get involved.'

'I thought you believed in reincarnation.'

'I don't believe in playing games with the occult.'

'Games?'

Wisps of dry ice were curling through her veins. Hugh was looking around uneasily. 'Sorry about the car,' he said, abruptly changing the subject.

Car. Triumph. Car. Gum. She put her hand out to her glass and it was shaking so much she nearly knocked it over. Her cheeks felt red.

'I ought to pay you a fee for parking,' he said.

'No. Not at all. It's — you can leave it, really.' There was a minty taste in her mouth. Gum.

There was a thud. A clatter. Hugh bent and picked up her fork.

'Oh, thanks —' She wiped it with her napkin. 'Please, leave the car for as long as you like.'

'A few more days would be helpful.' He lit his pipe with an old Zippo. A gust whipped hot ash from it and he clamped his hand over the bowl. 'Have you done much exploring around the area yet?'

'No, not really.'

'This is a very interesting part of the world. It's riddled with old energy lines. Used to be considered quite fey.'

'Witches on broomsticks?'

'That sort of thing.' He grinned and sucked on his pipe. 'Have you been to the Wishing Rocks?'

'Where are they?'

'It's a pretty walk. You go up through the woods the far side of the lake, take the right fork after the marshy bit and carry on.'

'Why are they called Wishing Rocks?'

'They're pagan holy stones — I don't know how they got them up there, unless they were hewn out of the hill — and the locals had a superstition that if you wanted something really badly you took the rocks a present.'

'A sacrifice?'

His pipe had gone out. 'No, not a living sacrifice, but it had to be something personal.' His lighter clanked and he sucked the flame down into the bowl of the pipe. She sniffed discreetly as the thick blue smoke drifted over her head. 'And if you wanted your love to be eternal you engraved your names on the Sweethearts' Rock. If your love ever faded, you took the rock a token and it made everything OK again.'

She was silent for a moment. 'What does that rock look like?' she asked.

'You can't miss it. It's shaped like a heart.'

Chapter Fourteen

Charley slept badly. The cacophony of birds and the roaring of the water and the churning thoughts in her mind kept her awake.

Tom lay awake too, tossing beside her. He got up and went to the lavatory. A while later he got up again, went into the bathroom and came back with a glass that was fizzing.

'You OK?'

The bed sagged as he sat down. 'Jesus. It was quieter in London. Can't we shut those bloody birds up?'

The sky was grey, stormy, and a strong wind was blowing. There was the clatter of a bicycle and tyres scrunched on gravel. Ben ran to the bedroom door, barking.

'Newspapers,' Tom said.

'Did you enjoy last night?'

'Good fun.' He screwed up his eyes.

'You and Laura were talking a lot.'

He stirred the Alka Seltzer with the handle of his toothbrush, drank some and grimaced.

'What were you talking about?'

He was silent for a moment, then mumbled. 'Nothing in particular.'

The window rattled and a gust of chilly air swept across her face. 'The weather's not so nice for your cricket,' she said.

'It might clear up.'

'What are you doing this morning?'

'I thought I'd start stripping the drawing room. There's no point in painting anything while they're messing around with the floorboards.'

Charley yawned and looked around the bare walls and the raw beams and the low, uneven ceiling. It still felt strange in this room, felt each morning as if she were waking in a hotel and not *home*.

'Back to work for you tomorrow,' she said. 'End of holiday.'

Tom nodded. 'Are you in London this week?'

'Tomorrow. I'm going to see mother, and I said I'd help Laura for a couple of hours. The money's useful,' she added defensively.

'It doesn't even cover your train fare.' He went to close the window.

'I've seen some very inexpensive kitchen units. I meant to tell you.'

'Is there any point at the moment? We might as well wait.'

'It's so dreary in there. It's going to be years before —'

He ducked through into the bathroom. The bath taps gushed then the sound changed to the hiss of the shower.

She raised her voice. 'I really wish I was still working.'

'Why?'

'Because I'm fed up not having any money. I'm guilty all the time about spending anything.'

He poked his head through the door. 'It's not forever. After we —' He hesitated. 'You know, have kids, you can go back again.'

'Not to my old job.'

'Your old job was killing you.'

'I liked it.'

She had liked the pressure. Her boss, who designed fashion accessories, had been a workaholic and it was infectious. She was expected in the office at seven and rarely got home before eight. They travelled somewhere in Europe at least once a fortnight, to the States twice a year and occasionally to the Far East, buying, exhibiting, looking. It had been fun. And well paid.

'A couple of new units and a lick of paint and the kitchen'll be fine until we can afford to do it properly.'

'If you put your mother somewhere cheaper, we could afford to do a hell of a lot more now.'

'I hope you remember that one day when your father's old and infirm,' she said angrily.

The first rock loomed out of the woods above her. She climbed over a fallen birch and stopped at the edge of a small clearing to get her breath back. The woods were dark and hemmed her in; they spooked her. Ben stopped, maybe sensing something too, and nuzzled his head against her leg.

She was the furthest she had been up here, beyond the point where she had met the old man, Commander Letters ... or imagined him ... or seen a time warp, a freak of the atmospherics. Or had met someone totally different, an innocent old codger with a fishing rod and had passed on his message to the wrong person.

She was nervous of meeting him again.

A shadow moved in the darkness through the trees, moved steadily, came out to greet her and she shrank back, goosepimples creeping over her flesh, until she realised it was just a bush behind a tree moving in the wind.

Two eyes watched her from under a dock leaf. Then the rabbit turned and scuttled through the undergrowth. Ben did not notice. She patted the dog, felt comforted by his company, by his hair, his warm body.

'Good boy,' she murmured.

The track ahead was through bracken. She climbed on, under the overhang of the rock, past a narrow fissure which reeked of urine and where there was a used condom lying on the ground. Behind, a long way back, she thought she heard a child shout and a woman's voice reply.

Then she could see the second rock a short distance above, and she stopped. There was no mistaking this rock, no saying it was just another rock and maybe ...

Heart-shaped, distinctly heart-shaped. It sat at the top of a short escarpment silhouetted against the boiling sky.

It was the rock she had seen in her regression.

She stared for a long while, trying to remember, to think back to childhood, to the outings in the country she had had with her mother. On Sundays they took a bus or a train to the country. However hard up they had been, her mother had insisted on a weekly treat. Maybe they had come here one Sunday? Or seen it in a film? Television? A book? Hugh said it was an ancient monument, a religious stone. Maybe she'd seen it in a magazine? A documentary?

She bit her lip and climbed a steep narrow gully up through the escarpment, scrambling over several smaller rocks. She reached the top and stood in the open, on a bracken-covered knoll with the heart-shaped rock in front of her and shrubbery behind.

She gulped down air, staring at the view; the buffeting wind made it hard to stand still. There was a panorama across the treetops in every direction except straight ahead which was obscured by the rock. Fields and woods and spires, pylons, farms, several large houses, a glinting swimming pool in the garden of one, a tennis court. She could see part of the lake, and the

110

white columns and conservatory of Yuppie Towers.

The rock was a massive granite lump, with deep cracks and patches of lichen, rising out of a bed of dried bracken. It was covered in names and initials and messages, crudely carved, mostly weathered and barely distinct. P loves E. Chris l. Lena. Kenneth/Elizabeth. Anna l. Lars. Mary-Wilf. Arthur Edward loves Gwennie. D loves BJ.

D loves BJ.

She looked closer.

D loves BJ.

The initials she had stared at in the regression as if she had known them.

She touched the rock; it felt, smooth, cold. Silent. Ben loped around below, crunching through the bracken. Up here was silence. Only the wind. She read the initials again.

Coincidence? Tricks of the mind? Like the chewing gum? The stables? The man with the fishing rod?

D loves BJ.

The tin. The tin she had carried up here in her regression. If that was here too? Her heart was hammering.

Chinese box, Tom had said with a grin. The Chinese box was a delicacy. You buried a tin full of maggots in the earth, with no food. When you dug it up a fortnight later the maggots would have eaten each other and there would be one left, fat, juicy, the survivor. You ate him.

She could remember the spot. There, barely ten feet away in the shrubbery. She went over to the dense undergrowth. Something was glinting. Excitement rose as she parted the bushes then fell as she saw it was just glass from a broken bottle. She cleared it and knelt down.

This spot here.

She stood up and walked away, feeling foolish. She gazed at the view, tried to fight, but slowly she was drawn back, slowly she walked across and knelt again. This time she began to dig with her hands, the sandy soil packing under her nails. Ben arrived and licked her face, thinking she was playing some great game.

'OK, boy, help me dig! Big bones buried!'

He sat and scratched himself.

She dug down several inches, felt something hard which grazed her finger, and she clawed the soil away around it until she could see that it was a piece of flint.

She widened the hole, winced as she scraped her hand on a sharp stone. She dug beneath it, felt the cold slime of a worm stuck to her fingers and shook it free with a grimace.

Stupid, she thought, standing up. Daft. Should have brought a spade. Need a spade. She shook some of the sandy mud from her hands and stared at the small molehill she had made. Her watch said quarter to eleven. A spot of rain struck her face. With her boot, she shovelled the earth back into the hole and trod it flat, then hurried, half walking, half running, back to the house.

It was past twelve when she got back to the rock, her lungs aching, perspiration guttering down her body.

She sat for some minutes listening to the silence, the wind. Blue crevasses were appearing in the grey sky and it was getting brighter. She turned the trowel over in her hands; the rusted old tool was slightly bent and there was a crust of earth on the blade.

She glanced round. Ramblers in orange waterproofs had trudged up the track behind her, but they had turned off at the fork. Her hair thrashed her face. A voice inside her whispered *Go back! Forget it!*

She went to the shrubbery and knelt. Her pulse tugged at the base of her right thumb, as if someone was

112

pinching at the skin. She felt a weird throbbing up her right arm and a tickling at the back of her throat. She glanced around once more, then began to dig.

Half an hour later the sky had brightened a little more. She had dug a crater eighteen inches deep and was wondering whose land this was and whether people were allowed to come along and dig holes. Did it belong to some farmer? The National Trust? Was an irate gamekeeper going to march out of the trees?

Ben had gone off somewhere and she felt very alone. Exposed. The silence was eerie. Forget it, there's nothing. No tin. She rammed the trowel into the earth, more in frustration than an intention to go on digging, and a metallic clank rang out.

She froze.

She raised the trowel an inch and pushed down again. The clank again. Duller.

She began to dig more carefully, feeling her way around the object, then dumped the trowel and used her hands. Something sharp grazed her finger and there was a trickle of blood in the mud. She dug with the trowel again, cutting the soil away on each side.

Then it was free, and she levered out a small mud-caked object. It was light, weighed scarcely more than the earth that was stuck to it. Something inside rattled, rattled again because she could not hold it steady.

She scraped the mud away with the blade of the trowel. Pitted metal showed through. A small square tin, three inches across and an inch deep. In parts the rust had eaten almost through it. She closed her hand around it, felt the edge. She could hear Ernest Gibbon's voice, probing.

What are you carrying? Why are you burying it?

It was this tin she had been carrying. Shiny and newer, but this tin. She was certain. And she was afraid to open it.

She looked into the crater. Two halves of a worm wriggled at the bottom.

Sometimes when you open the tin the maggot's bigger than you think.

The lid was held on by pressure. She tried to pry it off with her hands, but it would not budge. She used the blade of the trowel as a lever and twisted. The edge of the lid curled upwards then came free with a pop and a faint hiss of trapped air and fell into the hole.

A heart-shaped locket lay in the tin.

She stared at it, transfixed. An inch-high enamelled heart, ruby red, with a tarnished gold chain which spilled out and slithered down over her wrist, icy cold. It glinted dully in the sunlight that broke through the cloud. She blinked.

She knew this locket.

Knew that inside it she would find a note, carefully folded. Her head throbbed and her vision became blurry. Slowly, with fingers that felt like hams, she lifted the locket out. There was a tiny hinge and an even smaller clasp which, though rusted, moved under the pressure of her thumbnail. A minute piece of paper nestle inside, yellowed, brittle, folded several times. The wind fluttered it and she shut the locket, scared it would blow away. She felt giddy.

She wet her fingers with spittle and wiped them as clean as she could on her jeans then, shielding it from the wind, she took the tiny square out, and unfolded it. The ink was blurry, smudged, brown with age, and the paper so brittle she was frightened it would disintegrate. The handwriting was just legible.

'Dear Rock, I love him. Please bring him back. Barbara.'

'What are you doing?'

It felt as if a lever had been pulled inside her, switching her blood flow from slow to fast. A small boy was watching her, brown-haired, an earnest freckled face. He was about seven.

'Are you making a wish?' he said.

She nodded and managed a weak smile. A voice called out. 'Timothy! Come on, darling!'

He scampered out of sight. 'Mummy! Mummy! There's a lady up there making a wish!'

Her face was burning red with embarrassment. And guilt. This was someone else's locket, someone else's note. She had no business digging it up, reading, prying.

She refolded it, placed it inside the locket and snapped it shut. Then she laid it in the tin, closed the lid firmly and put it in the hole. She scooped the earth in and stamped it down with her foot. When she turned around, the boy was there again.

'Is that your doggie?' he said.

'Yes.'

'What's he called?'

'Ben.'

'I made a wish here,' he said.

'What did you wish?'

'I wished that the rock would make my daddy better.'

'Did it work?' she said smiling, almost relieved to have company.

'No.' His face puckered. 'He died.'

Chapter Fifteen

Tom hit a four off the first ball.

'I knew he could bat,' said Vic, the landlord from the George and Dragon, as glumly as if he had been clean bowled. 'I can tell a good bat when I see one.'

'Well done, darling!' Charley yelled, applauding the loudest. She stood beside the tea table, watching as the bowler paced out his run, rubbing the ball on the left cheek of his buttock. He started his run, slow, quick, slow, quick. The ball sailed through the air, Tom lunged out, missed, and it passed the wicket keeper.

'Yes! Go!' yelled the batsman the far end, already halfway down the crease. Tom ran, made the far crease long before a fielder ever got to the ball. There was more clapping. Fielders waited as the second batsman took his guard.

Charley felt a spot of rain on her face. The doilies under the cakes on the trestle tables flapped in the wind. Viola Letters's terrier ran in and out of the table legs yapping.

Charley squatted, patted the dog and tickled its chest. 'Hey, chappie, are we going to make friends?' It licked her hand tentatively.

Hugh Boxer came over, padded up, a weathered bat under his arm, cap tugged down over his head, wearing an old-fashioned college cricketing jumper and baggy white trousers. The outfit suited his aura of faded nobility.

'That was a bloody fine hit,' he said. 'Bold shot for an opener. He looks like rather a useful player.'

'He used to be very good.'

'Still is. Thank you for last night by the way,' he said.

'I hope you enjoyed it.'

'Very much. It was a good evening. Laura's a bright girl.' His eyes were probing.

'Yes, she is,' she said. 'I went up to the rocks this morning, the Wishing Rocks.'

'Oh yes?'

'You're right. It's a pretty walk.' She glanced at her nails, which were not completely free of mud, then back at Hugh. 'This custom — of burying things — does it still go on?'

'You might get the odd kid doing it occasionally. I think people have got more cynical about things like that these days.' He stretched down to tighten a strap on one pad.

There was a crunch and a silence on the pitch. The middle stump was bent backwards behind the batsman. Tom was at the other end she saw, relieved.

'I'm on parade,' Hugh said, and grinned.

'Good luck!'

'I'll need it.' He strode out, tugging on his gloves, pads flapping.

There were a couple of hundred people, Charley estimated, crowded around the jumble stall and the tombola and seated on the benches in front of the tiny pavilion. Several families lay sprawled on picnic rugs around the boundary, and two old buffers sat in front of the wooden scoreboard in deck chairs, surveying the match from under their green sun visors.

A batsman stood at a practice net while two others alternately bowled at him. He returned the ball each time with a proficient *snick*. A group of children played their own game with a tiny bat and a rubber ball. Hamburgers and hot dogs sizzled on a griddle, and the banner 'NSPCC CHARITY MATCH' shook precariously in the wind.

''Ow much is the cup cakes?' a child asked.

'Twenty pence,' Charley said.

He handed her a grubby coin, which she dropped in the tin, and helped himself to a pink one.

Viola Letters stood on a milking stool behind a trestle table covered in upturned cups on saucers, and peered into a massive steel urn. There was a half-hearted ripple of applause as Hugh reached the crease, and the unfortunate opening batsman arrived back to face his team mates.

'Bad luck, Johnny!'

'Got me on a Yorker. He used to bowl for Kent, that one.'

Charley watched Hugh and Tom. The ball came hard at Hugh and he blocked it neatly. An umpire called, 'Over!'

Cricket. Lazy days. It brought back good memories. Tom played regularly when they first went out and she had spent happy hours lying with the sun on her back, watching, reading the same page of a paperback over and over, chewing sweet blades of grass.

The urn hissed steam. Viola Letters lifted a huge metal teapot from underneath the table and filled it with boiling water from the urn. 'Be a dear, Charley. Give it a couple of minutes and start pouring.'

Charley staggered under its weight. She put it down on the edge of the table and waited for the tea to steep. Tom hit another run. Hugh hit a four. It was a pretty village green, bounded on two sides by houses, and a wilderness of common land on the other two. She was glad Tom was playing, glad to be here herself, helping with the teas, a part of it. Belonging. She was glad Tom was doing well.

The tin and the locket suddenly swirled through her mind, and fear followed like a wave, crashing through her. The terrier yapped.

'Oh, Peregrine, I'm sorry! I didn't mean to frighten you.' She put her hand down to stroke it, but it scuttled away and yapped again.

Dear Rock, I love him. Please bring him back. Barbara.

It was coincidence: the gum, the stables, the old man. But not the tin.

A cold gust blew through her and she smelt a strange, musky perfume, strong, so strong, as if the woman wearing it were standing next to her; then it was gone like a snatch of smoke whipped away by the wind. She glanced around, wondering where it had come from, then picked up the heavy teapot, holding the handle with both hands, and tilted it towards the first cup.

It happened quickly. Just a jerk, that was all, and the handle became weightless for a fraction of a second as the top of it sheared away from the pot, which swung upside down dumping two gallons of scalding tea straight on the terrier.

She heard the howl almost before she realised what had happened, before the hot metal banged into her legs, before she even felt the sting of the scalding liquid on her own feet.

The dog fell sideways, rolled on to its back, twitching, steam rising around it. Its howl constricted into a tight screeching scream.

Viola Letters dropped to her knees to help it, and it twisted its head, bared its teeth and bit her hand savagely. Then it slithered a few feet across the grass on its belly, tried to stand and fell, howling, snapping at the grass, snapping at one of its legs. It rubbed its face on the grass and most of the skin of its nose came off.

A child screamed.

'Peregrine!' Viola Letters bellowed, desperation in her voice, blood streaming from her finger as she ran after it.

The tiny dog rolled in agony, thrashing one way then the other, frothing, steam rising from its coat, like some grotesque beast from the pit of hell.

The shower was running upstairs, the plumbing creaking, water spurting up the pipes. The kitchen was snug from the heat of the Aga. The wind had died and a steady drizzle fell outside.

The cricket had gone on in the way games always went on, with a barely perceptible change in the tone, as if someone had tweaked the volume control and maybe the contrast knob. The children went back to their own games of cricket, except for a couple of tots who had leaned against their mothers, crying, their thumbs in their mouth.

The dog had been wrapped in towels to prevent it from biting anyone else, but by then it had given up struggling and lay helpless, twitching and whimpering. A girl from St John's Ambulance had bandaged Viola Letters's finger and someone had driven her and the dog to the vet. Charley had offered to go with her too, but Viola Letters had stoically told her to stay and carry on with the teas.

'It's not your fault, old girl,' a man with a handlebar moustache had said to Charley kindly. He held up the teapot, its handle twisted and hanging on by one bent bolt, and pointed at the jagged holes where the top bolts had sheared. 'Metal fatigue. Happens in aircraft.'

Later a tall woman in galoshes announced they had raised three hundred and forty-two pounds and eleven pence for the NSPCC. There was a ragged cheer. Tom had scored forty-two runs and bowled two of the other side out. He was voted man of the match and presented with a pewter tankard, and Charley's eyes had felt moist as pride broke through the cloud of shock and doom.

There were two messages on the answering machine, one from Holly Ohm thanking them for the party, the other was from Tom's squash partner, Paul Lerond. 'Tom, I got your message about cancelling tomorrow. How about Wednesday evening at six fifteen?'

Charley dropped a couple of pinches of food into Horace's bowl and chopped up the ox heart for Ben's supper, wrinkling her nose at the stench of dried blood.

Tom was lying on the bed wrapped in a towel, the Sunday papers strewn around him. The television was on: *Only Fools And Horses.*

'What do you want for supper?'

He combed back his wet hair. 'What have we got?'

'Tons of leftovers.'

'Fine. You look frozen.'

'I am frozen.' She peeled off her clothes, and examined the blotches of brown tea stains on her white trousers. There was a rash of small blisters on her feet from the scalding tea, and a larger one on her heel from where her wellington boots had rubbed earlier in the woods.

She went through into the bathroom. 'Do you think I should call Mrs Letters, or go round?' She stared at herself in the steamed mirror. Her face was sheet white, her eyes like dark beads.

'Call her.'

'If it's died — I —' She bit the skin below her thumbnail. 'Perhaps I should send her some flowers.'

'Or donations to its favourite charity.'

'Don't. That's horrible.'

Fatter. She was definitely getting fatter and losing

some of her muscle tone. Her breasts were larger. Maybe that was going to be a perk of growing old? Tom always complained they were too small.

'Bernie the builder said he'd keep an eye on Ben tomorrow. Want to meet up in London?' she said.

'I won't have time. It'll be hectic after two weeks away and I'm playing squash.'

'With Paul?'

'Uh huh.'

There was a roar of laughter from the television.

'There's a message on the machine from him, about cancelling.'

Another roar of laughter, more feverish.

'Oh, ah — yes,' Tom said, his voice sounding rather odd, she thought. 'I forgot. We've got a partners' meeting.'

Her birthmarks stood out tonight, two fine straight lines, each a couple of inches long, one on her stomach, the other on her right thigh. They were red, livid, like weals. They seemed more pronounced than usual. She touched them gingerly.

She heard the rattle of the locket, saw it again, in her mind, lying in the tin. Something inside her rattled too, something dark and cold and ominous. She looked again in the mirror. Her eyes stared back.

Afraid.

She could not sleep. Her mind was alive, crawling, echoing with the pitiful howling of Viola Letters's dog and the image of it thrashing on the grass with the steam rising.

She tried to think of something pleasant, but instead recalled the Chinese box. She could hear the maggots, smell them, wrestling, sweating, climbing over each other with their sharp claws, their concertina bodies heaving, eating through days and nights of never-ending

122

darkness. Eat or be eaten. Their jaws chomping, chomping, each chomp echoing around the tin, a dull boom.

The biggest one had the blunt face of a snarling pug. It was faster, uglier, greedier than the rest. It twisted in the darkness, its body bulging, chopping the rest up until it was surrounded by writhing white shapes that waited, helpless, to be sucked into its mouth until there was nothing left for it to eat, nothing left but to lick the tin shiny clean and wait.

For her.

Inside the folded piece of paper inside the shiny ruby heart inside the tin was a tiny speck of darkness. It was a speck only because it was far away in a dimension she did not understand. A vanishing point on a far horizon. As she opened the tin, opened the heart, unfolded the paper, the speck came at her. Huge, dark, its teeth like rusted blades, fire hurtled out of the dark tunnel of its throat, fierce volcanic flame that stank of Doublemint and melted away the skin of her face.

Tom rolled over and snorted air.

The killings of the night went on out in the darkness, under the light of a moon shrouded in mist. The shrieks, the cries, the crackle of undergrowth. The ecosystem taking care of its own.

Water tumbled down the weir. Boiling water tumbling from the kettle. The howl of Viola Letters's dog joined the screams of the night.

The teeth of the maggot closed, severing her in half below the shoulders. She tossed, twisted, trying to shake the image from her mind.

'Christ, you're restless,' Tom said grumpily. She snuggled up to him, put her arms around him, held him tightly, kissed him, slid her hands down his body.

'Charley, for God's sake! I have an early start. Let me sleep.' He turned away.

She laid her head against the small of his back, smelled his skin, felt its heat, pressed her cheek against him as warm salty tears slid down past her mouth.

Chapter Sixteen

The marigolds had wilted. Charley dropped them in the bin and changed the water in the cut glass vase. 'I'm sorry I didn't come last week, mum, but there was a lot to do in the house. It's in pretty bad condition — worse than we realised. The builders say we should really have a new roof.'

She held the flowers before the blank gaze of the old woman in the bed.

'Michaelmas daisies. They're from the garden.' She arranged the daisies and ferns in the vase by the window. 'We're planting lots of flowers.'

A blind girl with a guide dog walked across the park below.

'Lies death.'

She spun round, but her mother was staring motionless into space. She did not look as if she had moved or spoken. 'What was that?' Charley said. 'What did you say?'

The old woman blinked once and continued her eternal motionless stare.

'Lies death?'

No response.

'Is that what you said, mum?' Charley sat down beside her, took her bony hand. It was the first time she had heard her speak for months. Since before Christmas. 'Lies death, mum? Where does it lie?'

Silence.

She rubbed the old woman's hand. 'What did you mean, mum? Please tell me.'

There was no reaction. Charley waited. Five minutes passed, ten, half an hour. Her mother did not move. Charley stroked her hand gently. 'I went to a hypnotist the other day. To go back into my past lives. Have you had any past lives? Do you believe in that?' She didn't expect a response. There was a faint smell of urine.

'I don't think I believe in it,' Charley said with more conviction than she felt. 'But what was strange was that he made me go back through childhood. I had to tell him what I'd done on my sixteenth birthday, and my tenth. You took me to the zoo, do you remember? I had a ride on a camel. And my fourth birthday. I could remember it in such incredible detail. Daddy spanked me because I rode the bicycle you'd given me into his rhododendron bush. It was a red bicycle, a Raleigh, with whitewall tyres and a white saddle and it had a horn instead of a bell and little fat wheels, and two extra ones on the back for balance. He'd never spanked me before. You said it was his medicine that made him do funny things.'

She thought she detected a faint pressure from her mother's hand, but it might have been her imagination, her own wishful thinking.

'I've been thinking about childhood a lot recently. Maybe because I'm trying so hard to have a child of my own, maybe it's the move. Everyone says moving is pretty traumatic. I've had so many bizarre thoughts. It's noisy in the country, you know? Much noisier than London. Most nights I've lain awake, listening to the animals, watching the moon, thinking about how I used to sit on the floor with you, playing with Florence Doll, packing the bows. I used to feel safe then, with you.' She looked at the bedclothes, at the loose knit of the blanket that heaved gently up and down like the swell of a calm sea. 'I don't feel safe any more.'

As she was leaving she heard the voice again behind her.

'Lies death.'

'I think you should go back to him.'

'I'm frightened.'

Two women stared in through the window of the boutique and pointed at a coat. One said something and the other nodded. They moved on.

'I think this is incredible!' Laura said. She pressed the stop button on the cassette player.

'Sure you do,' said Charley. 'It's not happening to you.'

'Let's hear that bit again.' The tape rewound for several seconds, then Ernest Gibbon's voice:

'Why are you crying? Where are you?'

There was a long silence, while the tape hissed. A girl in culottes opened the door of the shop, changed her mind and went out again.

'Dunno.' The voice was strange, not her own voice. It was a rural working girl's accent.

'Where are you going?' said Gibbon, his voice steady, lethargic.

A minute passed.

'Up an 'ill. There's a rock.'

'Can you describe the rock?'

'Like an 'eart. It's got initials. Like lovers' initials.'

'Do you recognise any of the initials?' said Gibbon.

'D loves BJ. 'E wrote 'em.'

Laura stopped the tape. 'BJ! You said the piece of paper in the locket was signed Barbara, didn't you?'

Charley nodded.

'You see?'

'It doesn't mean anything.'

'It's working, Charley. Don't you see?' Laura seemed irritated.

'See what?'

'Oh, come on! *Barbara J.*'

'Laura, I just dug up someone's locket.'

'Your locket! It's your locket!'

'It wasn't my handwriting.'

A woman came into the shop. She made for a rail of blouses and began flicking through them.

Laura lowered her voice. 'You're not going to have the same handwriting.'

'I don't want to go on any more.'

'Why not? Christ, Charley, you must! Really!'

Charley looked at the customer. 'Can I help you, madam?'

The woman held up a blouse as if it were a mouldy cabbage. 'Hrumph,' she said, hung it back and hoicked out another.

Charley turned to Laura. 'What are you doing after work? Want a quick drink?'

'I — I'd love to, but I've got —' She hesitated. 'Dinner party. I'm having a dinner party.'

'Anyone interesting?' Charley wondered why Laura was blushing. Because she had not invited herself and Tom?

'No, just some friends I haven't seen for a while — people I met on holiday. I don't think you know them.'

'How about Wednesday?' Charley said. 'Maybe catch an early movie. There are several films I want to see.'

'Wednesday? Yes, that sounds great. I'll check my diary.'

The customer held several blouses up to her face, comparing the colours against her skin. She hung them back untidily; one fell on the floor and she ignored it.

'Why don't you want to go on with your regression?'

'Something's telling me to stop, that's why. I had this strange feeling' — she shrugged — 'that I hadn't any business digging it up.'

'But don't you see?' Laura said.

The customer marched over to a row of dresses.

'What has Tom said about the tin?'

'He's sceptical, even more than I am.'

'You're *still* sceptical? Come on!'

'Maybe I imagined it. I don't know. I'm sure there's a perfectly rational explanation.'

'There is.' Laura smiled and looked at her intently. 'You've lived before.'

It was just before seven when Charley turned into the lane. The Citroën bounced through a deep pothole, springing her up and down in her seat.

There were stories of sportsmen who carried on playing to the end of a game with broken legs. The mind was a strange thing. You could carry on, you could believe anything if you tried hard enough; for a while.

The Indian summer was ending. The evening sun shone through the open roof, but the air had an autumnal chill and she felt a coldness that would not go away. Charley knew she believed the discovery of the tin was coincidence the way a footballer believes his broken leg is just bruised, the way a drunk believes he'll feel fine in the morning.

She was frightened.

As she passed Hugh Boxer's house, she heard the sound of a power tool in his workshop. Viola Letters was in her front garden dead-heading her roses. Charley stopped the car, and climbed out.

The old woman came to the gate, her eyes red, a smile mustered on her pallid face and enough gin on her breath to anaesthetise an elephant. Her finger was still bandaged. 'Thanks awfully for the flowers,' she said, 'it was jolly sweet of you.'

'I'm sorry,' Charley said. 'I'm so sorry.'

'Like a snifter?'

'Thanks, but I've got some chores. I must get home. I've been in London.'

'Hardly ever get up there these days. All my old chums are dead or gaga.' She smiled sadly. The cat glared at Charley and kept its distance, as if Charley carried some pestilence. 'It wasn't your fault. I'd noticed the handle was a bit wobbly. I hope you weren't hurt.'

'A few splashes. Nothing. I'm sorry, I really feel awful.'

'You mustn't. I should have thrown the bloody teapot away.' She gazed around her garden. 'The Alexanders have done well this year, don't you think?'

'They're pretty. What's that one?' Charley pointed to a pink tricorn-shaped bud.

'An Admiral Rodney. No relation, I'm afraid.'

There was a silence.

'I — I don't suppose I could rope you in for something else?' the old woman said.

'Yes, of course.'

'It's this Wednesday afternoon. We have a jumble sale in the church hall. Doreen Baxter usually does it with me, but she's ill.'

'I'm meant to be helping a friend with her shop in London on Wednesday, but I could probably change that. I'll give her a call when I get home and ring you back.'

'Very kind of you, dear. Don't worry if you can't.'

'I'm sure it'll be all right.'

Viola Letters blinked. 'Kipling was right you know. Never give your heart to a dog to tear, but we always bloody do.' Her face crinkled as she fought to keep her composure. 'Still. I shan't get another one, not at my age. Wouldn't be fair. Peregrine was thirteen. Kipling said a lot of wise things. Shame he's gone out of fashion.' She mustered a smile again. 'I'd like to invite you and your husband to supper one evening.'

'You must come to us.' Charley ran her finger along the top of the fence. 'I don't seem to be terribly good news for you, do I?'

Viola Letters gave her an odd glance, as if she were about to say something, but changed her mind. In that moment, Charley had the sensation that she had stood at this fence talking like this to the woman before. She looked up at the dark stone wall, at the crenellations against the metallic blue sky, at the small mullioned windows, like the windows of a keep, and the feeling grew stronger.

'I suppose I'd better get on. I'll call you about Wednesday.'

'Thank you, dear,' Viola Letters said, and Charley had the feeling that she felt the same thing. 'And thank Tom for the flowers, will you?'

Charley promised she would.

The phone stopped ringing as she fumbled with her key, and Ben, inside, was barking excitedly. As she pushed open the door, picked up the groceries she had bought on the way home and stumbled into the dim hall, she heard the click of the answering machine. Half the floorboards were up, and lengths of unconnected piping lay around.

A voice in the kitchen echoed around the house. She ran down the passageway.

'... marvellous fun, great food. Great party tricks! Talk to you soon, bye!' It was Richard Howorth. There was a clunk. She dumped the groceries on the kitchen table and rushed over to the machine and lifted the receiver, but he had already hung up. The light winked busily, six messages. Ben was thrashing his paws against her waist.

'Hallo boy, hallo boy! Yes, yes, yes, it's good to see you too!' She knelt and hugged the dog while he splashed her face with licks. 'Have you had a lousy day? Have you? Yes, I know, it's no fun being locked in. Did Bernie let you out? Take you for a walk? Let's go, shall we?'

Ben raced out of the front door and over to a duck that was waddling beside the mill race. The duck took off in panic.

'Ben! Wicked! Wicked boy!' she scolded.

Ben wagged his tail. Long shadows lay across the grass and the drive. It would be dark in an hour. She stared up at the woods. At the hill. The hill with the heart-shaped rock on top and the locket buried in the sandy soil.

A flicker of recognition sparked deep inside her and faded. The roar of the water seemed gentler. The chirruping and trilling and distant cawing of the birds sounded like an orchestra tuning up for the evening's performance. A thrush swooped down near her and pecked at the grass.

She crossed the wooden bridge, pausing to look down into the clear water, brown in the fading light, then climbed up the short mossy bank on to the level patch where the stables had once been. She rummaged around with her feet through the long scrub grass for a sign of stones, foundations, but could see nothing. She sniffed as she thought she noticed a smell of burning, but it had gone, and she walked the width and length, criss-crossed the patch, but there was nothing there, no hint that there ever had been anything other than grass and weeds and earth.

On the opposite bank, across the stream, the house was bathed in a glow from the setting sun. A pile of bricks and building materials lay near the bottom of the steps, covered in plastic sheeting, with two long ladders laid out on the grass next to them.

Up above, at the edge of the woods, was the row of old sheds, a donkey shed, a privy, and an open-sided woodshed. Next to them, running along to the paddock, was the hen run and the kitchen garden.

Cattle lowed and a sheep gave out a single bleat as she walked back over the bridge and along the gravel past the barn. Viola Letters had been so sad. She wished there was something more she could do for the old woman.

The blisters from her wellingtons and the scalding tea made her limp slightly as she climbed the bank. In the paddock beyond the fence two chestnut mares stood silhouetted against the red ball of the sun, and she would have liked to have taken their photograph; except her camera was somewhere at the bottom of a packing case. Time, though. There was all the time in the world for photographs.

The hens clucked and tutted inside the compound that Gideon had fixed. Molly, the white hen, ran in a small circle clucking in fright at Ben. Daisy, white with black speckles, strode out of the henhouse rocking from side to side like a fat lady carrying shopping and pecked at some corn. Clementine, the prettiest, brown with a gold collar, poked her beak through the mesh as if she wanted to have a private word. Ben stared, uncertain still what to make of them.

Charley filled the hopper with feed pellets, ran some water from the stand pipe into the watering can, and filled the drinking bowl. She went to the back of the henhouse, squatted down and unlatched the flap of the nest boxes and slid her hand in. The red bantam they had christened Boadicea gave an outraged squawk and flapped away. Where she had been were two brown eggs, still warm. The other boxes only contained the plaster dummy eggs.

She relatched the flap and went into the run. 'Bedtime, ladies!' She herded the hens into the henhouse, closed the door, carefully shooting the top and bottom bolts, and walked away with a feeling of satisfaction, putting her hand into her pocket and touched the two eggs nestling there. She liked eating their own produce. Early days, but a start.

The kitchen clock said seven forty-five. She put the eggs in the basket on the table, picked up the phone and began dialling.

Chapter Seventeen

Tom lay on top of her, breathing heavily, his chest heaving, heart thumping, sweat running down his body. He rolled gently off, cradling her small shoulders in his arm and ran his fingers through her short razored hair.

She turned to face him, and he wondered what she was thinking. Her eyes looked serious; she opened her mouth, then closed it and studied him further.

He glanced past her at the darkening sky through the window. Going to rain, he thought, watching the winking lights on the roof of Chelsea Harbour Tower in the distance. The room was snug and pretty, white shag carpet, white wicker furniture, all white except for a few green plants; another woman's bedroom; the pleasant unfamiliar smells, different soaps, talcs, perfumes; sensuous; forbidden ground.

He felt the soft skin of her back, his fingers following the contours of her shoulder. 'On Saturday, at dinner, you said we had been lovers in another life. What did you mean?'

She gazed into his eyes. 'I think we've been lovers before. We might meet up in another life and be lovers again.'

Tom wasn't sure what to say. 'I hope you have such lovely skin again,' came out.

She kissed him lightly. 'Charley's a very lucky lady.'

'Oh yes?'

'To have you as a husband.' She pulled away and rolled on to her stomach. He traced a finger slowly down the small of her back and was about to reply, then realised what he was going to say would sound banal.

She kissed him softly on his eye. 'You shouldn't be here. We shouldn't be doing this.'

Tom said nothing.

A compact disc played on the far wall. Tiny columns of blue lights beside it rose and fell in tune with the music, which came out of thick padded speakers. The assured voice of Tanita Tikaram. Meaningless words sung with meaning. Tom heard those kinds of words in his office all day. His mind tuned out of the music and into the traffic noise from the King's Road below. There was a dull ache in his dried-out balls.

Guilt ate him up.

Every day of the week someone like him sat on the other side of his desk in the office. Good-looking guys and ugly guys, smart guys and dumb guys. Nice guys and creeps. He'd never thought that one day he could be in the same equation. Never start something you can't finish was a rule, a maxim, by which he had always lived. You kept order and control over your life that way. The divorce courts were full of people who had started things they could not finish.

A bead of sweat trickled down his back. Laura tidied his hair, tousled it, tidied it. 'Have you ever sensed anything odd in your new house?' she said.

'What do you mean, *odd*?'

'A presence.'

Tom grinned. 'Only this strange rapist at the barbecue.'

'I mean it. You don't think there's anything there?'

'No. Why?'

'When I went to the loo upstairs I sort of — felt something.'

136

'Has Charley been feeding you some claptrap?'

She slipped out of bed. 'No. I don't know what it is. I don't think I'd particularly want to spend a night there on my own.' She went through into the bathroom. As she closed the door there was a warbling sound beside him that made him jump. It paused, then warbled louder.

'Answer it, Tom, it'll be the plumber,' Laura shouted.

He fumbled, picked up the receiver and pulled it to his face. 'Hallo?' he said breezily. 'Laura Tennent's phone.'

'Tom?'

It was Charley.

He felt as if he was sinking in an express elevator. For a moment he toyed with slamming the phone down. Christ, she'd never know for sure — not absolutely for sure. But it was too late, he had hesitated too long. 'Darling, hi.'

'Tom, what are you doing?'

'Just popped in to have a look at — a letter — rather nasty letter Laura's had. Ah. From Bob.' Bob was Laura's husband.

'Bob?'

'Yes, he's creating a few problems — the house. I'll get her for you. I think she's outside with the plumber.'

'Isn't she having a dinner party?' she said, with faintly disguised hostility.

'Dinner party? No — I. No, I don't think so.'

There was a silence.

'I thought you were having a partners' meeting?'

'I — Laura rang, rather distressed. I —'

'What time will you be home? Are you going to want any supper?'

'Yes, I'm on my way now. Be on the next train, whenever it is.'

The bathroom door opened and Laura came out.

137

'Hang on, I think I can hear them.' He jammed his hand over the mouthpiece. 'It's Charley,' he hissed. 'I told her I'd popped in to look at a letter from Bob. About the house.'

Laura took the receiver. 'Charley, hi. Dinner party? Oh, yes, I am. It was really sweet of Tom to pop over. I got home and found this absolutely stinking letter from Bob.'

Tom went to the window and stared out. Shit, he thought. Warm air and fumes from the King's Road traffic below wafted around him. A taxi rattled up, a stream of cars, a bus. Shit. Shit. Laura rattled on.

Doing OK, keep it up, girl. Keep it up.

'No, he's on his way now. He's been so sweet — so helpful. Plumbing? Plumbing, did you say? Plumber here? No, I thought you were the plumber phoning.'

Tom's heart sank.

'Want another word with him? OK, see you on Wednesday. No? Oh, all right. Bye!'

She sat down on the bed beside Tom, and lowered her head. Neither spoke for a moment. He put his arm around her.

'How did I do?' she said, turning to look at him.

He stared gloomily back. 'Great,' he said. 'Just great.'

Chapter Eighteen

'Is she a good screw, the bitch?'

Perfectly reasonable explanation. Of course there'll be a perfectly reasonable explanation. Of course.

She forced a smile on her face and tilted her head. 'Hi, darling! How was your meeting?'

Ben looked up at her, puzzled.

It was dark outside now. A cloying blackness pressed against the window panes. Laura had warned her about that, been right about that: the countryside was dark, black, a million times blacker than London.

Laura's flowers were in a vase beside Horace. He drifted in his water, mouth opening and shutting, gawping at the endless movie he watched through the curved glass. Charley wondered if he realised that he saw everything distorted, as if he were watching life through a hall of mirrors reflection. She wondered if she saw it distorted too.

There was a faint smell of laundry in the kitchen, from the dishcloths and socks and underwear and Tom's striped shirts hanging on the drying rack above her. 'How was Laura? OK, was she? I mean she was fine when I saw her, just fine. But that was five o'clock and she couldn't come for a drink because she was hurrying home to organise a dinner party.'

Ben's tail wagged. He dropped the bone he had been chomping on and padded over expectantly. 'Not for you, boy,' she said, staring at the lumps of steak on the chopping board. Nothing. Nothing. Nothing to worry about.

It was really sweet of Tom to pop over. I got home and found this absolutely stinking letter from Bob.

Why the hell shouldn't Laura have had a letter from Bob? Bob was always causing Laura trouble. Perfectly reasonable. Yes-yes-yes. Tom had gone round because . . .

Is she a good screw, the bitch?

Charley stood still for a moment. The thought slammed through her; the words; as if someone else were speaking them, whispering them into her ear. They repeated louder, more insistent. She shook her head, trying to clear it. Not Laura. No. Maybe others, but not Laura. Definitely not.

Never.

Friends didn't do that. Not friends who went back twenty years.

The kettle boiled and she poured some water into her mug. She stirred the coffee. Tom's steak was thick, red, huge; she had asked the woman to cut it thick and she had, a massive T-bone. She prodded it and felt squeamish suddenly at the soft slimy texture.

A navy blue sock fell silently on to it.

She looked up at the drying rack. It was motionless. The other sock still hung from one of the wooden rails. Ben let out a low rumbling growl. Her eyes narrowed, her heart was beating a little faster than it should. She picked the sock off the steak and saw that some of the cotton fibres had stuck to the meat.

She didn't feel squeamish any more. It looked good as it was, raw. Flesh. Red meat. Bloody. She wanted to eat it, to cram it into her mouth and chew it raw, like an animal. She remembered, vaguely, a book she had read where a woman had a craving for raw meat.

She picked up her piece of steak, cut thinner than Tom's, and bit a mouthful off it. Her eyes screwed up and bile heaved in her stomach. She leaned forward, spat the chewed meat out into the sink, ran the tap, held her mouth under it, swilled the water around and spat it out.

Ye gods.

Why on earth had she done that? The taste lingered, of blood, flesh, something rancid, something — She gulped at the coffee and spat that out too, then, feeling sick she ran upstairs into the bedroom, through to the bathroom and brushed her teeth.

She leaned against the basin. In the mirror her eyes were red and puffy from crying. Crying because she knew ... knew that he had not gone there to look at a letter from Bob.

Her mouth tasted better, minty. She went into the bedroom, sat down at her dressing table and dabbed some powder on her face, then tidied up her smudged mascara. Anger welled inside her again.

The front door opened and closed and she was surprised not to hear Ben barking. Still absorbed with his bone, she assumed, and tried to prod some life into her hair.

The stairs creaked; Tom's footsteps up it, slow, as if he was tired, or nervous of a confrontation.

Stay calm. Cool. She tossed her head and tried to concentrate on her hair, tried to ignore him as she heard him come in the door, heard him walk across the slanting floor and felt him standing behind her.

Cold air had come in with him. Bitter cold air. The room felt like a freezer. She stared in the mirror.

But could not see him.

She felt the icy breath down her neck and smelled a musky perfume. She spun round.

There was no one. The room was empty.

141

But a smell of perfume hung in the air. Strong. Shivers ran down the small of her back. It was perfume she had smelled before, knew from somewhere. The room reeked of it, as if someone wearing it was there. Her eyes darted around.

'Tom?' she called out. 'Tom?' She walked across the floor, peered into the bathroom, stared at the bath, at the shower curtain, walked back into the bedroom, stood and listened.

She went out on to the landing. The cold air seemed to follow her. 'Tom?' She sniffed, but there was nothing now, no smell. Goosepimples prickled her. 'Tom? Is that you?'

Slowly, nervously, she went downstairs. 'Tom?'

She walked along the dim passageway, past the cellar door and into the kitchen. Ben was gnawing busily. She stopped, listened again. The door; she was certain she had heard the front door, footsteps up the stairs. Smelled the perfume. She stared at the drying rack, nervous of it for some reason, stared at the single blue sock, then lowered the rack slowly, creakily, paying out the cord and hung back the second sock.

Bright lights flashed against the window. A car scrunched down the gravel outside. Tom's car.

Instead of anger, as she walked down the passageway to greet him, she felt only relief.

Charley gazed through the curtainless window at the black starless night. Tom slept beside her, breathing heavily, smelling clean, squeaky clean, exuding a faint odour of pine shampoo.

She'd cooked him his steak, exactly as he liked it and he'd sat at the kitchen table opposite her and eaten his way through it silently, mechanically, not dining, merely refuelling.

Throughout their marriage there had been many

times before when they had eaten in silence, when Tom had been in one of his moods, moods that had often lasted for days. But tonight it wasn't one of his moods, and Charley wished it was because she understood those, knew that with a mood it was a matter of waiting and everything would be OK again.

Tonight something had changed, in both of them.

She wished they were back in London, in their small house with the streetlights and cars outside and neighbours around, the house where they had begun their married life, where they had made their home. Where they had been happy.

Ben padded around the room, his name-tag jingling from his collar, restless.

There was a cry outside, like a woman in distress. Ben barked and Tom stirred slightly.

Ben whined and pawed at the door.

'Foxes,' Tom grunted. 'Vixens.'

She dozed. Images flashed in her mind, and she could not sleep. She listened to the roar of water, heard the hissing of the urn, the howls of Viola Letters's dog. Howls. Shrieks. Screams.

'Jesus Christ!'

The bed moved, creaked. She opened her eyes. Tom stood silhouetted at the window. Her clock radio said 4.35. Then she realised.

The sound was real.

It was coming from outside. Dreadful panicky squawking, screeching. Ben was barking frantically. Tom pulled on his dressing gown. She ran downstairs after him, into the kitchen and jammed her bare feet into her wellington boots.

They ran across the wet grass, under the streaky back-lit sky, the noise getting worse the closer to the hen run they got, a hideous cacophony of clucking and beating wings and croaking and clattering wire, and a lump swelled up inside her throat. Ben stopped, unable to comprehend what was going on.

At first she was unable to comprehend also. She thought they were panicked, that was all. They were flapping wildly, Boadicea and Daisy and Clementine and Molly, rolling around as if they were drunk, crashing into each other, into the wire, falling over, pulling themselves along the floor of the run by their wings like old people on crutches. It was as if someone was shaking the run like a box. Boadicea rose up in the air, crashed into the netting, fell upside down, her neck twisting, her beak opening and shutting, her legs kicking, two bloody feetless stumps.

Charley clutched Tom's arm. Molly cartwheeled over and over, blood smeared across the white feathers of her stomach. She crashed into the mesh in front of Charley, trying to push her head through as if she was screaming for help.

'Jesus,' Tom said. 'Bastard. Bastard.'

Charley stared in horror at a twig on the ground, a thin grey gnarled twig, except it wasn't a twig, it was the foot of one of the hens. Then she saw another.

All the hens' feet had been severed.

Boadicea tried to stand on her bloody stumps, Boadicea who had been so proud now fell over sideways, chewing at the ground with her beak.

The bile slid up and she turned away and was sick on the ground behind her, her ears filled with the pitiful agony of the clucking and flapping. Tom marched into the run. He knelt and grabbed Boadicea firmly, gave a sudden sharp twist of his hand, there was a crunch and the hen went limp. Blood dripped down.

The cacophony of sound seemed to be getting louder. The wings of a hen thrashed against Charley's face, blood sprayed over her. It was Clementine. Charley picked her up, but she wriggled free and fell to the ground showering blood and feathers. She tried again, holding on harder, and put her hand on the hen's neck. For a moment Clementine was motionless, staring her straight in the eye, her beak opening and shutting as if she were trying to speak. Charley put her down and turned away.

She stumbled out of the run and sat down on the wet grass of the bank, listening to Ben barking and the cries of the hens quieting as Tom worked through them, the same pattern, a flurry of squawking, a crunch, a brief silence. Then a final silence, complete silence, even from Ben, even from the dawn chorus of birds, even, it seemed, from the weir.

Tom sat beside her, his face and dressing gown spattered in blood and excrement and feathers, and wiped his hands on the grass. 'I thought humans were the only creatures that killed for sport,' he said.

The air was full of the coppery smell of blood and the stench of damp feathers and the sweet morning dew. The sky above the lake was streaked with brushstrokes of pink and yellow and grey. She stared at it dully through her haze of tears. It was going to be a beautiful day.

Chapter Nineteen

Charley sat in the morning sun holding her mother's hand as she always did, staring at the flowers in the crystal vase and the oak chest of drawers on which they stood that contained most of her mother's possessions.

A few clothes, some photographs, trinkets, a passport with its one single purple stamp on its blank pages, '10 Jul. 1978, Entrada A Barcelona', the only time her mother had ever been abroad. Charley and Tom had taken her with them on holiday to a villa they had rented in Spain. Her mother hadn't liked it much — too hot, she had said apologetically, and the toilet had a peculiar smell.

'We lost our hens on Monday night. It was horrible. The fox didn't kill them, he just bit off their legs. I wanted to bury them and Tom said that was ridiculous and got angry. He said we'd have eaten them anyway.

'I couldn't do that. I buried them up in the woods, then I bought four chickens from Safeways and put them in the freezer, so he won't know.'

Her mother's nails were getting long, would need cutting soon. 'I think Tom's having an affair. But I can't say anything in case I'm wrong. I'd look a bloody fool.' She hesitated. 'You know who I think he's having it with? Laura.'

Laura. The name stuck in her gullet.

'Did daddy ever do anything like that?'

There was no reaction; they sat in silence for a while.

'What did you mean, mum, on Monday when I was here? You said "lies death". At least, that's what it sounded like. *Lies death*. What did you mean?'

There was a rasp of breath, different to the normal pattern. Her mother was trembling and perspiration was trickling down her face. 'What is it, mum? Are you OK?' A child shouted outside and there was a burst of music from a car radio that was too loud. Her cream gabardine dress was feeling too tight and stuck to her skin. It was always like a hothouse in here, summer and winter.

'I wish we could talk, mum, like we used to. There's so much I need to know from you. So much advice I'd like. I don't have anyone else to ask.'

There was another silence. After a while Charley said, 'Horace is still going strong. My goldfish. Remember him? He's eleven now. Tom won him at a funfair by shooting at ping-pong balls. He was in a tiny plastic bag and we never thought he'd make it home, let alone live for eleven years.' She scanned her mother's face, seeking a glimmer, but saw nothing. She stroked her hand gently. 'Funny how you get attached to things. Even a dumb fish in a bowl can be your friend.'

'Truth,' her mother said suddenly. 'Go back.'

Charley looked at her, startled, but she was staring blankly ahead again. '"Truth", mum? "Go back"?'

There was no reaction.

'What do you mean *truth*?' She leaned closer. 'What truth? Go back where?'

Nothing. Charley listened to the traffic outside. A telephone rang in another room. Her mother still trembled.

'I helped out at a jumble sale yesterday in the church hall in Elmwood. There's an old lady down the lane —

147

Viola Letters — that's an old-fashioned name, Viola, isn't it? She's getting me involved in the local community. A nice old stick. She doesn't have any children either. Been a widow for years. You've been a widow for years too, haven't you? Would you have liked to have remarried? Did I stop you, make it harder for you?'

Charley chatted on, trying to sound jolly through her heavy heart, about the party they were going to on Saturday, colours they had chosen for some of their rooms and the carpets they were going to look at. They thought a rug for the bedroom floor, keeping the bare wooden floorboards either side, would be more in character than wall-to-wall carpeting.

Her mother made no further sounds and gradually the trembling subsided during the next two hours. She was still staring vacantly ahead as Charley left, blowing her one final hopeful kiss from the door.

'Tom, if I wanted to trace my real parents what would the procedure be?'

He dug around disinterestedly in his salad bowl, elbows on the kitchen table, his striped office shirt opened at the collar and the cuffs rolled up. He lifted a forkful of mung beans and alfalfa sprouts and gazed dubiously at it. 'I thought you weren't interested in tracing your parents.'

A light breeze came through the open windows and a late bird twittered. She speared a couple of pasta shells. 'I used not to be. I suppose I am a bit now. I thought if we ever did have children it might be nice for them to know their ancestry.'

'Your parents are dead.'

She ate a mouthful. 'There might be aunts and uncles.'

He chewed his sprouts and screwed up his face.

'Christ, these taste like an old sack.' He had a pallor of grease on his skin from London that a quick dab from the cold tap had not cleaned away. He looked tired, strained. The way she felt. 'Charley, when people are adopted it's usually because there aren't any relatives who can — or want to — care for the baby.'

'I'm not saying I'm going to contact anyone. I think I'd like to know. I mean it's not as if I was the result of a one-night stand or anything like that. My parents were married.'

'Your mother died giving birth to you and your father died of a broken heart. Right?'

'That's what mum always told me.'

'He probably died of something else.' He frowned. 'How would your mum have known that, anyway?'

'That he died of a broken heart?' She shrugged. 'No idea. I've never thought about it.'

'You were adopted within a few days of being born, weren't you?'

'Yes.'

'People who die of broken hearts don't die immediately. And adoptive parents never usually maintain contact with the real parents.'

'Maybe he had a heart attack or something,' Charley said.

'Has your mum ever told you anything about them?'

'Not really. They were young, hadn't been married very long — about a year.' She drank some wine but it made her feel queasy.

'Do you know their name?'

'No.'

'The hospital where you were born?'

'No.' She saw her adoptive mother trembling in her bed.

'If they had a common name, it can be very difficult. I've known it take years — and cost a fortune.'

'What's the procedure?' she said. Her voice was barely more than a whisper.

'You have to apply for your original birth certificate at St Catherine's House in London.'

'Is that a long process?' It seemed as if it were someone else speaking.

Lies death.

Lies.

Lies about her parents' death? Was that what her mother had been trying to say? That she had told lies about their death?

Truth. Go back.

She remembered her mother trembling when she first told her they were moving. Had she started trembling because they were moving?

Or because of where they were moving to?

Go back.

Where?

A fat hamburger slid past, leaking gherkins and ketchup from its midriff like an open wound. It was followed by a plate of bacon and eggs, then a girl tossing her long brown hair in the wind.

'Alpha Temps. Join the smart set!'

Charley stood wedged in the crowd as the escalators carried her upwards like flotsam on a wave.

The rush hour. A few weeks of country living and she was feeling increasingly an alien in London. She stepped out into the daylight, found her bearings and turned right down the Strand.

She had not been back to the boutique, had not spoken to Laura since that Monday night. The thought of Laura at the moment made her uneasy. She was certain last night, when Tom had arrived back late again, that she had smelled Laura's perfume on him.

The words 'ST CATHERINE'S HOUSE' were clearly

visible on the other side of the Aldwych. The building had large glass doors and a sign 'Wet Paint — Use Other Entrance'.

Inside were two enquiry desks, a felt board with several blank forms pinned to it and some steps up to a large modern room filled with rows of metal book-shelves. Although teeming with people, the place had the studious quietness of a public library.

She joined a small queue for the desk marked 'Enquiries only', and waited her turn.

'I'm adopted,' she said, feeling as if she were saying *I'm a leper*. 'I want to get a copy of my original birth certificate.'

The clerk, a small man with a cosy smile, pointed round to the right. 'You'll need the reference number,' he said. 'Those rows there are Adoptions.'

She walked along the brightly lit corridor between the rows of files. It was strange to have your identity hidden behind a reference number. There was a rack of metal shelves against the wall with 'Adoptions 1927 onwards,' printed above.

She half wanted to turn away, forget the whole thing. What if? If?

Lies death. If what her mother had told her had been a lie?

So what if it was? If the truth was different, would it matter? She had met an adopted woman who had traced her parents and discovered she was the product of a one-night stand in the rear of an army truck. But that hadn't made any difference, had not brought her world crashing down. She always said she was pleased she knew, felt more comfortable with life for knowing.

And if she had been the product of a one-night stand she wouldn't have to tell her children, or anyone else (unless, maybe, it had been a duke). And if she was the daughter of a hooker or (please not an escaped loony) a criminal, well, that would be a shock. And maybe a secret. But at least she would know.

'1952. 1953. 1954.'

She lifted the ochre fabric-bound volume out. It was heavier than it looked. She laid it down on the flat writing surface and opened it. The pages were dry and turned with a sharp rustle; she was wary of tearing them. Boone. Boot. Booth.

There were about fifteen Booths, typed on old black typewriter ribbons. She ran her eyes down them, then stopped, feeling a sense almost of embarrassment at seeing her own maiden name there in print.

'Booth. Charlotte Lesley. 12.8.53. No. of entry: 5A0712. Vol No. 388.'

That was all. Somehow she had expected there to be something more, something that might make it feel special. But there was nothing special. The ink was thicker on some entries than others, where errors had been corrected.

She read it several times, glanced at the rest of the Booths, wondering who they were and where they had ended up, wondered how many others had made the same journey here and had stared at the same page and felt the same flatness when they should have been excited.

She took the book back to the clerk's desk.

'You have to fill in one of those.' He tapped a buff and yellow form on the felt noticeboard. 'They're out on the counters. Were you adopted before 12th November 1975?'

'Yes.'

'You have to send one of those to the CA section of the GRO. General Register Office,' he translated, seeing her blank face. 'The address is on the back. They'll send you an adoptee's application form and get in touch with you about counselling.'

'Counselling?'

'It's the law, I'm afraid. You'll have to be counselled. You can fill in the form I've given you here, if you like, and we'll send it off for you.'

She went into a stall, pulled out the antique Sheaffer fountain pen Tom had given her for her birthday, and pressed the nib lightly against the form.

There was a sudden tang of musky perfume. She began to write. The smell became stronger, engulfing her, as if the wearer were leaning over her shoulder. She turned, but there was no one behind her; nothing but the empty stall across the narrow corridor.

Chapter Twenty

The remains of the simple picnic were spread beside them and she lay back contented, her head nestling against his chest, smelling the sweet scents of the flowers and grasses.

His fingers ran through her hair, and the sun beat down between the trees. She closed her eyes and watched warm red spots dancing in the darkness. The chattering of the birds felt lazy, too, and the breeze rustled the leaves like the sea lapping on a shore. The ground seemed to sway a little, and she imagined they were castaways on a raft on a flat blue ocean.

Somewhere in the distance she heard horses' hooves.

The fingers touched her cheek and then her lips, and she bit one gently with her teeth. His stomach rumbled loudly and the baby inside her own belly made a few tiny jerks. She opened her eyes and saw a tortoiseshell butterfly skim the bluebells that were all around them.

He shifted his position and his face was over hers. He kissed her and she could taste the beer and sausage on his breath. She put her hand up to his chin, felt the rough stubble, and stroked it.

'Your name? Can you tell me your name?' a voice said.

He traced a line down her neck, then slid his hand inside her frock, inside her brassiere and began to fondle her breasts. He took hold of a nipple between his finger and thumb and she flinched.

'Ow! Careful! It's sore!'

'Your name? Tell me your name!'

Not far away a horse whinnied.

'Dunno.'

'Who is the man you are with? Your boyfriend? Husband?'

A hand was on her knee, sliding up her thigh, coarse fingers moving up her bare flesh.

'Do you know where you are?'

'Bluebells,' she murmured, irritated by the intrusion, wishing the voice would go away. The branches swayed above her, sunlight dappled through the leaves. A bee buzzed past them, a bird flew overhead, then the man's face blocked out the light as his lips pressed down again, his tongue ran along her teeth and searched hungrily inside her mouth. His fingers slid inside her knickers, tugged their way through her pubic hair. She tightened, pushed his hand firmly back down, said, 'No. The baby. We mustn't.'

'Course we can.'

The hand pushed its way back up.

'No!' She giggled. 'Stop it.'

'Won't do any harm.'

'It will. We mustn't.'

'Don't be a stupid cow.'

'Dick, please.' She closed her knees together. He rolled away from her and she sensed his anger.

She lay still. Her heart felt heavy and she did not know why. She lifted the locket that lay on her chest and stared at it, the heart-shaped stone glinting in the sunlight, ruby red, the gold chain sparkling. Then a shadow fell across the locket. A horse stamped its right foot behind her.

She looked up.

A woman on a chestnut horse, silhouetted against

the sky, stared down at them. She had fine features, handsome but severe, jet black hair tied back below her hat, and an elegant hacking jacket, smart breeches and shiny boots.

The woman's eyes were shadowed by the peak of her velvet riding hat, but they seemed to burn like sun through a mist. She could feel scorn, disgust, and something else — something that made her afraid.

Before she could react the woman had turned and ridden off, but the stare of the eyes remained and burned into her own retinas like sun spots.

Her dress was up over her stomach, and she tugged it down and giggled, a solitary giggle that fell away into silence. 'She must have seen. Why didn't she say nothing?'

He stood up abruptly, brushing the grass from his trousers.

'She was dressed fancy,' she said. 'I ain't seen her before. She must be stayin' at the manor.'

'She's from London,' he said brusquely. 'A lady. She's rented old Markham's place for the summer.'

'The mill?'

'Wants to buy it, I'm told.'

'That's 'er? The one they talkin' about? She ain't no lady from what they say.' The venom in the woman's eyes was vivid. 'Was that Jemma she were ridin'?'

'She's paying good money for me to saddle her.'

'Jemma's *my* 'orse. You promised.'

'After the summer. Anyway, you shouldn't be riding at the moment.'

'They say she's loose.'

'She's a lady,' he said, his voice rising.

'Do you think she's pretty?'

He did not reply and she put out her hand to him. 'Dick, you love me, don't yer?' It was dark suddenly. She was cold, shivering. 'Dick?' Dick?'

156

She smelled burning. Flames licked the darkness. Flames all around. Horses whinnied. There was a splintering crack above and a burning beam was tumbling down on her.

She screamed. Ran. Another beam fell in front of her, more beams were falling. Flames everywhere. A figure staggered towards her, a human being burning like a torch. She screamed again, turning, running, running into a wall of flame.

The flame dissolved into a red glow.

Eyes looked at her, myopic eyes through thick lenses. Anxious eyes. A voice intoned, 'Charley, wake up now please. You are back in the present. You are no longer in trance. You are back with us. You are safe.'

She saw the sad hang-dog face, the centre parting, the mutton chop sideburns, the cardigan the colour of dried mustard. Ernest Gibbon's crows' feet crinkled into the hint of a smile and his baggy jowls heaved. The microphone in its foam padding peered down at her like an inquisitive bird.

'You are quite safe, Charley,' he said in his soporific monotone. 'You're back with us.'

Tight bands of anxiety seemed to be cutting into her skin. Her heart thumped and her pulses throbbed.

'Dick,' the hypnotist said. 'You called him Dick. Can you remember your name?'

She lay motionless for some while, then shook her head.

'Do you know where you were? Did you recognise it?'

She thought hard before answering, trying to clear her mind, trying to work up the energy to speak. 'Woods near where we live. I think I was asleep — dreaming — just a bad dream. There's a girlfriend who —' She paused, partly from tiredness, partly from embarrassment, and smiled lamely. 'I — I'm jealous of.

157

Probably nothing in it. I keep thinking she's making a beeline for my husband. I think I was dreaming about her.'

'No, you were in a previous carnation,' he said, as blandly as if he were talking about the weather. His jowls heaved up and down as if he were chewing a cud.

A vague smell of cooking was seeping into the room. Meat, potatoes, gravy. It made her feel queasy. Outside she could hear the wail of a siren and rain tapped on the window. Smells and sounds that should have been normal seemed alien.

'What can you remember about the man you were with, Charley?'

'I — I've seen him before.'

'Would you like to tell me when?'

'I told you I was regressed once before I came to you. I think it's the same person.'

'Can you describe him?'

'Quite nice looking. Rugged. He had short brown hair. Stocky, wiry. A bit like — I suppose he looked like that actor Bruce Willis but rougher. He was attractive.'

Gibbon pulled out a large polka dot handkerchief and began wiping his glasses. 'Was he a farmer?'

'Yes.' Her voice tailed off. 'I'm not sure. I think so.'

'Were you living with him?'

'Yes.'

'Did you have a wedding ring?'

'I don't know. Locket,' she said. 'I had the locket, the same locket I found in the tin I dug up. The tin I buried last time —'

He studied her. 'And you were pregnant?'

She nodded.

'Is there anything else you can remember about yourself? The clothes you were wearing?'

She thought. 'A frock. A sort of muslin frock.'

He finished cleaning his glasses, and put them unhurriedly back on, settling them comfortably, adjusting first one side then the other. 'Do you know what time period? Which century?'

'It didn't seem that long ago.'

'How long ago?'

'It felt quite recent.'

'All past lives feel quite recent, Charley.' He breathed slowly, steadily; the wheezing made him sound as if he were asleep.

'It had to be recent,' she said, hope dawning. 'The woman was riding astride. She wore breeches. So I could have gone to the Wishing Rocks and watched someone bury it years ago and have forgotten. Cryptic something, isn't it, when you've forgotten something you've done or read as a child?'

'Cryptomnesia,' he said, with a faintly glazed look, as if he were used to trotting out the same old defence against the same old hoary argument. 'How much proof do you require?' His voice sounded testy.

'I don't know,' she said, deflated.

'Are you frightened?'

'A little.'

'What of?'

'I'm not sure.'

He smiled a smug teacher-knows-best smile. 'Are you frightened of the idea of having lived before?'

'I've always been sceptical about the supernatural. I still don't believe that ...' The self-satisfied smile on his face distracted her, irritated her.

'Don't believe or don't *want* to believe?'

She said nothing.

'People who come to me are often full of traumas they don't understand. These are caused by unpleasant happenings in previous carnations. Once people understand the reason for the trauma, the trauma goes.' His dreary voice could as easily have been reading out the instructions on a washing machine. 'You want to have children, and are not conceiving. Now in this previous carnation we find you have been pregnant and some trauma has occurred — something which frightens you so much you can't face it and I have to bring you back out. It could be the memory of this trauma that's blocking you from conceiving.'

The words stirred something. A tiny frisson of doubt tapped its way down her corridors of nerves.

'I've regressed many thousands of people, Charley,' the hypnotist continued. 'There are others who have found some sort of evidence to prove their regressions have not just been cryptomnesia, names in books ... landscapes ... But to go out and find an object, a buried object ... This hasn't happened before, you see. We need to continue, to have another session. It's very important.'

'Do you think we might find more buried treasure?' she said more cheerily than she felt. He did not smile back.

'It's not the locket, Charley. It's what we've dug up inside you. It's the connection.' His face tightened into trembling concentration. 'There's something in your past that ...'

'That what?' she prodded, his expression making her nervous.

'That's more than a memory.'

'I don't understand.'

'It's — it must be something malevolent you've done in that carnation and I believe you have brought it with you, into this present life.'

'Brought what with me?'

'It's that we need to find out.'

'I don't want to go on any more.'

'I don't think it's up to you to decide,' he said.

'What do you mean?' Anger arose at the smug, weird man. Creep.

'You could bury the locket back on the hill, but you can't bury this back in your mind. You see, it's very strong. We had better make another appointment.'

You bastard, she thought. This is all a trick; a great con. 'I'll think about it.' She opened her handbag and took out her purse. 'Thirty-five pounds?'

He shook his head and waved a hand dismissively. 'Give it to a charity. I support Guide Dogs for the Blind.'

She stared at him in amazement. 'Why?'

'Because I don't want you to think I'm a confidence trickster.' He smiled another teacher-knows-best smile, then stood up wearily and walked towards the door.

Chapter Twenty-One

'*Surprise him! Greet him at the front door in a sexy negligee with a glass of his favourite drink in your hand and music playing. Give him a candlelit dinner of his favourite foods; pamper him at the table; cherish him. Don't break the spell ... leave the washing up till morning!*'

Charley glanced around the crowded train compartment, trying to keep the cover of the magazine as low in her lap as possible so that no one could see the lurid teaser that had made her buy it at the bookstall.

HOW TO KEEP YOUR MAN TURNED ON!

The train rattled south, rain streaking the windows, through Gatwick Airport, backpackers waiting on the platform like refugees, past the hangars, the parked aircraft. A Jumbo was coming in overhead and she watched it until a tall warehouse blocked her view, regretting they'd cancelled their holiday in Greece because of moving; holidays were the only times these days she and Tom seemed to get remotely close.

She had played the tapes of her regression over and over when Tom had not been around, not wanting him to know she had been again, had spent more money. Each time she played them, part of her grew a little more sceptical and part of her a little more afraid.

She had worked in the boutique today, but had not seen Laura who had gone to France for two days, buying. They had not seen each other since her phone call to Laura which Tom had answered; when they had spoken on the phone a couple of days ago, Laura had chatted gaily; too gaily.

She had left the boutique at four, leaving another part-timer there, and gone to the nursing home to visit her adoptive mother. She had told her she had started the procedure for finding her real parents, and had half expected some angry reaction, but that had not happened. If anything (although she knew she might have imagined it) she thought she noticed a small expression of relief.

Sussex countryside was sliding by, and darkness was falling fast. A good-looking man in his mid-twenties was eyeing her. Being eyed always made her feel good, boosted her confidence. Right now it needed boosting.

Then she wondered if he had seen the cover of the magazine, if that was why he was smiling.

Her heart felt heavy again. She and Tom had made love once since they'd moved in, on the first night. For a long while they had only made love once a month, but that had been deliberate, on the instructions of her acupuncturist. The acupuncturist Laura had recommended, whose needles hurt like hell (even though Laura insisted they didn't), who assured her she would become pregnant very quickly.

Nothing wrong ... nothing wrong ... nothing wrong. Her brain beat to the rhythm of the train, to the rhythm of the specialists they had seen over the years.

Nothing wrong, nothing wrong, nothing wrong.

She had ditched the acupuncturist, the funny little man with his strange ideas on celibacy and body balance and energy, and the pungent herbs he burned from time to time and applied against her body. '*What are you trying to do? Conjure up a baby from black magic?*' she had said jokingly to him once, but he had not been amused.

Now she wanted to make love with Tom, wanted it more than at any time in years, and he was not responding.

On Sunday he'd gone off for the day, told her he had to go to the office to deal with an urgent problem. On Sunday night he'd smelled of Laura's perfume.

The rooftops of Haywards Heath appeared and the train slowed. She stood up and lifted the smart Janet Reger bag down from the luggage rack. It weighed nothing, and for a moment she was worried the negligee had fallen out. She opened it and peeked in. She could see the black lace and the receipt and her Access slip lying loosely down the side. £145.

She began to smile as she stepped off the train and joined the queue at the ticket barrier. Tom would be mad as hell. Good. He hadn't lost his temper for ages. Maybe it was time. Sometimes their lovemaking was at its most tender after Tom had come out of one of his tempers.

Outside the station a line of cars waited, engines running, wipers shovelling away the rain, dutiful wives in their Volvos and Range Rovers and Japanese runabouts with their *Baby on Board* stickers and children's faces pressed against the windows.

She felt a twinge of sadness, as if there was some cosy family club from which she was excluded, barred.

It was nearly a quarter to eight as she turned into the lane. She'd had to go to Safeways in Lewes to get steaks, and she'd bought scallops there as well. His favourite foods, as the article in the magazine had told her to do.

Scallops, steak, then vanilla ice cream with hot fudge sauce.

And sod the cost.

The memory of Apstead Road, Wandsworth, was beginning to fade. The new woman in there had rung up a couple of times relaying phone messages, but she hadn't been very communicative, hadn't said how much they loved the house. In fact, she'd sounded a little pissed off. Maybe they'd found damp or rot, though Charley knew there was nothing much wrong, apart from the leak in the roof of the utility room which she'd kept guiltily quiet about. It only leaked in heavy rain. It was probably leaking now.

Headlights came out of Yuppie Towers. It was Zoe in her Range Rover. 'Charley, hi!' She wound her window down and made a face against the weather. 'We're going to the George tomorrow. Do you and Tom feel like joining us?'

'That would be nice, thanks — if he's down in time.'

Zoe shielded her face with her hand. 'See how you feel. Got to pick up the kids. Bye!'

Charley drove on down the lane. Hugh's workshop doors were battened tightly shut, and a television flickered through the drawing room window of Rose Cottage.

She felt lonely as she drove down the steep hill, under the shadowy arches of the trees of the wood. Tom was playing squash and wouldn't be home until after nine. Her headlights picked out the green hull of the upturned skiff, and the sign 'PRIVATE. MEMBERS ONLY. NO FISHING', nailed to the tree. They'd seen a few people fishing at the weekends, and one or two in the early evenings. There was a small card in the window of the grocery shop in Elmwood village with details of a name to phone for membership.

The surface of the lake was spiked by the rain, and an arc of grubby froth slopped against the bank. There was straw lying on the gravel and she looked at it, surprised for a moment, then remembered that today Hugh had been moving the old car out. The rain increased, stalactites of water hurtled down from the sky and shattered in tiny sprays on the ground. She sprinted with her carrier bag for the front door. She could hear Ben barking. 'OK, boy!' she shouted as she went into the hall and switched on the light. Then she stopped, staring at the hall table.

It was lying on its side in the middle of the floor, the mail scattered around it.

Ben? Had he knocked it over? She peered down the dark passage. There was a tremendous bang behind her. She spun round. The wind had slammed the front door shut.

Christ. Her nerves were shot to pieces. She switched the passageway light on, and, water running down her face, her clothes drenched, went into the kitchen. Ben barrelled out, jumping up. 'Did Bernie look after you again? Take you for a walk, did he? Let's go, outside!'

He loped down the passageway. She followed and stared uneasily at the table in the hall. How had it fallen over? Surely Bernie, or the other builders, or the plumber or electrician would have had the nous to pick it up? Clumsy fools. She would speak to them about it in the morning.

She let Ben out; he ran down the steps and cocked his leg on the polythene sheeting the workmen had left over their materials. She grabbed the groceries from the boot of the Citroën and rushed back in, Ben following.

A buckshot volley of rain struck the windows. Wind yowled down the inglenook and something scuffled about inside it, rapping against the chimney breast.

Twigs of a bird's nest dislodged, she thought, breathing out a little as whatever it was fell and rattled against the sides. The wind moaned like breath against a bottle top.

Ben pattered along the passageway unconcerned, his collar jingling. She heaved the heavy table upright and examined its sturdy legs. They were fine. It hadn't fallen over of its own accord, and no one could have knocked it over without noticing.

She heard a scrape upstairs, and froze. She looked up the dark stairwell, listening. Ben drank from his bowl with a loud slurping. There was another volley of rain. A clank.

Kerwumph.

Just the new boiler. Water flowing through the pipes. The plumber wanted to leave it on for a few days, to check the system. It must be on low because there was a damp chill in the house. She replaced the mail on the table, another wodge of redirected letters from London, bills, circulars, a handwritten enveloped which she opened; it was a belated thank you from the Orpens.

She carried the groceries through into the kitchen and put them on the table. It was warm in here from the Aga. The red light on the answering machine was static; no messages. The goldfish drifted around in its bowl. She fed Ben, then boiled some water and took out the mug Tom had given her a few years back with 'Happy Xmas Charley' printed on it. She heaped in a larger spoon of coffee than usual to try to stop herself yawning, poured in the water, then put the steaming mug down on the table and emptied the scallops out of the white plastic bag into the sink.

Ben let out a low, rumbling growl.

'What is it, boy?'

A blast of cold air, colder than a midwinter draught, engulfed her.

Ben barked at the ceiling, back at her, then at the ceiling again. The drying rack swayed. The chill passed as suddenly as it had come, leaving her hugging her arms around her body.

'Shh, boy!' she hissed, trying to keep her voice low, like a child keeping its eyes tightly shut in the dark. Her hand went to her mouth and she bit at the skin on her thumb, staring at the ceiling, at the drying rack, at the pulleys, listening, listening. She could hear nothing.

She picked up the mug, sipped, and jerked it away from her mouth with a start: the coffee was stone cold. It was the right mug — Happy Xmas Charley.

Ben sniffed the floor and the skirting board, making a whining sound. She touched the side of the kettle. It was hot. She lifted the lid and steam rose out. She dipped her finger in the mug to make sure she was not mistaken, but it was cold, so icy cold she could not leave it there. Nuts. Going nuts. Must have filled it from the cold tap. She frowned, tried to think clearly, but her mind felt fogged. Poured from the kettle. Surely she had. Surely —?

Ben growled. He was staring down the passageway, the hackles rising down his back. She felt the hairs on her own body rising too. He padded out of the kitchen and she followed. He stopped at the foot of the stairs, glared up and growled again.

'Tom?' she called out, knowing he wasn't there. 'Hello?' Her voice had risen an octave.

Ben's gums slid back, his ears lifted. She switched on the light and the stairs became brighter.

Kerwumph.

The boiler again. She picked up her carrier bag and climbed the stairs, trying not to move too slowly, not to seem scared, but slow enough so she could hear if — *if?*

If anything was there?

She reached the landing. The bulbs in the sconces threw their shadowy light along the walls. The floorboards creaked and the beams seemed to creak too, like an old timber ship sailing through a storm.

The doors were all shut and she went into each room in turn. Nothing, nothing, nothing. Each time she turned the light off and shut the door with a defiant slam. She checked the attic too, quickly, attics always spooked her, then went down into their bedroom.

She thought vaguely that something seemed to be missing; it seemed tidier than usual. She checked the en suite bathroom, then lifted the black silk negligee out of the carrier, went to the dressing table and held it up to her neck.

As she did so she noticed the envelope lying flat on the table weighted down by her hairbrush. It had not been there this morning. It was marked simply 'Charley', in Tom's neat handwriting.

She picked it up, and it fell from her trembling fingers back on to the table with a slap. She tore it open with her index finger.

Darling,

I love you very dearly, but it doesn't seem to be working out too well down here.

I need a few days on my own. I'm sorry I haven't been brave enough to say it to you face to face. You've got a cheque book and credit cards and there's money in the account, and £500 cash in the drawer under my socks. I'll give you a call.

Sorry if this letter seems clumsy, but you know I've never been very good at expressing how I feel. I need to think about my life and what I really want.

I know it's going to hurt you. It hurts me too,

more than I can write and you don't deserve to be hurt. I've taken a few things I need.

    Love you,

Tom

Chapter Twenty-Two

Sunlight streamed in the window, as Mr Budley had solemnly told them it would, and she felt good for a moment, for a brief moment, smelling the sweet air and listening to the early morning chit-chit-chit of the birds before the memory lying asleep inside her began to stir.

There was a smell of burnt paper in the room.

She sat up, disoriented and drenched in sweat. Tom's pillows beside her were still plumped, undented, his side of the bed undisturbed. A swell of gloom rolled through her.

Darling, I love you very dearly.

She had dreamed it. It was a bad dream. Everything was fine. Tom was in the bathroom shaving, brushing his teeth.

'Tom?' she called out. There was no answer. Her hands were stinging and she pulled them from under the sheets and looked at them. Her eyes widened.

They were caked with mud and covered in lacerations.

A cut ran right the way down one finger and there was muddy, congealed blood around it. The skin was scraped off the top of three of her knuckles. More cuts criss-crossed the backs of her hands. They were hurting like hell. She turned them over. More cuts on the palms. Tension pulled her scalp. Ben? Had Ben attacked her? Never. A dream. Just dreaming. Just —

She swung her legs out of bed, put them on the wooden floor and then blinked in astonishment as she noticed her feet. A squall of undefined fear blew through her veins. Her feet were caked in mud, dried mud packed between her toes, spattered up her legs. She leaned over, touched them. The mud was damp; some came away on her finger. Her nightdress was filthy too, mud-spattered, sodden and streaked with blood.

She tried to think, think back to last night. Sitting at the dressing table; she had been sitting at the dressing table. Then — nothing. Blank.

A muscle twitched inside her throat. She stared hopelessly around the room as if somewhere in it she might find an answer. Dressing table. Hours. Crying. Maybe she had broken something, a mirror, a glass, was that why —? She shook her head. The mud, where had the mud —? Her hands and feet so sore, painful.

She looked at the dressing table, and it was then she noticed the small muddy object next to her hairbrush.

She staggered over. Rusty tin showed through the mud. She put her hand out slowly, hesitating, as if she were reaching out to a poisonous insect, and picked it up.

Something inside it rattled, slithered, clanked. She scraped away the mud with her raw fingers, ignoring the pain, until she could see enough to know what it was, to be certain what it was.

She waited, afraid, numb, then she pressed her thumbs up against the lid of the tin. It came off with a quiet pop, and there was the heart-shaped locket nestling inside. The same locket she had dug up then reburied at the Wishing Rocks.

Ben came over and stood beside her. The locket rattled as her hands shook. She put the tin down, knelt and patted the dog, squeezed him, put her arms around and hugged him, needing to feel something real, alive.

His coat was wet. His paws were wet too; wet and muddy. He wagged his tail. 'Good boy,' she said absently. 'Good boy.' She stood up. Her head was muzzy; the locket was muzzy too, a blurr. She lifted it out of the tin and the tarnished chain slithered down her wrist. She pressed the clasp, and prised the heart open.

A trail of fine black powder fell out. At first she thought it was earth, finely ground earth; then slivers of blackened paper floated out, zigzagged to the floor.

Dear Rock, I love him. Please bring him back. Barbara.

Someone had burnt the note.

The TCP stung her hands. The paint stung her eyes. She dunked the roller in the flat tray of paint, pressed it against the wall, ran it up, down, covering a little more of the lining paper on the panels between the oak beams with cream paint. Because she needed to do something. Anything.

'You oughter do the ceiling first.'

Laura. Bitch Laura.

She'd rung Laura, got her answering machine at her flat, got her answering machine at the boutique, rung Tom's private line which had not answered, rung his main number then hung up as the telephonist answered. Was he in Paris with bitch Laura?

'Otherwise it goin' run down the walls, innit?'

Bernie the builder stood in the doorway in his grubby overalls and his single gold earring, grinning cheekily.

'Ceiling? Yes — I — I should, I suppose.'

Bernie ran his hands over the lining paper. 'Not bad. You could turn professional. We'll give you a job any time.'

She forced a smile.

'Yeh, s'orl right it is, for an amateur!' He rubbed his finger on the crack between two joins. 'Got an overlap, want to avoid overlaps. Makes the paint bumpy.'

'I don't think it matters on these walls.' Her voice sounded weak. She squeezed her hands together, trying to stop the pain.

'Christ, wot yer done to yer hands?'

'Glass. I broke — some glass.'

He glanced at the beams. 'There's some good stuff you can put on those, bring their natural colour right back. Can't remember the name. I'll ask Pete.' He tugged his earring. ''Bout your table.' He jerked a finger towards the hall. 'The one what you said was knocked over. I remember the second post come, and I stacked it neat on the table.'

'Who was here after you left?'

'There wasn't no one. I locked the dog in the kitchen like you said.'

'The plumber wasn't still here?'

'No.'

'Are you sure?'

'He went early.'

'Did you see my husband when he came?'

'Yeah, 'bout three. Going off on a business trip. Orl right for some, innit? Where's he gone? Somewhere exotic? Leaving you to do the work, that's typical men, that is.'

There was a rap on the knocker. Ben barked. Charley wiped her hands on a rag and went to the front door.

Gideon stood there, well back, looking edgy. He touched his cap. 'I'm afraid I won't be coming any more, Mrs Witney.' He handed her a grubby envelope. 'That's me hours for the last week.'

She took it, surprised. 'It's not because of the hens, is it? We don't blame you for the hens, Gideon. It's not your fault. You did a good job with the fencing.'

He shrugged and avoided her eyes. 'I thought it would be different with 'er gone, but it's not.'

'What do you mean?' Mechanically she opened the envelope.

'I'd rather not say, if you don't mind.'

'I'd rather you did say.'

His edginess increased. 'You won't have no problem finding anyone,' he said as she took the handwritten sheet out. 'Eight and a half hours last week.'

'Have you been offered more money somewhere else? I'm sure we could perhaps give you a raise.'

He shook his head, and gazed at his boots. 'No, that don't come into it.'

'I don't understand. What's the problem?'

'I've made up me mind. I really don't want to say.'

'I'll get my purse,' she said, bewildered and angry.

She stood by the hall table and sifted through the morning post. There was a formal buff envelope addressed to herself and she opened it. Inside was a short letter, a leaflet entitled 'Access to Birth Records — Information for adopted people', and a form. She read through the leaflet, glanced at the form, then folded it back into the envelope, a thin stream of excitement, of hope, trickling through her gloom.

The electrician came down the stairs, a short chalky man with a goatee beard.

''Scuse me, Mrs Witney. Are you usin' any unusual electrical apparatus in the house?'

'Unusual? In what way unusual?'

'Something not domestic. Very high powered.'

'The man who came to read the meter said too much power was being used. He thought there was a short circuit somewhere. Didn't my husband tell you?'

'We haven't found no short anywhere. We've rewired and tested it all.' He tapped the small screwdriver clipped to his shirt pocket as if to underline what he had said, then tried to work a splinter out of his finger.

'There's somethin' being used here that's too powerful. Some of the new wiring we've put in is starting to melt.'

'*Melt?*'

He tugged a bit of the splinter out with his teeth. 'I've checked your appliances. They're fine. I'm goin' to have to replace some of the new wirin' I put in.' He shook his head. 'Something's funny. I'll give the Electricity Board a bell, make sure there's no underground cables round here.'

'Is there anything else that could be causing it?'

'Like what, do you mean?'

'I don't know. Damp, heavy rain.'

'Electricity can be affected by a lot of things. I'll keep looking.'

'Thank you.' She went into the kitchen, put the kettle on, sat down at the table and studied the application form for her birth records. She picked up a biro.

The form blurred; her mind blurred. She began to write, to fill it in, determined, oh yes, determined. She wrote in big letters, huge letters; twice the biro scored the paper, and she had to stop and press it back down around the punctured hole.

The kettle boiled, clicked itself off and the form came back into focus. She stared wide-eyed at what she had written. Except it was not her handwriting.

The lettering was bold, large, scrawly.

'LEAVE IT ALONE, BITCH.'

'Hello?'

Hugh Boxer stood in the kitchen doorway, holding a plant the size of a small tree. She turned the adoption form over, trying not to look obvious.

The top of the plant was bent, and leaves straggled in all directions; it was as untidy as Hugh's hair. 'A little thank you for keeping the car in the barn,' he said. 'And a sort of welcome-to-the-neigbourhood present,' he added.

LEAVE IT ALONE, BITCH.

Her insides churned. She stood up unsteadily. 'It's lovely. What is it?'

He looked down at the plant as if trying to remember what he was meant to be doing with it. His face was streaked with grease and he was wearing grimy dungarees over a frayed collar and tie. 'It's got a Latin name, and there's special food in a pack you have to give it. Red meat, or something.'

She smiled faintly and touched one of the leaves. It was soft and furry. 'Thank you, it's lovely. That's really nice of you.'

'What have you done to your hands?'

'Oh, it was — glass. Just scratches.' She looked away from his questioning stare. 'It's a beautiful plant.'

'I'll put it down for you somewhere. It's heavy.'

'The table will be fine.'

'It needs light,' he said.

'Maybe it'll like the view,' she said, trying to muster cheeriness.

He grinned, 'Particularly partial to views, I'm told.' His eyes fell lightly on her and she noticed his almost imperceptible frown.

'I was going to make some coffee.'

'Great, thanks, but don't let me —'

'It was going to be instant but I'll do proper in your honour.'

Company. She did not want him to see her misery, but wanted him to stay, to talk. Something was comforting about him — about his face, his manner, she was not sure what. He seemed even taller in here, barely had any headroom below the ceiling.

She put the adoption form on the windowsill and weighted it under a perspex picture frame of various snapshots of herself and Tom; Hugh put the plant on the table. There was hammering directly above them.

He wandered over to the dresser. 'I like goldfish.' He leaned over Horace's bowl and opened and shut his mouth, apeing the fish. Charley smiled, trying to prevent the welling tears. He made her feel sad. Sad because he was nice.

The blade of his frayed tie swung out of the top of his grimy boiler suit and dipped into the water. He left it there as the fish swam up to it. 'He likes my tie; this is obviously a sartorially aspirational goldfish.'

'You can take him anywhere,' she said, then had to turn her face away so he did not see the trickling tears. 'Do you always wear a tie?' she asked, her voice cracking as she spooned coffee into the percolator. She dabbed her eyes with a dishcloth.

'Yes.' He squeezed water from the end of his tie. 'Old habit. My father was always obsessed with respectability.' He smoothed the blade out and tucked it back inside his dungarees. 'He was one of those Brits you'd come across in the middle of the desert. It could be a hundred and forty in the shade and he'd still be wearing a tweed suit and a shirt and tie.'

'What did he do?'

He rummaged his hand through his hair. 'He was an archaeologist. A sort of real life Indiana Jones, but not as dashing. Obsessed with the Holy Grail, spent a lot of his life digging up tombs.'

'And always in a tie?'

'He was worried people would think he was a bit potty, so he liked to appear respectable. He believed people would trust a man in a tie. Poor bugger was always trying to raise money for this expedition or that, trying to convince people.' He touched his tie. 'That's probably why I always wear one. Wearing a tie is in my genes.' He grinned. 'Prisoners of our past, you see.'

'Did he ever find anything?'

'Oh yes. Not what he was looking for, but he made a few discoveries.'

Discoveries. Digs. She wondered whether his father had ever dug up a locket. Spots of tiredness danced in her eyes, fluttered in front of her.

'Are you all right?'

She nodded.

'You look pale.'

Genes. Parents. People always took their parents for granted, and the little traits they adopted. She wondered what traits her own parents had had, whether her father had always worn a tie, too. What perfume had her natural mother worn? Details like that had never occurred to her before. 'I'm a bit tired. It's hard work decorating.'

'I hope I didn't leave too much mess moving the car out. The straw was pretty rotten. It must have been there for years.' The hammering got worse above them. He glanced at Tom's pewter tankard on the dresser. 'How's Man of the Match?'

'Oh, he's —' She felt as if a cloud had suddenly slid over her sun. 'Away, on business.' The tears threatened again and she poured the coffee into the pot, holding the percolator clumsily, trying not to close her fingers too tightly around it. 'How is Viola Letters?' she asked, opening a cupboard and taking out a biscuit tin.

'She's OK. She rather doted on that dog. I'm not crazy about Yorkies, but it didn't deserve what happened to it.' He pulled the cord of the drying rack. The rack raised and lowered a few inches with a squeak, then he went to the sink and looked out of the window. Two swans drifted on the flat water. 'Fine view.'

'Gideon's not coming any more,' she said.

'Oh?'

'He wouldn't tell me why. I think he's upset about

179

the hens — thinks we blame him.'

'He's not going to do the lane at all?'

She shrugged. 'I don't know. He rather took me by surprise.'

Hugh carried the tray of coffee and biscuits out to the small patio at the rear of the house. They sat on hard benches at the oak table. Ben wolfed down a digestive biscuit, then stretched out on his stomach on the flagstones beside them. Charley scratched an insect bite on her neck.

'Nice to be able to sit outside in October,' Hugh said, heaping a spoon of sugar into his coffee. 'Make the most of it. How's your friend Laura?'

'Oh, she's well,' Charley answered, too quickly.

He stirred his coffee, the spoon clinking. A bird in the woods above squeaked like a plimsole on linoleum.

'Hugh, at our barbecue you said you had evidence of people being reincarnated, but you did not believe in regressive hypnosis. Do you really believe in reincarnation?'

He pulled his pipe out of a pocket and checked the inside of the bowl. 'I don't disbelieve all regressive hypnosis. There have been some convincing cases.'

There was a tinkle from inside the house that could have been breaking glass or something being dropped on a sheet of metal. They both glanced up, for a second, then she looked back at him. There was an expression of concern on his face that disturbed her. 'It's what I said. I don't believe in playing games with the occult.' he added.

'You think regression is playing games?'

'It depends how it's treated. On who's doing it. Regression itself is valid. And very dangerous. There are a lot of hypnotists around who treat it as a game — and that's even more dangerous.' He stared into her eyes.

180

LEAVE IT ALONE, BITCH.

She blinked; her eyes felt raw; she wished he would stop looking at them. She touched her cup and the heat hurt her cuts. 'What is the danger?'

'Hypnotists are like mediums. They put people into altered states of consciousness, try to reach out to different planes, different dimensions, and contact things that don't necessarily want to be contacted, or even want to be disturbed. Things they don't have any business disturbing.' He clicked his lighter and held his hand over the flame, shielding it from the breeze.

Coldness seeped through her. 'What do you need in order to prove you have lived before?'

'Evidence.'

'What sort of evidence?'

He tapped the burning tobacco down in the bowl with his thumb. 'Like knowing something happened during a previous life that no one else living knows. Something you could not possibly have known any other way, unless you had lived before.' He raised his eyes. 'It doesn't have to be anything enormous. In a way, small things are more convincing because they are less likely to have been in the history books.'

Small things.

Like a locket.

A locket that no one knew was there?

'Can it help people to resolve traumas? That's what I was told.'

'You mean someone's afraid of water in this life because they drowned in a previous one?'

'Yes, that sort of thing.'

'Learning how to swim stops people's fear of the water, not finding out that they drowned in the Spanish Armada.' He picked up a biscuit, broke it in half, then quarters. She wondered if he was going to make a

181

diagram; instead he dunked each piece in his coffee and ate it.

He spoke between bites. 'I think regressive hypnotism has all kinds of dangers. It tampers with thoughts and emotions that are dormant in the mind, usually dormant for a good reason because the mind has managed to put them away. You risk stirring them up.'

She put her arms around her chest and hugged herself. A sharp breeze blew and a brown leaf rolled past.

'Anything that involves dabbling in the spirit world is dangerous,' Hugh said. 'It's not just people who have memories. Places have them too.' His eyes fixed on hers again and she looked away.

She sipped her coffee and nearly spat it out, a wave of nausea sweeping through her. Puzzled, she lowered her nose and sniffed. It smelled of good coffee, but the taste in her mouth was vile. 'Places have memories?' she said.

'I think they do. You know the way you get atmospheres in houses? What happens over a period of time affects how places feel. If there's been some great tragedy or sadness in a house, quite often it — or a room in it — will feel depressing, maybe even cold as well.' He shrugged. 'It may be quite scientific. Perhaps the atomic particles in the walls retain trace memories, like videotape, and some people can accidentally tune in and trigger off replays. That's one of the theories for ghosts — that they are replays.'

Hugh looked up at the house, his eyes flicking from window to window, first floor then ground floor, back at her, back at the house.

He offered to carry the tray into the kitchen, but she insisted she could manage. As he was leaving he said quietly, deliberately quietly, she thought, as if he did not want someone to hear him, 'Be careful.' He patted Ben and walked off through the garden and up the drive.

She took the tray into the dim boiler room and through to the kitchen.

Something crunched under her feet.

Horace's bowl was not on the dresser and for a moment she wondered who had moved it. There was another crunch. She looked down. The floor was covered in water, broken glass, tiny coloured pebbles, strands of weed.

She was barely conscious of the china pot sliding across the tray, jerking against the latticed edging before it tumbled out of sight and exploded at her feet.

Horace?

Her eyes scanned the floor, her heart straining on its mountings, searching the shards of glass and china for the small fleck of gold. Please be all right.

Be flapping around. Please.

She put the tray on the kitchen table and was about to drop to her knees to look under the dresser when her eye ran down a black rivulet of coffee that had pushed its way through the debris, carrying Horace with it for a few inches until he jammed between a leg of the table and the severed spout of the pot. His tail waggled in the remains of the coffee and for a fleeting moment she thought the fish was still alive.

'Horace,' she mouthed, scooping him up in her hand. He was motionless, already stiffening, the eyes sightless, mouth open. Light, so light, he felt like the tinfoil wrapper of a sweet.

There was another volley of hammering and the dresser shook, the crockery rattling inside. She put the plug into the sink, ran the cold tap and laid Horace in the water, watching as he swirled around on the surface, hoping any moment he might wriggle and dart down to the bottom.

But he continued swirling on the surface, rising with the water. She picked him out. The water was cold and hurt her fingers. The fish had become stiffer still.

The hammering continued and the wooden rack rocked on its pulleys, squeaking, and she rocked on her feet, cradling Horace, making a high-pitched creaking noise herself as she tried not to cry over a dead fish.

She buried him in a plastic bag on the same bank in the woods where she had buried the hens, and placed a small stone over the tiny mound of earth.

She walked back down the bank and the horses grazing in the paddock reminded her of the smart horsewoman in her last regression who had stared down at her so contemptuously. And the unease she had felt.

Lies death. Truth. Go back, her mother had said.

Go back where?

There must be someone, someone who would know. She racked her brains, thinking back. Her adoptive mother had no relations alive now. Perhaps she had confided in a friend? Irene Willis. She might have confided in Irene Willis. Hope flared and faded. Irene Willis had died of cancer four years ago.

She went into the kitchen.

LEAVE IT ALONE, BITCH.

She stared at the form she had defaced, still tucked beneath the perspex picture frame. Nuts. Talking to myself. Sleepwalking. I dig lockets out of the ground in the middle of the night. I write instructions to myself.

Rebirthing. Weird rebirthing she had done with Laura, where they had tried to teach her to be positive about herself, where they gave her things she had to say in front of the mirror for half an hour a day.

'It is safe for me, Charley, to feel all my cleverness and all my feelings.'

184

'I, Charley, am loved and wanted as a woman.'

Laura. Bitch. Cow.

She sat at the table and breathed deeply, choking back a sob, stared at the empty space on the dresser where Horace's bowl had been and at the damp on the floor. She fidgeted, waiting for as long as she could, waiting for the phone to ring.

For it to be Tom.

Upstairs, music blared from the builders' radio. She turned the pages of the morning papers, her eyes sifting listlessly through the columns, a meaningless blur of black print and photographs, IRA bombers, a divorcing billionaire, a starlet on a bike, a wrecked car. Then she stood up and wandered aimlessly around the house.

In their bedroom she picked up the locket and toyed with the idea of writing a note herself. *Dear Rock, I love Tom. Please bring him back. Charley.*

She dropped the locket in the tin, put it at the back of a drawer and closed it. She went into the small room which would have been ideal for the cot for their first child, and looked out of the window, at the barn and the mill and the woods; it was starting to cloud over. It clouded in her mind, too, and she began crying again.

She went down into the kitchen, composed herself, picked up the phone and dialled Tom's private line. It was engaged. She waited, just in case he was trying to call her, then rang again. It was still engaged. She rang his switchboard, but hung up as soon as the operator answered.

It was weak to call him. He wanted time, space, whatever, to think things over. It was what he said in his letter. Fine. Let him think things over. She'd think things over too. She was not going to be weak. No way. Somehow, she determined, she was going to cope, to be strong, calm.

185

She was not so calm when she saw Laura through the glass front of her boutique holding up a dress for a customer. She walked in, seething.

'The shape is terribly flattering. Try it on. You really —' Laura's voice died as she saw Charley.

Charley stood near the window and flicked through a rail of dresses.

'The cut on these is tremendous. So many dresses like this aren't good over the hips.'

Charley moved on to a rail of blouses.

'And, of course, if you accessorise with a scarf, and maybe a pair of gloves —'

Charley sat down at the till and tapped digits out on the calculator, multiplied them, divided them, square-rooted them. Another customer came in, touched the collar of a jacket, flipped over the price tag and went out again. Laura glanced nervously at Charley, then turned her attention back to her customer. But the conviction had gone from her voice and she was losing her.

'I'll think about it,' the woman said, and left.

Charley tapped another row of digits on the calculator.

'Hi!' Laura put on a smile the way she might have put on lipstick.

'What the hell's going on, Laura?' Charley said, without lifting her eyes from the display of digits.

'What do you mean?'

'Come on!' Charley said, warningly.

Laura shrugged. 'I'm sorry, Charley.'

'Sorry? You're sorry? Is that all you can say?'

Laura turned away and fiddled with a showcard. 'What do you want me to say?'

Charley stood up. 'Bitch. You fucking bitch.' She stormed across the shop, yanked the door open, marched out into the street and along the pavement. She kept on walking, angry at herself now, angry for being weak and going there, for doing exactly what she had determined she would not do.

Chapter Twenty-Three

She became aware she was walking through darkness; except it was not darkness, not shadow. She was walking between two tall hedgerows, down a crumbling lane. She stumbled on a loose stone. 'Darn!'

'Where are you?'

'Lane.'

'What is your name?'

'Dunno.'

'How old are you?'

'Dunno.'

'Tell me what you are wearing.'

'A frock. It's sort of cream with a pattern.'

'How long is it?'

''Alfway down me legs.'

'What shoes are you wearing?'

'Brown. Heels are too high. I shouldn't be wearin' heels.'

'Why not?'

'Cos I'm expectin'.'

'Who is the father?'

'Dick.'

'You sound frightened. What are you afraid of?'

'Dunno. It feels bad. Bad.'

She passed Thadwell's Farm, with its cobbled yard and the tractor and haycart in the tumbledown barn, and on past the stagnant pond.

A man she recognised was sitting in the lane in front of Rose Cottage, painting at an easel. He was well groomed, very correct looking, and stood up politely as she approached.

'Good afternoon,' he said in a crisp military tone.

'Good afternoon,' she mumbled in response.

'Who are you talking to?' said a voice in the background, a voice she no longer recognised.

'Jolly nice one, isn't it?' said the man.

He was in the Navy, she seemed to remember.

She reached the gate and stopped. She stared down at Elmwood Mill. A horse in the stables whinnied, as if it recognised her. Horse. A black cloud engulfed her. She took a packet of Woodbine cigarettes from her bag and lit one.

'You are bothered by the horse. What is bothering you?' said a faint voice, distant, like a radio that had been left on in another room.

'Jemma's my 'orse. She's got my 'orse. He promised me.' Her voice was breaking up; she was crying. She took a nervous pull on her cigarette, then opened the gate, and paused, searching for the dog, listening; she stared down at the kennel. No sign of it. She began to walk down the drive, scared, weary, the infant weighing heavily in her belly.

The car was there. His car. The black Triumph with its roof down, parked carelessly in front of the barn. The horse whinnied again and she gazed through eyes fogged with tears at the smart stables and saw the head of a chestnut mare looking out.

Everything was fresh, in good condition. The barn was newly roofed, the doors recently painted. The woodwork of the house was bright. She threw away her cigarette and walked across the gravel and up the steps, where she hesitated, daunted. She looked at the bell, at the polished brass lion's head knocker, then at the bell

189

again. She pushed the button.

There was a solitary deep bark from inside the house and the door was opened almost immediately, as if she were expected. A woman stood there, tall, elegant, aloof, in a hacking jacket, breeches and riding boots. Her black hair hung down across one side of her face with studied carelessness. She pursed her lips and glared witheringly, with fierce burning eyes.

'I told you not to come back here,' she said coldly.

'Please, I just want to see 'im. Please let me see 'im.'

The woman smiled, a cruel smile filled with menace. She turned, walked across the hall and opened a door. She clicked the fingers of her right hand once, and mouthed one word: 'Prince.'

The mastiff came into the hall and stared in hostile recognition; he lowered his head, his gums slid back and he snarled.

She backed away, turned and ran, almost falling down the steps, heard the dog snarling behind her. She felt a searing pain as his teeth bit into her leg.

'No! Get off!' she screamed, windmilling her arms and kicking out. The dog shook her leg in his massive jaw, like a bone. She lost her balance and, cradling her belly with her hands, crashed down the rest of the steps on to the drive.

The dog was over her. 'No! Get off! Get 'im!' she screamed, trying to roll away. 'Oh please get 'im off! No! Dick! No! The baby! Don't harm my baby!'

Above her she could see the face of the woman in the hacking jacket, watching, arms folded.

She clambered to her feet and tried to run, but the dog went for her leg again and sent her back on to the gravel. She screamed in pain.

'Prince, stop. Prince!'

The dog let go.

She lay there, weeping, her leg and hands in agony,

and saw Dick, in baggy trousers and collarless shirt, his face puce with rage. 'Clear off, I told you! Clear off! I don't want you coming back. Out!'

She looked up at the woman who was staring at her as if she was nothing. Nothing on earth, just absolutely nothing.

'You hear?' he shouted. 'You hear what I said? Next time I won't call him off.'

She climbed to her knees. 'Help me. You got to help me. Please, you got to help me.'

They stared in blank silence.

'Help me!' She was shouting now. 'You got to help me!'

Their faces faded.

A distant siren. Wind rattling glass. A chair creaking. Someone wheezing.

'You're all right, Charley. You are all right. You are safe. You are free in time. Stay with it. Move forward a little, move forward.'

She opened her eyes, saw Ernest Gibbon's face, almost without recognition. She closed them heavily again. She felt herself sinking into darkness.

There was roaring of water in her ears.

It was dark; night; the weir thundered. There was determination in her step. She had something in her left hand that was heavy and slimy. She walked on the grass, the wet dewy grass beside the gravel. The dog growled.

'Shh,' she hissed. She was trembling; afraid of the dog; afraid he might not be chained. The mill race flowed darkly. The dog growled again and she tried not to be scared, tried to think only of the hatred she felt. He barked and the chain rattled in the iron hoop. She looked at the silent silhouette of the house, expecting at any moment a light would come on or a torch beam would flash across at her.

Swift. Had to be swift. The barn loomed ahead. She flashed her torch straight on the kennel and the glint of red of the mastiff's eyes glared back at her. He snarled and strained at the end of his chain. Her heart pumped fast; the snarl seemed to fuel her anger, made her strong, suddenly; stronger than the dog.

'Prince! Shh!' her hissing voice commanded.

He hesitated at her tone, hesitated at another smell. The smell of the bone which she held out towards him as she called him softly, 'Good boy! Here, boy!'

She held it high, just out of his reach, and as he tried to jump up, his jaws snapping, the chain pulled him back and he lost his balance. She stepped forward, holding the bone even higher so he had to stretch his head up, exposing his neck.

As he took the huge bone greedily in his jaws, she sliced the serrated blade of the knife she held in her right hand as hard as she could across the centre of his throat, pushing with all her weight, feeling it biting in, razor sharp, cutting through flesh and muscle and bone.

There was a punctured sigh, and the dog seemed to sag. Blood sprayed over her hands, her clothes, her face. The mastiff made a gargling sound. There was a squeak of air, like a whistle. He whined, the bone fell out of his mouth and he coughed, lurched sideways, his paws collapsing, and fell forwards making sharp rasping sounds, blood spewing out of his mouth, flooding around his chest, his paws. The rasping sound began to die down.

She ran over the bridge across the mill race up the embankment to the woods; a prickly bush tore at her. She stopped, her heart thumping so loud she could hear it echoing around the woods, around the night, could hear it echoing a million miles away. She threw the knife into a clump of bushes, heard the rustle as it dropped. Somewhere close by an animal squeaked.

They could find the knife in the bush. Stupid. The lake. Why the hell not throw it in the lake? She tried to switch the torch on, but it slipped out of her blood-soaked hand and fell into the undergrowth. She knelt down, scrabbled for it, then was paralysed with fear as she sensed something behind her.

She turned. A light had come on in the house. The bedroom light. Someone was at the window, a shadow behind the curtain. The curtain parted; there was a creak as the window opened.

Except it wasn't a window; it was a mirror. She was staring at her face in a mirror, and a figure was looming behind her, blurry, indistinct. She smelled smoke; burning wood; straw.

Charred flesh.

She saw the eyes, just the eyes. Raw through the blackened skin. There was a loud bang. The mirror exploded into spidery cracks. A jagged shard fell away, landing at her feet, and she screamed as the figure moved towards her.

The darkness became red. A red light. Ernest Gibbon's face, myopic through his thick lenses; his jowls heaving up and down as if there were tiny motors inside operating them. She was drenched in sweat.

'It's happened again,' he said. 'The same every time.' He sat for a while, wheezing, studying her with the faint disconcerting trace of humour she had noticed last time. 'We need to get beyond it. The answer is beyond it.'

'There's a parallel,' Charley said. She felt drained.

'Oh yes?'

'My real-life relationship with my husband and my relationship here with this man — Dick. Don't you think that's too coincidental?'

'People often come back and go through the same situations as in previous carnations. Some people believe it is because they failed in the way they dealt with the situations before.' He removed his glasses and wiped them with a spotted handkerchief. The surrounds of his eyes looked naked. 'Who is this unpleasant woman? Do you know her name?'

'No.'

'Could she be the person who comes up behind you in the mirror?' He put his glasses back on.

'The person in the mirror looks hideous — disfigured — the face is burnt.'

'Is it a man or a woman?'

'I don't know.'

'How would you feel if I did not bring you out when that figure comes up behind you next time?'

She felt a current of fear. 'What — what would happen if you didn't?'

He thought for a moment. 'You might find you are able to deal with it. We should try. I think it would be dangerous not to try.'

'Dangerous not to try?' she repeated.

He nodded like a sage. 'When we open up the subconscious like this, there is always a danger of spontaneous regression.'

'What do you mean?'

'I try to do everything here in a controlled way. If you are getting uncomfortable or frightened, I can bring you back out, quickly. If you were to start regressing on your own, somewhere away from here, and the figure in the mirror took hold, then —' He shrugged.

'Why should it? It's only something in my memory.' She saw uncertainty in his eyes and that scared her. She wished she were not here, had not started this. She wished she had more faith in the man.

'I don't know why it should, Charley. I don't know if it is just memory. It's what I said last time. It's very strong.'

'But you didn't tell me what it was.'

The teacher-knows-best smile was fainter, had lost some of its confidence. 'I don't know what it is. I haven't come across this particular situation before. I don't know anyone who has. I'm going to do some research, to see if there is anything to compare, some other case history.'

'I thought you were meant to be an expert,' she said, more acidly than she intended.

He looked at her and blinked slowly, seriously. The smile was gone. 'In man's understanding of the supernatural, Charley, we are all amateurs.'

Chapter Twenty-Four

She walked along the station platform among the throng of commuters returning home from work, from London mostly, the smart and the shabby, the eager and the despondent, home to *her indoors*, to *she-who-must-be-obeyed*, to *the little woman, the little man*, home to noisy kids and empty dark houses, home to the loved, the hated, the infirm, the dying, the dead.

And the reborn.

If you kept coming back, you didn't die. You merely changed. You got reconstituted. Recycled. Even your knowledge, your experiences, got recycled.

She filed through the ticket barrier then walked, her shoes clattering on the concrete of the steps, down into the tunnel. The train moved off, rumbling above them. Did everyone else around her, all the hurrying people, have past lives? Had they come back many times too, back to this life each time they died, the way they came back to this station night after night?

If? If it was there? What then?

The thought spurred her to walk faster, to run up the steps the far side, out into the blustering wind of the clouded grey evening, almost to sprint across the car park to the little Citroën with its two-tone paintwork.

Her hands still hurt, but she barely noticed as she climbed in, started the engine and switched on the radio out of habit. There was a roar of laughter. Frank Muir was telling a story. Not now, she could not cope with humour now. She pushed in a tape. Rachmaninov, solemn, sombre, old, too old. She felt the violin string as if it were sliding down her own tight nerves and she punched the tape out and drifted into her thoughts again.

She drove out of Haywards Heath on to the country road, pressing the accelerator to the floor, wishing the car would go faster, almost willing it to go faster. To get home.

To find out.

The car lurched as she came into a bend too fast, the tyres squealing, saw a car coming the other way, the driver looking at her alarmed, thought for a moment she was going to hit it but somehow the Citroën hung on. Then the bend went the other way and she swung the wheel, foot stabbing at the brake, cut the corner and narrowly missed a cyclist who swerved, fist waving in the air. Christ, slow down. She gripped the wheel, felt her face steaming.

The sky was blackening as she pulled up in front of the barn. It looked like a storm was on the way.

She climbed out of the car and closed the door, crossed the bridge over the mill race and ran up the banked slope on the far side and into the woods, following the route she had taken in the regression. A gust of wind rattled the branches and spots of rain were coming down.

She trod through some bracken on to the mossy earth and looked up at the trees, the tall, thin hornbeam trees growing crookedly out of the wild undergrowth. Their branches were tangled, some of them supporting uprooted trees from past storms which lay across them like spars, lay where they would stay until they rotted, until they went back into the earth. Biodegradable. As humans were.

In the regression it had been dark, but she knew the way. There was a small indent in the ground, a ditch in front of a thick bramble bush that was covered in rotting blackberries. She went a few yards to the left and through a heavy undergrowth of bracken. A bird jumped in the branches of the trees above, chirping like a dripping tap. A distant dog barked. A tractor droned. The woods were darkening around her, melting the trees, closing in on her.

She was panting and shaking, covered in a clammy sweat. She did not want to be here any more, wanted to turn, run to the house and close the door on the night, close the door on the bramble bush that seemed to be drawing her in, that seemed to be growing as she looked at it, spreading around her ankles, rising up her legs. Switches were clicking inside her, changing the speed of her blood, re-routing it, churning it, pumping it over blocks of ice, sucking out the heat, refrigerating it.

She crawled underneath the bush, pushing up the branches, the thorns catching at her clothes, then something caught her eye. At first she thought it was a rotting strip of wood, or a flat root.

A stone. Might be a stone. Hoped it was a stone. It seemed to rise out of the brambles at her, bringing the bush with it. She scrabbled towards it on her hands and knees, oblivious to the stinging pain of the brambles, and she gripped the handle, gripped it as if it was the lever that would move the world, then backed out and stood up, pulling branches up with her, letting them rip through her clothes, through the skin of her arms.

She turned it over in her hands, touching the cold, rusted metal. A knife with a bone handle black with age and weathering, and a long serrated blade eaten with rust.

The knife she had carried in her regression. The knife with which she had killed the mastiff.

She felt pain in her finger, as if she had been stung, and looked down. A thin line of blood began to appear from the tip of her index finger down to the first joint. She dropped the knife, jammed her finger in her mouth and sucked hard. The cut had gone right down to the bone.

It seemed as if the thousand eyes of the falling night were watching her. The wind tugged at her hair, her thoughts tugged at her mind.

She bound the cut with her handkerchief, her mind racing, trying to find an answer that was better than the one she had.

She had killed a dog. With this knife. In another life.

She pulled herself free of the brambles, her linen dress ruined, and stumbled down through the woods towards the lake. An explanation. There had to be an explanation. Something.

A drop of water struck her cheek, then another. She reached the bank, heard the lap of a wave, saw the lake black and sloppy under the rising wind. She stared down at the knife, frightened it might cut her again, a deeper cut than her finger.

She made sure there were no anglers, then threw it as hard as she could out into the lake. Far enough and deep enough so she could not wade out in her sleep and get it back. It rolled over in the air, barely visible, then fell into the water with a plop like a rising trout. Gone. It no longer existed.

It had never existed.

She went towards the house, squeezing her finger through her handkerchief, thinking, hoping, trying to convince herself that maybe she'd cut it on a thorn; not a knife. You didn't find knives under bushes. No one *ever* left a knife under a bush.

She took her handbag out of the Citroën and stared at the barn wall where the mastiff had been chained in her regression. She walked over, her feet dragging through the gravel, and scanned the wall. In the falling darkness it blended in with the bricks and she took a moment to spot it. She went closer, put out her hand and touched the hoop. It had almost rusted away; a chunk flaked off and crumbled into dust in her fingers.

Mad. Going mad. I have lived previous lives.

I killed a dog.

It was raining harder, but she hardly noticed as she stood gazing at the barn; the barn with its bats and spiders and the old car which it had held, like a secret. And which in turn had held its own secret. The chewing gum.

She looked down, just in case, although she knew she would never find it because it was not there, had never been there; it had been her imagination, like everything else. That was all.

She unlocked the door of the house and stepped into the tiny dark hallway, switched on the light and closed the door behind her.

The wind had stopped howling, the mill race was silent. It felt as if time had stopped.

'Ben! Hello, boy!' she called out. 'Ben?' She walked down the passageway, into the kitchen. Silence. 'Ben?' The red light of the answering machine winked frenetically out of the gloom. Rain spattered against the windows.

She jerked open the boiler room door, saw the dim blue flame of the boiler 'Ben?' She switched on the light.

He was cowering against the far wall, whimpering, his hair standing up along his back as if it had been brushed the wrong way.

She ran over, knelt beside him and put her arm around him. 'Boy? What's the matter?' He was shaking and a puddle of urine lay beside him. 'It's OK, boy, it's OK.' She stroked his head and rubbed his chest.

The boiler sparked into life and she jumped. The flame roared, the air hissed, the sound of metal vibrated. 'What is it? Aren't you well? Why are you shut in here? Was it one of the workmen? Let's get you supper.'

She went into the kitchen, took his meat out of the fridge and put it with some biscuits in his bowl by the basket. He stayed cowering in the boiler room, watching her, then slowly, warily, came out. The answering machine continued its winking. The windows shook, a volley of rain struck the glass. The drying-rack swayed in the wind, its pulleys creaking, its rails casting shadows like prison bars.

She cleaned up Ben's puddle and patted him again. He began to eat. She pressed the message play button on the answering machine, heard it rewind and went over to the sink and washed her hands carefully. She rinsed her finger under the cold tap, worried about the rust on the knife, trying to remember when she'd last had a tetanus jab. Her hands looked awful, felt awful; every time she moved a finger the skin parted on a wound, layers of it pulling apart.

The answering machine finished its rewind and began to play. There was a bleep, then a hiss, then a message-end bleep, and another hiss. She frowned. The bleep again. Another hiss. Silence. Hiss. The shuffle of the tape in the machine. Another bleep. Wind shook the house, shook the shadowy bars of the drying rack across the table. Ben looked up at her, then down at his food. He was still trembling.

Bleep. Hiss. The tape shuffled. The wind hosed the rain against the house. Bleep. Hiss. Again, as if someone demented was phoning, someone who refused to speak, who just listened, listened.

Tom. Was it Tom, phoning then hanging up, not having the courage to speak? She turned the volume up, listened to see if she could hear any background sounds, an office, other people talking, to see if she could tell where the caller was.

Ben's ears pricked and he let out a deep rumbling growl. All she could see in the window was her own reflection against the blackness. There was a final long bleep, the messages-end one. A cold draught of air blew through the old tired glass. The house was vulnerable, easy to break into, easy if someone wanted to —

She picked up the phone, listened to the hum of the dial tone and felt reassured, but she wished they had curtains, blinds, anything. Someone could be out there, looking in, watching. Ben half-heartedly chewed a chunk of meat.

She took the cassettes of today's session, which Ernest Gibbon had given her, out of her handbag and put them on the kitchen table. At least Tom wouldn't see them, wouldn't be able to get angry about her spending money.

There was antiseptic and dressings under the sink; she anointed the knife cut and bound it with Elastoplast. Ben shot into the hallway and started barking. The doorknocker rapped, flat dull thuds. She hurried down the passageway. Through the stained glass panel in the front door she could see a short figure in yellow. 'Yes?' she called out. 'Who is it?'

'Viola Letters,' shouted a muffled voice.

Charley opened the door, holding Ben's collar. The plump diminutive figure of her neighbour was parcelled in sopping yellow oilskins, sou'wester, red wellington boots and held a large rubber torch. She looked as if she'd just stepped out of a lifeboat.

'I say, frightfully sorry to bother you on a night like this,' she barked in her foghorn voice. 'You haven't by any chance seen Nelson, have you?'

There was a spray of rain, and Charley smelled the

202

alcohol fumes on the old woman's breath. 'Nelson? Your cat? No, I haven't I'm afraid.' She stepped back. 'Please, come in.'

'Don't want to make your hallway wet.'

'Would you like a drink?'

'Well, if you —' She strode forwards. 'Rage, roar, spout — always reminds me of King Lear this sort of a night,' she barked. 'Damned bloody cat. Been gone over a day now, not back for his food. Never usually wanders very far — can't see much having the one eye.' Ben trotted up to her with his chewed rubber Neil Kinnock head in his mouth. She patted him. 'Thank you, chappie. Dreadful bloody man, Kinnock, but very kind of you.'

'What can I get you?'

'Rather feel I'm barging in.' Viola Letters squinted at her and began tugging the knot of her sou'wester.

'No, not at all. I'm not doing anything. Whisky? Gin? We've got most things.'

'Went to Evensong on Sunday,' the old woman said, following Charley into the kitchen. 'Have you met that vicar chap? Damned good mind to write to the bishop about him. He's off his trolley. Either that or he was sloshed. Gin and tonic, dear, no ice.' She tugged off her wet overclothes and Charley hung them on the rail on the Aga.

'He was rabbiting on about organic farming; said that if Christ came back today he wouldn't be a priest, he'd be an organic farmer. Said it was better to have the odd maggot you could see, and pluck it out, than to eat a ton of invisible chemicals. Some analogy to casting out the moneylenders. Beyond me.'

Charley poured a large dollop of gin. 'I'm afraid we don't go to church.' She unscrewed the tonic cap; there was a hiss.

'Can't blame you, the way it's going. Quite mad.

Barmy.' She took the glass. 'Cheers!'

Charley poured herself a glass of white wine. 'Cheers,' she replied and sat down.

Viola Letters looked around. 'You've done a lot of work here,' she commented.

'It needs a lot more.'

The old woman sipped her gin and tonic. 'I gave my poor boy his breakfast yesterday morning, and I haven't seen him —' She stopped in mid-sentence as her eye caught the perspex photograph holder on the window-sill. There was a montage inside which Charley had made up from various holiday snaps: Tom in a suede coat and herself in a camel coat, looking very early seventies, in front of the Berlin Wall. Tom at an outdoor café in dark glasses, the two of them in the cockpit of a yacht in Poole harbour. A shot of herself having a go (her one and only go) at hang-gliding. Tom on a beach in scuba gear. The two of them amid a drunken gaggle of friends around a restaurant table.

Viola Letters blinked and leaned closer, then pointed a finger at the picture of Charley and Tom in front of the Berlin Wall. 'That's you?'

Charley nodded. 'Yes. I've changed a bit since then.'

She gazed at Charley, then dug her pudgy fingers inside the neck of her jumper and pulled out an eyeglass, closed one eye and studied the photograph.

She looked back at Charley. A strange wariness appeared in her crab eyes. 'It's uncanny, dear. Most uncanny.'

Charley felt edgy.

Viola Letters dabbed her forehead. 'I — if you don't mind dear, I'm really not — don't think I'm feeling very well.' She put her half-full glass on the table and glanced at the ceiling, as if she had heard something.

'Can I get you anything?' Charley said. 'Would you like me to call a doctor?'

'No. No, I'll be all right.'

'I'll walk you home.'

'No — I'll —' She stood up. 'I think it's just — bit of a chill.' She looked at the photograph again.

It had been taken by another tourist, an American. He'd had difficulty with the camera, kept pushing the wrong button and Tom had got exasperated. Strange the details one could remember over the years. That was taken before they married, when she was about nineteen. She could remember the American. He looked like Jack Lemmon with a beer belly.

'What is it that's uncanny?' she asked.

The old woman put on her wet oilskins and pushed her stockinged feet into her wellingtons. 'The resemblance,' she said. 'I'm sorry. It's really given me a bit of a shock. I'll be better tomorrow.'

'What do you mean, resemblance?'

Ben growled, his head tilted upwards, and the old woman's eyes slid up to the ceiling again, then at Charley, and she managed a weak smile. 'Nothing really, dear. Me being silly. The brain's not so clear as it was. It's just that you —' She paused. 'Perhaps another time, dear. Pop round and we'll have a chat about it.'

'I'll come tomorrow,' Charley said. 'See how you're feeling. I could get you something from the chemist.'

'It's only a stupid chill,' Viola Letters said, knotting the sou'wester strap under her chin. 'It's this damned change in the weather. Boiling hot one day, then this!'

'Is it someone who you know who I look like in the photograph? A resemblance to someone you know?'

They stopped by the front door and the old woman shook her head. 'No, I — I'd prefer to talk about it — another time.' She leaned forward, dropping her voice almost to a whisper. Her mouth became a small, tight circle. The eyes slid down out of sight, then peeped warily at her again. 'The first time we met, when you came with that message from my late husband. Did I tell you I'd had that same message before? On the day he died?'

'Yes,' Charley said. 'You did.'

'That photograph of you — there's a most extraordinary resemblance to the girl who brought me the message. I thought for a moment it was her.' She opened the door. 'Another time, dear. We'll talk about it another time.'

Chapter Twenty-Five

That photograph of you — there's a most extraordinary resemblance to the girl who brought me the message. I thought for a moment it was her.

Viola Letters's voice sounded crystal clear. As if she were in the room. Sunlight streamed in. Her finger hurt and her head ached. She climbed out of bed and walked to the window.

The storm had died sometime around dawn. Birds were out in force, thrushes and sparrows and blackbirds and robins prospecting for worms. Water dripped from the trees. The weir and mill race seemed louder this morning.

That photograph of you —

It was half past seven. The workmen would be here soon. She put on her towelling dressing gown and moccasin slippers and went downstairs.

As she bent to pick up the newspapers she heard a rustling sound coming from the kitchen, a crackling like shorting electricity. There was a smell of burning plastic. She ran down the passageway.

'Ben!' she yelled in fury.

But it was too late. Ernest Gibbon's two cassettes were lying on the floor, their casings split, the thin tapes unspooled, crumpled, twisted around the table, around the chair legs. Ben was having a great time, rolling in the stuff, burrowing, rustling, scrunching it up, tangling it further all the time.

'Ben!' her voice stormed out, deeper and louder still. 'Wicked!'

The dog stopped and looked at her. He stood up, brown tape draped around his head like a wig, and shook himself. The tape fell free and he slunk out.

She stared at the mess. How the hell had Ben knocked the cassettes off the table? She knelt and began to scoop the tape up into bundles, wondering whether it was still usable. But it was twisted, creased, knotted. Hopeless. She stuffed it into a garbage bag and tied the neck, ready for it to go to the large bins at the end of the lane. Then she noticed the smell of burning plastic again, getting stronger. It was coming from the Aga.

The lid of the hot plate was up and the picture frame of their holiday snaps, or what was left of it, was lying on the flat top, soggy, melting. The photographs inside were frosted globules of washed-out colour.

As she snatched out her hand to rescue it the frame burst into flames and she jumped back as filthy black smoke rose, twisting savagely upwards. She grabbed a dish cloth and whacked it. Bits of molten plastic and burning photographs scattered around the kitchen. One tiny piece landed on her hand, clung to it, burning, and she shook it and rubbed it against her dressing gown. Patches of lino were melting. She ran the tap into the washing up bowl, lifted the bowl out and poured it over the burning plastic on the Aga, then dowsed the rest of the tiny fires.

She opened the windows, coughing, her throat full of the filthy cloying smoke. The remains of the frame hissed and sizzled on the oven. She scraped it off with a metal spatula, dropped it into the sink and ran the cold tap. More steam rose and the blackened perspex curled as if it had a life of its own. The charred photographs inside it curled too.

* * *

The new application form for her birth certificate had arrived in the post. She read through it as she ate her muesli, chewing with no appetite, leaving the newspapers untouched beside her on the kitchen table.

The stench of the burned plastic and wet charred paper hung thickly in the room, and the floor was damp from where she had washed it down. The new wound on her hand ached along with the others. She finished her cereal and was having another go at scraping the remains of the perspex off the top of the Aga when the phone rang. She answered it mechanically, almost absently.

'Yes, hello?'

'Charley?'

It was Tom.

She slammed the receiver straight back down and sat, quivering, as it rang again. Three rings, then the answering machine clicked and Tom spoke as the tape revolved.

'Charley? Darling? I want to speak to you, please pick up the phone.' There was a pause. 'At least call me back. I'm in the office all day.' Another pause 'Darling? ... Charley?' Then the sound of the receiver being replaced.

'Go to hell,' she said.

She made the workmen their morning tea and walked with Ben up the lane to see whether Viola Letters was better. To see if the old woman would explain why a photograph had freaked her out so much.

Charley was pleased she had hung up on Tom, pleased she had been strong. She wondered how long she could stay strong.

The curtains of Rose Cottage were still drawn, which surprised her; it was after eleven. There was a mournful miaow and Nelson, the one-eyed cat, was rubbing itself against the front door.

'You're supposed to be missing,' she told it.

There were two bottles of milk on the step and the *Daily Telegraph* stuck out of the letter box. Charley closed the front gate behind her, tied Ben to the fence and ordered him to sit. She rang the brass ship's bell. There seemed something idiotic about it, she thought, as the clang rang out. Nothing happened. She rang it several more times, then rapped on the door as well.

She looked at the cosy yellow Neighbourhood Watch sticker in the frosted glass pane beside the door, then pushed open the letter box and peered through. She could see the carpet, the stairs and a picture on the wall. Everything looked very still.

She walked around the side of the house. There was a fine view from the rear beyond the fence at the end of the neatly tended lawn, over the valley and woods. The cat followed her, miaowing insistently.

A fan vent in the kitchen window was spinning. She could see a tray, laid with a crystal glass and an unopened bottle of wine, a napkin in a silver ring, *Country Life* magazine, a peach and a knife on a small plate. She rapped on the glass pane of the back door, gently at first, then louder. 'Hello? Mrs Letters!' She called, then hesitated. Maybe she was asleep and did not want to be disturbed?

She walked to the front again and stared at the grey stone wall and the crenellations along the roof. Wrong. Something was wrong. A high-pitched whine cut through the still of the morning. Hugh working on one of his cars, probably. She untied Ben and went up the lane.

Hugh's Jaguar was parked in his yard and the doors of his corrugated iron workshop were open. He was bent over the engine of the Triumph, which was sitting, minus its wheels, on metal jacks. A bright light hung down from the ceiling above him, its bulb inside a wire mesh cage. The place smelled of oil and old leather, and there were acrid fumes of burnt electricity.

She gritted her teeth against the banshee din.

There were two other cars crammed into the small area, both under dust sheets. Tools and bits of motor cars lay on the floor, the work top, the shelves. There were boxes, tins full of nuts and bolts, loose spark plugs. More tools hung from racks. Old wheels, tyres, were propped around. The bonnet of a car was suspended on wires from the roof girders and there were several metal advertising signs fixed to the walls, Woodbine cigarettes, Esso Extra and battered licence plates, mostly American.

The noise died. There was a clank and something metal rolled along the grimy concrete floor. Hugh lifted his head out of the engine compartment and saw her. 'Hi!' He gave her a welcoming grin and laid the tool on the ground. The two halves of the hinged black bonnet sat up in the air like claws behind him.

'How's it going?'

'I got the head off.' He wiped his forehead with the back of his oily fist and nodded at the engine compartment.

She peered in; car engines always baffled her. She saw a tangle of wires, rubber tubing, several thin metal rods sticking up beside elliptical holes in what looked like the main part of the engine.

'Considering she hasn't been run for years, she's not too bad. I need a couple of gaskets, and I might get her started up. Take you for a spin.'

She smiled thinly, feeling the odd recognition stirring again.

Chewing gum.

'How much do you know about its history?' she asked.

'I'm going to try and trace the provenance. I don't

211

think Miss Delvine was the original owner.'

No, she wasn't, Charley wanted to say. *His name was Dick.*

Her fingers felt as if they were touching ice.

Touching an old knife.

'I've written off to the licensing people in Swansea.' His eyes stared at her, penetrating, a deep curiosity in them, and she looked away uneasily.

'Have you seen Viola Letters today?' she said.

'No. She came round yesterday evening searching for her cat.'

'She came to me as well. She wasn't well. I've just been to see her. The cat's on her doorstep, and it doesn't seem like she's got out of bed. I hope she's OK.'

'Maybe she's asleep. Taken some pill. All that booze she knocks back, I should think a couple of aspirins and she goes critical.'

Charley smiled.

'Let's try phoning her.'

They went into his house, Ben was invited too. In contrast to the neat exterior it was a ramshackle chaos, mostly of books and manuscripts, among them, she noticed to her surprise, a row of James Herbert novels. The walls were hung with old framed maps; there wasn't much furniture, and what there was looked masculine and slightly dilapidated. Comfortable, in a lived-in sort of way, none of it would have looked out of place in a student room at a university.

He picked up the phone from under a pile of papers on his massive desk, rummaged through a book for Viola Letters's number and dialled. He let it ring a dozen times, then redialled.

There was still no answer.

'I'll pop by later on and see if she needs anything,' he said. 'Actually, while you're here, I was wondering if you and your old man would like to come and have supper on Saturday, if you're not doing anything.'

She blanched. 'I — we'd — he's away — business. I don't know when he's coming back.'

'So you're on your own?'

She nodded.

He was quiet for a moment. 'I'm going to the pub this evening. Why not come? There'll be a few people there.'

'I —' Cheery faces. No, no thanks, couldn't face it, could not face lying about Tom. Could not face —

Being alone in the house. Waiting for Tom to call. Tom could go to hell.

'Thanks. That would be nice.'

A police car was parked on the grass bank by the upturned skiff, and two policemen were standing on the footbridge with a local farmer she vaguely recognised, peering down into the sluice pond. She walked through the gate pillars, wondering what they were looking at.

Then she saw it herself. For a moment she couldn't make out what it was. A carrier bag blown by the wind, maybe?

It was wrapped around one of the blades of the mill wheel, flapping like a trapped animal in the water that surged over it.

Bright yellow.

Her heart came up into her mouth. Yellow. She began to run. Ben ran with her, thinking it was a game. Yellow.

Viola Letters had been wearing a yellow sou'wester last night.

It was a yellow sou'wester that was wrapped around the blade of the mill wheel.

Then she saw the huge chunk that was missing from the bank the other side of the footbridge. The path and the shrubbery had gone, collapsed into the sluice pond, leaving raw earth like a wound from which the dressing had been ripped.

The yellow sou'wester flapped again.

Charley screamed.

Chapter Twenty-Six

The man from the Water Board cranked the small round handle at the side of the wheel; the rods and gears it was attached to were rusty and creaked. One of the policemen cranked the opposite handle. The two corroded steel gates moved slowly, inches at a time, until they locked together.

Charley was aware of the new silence, as if a tap had been turned off. A bizarre silence.

The last of the water slid down the slimy concrete blocks of the weir and the level began to sink rapidly down the circular wall of the sluice pond.

The man from the Water Board knelt, peered over the edge of the bank and took out a measuring stick. 'Four inches,' he said. 'The level's high. It'll rise that in an hour. I can give you forty-five minutes then I'll have to open the sluice again.

Charley barely heard them talk as she stared over the parapet at the slime rising around the brick walls and the dark shapes becoming visible below the surface.

Be an old sack. Please be just an old sack, or plastic sheeting.

The top of a gas cooker appeared first; but by then the shape beside it was clear to them all, and their expressions tightened as the water fell further and they gazed at the dark sludge and the body wearing yellow oilskins and red galoshes that lay face down in it, between the mangle and the bicycle and the rusted bedstead.

'To look for her cat? You think that's why she went up there?' Constable Tidyman's notebook was in front of him on the kitchen table. His face was puffy, the smooth skin, on the turn from youth to middle age, streaked by red veins. He had the eyes of a small bird.

The kitchen still smelled of molten plastic. Through the window she could see two policemen stretching white tape around the weir. A Scenes of Crime officer was walking around with a camera, taking shots.

'Yes. She seemed in a bit of a state about it.' Steam from her tea rose. She saw Viola Letters sprawled in the sludge, arms outstretched as if she had been dropped from a great height. She had not been able to watch her body being hoisted out.

The policeman tapped his pen on his notepad, his nose twitching at the lingering unpleasant smell. Hammering echoed around the house and there was the whine of a drill. 'You saw her last night?'

Charley nodded.

'What time?'

'About nine o'clock.'

'And you gave her a drink?'

'A gin and tonic.'

'A large one?'

The question disturbed her; he was trying to lead her somewhere and that angered her suddenly. She didn't fall, for Christ's sake! It was a landslip. She contained her anger. 'No.'

'Do you think she might have been tipsy when she left?'

'No.'

'Had she been drinking before she came here?'

'I wouldn't know.'

216

The beady eyes stared at her accusingly. 'The dam wall was not maintained properly. Water must have been seeping through, undermining the path. It only needed one heavy rainfall to sweep it away.'

Charley shook her head numbly. She did not like the way the policeman had suddenly changed tack, as if he were determined to lay the blame on her.

'The wall is the Water Board's responsibility. I understood that it's checked every year,' she said.

The policeman heaped a spoon of sugar into his tea, stirred it, then tapped the spoon dry on the rim of the cup, more taps than were necessary. 'Did her cat stray often?'

'I don't know. We've only been here a few weeks.'

'Do you suppose there'd be any other reason why she might have gone up there?'

'No, I —' Her brain fogged.

I wonder if you'd mind terribly nipping down and telling Viola I'll be a bit late. I've lost my damned watch somewhere and I must go back and look for it.

The voice of Viola Letters's husband rang around inside her head, and she felt her cheeks getting hotter. Constable Tidyman leaned forwards, as if he had picked up a scent.

'Was there anything odd about Mrs Letters's behaviour last night?'

Yes, officer, she was very distressed by a photograph. Unfortunately it got burned this morning.

'She wasn't feeling very well. I did offer to walk her home.'

The first time we met, when you came with that message from my late husband. Did I tell you I'd had the same message before? On the day he died?

'Is there something else you'd like to tell me, Mrs Witney?'

'No. No, I'm sorry. I feel very upset; she was a nice

woman; she was kind to me.'

The beady eyes did not leave her. 'I understand she lost her dog recently.'

The eyes drew her like magnets. Bored into her. She nodded.

'Accident with a kettle?'

'Teapot,' she mouthed.

'Another accident,' he said.

She bit her lip. Tidyman looked solid in his serge jacket with its polished chromium buttons. He looked like a man who enjoyed afternoon cake in front of the telly and a pint with his mates, a man who was happiest dealing with shotgun licences and lost property. He asked a few more questions, finished his tea and prepared to leave. She let him out of the front door. At the top of the drive two men were loading a large black plastic bag into a white van. The Scenes of Crime officer was changing a lens on his camera. Water was tumbling down the weir once more.

Some people thought death was OK, they could accept it, some religions thought it was OK too. She could not. Death of people she knew always affected her badly. Death was evil. It disturbed her, disoriented her, as if the world had been given a half rotation so that instead of looking up at the sky she found herself looking down into an abyss.

She wondered sometimes what it felt like to die; what Viola Letters had felt plunging down the bank, into the water, being sucked under the water. Some man on a television programme about death, a jolly, earnest fellow whose name she had forgotten, said drowning was quite a pleasant way to go, actually.

It hadn't seemed very pleasant from where she'd stood at the top of the sluice.

It hadn't seemed very pleasant when they'd put Viola

Letters's body into what looked like a bin-liner.

The application form for her birth certificate was missing from the table. She searched the kitchen but it was gone.

She thought back to last night, to when Viola Letters had come into the kitchen. The cassettes had been on the table then, the old woman had noticed them. Had she moved them? The frame? Her mind was fuzzy; her sense of recall seemed to have gone. ·

Another time, dear. We'll talk about it another time.

That had gone too.

Hugh picked Charley up at half past seven in his elderly Jaguar saloon which felt solid and rather quaint. The ignition was on the dash and there was a starter button. She groped around for the seat belt.

'Afraid there aren't any.'

'Oh, right,' she said, feeling slightly foolish, as if she should have known there wouldn't be. There was a low whine from the gear box as they moved off and a gruff roar as he accelerated up the drive. The instruments flickered, the speedometer bouncing around the dial without settling.

The beam of the headlights picked up the white tape that cordoned off the sluice pond and the weir, and was staked across the footpath with a large sign in front, 'POLICE DANGER'.

She said nothing until they were past the old woman's cottage. 'Lovely car.'

He smiled. 'She's getting a bit tatty.' He changed gear, then slowed for a pothole outside the driveway of Yuppie Towers, stopped at the end of the lane then pulled out on to the road. He drove gently, rather sedately, as if he were nurturing the car along, respectful of its age, tilting his head for a moment and listening like a doctor to the note of the engine. She found herself comparing his driving to Tom's frenetic pace.

'Where's your hubby gone?'

Hubby. Sounded cosy. The acid in her stomach rose as steadily as the sluice water had fallen. 'He's — in the States.'

'Does he travel a lot?'

Never. 'Yes. Quite a lot.'

'He does international law?'

'Yes, a bit. Child custody and things.' She was uncomfortable at lying.

'Do you mind being on your own?'

'No, it's fine,' she said too hastily. 'I suppose I'm more used to being on my own in a city than in the country. I don't think I've quite got used to it yet.'

'You haven't had a very good start.'

'No,' she said. 'I haven't.'

The pub was quiet; she was glad not to see Zoe and Julian and to have to listen to how well the girls had ridden and how *sooooooper* Elmwood Mill was and weren't she and Tom simply *adoring* it?

Two wizened men sat at the bar with their own personal tankards, one smoking a pipe, the other tapping his cap which was by the ashtray in front of him. Hugh nodded at them and the one tapping his cap nodded back without interest. A youth was playing the fruit machine and a plump girl in her late teens sat eating a packet of crisps behind him. The fruit machine bleeped and there was a clatter of money.

Hugh ordered her a drink and exchanged a few words with Vic, the landlord, about Viola Letters.

'That path been goin' f'years. Any fool could a see'd it,' the old man with the pipe said to Vic.

Vic nodded, his dark funereal face ideally suited to the gloomy atmosphere.

Charley sat on a bar stool. Tom had rung again, left another message sometime in the afternoon when she had been out, gone for a long walk with Ben, tramping across the fields. She had not rung him and she was pleased, took a certain bitter satisfaction in playing his voice back. It would not last, she knew that; it came in waves, and when she was at the top she was fine, but each time she sank down into the trough she wanted to pick the receiver up and dial him and hear his voice telling her all was fine, he was coming back.

She thought of Viola plunging with the landslip into the water. Was it the cat that had made her go up that path in the darkness? Or her husband? Had she gone to try and communicate?

'Charley must have been the last to see her,' Hugh was saying.

'That path been goin' f'years,' the man with the pipe repeated. 'F'years.'

Hugh handed Charley her spritzer and clinked her glass lightly with his beer tumbler. 'Cheers,' he said.

'Cheers. Thank you.' She sipped the drink; it was cold and rather sharp. Vic walked down the bar and began to tidy some glasses.

'How are you feeling?' Hugh said.

'Pretty shitty.'

'Blaming yourself?'

'I offered to walk her home. She wouldn't let me. If I had insisted ...' She was silent for a moment. 'She didn't have any children, did she?'

'No.' Hugh was wearing a battered jacket, crumpled shirt and a vivid red tie with vertical stripes that reminded her of toothpaste. He ran his eyes across her face, searching for whatever it was he looked for.

Right now, she was not missing Tom. She was glad to be alone with Hugh, to have a chance to talk.

'Hugh. If — If I told you I had proof I have lived before, how would you react?'

The serious expression on his face did not alter; he

studied her a little more intently. 'What sort of proof?'

'Didn't you say that to prove you have lived before you need to know something that happened during a previous life that no one else living knows? And which you could not possibly have found out any other way, unless you had lived before?'

'Yes,' he said. He took his pipe from his jacket pocket.

'You said it could be something small.'

He rummaged in another pocket and pulled out a leather tobacco pouch.

'I have two things.'

He unzipped the pouch and pushed the bowl of his pipe in. 'Tell me.'

She told him: about her background; everything she could remember about her regression sessions; about the stables, Viola Letters's husband, the Triumph and the chewing gum, about the locket, and the note inside it, the inscription on the rock and the knife.

She did not tell him about digging the locket back up again, and burning the photographs; nor that Tom had left her. She did not want him to think she was nuts and dismiss everything as her imagination, because she was not nuts, not really — well, maybe just heading a little that way. But not the whole hog.

'D loves BJ?' He tapped his teeth with the stem of his pipe. 'Do those initials mean anything to you?'

'His name is Dick.'

'And what's yours in these regressions?'

'I don't know.'

Hugh struck a match and lit his pipe; the blue smoke drifted towards her.

'You're adopted and don't know your real parents?'

'I'm trying to find out now.'

'So cryptomnesia would be the most likely explanation.'

'Cryptomnesia is things one knew as a child and have forgotten, isn't it?'

'Totally forgotten, as if they never existed.' He sucked on his pipe. 'Memories of the ages one and two, for instance. Very few people can remember anything at all, without the help of hypnosis.' He peered at the bowl and prodded the tobacco with his finger. 'Maybe you were down here with your natural parents, before you were adopted.'

'I was adopted at birth.'

'Are you certain?'

'That's what my mother's always —' She stopped.

'Mothers often shield their children from bad memories. Is there any chance she's been shielding you from something?'

Lies death. Truth. Go back.

She glanced around. One of the old men at the end of the bar was staring at her. She looked back at Hugh; out of the corner of her eye she saw the old man tug the sleeve of his companion and mumble something.

'Surely if — if I had been in this area with my natural parents — or my adoptive parents — I would have some memories?'

Hugh took the pipe out of his mouth and twisted the stem around, adjusting it. 'You do have some memories. You knew where the stables were. You knew where the locket was buried, where the knife was.'

She nodded.

'You're pretty certain your adoptive parents were always in London. Do you think it might be possible that your natural mother was from around here? That you spent your first year or two here before being adopted? Or maybe, if you were adopted at birth, your adoptive mother has some connections here?'

'I suppose it's possible,' she said. 'But wouldn't I have remembered more than this?'

'You're remembering more all the time. You lost your natural father, then your adoptive father. That's a heavy trip for a small child. You've coped with it by burying it away. You needed a hypnotist to dig it up.'

'I thought philosophy was your subject, not psychiatry.'

He tamped the tobacco in the bowl with his finger. 'I'm playing devil's advocate, that's all.' He shrugged. 'There's usually an explanation for these things. If your mother won't tell you — or can't — what about any of her relatives?'

'There aren't any alive.'

'Friends?'

'No. I should have started this ten years ago.'

'You don't know your real parents names?'

LEAVE IT ALONE, BITCH.

'I'm hoping to get them.'

'It still might not help much, but it may tell you where they're from.'

She drained her glass and ordered another spritzer and a pint for Hugh. Just memories. Across the room the fruit machine made a demented wailing sound and sicked up a bucketful of coins. Memories. The minty taste of the chewing gum. The woman on the horse. The locket. Blood gouting from the mastiff's neck. She looked down at her hands, scratched and cut to ribbons. Wounds were memories. Wounds made the body remember that certain things were painful and not to do them again. Her mind was full of wounds. They hurt too much to belong to someone else.

She could see from Hugh's expression that he knew that as well.

They ate in the small restaurant at the back of the pub. Charley picked at her prawn salad, wishing she had not ordered it. The prawns disturbed her, something about them seemed too intense, the fishy flavour, the texture. It felt like eating maggots.

A low mist smudged the beam of the Jaguar's headlamps as they drove back down the lane, just after eleven. Rose Cottage slid by, dark under the marbled moonlight. A tiny red dot winked by the front door.

Hugh braked. She climbed out unsteadily, more drunk than she'd realised. Nelson miaowed mournfully. Hugh stood beside her. She opened the gate. The engine of the Jaguar ticked behind them. 'Nelson!' he said. 'Good boy!'

The cat miaowed again and the cry echoed through the night.

'I'll give him some milk,' Hugh said.

'I've got dog food, if he'll eat it. What's going to happen to him?'

'I'll tell the police in the morning,' Hugh said. 'They'll probably take him to a home or something. Unless you'd like him?'

'I don't think Ben would. You don't want him?'

'He gives me the creeps.'

Nelson wailed again, his solitary eye glowing.

'I'll run you down.'

'I can walk.'

'It's no problem. All part of the service.'

As he pulled up behind her Citroën a feeling of gloom enveloped her; she didn't want to be alone, did not want to go into the house alone. She stared through the windscreen at the dark shapes of the night.

'I keep thinking about Viola Letters all the time.'

'You mustn't blame yourself.'

'Would you like some coffee?'

'I ought to get back. I'm behind on my writing.'

'What are you doing at the moment?'

'Oh, I'm kicking around with the philosophical aspects of ghosts.'

She raised her eyebrows at him. 'What's that to the layman?'

He smiled. 'Maybe a quick coffee.'

She opened the Jaguar's door and the weak interior light came on and made the night beyond the windscreen even darker. The house seemed to be tilting in different directions above her. Lights burned inside; she had left plenty on, had not wanted to come back to darkness.

Hugh got out and closed his door. The weir roared, the water tumbling as if it had never been disturbed. The moon was sliding slowly through the sky, making the same journey it had made a million billion times before she'd ever been born and would go on making aeons after she was dead.

'Weird things, stars,' Hugh said.

'Do you know them all?'

'Ghosts,' he said. 'I always wonder how many of them are ghosts.' He pointed up with his pipe. 'You're not seeing the stars as they are now, you're seeing them as they were hundreds of years ago, millions of years ago; some of them don't exist any more. You are looking at light they emitted, images of themselves. That's what I think a lot of ghosts are. Images of dead people, like video replays.'

Ben barked as Charley unlocked the front door. They walked down the passageway and into the kitchen. She switched the light on and was startled by a sharp crackle from the switch. The light flickered, then steadied. 'There's some problem with the electrics, still,' she said.

'I thought you'd had it rewired.'

'We have.'

Ben was jumping excitedly and she let him into the garden. She filled the percolator with water and took a coffee filter out of a pack. Hugh stared around the room and up at the ceiling with a worried frown. The answering machine winked and she wondered if there was another message from Tom. She hoped there was. Sod him.

'Do you really believe in ghosts, Hugh?'

He prodded inside the bowl of his pipe. 'Yes. I believe in ghosts, but I don't know what they are. I don't know whether ghosts have any intelligence, any free will, whether they can actually do anything other than keep appearing in the same place, going through the same movements, like a strip of film replaying. I'm not sure whether a ghost could really harm someone, apart from giving them a fright by manifesting. That's part of the thesis in my book.'

'Have you ever seen one?'

'No.'

'Would you like to?'

'Yes. Would you?'

'No.' She let Ben in and sat down at the table. 'I'd be really freaked.'

'I don't think it's that frightening. We talk about reality and the supernatural as being two different things. But they aren't.'

'How do you mean?' The percolator gurgled and spat; a steady dribble of coffee fell into the jug.

'We know what corpses are, but I don't think we know what death is. I don't believe in death any more than I believe in life.'

'You don't think Viola Letters is dead?'

'They pulled her corpse out of the sluice pond.'

'But her spirit is the thing that matters?'

'Bodies matter too. All the cells in them, all the tiny particles, the atomic particles and the sub-atomic particles. Genes. Electricity.'

'Electricity?'

'The particles in our bodies have electro-magnetic charges. When our corpses break down, either through

227

cremation or burial, it all goes back into the earth one way or another, gets recycled. Each particle keeps its memory, like a tiny piece of a videotape. It's possible that you and I are made up of particles which have been in hundreds of other people. You might have particles that have been in Einstein, or Michelangelo, or Boadicea.'

'Or a mass murderer?'

'We don't necessarily get reconstituted as human beings. We might — or bits of us might — come back as humans, bits as dung beetles. Might even come back as a tree and get made into a table.'

'Or an encyclopaedia.'

Hugh grinned and relit his pipe.

She tried to fathom out his argument. 'You said the other day that places could retain memories of things that had happened.'

'There is a view that if there has been an intense emotion in a place then somehow the electro-magnetic particles in the atoms in the walls have absorbed this — and either some people, or certain atmospheric conditions, cause the replay effect.' He shrugged. 'That explains a large percentage of ghosts.'

Charley put two mugs on the table. 'Sugar?'

'Thanks.'

'What about the others?'

He rolled a spent match between his fingers. 'Intelligent ghosts? They seem to use the same electro-magnetic energy, but they need other energy too. They take the heat out of rooms, which is why rooms go cold; they draw energy off people; they even draw it off the electricity in a house.' His eyes glanced around the room again, over at the switch, up at the light bulb.

She noticed him. 'What — what do ghosts do with this energy?' she said.

'They can't do very much themselves. They are

energy forces but they don't have voices or bodies or limbs. They can move objects around — poltergeist activity — and they can manifest, but if they want to do something they have to do it through a human — or maybe sometimes an animal.'

'How?'

'By using their physical energy.'

She stared into her coffee; dark brown, swirling, like the sluice pond; like the sludge; the old woman lying face down. 'Can ghosts make people do things?'

'It's possible. There is evidence.'

'Viola Letters was going to tell me something. Last night, when she was here, she saw an old photograph of me that she said reminded her of someone. She got quite distraught — wouldn't finish her drink — and left.'

'What did she say?'

'She said she'd explain another time.'

'That was all?'

'She said that on the day her husband died, someone brought her a message. A girl. She said in the photograph that I looked like that girl.'

'Can I see it?'

'It — I — burned it.'

'Why did you do that?'

He looked harder at her, and she felt her face reddening. 'I don't know.'

He did not take his eyes off her while he spoke. 'Sometimes people do get spooked by photographs; the camera catches someone at a particular angle, in a certain light, and they look like someone else.'

'Do you really in your heart believe it is possible people can be reincarnated, Hugh?'

After a long while he nodded. 'Yes, I do.'

'I used to believe death was the end,' Charley said. 'It was easier that way. Do you think we come back time after time and go through the same things?'

'Life's not some slot machine in an arcade with a sign that flashes up saying "I'm sorry, you have been killed. Would you like another go?" But we might get put through the same tests each time, get faced with the same situations until we've learned how to cope.'

Charley felt for a fleeting instant as if she had pushed her fingers into an electrical socket. She was startled by the shock, by the jolt to her mind. 'Do you think that the past can repeat itself?'

Hugh smiled. 'You needn't worry; you're not pregnant, are you?'

She shook her head.

'The character in your regression is pregnant. So it's different, isn't it?'

'Yes,' she said reluctantly.

'Even if your husband has left you.'

She sprang upright in the chair, her eyes opening wide in astonishment. 'How? How do you —?'

'Am I right?' he said.

She sank down on her elbows, squeezing her eyes tightly shut, felt the tears trickle down her cheeks. 'Yes.'

'You're going through a lot.'

She sniffed, and felt angry suddenly, angry at herself, at the world. 'And no doubt I'll have to go through it again in some other bloody life; and again; and again.'

Hugh poured more coffee into his cup. 'I don't think we're doomed to go on forever round and round in the same spot, like some goldfish in a bowl.' He frowned. 'Where is your goldfish?'

'Dead.'

'I'm sorry.'

'You needn't be. It's going to come back as the next Pope.' She blew her nose. 'I'm sorry. I didn't mean to be trite. I just find this whole thing so freaky. These regressions. I really don't want to go on with them.' She sipped her coffee. 'Do you think I should go on with them?'

His eyes rested on hers, probing, still probing. He shot a brief glance around the room, then leaned closer and lowered his voice. 'I think you're close to discovering something; it could be very important, because you are intelligent and articulate and willing to talk about it.' He was quiet for a moment then added, 'I also think you are in danger. Quite serious danger.'

'Danger of what?'

He said nothing.

'Danger of going mad? Is that what you mean?'

'The paranormal,' he said. 'The supernatural. Occult. Whatever you want to call it. It's always dangerous to dabble.'

Chapter Twenty-Seven

She drove to the George and Dragon the next morning, trying to work out what time Hugh had finally left. Four? Half past? Must have been even later than that because it had been starting to get light.

They had talked through the night. About life after death. About religion. About themselves. Talked as if they had known each other all their lives. Hugh had a son who lived in Canada with his ex-wife and she was surprised; it had not occurred to her that he might have had a child. He hadn't seen the kid for two years; a custody fight slogged on. Tom might be able to help him, she said. Tom. She had mentioned Tom as if he was some third party, a casual acquaintance.

It was strange when Hugh left. Letting him out of the front door into the dawn chorus, the way she used to let Tom out of the front door of her mother's flat when they were dating. They used to come back after a night out and cuddle on the sofa until they were sure her mother was asleep, then they'd make love, trying to be quiet and ending up giggling, terrified her mother would wake. Sometimes they dozed, and when he left it would be first light and the milk floats would be starting their rounds.

She had felt comfortable with Hugh last night; so comfortable that if, instead of opening the door for him, they had gone upstairs to bed it would have seemed just as natural.

Get a grip girl, she thought. Fancying other men already. They say it doesn't hurt if you are shot, not for a few moments until the shock and the numbness wears off. Then it hurts. Maybe she was still in shock, still numb? No. Then a seething pang of pain twisted inside her at the thought of Tom and Laura waking up together, and Laura making him breakfast.

The pub was empty. Vic the landlord was behind the bar reading the *Sporting Life.* The fruit machine was silent, its lights off; a faint smell of coffee cut through the background odour of beer ingrained in the walls and the beams. The room was cool.

She stood patiently in front of Vic as he ringed a selection in a horse race. Then he looked up at her and smiled like a man caught leafing through a dirty magazine in a newsagents.

'Any good tips?' she said.

'Not usually.'

'Those two old boys in here last night, sitting just there.' She pointed. 'Who are they?'

'Regulars,' he said. 'Arthur Morrison and Bill Wainwright.'

'Which was the one with the pipe?'

'Bill Wainwright.'

It had been the other one who had stared at her the most. 'Do you know where Arthur Morrison lives?'

'On Crampton's farm. Saddlers Cottages.'

'How would I find those?'

'Simple enough.'

The sign was less than a mile down the road. Charley turned on to a rutted farm track which went across an open field, past a large barn and through a farmyard. A black and white dog ran out and barked at the car. A few hundred yards further was a row of dilapidated brick cottages and she pulled up outside the end one, behind an old van, and climbed out.

The garden was scrubby, overgrown and largely filled with rusted junk. An old black bicycle was propped against the wall and hens clucked somewhere round the back.

She stood, her head stinging from tiredness. For a brief instant she felt she had been here quite recently, and wondered if it was with Tom when they were looking for a farm shop, or maybe Gideon when they had bought the hens.

Arthur Morrison. Arthur Morrison with his wizened glum face and half his teeth missing who sat in the pub sipping his beer from his private tankard. Staring at her. That stare.

She walked down the path, stood in front of the faded blue front door and looked for the bell. She could not see one. There was no knocker either, so she rapped with her knuckles and winced with pain from the raw wounds that were only just starting to scab over.

Silence, then she thought she heard the shuffle of feet and the clink of crockery. She knocked again, using her car key this time. A curtain twitched in the window beside her.

In the farmyard the dog barked. The door opened a few inches and a face peered out of the gloom inside, a shrivelled, suspicious face that looked even older than last night, his scalp visible through his hair like a stone floor through a worn carpet. A smell of age came out of the door with him; of mustiness, tired furniture, tired people; decay.

'Mr Morrison?' Charley said, trying to smile politely.

His expression became increasingly hostile, his gnarled hands trembled. Yet through the hostility and shaking she saw sadness welling in the small yellowing eyes; sadness and tears.

'Go away,' he said, his voice quavering. 'Leave us

alone. Go away. We don't want you here.'

He stepped back smartly and shut the door.

Tom came home that night. It was late, past midnight, dark, and Charley was sleeping lightly, fitfully, when the door clicked. Ben barked.

'Hi, darling.'

Her heart trembled as she heard him walk across the floor, felt him sit on the bed, take her hand. His hand was cold, as if he had been out walking in snow, and she squeezed it.

'I'm sorry,' he said.

'That's OK,' she murmured sleepily.

He leaned over and she smelled strong, musky perfume on him, smelled his breath, which was foul and stank of smoke, not cigarettes or cigars but of burnt straw and wood. He kissed her.

His lips were hard and cold.

She recoiled in shock. The smell of burning and perfume got stronger, more pungent, filled her nostrils. The cold, hard lips pressed into hers, as if they were trying to grind them to pulp. She tried to pull away, pull back, but his arms gripped her around the neck, pulling her in towards him, tighter, tighter.

She shook her head, cried out, heard Ben snarling, cold pins and needles stabbing her body. The room was freezing. She smelled his breath, foul, the ghastly burned smell; the pressure of his hands was getting tighter, tighter. She tried to get out of bed, then realised she was out of bed, was standing up; smashed into something.

His hands tightened more. 'Tom!' Her voice emerged as a gargled cry. She thought her neck bones were going to snap. It was getting harder to breathe, Ben's barking was deafening. She kicked out, but her feet were barely touching the ground. She was breathing in short gasps, standing on tiptoe. She threw her hands up, spun round,

235

fell forwards, cracked her head against something; fell sideways. The pressure around her neck got worse. She stared wildly, looking up, but could only see the moon through the window.

The moon.

The window.

The window was in the wrong place.

Then she was aware of the silence. Of the breeze of cold air. The fierce grip around her neck.

Not hands. It was not hands around her neck; it was something soft that felt hard, was cutting into the skin. It was all right if she stood upright, stood upright on tiptoe and did not move, then it was just all right, just bearable.

The grip around her neck tightened.

It was silk. She tugged at it. The smells had gone. Something silk was knotted around her neck. She stood on tiptoe, as high as she could and tried to loosen it. She found a knot and tugged, but it was too tight. She stumbled and the knot choked her again. Ben barked in fury.

'Help me.'

She put her hands up above her head, felt the silk stretched taut. Where the hell am I? I want to wake up now. Please wake up.

But she was awake. She knew that. She was awake and dangling on the end of a silk noose. Someone had tied it around her neck. Someone in the room.

Her eyes were becoming accustomed to the moonlit gloom. She could see the bed, empty; the archway to the bathroom; Ben. She was standing with her back to the wardrobe. She tried to move away, but the noose around her neck jerked sharply. She clawed at it with her fingers, tried to loosen it but it was getting tighter all the time and she was shaking in panic, gasping for air, having to force herself up on tiptoe to breathe.

She pushed her hand out behind her, found the wardrobe door handle and pulled it. It swung open, thumping her, and she stepped back a few inches, grabbed at the dresses she knew were behind her, felt the polythene covers, heard the rustle of the clothes, the clatter of the hangers. She ran her hand down towards the floor of the wardrobe. It was high, several feet off the ground, with drawers below, but she could not reach down far enough, the noose would not let her, jerked her back up.

She tried again, stretched her arms as far as she could reach, the noose choking her; her fingers touched a shoe, knocked it a few inches sideways, out of reach. She tried again, found it again, was just able to grasp it with the tips of her fingers. She had to fight for breath and for one moment thought she was going to black out. Then her fingers touched the shoe again and she lifted it up.

Holding on to it carefully, gripping it hard, she hammered the heel against the inside of the wardrobe door. She heard the tinkle of breaking glass, transferred the shoe to her left hand in case she still needed it, then cautiously raised her right hand up to the shattered mirror and felt around until she found a loose shard.

With her forefinger and thumb she broke it away, lifted it above her head and started sawing through the twisted silk.

The grip slackened, just a fraction. She carried on sawing, then suddenly the last strands snapped, and she fell forward on her face.

She lay there, shaking, gulping down air, lay there for several minutes before she was able to move, to crawl to her knees and turn on the bedside lamp.

Blinking against the brightness, she stared fearfully at the wardrobe. Part of her black silk negligee hung limply from the latticed carving on the top of the wardrobe. The rest was knotted around her neck.

She shivered with shock and with fear, as she realised what had happened, what she had done.

She had tried to hang herself in her sleep.

She had taken the negligee out of the bottom drawer, out of its carrier bag, had stood on the small chair Tom usually folded his clothes on, tied the top of the negligee around a carved scroll on top of the wardrobe, tied the other end around her neck, then kicked the chair away. It was lying on its side.

Going mad. Did all that in my sleep. Mad. I dig up lockets in my sleep. I killed a dog in a previous life. I try to hang myself. Maybe I am dead now. A ghost.

Can ghosts make people do things?

It's possible. There is evidence.

Her blood flowed slowly, so slowly it felt as if it had stopped; droplets fell through her veins one at a time like condensation from the roof of a cave. She put her hand out and stroked Ben, needing to touch something alive. He felt like a statue.

Steam came out of her mouth. The room was as cold as a deep freeze and getting colder. She walked across to the open window, pushing her way through the coldness as if she were walking underwater. She put her hand out to close the window and realised it was mild outside.

It was only cold in the room.

A creature shrieked in fear, its cry echoing around the darkness. It was half past three. Tiny ghosts glinted in the darkness above her, and the big moon ghost slid silently in the track it had long ago etched in the sky, coating the lake with a sheen, like ice. Fear etched its own track silently down her back.

She shoved the broken glass from the mirror carefully under the wardrobe so Ben would not tread on it, then dressed in jeans, a fresh blouse and a sweater. Ben's tail wagged.

'No, we're not going walkies, chappie. Come on!' She spoke more cheerily than she felt, grabbed her handbag, walked out of the room leaving the light burning, and down the landing, snapping on lights as she went downstairs, picked up Ben's lead without stopping, opened the front door, went out, waited for Ben then shut the door behind her, walked over to her car and held the door open for Ben.

She scraped the dew from the windows, started the engine, and drove up the drive, fast, bounced along the lane, the car lurching, the suspension bottoming. Rabbits scattered as she rounded the bend past Rose Cottage and she noticed Hugh's Jaguar parked outside his barn.

She stopped at the end of the lane, the Citroën's feeble headlamps picking out the hedge across the road, and massaged her neck; the muscles were agony. She pushed the gear lever forward and pulled out into the silent road.

Chapter Twenty-Eight

A street-cleaning truck droned past, its brushes swirling against the King's Road kerb. The mannequins in the shop window opposite stood in arched poses, clad in street-fashion clothes in acid-house hues, glaring demonically out at the darkness through their Ray Ban sunglasses.

A trickle of crimson light leaked from the dark sky and dribbled down the grey precast walls of the high-rise block that towered above. Laura's windows were up there. Seven floors up. She tried to work out which they might be, but it was still too dark.

A spiky-haired girl in Gothic clothing, bombed out of her mind, stomped down the pavement repeating to herself 'Manic-manic-manic-manic', as if it were the key to the universe.

A police car drove by, the two policemen peering in through the Citroën's windows, and Charley remembered she had been drinking last night. The car drove on.

She climbed out of the Citroën, walked to the entrance of the apartment block, looked down the name panel and pressed Laura's bell. They might not be there; might be away for the weekend. There was no response. She was about to press the button again when there was a crackle, and Laura's voice, barely recognisable it sounded so tired: 'Who is it?'

'Charley,' she said.

There was silence, then the click of the lock and the buzz of the mechanism. Charley pushed the glass-panelled door and went in, across the foyer and pressed the button for the lift.

The lift door opened immediately with a clang that echoed in the stillness. The door shut and the lift moved upwards, clanking past each floor, and stopped at the seventh. She stepped out into the corridor, went to Laura's front door and knocked softly.

There was a rattle of the safety chain, and the door opened. Laura stood there in a limp nightdress, her hair dishevelled, her skin the colour of porridge.

'I need to speak to Tom,' Charley said.

'He's not here,' she said.

Charley looked at her disbelievingly.

'Want to come in?'

Laura closed the door behind them, and they went through to the kitchen. Charley looked down the passageway to the open bedroom door for a sign of movement, a sound. Was Tom hiding in there some-where, silently?

'Coffee?'

Charley nodded. Laura switched on the kettle. 'He's not here, I promise.' The kettle hissed.

Charley sat down wearily at the kitchen table. Laura sat down opposite; they stared at each other in silence for a moment.

'I need to speak to him,' Charley said.

'I don't know where he is.'

'I thought —' Charley twisted her wedding ring. 'I thought you —?'

Laura wiped her face with her hands. 'God,' she said. 'I feel awful.' The water boiled and the kettle switched itself off. 'What a mess.'

Charley watched her, anger rising up now through

her fear and tiredness. Laura poured coffee and took a milk bottle from the fridge. Charley glanced around the kitchen, hoping she might spot some evidence of Tom; a pen or a tie or something.

'I don't know what the hell you must think,' Laura said, handing Charley a mug and sitting down again.

Charley did not reply.

Laura looked into her coffee. 'I'm sorry. I didn't mean it. I don't think either of us did. I don't know how I can explain it.' She rested a finger on the rim of her mug. 'I've been so unhappy recently — the last few months — everything's so bloody shitty. Bob's been a bastard, and the boutique's going badly.' She sniffed. 'I've made a real fool of myself. So's Tom.' She shrugged. 'Not much of an excuse.'

'Where is Tom?' Charley eyed her coffee but did not feel like drinking any.

'I don't know. We spent two nights — Wednesday and Thursday — after he — left you.' A smile crossed her face like a twitch. 'It was pretty disastrous. I'm sorry. I'm really sorry.'

Charley stood up; too much was whirring through her mind to cope with. She saw Laura looking at her neck, and turned away, examining a postcard of Tangiers clamped to the fridge door with a Snoopy magnet. She did not want Laura to think she could not cope, that she might have tried to — hang herself?

She stumbled on her own thoughts; could not think of anything to say. She did not want a row, not now, nor a confession. She felt a sense of relief that Tom was not here. Apart from that she was numb. 'I'd better go,' she said, and walked back down the passageway.

Laura followed her to the door and laid a hand on her shoulder. 'I'm sorry, Charley. I'm really sorry,' she repeated.

* * *

Charley pulled up outside the nursing home and let Ben out of the car. They walked into the park opposite under the crimson veins of the breaking dawn.

Ben ran happily around and she sat on a dewy bench, closed her eyes and hugged her arms around herself. The air was mild, but she felt a deep coldness that would not melt away. Her head dropped and she dozed for a while, and woke to find Ben's damp nose rubbing her hands.

Her feet were wet from the grass, her white slip-ons sodden through. She stroked Ben, lolled sideways and slept more. Someone walked by with a dog, but she kept her eyes shut, trying to rest, to savour the drowsiness which for the moment blotted out the fear and the pain.

At half past seven she stood up, clipped Ben's lead on, put him back in the Citroën and crossed the road to the nursing home.

The night nurse was surprised to see her, and Charley smiled back lamely, knowing she must look a wreck, then climbed the stairs with an effort, walked down the landing and went into her mother's room which was silent and dark, with the curtains still drawn.

She closed the door gently and stood listening to the quiet breathing, so quiet it sounded like the whisper of an air-conditioning duct.

She wished the bed was bigger so she could lie on it too and snuggle up to the old woman, the way she used to as a child when she was afraid of the dark, when she used to go into her room and sleep with her arms around her. Safe.

She sat in the chair beside the bed, breathed the familiar smells of freshly laundered linen and stale urine. Safe. She slept.

A tray clattered, Charley stared around, disoriented, coming awake slowly, her neck in agony, her back in agony too, stiff, so stiff she could barely move.

Bugger. The stove. She had forgotten to fill the Aga with coke. It would go out and she'd have to relight it; it was a bitch to light.

A nurse was propping her mother up in bed, the breakfast tray on the table beside her. The nurse turned towards her. 'You've come early,' she said breezily. 'Missing your mum?'

She nodded.

'My mum was in a hospice. I used to sleep in the room with her sometimes.' She smiled. 'You never think that time's going to run out until it happens. Would you like something to eat? I could get you some cereal, eggs.'

'Juice,' Charley said. 'Juice would be nice.'

The nurse held the glass of orange whilst her mother drank, tiny little sips. 'Nice having company for breakfast, isn't it, Mrs Booth?'

She stared blankly ahead.

After the nurse had gone out, Charley went through into the small bathroom and looked at her face in the mirror. Christ. Like a ghost. Her colour was drained, her eyes yellowy and bloodshot. She raised her head and looked at her neck. There were red marks and bands of blue bruising. Somehow she had been hoping that it was a crazy dream. That she'd wake in the morning and the negligee would be back in the carrier bag and everything would be fine and there'd be no marks around her neck.

She washed her face with cold water, dabbed it dry and turned the collar of her blouse up. Elmwood. She had fled from the house. Fled because of — madness? All part of the madness?

Poor thing; of course she couldn't cope with her husband leaving her; pushed her over the edge.

Must be a terrible way to go, to hang herself in a room on your own, like that.

Voices murmured inside her head, snatches of conversations as if she were sitting on a bus.

She went out and kissed her mother, stroked her downy white hair, tidied the loose strands. 'Talk, Mum, talk to me. Let's talk today, have a chat. It's Sunday. Remember we used to go to the country on Sundays?'

The nurse brought in a tray. 'I've popped some cereal and toast on, in case you're hungry.'

Charley thanked her, and ate a little and felt a bit better. She drank her juice, sat beside her mother again and held her hand. 'Who am I, Mum?'

There was no flicker of reaction.

'Who am I?'

There was a yelp outside, then another. Ben in the car, maybe. She would have to let him out soon. 'Who are my real parents?'

Silence. Another mournful yelp.

'What did you mean, *Lies death! Truth. Go back?* Did you mean you haven't told me the truth before?'

The old woman moved a fraction more upright. Her eyelids batted and her eyes widened. She opened her mouth, stared straight at Charley for a brief moment, then looked ahead again and closed her mouth, her jaw slackening, the way someone's might after they have finished speaking. She sank back against the pillow as if she were exhausted by the effort.

Charley wondered what was going on inside her mother's head. Did she in her confused state believe that she had actually spoken. 'I didn't hear what you said, Mum. Could you repeat it?'

But the old woman was still again, her eyes back to their normal intermittent blink; as if an aerial inside her had been unplugged.

245

Chapter Twenty-Nine

'I don't have an appointment,' Charley said. 'Is there any chance Dr Ross could see me?'

'I'm sure Dr Ross could fit you in, Mrs Witney.' The receptionist was a well-preserved blonde in her forties who always reminded Charley of James Bond's original Miss Moneypenny. She shook her wavy hair and gave Charley a warm smile. 'He won't keep you too long.'

Charley walked across the dark hall into the seedy opulence of the waiting room. A mother sat with a small boy just inside the door. The room had not been redecorated in all the years Tony Ross had been their doctor. The plaster moulding was chipped and cracked; an ugly chandelier hung above a mahogany dining table spread with magazines, and the walls, which needed a lick of paint, were ringed with a jumble of chairs that did not match. The open sash windows behind the grimy lace curtains let in the fumes and the clattering roar of the Redcliffe Road traffic.

'No!'

'Oh please!' The boy punched his mother's chest and she shushed him, giving Charley an embarrassed glance.

'No!'

'My friend Billy's got a four-foot willy —'

'That's vulgar.'

The boy giggled and looked across at Charley for approval. But she only noticed him dimly, her thoughts closing around her like a cocoon. She felt grungy, still in the same clothes she had put on early on Sunday morning. She had not been home. Her jeans felt heavy and prickly and stuck to her legs.

She had stayed at the nursing home all Sunday, too drained to drive back home, to face the emptiness of the house; to face whatever it was that was in her mind.

Or in the house.

She had to go back, she knew that. She had to be strong right now if she wanted Tom back. He hadn't gone just because they only slept together once a month at the moment; maybe that was part of it, but there were other parts as important. Probably the most important was that he thought she was going nuts.

Her regressions irritated him, all her alternative treatments for infertility. Seeing the ghost of Viola Letters's husband had tipped him further over the edge. The stables. The car in the barn. The locket. He even felt her increasing mental instability was in some way contributory to Viola's dog being scalded to death.

If she moved out now and did not supervise the workmen it would be the last straw for him. *Sorry, Tom, had to move out, check into a hotel, because there's a ghost in the house which tried to hang me.*

She had to go back, stay there and brazen it out. She had to prove it to herself as well as Tom.

The receptionist called in the child and his mother. The staff at the nursing home had been good about Ben, hadn't minded him coming in, and the nurse had brought up a water bowl, then later some biscuits and a tin of food for him.

In the evening the night nurse had brought a camp bed into the room. It had been strange sleeping in the room, comforted by her mother's breathing; she could have been a child again.

She had wondered, all yesterday and all last night,

whether Laura had been telling the truth. If Tom and Laura were not together, somehow it made Tom's leaving her easier to accept.

She was glad he had not been in Laura's flat when she had turned up, glad in retrospect. It had been a stupid, dumb thing to do. Wanting to seem strong to him, to show him you did not care — and then turn up on his doorstep in the middle of the night. She was going to be strong, however tough that would be. She felt almost more bitter at Laura than at Tom.

Outside in the hallway Tony Ross was saying goodbye to the boy and his mother, his rich caring voice inflected with interest and enthusiasm; he put much effort into making his patients feel a little bit special.

'Charley! Great to see you! Come on in!'

He was wearing a grey Prince of Wales check suit, a tie with crossed squash racquets, and Adidas trainers on his feet. He had a lean face with twinkling grey-blue eyes and a mouth that almost permanently smiled. His hair was grizzly grey, cropped neat and short at the sides and almost bald on top, except for a light fuzz. He exuded fitness, energy, bonhomie.

'How are you?' He held her hand firmly for several seconds. 'Good to see you! It's really good! How's Tom?'

'Fine.' She swallowed.

'Great!'

She followed him across to his tiny office.

'Thanks for seeing me,' she said.

'It's been a while,' he said.

'We've moved to Sussex.'

'Yes, I got your note. Country life, eh? Lucky you.'

'We still want you to be our doctor.'

'Of course, I'd be delighted to carry on — although you should register with someone local for emergencies. So Tom's a squire now and you're lady of the manor? How are you finding it?'

She shrugged. 'OK.'

'Only OK?' His forehead crinkled and one eyebrow lifted.

'What's the problem?'

'There are several things.' She looked down at her lap. 'One is that I keep noticing a couple of smells, either a very strong smell of perfume — as if someone's come into a room wearing it — or a smell of burning, a really horrible smell of burning.' She frowned. 'I read somewhere smelling burning is a symptom of a brain tumour.'

His eyes studied her, giving her no hints. 'Any particular times when you smell these things?'

'It varies.'

'Do you get any dizziness? Blurred vision? Headaches?'

'Headaches.'

'Sharp or dull?'

'Dull. My head sort of stings.'

He took a silver fountain pen from his breast pocket and scribbled on an index card. 'What else?'

'It feels like my thermostat's gone haywire. I'm freezing cold one moment, then boiling hot the next. It doesn't seem to matter what the temperature is.'

He made a note.

'I also feel queasy a lot of the time.'

'Anything else?'

'I've had some very odd feelings of *déjà vu*.'

'Thinking you've been somewhere before?'

'Yes.' He had noticed the marks on her neck, and was leaning forward a fraction, studying them. 'It's quite strange. I've also been sleepwalking.'

'Have you had any change of diet?' he asked.

'Not really.'

'You haven't wanted to eat different foods to normal?'

The raw steak she had taken a bite out of.

The Chinese box. Why yes, Tony. I wanted to bury a tin full of maggots and to dig it up in two weeks' time and find one big maggot left. Yummy.

'Not especially. I go on and off tea and coffee a bit, I suppose.'

He made another note. His silver fountain pen glinted and a tiny white ball of reflected sunlight danced around the walls. 'How often have you done this sleepwalking, Charley?'

'I'm not sure. Three times, I think.'

'And do you wake up?'

'No.'

'Does it wake Tom up?'

She hesitated. 'No.'

He was silent for a moment. 'It's not in your imagination?'

'No. Definitely not.'

'How are you sleeping otherwise?'

'Badly.'

'Do you feel tired when you wake in the morning?'

She nodded.

'Afraid?'

'Yes.'

'Do you feel afraid in the daytime too?'

'Yes.'

'How are your bowels? Are they normal?'

'They're OK.'

'Are you urinating any more than usual?'

She shrugged. 'I'm not really sure.'

'How about your weight?'

'I've put on a little since we moved down. I haven't been going to my exercise classes, and I haven't bicycled at all.'

He smiled reassuringly at her. 'How are your periods?'

'The same.'

'Still as irregular?'

'Yes.'

'When did you last have one?'

Charley tried to think back. 'About a month ago.'

'Weren't you on pills at one time to regularise your periods?'

'My acupuncturist wanted me to stop those.'

'You've been having acupuncture?'

'Yes.' She blushed.

Ross smiled. 'Why not, Charley? Try everything. I've heard some very good reports about acupuncture.' He glanced through her notes. 'How many periods have you had over the last six months?'

'I'm not sure. Two — maybe three.'

'Are you and Tom still trying to start a family?'

Tom. Tom. The mention of the name was like a sting. 'Yes.'

'Are you going to try an *in vitro* implant again?'

'I don't know. I don't think I could bear the thought of another ectopic.'

'You were unlucky, Charley. The chances of a second ectopic pregnancy are small.'

'But I only have one tube left.'

'You've got some time still; you don't have to rush into any decisions.' He put his pen down and pushed his sleeves up his hairy wrists.

'You've been through a lot over the past few years, haven't you?' he said.

She felt weepy, suddenly, struggling to hold back her tears. She stared out of the window at the small garden, a lawn with a rose bed border beneath a high brick wall and the fire escape of the building beyond. It was quiet and she could barely hear the traffic.

Ross was looking at her neck again.

Tell him. Tell him.

251

Tom, it's Tony Ross here. Thought you ought to know that Charley's gone nuts; tried to hang herself.

'Moving home is a very traumatic thing, Charley. It's likely that these symptoms you are having could just be down to stress, but I'd like to have a few tests done. I'll take some blood and urine, and I think it would be sensible for you to see a neurologist and have a electro encephlogram — and EEG scan.'

'Tony,' she said, 'could I ask you something?'

'Sure, of course.'

She reddened. 'Have you ever had any patients who — who think they have been reincarnated?'

'Yes, I've had several over the years,' he said, replacing his pen in his pocket. 'I have a woman at the moment — bit of a fruitcake — who has back pains for no apparent reason. She's convinced it's because she was in a stagecoach accident in a previous life.'

'Do you believe her?'

'I'm a doctor of medicine, Charley, not a parapsychologist. I think it's a load of phooey. Why do you ask?'

'I — I'm just curious. Do you think there's something that could explain — medically — all these things I'm getting?'

'Yes, indeed, and a lot more convincingly than a past life.' He smiled confidently. 'It's not a brain tumour, you don't need to worry about that, but there's one possibility I'd like to eliminate. You wouldn't know if you have any history of epilepsy in your family, would you?'

'Epilepsy? No.'

'Of course not, you poor thing. These bloody adoption laws are so stupid. There are so many hereditary things which it might be helpful to know about.'

'Epilepsy,' she repeated.

'Trust me, Charley. You don't have anything serious to worry about.'

'Isn't epilepsy serious?'

'Not these days. I don't want to worry you, Charley. All your symptoms are consistent with stress and that's by far the most likely cause, but I have to eliminate other possibilities. You've always suffered from stress and moving house is bound to have made that worse. I think that's almost certainly all that's wrong with you, but some of your symptoms are also consistent with a very mild form of epilepsy — temporal lobe epilepsy. Temperature changes in the body, sensory delusions, olfactorial illusions — the perfume, the burning — *déjà vu*, your feelings of fear, depression, sleepwalking. Temporal lobe epileptics often carry out functions unconsiously, either sleepwalking or doing things when they are awake without realising it.'

Charley stared at him, her mind churning. 'Doing things without realising it?'

'We do things without realising it all the time. Haven't you ever driven down a motorway and suddenly found you've gone ten or fifteen miles without being in the slightest bit aware of it?'

She wiped some stray strands of hair off her forehead. 'Could you do something harmful to yourself without realising it?'

The corners of his eyes crinkled and he shook his head. 'The human body has a strong sense of self-preservation. If they're heading into danger, sleepwalkers usually wake up.'

'But not always?'

'There have been the odd instances of people falling down staircases or off balconies. There's no guarantee people won't hurt themselves. But it doesn't happen very often.'

'Have you ever heard of' — she hesitated — 'of anyone trying to kill themselves in their sleep?'

Their eyes met, his kind grey-blue eyes crystal clear,

as if he took them out and polished them.

'No,' he said.

'Do you think it's possible somebody could do that?'

'No, I don't.' He looked at her neck, more obviously this time. 'Why are you asking me this?'

'No reason. I was just curious.'

He stood up. 'Let's go to the examination room and do those tests.' He came round the desk and rested his arm on her shoulder. 'Is there anything wrong, Charley? You've got some nasty marks on your neck.'

'Oh —' she shrugged. 'I got it caught — a trunk — I was unpacking some stuff and the lid came down —'

He squeezed her shoulder gently. 'You'd tell me if there was something wrong, wouldn't you?'

She nodded but was unable to look him in the face, was unable to speak for a moment in case the tears exploded. She could feel his eyes on her neck again; she could feel them as if he were probing the marks with his fingers.

Chapter Thirty

Charley followed Ernest Gibbon upstairs, his feet plodding, the stairs creaking and smelling of boiled cabbage and scented air freshener. She looked at the familiar Artexed walls and the wooden plates with scenes of Switzerland whilst he paused to get his breath back on the first floor landing.

His skin hung slackly from his face, and his eyes, behind the thick lenses of his glasses, had sunk a little further into their sockets. He breathed in short wheezy gasps like a punctured squeeze box, walked across to his mother's room, rapped on the door and went in. 'Got a client, mother. I've put the lunch on, and locked the front door.'

They went on up, and Charley lay down on the couch in the attic room under the microphone. 'Thank you for seeing me so quickly.' she said.

He lowered himself into his chair, leaned over and checked his recording equipment, then made Charley do a brief voice test which he played back. 'How have you been?' he said.

'Not good.'

'Do you feel up to going through with it — all the way?'

'I need to.'

'Yes. You do.' He looked at her as if he knew exactly what had happened. 'You're going to have to be strong.

When you start screaming, that's when I've always brought you out before. I shan't bring you out this time. Are you happy with that?'

She tore at the skin above one of her nails, and felt a lump in her throat.

Gibbon switched out the overhead light.

She stopped, hot, tired and thirsty from her long journey, leaned against the brick parapet of the roaring weir, and gazed down at the house in the hollow, a hundred yards away below her. The house of the woman who had ruined her life.

She wiped the perspiration off her brow with the back of her hand and was grateful for the cooling spray that rose up from the weir as she scoured the property with her tear-blurred eyes for signs of life. She looked at the disused watermill, at the stable block, and warily at the barn with its silent empty kennel outside, and the brass ring beside it.

The black sports car was parked in the drive. Good. He was here. Somewhere. She slipped her hand inside her bag and felt the cold steel blade of the knife.

Talk. Just want to talk. That's all.

She stared again at the house, looking for movement in the mullioned windows, for faces, for the twitch of a curtain.

'Do you recognise where you are?' she heard a voice say, a flat distant voice.

The sun was setting directly behind the house, the rays of light stinging her eyes, making it hard to see, throwing long black shadows up the bank towards her.

'Are you in the same place as before?' The voice was faint, a distant echo. She vaguely wondered where it came from as she walked slowly through the gateposts on to the scrunching gravel of the driveway. The unborn child inside her kicked sharply, as if it could sense her fear, as if it were trying to warn her not to go on; she pressed her hand against her swollen belly, and patted it. 'It's all right,' she said. 'Talk. Just want to talk. That's all.'

She stopped at the bottom of the steps to the front door, and dabbed the perspiration on her forehead with the back of her hand. The house seemed much larger from here, forbidding. She looked up at each of the small dark windows in turn, and listened, trying to hear a sound in the motionless air of the warm summer evening that was not her own panting or the roaring of water.

She looked across the mill race at the stables, down at the barn, at the mill; and then at the car again. A thrush took off with a worm trailing from its beak. She heard the distant bang of a shotgun, then another, the bleat of a sheep, the barking of a dog.

She climbed the steps up to the front door and paused, nervously eyeing the shiny lion's head knocker which glared menacingly back at her. The door was slightly ajar and she pushed it further open and peered into the hallway.

There was no sign of anyone. She hesitated, then walked in, stopped and listened again. Her shadowy reflection stared back through the gloom from a spangled mirror on the wall. There was a staircase ahead with a passageway beside it, and doors to the left and right of her. The house smelled of furniture polish and a rich musky perfume; it felt feminine, elegant, alien.

There was a creak upstairs and she froze.

She stood for a full minute in silence, listening, but heard nothing more other than the tick of a clock and her own heavy breathing. She lifted the iron latch handle on the door on her left and pushed it open.

The room was empty. The diffused rays of the setting

sunlight through the French windows bathed the soft eau de nil and peach colourings. It felt so sumptuous, so beautiful; it almost made her turn and run out in hopelessness. The furniture was grand, graceful Art Deco, the pictures on the walls were mostly of elegant women in fine clothes, the lamps seemed to be ornamental. It was another world.

On the mantelpiece above the empty fireplace an alabaster court jester's face in a bronze bust smiled menacingly at her, as if he were encouraging her to turn towards the sofa, to look at the dents in the plump cushions. It seemed to be smirking at her knowingly.

There she saw a notepad on a writing bureau, with writing on it, a large feminine scrawl, in black ink.

Hector and Daphne, cocktails, Aug 20th?

Cow. Going to parties whilst she ... The handwriting was familiar. She had seen it before.

'Is it a woman's handwriting?' said the distant voice. 'Can you read me what it says?'

The voice faded. She went across the hall, down a dark passageway, to a kitchen with smart brown linoleum on the floor, bright yellow paintwork and an Aga set into a tiled surround. There were dirty plates on the table, and dirty dishes piled around the sink.

Slut, she thought, walking back down the passageway. Two places were laid on the large refectory table in the dining room for a meal that had been eaten and not cleared away. A half drunk bottle of claret, unstoppered, lay on the sideboard, two glasses, both with a small drop of wine left, were still on the table. The room smelled of cigar smoke. His cigars.

She climbed the steep staircase and stopped at the top, panting from the effort and fear, and listened. The house was silent. She looked up and down the dark landing, then turned to the right and went into the room at the far end.

There were two dressmaker's dummies on pedestals, one bare, with the word *Stockman* stencilled to its midriff, the other with a partially sewn dress in shiny turquoise taffeta pinned to it. There were four bald shop window mannequins in there also, two of them naked, two of them dressed in stunning evening gowns, one in a strapless black sequinned gown and wearing black gloves, the other in shimmering black moiré silk. She was awed by their elegance, awed because she'd never seen anything like them outside of a shop window in one of the smart London streets.

Her heart sank. London. The name itself brought a feeling of gloom. London. Where she lived, in the grimy building. London. A prisoner.

She walked down the corridor, past a second flight of stairs and hesitated outside a closed door. She opened it slowly, and saw a bedroom with a huge unmade bed, the sheets tousled. There were strong smells of musky perfume, stale cigarette smoke and scented soap. A shiny black telephone sat on a bedside table, an ashtray full of lipsticky butts beside it.

Slut.

She opened the doors of a huge maple wardrobe. Luxurious dresses were hanging there, coats and furs. Finery. The magnificence. Something she could never have known how to buy.

She went to the dressing table and stared in the mirror, ashamed of her own dowdiness, her dumpiness, her pudgy skin, her tangled hair, her cheap muslin maternity smock.

A thick crystal bottle of perfume was on the dressing table. She touched it, ran her fingers over the contours of the glass, picked it up, feeling its weight, pulled out the glass topper, tipped some on to each wrist and rubbed it in. It stung her finger and she noticed a slight graze. Must have cut it on the knife, she thought, but did not care; the pain felt good. She dabbed some on her neck as well, behind her ears, and rubbed more on her chest. The smell engulfed her. She shook more out, then more still, wiped her face with it, shook it over her clothes, her hair, shook it out until it was empty.

She took the bottle through into the en suite bathroom, stood and listened. Still silence. She removed the toothbrushes from a glass on the washbasin, lowered her knickers and urinated into the glass. Then, carefully, over the washbasin, she filled the perfume bottle with the contents of the glass, restoppered it, wiped it with a face flannel and put it back on the dressing table.

She felt a little better, stronger.

As she went downstairs, a horse whinnied outside. She hurried over to the front door and looked out. Two horses were tethered outside the stables, still saddled. Her heart pounded. They had not been there when she had arrived. One whinnied again; Jemma.

She ran down the steps, over the drive, across the grass and the ornamental wooden bridge over the mill race and up the slope to the stables.

There was another sound now, above the roaring of water, something that was half shout, half moan, coming from the stables. Another moan, then a woman's voice screaming out:

'Oh yes! Your dagger! Give me your dagger!'

She stopped. The sun had gone down further and a dark shadow hung over the hollow. She felt a chill spreading through her body and with it a sickness in the pit of her stomach.

'More! More! Oh God, more!'

For a moment she stood paralysed, unable to move. Then she began to run again.

'Oh God, yes! Your dagger! Your wonderful dagger. More! More! Give more! Oh! Oh!'

She reached the door and pulled it open.

'Dagger me! Dagger me! Dagger me.'

The woman's voice screamed out, echoing through the straw, the smell of horses, of petrol, of musky perfume. She went inside, into a dim tack room, with a lawnmower and a jerrycan and several smaller tins of petrol and paraffin, sacks of feed, a stack of hay, riding tack hung on hooks on the brick wall, and a pile of logs with an axe and a saw leaning against the wall beside them.

Through the doorway ahead into the dark stalls, she could see what she thought at first were two logs, then as her eyes adjusted she realised it was a man's legs sticking out from the end of a stall, his trousers and underpants down around his ankles, his shoes and socks still on his feet.

'Oh, oh, oh, that's so good!'

She felt something drain out of her. She began to quiver with rage, harder and faster, until everything was a blurr. She fumbled with the clasp of her handbag and slid her fingers along the blade of the knife.

No. She pulled her hand out and closed the bag. Talk. Just want to talk. That's all.

'OH YOUR DAGGER! OH! MORE DAGGER! MORE DAGGER!'

She walked through the doorway, past the first empty stall. She could see them clearly now, Dick's naked hairy legs and his buttocks, thrusting out at her, his shirt halfway up his back, the woman's slender white legs rising up either side of him, her knees bent, angulated, varnished toenails scrabbling against the loose straw, her head tossing wildly, her black hair flailing around, her fingernails buried into the base of his shoulders, Dick's bottom pumping, thrusting, faster, faster.

'OH! OH!'

She could see between his legs, the testicles flailing, the black bush, the red lips, the thrusting shaft. She looked at the woman's face, her hard beautiful face, eyes closed, hair thrown back, saw her eyes open suddenly, stare straight into hers.

For an instant time stood still. Then the woman's eyes flashed with a venom that startled her.

Dick suddenly sensed her presence as well and swivelled round, his hair tousled, his face, already flushed with exertion, turning puce with rage. 'Jesus Christ!' he shouted. 'What the 'ell you doing here?' He scrambled to his feet. 'You git out of here, you! Bugger off, you! You cow! You ugly cow! You hear me?' He staggered towards her, making no attempt to pull his trousers up, and slapped her hard across the face; then he slapped her again.

'No! Please — please we must —'

He shoved her, sending her tripping back through the doorway into the store room. She fell backwards and her head smashed into something hard.

'Go on, get out, you cow! Just bugger off, will you? Bugger off! Leave us alone!'

She stared up at him, dazed. 'Talk,' she mouthed but nothing came out. Talk. Just want to talk. That's all. We must talk, look at me, look at my stomach, eight months, please, you have to help me. Please —

The woman came out of the stall, wearing nothing but her unbuttoned silk blouse. 'If you ever come here again, I'll have you flung into prison,' she said.

She put her hand down to push herself up, and something gave. She felt a pain and heard the clatter of the lawnmower's blades rotating and fell back into the machine.

The woman laughed.

She staggered to her feet and spat in the woman's face, then in a sudden frenzy she threw herself at her and began pummelling her. The woman clawed at her with her nails and there was a searing pain as they tore through her flesh. Blood dripped from the woman's fingers, then she felt herself being dragged backwards by her hair. She wrenched herself free, rolled across the floor, hit a can, grabbed it wildly and threw it. It hit the wall behind Dick, the cap flew off and it fell to the ground with petrol gurgling out.

'You crazy cow!' he shouted, kicking her in the ankle, then in the hip, as she curled up throwing her arms around her belly, desperately trying to protect the baby. His foot slammed into her ribs, her shoulder. She scrambled away and somehow regained her feet, then grabbed the saw beside her and swung it wildly at him. Its huge jagged teeth dug into his neck, sending blood spurting out and knocking him to the ground. She swung at the woman, smashing it into her face, slicing deep through her cheek, cracking her against the wall.

Dick clambered up. The woman was on the floor, screaming, one hand pressed against her cheek, the other reaching for the axe. The saw sliced into her arm, then into her stomach. She saw Dick coming and took the axe, hit him in the chest, then she swung again, aiming between his legs, and he doubled up, screaming, clutching his groin, blood spraying like a burst pipe. She swung the axe again, missed him, smashed into the electric socket on the brick wall behind. Sparks shot out, there was a fierce crackle, then a *wumph* like a gas fire igniting and a trail of flame raced across the floor and into the hay, which exploded in a ball of fire.

He fell backwards into it, screaming, kicking his legs. The woman tried to crawl away, but the fire caught her silk blouse, ignited it and suddenly the whole place became one solid sheet of flame.

The horses whinnied outside. She ran to the door. Jemma and the other horse were rearing, pulling at their tethers, trying to get away. She dodged their hooves, untethered them, the reins whiplashing in her hands as they galloped down the bank.

The noise behind her was deafening. She stumbled down the bank towards the house, across the gravel, up the steps and in through the front door.

Phone.

She ran into the drawing room, stared around, could not see one.

Phone. There was one; somewhere. She remembered, staggered up the staircase and down the corridor into the bedroom. It was on the bedside table. She grabbed the receiver and tapped the rest several times. Please. Please. Quick. Answer. Oh God, answer.

She could hear the roaring and the crackling of the fire outside. Tapped the rest again. Please. Emergency.

She caught sight of her reflection in the dressing table mirror. Her face was streaked with blood and black smears.

A woman's voice said, 'Operator.'

'Fire! Elmwood Mill! Fire! Please come quickly.'

'I'll connect you with the fire brigade.'

Her vision was blurring. A figure came in through the door behind her. She smelled smoke; burning wood; burning straw. Charred flesh. She saw the eyes, just the eyes. Raw through the blackened skin.

There was a bang. The mirror exploded into spidery cracks. A large jagged shard fell away, landed at her feet.

She screamed.

'Stay with it, Charley.' A voice, dim, faint. 'Try and stay with it.'

She turned. The woman stood with a rifle, struggling to open the breech. Patches of her hair had been burned away to stubble. Her face was black, blistering; her blouse was stuck in smouldering blotches to her blackened flesh. A single wail like a siren was coming from her mouth. Blood dripped from her arm.

She dropped the phone and backed away.

The woman was struggling, swaying, could barely stand. The bullet rattled in the open breech then fell with a thud to the floor.

She scrabbled on the dressing table behind her for a weapon, knocked a hairbrush to the floor, knocked over the perfume bottle, then saw the shard of glass at her feet. She picked it up and lunged forward, smashing into the rifle, knocking the woman over and falling with her.

The woman's fingers gouged into her eyes, blinding her for a moment. The woman was stronger than she realised, seemed to get some new strength, tearing at her with her nails, spitting, pressed her hideous blotched, burned face down close against hers, and she smelled the foul stench almost as if it was coming from inside the woman's lungs. The woman climbed on to her, pinning her down, twisted the shard out of her hand.

She struggled, tried to free herself, saw the red eyes, crazed, saw a glint of the shard in the woman's charred hand. It flashed down and she felt an agonising pain deep in her groin.

'Baby!' she screamed. 'My baby! My baby!'

The flash again. The glint.

'Don't. My baby! *My baby!*'

The charred arm came down. The pain was as if a red hot poker had melted its way through her stomach and was now twisting around inside her.

A thin strip of white appeared in the blackness of the woman's face.

She was smiling.

The face blurred.

The pain blurred with it, then came searing back, and

she rose up and let out a scream she thought would tear out the lining of her throat.

She passed out.

Chapter Thirty-One

The interior of the ambulance shook and rattled. The boom of the exhaust drummed around the steel walls and the fumes that seeped in pricked the noses of the crewman and the policeman who were struggling to keep her alive.

Bottles vibrated furiously in the metal racks, a leather strap swayed above her head, hitting the stanchion each time with a soft smack like a boxing glove. She slid forward as the ambulance braked sharply, then up against the side as it cornered, the tyres wailing beneath her with their own pain.

Four minutes. After a pregnant woman dies, four minutes is all you have to get the baby out before the baby dies too. That's what the crewman was thinking. She knew because she could read his mind; she could read all their minds as she floated up near the roof of the ambulance, looking down at her body as if she were watching a play from a balcony. Everything seemed far away below and yet she could hear every word, feel every thought. Feel everything except the pain. There was no pain any more, up here, and that was good.

Don't bring me back, she thought. Please don't bring me back into the body. Save the baby, but let me go. No more pain.

The crewman held her pulse, stethoscope swinging from his neck. The policeman kept an oxygen mask pressed over her nose and mouth with one hand and a thick wad of dressing against her groin with the other. Strips of gauze lay across her chest, swollen abdomen and the top of her right leg, each with a spreading red stain, and rivulets of blood from the wound in her side ran into the bedding beneath her.

'Getting weaker,' the crewman said quietly. 'She's going on us.'

No pain, she thought. That was the best thing.

The policeman slackened the pressure for a brief instant and a fine spray of blood jetted on to his sleeve. He pressed hard again, startled.

The ambulanceman listened to her heart and placed another piece of gauze on a wound. 'How come she'd been left so long in the house? It's two hours ago we picked up the woman with the burns,' he asked.

'Didn't realise there was anyone else in the house until I searched it,' the policeman said. 'The burnt woman was in too bad shape to say much — she was lying at the bottom of the stairs.'

A contraction ripped through her and her eyes opened momentarily, stared up at him blank, unseeing, like the eyes of fish on a slab.

The policeman managed a weak smile. 'It's all right, love, you're going to be all right.'

'She's still fighting.'

Another contraction, then another, much fiercer, and water suddenly sluiced out between her legs. The ambulance lurched.

'Pail. Put the pail under,' the crewman said without taking his eyes from his watch. He leaned forward and put his head through the driver's partition. 'Contractions every three minutes and she's broken her waters.'

'I'm doing me best.'

He felt her pulse again and a surge of panic swept through him as he had to search several times to find anything at all. Her eyes were closed and her face was the colour of chalk. Going, he thought. She's going on us. The pulse was scarcely stronger than the tick of a watch; no blood, Christ, she was almost drained dry of the damned stuff. The ambulance slowed, stopped. The back doors opened; a trolley was already waiting.

She watched as they slid her body out and on to the trolley, and stayed above them, floating as if she were in a warm pool, as they wheeled her through into the pale green admitting room of the hospital.

'Stab wounds,' the houseman said. 'Some of them are very deep and she has heavy internal bleeding. She needs at least six pints.'

'We've only got two O negative cross-matched,' the sister said.

'That's all?' He walked away from the trolley, across the room. The sister followed him. 'She won't make it,' he said quietly. 'Not on that. Contact London and get some down. An ambulance or the police might bring it. Get the two in as fast as you can, and put her on a five per cent dextrose drip right away.'

The door opened and a man came running in, white jacket over his squash shirt and shorts. He stared down at her pale clammy body, his eyes wide open, caring eyes trying to comprehend for one brief instant, staring at each of the bloody dressings in turn. He carefully lifted the one on her groin and more blood spurted out. He nodded for the nurse to hold it while be examined her vagina.

'Breech presentation,' he said calmly, as if he were reading from a notepad. 'Baby's premature, a tiny mite. Breech presentation with breech impact into the pelvis, cervix four fingers dilated.' He put his foetal stethoscope to her uterus and listened. 'The baby's alive. Placenta posterior. The blade might not have penetrated, but we can't chance it. We'll do a full laporotomy immediately. She's very short of blood — she'll need at least six pints before the anaesthetic.'

'We haven't got it,' said the houseman. 'We've only got two pints. We're trying to get some more.'

'Anaesthetic will kill her.'

'So will the baby.'

'Can we have a word in private?'

She watched from above as the obstetric registrar and the houseman went into the corridor and closed the door behind them. 'I don't think we're going to be able to save both of them,' the registrar said.

'What does that mean?'

'We have to make a decision. Between them.'

'The mother or the baby?'

'Yes.'

The houseman shook his head. 'At what point?'

'Now. If you want that woman to live, we've got to terminate the baby.'

'We can't do that.'

'If we deliver, the mother's got an eighty per cent chance of dying. You want that on your conscience?'

'Which do you want?'

Their eyes met and each knew what the other was thinking. She's probably too far gone already. Let her go. Let her go and save the baby. Except they knew that they were not equipped to make that decision.

'Get the duty anaesthetist,' the registrar said.

The baby's bottom came out first in a film of membrane and blood. The houseman clamped the cord and the midwife sucked out the baby's mouth.

'Seems healthy and normal,' said the obstetric registrar. 'Doesn't appear to have been affected by the mother's blood loss. Two surface cuts to be sutured from the stab wounds.' He pointed to the gashes in the left side of the baby's stomach and in its right thigh, then looked down inside the massive incision in the mother's stomach. 'More clamps, Swab.'

She became aware that the bleeding was stopping, and what was there was dark blue. Her body was starting to palpitate and her face changed colour, to puce then to deep purple. The surgeon looked at the anaesthetist, who shrugged. The purple was fading, turning to slate grey, the pupils of her eyes dilating widely.

'More blood. Another pint.'

It was too late.

The people below her in their green gowns and cotton masks stared at the level in the glass bottle, watching it sink down into the red rubber tubing that ran to her vein. The blood pressure needle fell against its rest and flickered, twice. It was almost as if the people in the room could feel her life slip out of her.

Free, she thought. Free now. No more pain. Darkness closed in, soft warm darkness like a summer evening. It became a long dark tunnel with a tiny pinprick of light at the end. The light drew her, getting slowly brighter, warmer, deep golden, filling her with an intense sensation of joy, of welcome. She reached out her arms, the light blinding her now, smiling, laughing like a child. Then there was a draught of cold air and she felt herself slipping back, felt something pulling her back down.

No. Please. Let me go.

A dark icy tornado swirled, spun her around, drew her hurtling down like an express elevator. Please, no. She was plummeting. The light above her shrank into a tiny spot, then was gone.

Fear rose up through her, froze around her, encasing her, blurring her mind. Light began to seep into her eyes, harsh blurred light, cold, hostile, filled with hazy green shapes, strange sounds. She felt a prick in her stomach, then another. She screamed in terror.

'There, there! It's all right! It's all right!'

Faces. Eyes behind masks.

'There, there! It's all right!'

Someone held a needle in the air. A man took it. Brought it down. There was a fierce stabbing pain in her groin and she screamed out again.

'It's all right! It's all right!'

The faces dissolved. They became one face. Eyes behind thick lenses. One face bathed in dim red light, motionless, unblinking, studying her. Ernest Gibbon.

It was as if she were underwater, miles underwater and the weight was pressing down on her. She tried to move, but her body was leaden. Dead. She was dead. He knew that she might die and she had.

He continued studying her motionlessly. She looked at him, the person that could make her undead, somehow. He knew the key, knew how to make her live again; knew the command, the nod, the twitch, the words that would bring her back, bring her out. He stayed silent.

She wondered what the time was. Dark, it seemed so dark. Her brain was fuzzed and she could not remember when she had come, how long she had been here. She wished he would speak, or smile, or nod.

It was a full minute before she realised that he was the one who was dead.

Chapter Thirty-two

Charley sat on the pew, at Viola Letters's funeral, sandwiched between Hugh and Zoe. Vic and his wife sat further along in the same row. Several other faces in the church looked familiar as well, from the cricket match, from shopping in Elmwood village.

She stared at the printed words of the funeral service and fought back a yawn. She'd had only two hours' sleep. Her dress, a navy two-piece she had bought last year was tight; she hoped it was sombre enough.

The particles in our bodies have electro-magnetic charges. When our corpses break down, either through cremation or burial, it all goes back into the earth and one way, or another, gets recycled. Each particle keeps its memory, like a tiny piece of videotape.

Hugh's words echoed in her mind.

Ernest Gibbon's face stared back. Motionless. Ashen.

She looked at the oak coffin with its brass handles and the flowers on top, wondering. Wondering if there was a connection between what had disturbed Viola Letters in the photograph and her death.

Ridiculous. Just an accident.

For a moment she was confused, thought maybe it was Ernest Gibbon in the coffin on the trestle in front of the altar, in the small church with its frescoes on the wall dating back to Norman times, someone had told her.

They were singing 'Jerusalem'. Charley held the hymn book and sang the words quietly. It was her favourite hymn; normally she found it rousing, but today it was as if they were playing it in another room.

The regression had started just after one p.m., and should have lasted two or three hours. It had been ten p.m. when she had come round, out of her trance, and seen Ernest Gibbon sitting there, dead. She had touched him and whimpered in fear, in the knowledge that she had been in a trance for an hour, maybe two, three, or even more, while he had sat there, dead. She had wondered if she was fully out of her trance and was still scared she had not been brought properly out.

She had gone downstairs and knocked on the door of his mother's room. There had been no answer and she had gone inside, and seen an elderly frail woman in bed, eyes glued to the television.

'Mrs Gibbon,' she had said, 'we need to call an ambulance.'

'He's with a patient. He must not be disturbed,' she had replied, not turning her head. 'Nothing must disturb him.'

'It's an emergency.'

'He is not allowed to be disturbed. It is too dangerous.'

The old woman was like her adoptive mother in the earlier stages of the disease; Charley knew the signs. She had gone downstairs, found a phone in the sitting room and called the ambulance. Then she had let Ben out of the car and was amazed he hadn't made a mess.

The ambulancemen had been disgruntled when they'd arrived. Ernest Gibbon had been dead for at least six hours and she should have called a doctor to issue a death certificate. Not them.

Gibbon's mother had come out of the room, one shrivelled breast hanging out of her nightdress, and told them her son was with a patient and must not be disturbed.

When Charley had tried to explain to the ambulance-men that she had been in a hypnotic trance in a room with a dead man, they had thought she must be as barmy as the old woman and had called the police and a police doctor and left.

She'd waited for the police, aware that Gibbon's mother was beyond coping with the situation, and had to deal with the woman's hysterics when she saw her son's body and the truth registered.

A policewoman had turned up to handle the woman and Charley had finally left some time after five in the morning. It had been light when she'd got home and she had been glad about that.

There had been three messages from Tom on the answering machine. One early on Sunday morning leaving a phone number and a room number; a hotel, she thought. The second was on Monday morning. He was in the office all day, he said. The third was Monday night. He was going to Scotland on a custody case; he would call with his numbers when he got there.

She had gone to bed and tried to sleep, but the events of the past two days had replayed in her mind, over and over, and her regression had too, so vivid that each time she awoke, bathed in sweat, she was convinced it was still going on. Convinced that the woman with the hair burned to stubble and the blackened face was standing in the doorway watching her. Then convinced that she was in an ambulance and was dying, but they would not let her die, would not let her go.

Epileptic. *Some of your symptoms are consistent with* ... fine; that was all it was. Temporal lobe epilepsy. Delusions. Hallucinations.

The congregation knelt for the final prayers, and the service was over. The family came down the aisle first: a tubby elderly man, who bore a vague facial resemblance to Viola Letters led the way stiffly down the aisle, arm in arm with an elegant, ashen-faced woman. An assortment of age groups followed from the front pews, smart little children and pukka adults, different to the locals, who had come to say goodbye to a friend. The locals looked sad; the family mostly looked merely dutiful.

'Hallo, it's Mrs Witney, isn't it?' said the vicar, with a jollity in his voice that Charley thought would be more appropriate at a wedding. He shook her hand vigorously. 'You're new arrivals in the village, aren't you? I've been meaning to come and introduce myself.'

Charley stepped out of the porch into the dull grey morning, into the knot of people and the babble of voices.

'Rattled through the service a bit quickly, didn't he?' Zoe murmured to her.

She nodded absently, remembering Viola Letters's complaint to her about the vicar, and they joined the trail of mourners behind the pall bearers who were carrying the coffin up the path.

The sky was charcoal grey above them and a wind was blowing through the graveyard. The coffin sat on its ropes on the green baize carpet.

' . . . we therefore commit her body to the ground; earth to earth, ashes to ashes, dust to dust; in sure and certain hope of the Resurrection to eternal life, through our Lord Jesus Christ; who shall change our vile body . . .'

Change. Resurrection to eternal life. Eternal life here on earth. With eternal memories. Eternal change, eternal memories, eternally haunted by the past.

'The grace of our Lord Jesus Christ, and the love of God, and the fellowship of the Holy Ghost, be with us all evermore. Amen.'

Charley wandered away, thoughts drifting through her mind, away from the crowd, through the gravestones, past marble headstones with gravelled fronts, stones carved into scrolls, stones the shape of open books, stones with angels, new stones, bright and shiny, old stones, aged, stained, the writing barely legible, some leaning badly and some set in the ground and overgrown with grass and lichen. Some had vases of fresh flowers, or wreathes, some empty urns, forgotten, no one left to tend them.

She walked up the gentle slope, stepping around the slabs and the gravel, barely noticing anything except the occasional name or inscription.

'Ernest Arthur Lamb who fell asleep.'

'There's a land where those who loved when here shall meet to love again.'

There was a smell of autumn in the air; it suited the cold stones of death.

'John Rowe Buckmaster. Gentle in life, serene in death.'

'Barbara Jarrett. D. Aug 12th 1953.'

'Alice Madeleine Wells.'

Charley stopped. Stepped back, read the inscription on the plain tombstone again.

'Barbara Jarrett. D. Aug 12th, 1953.

The twelfth of August 1953.

She had been born that day.

She stood and stared at the plain headstone, dull, no other writing on it, so plain that she had nearly passed it without a glance.

Dear Rock, I love him. Please bring him back, Barbara.

The inscription on the locket. *D loves BJ.*

BJ.

Someone came up and stood beside her. It was Hugh. 'We're invited to the wake; they're having a little do at the George.'

'Right.'

'Would you like me to wait?'

'No. Go on. I might be a while.'

'Are you OK?'

She nodded.

'Can I buy you dinner tonight? Cheer you up?'

'I'll buy,' she said flatly, without taking her eyes from the gravestone. 'It's my turn.'

Hugh looked at the stone. 'Someone you knew?'

'Maybe.'

He walked away, and she shivered. Meaningless. Coincidence, that was all. She turned and watched as Hugh joined the last of the mourners who were filing through the lychgate. There was the scrape of a shovel and the rattle of earth. It sounded like a collection box. Mother Nature was collecting again.

'Know how to get there?' a voice boomed out. 'Follow us.'

Barbara Jarrett. D. August 12th, 1953.

There was grass in front of the headstone. No smart border to keep dogs off, no scrolls or cherubs or urn or flowers. No 'In loving memory of', no 'Beloved wife of'. Nothing. Just the name, the date.

Another time, dear, we'll talk about it, another time.

She thought of the old man in Saddler Cottages who had closed the door in her face. *Go away. Leave us alone. Go away. We don't want you here.*

Two old people. Viola Letters had noticed something in a photograph; Arthur Morrison in her face.

The stone suddenly changed colour, brightened, as if someone had shone a torch on to it. She jumped, then felt foolish. It was only the sunlight finding a hole in the cloud.

The electrician's rather dinky van was parked at the foot of the steps, and Charley was relieved there was someone in the house. White tapes were still stretched across the footpath; one had come free and jigged in a gust like a streamer. Constable Tidyman had told her at the wake that it was their responsibility to mend the bank. It was a public footpath and would have to be done soon.

It was hard to believe it was only four months since they had first seen the house. Since the excitement, the sense of peace, of hope. She could still remember the sensation that something was missing. The stables. Except they weren't missing any more. They were there, the other side of the mill race where they had always been, smart white stables. The head of a chestnut horse was looking out of one of the looseboxes. Jemma.

She blinked.

It was still there.

She whirled round. Her car was gone. The electrician's van was gone. The black Triumph was there instead, its roof down, its paintwork gleaming, its chrome shining. She looked up at the house. The window frames had been freshly painted, the brickwork repointed. She turned back to the weir. There were no white tapes, no chunk missing from the bank.

Her blood sifted through her veins like sand through a timer.

She closed her eyes, opened them again. A horse in the stables whinnied. The sand still poured but it was getting noisier and she could hear the faint hissing sound; then she realised it was the roar of the weir, that was all.

Come to the wrong house, she thought. I've come to the wrong house, took a wrong turning —

I try to do everything here in a controlled way. If you are getting uncomfortable or frightened, I can bring you back out, quickly. If you were to start regressing on your own, somewhere away from here, and the figure in the mirror took hold then —

Why should it? It's only something in my memory.
I don't know if it is just memory.

She blinked again. The black Triumph had gone. The stables had gone too. The white tapes were back, and half the bank was missing. The house looked old and tatty and plastic sheeting flapped over the builders' pile of materials. Two long ladders lay against the side of the house. Ben was barking inside.

She touched the side of the Citroën to steady herself; she was gulping down air as if she had just swum a couple of lengths of a pool underwater, scared, scared because Gibbon had not brought her back out.

You're OK, fine, came out of the trance naturally. You're tired now, that's all, tired and in shock; people often have weird hallucinations when they're overtired.

She went into the house. Ben came running up and as she bent to pat him she saw something move out of the corner of her eye, something coming down the staircase.

Her head snapped up. The electrician. It was the electrician walking slowly, strangely slowly, his face sheet white, his eyes open in shock; the short, chalky man who was normally so busy, so energetic, was treading his way carefully down the dust sheet, clutching on to the bannister rail like an old man. 'Was it you?' he said. 'Was it you what turned it on?'

'Pardon?'

He pressed his hand against his mouth. When he removed it, she could see a black mark running across the palm. 'The power,' he said. 'Did you turn the power back on?'

'I've just come in the door.'

'You in't been down the cellar?'

'No.'

'Some joker 'as. I turned the mains off, din't I, to rewire your bedroom sockets. Someone's switched it back on.' He held out his hand. 'See the burn.'

'God! I've got some dressings in the kitchen —'

'S'orl right.' His eyes darted around.

'Is it one of the builders who did it?'

'They ain't been here today.' He examined the burn. 'I dunno what's going on. I've changed all the wirin' and the fittins.' He sucked his hand. 'Let me show you somethin', Mrs Witney.' He walked down the passageway a short way and stopped by a wall switch.

'Take a good look at that.'

There were burn marks on the wall around the switch, and the plastic box had partially melted.

'It's the same in all the rooms. The wirin's melting again. Like last time. I thought it was the lad's fault before. Got a new lad and I left him to do most of the work. I thought he must have made a bodge-up, but it weren't him.'

'I left quite a few lights on over the weekend. I — I was away.'

'That shouldn't make no difference, leaving them on.'

He opened the cellar door and she noticed another smell above the coal and damp and mustiness, a faint acrid tang of burnt electricity. He turned on the light and she followed him down on to the damp brick floor and over, past the dark opening in the wall, to the fuse box. Several reels of wire lay beneath it and the large white box had brown scorch marks. There was a low-pitched humming sound.

The electrician gazed around. He went through the dark opening and she waited until he reappeared. The humming sound got louder and echoed around the room.

The electrician tapped the glass on the front of the meter. Inside a flat metal disc was spinning, so fast it was almost a blurr. Above it were several dials like miniature clocks; the hands of one were also rotating fast.

'See the rate the juice is bein' used?' he said. 'If you had every light and appliance in the house on, and then some, it wouldn't be using it at a tenth of this rate. And you haven't got nothing on. Just the fridge, and the timer for your boiler and a clock radio. Going to cost you a fortune on your bill — apart from the danger.' He reached up and pushed the master switch. There was a click and the cellar was plunged into darkness. He put on a torch. 'That's how I left it down 'ere.'

'Someone switched it on?' she said, her voice shaky. 'Are you sure it couldn't have thrown itself back on?'

The beam of the torch shone on the meter. The disc was slowing down now, the humming turning into a shuffling sound. 'I dunno what's goin' on.'

'You were going to speak to the Electricity Board. You thought there might be some cables or something, which were affecting —'

'I been had a look at their grid plans for this area. There ain't nothing round here.' He snapped the power on. 'We need an engineer from the Electricity Board to come down. Beats me. Never come across this before in all the years I been workin'.'

'What else can it be?'

He shrugged. 'I dunno. Maybe something to do with water — the lake — but I can't see what. Don't make no sense. I think to be safe we oughter switch off the power and leave it off until it's sorted out.'

'All the electricity?'

He nodded.

'I don't want to do that.'

'Could go up in flames, this place.'

'I thought you'd put in modern fuses. Tom said he'd asked you to put in the safest system.'

'I have. That's what I put in.'

'So why's there a risk of fire?'

'They're not tripping. And I dunno why not.'

'I've got to have some power,'

'You'd be best to stay in a hotel 'till we got it sorted.'

'I — can't do that. I need to be here. There must be something you can do.' She was aware of the desperation in her voice.

'I dunno what else I can do. I've checked everythin'. Rewired it, took it all out, rewired it again.' He grinned. 'Maybe you got a ghost.'

The grin dropped away and he looked uneasy, as if he had read something in her face that scared him.

'I'll try and get someone down in the next couple of days. Tell 'em it's an emergency. You'll have to be vigilant. If you're goin' out the house, turn the mains off. Have you got anythin' in the fridge or freezer what's going to go off?'

'Nothing that matters.'

'I'll have another try. But I dunno. I really dunno.'

'Thanks,' she said, her voice barely above a whisper. They went up the stairs. 'Would you like a cup of tea?'

'Ta very much.'

She picked up the small pile of post that had been dumped on the table and carried it through to the kitchen. It felt chilly in here. Because the Aga was out, she realised.

A late bluebottle buzzed by her. She filled the kettle and sat down, untied the blue and white scarf from around her neck and pressed the play button on the answering machine.

'Tom, you old bastard, what's all this about moving to the country? Got your very smart change-of-address card. Thought I might give you a good hiding at tennis one night this week. Give me a call. It's Tim — Tim Parker.'

'Er, good morning. This is Mr West from Fixit DIY, calling Mr Witney. The items you ordered are now in. Perhaps you'd be kind enough to let us know when would be convenient to deliver?'

'Darling, it's me. Please call me. I'm in Edinburgh. My hotel number is 031-556 7277. I'm in Room 420. You can get me in office hours on the same code, 332 2545. I'll be here until Wednesday.'

She let the tape play on without bothering to write the numbers down, a slight smile on her face. He was sounding increasingly anxious.

'Mrs Witney, it's Dr Ross's secretary here. Dr Ross would like to see you as soon as possible. Would three o'clock tomorrow afternoon be convenient? That's Wednesday, three o'clock. If we don't hear from you, we'll expect you then. Thank you. It's now twenty past two, Tues —' The voice stopped abruptly and the light on the machine went off. The power. The electrician must have turned it off again.

Tony Ross had not wasted any time getting the results of the tests. Was that because he had been more worried than he let on? Epilepsy? Or worse? Had he been lying about a brain tumour?

The bluebottle thudded against the window. The post was mostly bills. She tried to think what materials they had ordered from Fixit. Plans; she felt a wave of sadness as she thought about the plans she and Tom had made for the house. For their new life here.

Darling, it's me, please call me.

Sod you.

She ripped open the next envelope. It was another form from the General Register Office. Details of her adoptive birth certificate were required. Where was it? In an envelope with her passport, vaccination certificates and other bits and pieces. She had packed it somewhere safe when they moved. Shit. Her mind could not focus. In one of the large cardboard boxes. Which one? She thought for a moment. The attic.

Barbara Jarrett. D. Aug 12th 1953.

Who were you? Who were you, Barbara Jarrett?

Dear Rock, I love him. Please bring him back. Barbara.

You?

The kettle was silent; no power, of course, and the Aga was out. She went to the top of the cellar steps.

'Sorry, I can't make tea with the power off,' she called down.

'Be about ten minutes,' he shouted.

She climbed the stairs and pushed open the attic door. Just enough light to see by came in from a small window down at the far right end. To the left it became increasingly dark and shadowy. She could make out the water cistern. The holes in the roof had gone, and the light that had leaked in before was now sealed out. Dust tickled her nose and she stifled a sneeze. The ceiling was lower than she remembered and the walls narrower; the room seemed large and at the same time claustrophobic. She was acutely aware of the silence.

The wooden packing cases and large cardboard boxes had been dumped untidily by the removals men near the window, and it took several minutes of heavy work moving them before she found the one she was looking for. 'PERSONAL BELONGINGS' was written in marker pen across two sides.

She trod on something soft which made a crunching sound, and looked down. It was a dead mouse, its face partially decomposed. Her stomach churned, and she pushed it with her foot behind the packing cases so Ben would not get it.

The window shook in its frame in a gust, and something rolled down the roof. She ripped the tape off the lid of the box and opened it. The top half was full of old clothes, strange old clothes that carried with them in their plastic bags the smells of the past. They were neatly pressed, folded, with cleaning tickets attached

285

with safety pins, clothes she had not worn in years put away for — a rainy day? Fancy dress parties? Put away because they were her roots?

She found flared jeans, a miniskirt, a small wooden box full of beads and hippy bells, long white plastic boots, a corduroy cap, a plastic bag full of badges: CND, IMPEACH NIXON! LEGALISE POT! I AM GROOVY!

There was a sound like the scrape of a foot and she stared into the shadows at the far end of the attic, the dark end, with the silhouette of the water tank; but she could not see anything.

She rummaged deeper in the box and found another polythene bag, bound several times with an elastic band which was dried out and broke as she unwound it. She turned the package over, the polythene getting longer, until she could see inside. Letters and cards. One card was bigger than the rest, a valentine with a glum little man on the front holding up an enormous red heart. Inside, in Tom's handwriting, it said: 'To my eternal Sweetheart.'

The tears slid down her cheeks and she closed the card and slipped it back into the bag.

Something caught her eye in the shadows. A movement. She stepped back. Something was moving in the shadows.

Then she realised it was herself; she was standing in the light from the window, throwing the shadow.

It happened fast, without warning. A crack like a whip and her right leg plunged through the floor. She fell forwards, smacking her chin on to the hardboard. The floor sagged beneath her as she landed. Her right leg had gone through up to the knee.

She lay still, startled, trying to work out what had happened. She pressed her hands down on the floor and it sagged further; there was another splintering crack.

She was breathing fast, panicking now. She yanked her leg out then without trying to stand up, she slithered across the hardboard towards the door where the floor felt solid, and clambered to her feet. She rubbed her grazed leg; her tights were shredded.

She noticed the smell of perfume, suddenly. The attic reeked of it. Strong, pungent, musky perfume. A cold draught dusted her skin. Downstairs the electrician called out, 'Mrs Witney? I'm going to put the power back on now.'

Chapter Thirty-Three

A candle burned in a glass holder on the table. They sat by a large unlit inglenook with a grey marble surround like a tombstone. The small restaurant was quiet. Only two other tables were occupied, both by couples who talked in murmured voices.

Charley raised her menu to hide a yawn; tiredness came in waves. Hugh looked less world-weary, less beat-up than usual. He seemed to have made a special effort with his appearance tonight: his hair was brushed, his nails were clean and scrubbed, and his clothes were pressed.

She had dithered for half an hour deciding what to wear, putting things on and taking them off, wanting to look good. She felt better after she'd had a long bath and washed her hair, made up her face and put on a black halter top, trousers, a white satin jacket, patent shoes and a large chain-link necklace. She felt better, too, after another mouthful of gin and tonic.

'You're very quiet tonight,' Hugh said. 'You must be shaken finding your hypnotist dead like that — pretty horrific.'

'It was. And Mrs Letters's funeral.'

'Are you still blaming yourself?'

She nodded.

'I shall miss the old girl. I really liked her.' He picked up his glass and rattled the ice cubes. 'But it was an accident. Nothing more.'

She wished she could believe him.

'Where are records about graves kept?' she asked. 'If you see a name on a gravestone, and you want to try to find out about that person, where would you look?'

'On a recent grave?'

'Early fifties.'

'I should think the County Records Office in Lewes would be the place.' He looked down at his drink then up at her. 'Is it the grave you were looking at after the funeral?'

'Yes.'

His eyes watched her carefully, but she saw behind their studiousness something else, a warmth, an interest. For the first time since she had met him she sensed he was looking at her for another reason than merely to try to probe into her mind. She blushed and he grinned and raised his glass and touched her own with a light clink, and she drank some more and began to feel good, began to feel safe, to feel that maybe it was going to be possible, one day, to be normal again.

'Did you ever try to patch your marriage up?' she said.

He rattled the ice cubes again. 'Someone once said that marriage is like a glass. Once it's broken you can stick the pieces back together, but you forever see the cracks.'

'Are you ready to order yet?' The waitress was smiling; she looked informal, like a college student.

'A few more minutes,' Hugh said, returning the smile, flirting with her, and Charley felt a pang of jealousy. He studied his menu for a few moments. 'Will you and Tom get back together?'

She shrugged.'I don't think I have any confidence in anything any more.' His large hand slid across the table and his fingers lightly touched the tops of hers. Then he gripped them gently but firmly.

'You have lots to be confident about.'

Strange emotions heaved inside her. 'Being adopted is an odd thing. You don't feel secure. You've been given away, for whatever reason, even if your parents have been killed, you have the knowledge that someone had to find you a home, give you away. It makes you feel all your life that everyone else in the world is going to give you away too. I think I fooled myself into believing that our marriage would be forever. Nothing's forever.'

He squeezed her fingers. 'That depends what you call forever.'

'Do you think that people meet again, in future lives?'

'Some believe that's what attracts people to one another. You know, you walk into a crowded party and you are immediately drawn to one person because it's someone you knew from another life.'

'But we're not aware of it?'

'Some people are. Not many.'

'And you believe it's possible?'

'Yes.'

She fiddled with her napkin. 'My doctor thinks I might be epileptic.'

'Doctors are good at thinking that sort of thing.'

Their eyes met and they both smiled.

'Did you find out who used to own the Triumph?'

'I haven't heard yet. I'm hoping to get her started tomorrow. I'm just waiting for some gaskets to arrive in the post. I'll take you for a spin.'

'That would feel very strange.'

'You know, somewhere like Edinburgh University might be interested in doing a study on you. They have a faculty of parapsychology.'

'No thanks,' she said shortly. She glanced down the menu. She wasn't hungry and did not care what she ate.

She searched for a new topic of conversation, one that would interest him.

'Tell me about ley lines,' she said. 'What exactly are they?'

'Narrow magnetic fields that run in straight lines. No one fully understands what they are. Ancient man used them as lines of alignment for sacred places. The Romans are credited with building straight roads, but they only built them along ancient leys. The electro-magnetic fields seem to come from mineral deposits, ore seams and underground streams.'

'Can they affect electricity?' she asked, her pulse quickening.

'The strongest force fields are on junctions between leys. You sometimes get electro-magnetic disturbances on those.'

'What sort?'

'The Alexandra Palace in London is built over a junction of two leys. It's burned down three times.'

'Really?'

'Yes. The most common thing over these junctions is ghost or poltergeist activity. There seems to be some evidence that spirits get energy from these things. Ancient man built all his ancient places of worship — burial grounds, barrows, sacred stones — along leys. The most important ones are on intersections. Stone-henge is on an intersection.'

She frowned.

He looked at her in a strange probing way that reminded her of the first time they had met. 'So is Elmwood Mill.'

A full moon burned brightly above them as they climbed out of the Jaguar, and the water fell steadily over the weir. Charley listened for Ben's barking, but could hear nothing.

Hugh stood still for a moment. 'Do you know what I see when I look at the moon?' he said.

'What do you see?'

'Three bags of American urine.'

'Urine?' She picked up the large rubber torch she had left on the back seat of the Jaguar, and they walked towards the steps.

'That's what they left up there — the first men, when they landed. Three bags of urine.' He put his arm round her.

'Why?' her voice had a falsetto tremble.

'The official reason was to see what would happen to it. I often wonder if it was something different: like dogs and cats pissing over new places to mark out territory.'

She laughed. His arm was snug, comforting. 'So man's technology still can't nullify our base instincts?'

'Something like that.'

The roar of water seemed deafeningly loud against the silence of the house. She put the key in the lock, twisted it and opened the door. The sharp white light of the torch shot across the hallway, bouncing up and down the stairs, great shadows dancing with it as if they were clipped to the beam. No sound from Ben.

She swung the torch in a wide arc and saw his eyes glowing red out of the darkness of the passageway. 'Boy! Hallo, boy!' He did not move.

She hurried to him, knelt and stroked him. He was sagging on his haunches, cold and shaking; his hair felt almost prickly. 'I'm sorry, boy. Didn't you like the dark?' She hugged him, 'Come on, boy, come outside!'

He slunk to the front door, then seemed to perk up as he ran down the steps and across the grass. Charley unlocked the cellar door, felt the cold draught brush her face, and went down, glad that Hugh was with her. The mains switch moved with a loud snap and the overhead light came on.

Hugh glanced around, his head almost touching the ceiling. Charley looked up at the disc of the meter. It was barely moving, 'Do you know much about electrics?' she said.

'It's a good system you've got here. This is the latest, safest technology. I've got it in my own house.'

They went up the stairs and she closed the door. Hugh took her shoulders in his large hands and held them gently; his eyes were smiling; her own smiled back. They kissed. It was strange, wicked; a good feeling. His mouth was softer than she had somehow imagined. They kissed again, longer, much longer, for five minutes, maybe more, until they were interrupted by Ben who came running up to them, barking and jumping, and Hugh laughed and said it looked like Ben had made a pretty good recovery.

They kissed again in the passageway, in the chilly draught from the front door that was still open and she felt Hugh's hands slide up under her jacket, under her halter top and gently across the bare skin of her back.

As she worked his shirt tail out of his trousers and ran her hands up his warm powerful back, she did not hear the low humming that had started in the cellar.

Hugh lay, breathing heavily, cold sticky sweat drying on his body, sensing vaguely that he was at the wrong end of the bed. The moonlight beamed harshly in on his face, strong enough to tan him, he thought. He could hear Charley's breathing, deep, rhythmic, could smell her perfume, her sweat, her animal body smells, and he was becoming aroused again.

His mouth tasted vile, of stale garlic and brandy and cigar smoke. He tried to move but something was holding him down, pinioning him down, a weight across his chest. He put his hand out and felt something hard, smooth. One of her legs. Gently he lifted it and slid out from under it, padded across the room to the open window, and stood listening to the night, to the roaring water, the squeak of some creature, the solitary hoot of an owl.

He walked through into the bathroom and fumbled on the wash-basin for the toothpaste. He unscrewed the cap, squeezed some out on to his finger and rubbed it on his teeth. It tasted sharp, fresh, minty. He ran the tap and rinsed his mouth out, and out of the corner of his eye saw a figure coming through the doorway towards him, an indistinct, hazy figure through the darkness.

Charley. He was filled with a sudden energy and burst of lust as he saw a sheen of moonlight bounce on her breasts, saw her long naked legs. He wanted her in here, wanted to sit her up on the washbasin and —

She ran a finger down his back, tracing over his buttocks, down his thigh, then up, slowly up, took hold of his erection and began to rub it with strokes of her slender fingers, long light strokes, so light she was barely touching it. He smiled at her and she smiled back, a strange smile. A freaky smile.

Then he saw a glint of steel.

Saw the shadow as her arm came down and the knife sliced into his erection, sliced with burning agony right through it and blood sprayed like a fountain, agonising dark squirts in the darkness, spattering him in the face, spraying over her, covering her breasts, her stomach, her thighs, spraying over her grinning sick face.

The knife flashed again, seared into his stomach. Streaks of pain shot up inside him, and the knife twisted, tearing a scream of agony from his throat.

'Stop!' he bellowed, dropping his hands and grabbing the blade, but she tore it back, slicing open the skin of his hand, and bones of his fingers. The knife plunged again into his stomach, twisted, turned, lifted him upwards with an incredible maniacal strength, then he fell down on the blade and it cut him open like a filleting knife.

'Stop! Charley! Stop! For God's —'

He was howling, pummelling with his fists, shaking crazily, trying to back away. He smashed against the wall, except the wall was soft, cushioned him, bounced him gently.

Charley's face burned white, brilliant white. Moon white.

The moon.

He was staring out of the window at the moon, gulping down air. The room was quiet. Silence. Just as the roaring of the mill race outside and the thumping of his heart. He felt for Charley, but touched only an empty pillow.

There was a strong smell of perfume, a heady, musky perfume. Charley must have put it on, he thought, to freshen herself up. The smell seemed to be getting stronger, as if she were in the room now and coming towards him. But there was no one. He heard the door open and turned and saw Charley walking in, a shadowy figure in the moonlight.

Something was glinting in her hand.

His skin tightened around him. He pushed himself back, pressed the palms of his hands against the mattress, tensing his muscles, drawing his legs up, blind terror surging through him. He started moving across the bed, slithering across it.

'Hi,' she said. 'I've brought you a glass of water.'

He stopped, his heart booming, resonating inside him, and stared warily as she moved towards him, as the moonlight glinted off the thing in her hand. He did not relax until the hard glass touched his teeth, the fresh water washed into his mouth, and he drank gratefully, drank like a child. Then she removed the glass and replaced it with her lips.

They kissed, and she pulled back her head playfully, ran her fingers through his hair, and said, 'You taste nice and fresh. Did you brush your teeth?'

In the morning they made love again. Hugh lay on top of her and she felt his crushing weight, felt the warm strength of his body, the hairs of his beard tickled her face. He took some of his weight on to his elbows and she gazed into the blue-grey eyes that were so close they were blurred.

She felt safe. Safe with him here. Safe and good. A bird outside pipped. There was the clatter of the paper boy's bicycle and Ben, downstairs, barked. 'I'm going to have to throw you out in a minute,' she said.

'Oh yes?' He nibbled the end of her nose.

'The electrician'll be here soon, and the builders. I don't think it would be too good an idea if —'

'Can I see you tonight?' He rolled over and heaved himself up against the headboard.

She smiled, 'Yes, please.'

His eyes became serious. 'Charley, would you mind terribly if I did something?'

The change in the tone of his voice alarmed her. 'What?'

His face reddened. 'You know what I was saying last night, about ley lines — intersections?'

She said nothing.

'I — I don't know what it is exactly, but there is something very strange in this house — there's some atmosphere —' He smiled, but the smile failed to dismiss the worry that had suddenly etched into his face. 'It's probably what I think it is — a bit of electromagnetic interference caused by the ley lines — and that's almost certainly what's causing your electrical problems.'

'Why have they only just started causing problems

now? Wouldn't they have done so before?'

'You don't know they haven't. Your predecessor here was mad as a hatter and she might not have been aware of the problems.'

'Or maybe they drove her mad.'

His eyes probed Charley's. 'Surveys don't reveal leys; not many surveyors believe in or are aware of ley lines. I know someone who is quite into these things, who might —' His voice tailed away.

'I thought you were the expert.'

'I know a bit about leys, but not —'

'Not what?'

He looked uncomfortable. 'He's a — what you'd call a sensitive.'

'What do you mean, a sensitive?'

'Well, he's like me, really, only where I tend to take the scientific view he takes a more paranormal view, I suppose.'

She frowned. He was being evasive and it made her feel uneasy. 'I'm not with you.'

He lifted a strand of hair off her forehead and kissed her. 'I think someone who knows about these things should have a look. And I don't think you should stay here on your own.'

'I have to,' she said.

'You can stay at my house. I'm sure I could get him to come round within a day or two.'

'Your sensitive?'

'Yes.'

A feeling of doom slid across like a storm cloud. Tom. Viola. Gibbon. Peregrine, the terrier. Hugh's semen trickled down her thigh. Betrayal. It had felt good a few minutes ago. So good.

'What would he do, this sensitive?'

'He'd be able to tell you.'

She bit at the hard skin below her thumb nail and

looked at the dressing table. The dressing table with the heart-shaped locket in the tin at the back of the top right-hand drawer. 'Tell me what?'

'Tell you what's going on in this house,' he said. 'Whether you have a presence here.'

Chapter Thirty-four

Charley parked in the pay-and-display below the castle walls, and walked up the High Street. She stopped at a signpost which indicated every municipal building except the one she wanted.

A man in a well-cut suit was striding briskly towards her, swinging his umbrella which was still tightly rolled in spite of the drizzle, and she asked him.

'County Records Office?' he said, swivelling on his metal-capped heels and pointing helpfully. 'Up to the top and round to the right, as far as you can go. The Maltings — got a blue door.'

She walked under a flint archway into quietness and climbed up a steep cobbled hill, past several well-preserved Sussex flint and red brick Georgian buildings, with the castle high up above. She was trying to think clearly, to sort out her thoughts, frightened, suddenly. Frightened to go on. In case ...

In case she found —?

The drizzle was worsening. Part of her wanted to go back to the car park, forget about the records office. Another part walked on, head bowed against the rain.

Ahead was a low flint malthouse with a high roof and a blue door. A brass sign read 'East Sussex County Council. Records Office'.

Inside was a small entrance hall that smelled of furniture polish and damp umbrellas. The walls were lined with pockets of leaflets and a cheery-looking girl sat at the reception desk in front of a floor-to-ceiling rack of leather volumes marked 'Deaths 1745–1803'.

'Where would I find burial records for All Saint's Church, Elmwood?'

'Room C. Straight ahead at the top of the stairs.'

Room C occupied most of the roof space of the building. It was a long attic with small dormer windows and bright flourescent lighting. To her right was a low counter, to the left were metal racks of index files and a row of microfiche booths; the rest of the room was filled with flat tables and metal-framed chairs.

It was only half past nine, and Charley was surprised at the number of people already there. It bustled with an air of quiet urgency. People were scrolling through microfiches, leafing through binders of old newspapers, unfurling yellowing architects' plans, scribbling notes. At the far end, a group of students were clustered around a woman who was talking intently in a hushed voice.

Charley dug her hands into her raincoat pockets, went up to the counter and waited until one of the clerks looked up from her index cards. 'Yes? Can I help you?'

'I want to see the records on someone buried in All Saints' Church in Elmwood.'

'The burial register? Have you filled out a form?' She held a small pad up.

Charley shook her head.

'You need a seat number.' She pointed at an empty chair. 'That one'll do. Tell me the number on that.'

Charley walked across and came back. 'Eleven.'

The woman handed her the form. 'Fill that in, and

300

your name and address. Do you have a registration number?'

'No. Do I need one?'

'Are you doing regular research — or is this a one-off?'

'A one-off.' Charley took a pen out of her handbag.

'You're only allowed to use pencil here,' the woman said. 'I can sell you one for twelve pence if you haven't got one.'

Charley paid for a pencil.

'Is it a particular year you want to look up?'

'Nineteen fifty-three.'

'Write "Elmwood Burial Register, nineteen fifty-three" then go to your place and someone will bring it to you.'

Charley sat at the table opposite a smart businesslike woman in her late twenties who was scanning through a thick leather-bound volume and jotting down notes on a shorthand pad. Next to her a couple in their forties were poring over a set of house plans.

She wondered how long it would take. She needed to leave by twelve fifteen to make sure she caught a train in time for her appointment with Dr Ross.

A woman reached over and placed a cream leather-bound volume on the table in front of her and moved on silently. It had a gold embossed coat of arms, a typed white tag at the bottom and the wording, also in embossed lettering, 'Register of Burials'.

She stared at it. Forget it, she thought. Take it back. Leave it alone.

She opened it, turned the thick pages carefully, heard them fall with a slight crackling sound. The columns were spread across the width of both pages, the headings printed, the entries beneath neatly hand-written in fountain pen, the style of writing and the colour of ink changing every few pages. There were

301

several church names she recognised, Nutley, Fletching, Danehill, and some she had not heard of. 1951 ... 1952 ... 1953. She stopped, glanced at the headings. 'Name'. 'Date of death'. 'Place or Parish where death occurred'. 'Place of burial'. Her eyes ran down the names. And found it.

'Barbara Jarrett. August 12th. Cuckfield Hospital. All Saints', Elmwood.'

That was all. She leafed on through a few more pages, but they were the same.

She read it again, disappointment seeping through her, then went back to the counter. The clerk looked up. 'Was that helpful?'

Charley nodded, not wanting to offend her. 'Thank you. I really want to find out a bit more about someone who is buried in Elmwood. She's in the register, but it doesn't say much.'

'What is it you want to know, exactly?'

'I — I — want to know who she was, see if I can find out a bit about her.'

'Do you know her date of birth?'

'No.'

'It's not on the gravestone?'

'No.'

'If you had that, you could go through the baptisms register, which would give you the names of her mother and father and when she was born. And you could go on from there and look up the electoral register and get their address.'

'I've no idea when she was born.'

'None at all?'

'All I know is the date of death.'

'There's probably someone in the village who might be able to help you, someone who might remember her. Have you tried that? Pubs are often a good source. Or some of the old shopkeepers.'

Viola Letters's face burned in her mind. The old man in the pub, Arthur Morrison, closing his front door.

'Of course, the announcements in the local paper might give you something,' the clerk said. 'You could check the deaths column. Do you know how she died?'

'No.'

'If it was in some sort of accident, it might well have been reported — that might give you her address and family.'

The woman's words resonated in her head. *Some sort of accident.* Her last regression. The burning stable, the fight. The ambulance. The room spun. Charley steadied herself against the counter; she felt a pounding in her chest. The entry on the burial register: Place or Parish where death occurred.

Cuckfield Hospital.

Hospital.

'Are you feeling all right?' she heard the clerk saying.

'Sorry,' Charley whispered. Hospital. Calm down. Nothing. Millions of people die in hospital.

'The *Sussex Express*,' said the woman. 'That was the local paper deaths would have been reported in then.'

Charley returned to her chair and waited, tried to relax, but her adrenalin was pumping now. The businesslike woman opposite gave her an irritated look; Charley wondered if the thump of her heartbeat was distracting her. It was loud. Like drums.

'There we are. It's heavy.' The clerk laid a massive volume down in front of her on top of the burials register.

Charley lifted the leather binder. A smell of old dried paper rose up from the yellowing newspapers inside.

'SUSSEX EXPRESS & COUNTY HERALD. Friday 2 January 1953.'

An ad in the top right corner read, 'Bobby's Plastic Macs — With Attached Hoods' and beneath were the headlines, 'KNIGHTHOOD FOR LEWES MAN!'

There were several columns full of the New Year honours list, then the rest of the news on the front page was local: a car accident. The success of a charity New Year's Eve ball. She glanced through, fascinated for a moment; the newspaper was so old-fashioned, its layout messy, its advertisements bland, its stories almost all local; there was something cosy about it. She turned several chunks of pages at a time, working through the months. It was a weekly paper. Local news always made the major headline, national or international had smaller prominence.

'CUCKFIELD WAR HERO WEDS.'

'Stalin Dead!'

'COUNTY COUNCIL DECISION ON BYPASS!'

'Rebel Fidel Castro Jailed!'

Friday 7 August.

'FIVE DEAD IN BOLNEY SMASH.'

She turned through the pages of news, advertisements, sports.

'Bobby's Beach Towels In Gay Colours!'

Then Friday 14 August.

The headlines said: 'NEWLYWED DEAD IN BLAZE HORROR.'

It took a moment for it to sink in. For her to realise she was not imagining it. She tried to read it again, but the print had blurred. She squeezed her eyes, but that made it worse. Then she realised it was blurred because she was holding it in her shaking hands, and she put it down on the table.

Beneath the headline was a black and white photograph of an unrecognisable burned-out building. The caption read: 'Remains of the stables.'

Inset beside was a smaller photograph of Elmwood Mill, taken from the side, showing the house and the watermill, with the caption, 'The historic mill house property.'

Then she read the story.

The charred and mutilated body of local man, Richard Morrison, 32, was recovered from the burned-out remains of the stables at his home in Elmwood village yesterday evening, after a frenzied knife attack by a woman believed to have been his former fiancée.

The woman identified by police as Miss Barbara Jarrett, 19, of London, died in labour as a result of wounds she herself received in the attack in Cuckfield Hospital. Doctors saved the life of her premature baby girl.

Mr Morrison's bride of less than two months, society couturier Nancy Delvine, 35, who was also savagely attacked was last night in a critical condition in the burns unit of East Grinstead Hospital where the police are waiting to question her.

The attack happened at Mr and Mrs Morrison's remote mill house home where less than two months ago they had hosted a glittering wedding reception at which some of the most famous names in British fashion, including royal couturiers Mr Hardy Amies and Mr Norman Hartnell, were present.

Mr Morrison, who ran his own livery business in Danehill, and was the only son of Elmwood farm labourer Arthur Morrison and his wife Maud, of Saddlers Cottages, Crampton Farm, married Miss Delvine after a whirlwind romance. They met only a few months ago, when Miss Delvine rented the idyllic Elmwood Mill for the summer.

Neighbour, widow Mrs Viola Letters, stated that she

had seen the heavily pregnant Miss Jarrett walking to the mill several times in recent weeks and that she seemed to be in an anxious and distressed state. Miss Jarrett, whose address was a hostel for unmarried mothers in London, came formerly from Fletching and was the only child of Hurstgate Park gamekeeper Bob Jarrett who was decorated with the DSO in the war. Mr Jarrett and his wife were too distressed to comment yesterday. (*Continued page 5, column 2.*)

Charley tried to turn the pages, but her fingers were trembling so much she could not grip them. She turned too far, flipped back, heard a page tear.

Then she saw the photographs.

The top one was a wedding photograph, a couple leaving Elmwood church, the bride in white, the groom togged in morning dress. The coarse grin on the man's tough face, the cold arrogant smile on the woman's. It was them. The two people she had seen in her regressions.

There were larger photographs of each of them beneath. The man sitting on a horse, the woman in finery, her black hair slanted over her eyes. The woman who had set the dog on her, the woman Dick Morrison had been making love to in the stable, who had come into the bedroom and shot at her and stabbed her with the shard of mirrored glass.

Then her eyes were drawn down to another photograph, smaller, less distinct. She stared in numbed silence.

'Barbara Jarrett. Jilted?'

A girl gazed out at her. A girl in her late teens. Pretty.

The heat seemed to go out of Charley's body. Prickles raked her skin.

The hair was different, long, curled, fifties style. But

that was all. That was the only difference.

It was as if she were looking at an old photograph of herself.

Chapter Thirty-five

Tony Ross was looking as fit and perky as ever as he squeezed himself behind his tiny desk. 'So, Charley, how are you feeling?'

'Very strange.'

'Oh?' He raised his eyebrows. His eyes were twinkling and she wondered for a moment if he was drunk; except she could not imagine him getting drunk. 'I have the results of the tests, the blood and urine samples I took.'

She nodded glumly.

'I want to do a quick internal examination, to make absolutely sure. I think you're going to be rather pleased with my diagnosis.' He jumped up and held the door open for her, then led her across the hallway to the examining room. Miss Moneypenny glanced up from her desk and she was grinning too. Charley wondered if they were both drunk, had just finished an after-lunch bonk, if that was why they were looking so inane.

He asked her to undress and lie on the couch. She kicked off her shoes, pulled down her cotton skirt, slipped off her knickers and unbuttoned her shirt, then lay down on the fresh sheet of paper on the couch. She watched him as he pulled on a surgical glove, squeezed out some KY jelly, felt his fingers sliding up inside her and winced at the coldness of the jelly.

She studied the concentration on his face, the movement of his eyes, looking for some trace of doubt or anxiety, but he just nodded and kept smiling. She sniffed to see if she could smell alcohol on his breath, but could detect nothing even when he leaned right over her. The fingers probed deeply, then he removed his hand, peeled off the glove and dropped it in a bin. He ran a tap and washed his hands. 'You told me you last had a period a month ago.'

'Yes.'

'Are you sure?' He dried his hands on a paper towel.

'Yes. Maybe five or six weeks. Things have been a bit chaotic, the move —'

'Put your clothes on and come back to my office.'

She dressed, irritated by this game he seemed to be playing. She went into his office where he was writing notes on an index card. He put the pen down.

'So you can't remember exactly when you had your last period, but definitely not longer than five or six weeks ago?'

'Definitely.'

He beamed even more broadly and leaned back in his chair. 'Well — you're pregnant!'

It took a moment before the word registered. Then it hit her like a breaker wave. Washed crazily over her, winded her. She stared back, speechless.

'It is quite possible for women to go on having periods well into pregnancy,' he continued. 'It's unusual beyond a couple of months, but it does happen. I'd say you are about sixteen weeks pregnant.'

Pregnant. Sixteen weeks. The words crashed about like surf inside her head.

'Everything feels fine in the uterus, all in the right place. We need to do a few tests, because of your age — but I really wouldn't worry. We'll arrange an ultrasound scan as soon as possible.'

'Sixteen weeks?'

'You haven't felt any movement inside you? You should start getting some soon.' He turned the index card over and tapped his teeth with his pen. 'Pretty surprised, eh?'

'How — how can it have gone on so long, without my knowing?'

'It happens. I had a very fat patient who got to seven months without knowing.'

Pregnant.

The word lay beached inside her. The sun beat down, drying it up, shrivelling it into a blackened carcass.

NEWLYWED DEAD IN BLAZE HORROR

'You don't look very happy. I'd have thought you'd be jumping for joy.'

'I don't understand. All these tests and things. We haven't been trying for months. The acupuncturist wanted us to wait until my body balance —'

The doctor waved his pen around. 'You know, Charley, medicine's a funny thing. It's a very inexact science. I can't tell you why you haven't realised sooner, any more than why you've got pregnant now instead of five years ago, or ten years ago. There are so many factors, psychological ones just as important as physical — sometimes more important.' He pulled a pad out of a drawer and scribbled on it. 'I'm going to give you some things to take, iron and some dietary supplements. Cut out alcohol completely and you must avoid all medication. You haven't been taking anything in the last few months, have you?'

'No.'

'I had a pretty good feeling what your symptoms were, but I didn't want to say anything and get your hopes raised.'

'You knew?'

'Not for sure. It could have been temporal lobe epilepsy, but I didn't think so. Tom's going to be pretty pleased. Want to call him?' He pushed the telephone at her.

She shook her head.

'Tell him later, eh? Give him a homecoming surprise.'

She said nothing.

'Don't look so glum! I don't think I've ever seen an expectant mum look so glum when I've given her the good news.'

'It's not good news,' she said. 'Not good news at all.'

He frowned and leaned forward. 'Not good news?'

She bit her lip, then tugged at the skin on her thumb. 'Do you mean that *all* the symptoms I had are explainable by my being pregnant?'

'Yes.'

'So I'm definitely not epileptic, or anything else?'

'I'm absolutely certain your symptoms are due to your pregnancy — and, of course, not realising for so long would make them puzzling to you. Pregnancy causes hormonal changes which can affect women both physically and emotionally.'

She picked at a nail on another finger. 'Medicine is very convenient,' she said bitterly.

'What do you mean, Charley?' he said, surprised.

'You can explain everything, can't you? Neat. Pat.'

'It's what doctors try to do.'

She stood up, unbuttoned her shirt and pulled it open. She pointed to the small, barely visible ribbed line, three inches long, on the left side of her stomach. Then she hitched down her skirt and indicated the similar line on the inside of her thigh, below her groin. 'How do you explain these birthmarks?' she said.

He came round the desk and examined them closely. 'They're not birthmarks,' he said. 'They're scars.'

'Scars? They're birthmarks. My mother always told me so.'

'They've been stitched, a long time ago. You must have had an accident when you were very young. Quite neat lines. You might have been cut by a knife, or glass.'

She pulled her skirt up and sat down, rebuttoning her shirt. 'Are you sure?'

He sat down again himself. 'Yes. Old-fashioned stitching leaves marks like that; modern stitching is much better.'

She was silent, aware of his worried stare. 'Tony, are unborn children able to register what's going on when they are in the womb? What I mean is — could we — sort of — live our mothers' lives as they live them and remember things later?'

'Remember things our mothers did whilst we were in the womb?'

'Yes.'

He pushed himself back in his chair. 'What is it, Charley? Something seems to be really bugging you. Last time you asked me about reincarnation, now you're asking about pre-birth memories.' His eyes narrowed and he nodded pensively. 'Unborn children can respond to stimulae, yes; tests have proved that.'

She still picked at the nail. 'So there's nothing — supernatural — about perhaps remembering things — that maybe happened when you were in the womb?'

'A five-month-old foetus can hear a door shut twelve feet away.'

'Do you believe in ghosts?'

He grinned. 'Listen, I'm going to get strict with you. I know pregnant women have abnormal fears, but you're going over the top. You must relax. You're a normal healthy person and I'm quite certain you have a normal healthy baby inside you. You've been very wound up about these things that have been going on that you haven't understood. Now you know the reason for them, you don't need to be scared any more. You have

312

nothing to worry about. Just enjoy your pregnancy. Otherwise your poor child's going to be born a nervous wreck.'

She heard a voice somewhere inside her head, faint, as if it were trapped like an echo in a vacuum.

Seems healthy and normal. Doesn't appear to have been affected by the mother's blood loss. Two surface cuts to be sutured from the stab wounds.

She felt a chill blast of air down her neck. It triggered a feeling of fear, fear so deep and strong that the tiny creature inside her womb could sense it too.

It kicked.

It was dusk as she drove down the lane. She'd left Ross in a daze and wandered around, trying to put it all together, to find some meaning. The Citroën jolted through the deep pothole past Yuppie Towers.

There had been times in the past when her period had been late, when she had hoped ... When she had imagined the look on Tom's face as she told him the news. Happier times.

As she drove up to Rose Cottage the falling light seemed to change, to flatten. Viola Letters's Morris had gone from her drive. Instead there was an old black saloon. She was so distracted she almost failed to see the figure in front of her.

She stamped on the brakes, the wheels skidding on the loose surface, and was flung against the seat belt. The car lurched to a halt and she touched her belly gingerly, worried about the child inside and blinking at what she saw through the windscreen.

A man sitting at an easel, erect, with fine posture, in a white shirt, cravat and cavalry twill trousers. He tilted his head back, oblivious to her, raised his brush in the air, closed one eye and lined it up against the cottage then made a mark on his canvas. It was Viola Letters's husband.

He turned, as if he had become aware of her, and stood up stiffly.

Then he faded. Was gone.

The light brightened a fraction. She looked at the cottage. The black car was no longer there. The old woman's Morris Minor sat in the driveway.

Gibbon. Hypnosis. Still under. She was barely aware of where she was and wondered if she had imagined her visit to Ross, if that had been a dream. Then she felt another movement in her belly, faint, like a scratch.

'Hi,' she said lamely. 'How are you doing in there? OK, is it? What are we going to call you? You going to be a boy or a girl? I think you're a boy. I don't know why — you feel like a boy.' She patted her stomach gently. 'You want to stay in there for as long as you can. It's the pits out here.'

A smell of smoke and a haze of acrid blue fumes was drifting across the lane, and there was the droning staccato roar of an unsilenced engine. She was about to put the car in gear when she saw Zoe and her pointer walking towards her.

Zoe pegged her nose with her fingers. 'God, what a fug!' She flapped away the fumes. 'Bloody Hugh, honestly!'

'Is that where it's coming from?'

'Of course. Polluting half of Sussex! I don't know how on earth he can work in that — any normal person would be asphyxiated. I haven't forgotten about having you and Tom over. I'll sort out a date in the next day or so.'

Charley drove on, past Hugh's house. He was in his workshop, bent over the engine compartment of the Triumph, blue exhaust rising around him. He seemed to be engrossed, as if he were trying to tighten a nut, and she wanted to stop, run across and tell him her news but she drove on, afraid the news might put him off her.

Pregnant. Who wants to be lumbered with a pregnant loony?

Tom's child. Was Tom going to care?

Was Hugh going to believe her when she showed him the photocopies of the newspaper article?

The builders and the electrician had gone and she was relieved to hear Ben's bark. She hurried across the gravel and up the steps, then she noticed something off about the barks; they sounded muffled, intense, not like his usual greeting.

Angry.

She unlocked the front door and pressed the hall light switch. Nothing happened. Bugger. She sniffed. There was a smell of rotting meat in the house. Fridge, perhaps. She ran into the kitchen. Ben stood in the boiler room, barking at the ceiling, gruff barks as if he had made himself hoarse.

He turned his head towards her, whined, then looked up at the ceiling and barked again, desperately, as if he were trying to tell her something. She stared at him, then up at the ceiling, the black ceiling with the lagged central heating pipes. 'What's up, boy?'

He ignored her, then twisted round on himself and barked at the wall beside him, then snarled and ran out through the kitchen and down the passageway. She followed. He stopped at the foot of the stairs, glared up at them and growled.

'What is it, boy?'

He took two steps back, his hair almost rising straight up.

She climbed a few stairs. The smell of rotting meat was stronger here. She climbed on up to the landing. A gust of wind blew outside; something slithered down a wall. Her bedroom door was ajar; some of the floorboarding was still up and a coil of the electrician's wire was resting against the skirting board. The smell of rotting meat was stronger still; she wondered if it was a dead mouse, like the one in the attic. Except it seemed too strong.

She walked towards her bedroom, the loose boards rattling beneath her feet, echoing in the shadowy silence. She pushed the door further open and looked in.

The tin was on top of her dressing table. It was no longer rusty; it looked brand new. As new and shiny as when she had carried it up the hill in her first regression with Ernest Gibbon.

Someone had polished it.

Her head turned in short snapping movements; the room seemed to be closing in on her. She snatched up the tin and pushed off the lid. Then she screamed.

The locket was not there. Gone. Instead a real heart lay in the tin. It was small, fetid, rotting, and mostly covered in writhing white maggots.

She tried to back away, but the tin came with her, in her hand, the foul stench that had been released from inside churned her stomach like a pitchfork.

She backed into the wall and the tin jerked. The heart shook and some of the maggots fell off it. Others wriggled over the side of the tin and fell on to her hand, cold, dry, their feet pricking into her skin, trying to grip on her trembling flesh before they tumbled to the floor.

One crawled out, bigger than the rest, and perched on the rim. It see-sawed, then rolled on to her wrist, bit her as if in anger at having its meal interrupted, then tumbled through the air as her hand shot up and the tin flew through the air, hit the ceiling, then hit the floor with a bouncing clatter sending the rotten bloody heart rolling against a leg of the dressing table, scattering the maggots around it.

But she did not see it; she was already out of the room, running down the stairs, running for the front door.

Ben thought everything had changed into a game and ran joyfully beside her up the driveway. As they neared Hugh's house, the blattering roar grew louder; the engine was sounding uneven now, as if he were accelerating then decelerating, accelerating, decelerating, and every few seconds it missed a beat and backfired.

She paused at the entrance to Hugh's workshop and coughed violently on the fumes. Ben stayed back, not liking them at all. The roar of the engine was deafening inside as it echoed around, still speeding up, slowing down, but sounding increasingly uneven. The air was a dense haze of blue smoke. A powerful torch with a metal grill suspended on a long flex shone down into the bonnet of the Triumph, which was opened on one side, the cover in the air above Hugh's stooped figure. He was examining something in the engine, adjusting something, and seemed to be nodding to himself. A screwdriver was about to fall out of the back pocket of his boiler suit. She walked over to him, but he did not hear her, could not have heard her above the din. Exhaust and steam rose around him and she wondered how he could breathe in this hell-hole of a fug.

'Hugh!' she shouted. He did not turn round; he carried on with his head down, listening to his engine, nodding. She stood beside him and peered into the bonnet then pulled back, alarmed at the heat, the searing heat that sent up a shimmer through the fumes and steam.

'Hugh!' she shouted, panic in her voice. 'Hugh!'

She tugged at his arm, but it did not move. Still he kept nodding.

'Hugh!'

His arm was rigid as if it was set in a plaster cast. She moved further round the wide black wing, trying to see his face, but his head was low, inside the dark searing cauldron of hammering metal and spinning pulleys and shaking wires and black concertina tubing that was vibrating, pulsing.

His tie was sticking straight down into the engine, taut as a hawser, the knot pulled into a tiny ball, his shirt collar bunched and screwed up around his neck. She leaned over further and could see the blade of the tie now, twisted around the fan pulley which was jammed.

Smoke was coming from his face, his hair. She grabbed his tie, but it was like steel. She pulled it upwards as hard as she could, but it would not budge, would not break. She dived for the Triumph's door, yanked it open and was conscious for a split second of the stale leathery smell, like fresh air against the fumes. She scanned the dash frantically, looking for the key, saw it, turned it off.

Nothing happened.

The engine continued its blattering roar. Through the windscreen she could see the back of his head. He nodded on, as if he was pleased, pleased that the engine was running, silently nodding to himself in approval.

As she ran back to him the engine coughed and missed, and his head jerked sharply. It coughed again, and then died. Smoke curled up, steam hissed and there was a purring rattle, a sweet stench of burning flesh, then a click and the gurgling of water. She looked around for a knife, for something sharp. A large screwdriver with a chipped blade was lying on the ground by her foot. She took it, hacked at the tie with it, and it bounced off. She scraped it across the surface but it barely made a mark and she threw it away, tears streaming from her eyes, from shock, from the smoke and the steam, from the horror.

Christ, there must be a knife in here. She tried to move him, tilt him forward so she could loosen the knot, but he would not move. A vortex of shivers swirled through her, tiny demon fish playing tag through her veins. She saw his blue metal tool box on the floor with several trays opened out, full of nuts, bolts, washers, ring spanners, a hacksaw. She grabbed the hacksaw and tried to pull the blade along the tie. It snagged. A row of threads came away, springy, like wire coils. She pushed the saw forwards then back and the bottom half of the tie fell away.

He slid a few inches only his head turning sideways towards her. His face was a mass of blackened pulp. His eyes were open, bulging, unblinking, almost out of their sockets. As she stared a strip of skin peeled away, curling upwards, like the skin of chicken that has been left too long on a barbecue.

Chapter Thirty-six

Charley ran out of the workshop, and threw up in the yard. Then she went to the front door of Hugh's house, a low moan of terror reverberating inside her, and turned the handle; it was locked. She went to the back and tried the kitchen door. That was locked too.

She stood for a moment in the stark white light that spilled out of the workshop into the falling darkness. Hugh's body still leaned over the bonnet of the car. Silence lay around her, pressed in on her. The taste of vomit made her stomach heave. She could hear herself panting. 'Hugh?' It came out as a whimper. An animal rustled the leaves of a bush behind her.

She took a step towards the workshop. The smell of roast meat came out strongly. She stared once more at Hugh's sightless blackened face, then ran back down the lane, Ben chasing along beside her, and burst in through the front door of her house.

She stopped in the hall, puzzled for a moment. It looked different; felt different. A menacing winged bust glared at her from the hall table.

Phone.

She ran into the drawing room, and stared, disoriented, at the colours, eau de nil and peach, rich and lush in the warm glow of the setting sun. The room was full of fine Art Deco furniture, Lalique lamps.

Phone.

She crossed the floor towards a walnut bureau, tumblers spinning in her brain, trying to hit the right numbers, to unlock the code. The room became dark, suddenly, empty, the floor covered in dust sheets; brushes sat in turps in an empty paint tin. The eau de nil colourings had gone; there was no furniture, no glow from the sun.

No phone.

She gulped deep gasps of air, smelling the dry dust sheets. Regressed. Just regressed. Relief pumped through her confusion. Hugh was fine. She had seen something that had happened a long time ago, someone who looked like Hugh. Freaked out, that was all. *Pregnancy causes a lot of hormonal changes.* Yes, good one, Dr Ross, sir!

A wall bumped into her, nudging her gently. It did it again, and she moved away, irritated, trying to concentrate, to get the image of Hugh's face out of her mind. So vivid, it had been so vivid. As vivid as the fetid maggoty heart in the tin. The polished tin.

Imagined that too. The tin was in her dressing table drawer, where she had left it. Sure it was. Pregnant. Everything's fine. Going to be fine. She climbed the stairs almost jauntily, Ben following her, and went into her bedroom.

The drawer was open. The tin lay on the floor, empty, the lid near it. Both were pitted with rust and caked with mud. No one had polished them.

As she took a step forwards she felt a lump under her foot, heard a crunch and looked down. It was the locket, on the floor. A fine uneven crack ran through the enamelled heart.

She knelt, and something clattered against the chain. Something she was holding in her hand. Oh God, no. She froze, closing her eyes. Opening them again, willing it to go, not to be there.

But it was still there in her hand. The hacksaw with the red and green threads in the teeth. The threads from Hugh's tie.

She ripped the cordless phone off the hook, dialled 999 and put the receiver to her ear. Nothing happened. She punched the numbers again, three electronic pips, then nothing. Dead. Electrics. She had not put the electrics on. Maybe the cordless phone wouldn't work without electricity?

There was a vile smell of stale burnt wood. Something moved in the mirror. A shadow in the corridor. Someone coming in the door.

As she turned, the phone fell from her hand, clattering to the floor. She backed away in terror, crashing against the bed, sidled her way around it, trying to get further away, staring in disbelief at the figure, naked apart from an unbuttoned silk blouse, her face blackened, her eyes red, raw, her hair burnt to stubble.

It was Nancy Delvine. Standing motionless, staring in pure hatred.

Charley's ears popped as if she were going up in an aeroplane. All sounds vanished except for the dull thuds of her own heartbeat.

I believe in ghosts. But I don't know what they are.

Shivers rippled through Charley. It was getting colder. Vapour poured from her mouth.

I don't know whether ghosts have any intelligence, any free will — whether they can actually do anything other than keep appearing in the same place, going through the same movements, like a strip of video replay. Hugh's words drummed inside the soundproof box that was her head.

I'm not sure whether a ghost could really harm someone, apart from giving them a fright by manifesting.

The apparition raised one of its arms. Something glinted in its hand. Charley covered her stomach protectively, backed away, tripped, fell and hit her head. She heard splintering glass; shards from the mirror fell around her.

Nancy Delvine's hand raised further.

Charley fought against her own fear, breathing in short bursts, fought her urge to scream, to turn away and curl up helpless in a ball.

You are just a ghost. A trace memory. You are nothing.

She got back to her feet without looking away. Manifestation. She took a step towards it. You are just a manifestation. The apparition did not move. Its hand stayed in the air. Ben was snarling. Another step.

It was getting colder with each step. She felt her skin creeping, lifting. A band tightened like wire around her skull, and it felt as if a million maggots were crawling over her head, their feet pricking into her scalp. She stared the apparition in the eyes. Nancy Delvine's livid eyes stared back.

Manifestation. You cannot harm me.

Everything blurred, frosted. Her pace seemed to be slowing down; each step took an age, as if she was pushing through a great weight, like a diver walking on the floor of the ocean. It was cold, so cold. Terror swirled inside her, wind blew her hair, her face, blew inside her clothes, inside her skin.

Must not scream, she knew, must not show fear. Most not stop.

Then suddenly she was out on the landing. The pressure had gone. She kept on walking, faster, down the stairs, across the hall, out of the front door. It was dark. Cold air blew on her back. Her skin was still crawling.

God help me. She cradled her stomach. OK, she mouthed silently to her baby. It's OK.

It was just the bedroom phone that was dead. Dead

because it was cordless, needed electricity; the kitchen phone would be all right. She stared into the blackness of the house, listened, then went down the passageway to the kitchen. The table was nearer than she realised and a chair slithered across the floor as she bashed into it, its legs screeching. She grabbed the phone, held it to her ear.

The line was dead.

She tapped the rest, looking at the doorway, fearful that at any moment the apparition might come through. The light on the answering machine was off. Electricity. Did phones use electricity? She ran into the hall and picked up the torch from under the table. Then she opened the cellar door, shivers pulsing through her, and clambered down.

There was a low steady hum. She raked the darkness with the beam, then shone it on the fuse box. The master switch was in the OFF position, but the disc was spinning in the meter. It should not be turning. She pulled the switch down with a click which echoed around the cellar. The humming grew louder. She tried to turn it off, but it would not budge.

Something on the wall hissed at her, there was a ripple of sharp bangs and the wiring erupted into blinding flashes, vivid as a lightning storm. Acrid smoke filled her nostrils. Something hit her hand that felt like a wasp sting; a tiny piece of burning plastic. She shook it off, coughing on the smoke. Then the crackling and flashes stopped as instantly as they had started.

She shone the beam back to the master switch. ON. There was a fizzle and a weak flicker as the ceiling light came on, a dull yellow glimmer like a candle in a draught. Again she tried to push the master switch off, but it was too hot to touch. She folded her handkerchief over it and tried again. It would not move. The humming was getting louder.

She staggered up the steps and into the kitchen. The answering machine light was winking. She grabbed the telephone receiver.

It was still dead.

She tapped the rest up and down. There was a hiss behind her, and a curl of blue smoke rose from the light switch; a brown blister spread outwards along the wall around it as she watched.

She ran into the passageway. Dense smoke was billowing out of the cellar, so dense she could not breathe. She smacked into a wall, blinded by it, flapping it wildly away with her hands, coughing, choking, trying to think.

Up the lane to Zoe, use her phone? Too long. Got to stop the fire first. Must stop it. Must get it under control. Water. Must get water. She raced into the kitchen, turned on the tap, and took out the pail from under the sink. The wall around the switch was burning fiercely. Water dribbled into the bucket. She looked frantically for something she could use. Got to get things out of the house. Possessions, save things, documents, valuables —

Ben.

'Ben!' she screamed, her throat in agony, running into the hall. 'Ben!' She flung herself up the stairs, down the landing, into the bedroom.

He was cowering behind the bed.

'Come on, boy! Have to get out.' She tried to pull him. He would not move. 'Come on.' She patted him gently, then tugged his collar. He looked up at her, whimpering.

The floor jolted as if someone had thumped it from below, and wisps of smoke rose through the floorboards. She yanked his collar, but he sat resolutely, frozen in fear. She pulled harder and his paws skidded across the bare boards. 'Come on!' she screamed.

A sheet of flame shot up the wall and blackened the window. The glass exploded. Ben broke free of her grip and bolted into the landing. She ran after him then stopped in horror.

Flames were leaping up the stairwell.

Ben turned in panic, snarled at the flames, at Charley. The sound of the fire was deafening, the heat scorching her face. The bedroom erupted into flame behind her and Ben fled up the attic stairs.

'Ben! No! No! Down, we have to go *down*!'

Tears streamed from her eyes as she went up after him. 'Come back, you idiot dog!' she bellowed. He was at the far end of the attic, barking at the small window. Smoke rose up through the hole she had made when she had put her foot through the floor. 'Ben!' she shouted. Then the whole house seemed to move, to twist, and the landing floor below fell away into flames.

She slammed the attic door shut, ran over to Ben and pressed the latch of the window, but it was rusted. She put more pressure on it and the lever snapped off. She rammed the glass with her shoulder and it exploded outwards, the rotted frame snapping with it, and she nearly fell. She grabbed the sill, steadying herself, feeling a draught, the air cooling her face. She gulped the fresh air greedily, then coughed; it was thick with smoke. She looked down but the smoke and the darkness and the tears in her eyes made it impossible to see anything.

Ben had his paws up beside her, whining, scratching. She leaned out, cupped her hands over her mouth and screamed: 'Help! Help! Fire! Help!' Her voice petered into a hoarse croak drowned by the crackling and splitting roar of the flames below.

The floor lurched and she was thrown off her feet to the boards. They were hot. Plaster and rotted wood rained down from the ceiling.

Out. Got to get out. She scrambled across the

slanting floor to the packing cases, dug inside the one she had opened. A pair of jeans, another. She knotted the legs together, tested them. It was getting hotter. She rummaged for something else, something strong, her old combat jacket, pulled that out, found an arm and tied it to a leg of the jeans.

Ben ran to the doorway, barking. Someone was standing there, just a silhouette through the smoke. It was help. Fire Brigade. She was OK, they were both OK. Relief flooded through her. 'Over here!' she shouted. 'Coming ov —' The smoke choked her voice, swallowed up the figure.

She dropped the clothes and ran to the door. Then she stopped in stark terror as the smoke cleared enough for her to see that it was a woman standing there, smart, elegant, in riding gear, hatless, her black hair hanging carelessly across her face.

Nancy Delvine.

Smart, elegant, Nancy Delvine.

Ben whined, pawing at the ground as if he was trying to back away but could not. Smoke jetted up around him. As she moved towards him, she felt the floor sagging. 'Ben!' she yelled.

There was a loud crack, then the sound of splintering wood. Ben looked at Charley for a brief instant.

'Ben!'

He lurched, drunkenly, one step towards Charley, then plunged through the floor into a volcano of flame.

Charley threw herself forward. 'No! Ben!' The floor dropped several inches. Flames leapt into the rafters, raced along the beams and streaked over her head, showering hot sparks on to her.

The floor rocked, sagged more, as if it were suspended on slender threads. Nancy Delvine was gliding towards her, the flames eating up the floor behind.

Charley yelled out in fury and in agony. 'My dog. Get my dog, you bitch!' She pushed herself on her hands and knees away from the flames and thumped into the wall. She scrabbled to her feet, crouched in terror, staring up into Nancy Delvine's eyes, hard, venomous. Even over the smoke and flames she could smell the sweet musky perfume.

Manifestation. Apparition. You are nothing. Nothing.

Nancy Delvine smiled, came closer.

'What do you want?' Charley said.

Closer.

Nancy Delvine spoke. It was the same cold arrogant voice she had heard before, in the doorway of Elmwood, in her regression. 'You killed my dog.'

Closer.

'And my husband.'

Closer.

'You destroyed my life.'

Pins and needles surged over Charley in agonising ripples, worse than the heat, much worse. She gritted her teeth against the pain. 'It wasn't me. It was my mother.'

Nancy Delvine came closer. 'You are your mother.' She smiled again. Then the flames swallowed her, and she was gone.

The floor tilted, tipping Charley forwards. Frantically she grabbed the window sill, hung from it. Flames stung her flesh like whiplashes.

She heaved herself on to the sill, her eyes bulging in terror at the ground, now lit by the glow of the flames through the smoky darkness. It was a long way down. Her clothes were smouldering. Gripping the sill with her hands, she began lowering herself down the outside, trying to shorten the fall. Her feet dangled, scrabbled, trying to find a hold on the rough walls, but there was nothing. The sill was hot, crumbling; she closed her eyes. Any moment she would have to do it.

Then a voice yelled. 'Charley! Wait! Darling! Don't jump. Hold on!'

Tom's voice.

Her fingers were slipping, her arms hurt, the pain, the burning, the choking smoke. Easier to let go, to drop, easier to die. Her grip slackened.

She heard the clatter of a ladder and Tom's voice again. The sill was burning her fingers. The ladder vibrated from his footsteps. She felt his hand on her leg, guiding it across and down, on to the top rung. Flames burst out of the window above her, leaping into the darkness as if they were searching for her, but she did not notice. She could see nothing except Tom's face in the flaring light.

Epilogue

Alice Hope Witney was born on February 14th. Charley and Tom decided on the middle name Hope because, in a way, her birth had given them both hope for a fresh start.

Alice splashed in the bathtub and gurgled. Charley lifted her out, dried her, and dressed her in her sleep suit. Then she carried her downstairs into the kitchen.

The kitchen was smart, high-tech. Charley had made it as different as possible from the kitchen she had planned for Elmwood. Everything had gone in the fire, every photograph, item of clothing, piece of furniture, book. It was as if her past had been eradicated. She did not mind. In a way, she was glad.

The insurance payout on the fire had been good and they had sold the land to a property developer. Their new home was a large semi-detached house in a tree-lined avenue in Barnes, close to the river. Neither Charley nor Tom had any hankering to live in the country again.

She switched on the television in the living room, sat on the sofa and gave Alice her bottle. Alice had Tom's hair and his seriousness; at times too serious as if she were already, at eight months old, trying to work everything out. Charley wondered if Alice would ever one day remember things from the past, the way she herself had.

It was a year now, almost exactly. Some days it seemed a long time ago, just a faded dream; others, it felt like only yesterday. Little things triggered off the memories: the smell of a pipe; a man under the bonnet of a car; the colour of a tie.

She often wondered in quiet moments like now, as night fell outside and the television flickered, what had really happened and how much more there was inside her, locked away, that a hypnotist could get out. But it would have to stay there. Where once she had been so curious to know, now she must try hard to forget.

Some nights she awoke from a nightmare screaming, reliving a part of the horror. Ernest Gibbon might be sitting at the end of the bed, holding Viola Letters's yellow sou'wester in his hand. Or Hugh, in his sawn-off tie, with an agonised expression on his blackened face. Or Ben padding towards her and, as she reached out, he would plunge through the floorboards into an inferno. Sometimes she saw Nancy Delvine through flames, and as the fire engines roared down the drive, she would clutch Tom and scream, 'Don't let them! You mustn't let them. Leave it; let it burn down!'

The inquests had been the worst part: Viola Letters's and then Hugh's. The same coroner both times. Viola Letters's death he had concluded was an accident. On Hugh's he had been less positive and recorded an open verdict.

Alice finished her milk and burped, then lay sleepily in her arms. Charley carried her upstairs and tucked her up in her cot. Alice woke up and stretched her hands towards the mobile that hung out of reach above her, plastic bumble bees and butterflies. Charley gave it a twirl and Alice watched the pieces swinging, light glinting off them. She was fascinated by anything that sparkled.

Charley switched on the pink night light and the baby alarm, and went downstairs to make supper. Tom would be home soon. She took some lamb chops out of the fridge and put a knob of butter in the frying pan. There was a crackle of static through the receiver of the baby alarm, a gurgle, then Alice's breathing, steady, rhythmic. Asleep.

The garden lit up suddenly. Harsh bright light. The intruder sensor. Charley's eyes scanned the lawn, the neat flower beds, the greenhouse. A startled cat jumped the fence at the bottom, and she smiled in relief. Butter sizzled in the pan and wisps of steam rose. She glanced out at the garden again; the light was still on, and she felt strangely comforted by the ordinariness of their garden. Normality. Elmwood had never felt normal and maybe that was part of it.

She wondered whether she had really seen the ghost of Commander Letters that day, and the ghost of Nancy Delvine in the burning house, or whether they had been trace memories of people her own mother had seen, that had been passed on to her. This had been Hugh Boxer's theory, and there had been an article in the press Tom had cut out for her, with a programme on television on the same subject. Science, it seemed, was favouring that same argument.

And yet. You never knew in life; you never really knew. She had been to a couple of libraries and read all she could find on reincarnation. But the more you searched, she began to realise, the larger the riddle became.

Forget it, Tom had said, and that was the right advice. Maybe nature was helping her in its own way. Life had been good the past year. The balance; always a balance. Positive and negative. Yin and Yang. The good seemed to have followed the bad. Tom was doing well in the partnership. Their marriage had survived, although Hugh had been right when he said that a broken marriage was like a broken glass: you could stick the pieces back together, but you would forever see the cracks.

Laura was getting married again. Their friendship had never recovered. They had exchanged Christmas cards with Julian and Zoe and Zoe had scribbled a note inside saying she would give them a call in the New Year and invite them down for dinner. She never did. Charley was quietly relieved to have had the last link with Elmwood severed.

There was another crackle of static through the alarm, then a sharp clatter, as if someone had given the mobile a push. Except that it was out of Alice's reach; safely out of reach.

There was a splintering crack. Alice cried.

Charley sprinted out of the kitchen, up the stairs, and into Alice's room, snapping on the main light. The mobile had broken and was dangling down into the cot. Alice was screaming, panicky, windmilling her arms which were tangled in the cotton threads and tiny opaque shapes.

As Charley leaned over the cot saying, 'OK! It's OK, Mummy's here,' Alice's right arm jerked straight up in the air. Charley felt a searing pain in her face and pressed her hand to her cheek, startled. She took it away and saw that her fingertips were smeared with blood.

Alice was motionless in her cot, staring at her. For one fleeting moment Charley saw something in those eyes that terrified her. It was in the blackness of the tiny pupils. As if they carried in them an evil that had come down generations, that had travelled through all time and had brought with it a cunning and a hatred and a sense of victory.

333

The room went cold as if the baby had drawn all the heat into herself. Claws spiked Charley's skin; someone stood behind her, pushing her forwards, to the cot. To the thing that was inside it.

'No. Let me go!' she screamed, turning.

There was no one. Just the wall. Perspiration fell from her skin as if from slabs of melting ice. Alice's eyes closed and her head lolled to one side; her tiny balled fist opened and a shard of splintered plastic fell on to the sheet, marking it with blood.

Fear held Charley's throat and she stood for a moment before she was able to move, to reach down and touch her baby. Then she took Alice's hand, terrified it might reach out and grab her like a claw. She examined it carefully, but it was unmarked. She picked up the shard, disentangled the remains of the mobile and pulled it free. Alice was sleeping again as if nothing had happened, her breathing settling back into a steady rhythm.

Charley went through to the bathroom and dumped the bits in the waste bin. In the mirror she saw a ribbon of blood trailing down her face. And she saw the fear that was in her own eyes. The disbelief.

She had imagined it.

Tony Ross had said the shock would go on, would manifest itself in odd ways, and strange symptoms, for years to come.

Imagined it.

She pressed a towel against her cheek and went back into the bedroom. Alice was sleeping, her lips curled into a contented smile. There was a calmness and serenity about her. As Charley watched, her expression altered, then again, her eyes blinking busily, her tiny mouth changing from a smile to a frown to a question, her face like an ever-revolving kaleidoscope, as if she was reacting to things going on deep inside her mind.

Trace memories in her genes. That was all.
Charley hoped.